A Mountain Man's Prophetic Words

"I don't pretend to be no genius. Me, I'm just a mountain hawg, destined to get scalped by some burnt-up Blackfoot. But even I can see the plain truth. Ye cut down trees like some o' these, and she's going to take a while to grow back. I counted rings on some of those stumps there on the Russian River an' I tell ye, it makes a man humble. A couple of the big stumps was nigh to a thousand years old—unless trees grew different in them days. *Them redwoods ain't goin' to grow back, no sir. Not unless we're willing to wait around for a thousand years or so. . . .*"

TO FELL THE GIANTS

A powerful novel that captures history
in the making—and explores how the achievements of
yesterday and the lessons of the past live in
our hearts today.

TO
FELL
THE
GIANTS

Bill Hotchkiss

DOMAIN™

BANTAM BOOKS
New York • Toronto • London • Sydney • Auckland

TO FELL THE GIANTS

A Bantam Domain Book
Bantam edition / November 1991

DOMAIN and the portrayal of a boxed "d"
are trademarks of Bantam Books, a division of
Bantam Doubleday Dell Publishing Group, Inc.,

ISBN 0-553-29323-0

Published simultaneously in the United States and Canada

Bantam Books are published by Bantam Books, a division of Bantam
Doubleday Dell Publishing Group, Inc., its trademark, consisting of the
words "Bantam Books" and the portrayal of a rooster, is Registered in
U.S. Patent and Trademark Office and in other countries. Marca
Registrada. Bantam Books, 666 Fifth Avenue, New York, New York 10013.

Printed in the United States of America

RAD   0 9 8 7 6 5 4 3 2 1

CONTENTS

PART THREE—THE CALIFORNIA TRAIL

PART FOUR—REDWOODS & SEQUOIAS

ED ABBEY: *In Memoriam*

No more. That was my final river trip,
Whichever one it was. And I'm back home
Resting at last, preparing to go to work
On my great book, working title Fat Masterpiece,
When the phone rings. . . .

My first thought is "No, it can't be true.
Legends aren't like the rest of us, not fated
To the same final darkness. Surely Ed Abbey will live
To be a hundred and fifty-seven, at least."

March 14, 1989. . . .

This particular death—is it possible?

Frail human substance, no matter how fierce
The flame it carries, is after all
Perishable clay. This man whose spirit soared
Like one of those great turkey vultures above the Southwest,
Taking us along for a greater view
Of sand and sage and intricate canyons and arches,
The mind that set itself against progressive civilization,
Grinning in the face of all spoliation
Fighting back, enjoying a game that couldn't be won,
Odin and Old Man Coyote at once, and bringing us awake,
Those who followed and will continue to follow
By little and little into the teeth of Ragnarok itself.

Somehow Emerson and Thoreau began the thing,
John Muir picked up the torch, and Jeffers after him,
Then Abbey, prophet of sage and desert sun,
Tough-minded revolutionary with a skull full of sunset.

I always hoped he'd try to blow that Glen Canyon Dam
Before he packed 'er in. Futile or not,
The contest isn't over quite yet—because,
As St. Edward was careful to let us know,
Hayduke lives, and quite a few have surmised
The enemy's nature. We know about dynamite.

TO FELL THE GIANTS

PROLOGUE

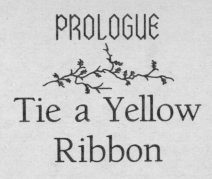

Tie a Yellow Ribbon

[1990:]

I SIPPED COFFEE at the truck stop in Canyonville and read my copy of the *Oregonian*. Clearly, matters of great significance were afoot. A columnist made astute suggestions as to how America, having won the cold war, ought to comport itself among the nations of the world, while the headline on page one read *Northwest Braces for Spotted Owl Ruling*. Official designation of this old-growth denizen as *threatened* would probably exempt from logging some very considerable portions of what remains of our once-magnificent Pacific Coast coniferous forests—with a predicted consequent loss of thousands of jobs over the next few years.

On the other hand, if we weren't sending billions of board feet of raw logs to the Orient each year and instead milled this timber Stateside, it's possible no jobs would be lost. But what do I know?

As I glanced out the window, I took note of several logging trucks heaped with Douglas fir. The Peterbilt and Mack diesel engines snored rhythmically, their exhausts fluttering like the hands of Homeric crones at work on vanished looms. The Doug fir logs, I knew, were most likely on their way to the port at Coos Bay, from whence they'd be loaded aboard Japanese merchant craft and sent westward, across the Pacific, to be milled en route. Balance of payments. Subsidized logging. Coast Range, Cascades, Olympics, Siskiyous, Sierra Nevada—all coming to look more and more as though some blind-drunk Bunyanesque barber had worked on them.

A banner on the far side of the parking area proclaimed in large red letters: *FOREST CELEBRATION*. The gathering of the clan, a "spontaneous" happening gotten up by the managers of logging conglomerates. On the counter, next to the cash register, rested a paper bucket stuffed with yellow ribbons. A truck driver, paying his tab, nodded to the pretty, dark-haired waitress, and took several ribbons—symbolic of the timber industry's opposition to *those damned en-vi-ro-meddle outside agitators* who oppose both clear-cutting and the harvesting of any more old-growth timber, period.

I finished my coffee, glanced over at a couple of rough-looking codgers who were apparently making assessment of me—a graybearded, spectacle-wearing individual in Levi's, brown shirt, and battered Oregon felt hat. Was I a redneck logger, some out-of-town turkey farmer, or *one of them thar outside agitators*? I rose, tipped my felt, and winked. A presumed truck driver instinctively lowered his eyes, while his companion glared at me.

The truth is, I like truck drivers—no matter the type of rig. In general these nomads of the American highways are good-natured enough. A week earlier, a couple of long-distance haulers pulled in at a Siskiyou rest stop where, at midnight, I was engaged in replacing burned wiring and distributor components on my '69 Jimmy pickup. Before I knew it, the truckers had taken over my project and had changed the wiring around and had installed a new set of ignition points.

And loggers? Well, I like them a lot, too, to steal a phrase from that eminent philosopher, George Foreman. Good-natured roughnecks, most of them, and working at what is very likely the most dangerous trade in America. There's a reason why falling limb ends are called *widow-makers*.

But right now I was on my way south to Williams, at the foot of Grayback Mountain, a big blue-green Siskiyou dome whose sides have been erratically shorn in the fashion of Pacific Coast logging. I paid my tab, tipped the waitress, and asked if I might have a couple of the yellow ribbons. She smiled and indicated that I should help myself. Thus encouraged, I grabbed a fistful, mumbled my thanks, gestured in the direction of the coffee-drinkers who, as I supposed, had been questioning my *good-old-boy credentials*, and strode out to my GMC. I roared south on the Interstate (a manifold gasket leaking on the left bank of my faithful 350).

> *Oh, tie a yellow ribbon on yore an-ten-ee,*
> *Yore an-ten-ee,*
> *Yore an-ten-ee,*
> *Tie a yellow ribbon on yore an-ten-ee,*
> *Yore an-ten-ee,*
> *An' cut the old growth down!*

One by one I freed the yellow streamers into the oppressive heat of late afternoon, leaving a trail of gold behind me. After all, America had just finished winning the cold war.

Close by the Grants Pass off ramp stood a burly hitchhiker, can of beer (Coors, no doubt) in one hand, fat thumb circling above his head.

"George Hayduke," I mused.

I waved, pointed to the off ramp ahead—in apology and in explanation.

Hayduke, if that's who it was, gave me the finger.

I responded by shaking my fist.

Once across Rogue River, I headed toward Williams, where I'd turn on my little workhorse of a Commodore 128 and begin a final revision of *To Fell the Giants*. Califia Beard was calling to me. She's the heroine of my novel, you understand.

Fictional characters have a way of coming alive.

It was odd, I reflected as I drove up Cedar Flat Road, that Hayduke could still be wandering about and looking for trouble, even though Ed Abbey had been dead for more than a year—buried, as I've been told, illegally in an unmarked grave out in the Utah desert he loved so dearly.

Trees. The biggest damned trees in the world. To cut down a tree twenty feet across the butt and three hundred feet tall—

that would take some doing. It was a matter of showing the wilderness, once and for all, just who was boss. Here in the Western mountains the drama began, really began, only when a New Englander decided to match wits with the trees—and that was something over a hundred and seventy years ago. In one of my reference volumes I take note of figure called Bill the Sawyer, an American ship-jumper who found his way to that little society of misfits and criminals who gathered near Santa Cruz during the second decade of the nineteenth century—in the year 1817, to be more or less exact.

A Yankee trader, *Baltimore Pride*, lay at anchor off Yerba Buena, the muddy Californio village that would one day become San Francisco. Aboard the *Pride* was William Beard, educated to be a schoolmaster but more at home in the forests of Vermont, where he'd spent summers working with his father, a logger by profession. Given the fact of this dichotomy in his nature, young Beard did the obvious thing and went to sea until such time as he could get the matter resolved—an interval of seven years.

On shipboard Beard dreamed of Vermont woods—of maples, oaks, pines, and spruces—of the solitude of walking amidst trees, rifle in hand—and the animals, sensing this new malign presence that had been on previous occasions merely a boy ambling through the forest, now fled from him. But there in a clearing stood an Indian girl, black hair gleaming in sunlight. . . . She wore an ornamented deerskin dress that emphasized what was under the dress, faintly rising and falling as she breathed.

Trees, yes, and even the smell of sap as the felling axe in his hands cut through sunlight and sliced pitchwood, while the chips, like oversized snowflakes, accumulated about his feet.

Along much of the coast of Western America north of the Los Angeles pueblo grew trees to challenge the imagination—such as those giants he'd seen when Captain Fairchild and half the crew took to dinghies and went ashore in search of tanbark oak, just south of *Pico Blanco*. Indeed, William Beard saw trees whose size and height were virtually beyond belief, huge columns of dark green foliage supported by boles sheathed in orange-red bark, serene monsters growing there in the *barrancas*, mysterious and undisturbed. In the glade, intrigued by the presence of *Bostons* and yet wary of them, as wary as though the sailors might have been either grizzly bears or cannibals, were bronze-skinned girls ranging in age, or so Beard presumed, from perhaps twelve to eighteen—and all of them bare-breasted, clad in nothing more than short skirts of either deerskin or woven tules. The Indian girls had long black hair, some braided and some not, and sunlight gleamed from their skin. A few were tattooed on breasts, arms, faces.

The seamen began to whoop and holler, setting off toward these children of the wild, even though Captain Fairchild had given no permission. The girls vanished. Indeed, it was as if some cave mouth had momentarily yawned open and the Indians had disappeared into it.

Captain Fairchild, sword instinctively drawn, stood there with blade raised high, and he was laughing, laughing. . . .

The old desire rose in Beard, and no doubt that was why, in his dream, he returned to the woods of Vermont and the lands first claimed by Samuel de Champlain and subsequently named New Connecticut—and to a boyhood vision of meeting a dark-skinned princess of the mysterious forest.

In any case, the Indian girls were gone—vanished as certainly as though they'd been nothing more than a momentary hallucination—and Fairchild's crew went on about appointed tasks. Yet that glade of redwoods, with ferns and azaleas just coming into bloom and down-slanting beams of sunlight: the place was haunted by a presence quite different from the loveliness of trees. Eden had come alive, and within the garden were many Eves. *Costanoans*. That's what the Spanish called these gentle, wild people who inhabited the coastal forests. Another term, as Beard learned later, and one sometimes used by the Indians themselves, was *Ohlones, the people, the people who live close by the sea.*

Half a dozen gray and white gulls and a pair of cormorants drifted over the blue waters of *Bahía del San Francisco*, coming close enough to satisfy avian curiosity and in the process to determine that no garbage or unattended food was lying about, then winging off, soaring on the wind. For a moment the birds were framed against the sprawling green of Mt. Tamalpais

northward, only to vanish in a mixture of sunlight and scud-
ding fog bank.

No doubt about it. The air smelled different this day in
1817, deliciously different, and randy March sun whispered
words that turned seasoned sailors into boys with troubles in
their breeches. Odors of pollen, odors of grass drifted across
the bay from rolling, oak-studded hillsides where new leaves
uncoiled in their own secret fashion from nubs of winter-gray
bark. In an area close by the settlement, bulls bellowed that
they might be allowed to mingle with the cows. Beard could
detect faint notes of guitars, and barely discernible on the air
were the sounds of female voices in song—but was that possible? *Courtship. Copulation. Gestation. Parturition.* Mother Earth,
bless her gaping thighs, was once again giving birth to the
perpetually recurring, ancient mystery of springtime. The longer William Beard thought about the matter, the more certain
he was of what he was going to do. Here lay a new world—a
brave new world, to use the good poet's phrase.

*Sweet land of Eden, which way shall I turn? Possess me, possess
me entire. . . .*

So William Beard jumped ship and, having severely wounded
an officer dispatched to return him shipboard, the man from
Vermont managed to acquire Spanish garb and proceeded to
the mission at San Jose, where he met Raymondo Olivo, an
Ohlone Mission Indian. Olivo was deemed a prodigy by his
overlords—for the man had not only mastered Spanish, English, and a bit of Latin and French, but he had become an
omnivorous reader and loved to expound on such topics as
religion, philosophy, geography, astronomy, and literature. Indeed, this Olivo managed to purchase his own personal copy
of Miguel de Cervantes Saavedra's masterwork, *Don Quixote*,
and somehow that very fact caused Beard and Olivo to steal
a herd of mission horses and to kidnap a corrupt priest and
his mistress and to flee into the mountains of Santa Cruz,
where they abandoned both the priest and his consort.

Beard and Olivo, vowing the bonds of partnership, led their
pilfered horses across the mountains and down into a long
canyon that drained toward the Pacific. Here, beside a running
stream, the brothers in crime spent the night. Awakening the

next morning, they found themselves surrounded by decidedly unfriendly Ohlone Indians—Pelican Doctor's men, from Hotochruk village.

Both Beard and Olivo, as well as the stolen mission horses, were taken into custody, and Bill and Raymondo were delivered to Pelican Doctor himself—the chief a short, barrel-chested, extremely powerful man whose face, arms, and breast were adorned with tattoos. The chief, as it turned out, had no wife—his mate had died of lung disease several years earlier. But he did have a family, for his wife had left him twin girls who had by now been transformed, in the way of nature's slow magic, from shapeless urchins into remarkably attractive young women. Their names were Seagull and Calling Owl.

Beard and Olivo were expected to live in the same lodge with the chief and his daughters and yet not, so they presumed, to look upon Seagull and Calling Owl as other than sisters. Matters progressed, however, and a strange kind of courtship was soon under way. Pelican Doctor agreed to the marriages, but the bride-prices he demanded couldn't be paid with horses. The chief wanted rifles and pistols so that he might arm his people against Californio Leather Jacket soldiers who sometimes attacked the Hotochrukmas even back within the fastnesses of the mountains. Therefore Bill Beard and Raymondo Olivo sold horses in Santa Cruz and farther south in Monterey, the capital city where Governor De Sola lived in a mansion. Here they met Jean Paul Martin, a highly successful French merchant, one who was ultimately to lend the partners money so that they might establish a shingle mill in the redwood forest north of Santa Cruz.

Beard and Olivo were permitted to marry Seagull and Calling Owl, respectively, and within a year twins were born to the man from Vermont and his Ohlone wife—Califia, a daughter, and Calvin, a son. At nearly the same time Calling Owl gave birth to a boy, one his father named Homer Virgil Olivo.

"With a moniker like that," Beard said to his friend, "the kid's got to write a book or two, doesn't he? You realize what you're doing to him, Ray?"

"Such, compañero," Olivo grinned, "is precisely what I hope may happen."

Beard nodded.

"And the next can be called *Miguel Cervantes* Olivo, right?"
Olivo laughed and performed a little jig.

"Only if he turns out to be a girl, Sancho my friend."

Beard pretended vexation.

"Had we not attempted to get that damned book of yours
back from the potbellied priest, we'd never. . . ."

"Have suffered the slings and arrows of outrageous good
fortune," Olivo laughed, completing his friend's sentence.

The period that followed didn't always bring good fortune, and
yet the partners, with their wild Indian allies as workmen and
with loans arranged by their *patrón*, Jean Paul Martin, prospered; the firm of Olivo & Beard established several shingle
mills and two lumber mills. Redwood, pine, and fir were abundant in the canyons of the Santa Cruz Mountains, and Martin
arranged for transportation of the finished lumber. Machinery
was brought in from the American East, and a small business
empire was firmly set upon the soil of Mexican California.
Again with the help of Monsieur Martin, Olivo & Beard purchased a cargo ship, renamed the *Don Quixote*. At Jean Paul's
insistence, the partners also applied for and ultimately received the first of three land grants—an extensive tract of thick
redwood forest along the San Lorenzo River, to the northeast
of Santa Cruz. With the founding of Rancho San Lorenzo and
the mill that was constructed there, a dynasty was set in place.

For their part, the two partners discussed the future and
worked endlessly to create the tangible components of the
vision they dreamed together.

"The land," said William Beard, "is very young. And our
redwoods are very tall."

"*Sí, sí*. Yes, it is so, Señor Bill. But in other ways the land
is old, very old indeed. The great redwoods here in this canyon, they didn't grow in our lifetime."

Pelican Doctor, standing with his sons-in-law, folded his
muscular arms across the bead-stitch tattoos on his chest and
stared upward among the branches of two big redwoods growing at the west end of Hotochruk village.

"Sisters," he said. "Twin sisters. Just like my daughters. The
spirits of the dead—sometimes they come back from across
the water and live among the people again, only now they live

inside the biggest of the trees. That is why you must not cut down such trees and turn them into shingles and boards. The spirits of the dead have power to cause the earth to shake."

"When the trees fall down, perhaps," Beard grinned.

"At other times also," Olivo added. "Last month the earth shook for several minutes, so that the water in Big Creek ran backward for a short time. Boulders of mudstone tumbled from the canyon rim. Our wives believed the world was ending."

"One day the ocean will rise from its bed and cover even the highest mountains," Pelican Doctor said. "That has happened before. The First People, those who lived here long ago, they were all drowned when the ocean came in to cover the land. . . ."

"Earthquake," Beard mumbled.

"Perhaps it is as you say, son-in-law." Pelican Doctor nodded. "But no matter. We mustn't anger the spirits who live within the giant trees. It's important to stay on good terms with the dead, for we must all go live with them at last."

From behind the redwoods came an eldritch screech. Then a long-haired little girl, nearly naked, darted away, her small legs churning through tall grass.

"My granddaughter Califia has a powerful spirit," Pelican Doctor chuckled. "And she can also run very fast. Neither of my grandsons can keep up with her."

I first conceived of and wrote *To Fell the Giants* as a much larger novel than the one you have in your hands, a book that drew a bead directly upon the present destructive and abominably ignorant and hypocritical practices of forest management in the American West—a sprawling volume, perhaps not sufficiently organized, and with one foot planted in the present and the other in the quicksand of California's past. As a result of such authorial sins, I was obliged to cut perhaps three hundred and fifty printed pages from my text—partly a long segment set in 1817–1822, partly a sequence of interchapters, polemic in nature, written from the perspective of the present, and partly from the series of chapters taking H.V., Goffe, and O'Bragh across the continent. However, gentle reader, I'm not done yet. "Waste not, want not," as my grandmother used to tell me. Both logging interests and ecological interests are in agreement on this one unfortunate truth: *The last of our old-growth Western forests will be gone within the next decade. And what will remain of the primeval magnificence will be those groves which are at least temporarily protected within national and state parks and various sanctuaries.* As I write these words, most of the remaining privately owned old-growth redwood is being logged, and clear-cutting of Douglas fir, red cedar, Noble fir, and so forth has extended to the very boundaries of such national parks as Olympic, Rainier, Crater Lake, Lassen, Kings Canyon, and Sequoia. There are places in the Sierra where I can no longer bear to go. From the air, doubtless, our mountains look like some vast, irregular checkerboard. And in Alaska? Believe me, you don't really want to know what's happening on our largest national forest, the Tongass.

A *preferred alternative* scenario proposes that such cut-over lands are to be replanted with breeds of super-trees, fast-growing monocultures, to the end of maximizing the take of timber and pulp during the next century.

A few days later the telephone rings. I depress computer keys in the sequence necessary to file to disk and get up to answer. It's my old Injun friend K'os Naahaabii, a.k.a. Don Jordan, in Bellingham, Washington.

"Thought you'd want to help me celebrate the owls," he says.

"The decision came today?"

"Sure as hell. Spotted owl, he's been declared a threatened species. I think the loggers are probably getting ready to have a revolution—Oregon, Washington, and Northern California'll withdraw from the Union, something like that. The boys with the saws think they're going to lose thousands of jobs."

"Losing them anyway," I say. "It's just a matter of when. Another eight or nine years, and the last of the old growth will be kaput—except for what's parked."

"Going to be a lot more of it *parked* now," Don says. "So maybe we've won one. . . ."

Don and I talk about other things, including an earthquake in Iran, at least forty thousand dead. George Foreman's comeback. The two Germanies getting together. Disintegration of the Evil Empire.

I hang up and fix a cup of coffee. Then Judy and I drive to the Williams Store to get a copy of the Grants Pass paper.

FEDS: SPARE THAT OWL. Fish and Wildlife takes rare bird under its wing. The U.S. Fish and Wildlife Service this morning listed the northern spotted owl as a threatened species under the Endangered Species Act, surprising few of those keeping a vigil on the old-growth forest debate. . . .

I return to my Commodore. I jot down these words and then allow my mind to drift backward through a frenzy of years—to Santa Cruz, California, 1836. In those days, without a doubt, life was both simpler and more terrifying. The human creature's numbers were much, much smaller, and the impact of Occidental civilization upon both Alta California and Oregon Country was as yet minimal. The interior of California was still essentially *terra incognita*, traversed only by a few groups of trappers, Americans and Brits coming and going, and inhabited by such peoples as the Wintuns, the Yanas, the Maidus, and the Miwoks, while to the north were the Shastas, Klamats, Takilmas, Umpquas, Killamooks, Clatsops. . . . Sierra Bigtrees had not as yet been officially discovered—nor had those magnificent redwoods of Klamath River Basin: Yosemite and Crater Lake were still myths, and very few Whitemen could claim to have seen the immense snow peak of Shasta.

The forest grew as it had always grown, rank upon rank of giants, from the lands of the Tlingits in Alaska to the region of the Ohlones and the Spanish missionaries in the south. Grizzly, mountain lion, elk, antelope, eagle, condor, goose, and loon pursued their time-honored business. Old Man Coyote howled at the moon, but even this primordial entity couldn't imagine the changes which were about to occur. It would be another eight years before the Donner Party, snowbound in the Sierra Nevada, would resort to cannibalism. Gold hadn't yet been discovered, nor had America sprawled westward to the Pacific. But the greatest gold rush, after all, would be that of the loggers, those individuals with peaveys and poles and axes and oxen and often far more bravery than brains.

Pelican Doctor stood silently as William Beard and Raymondo Olivo dropped a hundred-foot-tall redwood, the lashing top branches nearly striking the old chief. But he didn't move. Perhaps the Ohlone wiseman comprehended the full significance of what had just happened.

Were Califia, Calvin, and Homer Virgil close enough to have witnessed that little drama?

In any case, by 1836 a few of the giants had already been felled. In those days there were indeed giants upon the earth, and no one dreamed the forests would not last forever.

PART ONE

A TIME OF COURTSHIP

CHAPTER ONE

The Three Innocents

[1836:]

THE CHILDREN BORN to Pelican Doctor's twin daughters, Seagull and Calling Owl, were now seventeen years of age, soon to be eighteen—which is to say, young adults and in nearly all ways expected to act like adults, whether or not their actual natures conformed to this expectation. Califia and Calvin Beard and Homer Virgil Olivo had been schooled as thoroughly as circumstances might allow—a matter held to be of great importance by both fathers. In their leisure, however, the three young people were allowed to wander the forests of the Santa Cruz Mountains—or, when Pelican Doctor and the Ohlones returned to the site of old Hotochruk village, to tend sheep and cattle that grazed on the coastal meadows or on the grassy headlands above the heaving Pacific. All three had become skilled riders, somewhat in the tradition of California *vaqueros*.

The ocean, as well, exercised its lure upon their spirits, despite both undertows along the jagged coast and the occasional presence of white sharks. Like all Ohlone young people, the Beard and Olivo threesome loved to swim and to dive for abalones in the blue-green coves. As for sharks, those huge predators appeared to prefer the taste of seal flesh to that of human beings, but on one occasion the previous summer, when an Ohlone celebration was in progress at the place the

Spanish called Grayhound Cove, Jean Paul Martin's favored *doghole* for taking on cargo, a six-year-old boy was pulled under and then spit out, horribly mangled. Before Calvin could stop her, Califia had plunged into the swells and dragged the wounded child ashore, where he died from loss of blood within half an hour despite the best efforts of the Ohlones to stanch the hemorrhage. The shark had torn a foot-wide flap of muscle tissue from the child's abdomen, revealing his intestines without actually severing them.

A great pile of driftwood was gathered, and at sundown a funeral pyre was ignited. The child's spirit went up into the night air and, aided by the ritual chanting of Pelican Doctor himself, was presumed to have found its way onto the path which leads to Other Side Camp.

A few of the Ohlone children had also been lured into "school," but with less than complete success. In any case, Calvin and Califia Beard and Homer Virgil Olivo were all rendered admirably numeric and literate in both English and Spanish, with emphasis upon the former. William Beard and Raymondo Olivo could anticipate the future as well as other men, and what they saw was the great likelihood that California would one day be a part of the United States, an English-speaking nation—and hence the need for an essentially *Yengway* education.

The Beard twins were individual in temperament. Calvin, as was sometimes remarked upon, had grown to be the spitting image of his father, *Guillermo the Sawyer*, and had a keen, practical mind—New England in nature, if not by virtue of place of birth and maturation.

Califia was named in honor of that mythical Amazon queen whose domain, California, was a land which Montalvo had declared to possess streets paved with gold. Califia now appeared set on embodying at least some of the attributes of her legendary namesake. She'd grown, in fact, into a lanky tomboy, much given to competitions of one sort or another with both her brother Calvin and her cousin, Homer Virgil.

H.V., as young Olivo was called, was the most studious and meditative of the three, a youth with a basically poetic nature. He was fond of reading his father's books, and he was entranced by the sheer beauty of the world around him—a world in praise of which he occasionally composed verses characterized by their tone of celebration and wonder. He kept journals he never allowed Calvin to read—but which he was willing to share with Califia. Raymondo called him *Señor Ratón de Biblioteca*, the bookworm, the mouse of the library.

All three were expected to work at various aspects of the Olivo & Beard lumbering operations. Indeed, they were obliged to do so—and to accomplish responsibly whatever tasks were set before them.

The year was 1836, and far away from the California Mountains of Santa Cruz, the leaders of the United States and Mexico, President Andrew Jackson and *El Presidente Antonio López de Santa Anna*, respectively, were less than happy with one another. Ultimately, the political fate of a good portion of the North American continent was at stake. Early in the year a small Mexican army of less than four thousand laid siege to the Alamo, in San Antonio, Texas. The Americans resident there chose to fight to the end, and did. Among the dead were W.B. Travis, Davy Crockett, and Jim Bowie. Texas forthwith declared its independence, and Sam Houston was named commander of the Texas army. A few days after the Alamo, Santa Anna slaughtered an additional three hundred and fifty men at Goliad. But out of these two defeats came a grand Texas victory at San Jacinto (*Remember the Alamo!*), with the capture of Santa Anna himself. At Velasco, the Mexican tyrant signed treaties pledging both peace and recognition, treaties later to be repudiated by the Mexican Congress.

By July 4th, both the Senate and the House of Representatives called for official recognition of Texas, and by September the Texans held a referendum, electing Sam Houston as president of the Republic of Texas. Annexation to the United States was deemed inevitable.

In Alta California, American presence was also felt—as a relative handful of *norteamericanos* arrived, whether by ship or overland (Jed Smith and his men in 1826 and again in 1827, and then the Joe Walker–Joe Meek party in 1833, the time of the great meteor showers, or, as the Ohlones expressed things,

the year the stars fell), while other emigrants made their way
south from British-controlled Oregon Territory. New bands of
settlers came north from Mexico also, since the mother nation
was justifiably concerned with regard to the slimness of its
claim to Upper California, at least in terms of resident population, and by official decree the vast holdings of the Church
were broken up and the missions secularized. California was
growing, with a consequent steady market for building materials of every sort.

The logging and milling enterprise known as Olivo & Beard
also continued to prosper. Merchandise found ready markets
as far away as Astoria to the north and Cabo San Lucas and
Mazatlan to the south—all thanks to the offices of Jean Paul
Martin, the genial Frenchman who was, to be sure, himself
making a considerable profit out of the partnership he'd chosen to grubstake during its early months and years.

The mill on the San Lorenzo was a model of its kind—and
was indeed thus far the only member of its class in Alta California. Beard had engineered a low check dam of redwood
logs and concrete—the latter possible because limestone could
be mined right there on the rancho, to be reduced in a large
kiln Olivo constructed after the fashion of a similar structure
the priests had ordered built in San Jose, with the resulting
quick lime to be mixed with powdered clay to form cement.
Indeed, even cement proved to be a highly merchantable com-
modity.

A diversion flume carried water downstream for a quarter
of a mile, and there its energy was harnessed by means of a
large wheel, from whose spindle a wide canvas belt drove a
six-foot-tall circular saw at the end of a log carriage. At other
times power from the waterwheel was used for grinding or for
powering circular millstones utilized in the smithy, for honing
iron and steel, and for sharpening tools, felling axes included.

Redwood was converted into shingles, beams, rough planking, and even, upon occasion, furniture. Douglas fir (named in
honor of British botanist David Douglas, who first identified
this majestic *pseudo tsuga*, or "false hemlock," as a separate
species) provided structural timbers of great strength and
planking as well, while the wood of black oaks could be cut
into segments suitable for furniture, doors, and flooring.

The marriages of Beard and Olivo to the daughters of Pelican Doctor proved to be good ones, harmonious and stable, and for their part, the Ohlones themselves had even been persuaded, though with less-than-perfect success, to engage in herding and in the felling of timber. The old chief remained fiercely independent, however, and as a consequence, his people retained their freedom and the essential dimensions of their traditional ways. They were nearly as well armed as a comparable band of Leather Jacket soldiers, despite Californio laws to the contrary. For official purposes, they were *bound to Rancho San Lorenzo*, with Señors Beard and Olivo held officially responsible for their behavior.

"My name's Califia Beard," the young woman informed a luckless Leather Jacket who was so ill-advised as to make a pass at her that early July day in the village of Santa Cruz, "and don't you forget it."

Still smiling at the soldier, she produced and leveled a Deringer pistol at him. With her other hand, she waved a small American flag—thus, as it were, adding insult to insult.

Calvin Beard burst into laughter, and even H.V. began to grin. Ventures with Califia along never lacked excitement. One had to admit that much. The girl was a veritable magnet.

"Back off," Calvin suggested to the soldier. "Our fathers are friends with the governor. One word from Bill the Sawyer, *amigo*, and you're in the *calabozo*."

"Possibly the governor will have this ruffian hanged," Califia suggested, "or flayed alive."

The Leather Jacket stiffened into military posture, bowed from the waist, and turned quickly away.

As the three young people rode back toward Rancho San Lorenzo, Califia mused, *I've always wanted to say that, and now I have. My real point, however, is that most young ladies of seventeen—no, almost eighteen—wouldn't be able to carry such a handle, but then, I'm not like most young ladies. Great heavens, I suppose I'm already an old maid, by the accounting of some, at least. Alas and alack. . . .*

Calvin could guess, more or less accurately, what was going on in his sister's mind. However eccentric she might strike others, Califia didn't really seem all that strange to him. Pelican

Doctor had once insisted that, in another time and another place, she'd have become a *warrior woman*, one who wore men's clothing and who fought alongside the males. What was true (more or less): she could outride, outshoot, outcuss, and outspit just about any sonofabitch in the woods.

H.V. whistled as they rode along, made note of cougar tracks in the dust as they turned northward along the San Lorenzo trail, and toyed with the significance of wild creatures growing so used to civilized presence that they'd begun to adapt to that presence—the use the roadways, for instance, with every expectation of impunity.

Californios had hunted tule elk until their numbers grew small, and at the same time filled the grassy areas with long-horned cattle. *Hermano Puma*, perhaps with no great relish, began to dine on beef, thus adapting to a world in which herds of cattle were commonplace, herds of elk less so.

In a very real sense, Homer Virgil Olivo concluded, all creatures were at least partly responsible for the worlds in which they lived. But *humanidad*, this being had the powers of perception and foresight.

Or did the other animals also possess these powers, though to a lesser degree?

Geese flew north and then south once again. Deer and elk followed their own migratory paths. The great whales traveled north and south along the coast. Such actions could not be supposed the result of sheer happenstance. . . .

The time approached when the two families chose to celebrate the birthdays of Calvin, Califia, and Homer Virgil—an admitted approximation, inasmuch as Pelican Doctor's people hadn't precisely been following the Whiteman's calendar at the time. July 20th was close enough. Even though H.V. had been born two days ahead of the twins, one birthday for all three seemed just and appropriate.

Califia envisioned the festivities to come. It was time to load the wagons with shingles and lumber and then to follow the mule road across the mountains, down to Grayhound Cove, where *Monsieur Jean Paul Martin* and his cargo ship would be waiting. Pelican Doctor and most of the Ohlones had already removed to old Hotochruk village for the summer, and now the Indians who worked at the San Lorenzo mill would ride along, to rendezvous with their families at Grayhound Cove.

Califia glanced through a clothing catalog that had been published in Lisbon, Spain, three years earlier, and which had ultimately found its way to Monterey and then to Santa Cruz, where she had acquired the cheaply printed booklet. The drawings of expensively clad ladies were beautiful but hardly true to life. These were women like porcelain dolls—bearing little, if any, resemblance to actual human beings.

Califia showed the drawings to her mother.

"Yes, I have seen such women," Seagull admitted. "In Monterey, when once your father and Uncle Raymondo took Calling Owl and me to the great house where the governor lives. The governor's wife looked like one of these, and so did the lady who was with Monsieur Martin. That one, she was so lovely I believed her to be Monsieur Martin's daughter. But truly I believe now that he must have paid for her company. That is something the Espansh do. Ohlone women from other tribes sometimes do it too, Califia, but it is a bad thing. Tio Coyote wouldn't approve, though he approves of many things. Certainly the Jesus God wouldn't approve. Some women do it to make money, maybe even to feed little ones. And some of those women also dress like the ones in the book. . . ."

Califia nodded and turned away. Her mother had an odd way of thinking about the age-old practice of prostitution. Given the fact that Californio men tended to be slaves to their amatory urges, and given also the fact that men traditionally were the keeper of the purses, such an arrangement, upon occasion, was all but inevitable.

"Perhaps," Califia reflected, "I exaggerate. I'd never admit such a thing to Cal, but I'm afraid he's more than a match for me. The last time we fought was over two years ago, and that time he pinned me to the ground and would have made me cry *uncle*, which, of course, I'd never do. By pure force of will I managed to slip away. I can still outrun him, however, and I climbed up into our live oak and had to satisfy myself with shouting names at him and stepping on his fingers when he tried to come after me. I think it was decidedly unfair of him to have such a growth spurt. Now he's as tall as Father, four inches taller than I am and a good deal heavier, the lout. At any rate, that was when I decided it was time to stop tangling with the boys."

She stopped wrestling with her cousin H.V., however, for a different reason, one that was hardest for her to explain. Sometimes, when she was close to Homer Virgil, she felt weak in the knees, and her face turned hot.

Uncle Raymondo said she should study to be more of a lady, that the fair Dulcinea exercised greater power over the great Don Quixote than any number of hoyden tomboys, but Califia had read the book finally and now knew better than to believe anything Uncle Raymondo said.

Bill Beard only laughed. "It's the Yankee in her," he said one day. "Makes her rock-headed and straightforward as a young bull. Let her be, Raymondo, you'll only spoil her with your preaching. She'll be running the company before we're much older, and our two boys, and we as well, are subject to be taking orders from her. Best butter her up now, mark my words, old companyero."

Calvin guffawed and poked Homer Virgil in the ribs. Califia smiled prettily and then stuck her tongue out at her brother and her cousin.

But the partners were hot on the track of an argument and so chose to ignore their three offspring—proceeded to discuss Califia as though she weren't even present—as though none of them were there.

Uncle Ray said, "What is this *Yanqui* business, eh *amigo*? She is half Ohlone in her blood, she has grown up in this village, she speaks Spanish better than English and Ohlone better than either. It is not the *Yanqui* but the *Indio* that makes her strong. Look at Homer Virgil, *hermano mio*. He is a fine young man, *muy fuerte*, yet he has a love for the finer things, for poetry and song. When your young Amazon is bossing men about, and Calvin is sailing ships and selling lumber to the *Gente de Razón*, Homer and I will be in *España*, sipping drinks with ice in them and discussing the finer points of *The Aeneid* while you send us the money that will keep us in such a style. Ah, Guillermo, I am only trying to civilize my niece a little."

"Right. Just like the mission fathers *civilized* you, is that the idea? That's why I had to save your hide at the whipping post, because they were civilizing you so damned enthusiastically. Blood will out, Raymondo. I say the girl's a fine specimen of Yankee womanhood. Why, you never saw a finer figure hangin' out over the prow of a ship. Little rough around the edges, that much I'll admit, but she comes from damn good stock, and that's what counts. Next year, by Gawd, I'm putting her in charge of a crew."

At about this point Calvin and Homer Virgil and Califia went off in search of something more interesting than continuing to listen to the seemingly endless discourses between *Padre Raymondo* and *Padre Guillermo*.

In all likelihood, Beard and Olivo would die in the midst of yet one more unfinished discussion. Close as the two men had been over a period of many years, it was evident that they loved nothing better than argumentation. A particular discussion could go on for hours, with neither budging an inch from whatever position he'd decided to adopt. On another day, they might argue just as vigorously on opposite sides of the same question. Possibly stubbornness existed on both the Yankee and the Ohlone sides of the mix.

Seagull had long since given up on the idea of transforming Califia into a proper Ohlone maiden—and *gracias a Dios* for that, or so the daughter felt. In the girl's younger years there were times when the mother had actually kept Califia inside the big house William Beard had built, trying to initiate the girl into the mysteries of cooking or sewing or tanning leather—when all Califia wanted to do was go off with Calvin and Homer to race their horses in the flats by the creek or watch a big redwood come thundering to earth at one of the logging sites. By virtue of long and patient endeavor, Seagull was finally convinced Califia could burn anything from acorn cakes to salmon to plain water—and that she was truly dangerous with a sewing awl in hand. At length Seagull came to make only very rare and halfhearted ventures in that direction. More often the mother merely shook her head and sighed when Califia, in dungarees and flannel shirt, passed through the kitchen, Señorita Beard giving Señora Beard a quick kiss on the way out to the corrals.

Of late, however, there had been times when Califia wished she'd paid closer attention to certain aspects of feminine training, for indeed the attentions of her cousin H.V. had become a matter of some importance to her. Truly, she had not been around very many young men—and to know how to act in proper fashion was something of a mystery. But if young men expected *feminine* behavior, then no doubt H.V. as well could be made to *notice* her . . . if . . .

Was that what she wanted—for Homer Virgil to see, to see at least once, that she was worthy of the deep and, yes, *sexual* attentions that men gave to women? It was no more than that. Califia was virtually certain her intentions went no further. Besides, H.V. was her cousin, and so, as she had always presumed, no marriage was possible between them.

Marriage?

What in the Lord's name was she thinking of? No, it wasn't that at all. It was just that she, too, was female—and there were times, such as the present, when she wished to be paid attention to.

It absolutely sets my teeth on edge to see the Ohlone girls giggling and swaying their hips and looking at the boys with that fake-shy, up-from-under flirt of the eyes, but the whole sham has an amazing effect on the young men. Even Calvin drools all over himself and follows them around like an idiot, though that's no great surprise to me. I've never figured my big lump of a brother had much in the way of common sense. Oh, I like him—he's usually good-natured and even relatively intelligent in most matters, but what I mean to say is that he doesn't think too much about things, he just acts. But I've always believed Homer Virgil was different. He thinks about everything—always with his books and his philosophizing, enough to drive a sane person to distraction. I'd have expected better of him, but in fact he's gotten nearly as silly as Calvin, the two of them staring at the Ohlone girls, those little bare-breasted, simpering beauties, and poking one another in the ribs. At the last big clambake down on the beach, I watched H.V. flirting shamelessly with the worst of the lot, that hussy they call Butterfly. Yes, I expected far better of my cousin, but I guess the sad truth is that when it comes to women, all men are simply fools.

In looking back on events, it now seemed to Califia that H.V.'s ridiculous behavior with Butterfly on the beach that night was really the cause of everything to follow. It was a hot June day, remarkably so, for the weather was usually mild along the coast. The village was a couple of miles inland, and by afternoon it was quite unpleasantly warm. As if by some unspoken but instantaneously communicated agreement, the Ohlone workers at the old shingle mill began disappearing shortly after the lunch break, and by two o'clock or so only Bill Beard and Calvin and Califia were left in the woods, they and the small crew of genuine Maine loggers Beard had recruited on a trip back to the States a year earlier.

Father and daughter walked down to the mill to see what was going on. When they got there, they found Uncle Raymondo and Homer Virgil shutting down operations and getting ready to take a brief vacation themselves.

"Too damned hot to work," Raymondo explained in response to Bill's question. "Besides, there are a lot of clams in the cove right now. At least that's what Calling Owl told me last night. Our people have a sense of priorities, *Guillermo.*"

Bill Beard's face turned red, and Califia could tell he was getting ready to bluster, but then he shrugged and broke out laughing.

"What the hell, then, I guess we'll have a clambake. I'll send Calvin up to tell the fellas they've got the afternoon off."

After all these years, Beard told his daughter, he was finally beginning to accept the Ohlone attitude toward labor. "They'll work half a dozen Whitemen to death when they're in the mood," he said, "but if something more interesting comes up, you might as well forget about making them do what you want. I guess that's why I brought that crew in from the States, hoping some of the good old Yankee stick-to-it-ness might rub off. Hell, after all these years, though, damned if I'm not starting to believe your mother's people are right. You and Calvin, you're like me. You'll hang on to a thing till it kills you and never figure out that it might be just as easy to back off a little."

CHAPTER TWO

Too Close

[1836:]

WHEN WILLIAM BEARD and his daughter got to the modernized and more or less permanent lodge at Hotochruk, they found Seagull had already left for the ocean, and a perfunctory check at Raymondo and Calling Owl's lodge a hundred yards away in the same meadow below the spring suggested that Auntie Owl, as she was sometimes called, had accompanied her.

While Bill was cleaning up outside, Califia took time to stroke the fur of her two pet raccoons and her gray squirrel—the three animals scuttling to greet their mistress. Then she stripped out of her work britches and took a quick sponge bath. On some whim that she didn't bother to explain to herself, she put on the soft doeskin dress Seagull had made for her when the mother still had hopes her daughter might turn out to be a young lady, whether of Ohlone persuasion or in the fashion of Vermont, as Seagull imperfectly understood that fashion.

The dress was, Califia believed, very pretty, with abalone shell ornaments sewn into the seams and in several rows dropping down from the neck.

Then she turned to the small, gilt-framed mirror above the

crude washstand her father had fixed for her and unbraided her hair, which she commonly wore in a single plait in back, and that coiled and pinned to keep it out of the way when she was working.

But that day some demon seemed to be perched inside her skull, and she combed her hair out carefully, experimented with it in various ways, and finally caught it all over on one side and tied it in a leather thong ornamented with a cluster of blue-jay feathers. The tress, wavy from the braid, fell down over her left shoulder.

Her hair, she was careful to note, was almost black, but with red highlights most Ohlone girl didn't have, and her eyes were neither blue like her father's nor brown like her mother's, but rather a pale gray, rather startling in that her face was dark from being in the sun all the time. She stood nearly six feet tall and was probably stronger than many of the men—not at all like those drooping White heroines of the silly damned poems that H.V. was always reading.

Nonetheless, Califia decided that she rather liked the effect in the mirror. Then, as she was ready to go out the door, she began to feel so gawky and conspicuous that she'd have turned back and shucked the whole outfit and put on another pair of dungarees if Calvin hadn't begun shouting.

"What in hell are you *doing* in there, Califia? Dad and I are going to head on down without you if you're not ready to go in twenty-four seconds!"

Califia cast a last glance at the mirror, shrugged as if in despair, and then emerged into sunlight. She dropped to one knee to present *Nuts* the gray squirrel with a bit of acorn bread, and then stood up again. In an agile, fluid movement, she mounted her horse.

Bill Beard grinned and said to Calvin, "Son, I believe your twin brother's turned out to be a girl. Look at this, would you. . . ."

Calvin, sitting on horseback, whistled in mock appreciation and then began to laugh.

Califia ignored the men, at the same time subtly urging her mount over next to her brother's. Smiling but not actually looking at Cal, she managed to land what she knew was a paralyzing blow to his left bicep.

Uncle Raymondo and Homer Virgil met the Beards at the forks of the creek. H.V., who'd seldom seen Califia dressed in such fashion, stopped in his tracks, and his eyes flickered from Califia's face down to her feet and back again. She began to feel a bit warm, confused.

H.V. smiled broadly and, as if in a trance of some sort murmured, *"She walks in beauty, like the night.* I could almost believe Lord Byron wrote those words with you in mind, Califia. You're beautiful. . . . ."

She laughed at him, of course, and said, "Where do you get such tripe, H.V.? Byron, is it? *Night?* It's hardly past noon. You're blind as any bat."

Nonetheless, she could feel the corners of her mouth crooking into a sappy smile despite herself, and she kept her eyes down so no one could see how secretly pleased and confused she was feeling. She took care, however, to glance up from time to time to see if H.V. was still watching. He was. Then she realized she was acting exactly like one of the simpering Ohlone girls she despised, so she drew her pony up alongside his and whispered, "Come on, Olivo, I'll race you to the big bay tree. . . ."

Califia clapped her heels to her pony's sides and leaned low in the saddle as the animal broke into a full run. Down the meadows she thundered, hardly aware of the sounds of hooves behind her.

At the bay tree she pulled her mount about, stood waiting as H.V. and Calvin as well came hurtling toward her.

By the time everyone had made his way down the steep, rocky trail to the beach, the sun was hanging big and brassy out over the water, and the women had already gathered several large baskets of clams. A fire was roaring against a cliff face, and several of the *grandmothers* were tending to the roasting of *El Jabalí,* a luckless wild boar that had come foraging into Hotochruk itself.

Most of the married men were lying around, smoking, and the children ran loose across the sand, darting in and out of the surf and shrilling like the shorebirds that circled overhead,

attracted as always by human activity that avian minds invariably interpreted as an opportunity for possible food-theft.

Califia found Seagull and Calling Owl and went to work in
their company, hunting clams. Mother and Aunt had the good
grace not to comment on her clothing, but she didn't miss the
meaningful glances and smiles that passed between the twin
sisters. For a time she concentrated on clamming, an activity
she enjoyed. She liked the silent, intense attention, waiting for
the little bubbles to show in the wet sand, and then the quick
thrusts of the digging stick. . . .

"Why don't you join the others, Califia?" Seagull asked.
"Digging clams is for *old women*, those who have no other
interests except their own husbands. You've worked enough
already today."

Califia smiled at her mother, shrugged, and continued to
ply the digging stick. After a time, however, with the sounds
of the young people ringing in her ears, she turned aside and
began a solitary walk northward, along the base of the sea
cliffs.

Dressed as she was, she now felt herself very much an
outsider, a pariah among even these, her own people.

Butterfly was holding court. At sixteen the girl had full breasts
and a thin waist. Her hair was both long and lustrous, and
dimples adorned her cheeks when she smiled. Her lips were
full, and her laughter was said to resemble that of the mock-
ingbird when, on late summer nights, that creature of the air
chose to regale star-glittering darkness with wave after wave
of song.

That same laughter, in Califia's ears, was little more than
annoying and mindless noise. Miss Beard's judgment, however, had little or no effect upon either her own brother or
H.V., or indeed upon any of the young men of Hotochruk.
Consensus held that both Calvin and Homer Virgil would
probably end up marrying young Californio women, no doubt
the daughters of merchants with whom their fathers traded.
And yet, in terms of a bride-price for Butterfly, either Beard or
Olivo would have a distinct advantage. And it was apparent
to all that both Calvin and H.V. enjoyed the company of the
sensuous *Mariposa*, as she was sometimes called.

Ohlone bachelors talked much of her, seeing this particular young woman as a special prize. Her father, Spotted Fox, was quite aware of the particular attractions of his offspring, and for this reason he let it be known that the price for his daughter would be no less than a dozen shirts made of shiny Spanish fabric, an equal number of pairs of calf-high moccasins, a pistol, and a cap-and-ball rifle of American manufacture.

When *Mariposa* chose to splash along at the edge of the sea, all the other young females who'd been through the ritual of the moon lodge and were therefore eligible for marriage frolicked along with their acknowledged leader. Because the eligible young women ganged together, so too the bachelors formed a group of their own and followed along behind or sported ahead, often showing off by performing gymnastic feats on the wet sand or by diving fearlessly from jagged tidal boulders.

Calvin Beard, at such times wont to play the part of a mindless youth with no serious side to his nature, ran along with the other young men, laughing, tossing a pig's bladder stuffed with oak leaves back and forth, and in general exulting in the healthy strength of his male body.

H.V. ran also, but viewed the drama as from a point removed. Oh, *Mariposa* and the others were lovely to look at and fun to be around. Indeed, he found quite intoxicating the amazing energy the girls seemed to exude. Butterfly, he'd long since concluded, would be a good one with whom to share the first experience of mating—provided only that it were not necessary to enter into marriage as a consequence of this behavior.

Certainly, there were times when he actually dreamed of such a thing happening—he and the dimple-faced girl lying naked together, quiescent, with him stroking her hair and touching at her brow.

In one such dream, the girl with whom he lay in the naked embrace was not Butterfly at all—but his own cousin, Califia.

Califia!

He'd awakened, was unable to return to sleep, even though the dawn was several hours away. He felt—what? Guilty. He was the betrayer. He had violated a deeply embedded prohibition.

Amongst the Ohlone, he was aware, no such taboo existed with regard to marriage between cousins. But among both the Spanish and the Americans, his own cultural lineage and that of his cousin Califia, such a relationship was held to be highly suspect. First cousins were clearly not regarded as *kissing cousins*.

Well, marriage was hardly on his mind—not when he was just eighteen, for pity's sake. Yes, eighteen in a few days now. In his own mind H.V. was already mated to his studies—to the books, of which, seemingly, he could never have enough. His grand ambition, which he had but recently seen fit to share with his father, was to go away to study at a magical place called the *university*, perhaps in Mexico City—or perhaps in Boston—or perhaps even in Lisbon or at Oxford or Cambridge, in England.

The weight of his own given names, *Homer* and *Virgil*, was heavy upon his consciousness. Surely his father had so named his son for a good reason. . . .

An astonishing pipe dream! He, who'd never attended any real school at all. . . . Yes, that was true, but it was also true that he read endlessly and had long discussions with his father, something of a scholar in his own right at this point in his life, and with Uncle Bill as well—Guillermo, who'd graduated from teachers' college in Vermont.

Besides, had there not been others who, without prior schooling, attended universities? Well, it was little harm, he supposed, to entertain such a fancy. Neither was there any harm in dreaming about making love to *Señorita Mariposa*, provided only that his fantasy remained no more than fantasy.

But why had his own cousin intruded upon the mind's harmless game?

For now H.V. ran with the others, even joining in with the shouting, but at the same time he acted as observer—as would-be poet, *poeta, maker, creator of images, imitator of nature*. The half-understood pronouncements of Aristotle were with him, there in his skull, in his awareness. The old Greek—so long, so long ago. . . .

Once back at the lodge, his *Journal* in hand, perhaps he'd write something like the following:

Offshore wind and the odor of salt in the air, decaying tree-kelp left high on the sand by the waves of the previous night, gulls and cormorants and even flights of pelicans soaring and diving a few yards offshore, splashing into the waves and emerging, their movements uniting ocean and atmosphere. And the brown-skinned girls, dashing along in the surf like so many wingless scoters, drop-lets of water gleaming on bare breasts as the maidens ran and chanted prayers they could scarcely have understood, to whatever gods had been thoughtful enough to create days of sunlight and rolling waves and glittering beaches and the attentions of the li-cenciados who sported along behind.

Homer Virgil quickly grew tired of the scramble along the sea's margin and, shouting a last friendly insult at Calvin, gave up the chase. He shook his head, more in disapproval of himself than of the others, and walked back along the beach to where his father and Bill Beard and Pelican Doctor and a number of other adult males were overseeing the roasting of the boar—and where the women, his own mother included, were stu-diously searching the wet, packed sand for clams, as the surf rose and fell.

"Did that *Mariposa* tire you out?" Calling Owl asked her son. "The girl has great energy. Whichever bachelor wins her for his bride will have to be very fleet afoot. That's what I think."

"Yes," H.V. replied, "and he will have to be willing to in-denture himself, as well."

"Calvin says that you're interested in Miss Butterfly, Homer. Is that not so? All the other young men chase after her, but you return to help the old ladies dig clams? Perhaps you'll wish to help Little Salmon fill her basket. . . ."

The twin sisters laughed, almost in unison—their dark eyes gleaming. Little Salmon, digging close by, was Butterfly's mother.

"*La Mariposa* is indeed charming," H.V. admitted, "but I think she has more suitors now than she has any need for. Why would she be interested in *Señor Ratón de Biblioteca*? I'm afraid I'm not a potential husband. Mother, where's Califia? I thought she was here with you and the others, digging clams. . . ."

"The strange person to whom I gave birth nearly eighteen summers ago," Seagull said as she stooped to snatch a clam out of the wet sand, "she is all dressed up, and so naturally she has gone off by herself to brood—or perhaps to find yet another wild animal to have for a pet. No doubt she believes *Nuts* is lonely and wishes a mate."

Seagull pointed in the general direction Califia had gone, and H.V., thanking her, strode off up the beach, toward the north. Califia wasn't in sight, and that meant she had already passed beyond the big yellow sea cliff that jutted into the Pacific.

H.V. nodded and then walked across to where the boar had been buried in sand beneath what was now a roaring fire. The cooking pork gave off a rich, almost intoxicating odor.

In answer to his son's unspoken question, Raymondo shrugged, said, "Not too much longer. Pigmeat, it must be cooked thoroughly. That is what Guillermo says, and he should know. Americans all know about such matters."

"Eat the stuff raw, old friend," Bill Beard replied, "if it pleases you. A great deal of the world's sickness comes from eating half-cooked flesh. Be warned."

"If you cook the meat too much, all the *health* goes out of it. Then one must consume cabbage as well—so that one poison will balance the other."

H.V. nodded, glanced to heaven for sympathy from Tio Coyote or Hummingbird or some other benign entity.

Spotted Fox, who was said to be sixty winters of age but who looked much younger, smiled and nodded, then pointed to an arrangement of food just a few feet distant. Spread out on a deerskin blanket were various things to eat, including a heap of wild plums, a basket of blackberries, and a quantity of jerked deermeat. H.V. helped himself to some of the latter, thrust the leathery strips into the side pocket of his light canvas jacket, then turned away and began to walk northward, along the base of the sea cliffs.

"Califia!" he called out. "Little Cal, where are you?"

Then something, perhaps a pebble, struck him between the

shoulder blades. He turned about, uncertain. Had a gray gull inexplicably thumped him with its wing, possibly mistaking him for some sort of available perch? But as he stared back down the thin slip of sand that lay along the foot of the cliffs, he saw no one and nothing.

Then another pebble, this one missing, bouncing, rolling along the packed, wet sand.

"Up here, H.V.! Warriors are supposed to keep their eyes open—to be constantly vigilant."

There she was—Califia—perched thirty feet above him, on a narrow ledge upon which a large bush lupine was growing, a few clusters of yellow flowers still visible, even in July.

How in hell? Olivo scanned the high sandstone bluff—and then detected a faintly-visible avenue, a way up made possible by a fracture in the stone.

"I realized someone was following," Califia called as she worked her way down to the sand. "I hoped it was you, Homer V."

"Why'd you leave the—celebration?"

"Why did *you* leave?" Califia demanded. She'd scrambled down to beach level now. She was smiling, nervously pressing her hair back into place, adjusting the leather thong with its trailing blue-jay feathers. "I saw you and Calvin chasing off after that Butterfly girl, the one with the big . . . eyes. Did she reject you, H.V.? Yes, and so you came to find your old friend *Little Cal*, in the hope that I might console you."

Olivo shifted from one foot to the other.

"If you'd rather be by yourself . . ." He shrugged.

Califia stared at him. Such piercing, forthright gray eyes. What, H.V. wondered, did they mean? Califia was acting quite strangely—almost, yes, almost as though she were jealous of the empty-headed little *La Mariposa*.

"No, you may stay—if that's what you wish. I won't tell you to leave."

"I brought a bit of deer jerky," he said, offering her some. "Actually, the roast pig will be ready before too long—perhaps another hour at most. Pork and clams—a meal fit for a . . . queen. You're like a queen today, Califia. You're . . . very striking when you dress like . . . well, like a *woman*, to be blunt about it."

As she chewed on a strip of jerky, Califia was keenly aware of H.V.'s momentary confusion—and was glad, inasmuch as his uneasiness enabled her to mask her own.

"So you've already told me—or at least old Byron did."

"George Gordon's not old—he's a modern poet, and probably the most important of all of them, despite the irregularities of his private life. The affair with his half-sister, I mean, and . . ."

Califia burst out laughing. She reached down, grabbed a sand dollar, and tossed it at Olivo.

"Perhaps he's not *old*, then, but he's certainly *dead*. You yourself told me, H.V., that his heart's buried in one place, and the rest of him somewhere else. . . ."

"True enough, true enough. His heart was buried in Greece."

"Your great hero's a bit grotesque, I should think. Come along, let's go up to the little lagoon. The water's much warmer, and there are no sharks. We'll swim. Nothing to worry about but blue herons and mud turtles."

H.V. felt his breath come short—as though he'd been lashed across the face with a remembered dream. But nonetheless he followed Califia as she walked ahead of him, taking those long strides so characteristic of her. Today, he concluded, there was an astonishing difference in Califia's movements. He was used to seeing her in pants—not in some ornate doeskin dress.

Little Cal, where have you gone? Who's this stranger walking ahead of me? Or is it Homer Virgil Olivo—I'm suddenly a stranger to myself?

"Hurry, H.V.," Califia insisted over her shoulder. "Hurry, or we'll be late for the roast pig. . . ."

The Ohlones gathered about the fire pit. The women heaped baskets of steamed clams while Spotted Fox and Pelican Doctor cut up portions of roast pork.

Califia and Homer Virgil hadn't returned, and so Calvin, with a chunk of roast meat to chew on, began to jog northward along the beach, circling the big headland and continuing up the sand beyond.

H.V. and Califia were nowhere in sight.

"Perhaps," he thought, "the small lagoon—or perhaps

they've climbed one of the cliff faces and are walking across the headland, where the sheep are. Califia probably wants to console the lambs for the loss of their tails—and faithful H.V., of course, he'd have gone along with the scheme. Sometimes that sister of mine lacks reasonable judgment."

Calvin worked his way up a ravine overgrown with bush lupines and buckeye trees, emerging at length on a gently rounded foreland where bunches of pampas grass and occasional yuccas grew, and where a hundred or so sheep grazed contentedly, watched over by a fourteen-year-old boy named White Porcupine, who was assisted in his ministry by a one-eyed dog that appeared to be part otter hound and part wolf. The young shepherd hadn't seen either Califia or H.V. Calvin nodded, exchanged a few brief pleasantries, and promised to have some of the children bring up a portion of roast pork for the keeper of the *rebaño*.

"The pond, then," Calvin thought. Puzzled, he opted to walk northward a bit farther, and after a quarter mile or so he stood at the edge of a cliff, from which spot he could look down to a dark blue, crescent-shaped lagoon of fresh water—fed, as he knew, by two small creeks and dammed up, back away from the heaving ocean, by wind-drifted dunes, these overgrown by brush and grasses and spreading mats of purple and white flowering ice plant.

Far below stood a man and a woman. Half-dressed, they'd apparently just emerged from the water.

"Swimming," Calvin mused, "like a couple of silly children."

He dropped to one knee so as not to be noticed there on the skyline and continued to watch. But he was startled, if not truly surprised, when the two figures, rather than dressing hurriedly, turned to face one another—and then embraced in the fashion of lovers. Even from this distance, Calvin was left with no doubts. His sister and his cousin were kissing. The embrace was extended. They clung to one another.

Close. Too close.

Calvin felt—what? Jealousy? Certainly not that. The three of them had grown up together, and now they were virtually adults. When the body comes alive, he knew, when the loins begin to experience subtle and yet demanding fire, then the time of childhood is past—just as it was already past for him. Women tended to marry at an earlier age than men, both among the Ohlones and among the Californios, and Calvin did not have any particular reason to suppose his sister would be abnormal in this matter. He'd wondered, of course, wondered idly—and had even spoken of the matter with his father. Where would poor Califia be likely to find a mate? For it was only the occasional young Californio on a white horse, come to visit Bill the Sawyer and Uncle Ray, who commanded Califia's attention—at least, until the present moment. For both Calvin and Califia, no doubt, matters would be different than they were among their Ohlone age-mates—and, of course, different for H.V., as well.

Now Califia and H.V. seemed to be taking the issue into their own hands.

Homer Virgil—Calvin's best friend, almost his brother. How, then, should Calvin feel either anger or even surprise by what he witnessed on the sand dune below? The pairing was natural enough—other than himself, H.V. was the only male her own age to whom Califia had been genuinely close. The three of them, *en tres sin gracia*, as Uncle Raymondo called the trio, they'd been virtually inseparable throughout their lives.

Calvin felt relieved when Califia and Homer Virgil, after their too-familiar embrace, turned away from each other and hurriedly began to dress. But had the two of them in fact been meeting secretly for some time? More to the point, was this relationship that had now inadvertently come to his attention something he was honor-bound to remain silent about, or was it his duty to speak to the two of them—or possibly to Father or to Uncle Raymondo? As Calvin walked rapidly back away from the edge of the cliff, he realized he felt guilty—guilty of an act of voyeurism. Yes, and culpable both for knowing and for not wanting to know.

Half an hour earlier, without question, Calvin Beard's world had been far simpler.

CHAPTER THREE

To Rancho Vallejo

[1836:]

THE LONGER BEARD dwelt upon the subject, the stickier it got—
even though his first response to what Calvin told him had
been, *What the hell? Why not? Keep things in the family. . . .* But
with twin sisters for mothers, after all, the fact that the boy
and girl had been essentially brother and sister since they were
born, why . . . .

Bill and Raymondo urged their mounts forward across the
little San Lorenzo River. Once up the rocky stream bank and
into the broad meadows, they dismounted, tethered their riding ponies, and crossed the hundred yards or so of summer-
brown grass and occasional clumps of thistle, toward a thick
redwood glade beyond. The partners, both now in their mid-
forties, had been cutting and processing trees by one means
or another for more than eighteen years. Their goods found
ready markets in California and in Mexico, as well as in South
America and to a lesser extent in Oregon country, as well as
in Nova Archangelisk.

Eleven years earlier Russia had signed treaties with both
the United States and Canada, establishing 54-40 as the southern boundary of Russian territory in the New World—and

south of 60, in fact, inland only to the crest of the coastal mountains. Thus it was generally presumed to be just a matter of time until the Russian American Fur Company presence at Fort Ross, on the coast to the north of Point Reyes, was no more. Already the Russians were reportedly in search of a buyer for their California agricultural and trapping outpost. In the long run, or so rumor suggested, the Russian presence itself, the entire huge Alyeska operation, was destined to be part of Canada.

Whether Canada or the United States, however, was of little concern to the partners of Olivo & Beard, for their vision had not soared beyond the matters of bringing down trees, processing them, and selling that which was produced. In the extensive forests of the California Coast Range, redwood, Douglas fir, and to a lesser extent ponderosa pine were readily available, and free-running streams could be made to provide power sufficient to operate small mills. What remained as a genuine block to full commercial utilization of these forests was a lack of rivers large enough to provide avenues for log runs from the cutting areas down to saltwater—the key to success, after all, both in New England and elsewhere in the American East.

Here in California, many of the trees were immense, but transportation was a tough nut to crack. Thus far one answer had lain in milling near the cut site and then transporting the finished goods via ox-drawn carts, with consequent need for the building of wagon roads and the selection of cutting and milling sites as close as possible to places where the shingles and rough lumber might be taken shipboard.

Beard and Olivo had tried running small logs down the San Lorenzo to Carmel River, where they'd set up a mill near Branciforte, utilizing an Evans steam engine as a power source for their operations. After only two years, however, problems inherent in the ongoing social friction between the church and the merchants in Santa Cruz on the one hand and the irregulars of Branciforte on the other had led the partners to abandon the operation.

"We have created a very fine orchard of stumps," Raymondo said, gesturing toward a cut-over area to the south of where the men stood. "And now that we have our own schooner, *Don Quixote* of the triple masts, there's nowhere we cannot ship the redwood we cut."

Beard nodded.

"The craft's no better than its captain, though," the man from Vermont added. "We need the right *cahuna*—a man both skilled and trustworthy."

"Always in the past you have guided small craft up and down the coast," Raymondo said. "Can't you captain *Don Quixote* as well? If not, then why in the name of Tio Coyote did we agree to buy that old bilge-water tank?"

"Even if I could, I put that kind of life behind me long ago. For the most part, I'm as much a landlubber as you are, Ray. A venture to Yerba Buena or Monterey or even Pueblo Los Angeles—that sort of thing I don't mind. But my presence is needed here in the logging woods. No, I think we must find someone—not just *someone*, but a captain and a worthy crew. Martin has contacts, after all. Besides, he's the one talked us into this seagoing extension of our operations."

Beard and Olivo had on numerous occasions, whether jokingly or seriously, discussed old Pelican Doctor's *medicine vision* of many years past. And always they concluded that the scale of forest spoliation the chief had envisioned was certainly far beyond their capacity and beyond the capacity of logging *period*, for without question more timber was added to the forests each year through growth than they and the one or two other small companies engaged in timbering could cut and process.

"It's a beginning, though." Beard grinned. "In truth, trees don't grow back as fast as we can cut 'em, but in most cases all we're doing is thinning the patch a bit. We pull the medium-sized turnips and leave the granddaddies. That way we open up space for the little guys. Weeding's half the genius of having a good garden. Damned right."

"Pelican Doctor's vision," Olivo suggested, "it was simply a dream that indicated fear of change. Human creatures are too puny to alter the great order of nature. We are little more than the gophers and the bears in terms of what we do. No,

even less than that. We are like flies on the back of a great
long-horned bull."

Beard whistled.

"In New England," he said, "the boys have pretty well taken
care of big patches of forest. I mean, cleared 'er out and turned
'er into farmland, just the way the Good Fathers and their
friends have done to the oak woods here. But in the American
East, with cities like Boston, Hartford, and New York, there's
enough demand for timber to keep the lads humping all year
round. If California ever gets to the point where we've got
honest-to-Gawd cities, then logging'll be a business that
amounts to something. That day might come, too. I tell you,
Ray, there's everything here that's needed for California to be
a powerful nation all its own—or maybe the most important
part of Mexico or the United States, if it comes to that."

Olivo laughed.

"I don't imagine there will ever be that many people. If you
think about it, Guillermo, already there are too many. In any
case, *Señor Sancho del Barba*, when will we begin to cut down
the truly *large* trees? Perhaps we must first find oxen that are
five times as big as the ones we have now. The little redwoods,
they are common as dirt itself, *ser ajónjoli de todos los moles*."

"*Abundar como la mala hierba*, is it not so? Ah, Raymondo,
the redwoods on the mountain above us, they are lovely—
lovely to look at. But how shall we get them down to our mill?
By damn, it's easier to cut them, perhaps, than to do something with them afterward. Of course, we can quarter them
with gunpowder, possibly, but even then they are still too large
for us to handle. Besides, we've already used that method—
with no great success."

Olivo grinned.

"I have a better idea," he said.

"That so, is it?"

"*Sí, sí*, it is so. Now that we have our own schooner, we
are not restricted to operations here in the Santa Cruz Mountains only. We can take our crews wherever we want to, clear
up the coast into Oregon country. If we have no rivers such
as you say we need, then we must go to where there are rivers.
De la noche a la mañana, all of a sudden we have changed
things to the way we want them."

"Somewhere up the inland waterways, or over along the coast, where we've got Russians for neighbors? On Russian River itself, maybe? *Mala suerte!* So—it's inland you're thinking of, somewhere up that *Nem Seyoo* River, beyond Rancho Vallejo?"

"Yes, *sí, amigo,* that is what I am thinking."

The partners lapsed into silence as they continued to walk, making their way upslope for a time, then across a ravine where a grove of grand old patriarchs stood, and then back to the meadow where the ponies grazed.

"Been meaning to bring this up, Raymondo," Beard said, clearing his throat. "Except, hell, I'm not sure it's even worth discussing. No—let's head on back. We can palaver while we ride. Look, my boy Cal, the other day when we had the roast pig down on the beach, apparently he kind of spied on H.V. and Califia—accidental, as I take it. Caught the two of them playing kissy-face, as it turns out. . . ."

With the most promising local markets for timber products being in Yerba Buena at the tip of the San Francisco Peninsula and at San Jose and the clustered villages that had grown up near the mission and Pueblo, the possibility of locating stands of merchantable timber close at hand to the placid waters of the Bay seemed reasonable enough. The distance from Grayhound Cove to the embarcadero below Mission Dolores was no more than approximately seventy miles, but the coastal waters were treacherous, often rough and windy, and the problems with doghole on-loading at the cove were many, including jagged rocks capable of slashing through a hull, and the unpredictable force of tides and offshore winds.

Furthermore, one had to contend with the dangers inherent in winching a load down from the long-legged trestle and along a wooden chute, sometimes board by board or bound square by square, from the hundred-foot cliff to a waiting craft heaving against the stabilizing tension of half a dozen hempen lines. Over the years some three men had lost their lives at Grayhound, and numerous crewmen had been seriously injured or had lost fingers, while one of Martin's crew had his arm torn off, right at the elbow, the mishap due to a wildly whipping hawser on a storm-wracked day when no one with good sense would have been trying to take cargo aboard.

Monterey comprised the other obvious market, and to this end the partners gave serious thought to future operations on the Sur River, a stream which fed down out of the wilderness of the Ventanas. But the primary objective for expansion of the business, Beard, Olivo, and Martin all agreed, was the region around the *Bahía del San Francisco*. With large areas suitable for farming as well as for cattle operations, this land, with its extensive estuary system, appeared to be the zone of the future.

Jean Paul Martin put the partners in touch with an American named Thomas Larkin, the official consul to Mexican California, a wealthy Massachusetts Yankee who was interested in providing financial backing for a full-fledged sawmill somewhere to the north of San Francisco Bay. Larkin, a stiff-backed, balding gentleman with thin lips and dark, intense eyes, had contacts in the District of Maine in the American East and was intent upon engaging himself in the timber industry and in constructing permanent buildings in such growing communities as San Jose and Yerba Buena—an ambition which, in itself, would require significant amounts of redwood, pine, and fir. The American agreed to provide the full range of machinery necessary to setting up a mill, to be built and put into operation by Olivo & Beard, somewhere to the north of the Sonoma Mission—if, indeed, redwood or other merchantable trees were found to grow there, in locations sufficiently close to a tidewater inlet of the Bay itself so as to provide convenience of cutting, milling, and loading of cargo.

Don Quixote, with William Beard as captain, was to depart from Santa Cruz, bound for Yerba Buena and points inland along the estuarial system of the Sacramento and San Joaquin rivers. The schooner had been brought up from San Diego two weeks earlier, making port in Monterey with some fifty settlers aboard, as well as a cargo of tools and machinery of various sorts, quantities of corn, wheat, rolled oats, wine, whiskey, bolts of cloth, and articles of clothing manufactured in the best Spanish style.

The new emigrants to Alta California, consisting largely of

families, came ashore at Monterey. Some of the men had been promised employment on several Salinas Valley ranchos, while others were to work as carpenters in the employ of Thomas Larkin himself.

Jean Paul Martin also ordered a good portion of the cargo to be off-loaded, to stock his own mercantile and the shelves of several other retailers as well, and while the matter of trade goods was being attended to, the fore-and-aft-rigged schooner's name was changed (in accord with the expressed wishes of its new owners) from *Bribón* to *Don Quixote*—the latter so inscribed in large white letters boundaried in red to either side of the craft's prow.

Martin introduced Olivo and Beard to Thomas Larkin's younger half-brother, R.B.R. Cooper, a man who, at the consul's insistence, was to be foreman of the proposed lumber mill to the north of San Francisco Bay.

"*Salud!*" Martin said, raising his wine glass in a toast to the mutual enterprise. "*Monsieurs*, as you know, we will soon have genuine competition in our trade with the Sandwich Islands and with Chile and Peru. Here in the North American West we have the greatest forests in all the world, and now it seems that every day some new operation is begun. At Fort Vancouver on the Columbia River, for instance, Dr. McLoughlin, the Hudson Bay Factor, he has turned from fur trading to lumbering—and others follow his lead. When the gear-and-lever systems find their way to the Pacific, then everything will change. Consul Larkin is the one who will bring us such equipment."

"*Perdón, Señor Martin*," Olivo protested. "Bill the Sawyer and I, already we have such equipment at our San Lorenzo mill. We do not live in the Middle Ages. . . ."

"*En vraiment*," Martin replied, "but your equipment is insufficient and largely produced out of necessity. Larkin is prepared to finance mills that are completely modern. As it is, in most cases at least, you roll a log on top of a scaffold over a dug-out pit. With a sawyer below and above, you whipsaw the logs, up and down, up and down. And what do you produce? A hundred and fifty board feet a day? Two hundred?"

"And the bloke below, he gets a faceful of sawdust," Cooper said, lighting a cigar and puffing. "Well, old Thom, he'll buy us the machinery we need. Once he heads into a business, he goes in all the way. Growing up behind Thomas in the same family—well, it was exasperating at times, as you can imagine. Sort of like having two fathers."

Beard studied Cooper. The man was not precisely the sort of associate he'd had in mind when the Larkin plan was first put forward.

At the meeting's conclusion, Beard and Olivo excused themselves and went out for a constitutional.

"Señor Cooper, he's a good enough fellow," Raymondo said to Bill as the two of them walked together from Martin's house down to the embarcadero—for the purpose of examining their newest acquisition, "but not, I think, too quick between the ears. Do you believe, Guillermo, that this man will be a good foreman? Sometimes my judgment in such matters is not accurate. I was wrong years ago about Samson Flowers. As it turned out, we have never really been able to replace that one. So I leave the decision to you."

"What decision? *Hermano*, I don't know, I don't know— though apparently Cooper's part of the bargain. Mostly I think Consul Larkin's just looking out for the interests of his less-able kid half-brother. Well, we'll hope for the best. What else can we do? Look, Raymondo—thar she rides. Our own navy. Fit her out with some four-pounders, and you and I could conquer California itself. By Gawd, she's as pretty as I remembered from when she was here a year ago. Nice lines, I tell you. Damned nice."

"*Según el caso*, it all depends on how one looks at a thing. *Don Quixote* is a good ship if it will carry a cargo of redwood."

"Show some enthusiasm, old friend. Why'd you insist on naming 'er *Quixote* if you don't like 'er?"

"*Irsele a uno la onda*, I haven't the slightest idea. What do I know about ships? Only this much. One goes out onto the ocean in such a packing crate, and then it springs a leak and sinks, and then one drowns or is eaten by a big white shark with many teeth. But then, I am only a heathen Indian who has learned a bit of Spanish and English. What do I know of the world?"

With Captain William Beard at the helm, the *Don Quixote* made port at Yerba Buena and then proceeded northward across the waters of the Bay of San Francisco, past San Rafael and east-ward to Carquinez Strait, and then northward into the estuary of Napa River, setting anchor close by Rancho Vallejo. On board with Beard were Raymondo Olivo, H.V. Olivo, Calvin and Califia Beard, R.B.R. Cooper and a striking young Indio woman, Señorita Plumas, Cooper's fiancée, as well as a crew sufficient to an exploratory expedition, complete with a dozen saddle ponies lodged none too happily in the hold.

Mariano Vallejo received his unexpected visitors quite gra-ciously, insisting that they spend a day, thus providing time for a brief tour of his mansion and extensive holdings—stables and training arenas, barns, slaughterhouse, tannery and chan-dlery, vineyards, winery, orchards, and gardens. Nor, Vallejo insisted, could he possibly allow his guests to escape without participating in a grand barbecue, complete with guitar music and dancing.

Vallejo, uncle to Juan Bautista Alvarado, belonged to a fam-ily that had been quite important in California for a long time. Mariano was a man of medium height, round-faced, and with sideburns extending to either side of his mouth. He had a charming wife and five daughters, the eldest named Rosa, aged seventeen and in the first blossom of young womanhood. Liv-ing with Vallejo also, as Mariano explained, was his niece, fifteen-year-old Señorita Juanita Ortega—a young lady whom he regarded as virtually another daughter.

Calvin was smitten immediately. He could only take his eyes off Juanita by means of an act of will.

The somewhat frail Juanita, for her part, was hardly un-aware of Calvin's searching (and perhaps even pleading) gaze. At first Rosa was quietly annoyed that neither young Beard nor young Olivo was paying attention to her—and further an-noyed that Señor Cooper was, to the great chagrin of Señorita Plumas. At length Rosa concluded that she was interested in neither youth—and so she directed her energies toward teasing Juanita, while at the same time arranging matters so that her cousin and Calvin would find themselves together.

When such a chance meeting occurred, neither Calvin nor Juanita seemed quite certain what to do next.

Califia made quick assessment of the attractive daughters of Mariano Vallejo, took note that H.V. didn't appear to be overly impressed, and so was able to relax. Her own relationship with H.V., barely begun, had to be kept utterly secret—or so they'd both concluded. They'd agreed to—and had been able to—find brief moments during which they might be together.

Being apprised of Cooper's relationship to Thomas Larkin, Mariano Vallejo himself encouraged Beard, Olivo, and Cooper into his confidence. Political affairs were seething, and among the Californios resentment was growing toward Governor Nicolas Gutierrez. Indeed, many hoped that Juan Alvarado, who had the backing of the American Isaac Graham and his band of sharpshooters, might proceed against Gutierrez. Vallejo wished to know where Consul Larkin stood—and he wished to know as well whether Beard, Olivo, and Cooper might be counted on as potential allies.

"Your nephew, Juan Alvarado, is an old friend of mine," Bill Beard said. "Raymondo and I have gone deer-hunting and boar-hunting with him on several occasions. And while I can hardly condone a civil war, I appreciate the feelings of those who wish to see Alvarado as governor."

Mariano Vallejo appeared satisfied with this response and thereupon called for a bottle of imported whiskey.

"So," the aristocratic Californio continued, "you wish to secure sufficient stands of redwood and pine and set up a permanent sawmill, is that correct?"

"Yes," Cooper said. "My brother Thomas, he'll supply us with the most modern American equipment."

"How will you get the logs from the mountains where the trees grow down to the estuary, where you'll load them aboard? When I built the mansion, my crews did all the manufacture of timbers and boards by hand, with adze and axe and whipsaw. A very slow process, *por desgracia*, but effective. So how will you do all this?"

"Perhaps," Beard suggested, "we'll divert a mountain stream, build a flume, and float rough-cut lumber down to a planing mill. There are many possibilities. One can also build a check dam across a stream, then open the dam, and the resulting flood will carry whole logs to a good mill site."

Vallejo shook his head, winked.

"The Yankees," he said, "are a wonderful people. If they

emigrated to hell itself, they would somehow manage to change the climate."

The festivities at Rancho Vallejo continued well into the evening, with torches blazing. An *acompañadora*, however, managed to urge Vallejo's daughters and his niece away from the festivities at what was deemed a decent hour, but not before Calvin had been permitted to engage in the *baile de etiqueta*, once with Rosa Vallejo and three times with Juanita Ortega. As Juanita and her cousin were chaperoned away from him, Calvin Beard bowed from the waist and then, his joyous heart instantly turned to a lump of sodden mash within him, he stared mournfully after this sudden light of his life, this exquisite creature whom he had never met before the previous day and who now played so great and indeed central role in the drama of his being—so that already he found himself scheming to return to Rancho Vallejo, preferably on a regular basis.

Calvin turned away, thinking to pour out his feelings with regard to this delicious sensation of both joy and melancholy—*love*—using his friend H.V. as an audience. But Homer Virgil, as things turned out, was nowhere in sight.

And neither was Califia.

Calvin cursed himself for his inattention. Despite his best resolve to keep an eye on his sister and his cousin, and all for their own good and future sanity, as well as continued harmony within the families both White and Indian, his sister and his cousin had somehow managed to slip away.

Calvin took note of his father and his uncle, who were engaged in energetic conversation with Mariano Vallejo and several of his assistants, with Mr. Cooper also a participant. The fair Señorita Plumas, who had perhaps drunk a bit more wine than was wise, had fallen asleep in a fringed hammock slung between two small oaks.

Calvin moved about, patrolling even the areas of semidarkness at the perimeters of the torch-lit lawn and garden spaces, but H.V. and Califia were not to be discovered.

At the moment, however, Calvin's thoughts were not primarily preoccupied with the matter of his sister and his cousin. Indeed, the image of Juanita floated, wraithlike, before him. So near and yet so utterly distant! There in the great *casa*, a second-floor room at the rear of the house, a window on the south corner, just above a big climbing grapevine that was doubtless half a century old—perhaps one that grew wild and so was already in place when the house itself was built. No, all this was not simply Calvin's imagination. The room was shared by Rosa and Juanita, the two oldest girls—and Rosa herself had explained to him about the grapevine—and how she and Juanita had upon occasion climbed down the vine and so were able to sneak away from the house, undetected. Why had she bothered to provide him with this strange bit of information?

Surely, Señorita Vallejo did not suggest that he, Calvin, might wish to stand below that very window and gaze upward—might even wish to venture to climb the vine and so make entry into Juanita's room itself. . . . Adventure, an act both dangerous and prohibited, for to be apprehended might well have extremely serious consequences, a disruption of his father's business, indeed, possibly a round of lead squarely between his own eyes, and himself falling from that fatal grapevine, down, down into darkness. . . .

Hardly able to breathe, Calvin slipped around to the rear of *Casa Vallejo*, detected the corner window with the sprawling vine growing up to it. Two candles were burning within the room, and the window itself was open to the night air.

Cal approached the vine, looked upward. He thought to call out, but his voice froze in his throat.

He detected movement above, a shadowed form framed by the casement. . . .

"Juanita, I'm certain I heard something—a rustling among the leaves. Come, look. . . ."

Then there were two forms framed by the shadowed square of the window.

"Juanita?" Calvin managed, his voice half a whisper and half a croak. "It's me—I mean, it is I, Señor Beard. I . . ."

"Señor Calvin?"

"Yes."

"I told you he'd come to the window, is it not so?"

Rosa's voice.

"Calvin? You'll catch me if I fall? I'll climb down. Rosa, you must hold the candle so that I can see a little bit. . . ."

After what seemed an incredibly lengthy interval, Juanita Ortega was standing close beside him, the two of them pressed up against each other as well as against the thick foliage of *El Parra Abuelo*, the grandfather grapevine.

"We shouldn't be doing this," Juanita whispered. "Calvin?"

He was trembling. He could hardly breathe. But he took her into his arms, and their mouths sought each other.

"Hurry, *Prima Juanita*! Kiss your young man quickly and climb back up here before anyone comes."

Then he and she were apart again, and Juanita was scrambling up the grapevine.

"I . . . I think I love you, Juanita," Calvin said, and his words seemed to hang there in the darkness of summer.

CHAPTER FOUR

To Locate a Mill

[1836:]

ON HORSEBACK, THE Beard and Olivo contingent made its way through the land-grant holdings of Mariano Vallejo and into the Coast Range, where the partners indeed were able to discover considerable stands of redwood—extensive forests that lined the long, parallel swellings of mountains that rose off to the north, into *terra incognita*, lands still controlled by wild and warlike Pomo Indians.

Calvin, Califia, and Homer Virgil found themselves battling their own emotions—rather, they found their emotions virtually dominating and all but obliterating their rational beings—for all three were in love.

Sensing what they presumed to be resistance on the part of their families, Califia and H.V. chose to keep their feelings for one another quite to themselves—indulging only when a chance for privacy occurred, as had been the case at the conclusion to Vallejo's *grande soiree*.

The lovers drew solace from the present, whenever that immediate moment offered opportunity sufficient. Surely, during the course of this venture, there would come an interval when the two of them might embrace without anyone else knowing. If Calvin were indeed suspicious, it was clear that his attention was all with his memories of Rosa Vallejo—or was it Juanita, the cousin?

Calvin, for his part, had vowed to keep protective watch over his sister and his cousin. Yet, in all truth, he had no heart for playing moral *agente de policía*. Again and again, as the party proceeded northward, Calvin was on the verge of feigning illness so he might return to Rancho Vallejo. Memory of beautiful Juanita possessed his imagination. When he considered that, given the uncertainties of life itself, he might well never again so much as see the one who'd now become the solitary object of his amorous designs, he found not only such a thought but also life itself utterly unbearable. If he were required to turn the world on its very axis, he'd discover a way of seeing Juanita Ortega.

Indeed, he'd marry her. As the son of a wealthy businessman or merchant—whichever cognomen best fit Bill the Sawyer—he, Calvin Beard, couldn't be shunted aside. If he brought suit for the hand of raven-haired Juanita Ortega, that suit would have to be considered seriously. And while it was true that his age was against him, yet he was a man of eighteen, and his prospects were good. Mariano Vallejo had seen him as a mere boy, and so it would be necessary to demonstrate that, indeed, Calvin Beard had reached the condition of *manhood*.

The solution was simple in its conception, if not in its execution. The new redwood mill would produce lumber, and this lumber would of course have to be shipped to market. He, Calvin, would learn the art and trade of ship's captain—thus giving him ample access to Vallejo Rancho and hence the presence of fair Juanita. As captain of the *Don Quixote*, his position in the world of men would be well established.

At the earliest possible moment, he vowed to reveal his ambition to his father, who would, Calvin felt certain, be willing to teach him much of what he'd need to know.

Bill and Raymondo had built a thriving company, but one by now too large for the two old cronies to handle entirely by themselves. Enter *Captain Calvin Beard*. . . .

Now that he himself had been struck by the arrows of the goddess of love, Calvin began to reconsider the *too close* relationship between his sister and H.V. Was it possible those two indeed felt the same exquisite longing that now tormented him? That they themselves were scheming and dreaming to the end of turning themselves into a mated pair as husband and wife? Such conjectures, new as they were to Calvin, were both troubling and mind-befuddling.

Take Mr. Cooper, for instance. Cooper, so far as Calvin was able to determine, had learned the art of feeling nothing very deeply—and for this reason the man was in nearly all ways highly successful. Señorita Plumas, dark-skinned beauty that she was, adored the man—basked in his sight—gave herself over to pleasing him. Surely Cooper had discovered some ancient secret for success with the opposite sex—and was not that secret, after all, the art of feeling nothing too profoundly? To love deeply was to allow oneself to become highly vulnerable and hence susceptible to being hurt, should the object of one's affections decide to look elsewhere, having discovered, perhaps, some greater spirit.

Juanita was beautiful, and Calvin loved her. But to secure the person of the woman he loved, Calvin realized, he'd have to perform some great action—or rather, a sequence of actions both difficult and well-thought-out. If his vision were great enough, and if Señor Vallejo did not marry off his niece to a member of the God-cursed nobility, then he, Calvin Beard, had at least a small chance of winning the hand of Señorita Ortega. After all, hadn't she climbed down the big grapevine, to stand beside him there in the darkness? Hadn't they kissed? Surely all of this meant something—implied some sort of commitment.

The first groves of big trees seemed quite sufficient to R.B.R. Cooper, who was apparently a great deal more interested in exploring the charms of Señorita Plumas than in attempting to assess the extent of these dark forests the party now rode among. Bill Beard and Raymondo Olivo, however, insisted that the journey continue—and thus the group made its way through Napa Valley and on toward a peak Mariano Vallejo had inked in on the map as *Santa Helena*—and through the mountains beyond, passing a zone of sporadic and somewhat malodorous geysers and crossing through densely forested hills to a freshwater lake of considerable size.

Close by the big lake, a band of wild Indians began following along—never far away, and yet hardly ever within eyesight—a presence clearly felt, malign, threatening.

"Pomos, most likely," Raymondo said. "It's best, old friend,
that we do nothing to upset these people."

Bill Beard nodded agreement.

"I've heard tell the Pomos have attacked Fort Ross, and on
more than one occasion."

"Perhaps *attack* is not the correct word. The wild Indios,
they observe that Californios often kill the deer and the elk. If
long-horned cattle come wandering back into the hills, are
these creatures different from deer? They are the Whiteman's
deer, and so it is their fate to be killed and eaten. After that,
the Russians, they are said to hunt the Pomos. Then the Pomos
are obliged to go on a revenge-taking. It's as I have often said:
there's no hope for the human race."

"None, Ray? You're saying we're finished, then?"

"*Sí, sí, acabado, finito*, gone goslings, Señor Hairy-face."

Due to the wild Indians, Cooper was on the verge of panic;
for this reason, Bill and Raymondo elected to turn back to the
south, though without precisely retracing their steps—for they
angled toward the Pacific Ocean and the parallel series of hills
and ridges they'd been able to see from a summit above the
big lake. Here, they discovered, were additional stands of redwood, some trees of medium size, and some as large as any
that grew in the Santa Cruz Mountains.

The expedition reached a swift-running river at the bottom
of a canyon, and Beard, studying the crude map Jean Paul
Martin had provided and Mariano Vallejo had annotated, conjectured that the stream must be none other than Russian River,
which would eventually reach the Pacific Ocean perhaps a
dozen miles to the south of the Russian-American fur post and
agricultural station at Fort Ross—a colonial presence in Alta
California, as it were, tolerated none too gracefully by the Californios. The Russians, furthermore, cut logs and fabricated
these into sawn timber—primarily for the building needs of
their outpost and for the construction of ships.

Beard and Olivo were not at all interested in making contact with the vodka-drinkers, however; and so the party turned

southward toward San Francisco Bay. On the eighth day of their venture, the party made camp at the confluence of San Antonio Creek and Petaluma River. Here, Beard, Olivo, and Cooper decided, the first *modern* sawmill in California was to be constructed, with Consul Larkin to provide the machinery and Cooper to head up the operation. From the very spot where they stood, Bill Beard said, sawn lumber could be rafted down to deeper water and so loaded shipboard on the *Don Quixote* or on one of Martin's schooners, for export or for sale in Yerba Buena or in any other developing communities about the shores of the *Bahía del San Francisco*—or, for that matter, in Monterey or on down the coast at Santa Barbara, Los Angeles, or San Diego. Possibilities, Beard insisted, were virtually without limit.

"Because that's one thing we know for damned certain," Beard continued. "As long as human critters survive, there'll be a more or less constant demand for boards. What would civilization be without boards and dowels and nails? Mud huts and Greek temples, that's what."

"In Egypt," Olivo smiled, "there are pyramids—and these are also not built of boards. Many buildings all over the world are not built out of boards. And there are pyramids throughout the land of Mexico as well—the work of the Toltecs and the Mayas."

"You agree with my basic point, though?"

Olivo laughed.

"Of course, Sancho," he replied.

Bill Beard stroked his chin whiskers and raised one eyebrow.

"My learned colleague forgets," he said, "that Sancho was the shorter of the two. Yes—Cervantes himself says so. The gentleman from La Mancha, on the other hand, was both tall and bearded, just like me. You admit I'm right?"

Olivo shook his head.

"Only in the unauthorized edition, *hermano*. Those are the ravings of Arillaga. Besides, one must comprehend basic literary expression if one wishes to interpret a classic. *Good books have got to be read careful.*"

"I see, I see," Beard chuckled.

———

William and Calvin Beard left the remainder of their party behind and rode toward Rancho Vallejo—the intention being twofold: first, to retrieve *Don Quixote* from Vallejo's embarcadero, and secondly to enter into a working agreement whereby a dozen or so of Mariano Vallejo's men would be hired, short term, by Olivo & Beard to return with Bill the Sawyer to the mill site. Cooper would set the men to the task of putting in temporary barracks and constructing the mill building itself.

From Calvin's point of view, the prospect of actually seeing once again the young woman who had been the chief player in his dreams for the past few nights constituted cause sufficient for the undertaking of a journey of infinite distance and infinite difficulty, to say nothing of a single day's ride along the shores of the *Bahia*. Further, this time alone with his father would provide ample opportunity for the voicing of Calvin's ambition to be a merchant captain. The younger Beard would be able to converse with his father, man to man.

The company was flourishing, and with the acquisition of the schooner, here was the perfect opportunity for the son to find a useful—nay, a crucial—occupation within the framework that Olivo & Beard provided.

For Bill Beard's part, he hadn't failed to notice the apparent spontaneous attraction between his son and Mariano Vallejo's niece, and the man from Vermont had never been one to stand in the way of true love. A marriage between his son and young Juanita, should fate's filament unreel itself in such a direction, would hardly be the worst that could happen—certainly not in a political sense. To be linked through marriage to the powerful Vallejo could hardly be thought of as other than an asset.

When the senior Beard queried his son as to his feelings with regard to Señorita Ortega, Calvin stammered, grew red in the face, and then remarked as casually as he was able to that, yes, he had found the young lady *interesting*.

"Likely," Bill Beard nodded, "you'll be pleased to see her again, then. But what about the Butterfly Maiden, back in Hotochruk? A girl in every port, ehh, Son? Well, I was young once. At least I seem to remember something of the sort. Then I met your mother, and Seagull—well, she trained me, I suppose one would say. A good and faithful wife, Calvin—for a man, that's the difference between a life of eternal wandering and a life of purpose and contentment. A fellow who used to work for us years back, when Raymondo and I were just starting out, Sam Flowers—you've heard me talk about the old mountain man, Cal. Well, he was a wanderer, pure and simple. Couldn't stay put anywhere, not for the life of him. As I say, Samson and I were much alike in many ways—but I had the good fortune of falling in love with Seagull."

"Where's Sam Flowers now?" Calvin asked, knowing full well what the answer would be.

Bill Beard grinned. His son was humoring him.

"Somewhere between here and the Mississippi River, if he hasn't been scalped or burned alive long since. If the old coon's still kicking, I figure he'll show up one of these days. It's the way of things. Truth is, I could damned well use his help—getting the mill started, I mean. Mr. R.B.R. Cooper, well, his intentions may be just fine, but I'm not certain he's got the knack of working with a crew. Hope I'm wrong. I'm saying this in strict confidence, you understand. Now about little Juanita—a fine-looking filly, Son. I admire your taste in women."

"Come on, Pa, so I danced with her two or three times. . . ."

"A dozen would be more like it. I make it my business to keep an eye out for matters of . . . the heart. A man's got to learn to keep his eyes open, or sure as blazes there'll be someone around to blindside him. And if I'm not mistaken, Calvin me boy, I definitely caught the proper twinkle in your eye when Miss Ortega was close about."

"Well—she is *pretty*. I'll admit that much. How come she's living with Mariano Vallejo?"

"Son, you likely know more about that than your father does. You figure the two of us'll be able to navigate the *Don* back to Petaluma River—just the two of us and a dozen or so ranch hands?"

Calvin Beard nodded and then glanced sideways at his father.

"Son," Bill Beard continued, "do you realize—there's enough standing timber in these California mountains to rebuild all the world's cities? And the time's going to come when the trees are needed, too. But how in the hell do we get our boards

to London and Paris and New York and Boston and the like—
and still make a fair profit? If we can untie that Gordian knot—
well, it dumbfounds the mind. In all truth, Calvin, I do believe
Señorita Ortega was a tad taken by you, as well."

Califia and Homer Virgil spent the better part of a day engaged
in whatever preliminary tasks Raymondo and Cooper suggested—H.V. using axe, maul, wedges, and adze to split a cedar
log the high tide had brought into the tidewater channel of the
little Petaluma River from God-knew-where—to split it and
smooth the halves so that, set side by side in a cradle fashioned from three-foot sections of the same log, the result was
something that might pass for a camp table.

Benches to go along with the table, however, presented a
problem of a different order—for no other driftwood logs were
to be found anywhere along the banks of the estuary.

*Califia Beard, with two broad-bitted felling axes, one over
either shoulder, and her long dark hair, not braided as was usual,
in a storm about her shoulders, and those piercing gray eyes of
hers. . . .*

"Upriver," she said so matter-of-factly that no one could
possibly have questioned what she said, "that big grove of
cottonwoods. We'll take a pair of packhorses, and after we've
downed a couple of trees of the proper dimensions, we'll sling
the logs behind our nags—we'll fashion a harness out of rope,
and drag the timbers along."

H.V. put down his adze, took off his sombrero, and wiped
at his forehead.

"A lesser woman might think to roll the timbers into the
river and then use a line on them—float them to our landing.
But what do I know? I'm game for whatever you say."

"The problem with men," Califia said, suddenly not altogether pleased with H.V.'s droll sense of humor, "is that they
tend to be strong in the back and weak in the head. You read
too many books, Homer. Byron and Tomas de Iriarte and Voltaire and the others. You'd be better off reading the pebbles in
the streambeds, the odors of flowers, the flights of birds. Those
are the real things, not your precious *literatura*. Will you come
with me, or do I have to cut down the damned cottonwoods
all by myself?"

H.V. put his sombrero back on, tilted the hat forward.

"I'll do whatever my Lady Cunegonde wishes, as always. How else will we ever manage to build benches to go with this fine table? Where's my father gotten to? We've been working, and all the while Dad and Señor Cooper and *Señorita Maria Isabella Eleanora Plumas*, they have gone off to listen to the cries of the mourning doves—or else to catch some fish for supper."

Califia gestured with palms upward.

"They walked downriver, H.V. We must go the other way—then perhaps we'll have a few moments to ourselves. I hate this . . . being secret to everyone. What are we going to do, my . . . love?"

H.V. took her hand, held it for a moment, held it gently as though he grasped a young jay or sparrow, and then let go. Their eyes met, lingered.

"Tools," he said at length. "We'll need the small whipsaw as well, and a pair of lariats. Let's hurry, Califia, before our keepers return."

Once up to the grove they'd selected, the two young people unloaded their pack animals and set to work. They hewed down three young cottonwoods, each about a foot across the butt, and proceeded to buck off the limbs and divide the timbers themselves into twelve-foot sections. H.V. was sweating profusely in the late afternoon sun. He took off his sombrero and removed his linen shirt-coat.

"You're growing stronger every day," Califia laughed. "With the sweat all over you, you look as though you'd been rubbed down with bear grease. I have muscles, too, Homer Virgil. Shall I take off my shirt to show you?"

"You're shameless, totally shameless—though possibly I have sufficient virtue for both of us. No, no, that's not necessary—don't take off your clothes—not yet. Wait until we're finished cutting, at least. Califia, how can I keep my mind on my work when you say things like that?"

Maria Plumas contrived to produce an excellent dinner of catfish, wild parsnips, and biscuits smeared with the last of the jug of melted butter Mariano Vallejo had given them. Raymondo brought out yet one more flask of red, ropy-tasting

Salinas Valley wine, and Señor R.B.R. Cooper was persuaded once again to play his harmonica. A full moon rose, almost red at first due to some grass fires that were apparently burning somewhere or another—in any case, a faint odor of smoke was discernible. A cool, pleasant breeze brought with it a scent of the ocean—salt and scorched grass mixed in the pulsing air.

The evening was beautiful. In the darkness to the southeast, across the broad expanse of the *Bahía*, one could detect a few flickering lights—at least until fog began to form over the water, obscuring the spots of illumination.

"Must be Pinole village," Raymondo said. "North of there, not too far from the mouth of Napa River, in fact, where we anchored *Don Quixote*, close by Rancho Vallejo—that's where I was born and where I grew up, at least until the Spanish came and took me to the Pueblo, so that I could be civilized. In those days, the *padres* were very much interested in civilizing *Indios*. I think perhaps the good fathers believed there weren't enough servants in that heaven of theirs, and so they came in search of Indian children. But with me, I don't think they accomplished their purpose."

"Is the village still there, Uncle Raymondo?" Califia asked. "Or perhaps it has moved back up into the hills—as the Hotochrukma did—so as to be away from the Californios."

Raymondo Olivo tamped his pipe full of imported American tobacco, offered the pouch to Cooper, and then leaned over to pick up a burning splinter of cedar. He lit his pipe, sucked several times, and nodded.

"I don't think so, Cally. My people are all gone, I believe. There are no longer any truly wild Ohlones, and that includes Pelican Doctor's village. After all, the Hotochruks work for Olivo & Beard, do they not? And I myself have spent many years teaching the children, and some of the adults as well, to read and to use numbers. Our people dress in Mexican clothing and ride horses and use rifles for hunting. No, the world that existed when I was a young child, and the world that still existed when Bill Beard and I first went to live with Pelican Doctor's people, that world's gone. Much can happen during the lifetime of a single man, and always things happen more and more rapidly. You and Calvin and Homer Virgil, you three will see much change during your lifetimes. I hope most of it is good."

"The land of California," H.V. protested, "right now it seems sleepy, almost sluggish. The *real world* is very far away. We have no great cities. We have no universities. In all truth, there are but very few of us. What happens here in California isn't important to Mexico or the United States, and in Europe and Asia, surely those places have not even heard of us. We are nowhere, Father—at least in the eyes of the world."

Raymondo glanced over at Cooper, who had ceased to play his harmonica. Señorita Plumas sat on the ground beside him, her chin resting on his knee.

The fog, now, was beginning to drift up through Petaluma Valley, and the moon, moving higher in the sky, was but half visible from behind the mists. A mountain lion screamed in the silent darkness—screamed a second time.

"Goddamn, that's a weird sound," Cooper growled. "Don't guess I'll ever get used to it."

"El Puma," Califia laughed, "he would make a fine pet. I'd like to have a cougar for a friend. Perhaps a cougar and an eagle as well."

"Nowhere?" Raymondo asked. "Well, perhaps that's so, *in the eyes of the world*, as you say. But I believe this land of ours must be the most beautiful of all lands, even though I've never seen elsewhere so that I might make comparison. It's true that I see the rest of the world only through the eyes of my books— and yet, nonetheless, I believe what I say is correct."

"We have oceans and forests and grasslands and rivers," H.V. admitted. "Yes, and very large trees. I've never heard of finer trees than ours. But what about mountains, Father? I read of the great Alps, of the Andes and the big volcanos of Mexico, and of the huge Himalayas that are said to be greater than all others. What has California to compare to these?"

Raymondo Olivo laughed.

"No cabe duda, beyond all doubt you are right," he agreed. "And yet, do we not have our own mountains? The Ventanas and these we have just ridden through. . . ."

"Hills," H.V. replied, "mere hills."

"Well, my son, I tell you there are others also—even though we have not been there to look at them. Samson Flowers, an

American fur trapper who worked for Bill and me years ago, before you and Cally and Calvin were born, he told us of a great snowy peak far to the north of here, near the place where *Nem Seyoo* River, the Sacramento, begins—a mountain the Indios call *Waiiaka* and the British call *Shasta*. Perhaps that snow-covered giant is the greatest *montaña* in the world, I do not know. But I do know that far across the Big Valley there is a high, snowy range, *Sierra Nevada*. These I have viewed with my own eyes—one can see them, many miles away to the east, from the ridges high above San Jose."

Cooper stroked Maria Isabella Eleanora's hair and then puffed several times on his pipe.

"By heaven, I can tell you folks a thing or two about those *Sierra Nevada*," he said. "Three years ago it was—the summer of all the shooting stars. Joe Walker and his gang of thieves—American fur trappers, I should say—came riding into Monterey, hoping my half-brother Thomas would be able to put in a good word for them. Walker and a big fellow named Joe Meek and thirty or so others, including a young chap named Zenas Leonard, who was writing a book about how they got here. Zenas, he told me about those mountains, all right. Walker and his boys crossed 'em in the middle of winter and ended up having to eat their mules. A hundred miles of snow, more or less, and waterfalls half a mile high. That's what he claimed, and Walker himself agreed."

"Maravilloso!" Raymondo chuckled. "Yes, I too heard some of those so-called trappers speak of their crossing of the snowy mountains. Walker and Meek, they were part of a group called *Bonneville's Brigade*—they were sent here by the American military officer who pretends to run a fur company. Every few years, the Americans arrive. Soon the American government will come here and stay, and Californios won't be able to drive them off. Mexico won't stand up to the Yankees, and that's all for the best. There's a reason, after all, why I taught my son and all his friends to speak American English. That's the language my partner speaks, and hence I am already part American myself. Your brother, Señor Cooper, he's also a representative of the United States Government. Soon we will all be Americans, and I'll be able to vote for *el presidente*."

"Tell you what else, Olivo. Zenas claimed there was trees

up there even bigger than the biggest of our redwoods. These was redwoods, too, but different foliage—trees so damned big a man would have to see 'em to believe in it. If things go well, maybe someday we'll be building us a sawmill over there."

"We've all seen very large redwoods," Olivo replied. "Perhaps this Zenas Leonard didn't know a cedar from a redwood or a dog from a porcupine—perhaps he simply liked to exaggerate. But one day soon I'd like to cross the Big Valley and ride up into those mountains to see for myself what's there. Bill Beard and I have spoken of such a trip many times."

CHAPTER FIVE

Guilty Embraces

[1836:]

ROSA VALLEJO MANAGED to meet Calvin Beard at the edge of the great vineyard, for it was there that he had gone to walk while his father conferred with Mariano Vallejo.

"Señor Beard," Rosa called out. "May I speak with you?"

Calvin, momentarily confused, nonetheless was able to gather his wits about him. He turned, smiled, and bowed sharply from the waist.

"Señorita Vallejo—you startled me. Well, I'm at your service, of course. Your cousin's not with you?"

Rosa, flushing, stopped a pace or two short of where Calvin stood.

"It's in Juanita's behalf that I've come," she said. "My cousin wishes to have an audience with you, but my father mustn't know about it. Part of what she has to tell you won't be pleasant for you to hear—at least, I don't think it will be. Do you truly care for her, Calvin Beard? I think you do. No—don't speak. Just listen. Look there. You see the great oak between the mansion and the barns? Go there just at midnight, Calvin Beard. It's dangerous if anyone should see you. . . . My father's like a hawk, but Juanita and I have found this way to outsmart him. Be there at midnight, and I'll stand guard for the two of you. . . ."

Calvin would not have been able to answer even if he'd been able to think of a suitable reply, for the moment Rosa had finished speaking, she was gone.

. . . *won't be pleasant for you to hear.*

Calvin continued his solitary walk, but within half an hour he had returned to the guest cottage to which he and his father had been assigned.

"Well, Son," Bill Beard grinned, "Mariano's of a mind to go along with us. In exchange for preferred rates on lumber, he's going to give us a crew *gratis* for the remainder of the summer, at least until his harvest starts coming in. By then we'll be able to have our own lads up here, and after that. . . ."

Bill the Sawyer wasn't yet finished speaking when the door to the guest quarters opened. Two serving girls and a Spanish majordomo entered, the girls bearing brass trays upon which were plates laden with shredded beef seasoned with onions and chili peppers, tortillas, and sliced tomatoes. The major-domo presented them with a flask of wine and gave assurances that Mariano Vallejo would join them within the hour.

Calvin ate quickly, but his mind was hardly on food. He sipped a bit of wine and then excused himself, telling his father that he wished to go aboard the *Don Quixote* to acquaint himself with the ship's charts and running gear. During the ride back to Rancho Vallejo, Calvin had spoken of his desire to pilot Olivo & Beard merchant craft. The elder Beard had asked numerous questions and nodded thoughtfully in response to much of what his son had to say—without making any commitment.

Calvin was, he had assured his father, eager in all ways to learn the art of piloting the schooner—against a time, not too distant, he hoped, when he might presume to captain her.

"The lure o' the sea, ehh?" Bill Beard laughed now between mouthfuls of food. "Well, I suffered from that malady myself for a time. *Captain*, is it? By heavens, since it's our own craft, Cal, I see no reason why we can't manage—at least, if you're up to it. You'll have to learn, and learn good, mind you. A foul-up on the high seas can be, well, a tad fatal, and I've got no use for waterlogged offspring. Your mother would never forgive me, for one thing. Lad, I'll come aboard later. Vallejo and I still have a few things to settle between us. You can try the wheel on our way back to Petaluma River."

"Calvin, is that you?"

"Juanita? Yes, yes, here by the oak, just as Rosa said."

"It's dark—and I. . . ."

Then they were in one another's arms, locked in desperate embrace. They kissed and clung to each other and kissed again, this time for a long while, as if fearing that their moment of secrecy would too soon be gone.

Calvin stroked her hair and then touched his lips to her forehead.

"I feel all . . . funny . . . inside," Juanita whispered. "Oh, Calvin Beard, why did I ever have to meet you? But now that I have, how shall I ever manage to be happy?"

"I . . . I . . . Juanita? My God, I can't even think straight. Maybe I love you, Juanita Ortega!"

"Don't say so. You mustn't ever say that again, Calvin. Only kiss me once more."

"Why shouldn't I say it? I speak the truth. It's true, Juanita. I swear what I say is true. . . ."

"Then I'll confess as well. Kiss me, Calvin Beard. Please kiss me."

They embraced until their knees were weak and their lips had begun to go numb.

"Oh my dearest!" the girl cried out as she buried her face against Calvin's chest. "I do . . . I love you. It's just that . . . I never believed you could possibly feel the same. We've only just met. Calvin? How could this be happening to us?"

"It *has* happened, yes. We must accept it and be grateful. In the name of Jesus, I swear it—I've thought of you constantly, every moment since I saw you last. I've hardly been able to sleep. I'll find ways to keep coming back to see you until you're indeed my own wife. Will you marry me? Tell me that you will. . . . No, damn it, don't answer. I don't even know what I'm saying. Pay no attention. . . ."

She began to cry, clinging frantically, sobbing, sobbing.

"What is it, Juanita? Have I said something wrong? Tell me what I said, and I swear I'll retract it all. No—I won't retract.

I've asked you to marry me, and you must answer. You just said . . . said that you love me?"

"I do, yes. But I can't marry you. My uncle won't let me. Mother of God, I want to die. Dearest, I've been promised to another—my uncle's arranged for me to marry Señor Jose Albion. . . ."

"Your uncle's done *what*? Who is this . . . Albion? I'll kill the fat pig. I'll blast him with my bear rifle, and then I'll drive a stake into his heart. . . . Goddamn it, Juanita, you love me— you've said so."

"A rancher . . . Albion . . . that's what he is. I've never met him, so I don't even know whether he's fat or thin. I know only what Uncle Mariano has told me. Señor Albion's forty-five years old, and his first wife died three years ago, of the cholera. He has a daughter who's a year older than I am! How could my own uncle do this to me? I'll never marry that Albion, not while there are knives in the world. I'll kill myself first. . . ."

Calvin crushed Juanita in his arms, pressed his lips to her hair. Lights seemed to be exploding inside his head—everything was swirling, as though into a vortex, a dark, downward spiral toward the elemental zero which lies at the base of the cosmos itself.

Uncle Raymondo's words, often repeated, drifted into Calvin's consciousness: *"I have a better idea. . . ."*

"No," he said. "We'll elope. I'll kidnap you, We'll go away together. . . ."

"How can that be? My uncle would only follow after us, and then. . . ."

"Do you love me, Juanita Ortega?"

"Yes, oh yes, I do. I love you, Calvin Beard."

"In that case," Calvin began to laugh, "God has heard what you've said, and so you're honor-bound to come away with me."

"How can I argue with you and God both?" Juanita demanded. "God never makes sense, and now you don't either."

Their lips joined yet one more time.

The voyage of the *Don Quixote*, from Vallejo's embarcadero on the tidewater channel of Napa River and thence across San

Pablo Bay and up the barely navigable estuary of Petaluma River to the mouth of San Antonio Creek, was accomplished easily enough—with Bill Beard instructing his son in matters of nautical craft and at the same time attempting to turn a gang of vaqueros and vineyard workers into instant sailors.

Beard noted the grim determination on the part of his son— a kind of spiritual coldness that had come over the boy in the interval between dinner and the drinking of an evening glass of wine. Beard knew as well the cause—the reason sufficient for the change of mood from one of great expectation to one of fatalistic determination. In short, Calvin had shared with his father both his intense feelings for one Señorita Ortega and also the latter's having been *promised* to a mysterious Jose Albion, a wealthy man with a land-grant rancho which extended up into the mountains to the east of the San Diego Mission.

Calvin's was, indeed, to be a difficult introduction to the life of the *enamorado*. In the first place, the girl was young— altogether too young to be getting married to anyone, or so the elder Beard surmised. To hitch her up to a gent in his mid-forties, Beard's own approximate age, would be difficult—even painful—for the girl. Such a marriage was certainly not the kind of thing Beard envisioned for Califia. Young people, he'd observed, found the act of copulation, in general, to be far more attractive with those their own age as partners in crime. For one so young as Juanita Ortega, the arrangement could be seen as a matter *gross and rank in nature*, to use Will Shakespeare's phrase. As for Albion—well, that gentleman, doubtlessly just doing Mariano Vallejo a favor in relieving him of a not-altogether-desired obligation, would be taking on a headstrong teenager who'd never, in all likelihood, be satisfied to share the good man's bed.

Some gents, apparently, found such arrangements to their liking—rather akin to breaking in a horse. But then, some men were also utter damned fools. No one in his right mind, Beard had long since concluded, could possibly wish to have an empty-headed and probably bad-natured child for a companion. In bed she'd likely be nothing at all—sullen and hysterical. At other times she'd wish to be toadied to—to play the role of favored daughter, to be pampered, spoiled. If Señor Albion were wise, he'd reconsider before the moment of the fatal and permanent bonding occurred

But as a potential mate for his own son? Well, Juanita seemed reasonable enough—and pretty enough—and infatuated enough with Calvin. The time of her projected marriage to Albion had been set at two years hence. For this reason, Beard reflected, there was time sufficient—time to make an adjustment or two in the web of fate, if adjustment was what was called for. In the meanwhile, Calvin Beard was acting like the doomed hero of some medieval saga.

Now that Calvin had managed to complicate his own life—with a distinct potential for complicating the lives of quite a few others along the way—Bill Beard found it reasonable once again to give thought to the *kissing cousin* relationship that had, in its own sputtering way, begun between Califia and Homer Virgil. For good or for ill, Bill Beard had chosen to do nothing more than to hint about the potential problem to Raymondo—in a kind of good-natured, jesting fashion. In his own absence from the new mill site, Beard trusted, Raymondo would have kept a keen eye on the two young people. Thus far, at least, whatever was going on between Califia and H.V. had transpired entirely *sub rosa*.

Let sleeping dogs lie.

But when Beard thought about it, the image of *sleeping dogs* didn't particularly please him.

Raymondo had spoken on several occasions with regard to a notion that he might send H.V. to the American East for an education—inasmuch as the young man was quite obviously a scholar by nature, a philosopher, a poet, a dreamer. Perhaps even some European university was not out of the realm of possibility. The partnership of Olivo & Beard, after all, had flourished. Adequate funds were available—and what better way to spend money than to use it to set up one's offspring? Raymondo Olivo, Beard knew full well, had since childhood cherished the notion that he himself might eventually be able to go to such a place as the University of Madrid—or to Cambridge or the University of Paris. But the years had drifted out from under the two old partners. Good years, yes, and prosperous—but they passed all the same. The moments of one's

life were like the waters of a mountain stream—rushing heed-
lessly onward, flooding, dwindling, flooding. . . .

What the father could never do . . . perhaps the son would
be able to experience.

"I learned an interesting thing or two from Mariano," Beard
confided to his son, thinking to draw Calvin from the depths
of Aphrodite-imposed melancholy. "First off, our Russian
friends over at Fort Ross, they're not just cutting logs for use
at the compound, or for building ships, either. No, sir. According to Vallejo, those boys have got them a genuine mill,
though I think she's powered by Aleut Indians rather than by
any kind of steam engine, and what they're doing is cutting
up lumber for housing—and using the ships they build to send
off cargos to the colony in Alaska—maybe even over to Kamchatka."

Calvin nodded.

"We presumed something of the sort all along—you and
Uncle Raymondo did, at least. What else did Vallejo have to
say? Has he been matchmaking for his own daughters as well?"

"If it were me, Calvin, and I knew damned well I wanted
little Juanita, I suppose I'd be thinking of some dramatic way
to let my ambitions get known. In any case, just dwelling on
a thing isn't going to improve it any."

"Like what, for instance?"

"I can't solve your problems for you, Son, but I'll back
you—you know that. The other business Mariano told me
about—and I'm not even sure how good his authorities were—
it's about what's going on in Oregon country. The Hudson's
Bay Factor up there, a doctor named John McLoughlin, he set
up a logging and milling concern about nine years ago. But the
whipsaw method wasn't doing the job, and so now he's put
in a complete *modern* operation, just like what we're planning
on the Petaluma. Hudson's Bay sent in saw blades and gears,
and McLoughlin used water power to drive the thing, sort of
the way we did on the San Lorenzo. Word has it the mill can
cut three or four thousand board feet a day—that's Oregon
pine, though, and not redwood. No redwoods that far north,
apparently. At least, there's no mention of 'em. Anyway, this
McLoughlin's got a crew of twenty-five or thirty men at work.
Raymondo and I, we're hoping for better production than that

at our new mill. Hell, we can cut twenty thousand on a good day over at San Lorenzo. With the new equipment . . ."

"How would Vallejo know about any of this? I don't think he's ever been out of California, any more than we have—except you, of course. You were all over the world when you were . . . younger."

The father laughed. He'd never really thought of himself as growing old exactly, but Calvin's near-slip said *old* both loud and clear.

"However uncharitable you may be feeling toward Señor Vallejo, Son, he's nobody's fool. It turns out that a brigade of British trappers came wandering through his lands early this spring. You've heard me talk about Samson Flowers? Well, that old goat was with 'em, but he was planning to ride east, into American territory, once the H.B.C. brigade made its way back to Williamette River in Oregon. Apparently Sam's got a family among the Shoshones—the Snake River Indians—so he told Vallejo, anyhow. . . ."

Beard glanced at his son, intent upon steering the *Don Quixote*. It was certain that Calvin had ceased to listen—the young man's thoughts were doubtlessly concerned with a fifteen-year-old Californio girl who seemed destined to be the wife of a wealthy rancher.

At the mouth of Petaluma River, Bill Beard took the wheel, called for the furling of all but the rear mainsail, and guided the old workhorse of a schooner up to the confluence with San Antonio Creek. He set anchor within twenty feet of shore and landed his party of temporary laborers—Cooper's party, rather, for Cooper would have the task of converting the sketched plans of a mill into some semblance of a reality consisting of beam and plank and brace and roof.

After a big meal of roast elk (Cooper was proving an adept hunter) and a good night's sleep, Raymondo, Bill, Homer Virgil, Califia, and Calvin bid *adieu* to R.B.R. and Señorita Plumas and set sail for the open waters of San Pablo Bay and San Francisco Bay, past the presidio and into the ocean, thence south along the coast and into port at the embarcadero at Santa Cruz.

Calvin shared his misery as well as his wretchedly painful happiness with his sister and his cousin. Califia and H.V. listened attentively, asked questions at crucial moments, studied Calvin's woebegone and yet angry face, and glanced at one another.

As he spoke, Calvin recalled what he'd seen on that day earlier in the summer as he stood on the headland, gazing down toward the freshwater lagoon from whence two figures emerged—he recalled their long, even desperate and, as he'd presumed, *guilty* embrace. Now, with his own world at sixes and sevens, he was much less prone to pass moral judgment. Whatever conclusion Cal had reached too quickly at the time, he now regretted. But the present, he realized, was no proper moment to enter into *that* particular discussion.

"It's simple enough," H.V. said. "Can you not deduce the solution, old friend?"

"Short of changing about the entire social and political structure of California, no, I can't. To tender a suit of my own would be to enter into competition with an established and wealthy rancher. Damn it! Young people should be allowed to choose their own mates! Juanita has chosen me, and I've chosen her."

"Poor Mariposa." Califia smiled. "Forsaken, jilted by the fickle male heart! Already my brother has forgotten his first love. . . ."

"The solution to your problem, Cal," H.V. insisted, "is simple. It's called *kidnapping*. It's also called *eloping*. If your Juanita's got enough strength of character, she'll not flinch, not hesitate."

"Does he always talk this way?" Calvin asked his sister.

Califia shrugged.

"What he says makes sense, Cal. You must go back to the new mill—Dad and Raymondo say Thomas Larkin was able to obtain the saws and other machinery they need from a merchant in Mazatlan, and that the equipment's already been shipped. It's expected to arrive in Monterey any day now. Go back to Petaluma River—and then ride to Rancho Vallejo. If your Juanita cares for you and if she's got the *spunk* to do something about it, then she'll be willing to leave the security of her uncle's rancho. We Beards aren't exactly nobility, I guess, but we're wealthy. Dad and Uncle Ray are friends with Alvarado, and with Pico as well. What's that old duffer from San Diego going to do about it if you steal Juanita Ortega away from her captor? He can't exactly send an army up here, after all. H.V.'s right. Eloping is a good idea."

Homer Virgil nodded.

"A very good idea," he said. "You see, Calvin? I always end up agreeing with myself."

The previous evening Califia Beard had done quite a strange thing—for she'd approached Mariposa, who'd always presumed Califia didn't like her, and gave the Ohlone girl both her two tame raccoons and *Nuts*, the gray squirrel. These gifts were made on the condition that Mariposa would agree to take good care of the creatures and to see to it that the animals occasionally received the tasty tidbits to which they'd become accustomed.

Butterfly, who'd always coveted Califia's pet raccoons in particular, was astonished both at the honor that was being bestowed upon her and also by her good fortune. She thanked Califia several times—and was amazed once again upon finding herself being embraced by Señorita Beard.

Calvin himself had paid Butterfly but scant attention since returning from the place where the new mill was to be built, and Butterfly wondered if Califia's inexplicable change in attitude had something to do with that. If Calvin Beard were indeed smitten with some foolish Spanish girl, then he was not really worth possessing, or so she concluded.

But the actual significance of the gift-giving wasn't apparent until several days later—when a rider coming over to Hotochruk from the San Lorenzo River mill was surprised to learn that neither Califia Beard nor H.V. Olivo were in the village. Everyone in Hotochruk presumed Califia and Homer Virgil had ridden to San Lorenzo, since that's what the two had said they were going to do.

Bill Beard and Calvin and a number of experienced *timber beasts* had by this time already departed on the *Don Quixote*, their destination Monterey, where they were to take on a cargo of saws and gears and winches and pulleys and the like, as well as foodstuffs sufficient to last a crew of twenty-five for two to three months. As a result, only Raymondo Olivo and Pelican Doctor were in the village when the disappearance of Califia and Homer Virgil became evident.

"I do not think they have been robbed and killed," Pelican Doctor said by way of consoling Raymondo, Calling Owl, and Seagull. "I think they've gone off to be together—because they didn't suppose that we would allow them to be as man and wife. I've observed them together a number of times, and always they had the look of two who are in love."

"Bill was afraid of such a thing," Raymondo said. "I thought only that the two were close, just as they'd always been close, from childhood on. I didn't even yet have an opportunity to speak with my son about the possibility of his going to Europe to study—I know that's something he wishes."

"Everyone was concerned with Calvin and his Spanish señorita," Calling Owl reflected. "Calvin was very unhappy, and we all spoke of that—and didn't notice how it was between my son and Califia. Since Seagull and I are sisters, those two believe they cannot marry—and so maybe they've run away from their own people. But that isn't true, is it, Father?"

Pelican Doctor looked troubled—troubled and stern. He folded his big arms across his tattooed chest and bit at his lips before speaking.

"Bill Beard says that among his people such a mating would not be allowed except among *royalty* or those who are very wealthy. The Spanish, perhaps they would object, I do not know. But for Ohlones, only brother and sister are prohibited from being as man and woman—whether they're brother and sister by blood or because they've been adopted. Even though my daughters are twins, they married different men, and William and Raymondo are only blood brothers, not brothers from the same mother. For this reason, their children are free to marry each other if they wish—and if the young man is able to provide a proper bride-price."

"Do you think my daughter and Homer have run away for good, Father?" Seagull asked.

"Too much theory, and too much talk about marriage. I'll get some men together," Raymondo put in, "and I'll track the two criminals. Not a lick of sense between them. If they haven't gone to San Lorenzo, then where in the devil would they be? These two know very little of the world beyond the mountains of Santa Cruz."

"If you catch them," Pelican Doctor asked, "what then? Will you demand they return? My son-in-law forgets that Homer Virgil and Califia are now adults. Among the Ohlones, if a young man cannot produce a bride-price, then he and the young woman may run away—to one of our *secret* lodges. It's not the best way to do things, but when such a pair returns to the village, we all know them to be married."

"*Maldito sea*, I've waited so long to . . . send my son to a university. Why does this have to happen now? I have written applications. . . ."

"All things occur when Tío Coyote is ready," Pelican Doctor said. "It's true that he often makes mistakes, but that's a matter beyond our control. Old Man Coyote has whims, and we can do nothing."

"I refuse to accept Old Man Coyote's whims," Raymondo replied. "I'll get together a search party and find the two foolish ones."

"It's better to let them return to the village when they wish to do so," Pelican Doctor said. "After all, we cannot keep our own people prisoners—and we can't live their lives for them."

For a long moment Raymondo Olivo stared at his father-in-law's wizened face, made note of the expression of elemental acceptance. Raymondo shrugged and turned away.

CHAPTER SIX

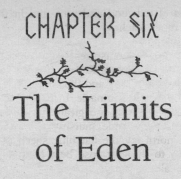

The Limits
of Eden

[1836:]

PERHAPS HOMER VIRGIL Olivo and his cousin Califia Beard actually intended simply to cross the ridges and continue only so far as the mill on the San Lorenzo, in accord with the expressed wishes of both fathers—but youth is impatient and susceptible to sudden emotional fevers.

They crossed San Lorenzo River a mile or two above the mill, close by the mouth of Zayante Creek. Here Califia broke off the intense conversation they were having, barked like a coyote, used her quirt on her pony, and thumped his sides with her heels. The young stallion, perhaps bored with the studied and monotonous pace the journey had taken, broke into a full run and inexplicably veered eastward along the Zayante trail. Nor did Califia seek to restrain her mount. Rather, she leaned forward against his mane, slapped him repeatedly about the shoulders, and *yip-yipped* into his ear.

Startled, H.V. nevertheless joined the chase—and within moments the two horses and their riders were laboring up the canyon, bursting through tangles of wild lilac and willow, lurching through thickets of oak, and pounding along into the graceful stands of redwood and pine and fir that grew along the canyon's upper reaches.

At length they found themselves high up among the grassy meadows along the spine of the mountains. Here the horses were left to graze as the boy and the girl walked together, hand in hand, toward a rocky pinnacle, from the top of which they could see the Pacific, vast and gleaming and far away to the west. Eastward was the wide, marshy basin of Santa Clara and San Jose. Due north lay the flat blue sheen of *Bahía del San Francisco*, while to the east rose Bear Mountain, Blue Ridge, and Mustang Peak.

"Across those mountains," Califia said, pointing, her voice nearly a whisper, "would we be able to find freedom, you and I?"

"A great valley lies out there," H.V. said. "I've heard that it's fifty miles across, perhaps even wider than that, and in places there's no water at all. But once one has crossed this *Valle del San Joaquin*, then the land begins to tilt upward toward the Sierra Nevada. On a clear day, one can see those mountains from the tops of the ridges beyond Santa Clara Valley. Our fathers have seen the Sierra Nevada from over there."

"Then why should we not see them as well, Homer Virgil?"

When H.V. remembered this moment later, he recalled that his first impulse had been to convince Califia that the two of them were obliged to turn around, to ride back down Zayante Canyon, and to get on over to the mill—since the hour of the late-afternoon meal was approaching. And yet he merely nodded and said nothing of the sort.

They turned and started across the yellow-brown slope to where their riding ponies were contentedly grazing along a band of greener grass. An ooze came from the deep black earth, which sometimes had seashells in it. But then they fell into one another's arms, and mouth sought mouth. They clung to one another. Califia's softness and fragrance were all about him—he had not believed she could be so soft. He kissed her hair and groaned audibly.

Then they pulled apart, and Califia bolted off, running downhill—at the same time challenging H.V. to a footrace.

This—this was more like the Califia he'd always known. But the instant alteration from the *unknown* to the *familiar* came nonetheless as a bit of a disappointment. He ran after her, knowing without question that over this kind of terrain, at least, he had no chance whatsoever. Califia could run like a jackrabbit or a fox. . . .

Laughing.

She stood between the two horses, laughing. She smoothed the hair back on her forehead and grasped her long braid with both hands.

"Homer?"

"My God you're fast, Little Cal! What . . . what is it? Your eyes look all wild. . . ."

"Are you going to be the kind of man who'll see what he wants and then take it, or will you wait forever?"

Her words stung his face. He knew, instinctively, exactly what she meant.

"Those Sierra Nevada?" he asked quickly, searching for words. "Well, yes, I think we should go see them. If we don't arrive at the mill until tomorrow, whom will we hurt? We don't have to be like the French—and do everything in accord with the hands on a pocket watch. You know—I've read it in books. But we haven't brought much food with us. I've got my Kentucky rifle, and we've both got pistols—so we can either hunt deer and jackrabbits or rob some honest farmer of his rightful toil. We could lay in wait along the wagon road and rob the true men as they pass by. . . ."

"Be serious, Homer. Look. I have some money. We can buy what we need at one of the villages in Santa Clara Valley— some cornmeal and dried beans, perhaps even some bacon or corned beef. We won't starve to death—we'll live the way the Ohlones live. But where will we sleep?"

"Together, of course. We don't need a hotel like the one in Monterey. We've got a good blanket, and we can skin a deer if we have to. We've slept together before, after all."

"Like brother and sister," Califia said. "We've been children. I don't want to be a child any longer, H.V."

They mounted their horses, and H.V. withdrew his long-barreled Kain-tuck from its sheath, fit a cap into place, and aimed at a limestone formation above them. He winked at

Califia and then fired. A puff of blue-gray went up, and the sound of the blast echoed far across the mountain.

"It's a good rifle," he said, suddenly feeling obliged to explain. He reloaded, tamping the wadding in place by means of a wiping stick, and then he slid the Kentucky back into its leather sheath.

"You think you can hit a grizzly with that gun—I mean, if we run into old *Pano* and he wishes to dispute our right-of-way?"

H.V. laughed.

"You've seen me shoot before. I can hit a gray squirrel up in a tree, a hundred yards off. . . ."

Califia reflected momentarily on the often-demonstrated fact that she was a better marksman than either her brother or H.V. Though the thought passed quickly, she regretted not having brought her own rifle.

The two of them proceeded, found themselves heading downward toward Santa Clara Valley, along a trail that had been used by both deer and sheep. Sundown found them moving along the main wagon road between Santa Cruz and San Jose. Near the village of Los Gatos they helped themselves to a dozen ears of corn from a peasant's garden, and farther along they departed the thoroughfare and, close beside a summer-low stream, they built a fire and roasted the ears—ate these and some jerky.

An owl called repeatedly from somewhere back in the tangles of toyon, buckeye, wild lilac, and manzanita—a screech owl, performing its mating cry: *kit-kit-kit-kit-twirrrrrrr, kit-kit-kit-kit-twirrrrrrrrrr. . . . .* And the stream, just a few feet from where they lay side by side, gurgled disconsolately in late August drought. Tree frogs chittered, perhaps clinging to the exposed roots of a big live oak that grew from the stream's bank, the penetrating force of living root tissue in constant conflict with the capacity of the stream, at winter flood, to excavate, to remove rock and sand and humus from the grasp of those roots. Dry leaves rattled in the close darkness. A family of quail, growing nervous under the protection of overreaching fragrant laurel, began to stir about—trilling noises, little strings of red question marks streaming out into the air.

The two horses, tethered short perhaps fifty feet from where the humans had chosen to sleep, stamped their hooves on the soft earth and whickered repeatedly.

A dozen or so pigeons, picking up the anxiety of the horses and of their small cousins on the ground, broke from their roosting spots in a live oak, wings clattering in panic. The moon, large and white and not quite full, turned the woodlands into a dream of silver and shadow, light cascading into the grassy margin beside the stream.

"Hold me tight," Califia whispered. "I have dreamed this moment over and over, and yet I don't know what to do. I want you to . . . take me. I am yours. . . . It's time for me to become a woman. A girl needs a teacher—you must show me what to do, Homer Virgil. I'll do whatever you tell me."

H.V., his hands trembling, began the process of unfastening Califia's clothing—lacings, buttons, ribbons in places he hadn't suspected. Then she was lying there before him, *unresistant victim, woman awaiting penetration, naked and burningly white in the glow of moon radiance, hardly real, hardly human at all.*

H.V., on the verge of wild confusion, began to remove his own clothing—had to fight back an impulse to turn away from her, to seek privacy. What, after all, did he actually know? What he had read of in books many times was of no use to him now. Those books, none of them ever told the truth— none of those authors had ever been with a naked girl beside a trickling stream in California moonlight. *She's watching me— her eyes, her insane gray eyes that are the same color by daylight as they are now, her eyes are on me, examining, making comparisons to . . . She's seen men unclothed before, many times—the Ohlones, swimming. She's seen me as well—but this is different. Why does it feel so strange? Because I'm pounding with excitement, because I'm stiff as a board? My God, what if I lose the erection before . . . ? What if it just goes away, and I'm humiliated? Then she'll wish to go back to San Lorenzo, and she won't be interested in me again? Or will she be relieved . . . because . . . I can't make love to her? Why am I thinking all these things? Why am I frightened to death?*

He sat down on a log to remove his riding boots—his stockings—finally his tight-fitting britches as well.

Slim and nude in the moonlight, naked and fully aroused,

H.V. stepped toward Califia Beard, kneeled beside her, spoke her name.

Califia laughed, sat upright, and reached for the little male implement that would very soon now tear through her maidenhead as she had always known would be the case, sometimes desiring, sometimes dreading. Califia had to force herself to take hold of him—she was half fearful his erect penis would scald her hand.

It feels different than I thought it would. . . .

A shudder passed through Homer Virgil's entire body—a warm, aching jolt of lightning.

"Is this for me?" Califia asked.

But then his mouth stopped hers, and neither he nor she spoke for a while after that.

Homer Virgil slept, slept deeply there at her side. She studied his face in the moonlight and finally drew their single blanket up over him.

Was it, after all, so different to have become a woman—to have made love for the first time, to have lost a bit of membrane that was the metaphorical equivalent, in the minds of both men and women, of *innocence*? No, she concluded, no, there was nothing much to the act at all, certainly nothing to account for the longing and confusion and terrible intensity. Great excitement, great longing, great anticipation and kissing and stroking and fondling, and then a little pain, a few droplets of blood, and the distinct sensation that there was more to feel, much, much more, sensations of pleasure coming on and carrying her to heights and to . . . but then it was over, over and H.V. holding her and kissing her and saying, of all things, that he was *sorry*, and that he hoped he hadn't *hurt* her. How could he have hurt her except by choosing not to hurt her? After all, he was certainly every bit as innocent as she—unless, that is, his father on one of those trips in to Branciforte had paid money to an Indio woman who would for her price have taken his virginity from him.

Califia had heard the men at the sawmill talking—their voices dropping to whispers when she came near. But she knew. Indeed, Calvin had told her much—about the *putas* who would do almost anything one could imagine for a few silver coins. And, yes, Califia had wondered if it would not be a good idea for young women as well, a male prostitute, trained so that he possessed great skill, one who would take a girl's virginity from her and at the same time explain to her the skills of lovemaking.

Society would never allow such a thing, of course. It was evident to her that Californio males all wished their brides to be virgin—so the women would bleed on their marriage bed, as homage to male sexual power—ritual sacrifice to *the little god of love*.

Among Ohlone girls, though, things were different. Once a young woman had gone through the time of her moon lodge, no ill was thought of her if she lay with a man, one whom she might meet at some secluded spot where the two of them might indulge in lovemaking. Such was the way of courtship, and there was no bad reputation involved, not unless the girl in question had decided to leave her sexual print on half the males in her village. Only then, perhaps, would no man wish to pay a bride-price for her.

Mariposa, though younger than Califia, had almost certainly experienced mating with at least one or two men—possibly even with Calvin or with . . . H.V. But the latter thought was repugnant, and Califia willed the supposition away.

In her girlish dreams, however, Califia had gone many times to see her imagined male *puto*, one who, once he had taken her money, was obliged to do whatever she told him. Dreams, however, were unsubstantial. Reality was something different. Now that she'd actually *slept* with H.V.—no, *made love* with him, *mated* with him—was she glad? Was she relieved?

Yes, to both questions.

Homer Virgil was indeed the man she wished rightfully to have taken her virginity, even if nothing beyond this single night should ever transpire. But how did he feel now? Would he soon find her repellent, odious? She'd heard stories of men who, once they'd possessed a woman, wished to have no more of her. And this man, sleeping the profound sleep of a child, and after all that had happened—their lives now forever bound, one to the other, and possibly their ties to everything they'd always known now severed, and yet he could simply lie there and sleep. . . . She'd known him all her life and couldn't imagine a time or a situation when he wouldn't be there, but did she actually know him at all? Understand what made H.V. or any other male act as he did?

The two of them, cousins, had they violated some deep law—by their actions, had they caused their families to turn against them? If they attempted to return, would they be shunned, cast out?

As Califia contemplated the phenomenon of cultural tradition and male nature and her own odd sensation of *nothingness* with regard to the loss of her virginity, a heavy sense of drowsiness came over her, stole upon her almost unnoticed, and she lay her head against H.V.'s chest and closed her eyes.

Morning light spilled from the eastward rim, and at first Califia wasn't quite sure where she was.

It is all changed, changed. . . .

She turned over, toward where Homer Virgil would be sleeping. But he was not there. She sat up, instinctively pulling the blanket around her, to cover her breasts.

"My lady awakens?" H.V. asked.

A camp fire was burning, and he sat before it, smoking a small cigar—one of those little Mexican cigars that Jean Paul Martin had given to Uncle Raymondo.

"Why did you let me sleep, Homer Virgil? You should have—"

"So, get up. Come on, Little Cal, we've got a long ride back to the San Lorenzo mill."

She felt her face flush. Would he cast her aside, after everything . . . ?

"You go there if you want, H.V. I won't. A certain young man lied—he told me he'd ride to the Sierra Nevada with me, no matter what the cost. But now he doesn't want me anymore. I'll go myself. Don't you worry about me, Señor Olivo!"

"You're impossible! You truly wish to journey clear over to those mountains at the end of the world? Off into the howling wilderness, halfway to the United States? Our families will suppose we're dead."

"Wolves and coyotes howl in the mountains of Santa Cruz as well. The sound cannot be much different in the Sierra

Nevada. As to our families, that's the reason why we decided to elope. But if you're afraid, then. . . ."

"Wretched girl! We'll be disowned. Even Pelican Doctor will pretend he doesn't know us."

"I don't want you to come, then, Homer, Not if what we did last night makes no difference to you. . . ."

H.V. puffed on his little cigar, blew smoke into the air, and stood up.

"All right. Get your clothes on, Califia Beard. I'm not going to ride across Santa Clara Valley with any girl pretending to be Lady Godiva."

"*Acciones son amores, no besos ni apachurrones*, Homer. Actions speak louder than words. Do you have enough nerve?"

Califia sat there a moment longer, tried to determine whether her cousin meant what he said.

Apparently he did.

They rode east around Sierra Azul and the Santa Teresa hills, and then stopped briefly at an adobe structure which served as a village post, close beside Coyote Creek. Here they purchased tea leaves and sugar, a few basic foodstuffs, and other supplies, including tallow candles, a burlap-wrapped flask of coal oil, and some lead and black powder. From the village they continued their trek across Pine Ridge and through the canyon of a southward-flowing stream they surmised to be a branch of Coyote Creek, then up Blue Ridge and across another drainage and finally onto a high and relatively barren rim which dropped away eastward to a welter of low, bare hills and beyond that to an immense and utterly flat plain, the Valley of the San Joaquin. No houses, no roadways, no ranchos were evident within their span of vision. In places oak forests grew on the floor of the big valley, while in other places there was only grass—a brown, sere land reaching toward hazy distance.

But the horizon lay far beyond that—high and blue above the haze of the valley, a final boundary to this world they knew as Alta California—the great mountain range they'd so often heard of in stories, *Sierra Nevada*, the Snowy Mountains.

"Now I suppose you wish to return," Califia said as she and Homer Virgil sat their ponies atop the windy crest of the mountains dividing the land they knew from an unknown interior—San Antonio and Valpe and Monte Diabolo and all the others. These mountains they'd been riding among were large—greater than the ranges of Santa Cruz.

Homer Virgil shook his head.

"We've cast our lot," he said. "I don't think there's any way back, Califia. Do you regret what we've done?"

She laughed.

"We haven't done enough of it yet for me to make a judgment," she replied.

Two days of riding took them across San Joaquin Valley—a trek that required them to traverse low, desertlike hills where sometimes a gray-green rattlesnake could be seen coiled about a clump of grass or stretched out in a bare area, enjoying the intense sunlight. Blazing yellow sun indeed poured down relentlessly, so that Califia and Homer Virgil were obliged to seek shade during the midday hours, shade and water.

Farther on out into the valley, they encountered sloughs and marshes whose shallows were populated by countless waterfowl—ducks of many kinds, geese, herons, cranes, egrets, mud hens, and others. When the birds went up all at once, there were so many that they appeared almost to be some kind of cloud formation.

The two lovers-in-exile forded their ponies across a dozen small river channels and one stream of considerable size before emerging onto drier land that sloped the opposite direction, toward the great mountain range distantly visible, its peaks evidently holding snow in places, even now, at the end of summer.

There was no sign of Mexican Spanish civilization, and indeed very little sign of human presence at all. However, H.V. and Califia did happen upon a deserted village site as they followed the course of a creek that was obviously a roaring torrent at certain times of the year but was by summer little more than a series of half-stagnant pools.

"Those who lived here must be the ones called *Yokuts* and *Chukchansi*," Homer Virgil said. "The ones sometimes called *dog people*. When they meet a stranger, they ask, *What is your dog?* My father has told me about them, but I don't know how good his information is. I don't think he's ever been out here."

Califia gazed about the village site—constructions sheathed with tules, some of the lodges quite long with separate fire holes, numerous doorways, steep-pitched roofs. A single such structure, she supposed, might well house up to ten families and was complete with what appeared to be a shade porch along one side. Farther out stood a series of round stone structures perhaps five or six feet tall and half that wide. These were found to be empty—excepting one, which was filled with dried acorns—storage cairns, proof against squirrels and birds, if not against field rats.

The entire village must have been as large as Hotochruk and yet apparently hadn't been occupied for at least a year.

"The houses are much different than the lodges of the Oh-lones," Califia said.

"Yes, yes. These are the Indios who have many tattoos and are always at war, or so my father says. They smoke *loco weed* and make ceremonies with rattlesnakes. The shamans dance before a rattlesnake den in the spring. They lure the snakes out and then do magic so that no one will be bitten during the rest of the year. Pelican Doctor told us about that."

"Not a bad idea, when you think about it." Califia smiled.

"I recall these words—though I'm not certain they're Yokuts. This is all I can remember: *Do not touch me, rattlesnake of the plains! You whose white eye the sun shines on, do not touch me!*"

Nearby the abandoned Yokuts village Califia and H.V. spent the night—building a small fire and hoping the smoke wouldn't drift so far their presence would be revealed to any of the local Indians. H.V. had no information as to how the Yokuts treated strangers, but under the circumstances, out in the immensity of this great valley, neither H.V. nor Califia wished to discover the truth at first hand.

They ate beans and corn mush and a few strips of bacon, washing their repast down with some hot tea laced with lumps of brown sugar. Afterward they were both eager to make love once again, and when they'd finished, they lay in one another's embrace and listened to the crackling of sandhill cranes perhaps a mile away and the shrilling of mockingbirds closer at hand.

The following day they passed over extensive dry, rocky areas of patchy grass. At this point, the stream they followed had a bit more water in it, and along its banks a few fading sweetpea vines bloomed, as well as an occasional stalk of leopard lily. Wild grapevines hung from the limbs of alder and cedar. The leaves of the big creek maples had begun to turn yellow, and the foliage of buckeye bushes was withered to pale brown.

"We've reached the Sierra Nevada," Califia said as they dismounted shortly before sundown to make preparations for the night's camp.

CHAPTER SEVEN

Star-Crossed Lovers

[1836:]

WHO KNOWS EXACTLY what these two had in mind? For surely they realized that the mountainous terrain ahead of them constituted a portion of *terra incognita*.

Jed Smith was the first American to cross the Snowy Mountains, and after him came Joe Walker and his bunch. There had been other penetration, of course, both before and after the Americans. A Spanish explorer, shortly after the turn of the century, was said to have ridden far back into the *Sierra*, and though no maps or much of anything else came of the expedition, he gave a name to the river whose course he followed, *El Río de los Santos Reyes*, the River of the Holy Kings, which was said to issue from a huge granite canyon in a land where gigantic cedars grew.

Such trees, if they existed, must be redwoods—or so Homer Virgil Olivo surmised.

As H.V. and Califia Beard continued their trek eastward, the land ever rising in the direction they traveled, oak and digger pine woodlands gradually altered into a dark forest of yellow pine and fir, a forest punctuated by a different variety of pine, with individual trees of extreme height, in excess of two hundred feet. The needles grew in bundles of five, the foliage a darker green than the *ponderosas*, and the high branches laden with enormous cones. Dried specimens, littering the ground beneath groves of these patriarchs, were up to a foot and a half in length.

Califia and H.V., who'd never had a plan clearly formulated, now ceased to worry about just how it was that they intended to survive. Instead, they were fascinated—hypnotized, so to speak—by the land through which they were passing. As the canyon walls grew higher, as the terrain became increasingly rugged, perhaps only then did their own vulnerable nature occur to them. And perhaps each had begun to think of reasons why it would be politic and wise to return to the mountains of Santa Cruz, to their own families and to Pelican Doctor's village. But how to do this and yet cling to the intense love that had only begun, so it seemed, to flower? The two wished passionately to be able to spend their lives together, and yet they were uncertain just how to go about turning their wishes into fulfillment.

At noon of their second day in the mountains, they rested their ponies and surveyed the canyon before them. A trail they'd been following was now all but imperceptible, indicating that neither Indian people nor deer very often came this way. Indeed, the canyon bottom ahead of them appeared to be nothing so much as a wild garden of boulders of gigantic proportion.

"I don't think the horses can make it any farther," H.V. said. "We'll have to turn back. . . ."

"Without really seeing the mountains? Then why did we come so far . . . why did we leave . . . home?"

Her astonishing gray eyes pierced him—caused him to search for words, for explanations. He felt weak, ineffectual, a guide who hadn't the slightest idea where he was going.

"That side canyon," he said, "about a mile or so back. It must lead down from the plateau above us. What we could see, at least, was nothing like this. We'll follow the tributary up out of this astonishing—hole. Well, isn't that what it is?"

Califia drew her pony up alongside his.

"We're going to have to go back, aren't we? I mean, all the

way back. We can't live here, Homer. I don't even think those Indians—the Yokuts—come up here. We're going to have to go home—and then fight for our rights. There's no one can tell us we can't be together . . . as man and wife."

"I don't want to think about going back, not yet," H.V. replied. "I promised you we'd see the Sierra, and we haven't done that yet—only from a distance. But we're close now."

They turned their saddle ponies downstream, returning as they'd come, and then moving off northward into the lateral canyon Homer Virgil had spoken of. Here, despite occasional cascades in the stream, the horses were able to move along easily enough, and by afternoon the two riders emerged into a dense forest through which the stream meandered.

Then, coming through a screen of dogwood and alder, they found themselves in the midst of a grove of gigantic trees whose heavy bark was the same red as the big trees of the coastal mountains. But the foliage was different, more like that of a cedar. And the girths were truly amazing—with some few individuals perhaps twice the heft of the biggest redwoods either Califia or Homer Virgil had ever seen.

"Great God!" H.V. exclaimed. "These . . . things . . . are astonishing. That tree over there—I'd say it's as large as our San Lorenzo mill itself."

"Impossible to cut one down," Califia said. "And even if we could fell such a tree, what would we do with it? Unless someday there were to be cities in the San Joaquin Valley, there's no reason why anyone would even think to. . . ."

Homer Virgil laughed bitterly.

"Remember," he said. "This is the human race we're talking about. The little creatures with the large brains and a yearning to be like gods. Shall we not cut these *maderas rojas*, these *arboles de gigantescoses California*? I think there are men who will find a way to cut them down for no other reason than to prove it can be done. Think of it, Califia. Think how many bundles of shingles such a tree as one of these might make."

"Such trees contain the spirits of those who've died and have gone to Other Side Camp. Perhaps there are giants who live in these mountains—and that's why the trees are so large."

"We could simply stay here," H.V. suggested. "In that giant—the one fire hollowed out. The space is large enough to build a home inside. You and I, Califia, we could live in a tree—we'd become friendly with the spirits of the dead who inhabit the redwoods. I speak seriously. Listen to me. There's a great deal of game—we've seen animals all day long. And we could plant things in an open meadow—raise whatever we need."

"Until we run out of gunpowder," Califia said, reaching toward H.V., taking his hand. "No, we'll have to go back, all right. But they can't separate us unless we're weak—and allow them to do it. What law says we can't be together? Perhaps we've created the entire problem—perhaps if we'd simply been open about it, if we'd talked to our parents, told them what we wished to do. . . ."

"There are other options," H.V. suggested. "Yerba Buena, San Jose, Monterey—we could survive in any of those places."

But the conversation was cut short when they became aware of a great golden-furred grizzly sow and two young ones—a trio oblivious to the humans on horses and seemingly not even curious. H.V. grasped his Kentucky rifle, and he and Califia watched as the mother bear and her offspring took their time, ambling the length of the giant grove and finally disappearing into the forest of pine and fir beyond.

The lovers slept the night, their camp fire at the base of one of the huge redwoods, the flames sending up a trickle of thin, gray-blue smoke that dispersed among the foliage of the great branches a hundred feet above their heads. Though Homer Virgil and Califia were troubled, uncertain which way to turn, what action to take next, whether to return to their familiar situation or to continue their trek into the great unknown, they fell gladly into one another's arms, finding both comfort and wild exhilaration in the full discovery of one another's bodies.

Homer Virgil nursed at Califia's breasts as though he were an infant, and she, for her part, embarrassed though she was, could not keep her hands away from his genitals.

"One was formed to fit the other," she whispered after he had slowly penetrated her. "Now that I have you inside me, I'll never let you out. I'll keep you prisoner until someone comes along and throws cold water on us, the way we do with the camp dogs when they get stuck together."

"If you get me to laughing, Califia, I'll wilt—and then we'll have to stop playing."

"Go ahead, Homer Virgil. Try to wilt. I don't think you could do it even if you wanted to."

"Then I suppose I'll have to ride this mare until I fall asleep from exhaustion. . . . "

"Stop talking and concentrate. Blow in my ear the way you did last night—that makes me tingle inside. Are you all the way into me yet?"

He thrust forward from the haunches, and she sucked in her breath, making a long moaning sound that verged on a giggle.

"Again . . . Don't stop, Homer Virgil. I want you to ride me all night long. I'll be your night-mare."

Sensing that she would go on babbling otherwise, he stopped her mouth with his. And then their two bodies began to move in unison, began to thrust and withdraw in a language that both of them realized was as ancient as the human race itself—no, as ancient as life.

He was collapsed over her when she opened her eyes next—and their bodies were slippery with love sweat. Again, she felt she'd been to the edge of something amazing but had then withdrawn—not in disappointment but in contentment. She'd heard the older women laughing and talking—*it* would take awhile, that was the wisdom of the Ohlone women—one should be patient. The men tried, but they needed to learn. Only when they were able to be patient themselves were they able to confer the gift they sought to present and the woman sought to receive.

High up, in openings between the great trees, Califia could see a handful of stars—like an Ohlone bracelet adorned with numerous dentalium shells—just those few stars, suspended, relentless and distant against a setting of perfect blackness.

They rode westward, and crossing a saddle between oak and pine ridges, they could see an immense distance, out beyond the big valley of the San Joaquin to the long, purple rims of the Coast Range, the solitary peak of *Monte Diabolo* distinctly noticeable. It was not that they'd given up their shared dream of living together, of being man and wife together, but rather that they recognized the only genuine possibility of fulfillment lay in a return to the world they'd always known. Indeed, would there be any real resistance at all? Who had spoken specifically against what they would propose to their elders? Perhaps no one had directly laid down such a prohibition, and yet H.V. and Califia knew—*knew* that this new set of conditions between them, their being not merely friends but lovers as well and ultimately man and wife, would not be gratefully received by those close to them.

Whatever you think, Califia, in the final analysis, you're not one of the boys. You and Homer have got to stop wrestling around that way. I realize that you and H.V. are thick as thieves, and that's all good and well, but . . .

Ah, little Califia, you must look ahead to a time when some handsome young man on a big white horse, perhaps someone like Alvarado himself, will come here to court you. The time of childhood will soon pass.

And you, Homer Virgil, don't you wish to go to a great university to study? How could you ever be happy to live the limited life your father has led? There are worlds of opportunity ahead, if only you will seize the moment. There's a tide in the affairs of men. . . .

You kids weren't raised to be kissing cousins, after all.

Sometimes H.V. and Califia talked as they rode and sometimes they were silent, with each laboring separately under a fog of despair and a sense of the world's inherent unfairness—especially with regard to the designs of young people in love.

They passed out of the zone of ponderosa pines and black oaks and down into a region where the vegetation more nearly resembled the lower portions of the Coast Range, except that the hills were rocky and spotted with ungainly pines with gray-green needles. They followed a little river now—a river that at times of winter storms was obviously a raging torrent, as evidenced by the water-worn boulders high up away from the bed and by logs and clots of dead brush that had been deposited by the most recent floodings. In places alder and willow grew close by the stream's banks, and a profusion of grapevines netted among the branches of these trees and also over the drifts of gravels close to the water's edge.

The sun dropped westward, at length vanishing behind the rims of the Coast Range and turning the few streamers of cloud above the summits a glorious wash of crimson and gold, so that H.V. toyed with the idea that the Divine Spirit had grown tired of the present world and, out of sheer boredom, had set it ablaze. They detected an odor of smoke in the air—possibly, they surmised, the result of wildfire out in the late-summer brown grasses of the San Joaquin Valley.

"You don't suppose we're about to stumble into some Yokuts village, one that's occupied, do you?" H.V. asked, trying to make his tone seem casual. "I'm not sure those folks would be particularly interested in welcoming strangers. . . ."

Califia breathed deeply, attempting to analyze the combination of faint odors. Was there also, along with smoke, a smell of meat being roasted? She pulled her young stallion to a halt, looked toward H.V. for confirmation.

"Cooking fires?" he asked, his voice now little more than a whisper. "Our luck's turning sour, Califia. . . ."

Then a coyote *yip-yipped* close at hand, and they knew they'd been detected.

"Upslope!" H.V. hissed.

Califia drew her pistol and leaned forward along her pony's back, urged the animal into a wild run through shadowed tangles of grapevines and willow brush and greasewood. She heard Homer Virgil cry out, his horse plunging along behind hers, but she couldn't tell what he said.

As twilight thickened, they emerged into rock-studded grasslands and were obliged to slow their mounts to no more than a brisk walk. Califia detected a trail that appeared to meander its way upslope—a pathway doubtless utilized by tule elk and deer and antelope.

"Can you see anyone behind us?" Califia called back to H.V.—but whatever his answer was, she couldn't hear it. Only when they reached the summit of a low ridge perhaps two miles from the place of danger beside the little river did Califia draw up her mount.

Homer Virgil, she realized, was slumped forward in his saddle.

"H.V. what?"

"Arrow . . . arrow in my damned shoulder," he replied. "It's bleeding pretty bad, I'm afraid. . . . But keep moving—we can't stop yet; they'd find us in the morning, sure as hell itself."

Despite intense pain, Homer Virgil was able to keep up with Califia as they took advantage of the rapidly dwindling light to put the greatest possible distance between themselves and the wild Indians with whom they'd come into unwelcome contact. They passed from one drainage into another, riding cautiously downslope, until they came at length to a rocky ravine coiled over by grapevines and tangles of blackberries. A meager flow of water whispered among the stones. Here they made camp—since near-total darkness made further riding a greater danger than remaining where they were.

In trying to dismount, H.V. fell—and let out a wordless cry of pain. Califia was at his side immediately, helping him to his feet and onto a nearly flat outcropping of stone.

"No fire, no fire," he said. "Califia, you'll draw them right in. . . ."

"I have to be able to see what I'm doing if I want to get that Yokuts arrow out of your shoulder, Homer. It has to come out or you'll die of blood poisoning. You know that as well as I do."

Within moments she'd drawn together a little pile of dead leaves and twigs, and with a patented fire striker and a bit of black powder, the flames jumped up.

"See if you can pull the goddamned thing out of me."

Califia placed a few larger pieces of wood on the fire and then knelt beside H.V. She cut open his shirt, placed one knee against his back and grasped the short-shafted arrow with both hands, counted out loud to five, and then threw her weight backward. H.V. uttered a long, wordless gurgle of agony, but the shaft remained embedded in his shoulder. The arrow had slipped through her hands.

"God help me, I'm going to have to dig the thing out. Maybe it's stuck in the bone—or down in the muscle. Or maybe I should just cut off the shaft and—"

"Could be poisoned for all we know. Is there a lump—can you feel the head?"

"Yes . . . yes. There it is—up against the shoulder blade. But I can't . . . cut . . . into you. . . ."

"You've got to, Califia. We're nearly a hundred miles from the San Lorenzo—three days of riding, if I could manage to stay on horseback. Three days with this thing in me, I'm as good as dead. Should have brought some *aguardiente*. A few swigs, and they say a man can't feel a damned thing. Go ahead. Get it over with. I'll try not to yell so loud our new friends'll find us."

Califia held the blade of her hunting knife to the flames, and H.V. moved around with his back to the fire, so that she'd be able to see what she was about, more or less.

She quickly cut away the arrow's spline, all but an inch or so. And then, bracing herself, she slipped the point of her blade into the ragged puncture wound the arrowhead had made and eased it down until she felt the head. She twisted her knife back and forth to position it in under the stone point.

Homer gasped in agony, went rigid, relaxed.

"Hold on, Homer Virgil. I've nearly got it. Oh sweet little Jesus, I hate this—I hate doing this to you! But I can get the head out—I'm positive. Can you bear it?"

"I . . . I . . . think so. . . ." he replied, his voice slurred by pain.

A moment later Califia was holding up the bloody point to him to look at, but Homer Virgil Olivo was no longer conscious.

Her sensation of triumph faded immediately. Blood was flowing out of the wound—and for a moment she couldn't think what to do.

Kerchief. . . .

She removed the bandanna from about her throat and used the cloth to stanch the bleeding. Then, having placed her blade into the fire until the steel was nearly as hot as a brandishing iron, she removed the kerchief and lay the flat of the blade to the open wound.

Olivo winced, his head shaking and his voice taking on the sound of an animal in intense pain. His shoulders hunched forward, and he sucked for air. Mercifully, however, he did not regain consciousness. Califia crouched beside him, strained to detect the rhythm of his breathing. Only when she heard that sound, and was certain of it, did she begin to weep—very quietly at first, and then more loudly, so that she had to bite at the insides of her mouth in order to stifle the outburst.

Homer's life, he dimly realized, was entirely in Califia Beard's hands—for an infection of some sort had possessed him, whether the result of a substance the Yokuts had applied to the point of the arrow or from some other cause stemming from his wound. He couldn't see clearly, and it was extremely difficult for him to vocalize. Desperately, he clung to his horse, using his entire energy to maintain balance as the creature jolted its way along.

Then it occurred to him that his life might already be forfeit, that he could very well be dying. Perhaps he had indeed sinned by lusting after his cousin—by violating the trust that those who loved him had placed in him. Worse yet, he'd corrupted her as well, seduced her, was cause sufficient for Califia's giving in to her own dark, sensual side.

How could he have stooped so low as to have done such a thing? How could he have been so blind, so appallingly obtuse as to have fallen in love?

Then it seemed to him that he wasn't on horseback at all, but rather striding high above, on the backs of those great Sierras which he hadn't in fact seen except at significant distance—a high, rocky landscape dotted with small blue lakes and punctuated by domes of gray-orange stone—a zone that might have been accidentally damaged in the time of creation, that or washed across by immense floods, as in Noah's time. In this mountain realm where he wandered, the air was different—more fragrant, almost intoxicating, as though volatile oils of various sorts were being exuded into a sun-drenched atmosphere.

From time to time Homer Virgil was half aware of Califia's voice. She was calling to him, calling out his name. But when he attempted to answer, incomprehensible syllables issued from his mouth.

He stood outside himself and watched his own actions. He saw himself pick up a felling axe and whipsaw and a whiskey bottle filled with lamp oil—he saw himself begin to hew away at a tree— not merely a redwood but one of the new giants they'd found, he and Califia Beard, the woman he loved and would always love, and she was there, watching.

Moments later she was gone, and he was solitary among these unbelievable red-clad giants that lived in the mysterious interior mountains of Alta California. The calm was immense, overpowering, yes, and hushed with a quiet almost tangible. Red trunks rose like the columns of some ancient Greek temple, but on a scale so much greater that comparison was absurd. Bars of light fell through curtains of foliage, as though God's own fingers were playing softly on the strings of an invisible flamenco guitar, music all the more intense and compelling for the fact that one couldn't actually hear it. Insects, when one gazed upward, winked in the spars of light, materializing, dematerializing, blinking like tiny, instantaneous stars. How old were such trees? Was it possible? They were ancient when Jesus the Nazorean was hung upon a cross—were already perhaps a thousand, two thousand years of age. Perhaps they were large when the world itself was formed—perhaps God had created them half grown.

Then H.V. perceived music he could indeed hear—wind drifting, gusting overhead, unfelt in the silence of the grove beneath, perhaps like the sound of that Niagara Falls he'd read of, perhaps like the hissings of great volcanos in a land of perpetual ice. And there were cries of blue jays and gray jays, of white and red-headed woodpeckers, small shrieks of angry squirrels and pip-pip-pippings of chipmunks and ground squirrels.

Quite suddenly, he perceived himself alone in a vast emptiness punctuated by gigantic stumps. Where were the trees? What astonishing force had worked its will upon the king-redwoods and left such devastation?

"It's wrong, it's wrong," he kept saying, "to murder such giants. . . ."

At the same time, he could feel an axe's heft in his hands, he could feel rhythmic movements of arms, back, shoulders, and he brought the wide blade into contact with a last remaining tree, one that had somehow escaped the devastation visited upon all the others. His shining blade bit deep into the wood, and the wound poured out red-colored sap—no, not sap, blood. For this wasn't a tree he was cutting down, he realized, but a person, a titan, the leg of some mighty presence, some god of the mountains.

Where was Califia? He could hear her calling to him, but her voice seemed to be receding into blue distance.

Then he could not hear her at all.

CHAPTER EIGHT

Courting Juanita

[1836:]

DON QUIXOTE WORKED its way north into the narrow channel
of Petaluma River, with Bill Beard and his apprentice navigator
dropping anchor just above the mouth of San Antonio Creek.
The ends of a pair of hawsers were dragged ashore and tied
off to bankside cottonwoods, so as to secure the schooner,
and immediately the men began the task of hauling to the mill
the machinery Larkin had secured. With both the new crew
recruited from Branciforte, San Lorenzo, and Monterey, and
Vallejo's retrained *vaqueros* working diligently, the task of
moving the heavy forgework was accomplished within the
space of a day.

Within another twenty-four hours various gears, pulleys,
and so forth were in place. Bill Beard and R.B.R. Cooper set
about positioning their prized Woolf compound steam engine,
in which (as Jean Paul Martin had earlier explained) steam at
high pressure was used in one cylinder and then, after expansion and reduction of pressure, it was ducted to another cylinder, allowing for further expansion. The Woolf people were
already manufacturing engines with three and even four cyl-

inders, as Martin had noted—and who knew how far such modern technology might ultimately go?

By nightfall the wood-burning steam generator was also in place, its pipes connected to the Woolf. Beard and Cooper were of a mind to await the light of morning before starting the apparatus, but Calvin argued there was nothing to be gained in postponing matters. The older men laughed, grumbled, and went along with Calvin. Wood was set to burning, and water was introduced. Then everyone stood around (including Maria Plumas, who'd brought out a big pot of steaming red beans for the men), waiting none too patiently for pressure to build to a degree sufficient for operation of the Woolf.

The workers scooped out pewter cups full of beans, half drinking and half chewing the highly seasoned concoction, and waited for the critical moment. At length Bill Beard threw the operating lever, and the steam engine came to life, whooshing and hissing and admirably turning its big flywheel.

"Hit the whistle, Cal!" Bill Beard yelled to his son.

A protracted, bellowing yowl went out across the waters of the tule-lined Petaluma River and into thickening twilight. High on the forested ridges to the west, deer, elk, mountain lions, coyotes, and a sleepy grizzly or two must have wondered what prodigy of the animal world it was that possessed so resonant and powerful a voice, but only the grizzly must have felt reasonable confidence in the face of this considerable potential adversary.

For the men, however, the steam whistle's howl marked a signal moment, one which justified minor celebration. Beard produced a keg of British rum, and members of both crews were allowed a drink.

"By the great horn spoon," Cooper sang out, "with this baby we'll power whatever saws we need. All right, Bill the Sawyer, let's get some damned big redwoods down here. We'll show these Californio sticks-in-the-mud a thing or two about making lumber, by damn!"

"With lever sufficient," Bill Beard grinned, "we can move the earth itself. But with the aid of noble Woolfie, here, that old Greek's damnable lever doesn't have to be quite so long. *Power!* That's the name of the human game. If a man's got sufficient power at his fingertips, there's hardly a thing imaginable he can't take a crack at. Calvin, my boy, I tell you it's a brand-new world! Set up a few mills like this one, and we can be purveyors of quality timber to half of civilization! Mr. Cooper, are you by any chance familiar with the pre-Socratic philosophers?"

"Can't say as I am, you windy barstard. Vermonters are all alike, that's what I say. Here, have another shot of rum before the mosquitoes and the night air get you. Maria Isabella, you stick close to me, now. Our lads haven't been in bed with a woman for a month, and with the demon run in 'em, they'd hump a bush if they thought it had a snake in it. If you're going to have anybody's litter, it's damned well going to be mine!"

The Spanish-Indian girl smiled, winked at Calvin Beard.

"Señor Cooper," Maria Isabella Eleanora Plumas replied, "you get drunk—pass out. After that then I will take care of the baby here, El Niño."

Bill Beard, with Calvin now at the helm of Don Quixote, transported Mariano Vallejo's men back across San Pablo Bay and then up the Napa River inlet to Rancho Vallejo.

Mariano had heard the wail of the Woolf engine—though the distance, straight line, from one point to the other was perhaps fifteen miles. Apparently the sound had carried quite well through the twilight.

For his part, Calvin was awaiting the appearance of Rosa Vallejo, but that young lady was not to show up. The news Vallejo had to relate, in fact, was utterly shocking. Nearly everyone at the Rancho had been hit by cholera, and half a dozen all told were dead—including the fair Rosa, who was buried among family members in the Vallejo cemetery, on a low rise dotted with Australian blue gum trees, a hundred yards or so from the mansion.

"And Juanita?" Calvin asked Vallejo himself. "I mean, your other daughters and your niece? Did they survive?"

"It's a very sad time, Señor Calvin. I have never felt old before—but now I am just that, el anciano. When sickness comes, not even learned doctors can do anything about it, and in such a place as this, far from the great cities and the places of learning, there is no doctor at all. There is only God, and so we must pray to Him and hope that extensions of our lives are included in His plans. My daughter is gone, and several of my servants as well. But the Lord has blessed me and spared the rest of those who are dear to me. My little niece, who will one day be Señora Albion, she was very ill for a time, but now she's well again and in good hands. Death is about us very often, Calvin Beard, and it is best that we never forget this unpleasant truth. No man has cause to celebrate, since death may come to him at any moment and in any one of a thousand ways. Only the dead themselves are truly fortunate—fortunate, at least, if they have lived well and in the spirit of the Good Book and the Holy Faith. Then they will go to be with the Father of All of Us."

A wave of utter relief swept over Calvin, this sensation followed a moment later by a terrible sense of bitterness with regard to Rosa Vallejo's death. And guilt—he had in the length of time it took Mariano Vallejo to tell the tale, Calvin realized, already come to see Rosa as a sacrificial victim, slain so that Juanita might live. If God needed victims, if that's what God was, then it was pointless to pray to Him, All-Powerful or not. Indeed, it was immoral to pray to such a Being.

"The Lord sends us these blows," Vallejo continued, "and we must learn to accept and to be thankful for what has truly been allowed to us. If we're given our health, and if most of our family is well, then we should be humble and thankful."

Juanita did not make an appearance in the main hall, and Calvin found himself reduced to a state of utter misery. Perhaps the young lady, in the aftermath of the tragedy of Rosa's death, had chosen simply to end her foolishness and to resign herself to the prospect of being the mistress of a great rancho, similar to the one her uncle controlled.

In the pleasant darkness of the guest facilities that night, Calvin couldn't sleep—not with the issue of his love for Juanita unresolved. However comfortable the bed might have been which Vallejo provided for his American acquaintance and that man's half-Indio son, there was to be scant rest this night. At length, candle-holder in hand, Calvin rose and went outside into the courtyard. He relieved himself at the latrine; but thereafter, rather than returning to the guest quarters, he found himself drawn to that place where *grandfather grape* grew up the side of the house, providing a ladderway that Juanita had once descended, into his own arms. What a raven-haired, almond-eyed beauty could climb, he reasoned, another (albeit less exquisite human creature) could climb as well.

He stared upward to a flickering light in the window. He waited a long while, attempting to summon the will (or gall) to climb to that window—to tap on the pane—to see the face which he, in the fever of his nineteenth year, had construed to be the aspect of an angel—a creature so lovely and so without mortal faults and disfigurements as to be almost beyond mortal possession.

No. She's constructed of human flesh, just like me. She's no prettier, say, than Mariposa—or even my sis, for that matter. Her nose looks as though some invisible finger were pressing back against the tip. That poem H.V. likes to quote—Shakespeare's, is it? His or Byron's. I grant I never saw a goddess go;/My mistress, when she walks, treads on the ground. *Shakespeare, that's who it is.* O, never say that I was false of heart,/Though absence seemed my flame to qualify. . . . *Absence. I am guilty of having been in the wrong place at the wrong time. And that's true, but I'm here now—here and afraid to act.*

Calvin carefully set down his candle-holder in an area of open soil and then grasped the heavy vine and pulled himself upward, found footholds, and within a matter of moments was perched like some oversized, ungainly bird outside Juanita's window. He stared in through the glass to where a pair of candles were burning. It was clear to him now that the room was unoccupied, the burning candles apparently votives for the benefit of the soul of the departed Rosa Vallejo.

Impossible to imagine Rosa dead—that good-natured, intense presence, taking delight in allowing for a tryst between her younger cousin and Calvin Beard. . . .

But where was Juanita?

The windows to either side, though he might well have gained access to them by means of crawling along a two-foot-wide ledge, were unlit—as would be appropriate if those within were asleep. But surely Juanita knew by now of his presence at Rancho Vallejo; and even if she'd been instructed not to make a public appearance, surely she'd be waiting for him to contact her. How else except by means of the big vine?

Disconsolate, Calvin Beard made his way back down the ropy tangle. Already, by late summer, the grape leaves were beginning to relax their grips in anticipation of the changing season—and Calvin's movements sent drying foliage sidling away into darkness punctuated only by light from the candle-holder he'd left below.

Mission Dolores, in the village of Yerba Buena? Apparently Vallejo had sent her there, partly because of the girl's grief over the loss of her friend, and partly because the mission would provide training to one who was ultimately to be the wife of a great and powerful man.

Over breakfast, Bill Beard remarked on the fact that none of Mariano's daughters seemed to be present about the rancho, and Señor Vallejo explained that, in the aftermath of the deadly cholera and in fearful anticipation that the disease might break out once again, he and Señora Vallejo had thought best to send the girls away for a time. For one thing, the nuns at the mission were reported to be very fine teachers—and school was a civilized nicety of which his girls had all too often been deprived.

During the brief voyage across San Pablo Bay to the Petaluma channel, Beard shared this information with his son.

Whereas the senior Beard had presumed his son would stay on at the Petaluma mill, for a couple of months anyway, remaining there now seemed to be utterly antithetical to Calvin's wishes.

Once last-minute business arrangements had been settled with R.B.R. Cooper, Bill Beard entered into an anticipated *deep discussion* with his son.

"Father, I have to see Juanita—at least one last time. I love her. Yes, I think that's true. How can I allow her to go off to San Diego if she feels the same about me as I do about her? She'll never be happy with anyone but me."

"Sure of that, are you?" Bill Beard asked, at the same time studying his son's intense brown eyes—brown, just like Sea-gull's eyes. Often happy-go-lucky, at other times Cal evidenced a terrible intensity, almost a sense of the tragic. Perhaps Raymondo encouraged all three of the kids to read too many of those translated Greek and French plays.

Pretend enough of a thing, and you start acting as though it were true. You turn reality into a dream. . . .

"If Pelican Doctor had chosen someone else to be Mom's husband," Calvin protested, "what would you have done? Kidnap her, I'll bet."

"It's that serious, then? Well, Son, I actually tried to get your mother to run away with me, but—"

"And you'd have done it, too. Everyone says I'm just like you—then how can you expect me to give up on Juanita? She's the one I'm determined to marry. Dad, I want you to set me ashore at Yerba Buena. I can handle things from that point on. Don't say otherwise—I'll just jump ship. You said you'd back me. . . ."

Bill Beard nodded, stroked his gray chin whiskers, nodded again.

Jump ship? Haven't I taught this kid any better than that? A man can't leap overboard and expect to solve his problems. Except in my own case, that is. Back then, things were different. Besides, fate was calling me. . . .

"What if the lass says she's decided to hitch up with that gent from down south—Albion, is it?"

"She wouldn't do it!"

"Good and well, good and well. All the same, what if she has? Do you care for her enough to respect her wishes, even if they don't include you?"

"Dad, Juanita wouldn't make such a decision. We—"

"You've got to learn to deal with reality, Calvin, my boy. Reality's a hard teacher sometimes, but it's the only one a human critter can trust. It's no good to make things up an' then start believing them. Set your feet on solid rock, and then. . . . What I'm trying to say is—maybe, just maybe, all you two ever had was a harmless little flirtation."

Calvin buried his head in his hands.

"I *hate* this goddamned world!" he said. "Juanita, she's not like that, not shallow. It's just that she's powerless—kind of a castoff, and your friend Vallejo's dealing with her the way he would one of his horses or cattle. If I show her a way, Juanita'll come with me—I know it. And then Mariano Vallejo'll be wanting you to return her to him so that he can complete his *sale of livestock* to the old geezer in San Diego."

"Albion?" Bill Beard asked. "I thought you said he was a young fellow, about my age. Listen, Son. I said I'd back you, but I'm sure as hell not going to hold the net while you're luring her to jump in. If the little gal decides to come on her own, however—why, that's a different matter. Mariano can understand a thing like that, just the same as I can. All right— you're eighteen and I guess that means you're a man now. You look big enough, anyhow. You up to what you're about? Cal, it's *man's work*, this courtship business you're undertaking, and I don't want to find out the *guardias del orden* have stretched your neck. Seagull'd stab me to death if she figured I let you go get yourself killed—and that would kill her, too. You stand ashore at Yerba Buena, then, and you buy yourself a couple of riding horses and a pack animal. If Señorita Juanita Ortega wishes to accompany you to Hotochruk village, why, fine. If she doesn't, you get on back down the coast. You hear me now?"

Calvin Beard stood up, touched his fingers to his chin, and squinted out to where *Don Quixote* was moored in the tide-water channel. A drift of gray gulls moved with the air, but then a pair of them floated down, alighting on the schooner's foremast.

"She'll come," he replied.

Once in Yerba Buena, Calvin Beard did as his father had suggested. First, he took a room in the boardinghouse, and secondly he acquired three horses—a pair of riding ponies and a pack animal, the three of them complete with saddles and saddlebags. In his pocket he carried a hand-drawn chart the elder Beard had sketched, a map showing the general features of the land, including wagon trails, major streams, and mountains. Much of the topography, of course, was already quite familiar to Cal, who'd been fascinated by maps and charts of all sorts since early childhood. As to the long *Península del San Francisco*, he fancied he knew the terrain virtually by heart. Even though he'd not traversed a good portion of the land, hadn't he seen it from shipboard, both from the one extremity and from the other?

The presence of a tall, young, and well-dressed stranger did not go unnoticed, of course, and indeed Cal made no attempt to conceal his identity. Carrying letters of introduction written upon Olivo & Beard letterhead, he made a point of circulating freely throughout the town. If everyone in Yerba Buena, he reasoned, was puzzled by his presence, then surely that presence would become known to a certain señorita housed within the confines of Mission Dolores.

On Sunday morning Calvin attended mass. While he neither received communion nor took confession, he was nonetheless able to make eye contact with the object of his dreams. In short, he'd been able to arrange to sit on the pew bench directly behind Juanita Ortega and the Vallejo girls. From this position he spoke her name, causing her to turn about, a startled expression on her face.

At the conclusion of the liturgy, as the two of them rose from their respective benches, he pressed a note into her hand. He exited quickly and made his way back to his quarters at the village boardinghouse, and there he waited, none too patiently, until the hour of the proposed tryst arrived. But would she come to him? Would the Vallejo girls alert some mother superior, who would then require that Señorita Ortega be confined to her quarters for the remainder of the Sabbath?

At the appointed hour of four in the afternoon, Calvin Beard rode past the mission complex, taking time to place himself within full view of any who might be watching. From there he proceeded the three miles or so down to the shore, sandy in some places, rocky in others, and everywhere swarmed over by gulls and cormorants and great-winged pelicans. Across the green, windblown waves, just a few miles northwest behind the dark green of Marin Peninsula, rose broad-shouldered *Monte Tamalpais*. At the moment, long bands of vapors were trailing from its slopes, and offshore, out over the Pacific itself, thick gray fog hovered like some sort of malign beast.

Calvin dismounted, tethered his horse, buttoned his jacket, and thrust his hands into the pockets of his trousers. September or not, the wind coming in off the sea was distinctly chill.

He took note of half a dozen Indian children fishing from a projecting ledge of black stone, most likely in the hope of taking rock cod—or possibly they were trying to lure in a few

of the large crabs common up and down the California coast—
to lure them with a strip of suet on a cord, tease them, bring
them up into shallow water, and then make capture with a
woven net.

Calvin paced back and forth along a well-worn pathway
amidst bush lupines and patches of bunch grass and broad
areas of white and purple blooming ice plant, while at other
times he walked the narrow beach, sandy areas interspersed
with jumbled rocks. He whistled as he walked—even forced
himself to hum a few bars of music, and again and again he
glanced upslope, across a scattering of adobe huts and makeshift barns and chicken coops, in the general direction from
which, he hoped, Juanita would appear.

Soon? Will she soon come to me?

But was it pretense, a wild hoping for something that was
simply fated not to be? What, after all, had he to offer? No
more than a boy, he had nothing of his own—no property, no
house to which he might bring a bride, no more than the
merest beginnings of a trade. Whatever it was that he was fated
to become, all that lay somewhere ahead, out in the fog-
shrouded future, stubbornly awaiting realization. And Albion?
While Cal knew virtually nothing of the man, it was clear that
the middle-aged Californio was one of the *Gente de Razón*, an
individual of means, of reputation, and possibly of genuine
power.

The whole thing was hopeless, except for one salient fact.
Fact? Calvin *hoped* for a clear and inarguable demonstration of
the truth—yes, that Juanita Ortega, magically, beyond all probability, *loved* him. But the hour was growing late. Before long
the mission church would toll vespers—a clangor of bells
echoing from the heights—the sun would begin its plunge toward heavy fog that lay offshore, and the glowing crimson
would be silently extinguished.

"Calvin? My dearest, I was afraid I'd never see you again—after
Rosa—and after Uncle Mariano sent me here—it's all coming
apart, everything, like shotten cloth that's lain out in the rain
all winter. What am I saying? This doesn't make any sense.
Will you hold me? Will you kiss me, Calvin? I'll never be able
to die happily if you won't! You aren't angry, are you?"

"Of course not—don't say foolish things. I followed you here because I love you and. . . ."

Then they were clinging to one another, desperately, hopelessly, and if the world itself had ended at that moment, they would neither have noticed nor cared.

Words were spoken, kisses given and received, and vows made. After a time Calvin assisted Juanita up onto his horse, and he proceeded to lead the animal back toward Mission Dolores. When they were within half a mile, Calvin helped Juanita to dismount, and the girl walked quickly away into the crepuscular hour, with the sky to the west a dull glowing orange hue.

At the place where they'd parted the preceding evening, they met again in the morning, just as matins bells were sounding. Juanita had brought only a precious few things with her, and these were stowed away in the saddlebags of the pack animal. Calvin then helped her to mount, and the two of them rode away southward, toward what they hoped might be a life together. From Yerba Buena the pair made their way across the San Miguel Hills toward the bare rim of San Bruno Mountain, thence across San Andreas Rift to Montara Mountain southward.

On the heights they drew their ponies to a halt and stared, wonder-struck, at the vast blue ocean, gleaming with light and curving away to the horizon.

Never, they told themselves, had they ever been so free.

Yet they would probably be pursued, and Calvin might be liable to charges of unlawful abduction. Mariano Vallejo, a powerful and influential man in Californio society, had friends, relatives, and political allies, all within a few miles, including those in command at the presidio. Word of Juanita's disappearance would spread rapidly—nor would it take anyone very long to fit the tall young stranger, one who advertised himself as a representative of Olivo & Beard, into the equation—indeed, Mariano's daughters knew well enough who he was, had seen him several times at Rancho Vallejo, and had seen him again at mass. In all likelihood, the deceased Rosa Vallejo had not been the only one of the sisters who knew something of Juanita's *infatuation*, since, as is widely accepted, sisters experience genuine difficulty in keeping secrets.

For these reasons, then, the lovers avoided the two commonly used roads, one generally following the ocean, and the other the western shore of the bay. It was possible, Calvin surmised, that a dispatch rider had been sent out—perhaps even a posse. The following morning would be a more likely time, however, and by then Calvin hoped to have vanished into the forested wilderness between their present position and Hotochruk village. They would studiously avoid such coastal villages as Pilarcitos, San Gregorio, and Pescadero.

Soon, Cal reflected, they'd be on *his* territory, in the midst of a land he knew intimately, and his possible pursuers would be at the disadvantage.

On San Vicente Creek, high in the hills above Half Moon Bay, they made camp for the night. By late afternoon banks of fog had begun to push in from the Pacific, and the night ahead promised to be uncommonly chilly. Calvin built a fire. Sitting side by side near the edge of the stream, the lovers ate jerky, parched corn, and unleavened bread. They talked for a long while—in unspoken understanding that they were postponing a moment of decision. Finally, when the fire died down for perhaps the fourth or fifth time, the subject had to be broached.

"You wish to sleep—separately?" Calvin asked. "I understand—until we're legally married, of course. That's only right. . . ."

"Perhaps," Juanita smiled, almost afraid to look directly at Calvin, "and yet it is already *frio*, quite cold. If you'll allow me to lie beside you this night, *mi marido*, I'll promise to be good. I won't even allow you to kiss me, if you think that is best. I won't allow you to put your hands on my *tetas*, though it pleases me when you do so. . . ."

"It would be all right? To sleep next to one another? Juanita, I respect you—I won't touch you until we're married, if that's what you wish."

"You are wiser than I am," Juanita Ortega replied, "and yet I think perhaps you're even more frightened. After all that's happened, though, and after you've come to the mission to rescue me, and after we've run away into the wilderness so that I won't be obliged to marry old Albion, I don't understand, not after all this, why we should worry about church rules. I don't think those nuns know about being in love—maybe they don't know about anything else, either. I'm old enough to be a woman, Calvin Beard! Rosa, she told me what to do."

"God bless," Calvin whispered. "She was a good friend to us."

"Yes, yes, that is so. She had become my older sister—she was so full of fun—she was. . . ."

"And now God has taken her."

Juanita was silent for a long moment, and then she said, "Please forgive me, God, but I don't like you very much. You cannot stand for people to be happy, and yet I'm going to be happy tonight. Will you make me happy, Calvin Beard?"

"Hush, Juanita—God may be listening. I'll try. What do you wish me to do?"

"Here," she replied, pulling their two blankets over them, and after that they hugged and kissed for a long while.

Then she said, "If I should begin to cry, Calvin, remember that it's because I'm happy. I chose my man. I chose you, Señor Calvin Beard, the first time I ever saw you."

The twigs and sections of pine limb Calvin had put on the fire blazed for a time and then died down. When nothing but orange-red coals remained in the dark, the two of them, tangled in one another's arms, slept close beside San Vicente Creek. A half-moon, rising late, was unable to penetrate the thick fog which had rolled up from the sea, but the light refracted through mists. Had the lovers been awake, they would have observed a glowing coyote, stepping almost on tiptoes, as it edged up to where the two of them were lying, sniffed momentarily at their blankets, and then melted away into moon-suffused grayness.

CHAPTER NINE

Raymondo's Decision

[1836, 1837:]

AFTER WAITING A day or two in the hope that Homer Virgil and Califia might return, Raymondo Olivo and Pelican Doctor and four other Ohlone men rode eastward, intent upon discovering the whereabouts of the love-struck cousins. The search party had no significant information, nothing to guide them except intuition and the fact that Raymondo recalled that his son had often asked questions about the big mountains on the other side of San Joaquin Valley and had been intensely disappointed that no substantial information was available concerning the area.

"How," H.V. had once asked in frustration, "am I to believe that any *considerable cordillera* exists, when all the evidence is hearsay and reports of those who have merely observed from a great distance? Perhaps you and Uncle Bill saw a mirage."

"Homer, my son," the father had replied, "I too am curious. I don't know why I've never taken time to go there. Perhaps we should explore those mountains, you and I."

Bobcat Who Limps, an Ohlone who volunteered for the search party, recalled several conversations with H.V.—times when H.V. had told him about the Lewis and Clark expedition, and about people named Charbonneau and Sacagawea and their son Pompey, and about how Clark was utterly appalled by what seemed to him the perpetual rains of Oregon. H.V. even speculated about the likelihood that the Sierra Nevada of eastern Alta California might be simply a portion of those Rocky Mountains that the American exploratory expedition crossed on their way to the Pacific. H.V. inquired whether Bobcat Who Limps actually knew anyone who'd ever been across the *Valle del San Joaquin* and up into the *Sierra Nevada*. Further, Bobcat insisted, young Olivo seemed at times almost obsessed with the idea of going to those mountains and possibly living there, once even suggesting that the Ohlones should migrate to the Sierra and live away from the Californios, as in the Old Times.

Raymondo shook his head.

"Me, I think my son and my niece probably rode south, perhaps to Monterey. Maybe they supposed Jean Paul Martin would give them a place to live—or put them on one of his ships and allow them to sail away to South America or some other such foreign place—perhaps to Puerto Villarta or to Mazatlan—or just some little village far down on the Baja, or to Cabo San Lucas."

"I didn't realize H.V. and Califia had eyes for each other," Bobcat said. "For a while Homer seemed interested in Butterfly, just like all the rest of us, even Calvin."

Pelican Doctor smiled.

"I've noticed that the young men seem to follow that girl as though she were a camp dog in heat. Does Mariposa have some kind of magic? Some of the other girls her age are prettier, I think."

Bobcat Who Limps grinned.

"Butterfly, she looks like someone who was born to make love. I think it's the way she walks. . . ."

"Yes," Pelican Doctor agreed, "some women walk strangely, as though they really wished to lie down . . . with someone. I'm old now, but I remember how it is, Bobcat. Calvin, so my other son-in-law tells me, is smitten with a Californio girl who lives on a great rancho, only she's been promised to another, one who can pay a large bride-price. Perhaps this man is even someone as old as Raymondo here, or me. Anyway, Calvin no longer competes for Miss Butterfly. Soon she will choose some-one."

"I hope she picks me," Bobcat laughed. "I'd pay a high price for that girl."

The other three Ohlones, all married men, grinned and made hooting sounds.

One man in his thirties, a warrior called Tunnel Spider, remarked casually that he was thinking about acquiring a sec-ond wife, a young, pretty one, and that he'd been hoarding valuable items so that he'd be ready when the time came. Perhaps, he said, he'd speak to Butterfly's father, old Spotted Fox.

"Mariposa will never wish to share a lodge—and a hus-band—with another woman," Bobcat Who Limps protested. "No, I think she'll choose me, and then I'll speak with Spotted Fox myself. Spotted Fox won't force her to marry against her will."

"It is better for everyone when a man has more than one wife," Tunnel Spider laughed.

"All this talk," Raymondo complained, "and yet none of it has to do with where we should search for my son and my niece. Pelican Doctor, how do you say? Should we ride south?"

Before speaking, the broad-shouldered head chief pursed his lips, so that they oddly resembled freshly dug root of leop-ard lily.

"South . . . but not to Monterey. No, if I were Homer and Califia, I'd go to the Sur Rivers and then into the Ventana Mountains. The redwoods are thick there, and the *barrancas* are deep and branch often. No one could ever find me in those mountains. If Homer Virgil and Califia wish to live together—and not return to their own people—then I think they'd go to the Ventanas. But I believe they'll come home of their own accord."

"I shouldn't disagree with the chief," Bobcat said, "and yet it's true what I said before. H.V. spoke often about how he'd like to cross the great valley and explore the inland mountains. Califia spoke of it, too. We all did, I guess, because H.V. made us think about it. He loves to speak of the things he's read in his books."

Raymondo glanced at Bobcat Who Limps and then said,

"The one direction we haven't thought of is north, toward Yerba Buena. For certain, H.V. and Califia haven't gone west, not unless they've acquired their own version of *Don Quixote*. Thus, it would seem only reasonable to suppose that—"

"Why would Califia and Homer wish to go to Yerba Buena?" Pelican Doctor asked. "To the Dolores Mission? Our two young people wouldn't find a good life there, even though you've told me the missions are now secularized, and not as they were long ago, when I was obliged to stay there. Those *fathers*, they wished to take my name away from me and force me to learn lessons from their *Holy Book*, just as they did with you, Raymondo. The priests tried to give me a number instead of a name. No, I don't believe my grandchildren would go near any of the missions. Perhaps they'd buy some cattle and build a small farm."

"*Maldito sea, maldito sea!*" Olivo said in obvious frustration. "There are too many possibilities. Nevertheless, I propose that we ride north, north on the bad wagon road along the crest of Santa Cruz Mountains. *El que no arriesga no gana*—if one makes no attempt, one will not succeed. So we'll inquire of everyone we meet, and if the God of Luck is with us, we'll find the rascals in time to save them from themselves."

Pelican Doctor pursed his lips once again.

"I am just an old man," he said. "What do I know? On the other hand, my son-in-law reads many books and knows of strange things in faraway places. But who is this *God of Luck*? Is he more powerful than the *Goddess of Love*? You see, I have learned a little about the Whiteman's world. Your son told me about the one called *Aphrodite*. I think Homer's been praying to her."

"The *niño* and the *niña* are cousins, Pelican Doctor, cousins! In any case, they're both too young. Besides, Homer has always said he wanted to go away to a university, and now that I have the money to send him. . . ."

"Such a pairing is allowed among my people, Raymondo. Surely you won't force your son to observe the traditions of the Spanish? Well, maybe you know best. Perhaps it's important for Homer Virgil to go far away and spend his time reading even more books instead of staying here and helping you and Bill Beard to run your empire of logs. I am only the grand-father, and so I'll stand behind my son-in-law."

Halfway to Yerba Buena, Raymondo Olivo changed his mind, and the search party changed directions, riding toward the southern terminus of San Francisco Bay. They forded Guada-lupe and Alviso sloughs and skirted the upper end of the much wider Coyote Creek estuary, passed through the little village of Milpitas, asked several questions, and rode on toward Ca-laveras Valley.

"I have a bad premonition," Raymondo told Pelican Doc-tor. "The valley of the skull. I think we'll find their graves in that place. . . ."

"If they were dead," Pelican Doctor replied, "I would have known about it in my dreams. No, I believe they're alive, but in some kind of trouble."

As the party followed Berryessa Creek back up into the hills, just where the trail passed between twenty-foot outcrop-pings of mudstone, they saw and at first didn't recognize the two riders coming toward them—one half slumped forward, the other leading his horse.

"Madre de Dios!" Raymondo cried out—and then spurred his mount ahead.

"Uncle Raymondo!" Califia shouted when she recognized the rider thundering toward her. "He's going to live . . . he has to . . . Indians chased us . . . H.V. took an arrow in his back . . . days ago, across the San Joaquin Valley. . . . Some-times he's too sick to ride. . . ."

Pelican Doctor ordered that a healing lodge be set up, and within an hour a makeshift structure had been erected. Homer Virgil was placed on a pallet of dried oak leaves and grass. He mumbled a few words to Califia and to his father, drank a concoction of herbs that his grandfather prepared for him, and then fell into a deep sleep. At one point, Califia, looking in, thought for a terrible moment that his spirit had left him; but then he coughed, sucked in air, moaned, and turned onto his side.

As the sun set across the Santa Cruz Mountains, smearing

scarlet light on bands of incoming clouds, Pelican Doctor began to chant, over and over, the words to a healing song:

> Condor wings
> Do not darken this sky
> Great bird
> Who flies back and forth
> From the land of the living
> To Other Side Camp,
> Do not come yet
> Great bird. . . .

Bobcat built a fire, and Califia helped to prepare an evening meal—but Pelican Doctor didn't eat. He sat, legs crossed, at the entrance to H.V.'s little healing lodge, and it appeared to those watching that, as time wore on, the old man's breathing slowed, slowed, slowed. Raymondo had seen Pelican Doctor conduct a healing before. At first Olivo was skeptical, but that response had passed. Whether he now believed what was happening could in fact happen at all was irrelevant. In the only reality that mattered, Pelican Doctor was in the process of willing his spirit to leave his body—so that he might go in search of Homer's spirit, which was presumed to be wandering in the space between the two worlds.

Califia sat next to her uncle, but the matter of relationship between cousins never came up—as if the issue were rendered meaningless by the drama being silently and motionlessly enacted before their eyes.

Bobcat Who Limps and his two Ohlone companions fell asleep at length, but Califia and Raymondo remained as mute witnesses to Pelican Doctor's *spirit quest*. Observing slight changes in the old man's wrinkled aspect, they presumed the search was continuing.

Sometime after midnight Homer Virgil cried out and then spoke a series of words—no, syllables—that made no sense whatsoever. Next Pelican Doctor uttered a series of sounds, as if in answer. After that both the sick man and the one who sought to heal him were utterly quiet, utterly motionless. One might well have supposed both of them had slipped over into Other Side Camp.

Califia fell asleep praying—sometimes to the Mother of Jesus, sometimes to Tío Coyote, sometimes to Great Dreamer. Her head was against Uncle Ray's shoulder. Olivo drew his blanket about her and sat that way for an hour or more, his mind dull, a blank, his awareness only that of despair so total that no resolution was sufficient to draw it from the depths to which it had descended.

Then he, too, slept.

Odors of coffee and manzanita tea, brewed together, awoke them.

In the interval between false dawn and sunrise, with the sky a shimmering silver-gray, Pelican Doctor was up and about—replenishing the fire and cooking a breakfast of possum meat and duck eggs, the latter found unattended in a nest amidst bunch grass close by the creek.

"Is Homer Virgil . . . ?" Raymondo asked quietly.

Pelican Doctor nodded, placed a big hand on Olivo's shoulder.

"I met your son high on a mountain. He was sitting on a great granite boulder in the midst of a slope covered with snow that had melted into a field of daggers—but the blades exploded, vanished as I walked through them. *Will you help me find my way back, Grandfather?* he asked. *I have come so far I can't remember how I got here. Where's Califia? That's why I climbed to the mountain—to find her.* . . . Then Homer jumped down from the boulder, and we walked away together. Your son will live, Raymondo. I think he would have found his way back even without his grandfather coming to find him."

Calvin Beard and Juanita Ortega proceeded toward Hotochruk village, moving southward parallel to the coast—but keeping well inland, high up, away from the likely paths of any possible Leather Jacket pursuit. They crossed stream after stream, each tumbling down through its respective *barranca* from out of the Santa Cruz Mountains—Pilarcitos, Arroyo León, Purisima, Lobitos, Tunitas, San Gregorio, Pomponio, Pescadero, Butano, Gazos . . . names, though he had to guess which was which, that were all familiar to him as he marked them off one by one on the chart his father had drawn for him.

Then they moved upslope, into redwood forests and across

into a formation his father and Uncle Raymondo had many years ago named *Big Basin*, where some of the largest redwoods grew—hundreds of great vertical columns almost seeming to support heaven itself. Cal and Juanita rode downslope just at sundown, crossed the stream some called Waddell Creek, found a sheltered glade, and tethered their horses for the night.

Winds had been driving heavy clouds all afternoon, and now a few raindrops began to spatter down, hissing against the foliage of redwood, fir, live oak, and bay tree.

"Equinox," Calvin remarked as he kneeled to utilize his fire striker to set flames dancing among dry leaves, weakly at first and then more briskly. "Sometimes rain comes heavy at the turn of the year. That's what Pa insists, at least. Storm clouds ride in over these Santa Cruz Mountains, and Coyote Man tells the rain to come down. Without moisture the redwoods won't grow—not so well, at least."

"You love to talk," Juanita replied. "*Uno capaz de empeñar la sabana sagrada*—first he drags me off into the forest, and then he talks me to death! What do I care about *madera roja*? It's time for you to kiss me until my lips go numb, Calvin Beard."

"*Á pedir de boca*, my lady, just as you wish. . . . Perhaps after we've made love, then we'll worry about dinner."

When Calvin took her into his arms, Juanita laughed, giggled, shrieked, and attempted to evade him.

"You've got too many hands," she said.

"My grandfather was *el pulpo*, the octopus. . . ."

"I'll catch cold if you take my blouse off—be careful, Calvin, don't tear it! Why does a grown man want to nurse like an infant? Do you suppose I wish you to do that?"

"Yes, of course. Pelican Doctor was right—women in love are perverse. When our child comes, Juanita, it'll be different. But for right now, both your small fountains are mine."

"Do you think . . . my breasts . . . are too *little*?"

"Which of us did you say talks too much? Juanita, *mi alma*, how shall I be able to *enamorar* if you keep chattering? I am told a man must concentrate if he wishes to do this thing right."

"Will you be *el caníbal* and devour me?"

"Does my lady wish to be eaten?"

They rolled back and forth over a bed of dry leaves, the boughs of redwood above their canopy and the smell of summer ending in the air. At one point, in the haste of their newly realized desire, they came very close to rolling into the fire itself, and yet neither noticed.

Rain began to increase in intensity, and finally a steady downfall was in progress. Time grew warm and soft and didn't hurt at all—only easy waves coming in, surge after surge.

Then, aware that Calvin's weight was off her, that she could breathe more easily, Juanita opened her eyes and looked up into diminishing twilight. Her skirts were about her middle, and droplets that fell from the boughs above her splashed onto her bare legs and her belly. She sat up quickly and attempted to pull her clothing back into place, to make herself decent.

She stared at Calvin, kneeling by the fire, trying to get the blaze going once more. Rain must have extinguished the flames. Except for his sombrero, the man with whom she had just now . . . he was completely nude, pale against near-darkness, pale in the light of small, dancing flames. Juanita began to giggle. She couldn't help it. The man, *her man*, naked but with a hat on, he looked so—awkward—foolish—undignified— primitive—like a big monkey she'd seen a picture of in a book at Uncle Mariano's rancho. And that silly little thing between his legs, the thing men all seemed to believe to be so important, how absurd it looked, how shriveled, lost, how forlorn!

Juanita remembered a year earlier, no, yes, when grapes were coming sweet, that pair of hunting dogs who, in their fit of amorous desire, got stuck together. She remembered the *vaqueros* laughing, pointing, whooping—and one of the hired hands fetching a wooden bucket full of water. . . .

She and Rosa had hid behind a hedge of grapevines, peering through a curtain of leaves where they'd been picking and eating mouthfuls of grapes.

When they reached Hotochruk village, the site was deserted— with all the signs of a recent exodus. The lodges were undamaged, and Calvin could find no telltale sign of struggle between the Ohlones and anyone else. A message had been left in full view, however, a sheet of oiled wrapping paper that had been inscribed on both sides with quill and ink and affixed to the bole of a young redwood directly in front of the Beard lodge. Cal, perplexed by the absence of Pelican Doctor's people, had simply not seen the message. Juanita pointed it out to her beloved, and he took the sheet down, stared at it.

Dear Son. If you come this way, be advised that we've all headed on over to the San Lorenzo mill. Martin's secured the company a large and profitable order for timbers and shakes, but time's short. The lumber goes to the Sandwich Islands, of all places, & we're under strict deadline. That's why Hotochruk's empty. I've hired them all, every one except Father Pelican, who prefers to watch others work—and a band of Branciforte thieves as well. On the other hand, Calvin, if you haven't come this way, with or without your señorita, then don't bother to read my note. Chances are we've set off looking for you, since I'm concerned the authorities may have you locked up & in chains. In that case, I'll have to buy your freedom & trust that experience has not proven too dear a teacher. Another possibility might suggest Olivo and Beard versus the Vallejo clan, in a kind of minor Californio civil war. Well, the odds are more or less even. By the way, Califia's had quite an adventure, she and Homer. Neither one's dead, but Homer came close, having taken an arrow in the back. They both claim it was a Yokuts arrow, so you figure that one out. Papa Raymond's not altogether happy, & neither am I, & neither are Seagull & Calling Owl. However, there's little point in writing an ungawdly long message that in all likelihood you'll never read, since you're probably in the Yerba Buena hoosegow, charged with disturbing both the peace and good common sense and decency & I hope nothing more serious than that, & so I won't.

—Yr. Pa, a.k.a. Bill the Sawyer

Both Calvin and Juanita read the missive, but then Cal felt obliged to translate portions, inasmuch as Señorita Ortega's English was not as perfect as it might have been. After she'd asked a few questions, at the same time studying Calvin's face as a means of assessing the full significance of the elder Beard's rambling directive *to go to San Lorenzo*, Juanita laughed and said, "Perhaps your father should write one of those *romans*. Rosa and I read several, without telling Uncle or Auntie. It's obvious that your father loves to go on and on about almost nothing at all. When I first saw him, I was afraid, but I'm not afraid now. He sounds more like a friend than a parent."

"Cousin Homer Virgil's the one who'll end up writing the books—he's the original *mouse of the library*. How in God's name he managed to take an Indian arrow in the back I don't know, but he and my sister . . . well, they're attracted to one another. Actually, they encouraged me to kidnap you, Juanita. Maybe they took their own advice and wandered into some wild Indian encampment back in the mountains, even though there aren't supposed to be any *Indios indómitos* anymore. Perhaps a tribe came wandering over into the Coast Range from somewhere else. Yokuts? Those Indians live out in the Big Valley, the San Joaquin—at least, that's what I always thought. Anyway, Califia and H.V. are both all right, so I suppose no great harm's been done."

Juanita studied the deserted village, several of the lodges rather obviously larger and more elaborate and in fact more like houses of Californio villagers than Indian abodes. She dismounted and walked across an interval of ground that would doubtless have been lush meadow if not for the humans who apparently lived there most of the time.

Juanita Ortega, who now considered herself very much a woman despite her mere fifteen years, stood beneath the great, outreaching branches of a pair of redwoods that grew side by side and had long since fused, so that for the first ten feet above the ground, the two huge trunks were essentially one.

Calvin followed her. The two stood in the presence of these *spirit* trees and kissed.

"Right here would be a very fine place for you to . . . make love to me. Couldn't we ride on to San Lorenzo tomorrow? Oh, Calvin, what if Uncle Mariano's there when we arrive? I've already vowed to take my own life rather than be made a slave to some stranger. I want to live with you, or I don't wish to live at all!"

"I have many friends amongst the Ohlones," Calvin replied. "I'll slip into the camp on foot, and someone will tell me if there's any danger. But it's impossible, Juanita—there's no way at all."

"You don't understand how my uncle is once he's set his mind to something. . . ."

"But I do know there simply hasn't been time for a messenger to reach Rancho Vallejo and for your uncle to ride clear down here. The danger, if it occurs, will come two or three days hence—presuming that the priests and nuns were able to figure out where we were likely to go. I made no secret as to my identity, and Olivo & Beard is well known. You've made your choice, Juanita Ortega—we've both made our choices. My pa and my Uncle Raymondo will back us all the way."

Juanita stood on tiptoes, and her mouth sought his.

"Is it possible, Calvin Beard, that I may indeed be able to have you as my *esposo*? Perhaps it's wrong to wish to be happy, but that is what I want. I desire that with all my heart, *querido mio*. Perhaps a good Catholic woman should be willing to cry all the time, like that Mary Magdalene, but I think it's better to laugh and to make love with a man whose soul is like one's own—to have his children and to be able to watch them grow up."

"And if we have daughters," Calvin asked, "will we allow them to choose their own husbands?"

Señorita Ortega gazed into the eyes of Señor Beard, and a moment later she burst out laughing.

"No, of course not," she replied. "They would not be able to choose as wisely as I have chosen."

Autumn came with a series of rain squalls, followed by a few glorious days of full sunlight, and then cinched with a two-week downpour. The San Lorenzo rose to flood stage, and in its fury carried away a recently constructed check dam built to divert water into a flume whose current ran the big circular saw and several smaller saws at the Olivo & Beard mill.

With the assistance of old Pelican Doctor's Ohlones, however, the contract to provide timbers and shingles for the Europeans who'd established themselves in the Sandwich Islands was satisfactorily fulfilled. The redwood was on its way, loaded into the hold of one of Martin's three-masters, to the operations of those who'd planted coffee and sugar plantations—and indeed had founded an English school at Lahaina, Maui. Jean Paul Martin had earlier visited the islands and had been astonished by the great volcanoes (one of which was in constant eruption while he was there), the fertility of the soil, the complexity of rituals and customs, and the impact of Congregational missionaries upon religious awareness. Pacific whalers, Martin said, also used Hawaii as a winter base for a fleet of more than four hundred whaling ships, primarily those from New England.

"Whale oil for the lamps of the world." Raymondo shrugged. "The Bostons kill the great creatures of the sea, but we are no better. After all, we hew down the mightiest of all the trees."

"Not quite, we don't, Herr Presidente Quixote," Beard said. "We'd have to weld three misery whips end to end to be able to put up any kind of *show* against some of the trees. Setting matters of local religion aside, I'd say the big fellas are safe, for the time being at least. Tell you what, though. Just as a matter of principle, I'm going to invent a method that'd do 'er if we want to. The way I see things, a fella'd have to bore holes about ten feet up—and slip in some kind of springboard with a steel nipple on it, to keep it in place. Use some device of the sort to put up scaffolding all the way around the tree. Then the boys with the broadaxes might have a chance—only we really need a different shape axe, something that'd cut through the ungawdly bark. I hear the timber beasts up along the Columbia have started using double-bitted axes, narrow and sharp."

"You'd cut down such a tree just to prove it can be done? This project is not worthy of you, Sancho Fur-on-the-Face."

"Raymondo, just think of the shingles we could get out of one of those *ungawdly great big red sonsabitches.* . . ."

In late November, a delegation did finally arrive from Rancho Vallejo—inasmuch as William Beard had sent word back to R.B.R. Cooper that Señorita Juanita Ortega had escaped from

Mission Dolores, thinking to elope with Calvin Beard, and that the two would-be lovers had arrived shortly thereafter at Olivo & Beard operations near Santa Cruz. The two young people were, Beard informed Mariano Vallejo, quartered separately, the young lady a guest of the Olivos and being tutored in English and Latin by Raymondo Olivo and his son, the scholarly Homer Virgil, who was now nearly recovered from being shot in the back by an arrow, possibly poisoned, and who was to leave shortly on a voyage to England, where he'd been accepted for matriculation at Cambridge University for the following year.

Mariano and his entourage arrived and were greeted warmly by William Beard and Raymondo Olivo.

"But where are the lovers?" Mariano inquired, at the same time making a curt bow. "Does Juanita Ortega not wish to embrace her favorite uncle? Where is the young lady—you must tell me."

"She's in her room, where she's weeping her head off," Raymondo replied. "Very passionately, this young woman does not wish to marry that *old man from San Diego.* When my wife and I invite young Calvin to have dinner with us sometimes, the two of them eat nothing at all—they spend their meal staring into one another's eyes. I suspect they're in love, though I know they seldom show any signs whatsoever."

Vallejo nodded.

"This match, it would not be completely without advantage," he said. "Tell me what your judgment is, Señor Beard. Would you be willing to have such a girl as Juanita Ortega as your daughter-in-law? She's of good blood, but unfortunately all her relatives excepting myself are dead and are now sleeping the long sleep with their ancestors. I'm certain you've both heard of Señor Albion—he who had offered to take Juanita as his wife. Well, unfortunately, I've learned that the man is dead. No longer does he graze in the fields of Alta California. I believe it was grazing, in fact, that killed him—for it's said that he died in the arms of another man's wife, possibly poisoned with four ounces of lead. *Ahi muerte!* This world, it's a most unpredictable and unpleasant place at times. What do you say, Señor Beard?"

Bill the Sawyer nodded.

"I suppose my kid could sort of take Juanita off your hands," he grinned.

"Then we shake hands on it. But you must understand that she has very little in the way of a dowry. As I say, however, she's of good stock."

"It's a pleasure doing business with a true gentleman," Bill Beard responded, extending his hand. "Now maybe we ought to roust out the young folks—an' tell 'em the bad news. Getting what you want—that puts an awful responsibility on anyone, male or female, human or otherwise."

Homer Virgil and Califia left their horses tethered among the yellow bush lupines that grew on the headlands, descended a steep trail, and walked on the sands of Grayhound Cove. In the aftermath of a January storm, waves continued to batter in against the coast rocks, and a strong wind was blowing, whipping chill sea spray through the air.

The two who had once been lovers did not even hold hands, nor did they walk close together, until they came to a place where they found it necessary to scramble up over a long, wet shelf of stone.

"Tomorrow," H.V. said. "My father will accompany me to Monterey, and after that . . . Will you ride along, Califia?"

She was silent for an interval, and when she answered, she did so with a question of her own.

"Will you return when you've finished your studies in England? I. . . ."

"Of course," he replied.

"That will be four or five years from now," Califia said. "Many things will change in that span of time. This intense little existence we've known, Homer Virgil, it's ended now. We might have made it work. We could have. . . ."

"I shouldn't have listened to my father," H.V. said. "Even when my mind began to agree with him, my heart was saying something quite different. I've never felt so confused and . . . empty . . . in my life. Calvin and Juanita will be married at the end of the month. You and I could have been . . ."

"Only what we are," Califia said, finishing H.V.'s sentence.

"Perhaps indeed it is better this way. When you return . . . if you return, I should say . . . then. . . ."

"I want to kiss you, Califia. May I?"

The two embraced, each knowing all too well that the time of innocence had ended. Great storms would pass over them before they'd meet again.

PART TWO

CALIFIA, BOOSHWAY

CHAPTER TEN

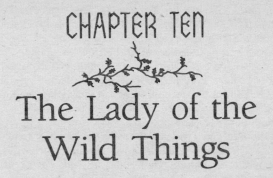

The Lady of the
Wild Things

[1845:]

SCENE: *CHALK MOUNTAIN, to the north of the site of the ancestral village of Hotochruk, Santa Cruz Mountains. The month was January, but in the mild region of the California coast, there was neither snow nor frost. A soft haze hung over the range, and the day was quite pleasant. A human figure, field glass in hand. This person was clad in black pants and jacket, red shirt, riding boots, and a sombrero—and was seated on a high outcropping and was engaged in making casual survey of rough canyon land below. Two black-plumaged birds, a vulture perched in the crown of a sapling madrone, the other a rooster with a bright red, bent comb, the chicken contentedly taking a dust bath, eyes closed, wings partially spread, feet kicking at dirt and leaves beneath.*

To the south and west, the vast blue shield of the Pacific reached to the far horizon. Northward and to the east rose the mountains. Hawks and eagles floated indolently on thermals high up, while across redwood-studded Waddell Creek Canyon below Chalk Mountain, a great blue heron winged its way from one fishing area to another.

The figure with the field glass: a female in male clothing, a young woman with fair skin and intense gray eyes. Califia Beard

*put her glass back into its case, removed her sombrero, loosened
the string tie at the throat of the shirt. She unpinned long, gleaming
dark hair and withdrew a comb from a leather satchel. She relaxed
in the warm sunlight and began to come out her mane.*

*A nearly full grown cougar appeared on the rim above Califia—
then a second cat, evidently the first animal's mate.*

*The vulture in the madrone began to fan its big wings and to
make a soft hissing sound.*

Califia turned, looked up.

*"Gatogordo and Ponchita! Where have you two been? I half
supposed some grizzlies had eaten you for dinner. . . ."*

*The rooster continued to dust-bathe, his body now turned over
onto one side, a spurred black foot kicking out into the air as the
seemingly jointless bird went into a spasm of feather-grooming.*

Bill the Sawyer liked to insist that it was just a matter of time
before the province of Alta California became its own country,
free and clear of Mexico, and Raymondo Olivo agreed. Thereafter, Bill insisted, California would become a part of the United
States, a full member of the Union. Olivo wasn't altogether
certain of the advisability of the latter arrangement.

As fate would have matters, entry into the United States had
nearly come about three years earlier. Commodore Thomas ap
Catesby Jones of the U.S. Navy sailed into Monterey Bay and by-
God seized the capital. Thereafter the good commodore concluded that a slight mistake had been made—inasmuch as the
United States and Mexico were not in fact engaged in a war at all.
With visible egg on his face, Catesby Jones departed Monterey
and proceeded to Los Angeles, where he met with the governor,
made apologies, and paid a fine.

The simple truth was that California was unable to defend
itself against even a modest naval assault, and Mexico was in
no position to protect the province. When the Yankees came
again, Beard presumed, they'd stay. As things were at present,
the community of Americans living amongst the Californios
was fairly large and seemed to be growing at what Californios
felt to be an alarming rate.

Califia Beard was an old maid. So she'd have been considered, at least, back in Vermont.

It wasn't that she ever actually intended to go tomboy, but

things had worked out that way nonetheless. In Alta California there was no disadvantage to being female—not if the female in question could outride, outshoot, outcuss, and outsmart the men she palled around with. Califia didn't make a point of flaunting her abilities, but she was confident of them. Her father had taught her how to ride and shoot, right along with Calvin, and she learned the rest on her own.

The issue of marriage didn't worry her. She'd had her fling with H.V., and that was long since over. Raymondo's son was still in Europe and not much more than a fond memory. Well, she'd get married someday, someday when she was ready for it—and that meant when she found someone she really wanted to live with and go to bed with. Mating, Califia believed, was something that didn't make much sense unless a girl really wanted to do it. Copulation, one might say, was actually rather a grotesque performance. Animals managed with infinitely greater style and dignity. In any case, Califia mused, things were better as they were. She was single and free—could come and go as she liked. If she'd had a husband, the men in her crew would be looking to him for directions. Males of the human species, she supposed, were generally hopeless traditionalists, and their chief redeeming feature was that they were obtuse—stupid, yes, was a better word. That's why she was glad she wasn't a man. Behind their bravado, men were as vulnerable as children—and in some ways just about as helpless.

In this one area at least, the matter of the mating thing, Califia's education had been incomplete. One runaway venture to the Sierra, and then God had struck back. Even now, however, she sometimes dreamed she was in bed with . . . yes, H.V., her cousin.

What a terrible, pathetic, irony. I loved H.V. until I was certain I couldn't love any more—and yet the flower died, no fruit came of it. Fate and Uncle Raymondo intervened, and Homer Virgil was sent away to England—to Oxford University. "Not kissing cousins," as my dad says. I never took my clothes off except for H.V., and that was because I wanted to—I wanted him to possess me, and I wanted to possess him. Dear Homer Virgil! We meant to do it— run away—and really we did do it. If it hadn't been for that Yokuts arrow, we could have forged a life for ourselves. I was ready, I was willing—but perhaps Homer wasn't, and so he listened to Uncle Ray.

Not even at the time, when H.V.'s departure was upon them and what had happened seemed like an utter catastrophe, not even then did Califia fully realize what the effect would be of the passing of time—the numbing. . . . Weeks and then months and then years—until those beautiful days in the sunlight together, the two of them walking arm in arm beside the Pacific, seemed no more than a pleasant dream with a sad ending.

I wanted you then, H.V., and I want you still, even though I know it can never happen. God made the world badly, though doubtless He had His reasons. But why in the devil does the Old Boy nudge us into falling in love with someone we can't have?

Yet such was the way of the world, and the wise person learned to accept reality. After all, what other options were there? H.V. had found a home in England, Califia reasoned, and she was here, halfway around the world from him. If there were a more effective way of keeping the bull away from the cow, she was certain she didn't know what it was. A girl had to learn—though perhaps her education had been terminated for the best. For all she knew, their children might have been born with two heads and no feet, or something of the sort. That's what Uncle Raymondo hinted, in any case—though she'd observed no irregularities among animals when even brother and sister mated. Perhaps humans were different, and perhaps they weren't.

So here she was, unmated and subject to stay that way, at least for a while. Instead of a husband she had a disgustingly domestic pair of mountain lions, Gatogordo and Ponchita by name—tame enough so that they'd forsworn killing and eating cattle, and tame enough to sleep in the same bed with her, if given the chance. For good measure, she had a pet turkey vulture named El Buzzardo and an as-yet-unmated fighting cock she'd dubbed Rory Sunrise. It wouldn't take long, she smiled, for anyone to figure out why she'd given him handle—except that he didn't restrict his roaring to that time of the day.

Raccoons, possums, owls, *Nuts* the squirrel, a couple of coyotes at one time or another, a bad-natured kingfisher that was intent upon nesting in her hair, and even a young wild pig that came wandering in out of the woods one day—these creatures had been a part of her family. A better way to put it: they'd been her nonhuman relatives.

For years now Aunt Calling Owl had insisted that Califia was going to turn into an animal or a bird—that instead of going to the Spirit World when she died, her soul would come back to inhabit the body of some creature or another. Califia surmised that one could do worse. On the whole, animals had a certain dignity that humans lacked.

Seagull, her own mother, referred to Califia as the *Lady of the Wild Things*, but the daughter believed the mother had missed the point—since none of her animal and bird friends were wild at all.

Calvin had become a ship's captain and a full-fledged junior partner in the Olivo & Beard lumber business. Cal and Juanita *née* Ortega remained married and stupidly happy. The children kept coming, something a skeptic might suppose strange, in view of the fact that Cal was away so much of the time. Raymondo claimed that Juanita managed to get in a family way merely by putting her private clothes and Cal's together in her hope chest. Inasmuch as Raymondo was known for his learning, who could doubt something he claimed to be true? Nevertheless, Califia harbored certain doubts with regard to the efficacy of the method. When Cal and Juanita *were together*, they doubtlessly spent a good many of their hours hooked up like a couple of grinning camp dogs.

Unmarried female or not, Califia had learned to handle a crew of men, and she knew the lumber business about as well as anyone. Her father and uncle trusted her judgment and had essentially given her free rein in the pursuit of business matters. She was of the opinion that no man could have done much better than she did in working out a potentially profitable arrangement with John Sutter, for instance, and by Hecate and Old Lady Coyote, she'd push the thing through to fruition.

She appreciated the prospect—that what her father and uncle had in mind was a kind of empire, something like Sutter's—only one based on timber, mills, log runs, boards, beams, and the like. John Sutter was a relative newcomer to California, but somehow he'd managed to generate trust among the old families, and a huge land grant had been awarded to him—out in the Big Valley. Sutter's dream was different, and in truth he was a great deal closer to realizing it—a country of his own, *New Helvetia*, with Sutterville, his capital city, close by the Sacramento River.

Sam Brannan the Mormon—he was another man of vision, or at least part of a vision. Bill Beard had explained the thing to her—Brigham Young and the inland nation-presumed of Deseret, with corridors to the sea that extended through California, either at Los Angeles or at Yerba Buena—and if the latter, that meant right across friend Sutter's land grant.

Word had it that Brannan got along better with John Sutter than he did with his patriarch, Brigham Young, however. So perhaps Brannan would set up his own church.

There was rebellion in the air—like a summer thunderstorm, but at the moment between episodes. Soon enough. . . . As Califia was well aware, Californios had a long history of fighting among themselves, north against south, and of getting rid of unpopular governors. That was true even before Mexico became independent of Spain, back in 1822. News of the victory hadn't reached Alta California until six months after the fact. Perhaps the authorities in Mexico City hadn't thought it was particularly important for the *Gente de Razón* to know, as remote as they were.

The Californios had deposed Governor Sola when Mexico became independent of Spain, and then came Manuel Victoria and Echeandia. Jose Figueroa, whom Bill Beard and Raymondo Olivo believed to have been an excellent governor, had unfortunately died in office about ten years earlier, when Califia was still a girl of sixteen. Thereafter Mexico sent up Nicolas Gutierrez, a lunatic who proclaimed Los Angeles Pueblo not only a city but also the capital. The shift southward wasn't popular, though, and the capital returned to Monterey, where most Californios thought it belonged.

After Governor Gutierrez came Hariano Chico, a genuine *malvado*, one who lasted just three months—largely because he rebuked the vigilantes, the *junta defensora de la seguridad pública*, but also because it turned out that the reprobate's niece was actually his mistress, his *puta*, only maybe she was both—and he had quite a few other sexual dalliances as well. It was said of him that he once attempted to copulate with a pet heifer who had her own private boudoir. Chico was run out of office, and Gutierrez presided over a provisional government.

That was when Juan Bautista Alvarado (an honest-to-God Californio with the backing of almost everyone, including Isaac Graham and his American riflemen) headed a rebellion and defeated Gutierrez. Alvarado dreamed of Alta California as an independent country, and furthermore he declared that Californians didn't have to be Catholics—or anything else in particular.

Alvarado, Califia Beard reflected, was a good man and quite handsome. She'd seen him on a number of occasions—like when he came to visit at the San Lorenzo mill, for instance, just after her fourteenth birthday. The man had not yet become governor and probably hadn't yet even thought of such a thing. He'd visited in behalf of his uncle, Mariano Guadalupe Vallejo, who wanted to purchase a quantity of finished redwood. Alvarado was very good-looking and wore a large black sombrero and rode a black stallion with a white crescent on its forehead. Califia remembered that once or twice she'd even forgot about her infatuation with H.V., and had asked Uncle Raymondo if he thought she'd turn out to be pretty enough to marry Juan Bautista when she grew up.

"I didn't, naturally," she mused. "Didn't marry Alvarado, I mean. About the other thing, who knows? In any case, *pretty* is how a girl thinks about herself—and that affects the way men think about her. Mariposa's pretty and knows it, and so the young men continue to follow her around, even though she has two young children. The endless flirtations drove Bobcat Who Limps crazy—she goaded him into beating her, and after that she moved his things out of their lodge and divorced him. Why men have a weakness for the demure eyelash-batters, I'm sure I haven't the slightest idea. . . . Well, maybe at least one idea. I think it must be something like what happens to male dogs when a bitch is in heat. The boys go completely crazy, poor dears, and can't help themselves. With humans, though, it's a bit different. Our males are crazy all the time."

Califia's thoughts returned to Alvarado—and to the unpredictability of politics in Alta California.

Two years earlier, Alvarado decided not to be governor anymore. He'd had some disagreement with Uncle Vallejo the military commandant, Calvin's semi-father-in-law; Califia was uncertain about the details. But after Alvarado resigned, Governor Manuel Micheltorena came up from Mexico City, and he brought with him his three hundred *cholos*. Nobody liked them (or him), and for good reason—the governor's troops, recruited from Mexican prisons, were a pack of rabid dogs, and power-mad. Presuming they enjoyed the governor's blessing, they'd visit Indian villages and even missions and ranchos and gang-rape whichever señoritas took their fancy or didn't hide quickly enough.

Twice Califia herself had been obliged to draw her pistol against a group of *cholos*. In the aftermath of the second incident, Bill Beard shot one Leather Jacket and said he hoped he'd killed the right sonofabitch but wasn't much concerned, one way or the other. The Leather Jacket's body was found floating in San Lorenzo River, about eight or nine miles downstream from Olivo & Beard mill number one.

Eventually Juan Bautista Alvarado resolved his differences with Mariano Vallejo and subsequently joined forces with Jose de Castro; in February of 1845, yet another battle was fought at Cahuenga Pass, the traditional place for resolving military imbroglios.

Calvin and Califia were attending to some business at Rancho Vallejo, delivering a quantity of redwood timbers from the Petaluma mill, and had anchored the *Don Quixote* at Vallejo's embarcadero, when word came in of what was afoot. Calvin wasn't certain that Olivo & Beard ought to get itself involved in the political squabbles of Californios, but the present instance, Califia argued, was no time for fence-straddling and other forms of calm reflection.

Shortly thereafter they were on horseback in the company of Mariano Vallejo and his men, heading southward, Califia with El Buzzardo either sitting on her shoulder as she rode or else flying along, trailing from up high and possibly exchanging greetings with hawks and eagles or with other vultures, though with hisses and wing-language, of course, since vultures don't have vocal cords.

Volunteers flocked to the rebel cause from nearly every village Vallejo passed through, and these volunteers included a handful of Americans, lads who were armed to the teeth.

Near Santa Barbara they joined forces with Juan Bautista Alvarado and his men, and the combined force thereafter moved inland, into the Tehachapi Mountains, crossing the Santa Ynez, the Santa Maria, and the Cuyama. As the rebel band rode northeastward, the mountains became ever more barren and grim, a narrow coastal forest of fir and pine giving way to scrub oak, madrone, toyon, digger pine, manzanita, and mesquite. They passed west of a considerable mountain named *Pinos*, upon whose slopes were indeed what appeared to be pines and other evergreens. Close by, a dozen condors (Califia had never seen more than one or two at a time before) took to following the formation of humans, as though the huge vultures had some uncanny sort of anticipation of a battlefield littered with dead soldiers.

As for El Buzzardo, he must have felt intimidated by his overgrown vulturine cousins, because as long as the king birds were in sight, Califia's bareheaded friend was content to ride on her shoulder or to skulk from one oak or madrone to another.

When Califia spoke to Calvin about a premonition regarding casualties and of a connection with the soaring condors, he merely laughed and offered to shoot one or two of the *carrion crows*.

"Someone has to look out for Buzzardo," Cal said. "Poor thing's afraid to climb the walls of heaven. . . ."

El Buzzardo craned his long neck sideways—though whether in an attempt to understand what was being said or because he *already* understood, who could say? Calvin Beard wouldn't have shot a condor, though, because he respected the ways of old Pelican Doctor and his people. The king birds were sacred.

From Pinos they began to move downslope and at length emerged from the mountains and onto the floor of a broad valley—the southern end of the San Joaquin. Visible to the north was a large lake, *Buena Vista*, quite full, as Califia surmised, owing to the heavy rains of the previous three months. One of Alvarado's men said the lake was fed by a river that flowed from the *Sierra Nevada*, a very high mountain range off to the east—mountains where snow and ice remained throughout the summer. But could those actually be the same mountains she and Homer Virgil had entered into, the place of great trees?

Joe Walker and his men had crossed through the snows of those mountains back in 1833, the year when all the stars fell down, as Pelican Doctor put things. She'd been fifteen that summer, and she remembered the big to-do when the news reached the San Lorenzo mill—a gang of American trappers had come to Monterey. Her father and Uncle Raymondo imagined an American invasion was in the wind.

Califia introduced both herself and El Buzzardo to Alvarado, and she spent an hour or more riding beside him. The man was indeed handsome, even more so now that he had a few years on him. But he was married, of course, a family man— and his features displayed the weariness of one who has wielded authority and attempted to lay the power aside and then been forced to take up the burden once again.

As it turned out, she discovered, Alvarado knew Bill Beard relatively well, though the Hero of California had no recollection of a certain fourteen-year-old who'd been too shy to do more than observe him from a distance. By that lack of recall she was not surprised, but she was somewhat taken aback when Alvarado expressed the wish that, before troops actually entered into combat with Micheltorena's forces, Califia and her pet bird should be kept to the rear, out of harm's way.

She informed the *great man* that in such a case, he would be losing a very fine rifleman, one who'd chosen to fight for the dignity of all Californios. With these words, she turned her horse and found her way back to Calvin. For his part, El Buzzardo went flapping off into the sky and was soon describing handsome arcs high above the human midges.

"Well, have you decided to marry His Excellency, or not?" Calvin asked.

Her brother had always had, she reflected, the maddening ability to keep a perfectly straight face while he was in the process of saying truly outrageous things.

Below Cahuenga Pass they made contact with a dispatch rider from Castro's force—a lanky, bearded, leather-garbed American named Samson Flowers. From the man's appearance, Califia presumed him to be somewhat older than her father and Uncle Ray, yet not a great deal older. More than that, she was virtually certain she recalled her father and her uncle talking about this individual, if not another with the same unusual name.

When Flowers had finished speaking with Alvarado and appeared, in fact, as though he were about to mount his horse and ride out in the direction from which he'd come, Califia grabbed her brother by the arm (somewhat against his will) and introduced both him and herself to Flowers—told him they were William Beard's children.

At first she wasn't certain the buckskin man even recognized the name. After so many years, how would anyone have recalled . . . a name? Or was it possible that this individual might indeed be a *different* Samson Flowers?

At length he grinned, winked, and extended a pawlike hand to Calvin.

"Brother an' sister—twins, ye say? Seagull's little ones, then, as I gather? By Gawd, it's a surprise, certain it is. How's Bill an' Raymondo? They still partners in the wood-thievin' business? Actually, I heard it were so."

Flowers wasn't exactly certain as to how he ought to embrace the tall, attractive young woman. For Califia's part, she could sense the confusion in his face. So she smiled (and damned if she didn't catch herself batting her eyes, just the way Mariposa did it), and then she extended her hand.

Samson Flowers grinned, nodded, and engulfed her hand in both of his.

"Don't get her riled, Flowers," Calvin warned, "or she'll be wanting to wrist-wrestle with you."

"Ma'am," Samson Flowers said, half whispering, "you sure are the purtiest thing these eyes have gazed on since the year the stars fell down. . . ."

"I'll presume that to be a compliment," she replied.

All of a sudden she didn't feel very certain of herself.

"When you wear 'em, Miss Califia, men's clothes just don't appear to be men's clothes at all."

Calvin gave Flowers a dirty look and motioned his sister away with him.

"Where are *Torrejon*'s forces encamped?" she persisted. "And where's Castro?"

"The general's already done attacked Los Angeles Pueblo, an' right now him an' the boys is movin' up the Tehachapis. Figger we've got the governor an' his bunch o' egg-suckers as good as surrounded. Colonel Sutter along with 'im, sad to say, an' a few Rocky Mountain trappers that has somehow got turned around an' ended up on the wrong side."

At that moment El Buzzardo came drifting down out of the blue and landed on the crown of Califia's sombrero. Samson Flowers squinted one eye, shook his head, and shrugged his shoulders—all at once.

"A pet carrion crow? Messenger from the other side, some say. Well, ain't that the damnedest thing I ever see? Dog my cats, looks like ye got plenty o' allies, Miss Califia. . . ."

Then the buckskin man was astride his mount and on his way back into the mountains, intending, doubtless, to make a wide sweep away from the road leading to Cahuenga Pass.

They moved ahead, encamping for the evening when, as their own scouts told them, they were little more than a mile from Micheltorena's force. The men were relatively quiet that evening. Not subdued, exactly. Thoughtful. Many, if not all, had fought in battles before, but for Califia, and her brother Calvin as well, tomorrow's experience would be quite a new one. If things went badly, she reflected, she could easily end up seriously wounded or even dead.

She had difficulty sleeping that night, though she hated to admit it even to herself. And when she did sleep, she found herself dreaming of the difficulties of battle—stories she'd gleaned out of her father's books or out of those she'd borrowed from Uncle Raymondo, volumes of fairy tales and histories and things like *El Cid* and *Le Morte d'Arthur*.

She was awakened by the notes of a bugle, and, with the

others, ate a hurried breakfast without benefit of firelight. Then, shortly after dawn on the 20th of February, 1845, a sporadic cannonade was begun by Micheltorena's force, and Alvarado returned fire. After a time this activity ceased, and Califia could hear cannon fire on the pass above—indicating that Castro had entered into the battle.

Aside from some ineffectual rifle fire at long range, nothing of note transpired at all. Shortly after midday, Samson Flowers appeared once again, this time in the company of perhaps fifty other Americans, all of whom were dressed in leathers, just as he was. Among them were Jim Beckwourth, a tall, powerful Mulatto, and Caleb Greenwood, rangy and given to laughter at odd moments. Both appeared to be friends with Flowers, and all three of them were about the same age, so far as Califia could determine. She presumed them to be old friends from the days when they trapped for furs.

"What's the news?" Calvin called out.

"The news?" Beckwourth thundered. "The news is—it's all over but the shouting. Colonel Price lost his horse, and that's the full count of our casualties."

Flowers and Beckwourth rode up to Califia.

"Jimmy," Samson grinned, "now ain't this'n the prettiest little rebel ye ever saw? Don't have a husband, neither, though I can't figure why. Thinkin' about proposin' to her myself. Truth is, I used to work for her pa before she was even born. She's got her a pet buzzard, too, though I don't see the varmint just now."

Beckwourth nodded, tipped his hat.

"Mr. Flowers forgets about names when he's making introductions. James P. Beckwourth, at your service, ma'am. . . ."

"Califia Beard," she replied with as much reserve as she could muster. She'd heard about Jim Beckwourth, after all, and Caleb Greenwood as well. Word had it that Beckwourth was actually an Indian chief for a number of years. One of the American crew members at the Petaluma mill claimed to have known Beckwourth in St. Louis and to have served with him in the Missouri Volunteers, an American expedition against some wild Indians in Florida. If Beckwourth had been an Indian chief, Califia wondered, then why on earth would he be helping government troops to subdue some other Indians? The story, she concluded, was best consumed along with a few grains of salt.

In any event, as for Samson Flowers—well, that individual was definitely beginning to get on her nerves.

CHAPTER ELEVEN

Russian River Encampment

[1845:]

THE BATTLE WAS over the following morning, February 21st. Micheltorena had been caught in a pincers, with Alvarado to the north and Castro to the south. The governor sent a flag of truce and asked for negotiations. Alvarado insisted on articles of capitulation, and as a result, Micheltorena and his despised *cholo* Leather Jackets were to lay down their arms and depart from the province immediately, at least as far as Guaymas, he and his men never again to be seen on this side of that dark river which divides the land of the living from the land of the dead.

Within a few days news came from Alvarado that Castro and Pio Pico were to share power, one to the north, the other to the south. Cal and Califia were on their way back to Mariano Guadalupe Vallejo's rancho to complete their business transaction and then to sail the *Don Quixote* south to Santa Cruz.

Brother and sister proceeded along the great Valley of the San Joaquin, and on the third day after reaching that stream, El Buzzardo discovered a dead tule elk, the animal just recently killed, perhaps by a grizzly bear. The pet vulture was soon crowding his way in amongst several others of his own kind and a couple of red-tailed hawks as well, and not even Califia's repeated calls to him made the slightest difference. He was determined to be one of the boys.

"Carrion eaters will be carrion eaters," Calvin reflected. "It's the Feast of St. Francis, and he's with his family. . . ."

They rode on ahead, and all afternoon Califia listened for those big wings descending above her, but to no avail. Shortly after she and Calvin encamped for the night, however, El Buzzardo showed up—quite as though nothing unusual had happened. Califia was half of a mind to ignore the feathered delinquent, but she couldn't. For one thing, even a skunk smelled better.

Califia managed to strike a deal with John Sutter, the *emperador* of the Sacramento Valley and the owner as well (on credit) of the former Russian fur post at Fort Ross. Sutter reached Vallejo's rancho just as Calvin was getting ready to weigh anchor. Possibly because of a sense of loyalty to the established government which had granted him his massive holdings, Sutter had exercised the bad judgment of backing *Torrejon*, as the American mountain men called him. In a way, Sutter was obliged to do so, since he was a colonel in the provincial militia. Yet it had been Alvarado who'd provided Sutter with his Sacramento land grant in the first place, and just possibly Herr Sutter should have kept this salient fact in mind.

In California, everyone changed sides at least once a year. Raymondo Olivo, straight-faced, insisted it was because the sun is closer to the earth in California than anywhere else. In any case, one way or the other, it was more or less understandable that John Sutter would have done what he did, even though he must have realized Micheltorena couldn't possibly emerge as the victor, not after what his *cholos* had done, and not with most of the Californios north of the Tehachapi Mountains against him. In point of fact, Mexico was relatively helpless in these matters, with Alta California remaining a part of Mexico only because of convenience. There were already so many Americans in the territory that full independence was virtually assured.

At one point John Sutter had actually threatened—not face-to-face, but by means of a messenger—to have Samson Flowers and Jim Beckwourth and the other American mountain men put before a firing squad—*at ten o'clock tomorrow*, unless they came over to the governor's side. This threat was made the day before the battle—that is, the day before Colonel Price lost his horse (which had been liberated from the Los Angeles Pueblo no more than three days earlier). Califia presumed that neither Flowers nor the other mountaineers took Sutter's threat very seriously, but when the mountain men had an opportunity for a measure of revenge, they took it. In the aftermath of Micheltorena's defeat, the American *irregulars* captured Sutter—and there was some talk of hanging the Swiss-American, threats made mostly (but not entirely) in jest. Califia supposed that was the case, though from what she was eventually to learn of these mountain men, they might well have gotten blind drunk and then gone on to hang poor John of Switzerland and a few other people and possibly one or two pigs and geese as well, all in the spirit of good-natured fun.

At length, Caleb Greenwood proposed that, since Sutter was in all other ways a generally good sort, he should be given his freedom, on the condition that he provide free rum to any *coon what shows up at the old barstid's abobe fort*. Even with the rowdy Americans more or less back on his side, however, Sutter must have felt it in his own best interest to strengthen connections with persons whose relations to the new government were somewhat better than his own. Though the owner of Fort Ross and New Helvetia and other real estate had not always gotten on well with Mariano Vallejo, it was to his neighbor seventy-five miles to the west that he first turned—and Mariano, for his part, accepted the peace offering.

Hence, when Califia subsequently arranged to meet with John Sutter at San Jose and approached him with a proposition from Olivo & Beard, the empire builder was very much of a mind to listen. When the scheme appeared not only reasonable but also potentially profitable, Johann Von Sutter was willing to affix his name to a sheet of paper, right alongside Califia's (as official agent for Olivo & Beard).

Apparently the tame Pomo Indians Sutter had hired as a logging crew were more than just a little unreliable during the best of times. When one worker was killed by a *widow-maker*, a falling limb, the Pomos returned to Chalanchawi village to cremate the man's remains, while his wife burned off her hair and smeared her forehead with pitch and ashes. After that incident, the Pomos had no heart for the cutting of trees.

In brief, the arrangement Califia worked out was this: Olivo & Beard was to supply redwood, fir, and pine timbers, as well as redwood and cedar shingles, both to Sutter's operations at New Helvetia and at Fort Ross, perhaps a dozen miles or so north of the Russian River mouth.

After conferring with Bill and Raymondo, Califia proceeded to recruit a reliable crew. Her father suggested that she take along Juan Pescadero, a Spanish-Indian half-breed who'd been employed by Olivo & Beard for several years. His fellow workers respected Juan and could likely be counted on to follow him in time of crisis. For his part, Juan's long association with Olivo & Beard would see to it that the man didn't act entirely on his own. If anything, he'd be likely to defer to Califia, even if he knew she was wrong.

Once the venerable *Don Quixote* was loaded and shipshape, Calvin would transport crew and sister and her mountain lions and two birds and all necessary equipment north from Santa Cruz to the redwood forests near Fort Ross. That her father and uncle should trust her and her judgment to this extent, Califia reflected, pleased her a great deal—and she resolved to conduct operations in such a fashion as to justify the faith placed in her.

In April they made their way north from Santa Cruz, the ship's cargo consisting of one logging-camp boss lady, one crew of loggers, one zoo in the making, a three-month supply of staple foods, clothing, axes, peaveys, saws, skids, harness, a pair of wagons, and eight of the largest oxen money could purchase. According to the hand-drawn map John Sutter had given Califia, a considerable redwood forest covered the coastal ridges, the big trees beginning just a few miles back away from the Pacific, as was also the case, in fact, to the north of Santa Cruz and south of Monterey as well, beyond the Sur Rivers. Bill Beard's advice was to establish a cutting area adjacent to Russian River and to use that stream as a means of getting timber down to tidewater, where a mill might be established and where *Don Quixote* or some other Olivo & Beard craft could work its way in to quiet water to take on a load—some of which presumably would go to Fort Ross, but some directly to Sutter's Fort on the Sacramento River, and the remainder to find markets in such places as Yerba Buena, San Jose, Monterey, and even Los Angeles Pueblo or Mission San Diego.

In Alta California, the market for lumber was growing rapidly, in part due to the initiative of John Sutter, whose fort provided a point of arrival for emigrants from across the continent. Newcomers increased the need for boards. Such timber as might be produced in excess of Sutter's needs, if any, was the company's. But Sutter had first option, and his price was lower than might have been commanded elsewhere—this in exchange for cutting on *his land*, though Bill Beard and Raymondo Olivo were virtually certain the forests along the Russian River were in no way included within the boundaries of those properties Sutter had bought from the Russians. But Sutter's prices would be more or less fair, generally in keeping with Monterey values; and with a guaranteed market for whatever Olivo & Beard might produce, success in the venture seemed certain.

Calvin Beard used the high tide to get his craft in across the bar at Russian River's mouth and proceeded upstream past a couple of Pomo villages, one to either side, Chalanchawi and Ashachatiu. Calvin nosed his craft inland for perhaps three miles or a bit less, to a point where redwoods began to line the banks and the river grew narrow and shallow. After momentary difficulty with a sand-and-mud bar, Cal maneuvered the *Don Quixote* around, and dropped anchor. With the help of two large landing craft constructed before leaving Santa Cruz, he was able to get the equipment, half a dozen horses, and the oxen ashore. In prospect the task had seemed herculean, but in point of fact no more than four hours of labor were required.

Gatogordo and Ponchita, perhaps fearing that they were to be left permanently aboard, took it into their feline heads to leap into the river and swim ashore. El Buzzardo was already circling far and wide over this new territory. Poor Rory Sunrise, however, not able to fly so far and quite averse to swimming, came squawking over when Califia returned to the ship, doing an impressive little threat-dance for her and then complaining loudly. She picked up the rooster and held his head under her chin, at the same time assuring him that she couldn't get along without her prize bantam.

They set up camp among a grove of large redwoods—supposing that the high canopies would at least partially shield them from the rainstorms that were still certain to come. The overgrowth, however, proved no protection at all from chilly mists that blew in along the river. But with the men grouped in threes and fours against the larger trees, and with a roaring fire for each of the groups, they felt quite at home—at least once the chuck wagon was set up and beans and bread and venison could be cooked.

Darkness flooded the canyon, and after dinner Califia announced a ration of wine for the men—in honor of . . . well, in honor of nothing in particular except that they'd be ready to fell timber within a very few days.

"Hoorah for Miss Califia!" the lads sang out. *"Maraviloso!"*

The men sat about their respective fires, talking and nursing their wine; the oxen huddled together, groaning softly in the meadows below the encampment; and the mountain lions sprawled out near the fire, sound asleep but with an occasional twitch of a tail. Rory Sunrise perched at the base of Ponchita's neck, awakening for a moment, emitting a vigorous crow, and then drifting back into galliform dreams.

"Sis," Calvin said from across the dwindling camp fire they were both crouched beside, "I'm beginning to think this project may just be a bit more than you can handle. No—don't get riled; I put that badly. I mean, more than you can handle *gracefully*. Even without help, you'd manage. I'm not questioning your ability. But do you want me to convince Dad that he needs to get one of his honest-to-Yahoody experienced foremen up here—Thompkins, maybe, from San Lorenzo number two? This Russian River's a damned howling wilderness, and that's a fact. To tell you the truth, I was expecting a few cabins, little farms up in the *collados*, that sort of thing. I ought to stay with you myself, but. . . ."

Califia pretended not to have heard most of what her brother had just said. Calvin was born with a look of male smugness on his face. But he was a good soul, and in fact she could hardly have asked for a better and more loyal brother—though after all these years, one would suppose he'd have begun to get the idea. Califia Beard didn't need looking after—not while she was wearing a gun on her hip. Lead pellets were wondrous equalizers.

"No need, Cal, no need. The lads are proficient. Pa and Uncle Ray trained all but a few of them, so they know what they're about. And Juan Pescadero, he'll keep the others in tow."

"At least you've got Juan." Calvin nodded—and then took a pull from the wineskin they'd been passing back and forth—wine from Salinas Valley. Sour, but potent. . . .

"Drinking contest, Cal? See which one of us outlasts the other?"

He laughed, shook his head.

"The skin's virtually empty, Sis. Besides, I've learned my lesson. The thirteenth commandment says, *Thou shalt not be stupid enough to attempt to outdrink thy sister, who has a hollow leg.* . . .

"You take the fun out of things."

"Your compulsion about wanting to compete with men—it doesn't make sense. And those drinking contests you're so fond of—some night you'll try it with a stranger, and he'll end up taking advantage of you. Califia, you've got to learn to exercise better judgment."

She broke out laughing, though perhaps the laughter had a touch of bitterness in it.

"Why in hell do you think I drink?" Califia asked. "I'm almost twenty-seven, for God's sake—the heifer's twenty-seven and hasn't been humped since . . . I tell you, I'm damned tired of waiting for the right male to come along. Maybe it'd be better for me just to have a man when I want one and then chase him off—nothing permanent."

Cal shook his head.

"A child with no father—that's permanent, whether you like the idea or not."

The sister laughed again.

"We ladies have means to avoid getting pregnant—if a family way isn't what we want. Besides, I might actually enjoy raising a little *Jesús* all by myself."

Calvin raised the wineskin.

"You're an original, Califia Beard," he said.

"Coming from you, I'll take that as a compliment."

With the next tide, Calvin was gone, and she was alone except for her animals in the godforsaken Russian River woods. Well, not precisely alone—for, after all, she had several tons of equipment and supplies, six horses, eight oxen, two wagons, and twenty-three would-be loggers, gentlemen of varying dispositions and backgrounds, several of them skilled axemen, a few experienced workers from the mill on the San Lorenzo.

She was not alone for another reason—without question, she realized, more than just those two Indian villages were fairly close about—Pomos and possibly even Miwoks, both peoples said to be sometimes taciturn and sometimes as belligerent as the very devil. Whatever their inclinations, Califia could think of no particular reason why the native peoples should welcome a gang of rowdy tree-butchers. It was clear to her that she didn't wish to incur the ill will of the Pomos or anyone else, not if she wanted to succeed in her endeavors. Pescadero, her presumed number one man, had even advised her of a mysterious race of hairy giants who were said to live in these forests, though Juan thought perhaps the creatures didn't venture as far south as Russian River. Farther north, or so he insisted, *Bigfoot* was positively and without question known to exist—and to be responsible for random raids against *civilized humans* and *Indios* alike.

Possibly Juan was merely testing her gullibility, for as he spoke, his voice had in it that slight and telltale change of inflection the male of the species so universally adopts, whether he knows it or not, when attempting to blow smoke into a lady's ear. And yet, certainly, Califia had heard rumors of such apelike bears before, and she remembered Seagull speaking of someone who'd actually *seen* Bigfoot back in the recesses of the Ventanas, south of the Sur Rivers.

The two wagons piled high with goods and drawn by teams of four, Califia Beard and her men struggled inland, in most places being obliged to cut a roadway as they inched along for another two miles or so—while the cougars frolicked ahead, sometimes disappearing into the forest for an hour at a time.

A considerable meadow stretched along the river's northern bank, and a good-sized tributary stream joined with the *Rio Ruso* from the south. Back away from the coiling torrent rose high ridges cloaked in dense forest, some of the trees, as Califia and Juan Pescadero soon realized, having grown to genuinely monstrous proportions, noticeably larger than the specimens in the San Lorenzo groves.

This site seemed destined for the uses and abuses of a logging crew, and so Califia gave orders to set up a temporary camp at the mouth of the stream—Dutch Bill Creek, according to the rough chart the estimable John Sutter had provided. The choice of a permanent site, however, would have to wait upon Califia's meeting with the King of New Helvetia, a few days hence.

Once the basic needs of organization—of survival, rather—had been attended to, Califia rode out early in the morning, Gatogordo and Ponchita following. She told her leonine friends they should return to camp, but the cats were having no part of that. Not even the argument that neither El Buzzardo nor Rory Sunrise was along for the jaunt had any effect. She had long since observed that human pronouncements with regard to behavior had little effect upon cats of any size.

Califia intended to make her way downriver to the Russian's mouth, keeping to the north bank. From there she'd ride on toward Fort Ross. With luck she'd arrive at the former Russian-American fur post about noon, just in time to have lunch with John Sutter.

A light rainstorm had passed over during the night, leaving behind trailing bands of mist above the river's strong, gray-green current—and leaving behind vapors as well to drift among the thick gray-brown boles of redwoods along the water's edge, boles which vaguely reminded Califia of pictures she'd seen of columns of Greek temples, except that the shafts of the redwoods disappeared high overhead into tangles of green. The sensation was uncanny, and for a moment she found herself transported some nine years backward—so that she was there with Homer Virgil in the wilds of the Sierra, among those other huge trees. . . .

Early-morning sunlight, spilling down the eastern rim of the densely forested canyon, produced the sort of landscape that might have been purely a dream—light refracting through mists and suffusing the air with a seductive, luminous glow. It was one of those mornings when simply being alive was almost more than she could bear, and she half supposed she might at any moment come upon Pan and his attendant satyrs and nymphs, straight out of one of her Uncle Raymondo's books—for the soft, sun-bitten music of slow-moving wind through the redwoods, cascades leaping over cutbanks, and even the heavier sound of Russian River itself, all these blended into an orchestrated music that was played more certainly to the inner ear than to the outer.

When a cow elk and her two new arrivals started, matriarch glaring silent warning and then moving off into a dense growth of young redwood and fir, Califia toyed with the idea that she'd just come upon a sort of mystery—the wonder of all procreation, all generation. Azaleas bloomed along the river's margin, and the odor of the yellow-and-pink-throated blossoms was all but intoxicating.

As Califia's little sorrel mare plodded along, Gatogordo and Ponchita came streaming down from a tangle of alder and willow, their bodies like two tawny arrows. The mare gave a lurch, even though she was used to the big cats and their whims. But in the mare's mind, Califia strongly suspected, the notion of a pair of disgustingly tame cougars simply wasn't *natural*. In all truth, the same thought had crossed her own mind on more than one occasion. Then the pussies, drunk with their own physical prowess and the magic of the spring morning, were gone again, out of sight amongst a copse of young redwoods and firs.

At tidewater, the Russian River widened considerably—its surface this glorious morning an almost perfect mirror except where trailing mists still hovered.

Across the water from Califia was Ashachatiu village. The Indian people, she noted, were engaged in their ritual morning swim—nude bathing, women and girls on the upstream side, and men and boys perhaps a hundred yards downriver.

Possibly, Califia thought, she too would take a dip—but later in the day, in the surf a few miles up the coast, as she drew closer to Fort Ross. The Pacific would be icy cold—but with luck the sun would keep fog away from the beaches, and she'd at least find some warm rocks to retire to after plunging into the restless water.

CHAPTER TWELVE

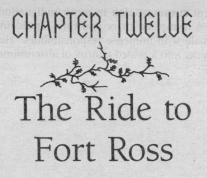

The Ride to
Fort Ross

[1845:]

FROM THE RIVER'S mouth, Califia turned north, riding across
hard-packed sand where possible, guiding her pony onto
headlands wherever that course of action was necessary. For
a time her two mountain tabbies followed, occasionally paus-
ing to sport with the seabirds and at one point actually beginning to stalk an old bull sea lion, a huge creature with perhaps
a dozen females in his harem, a brown monster who alternated
between glaring at the cougars and ignoring them utterly. Gatogordo and Ponchita persisted, forgoing their dangerous game
when the big fellow began snorting and roaring and lurching
toward them. Thereupon the two cats, as though struck by
lightning, went racing across glistening tide wash and up
amongst a series of dunes the incessant sea winds had created
and would in due course destroy—a process that seemed to
Califia a metaphor for her entire cosmos.

> *Change, change, it is all changing,*
> *Forever this way and that, forever*
> *Swallowing itself and giving birth to itself.*

Gulls went streaming aloft in mock indignation, while the great sea lion trumpeted twice and then lapsed into the fitful sleep of a male with immense responsibilities. His ladies, for their part, went into a muted chorus of absentminded braying and then subsided to snuffling for mussels or to looking after errant offspring. This society of sea lions, it seemed to Califia, in some ways quite accurately reflected the overall human condition—not as things should be and perhaps in the future would be, but as they unfortunately were. Large, posturing, aggressive males and self-absorbed females with young. . . .

The day was lovely, and the earth itself fairly shouted (silently, silently) of procreation, gestation, revelation. As Califia rode along, she found herself drifting into thoughts of H.V., dear H.V. who'd been her first love, and who, as matters were presently constituted, figured to be her only love.

The two of us, he and I together, high on the grassy rims above the headwaters of Big Creek and Pelican Doctor's Ohlone village where we both grew up, cousins who fell in love but who were denied the fruition of that love and who were drawn apart, separated, H.V. thrown halfway around the world and into the decadent civilization of European England. . . .

H.V., goddamn you, can't you hear me? Don't you realize what they've done to us? Yes, the very people who always insisted they cared for us. . .

Perhaps halfway to Fort Ross she drew her pony to a halt at the mouth of a fair-sized creek. Recent rains had swollen the stream to the point of allowing it to clear its throat—that is, to erode through a considerable accumulation of wind-driven sand at its mouth. Now, even though the stream's volume had significantly diminished in the aftermath of the rains, a torrent was racing down to join with surging saltwater.

Califia dismounted, treated her pony to a bit of bread smeared with molasses, left him to graze at will on bunches of coarse grass lining the stream banks, and walked across loosely compacted dunes toward the ocean. Sunlight gleamed from gray-green waters—configuring a wide sheet of silver fire that diminished to a point on the horizon.

"God's in the air today," she said, not at all concerned that she herself was the only one capable of hearing the words or of answering them. "God's in the air and the water and . . . in me, too. All this glitter's enough to unsex me—no, to get me with child. I'll be the Virgin Mary, then, and conceive our Holy Father's demon offspring. . . ."

Unable to control herself, and only partially responding to the wild words she'd just spoken, she began to laugh. Hat in hand, she began to run—stumbling through mounded sand, sea wind blowing into her face and causing her long hair to stream out behind. She felt giddy—almost drunk. Yes, drunk, the way she'd been that day at Grayhound Cove, years ago, when she and Calvin built a fire out of driftwood and proceeded to polish off a flask of Bill Beard's best tequila, at the same time discussing matters of religion and philosophy and the ultimate meaning of life.

They must have been—what? Nineteen? Yes, so young, and at the time she was so pitifully and foolishly ignorant of nearly everything around her except what she was feeling at the moment—melancholy, philosophic melancholy because her one true love had been sent away, off to Europe to be educated— and to get him away from her. . . .

Years ago. . . . very long years, and she had gone from being a proper young Californio señorita to the questionable status of old maid, twenty-six now, almost twenty-seven, and hardened and therefore old, whether she happened to feel old or not. An unmarried woman of her age was likely to remain so, since no self-respecting señor was likely to be interested in a woman who'd half changed her gender and was running a logging camp full of maniacs and partially reformed criminals.

But this day's sun was warm, inviting, almost seductive in its power—and so her reflections dropped away, the heaviness absorbed by wind and smooth-swept sand and brilliance glittering from green sea waves. She threw back her hair and laughed. Salt air filled her lungs, and for the moment her world was indeed the best of all possible worlds, just as the philosopher Pangloss asserted in *Candide*, a delightful little book H.V. had sent her from England, translated, fortunately, into English—the French she'd learned under the tutelage of Uncle Raymondo was hardly sufficient to the reading of literature. Nor did the fact that Voltaire discredited so completely the position of his esteemed philosopher make any difference to Califia—not on a day like this one.

Sweet music (that she couldn't hear but could feel down deep in the marrow of her bones) came drifting in over the God-struck waters, and she could almost have sworn she detected her name being called. With the wind blowing about her, Califia was unaware of the cats approaching. She was struck just below the knees as Gatogordo swerved into her and Ponchita gave her a less-than-gentle nudge, so that she was spun about and flipped to one side as if no more than that rag doll she'd had for the two of them to play with when they were kittens. A gust of wind caught her sombrero and sent it sailing down the beach. Startled though she was, she howled a protest and, scrambling to her feet, hurled a handful of sand toward their retreating forms, then went to fetch the hat.

Malicious cats. . . .

One cougar after the other, Ponchita in pursuit now, the two of them streamed down the beach, sending sandpipers aloft in a flurry. The lions, suddenly disdainful of wetting their paws, skidded to water's edge as a wave rushed up the beach. Then they turned and set off at a full run toward their mistress, one passing to either side. Tails to the wind now, they vanished among the dunes.

Califia was alone on the beach, the ever-present gulls her only companions. She sat on dry sand above the tide line and pulled off her boots. She rose, took a few steps, savoring the gritty sensation of coarse sand underfoot. She walked to the water's edge, heedless as the surf streamed up around her ankles, heedless and yet drawn to the power and serenity of the immense gray-green ocean.

She remembered Seagull's tale about a land across the water—her mother's insistence that this *land of the dead* was also a real land where real people existed, and that it was not merely some small island a few miles off the coast. No, the mysterious place was far away. The journey there required numerous days by big canoe, and was extremely dangerous. Many who went that way never reached their destination, while some who were successful in reaching the land in the west were unable to find their way back to the *barrancas* where redwoods were rooted in the earth.

Well, if God was in the air and in the water, then she'd swim out to meet Him. If He drowned her in the process, why certainly even drowning would be a good thing. In truth, though, Califia had no fears along such lines. The sea was relatively calm, its swells of no great height and nearly uniform as they marched in to meet the land. Besides all that, she prided herself on her swimming ability. Hadn't she always been able to outswim and outdive both her brother and dear H.V.?

In short, with no more than a casual backward survey of the upper limits of the beach whereon she stood, Califia Beard built a small fire out of scraps of driftwood—in a place where the wind had formed a declivity about the half buried form of a water-worn redwood stump, a tree probably washed down one of the rivers in a time of flood, bole broken away perhaps when storm waves hurled the tree's skeleton against protruding black coast boulders—and, hanging her sombrero from a root, undressed.

Califia stood in the wind, felt the flow of air about her face and breasts and thighs. She laughed in pure joy and then, remembering how the cougars had streaked toward the waves, only to pull up short, shook out her hair once again, and then ran like a madwoman directly into the incoming array of green breakers.

Unlike her friends, however, she steeled herself against the expected shock of cold water and at the same time lunged out into the oncoming waves. Seagulls flowed up into the air before her as she felt the coldness of saltwater about her ankles. Then she was all the way in, the ocean completely about her— as though she were in the embrace of an immensely powerful lover, one with the capacity to touch her all over in a single instant, a god whose touch burned cold and tasted of salt. . . . Califia struggled to the surface, gasped for air, and howled with pleasure as she spat brine.

Then, oblivious to the depth or the rolling waves about her, she was stroking outward, away from the shore. The insane notion of swimming all the way to that so-called *land of the dead* crossed through her mind, but then a particularly large wave quite unexpectedly coiled over and disabused her of the idea.

She treaded water, rose and fell with the passage of each wave as it moved past her. A gull swooped close, and she called to him. He ignored her and continued his irregular, wind-buffeted flight. Sunlight gleamed around her. She squinted toward this other god, the Being of Light—and she was on the verge of calling out in a kind of insane frenzy when a wave crested behind her and came pouring down, sending her spinning toward the beach.

Despite the violence of churning water, once she was beneath the surface she entered into a realm of disconcerting calm, a gentle rising and falling whose rhythm seemed strangely familiar and at the same time primeval, ancient, mysterious, and comforting. She knifed through the brine, eyes open as she passed a zone of drifting kelp trees that previous rough seas had ripped loose from moorings on reefs half a mile out.

For a moment Califia was face-to-face with a large harbor seal—the creature as startled as she. They both turned in the same direction and so for a few seconds moved through the water parallel to one another. Then the seal was gone, and she was stumbling to her feet in shallow water, thrown off balance and headlong by the surges as they rolled past.

Coarse sand beneath her feet, the water knee-deep, she twisted the moisture out of her long hair and exulted at the same time in sunlight and the intertwined odors of seawater and sand and iodine smell of kelp left high on the beach and drying out in an easy breeze that pulsed from the ocean. She licked the salt from her lips and waved at a large gray pelican.

Gatogordo and Ponchita came strolling down the sand— and suddenly, as though they were house cats that had caught sight of a hapless mouse, they shifted their postures to a slink and, now on tiptoes, continued to approach their mistress. In whatever game this was they were intent upon playing, Califia was the apparent prey. She called to the cougars and even shook her fist at them, but to no avail. They continued to stalk her—the two big felines spreading out so as to make a final mad dash at her and have her in effect pinned between them.

Without other alternative, she decided to mimic their attitude. She began her own stalking procedure, ignoring Ponchita and slouching directly toward Gatogordo. For a moment the cougars lost their nerve, but after sidelong glances at one another, they once more took up the hunt. Califia turned quickly and dashed toward Ponchita. The lioness, in turn, decided the game had gone far enough—and, tail streaming behind her, she went gliding toward a covey of scoters, sending the small birds whirring upward in a rush.

With his mistress' back turned toward him, however, Gatogordo leaped forward, the full force of his two-hundred-pound body striking Califia as she was in the act of chasing Ponchita, and Califia went sprawling face-first into the sand, the wind half knocked out. Then Gatogordo was over her, his big jaws clamped about her arm.

You realize, Mistress Beard, that I could have you for dinner if I chose to do so. Mountain lions are much stronger and faster than people, yes, and much more intelligent and handsome, too. . . .

Gatogordo and Ponchita, once their fun was behind them, went skulking off to whatever variety of business it is that occupies mountain lions during their working hours. Califia dressed, donned her sombrero, and walked across the dunes to where she'd left her trail pony. Once in the saddle, she proceeded northward to Fort Ross, where the honorable Johann August Sutter was in temporary residence, with the general blessings of the Californio government, since Sutter's acquisition had put an effective end to Russian presence in California—though rumor had it that Mariano Vallejo was not altogether pleased.

Sutter, her father had told her, claimed to have been an officer in the Royal Swiss Guard of France—and had arrived in Monterey in 1839. At some point along the line, between his native Switzerland and California, Sutter had been a trader on the Sante Fe Trail.

"Sí, sí," Uncle Raymondo had said, *"it's simple. Señor Sutter, he wants his own country, that's all. He wishes for self-government. That is to say, he wishes to be the only government, and so he convinced the admirable Juan Bautista Alvarado to give him a huge land grant along the Sacramento River. Alvarado may be handsome and a very brave man, but he doesn't always use good sense. Perhaps one day we will all be citizens of New Helvetia. . . . With Isaac Graham and the American riflemen, Sutter even managed*

to assist in removing Nicolas Gutierrez. Indeed, Herr Sutter had very good luck until he got onto the wrong side in our last little revolution. . . ."

"Well, so it is." Bill Beard had shrugged. "Sutter's Empire of New Helvetia's in need of timber, and he's got nothing close to him the likes of our coastal redwoods and firs. With a bit of luck, Califia, Mr. Sutter should prove to be a profitable friend. He's said to be long on civility, and if approached properly by an attractive lady such as yourself, he's likely to draw up such papers with us as may be of great future value. With this in mind, Daughter, I hereby instruct you to forego challenging the gentleman to either horse racing or pistol shooting."

The remembered conversation with her father and uncle faded away as Califia reached a crest in the coast trail and stopped to survey the cluster of barns, workshops, barracks, and headquarters of Fort Ross—the flag of Mexico flying proudly from a tall staff at the center of an open courtyard. Gatogordo and Ponchita slunk along beside her, and now she dismounted and proceeded to lecture them as to the dangers of approaching any human beings whom they didn't know on an intimate basis.

The cats had heard this speech before, but nevertheless they listened quite impatiently. Whether they understood what she was saying was another matter altogether, but certainly the gist of her warning was comprehended. Had the felines not been well trained, they'd never have survived. El Puma was hardly the most popular of wild animals in areas where cattle were being raised—and the raising of cattle was the principal agricultural endeavor throughout Alta California. Cats that made an attempt to approach the herds, in the hope of making off with a fat calf, were as good as dead—if the marksmanship of the vaquero proved sufficient to the task at hand.

Ponchita indicated that she was more interested in the possibility of a wrestling match with her mistress than she was in being banished to the forest, but Califia shook her finger at both lions and was otherwise extremely forceful. Gatogordo nuzzled her hand, and then the two lions, as if on cue, turned and loped off, moving with astonishing liquid grace.

Califia smiled as she watched them disappear. In her mind, the lions were indeed soft, malleable to her will, and harmless—and yet she knew well enough the various stories of big cats killing horses and cattle. Juan Pescadero insisted that he'd once witnessed a confrontation between a grizzley and a she-lion—the cat having killed a deer, the bear intent upon taking the prize. Since a grizzly may weigh five times as much as a lion, one would expect such a contest to prove no contest at all. However, according to Juan, the she-lion was not only able to hang on to her capture but, after delivering several astonishing blows to the grizzly's nose and ears, managed to drive the bear away in most dramatic fashion—a complete rout.

Califia tried to imagine Gatogordo or Ponchita in the process of such heroics but was unable to stretch her imagination that far. She laughed, reached into her saddlebag for the lovely gold comb H.V. had given her before his departure for England and Europe and the various other wonders of civilization, and attempted to straighten her hair—which, she feared, was somewhat tinged with sea salt and greatly in need of washing. No doubt she should have considered the matter more seriously before deciding to play mermaid.

Well, Herr Sutter would have to deal with her, no matter what her appearance. In his mind, almost certainly, Califia was that *gnädiges Fräulein* who was convinced she was a man—for who else would be involved in business dealings and the operation of a logging camp? But when it came to business, as a matter of simple fact, Califia was determined to be no more a woman than the next man—and if Sutter wanted timber, then he'd be obliged to deal with her as a professional equal.

She urged her trail pony forward and proceeded downslope toward the fort itself, dipping her sombrero in the direction of a pair of young men, bare to the waist, who were engaged in splitting cedar rails.

Healthy specimens of the male animal—probably not particularly bright, but no doubt serviceable enough in other ways. . . .

She smiled, glanced back at them. To continue in her present *unhumped* condition, she decided, was untenable, against nature. There were tales of women who went crazy because of a lack of sex. Perhaps she should purchase a fifteen-year-old Panamanian and keep him on a leash. . . .

Califia noted that Fort Ross and all the outbuildings were

constructed almost totally of redwood poles—as well as some larger logs, these split into half rounds.

"*Ach ja*, Fräulein Beard, come in, come in. Sit down, *bitte*. You have had a long ride. Two of my *Arbeiters*, they rode up from the mouth of *Der Russisch Fluss* just yesterday, and they say the *Indios* tell them you and your crew are camped upriver a few miles."

Captain Sutter—or General Sutter—or King Sutter, whatever he was, wore no military garb this day. Instead, he was clad in expensive silks and linens, with a brilliant maroon choker protruding from beneath a green blazer. Califia would almost have supposed the good gentleman dressed for the purpose of attending a festival or even an opera, but no such entertainment was available here at the former Russian fur post. The elegant garb, she surmised, was in fact Sutter's trademark. He looked very much the dandy, except that his large, calloused hands were clearly those of a man who was fairly well acquainted with manual labor.

For a moment Califia was nearly overcome by the urge to curtsy—and then it was all she could do to avoid bursting into laughter.

The gentleman's married—a family back in Switzerland—married but fond of the company of Californio ladies and Indio women—and fond of his whiskey as well—how do Dad and Uncle Raymondo know all this about him?

"A good day for a ride," she nodded, sitting down and removing her hat, placing it on the floor beside the chair. "Yes, yes, Señor Sutter. My crew's in position, ready to begin cutting timber. So, John—may I call you John?—where are you planning to set up this mill? Possibly that's something I should handle—the milling operations, I mean. We have many years of experience with all kinds of equipment. Then Olivo & Beard delivers whatever timber you need, cut to specifications, either here or inland, at Sacramento—the Oregon fir, yellow pine, or redwood."

Sutter lit a cigar, and Califia could see that he was on the verge of offering her a stogie as well—then hesitated on account of her gender.

She smiled, shook her head.

"No thanks. I don't smoke. My mother's people—in their minds, tobacco shouldn't be touched by a woman. I'm half Ohlone, you see. . . ."

Sutter studied the handsome, gray-eyed woman, puffed on his cigar, allowed his eyes to drop to the leg harness that held Califia's prized Elgin gun knife, a hefty forty-five-caliber pistol with a nasty-looking but actually somewhat awkward bayonet attached. At least Califia presumed that's what the good man had his eyes on.

She glanced about the captain's well-appointed office, complete with two large bookcases half filled with volumes, some of them appearing to be quite old.

"*Ach ja, ach ja, Fräulein.* The *Schneidemuhle*, indeed. At the mouth of Russian River, *Russisch Fluss*, that is where I will place the mill. You will float the logs down to my mill, and when the boards have been sawn, then your brother and his *Schiff* will take on the cargo we have created. Yerba Buena, Monterey, New Helvetia—there's good profit to be made, *Fräulein Beard*, good profit. You'll keep whiskey away from your men, *ja*? Once such men begin to drink, no more work is done."

Califia glanced about the room, nodded.

"You must understand that this isn't my first crew, Señor Sutter," she smiled. "You may count on a good supply of timber, and on a regular basis. How soon can you have your mill up and operating? There's an island about a mile in from Goat Rock—we can tie the logs into rafts at that point. When the milling actually begins, we'll already have laid in a considerable supply."

"Your father and uncle, *Fräulein*, they will . . . send additional men if that should prove necessary?"

Califia smiled and winked at Sutter, apparently disconcerting him, at least for the moment.

"When will your saws arrive?" she asked. "No sense in cutting the entire forest if the logs are going to lie in the water for months at a time. . . . Possibly we should bring in Mr. Cooper from our Petaluma operation—I mean, to give expert advice on setting up the mill."

Sutter nodded, coughed, and poured himself a shot of whiskey—offered the same to Califia, who accepted. She was hardly used to drinking whiskey, but there was no sense in letting Sutter know that. She sipped at her drink and studied her well-dressed new business associate. Sutter was indeed a distinguished-looking man, and she could understand how it was that even women her own age might find him attractive.

"You fought on the wrong side in the last skirmish," Califia observed. "My brother and I were both there, with Alvarado's force. Since Alvarado's said to be the one who pushed through your application for a land grant, why didn't you fight on his side, if I might be so bold as to ask?"

Sutter sipped the remainder of his whiskey.

"Ah, *Fraulein Beard*, that thing is unfortunate—for I consider *Herr Alvarado* to be a very good friend. But you must remember that I was then, as I still am, the *Comandante militar de las fronteras del norte y encargado de la justicia*, and so I was duty-bound to fight to protect whatever government had been duly authorized by Mexico. That government was headed by Micheltorena. Now that he's gone, I am glad. Pio Pico and Jose Castro are able leaders, and I trust that all will go well."

"In California, wars are fought differently than anywhere else in the world." Califia smiled.

"*Ja, jawohl, du hast richtig.* I fitted out most of the men at my own expense, and failing in my purpose, I lost it all—money, horses, arms, and provisions. I returned to the north with Jim Bidwell, Dr. Townsend, and my good friend Juan Vaca, along with my Sandwich Islanders and of course my Maidu Indians. We rode up the San Joaquin Valley, just as you and your brother and Vallejo did."

"But surely, things are going well for you now?"

"*Nein*, no, the war has thrown everything into chaos. You have heard of Pierson Reading, no doubt? He commanded my fort while I was gone, but he was unable, with the small force I left him, to see to it that my crops were planted as they should have been. No plowing, not so much as an acre sown in *Samen*, to seed. *Ach ja*, and one band of Indians raided two ranches near my fort and stole a number of horses and cattle— then, after my return, they killed a rancher. As *Comandante*, however, I have already addressed that problem. Unfortunately, I had counted on this year's harvest in order to restore my credit with the Russians."

"Perhaps," Califia said, "our lumber arrangement will help to make up for the other losses. Once we're in full operation, the business should be quite profitable—for the owner of New Helvetia and for Olivo & Beard as well."

Sutter rose from his velvet-lined chair, strode to the liquor cabinet, and poured himself another shot of whiskey—at the same time making an offer to Califia.

"Why, yes," she replied, "I don't mind if I do."

John Sutter, she concluded, was quite charming—without genuine guile—and one in love with the sound of his own voice. Her latter observation, however, in no way amounted to an indictment—since virtually all males suffered from the same affliction.

CHAPTER THIRTEEN

A Hunter for Miss Boss

[1845:]

JOHN SUTTER ACCEPTED assurance that a sufficient supply of logs would soon be floating down the Russian River, and Califia was convinced that the patriarch of New Helvetia had both the intention and the capacity to set up the necessary mill at or near Russian River's mouth, to get the project under way forthwith, and most importantly to pay for services rendered and goods received. Both their signatures were penned to several documents binding New Helvetia and Olivo & Beard.

Thus, despite Sutter's tempting invitation that she should join him for supper and also take lodging for the night, Califia declined (in deference to appearances and to the presumed feelings of an absent Mrs. Sutter, who was on the other side of the world and hence unable to defend her territorial rights) and opted instead to utilize the remaining hours of daylight to make her way back toward her logging camp. Whatever the good intentions of Señor Juan Pescadero, Califia half suspected her men of all being gloriously drunk in their mistress' absence. While she'd taken some care to see to it that no sufficient stores of spirits had been brought along, no amount of diligence (since the dawn of time) had ever been sufficient to

separate the dedicated woodsman from his grog. In the vicinity
of logging camps, whiskey was known to appear as if by magic.
Some said gnomes were responsible, while others blamed the
ghost of the infamous Maine woods logger, Johnny Applesnort.

Gatogordo and the faithful Ponchita saw fit to rejoin Califia
four or five miles south of Fort Ross—and from the expressions
on their feline faces, their mistress strongly suspected they'd
been up to no good. With neither range cattle nor farmhouses
(and hence poultry) about, however, she couldn't even guess
as to what the mischief might have been. Possibly the lions
had been back at their trick of harrying sea lions or had been
baiting an old and hence not altogether spry black bear or
grizzly.

With the lions padding along ahead of her, Califia made
her way toward what would pass as home for good portions
of perhaps the next two or three years. The moon, very large
and very white, was nearly to full and would provide light
sufficient for the last half of her ride upriver from tidewater—
or so she thought.

As matters turned out, luck wasn't with her. As she neared
the place where she'd gone swimming earlier in the day, her
pony went lame. A sharp piece of slate had lodged itself into
a forehoof. The mare was extremely reluctant to have a human
working on her foot, and even after Califia threatened to hit
her over the head with a club and feed her remains to the
mountains lions, the trail pony still wasn't altogether convinced. When Gatogordo whipped his tail, however, the horse
gave in, and Califia was able to pry out the stone—a chipped
flint arrowhead, oddly enough, one that had apparently been
lying in the trail, waiting for the right hoof to step on it.

It was now clear that Califia was fated to lead her mare
back to the logging camp, and since the sun was hanging low
and red above a slate-gray Pacific, Califia decided that wisdom
lay in making a camp for the night and proceeding back to
home base in the morning. Pescadero and the others would
presume that she'd stayed at Fort Ross, so no one would be
out on the trail searching for a maimed or murdered boss lady.

By twilight she'd led her horse out through the dunes, to
the edge of a small freshwater stream the beach swallowed.
Here was grass for the animal to graze. By means of a long,

braided lariat, Califia tethered the mare to a big bush lupine. The horse, limping conspicuously but probably more for show than for any other reason, hobbled about and began to lip coarse grass.

The lions were off on another jaunt—possibly in search of an evening meal. Handouts from human beings were agreeable most of the time, but people were no predictable source of red meat. Sometimes yes, but sometimes no. And so the big cats hunted for jackrabbits, possums, squirrels, mice, and occasionally even deer, as the luck of the hunt or the degree of hunger decided.

Califia built a fire in the sand above the stream and rolled out her bedding, used saddlebags to form a pillow. But it wasn't time for sleep as yet, not with a full moon hanging amber above the eastern skyline; and besides, she was hungry. With sugar to sweeten her coffee, jerky to chew on, and a pan full of peas and cornmeal to eat, Califia stared at a final, fading bar of crimson out across the gray-black Pacific and relaxed. An offshore breeze brought in odors of salt and of iodine. A night heron crossed the still-glowing portion of sky—almost, she thought, like some grotesque messenger from the other world.

She could hear the sound of the mare drinking from the stream—a snorting, sucking noise. Somewhere, beyond the dunes, a horned owl was crying—silent hunter of the crepuscular hour, perhaps attempting to cause a cottontail or a wood rat to lose nerve and bolt from cover, perhaps merely letting its mate know its whereabouts.

If Califia listened very carefully, she realized, she could actually detect the sound of grains of sand streaming across the beach, driven by that constant flow of air off the Pacific. As the moon rose higher, it cast out a broad swath of light and turned the restless surface of the ocean into a seething dull metallic radiance.

Califia sipped coffee, chewed jerky, and reflected on her general impression of John Sutter. The thought of spending a night with the man crossed her mind. She toyed with the notion—was Sutter not *distinguido*, powerful, respected, extremely wealthy? Furthermore, she enjoyed the tenor of his voice, the modulations and flowings of vocables, these punctuated by an occasional Germanic growl, cough, or sputter. But no. Perhaps it was true that, as a man of the world, John Sutter was highly adept at making love, knew what to do, would be gentle and demanding by turns—and yet Califia had known all along that this was simply not a man with whom she wished to share her body. She vowed to keep the association with Sutter on a totally businesslike level.

The man she wanted, had always wanted (aside from Juan Bautista Alvarado, who'd insulted her before the battle and so had been crossed off her list), was that wretched cousin of hers, Homer. Why had the two of them long ago not found the courage, the strength to fly in the face of convention and simply ride off together to whatever sort of life they were fated to live? Instead, a Yokuts arrow intervened—even as, right now, the point of an arrow, lying there in the trail for God-knew how-long, had managed to lodge itself into her mare's hoof, thus preventing her from getting back to the logging camp.

In all likelihood, however, matters had turned out for the best. Homer Virgil had long since graduated from Cambridge University and was teaching in what he called a *preparatory* school for the sons of the well-to-do. Naturally he'd found someone with whom he might share his dream of civilization and learning, and so he'd married her. H. V.'s life was there in England, and Califia bore him no ill will. Indeed, she wished him great happiness—even as she treasured and would always treasure those few days they'd had together long ago, the wonder and the horror as well.

Furthermore, in most ways her own life's pattern had worked out quite profitably. She was happy with her lot, and she enjoyed immensely the role of being a woman fully able to compete with men in the world of logging and milling. In a sense she was her father's *right-hand man*, yes, and Uncle Raymondo's as well. Brother Calvin's realm was that of the sea, while hers was the forest, the great trees, and her collection of animal friends, both wild and domestic.

Her gruel of cornmeal and peas was puffing and sputtering in its pan. Taking this as a sign the concoction might have been rendered edible by means of the fire's subtle alchemy, Califia removed the mush from the flames and set it to cool.

She sipped hot coffee and gnawed at yet another strip of jerked beef.

"An ocean of brine right beside me," she said, addressing the night, "and no salt for my meal. . . . Little Cal, is that what they call you? Well, I'd say this omission in preparation constitutes a small instance of lack of foresight, and that proves it: a woman's got no beeswax trying to run a logging operation."

Out of the darkness and into the irregular circle of firelight came Gatogordo and Ponchita, their tongues lolling to one side. They drank from the stream, and the male gave thought to grooming the female's neck fur. But Ponchita hissed, and Gatogordo instantly lost interest.

The cats came up into the circle of firelight once again, tails whipping back and forth. They sniffed at the pot of mush.

"I suppose I could share," Califia said. "It's not much, but it's more than I want, I'm sure of that. It's hot, though—you'll burn your tongues."

She used her hunting knife to remove a portion from the container, then blew on it before offering it to the lions. They, in turn, licked cautiously before deciding they enjoyed the taste. When the treat was finished, they lay down on top of Califia's bedroll, side by side, bit at their paws for a few moments, and then lowered their big heads and slept.

Califia took a lump of brown sugar to the horse. It was only common justice, after all, that mares with sore feet should be given sugar.

After sitting by the fire for an hour or two and mulling her thoughts, Califia struggled to persuade Ponchita to move over so that she, the person in authority, might be allowed to slip under the blankets. The lioness got up, sat on her haunches, and sulked until Califia stroked neck and ears and apologized several times. Then Ponchita lay down, side pressed against the human's body.

Morning sunlight filtered through running fog, and the waves thrashed about, booming at times. Califia awoke and was immediately aware that her cougars had left her—probably, she thought sleepily, off on a foraging expedition—either that or chasing surf birds or disturbing harbor seals. The fire was still burning, but how could that be? She tried to recall if she'd even bothered the previous night to pile extra chunks of driftwood over the coals before falling asleep. But her last remembered image was of nothing more than a bed of embers, these glowing with the magic of heat, and yet allowing for no more than a few wisps of flame.

So why's the damned fire burning? And the odor of coffee?

She opened one eye, glanced to where she'd left her pony tethered.

A mule?

Suddenly she was wide awake. Without appearing to do more than move in her sleep, she unholstered her Elgin gun knife, slipped barrel and bayonet carefully free of her blankets, and then sprang up into a crouch, her weapon before her.

What in hell's name?

On the opposite side of the campfire, squatting Indian style and sipping from a tin cup, was a large, leather-garbed individual, his reddish beard tinged with gray, a grease-matted beaver cap punctuated by three hawk feathers. A pair of blue eyes beneath shaggy eyebrows that might once have been brown but now were silver. . . . The man lowered his cup of coffee, grinned (revealing one front tooth missing), and nodded.

"Mawning, Mizz Beard," he said. "Heard you was up in this neck o' the woods, and since I need a job, I paid your camp a leetle visit. Sure enough. But your foreman, John the Fisherman—*Pescadero*—he said ye was off to shoot the breeze with John Sutter, over to the old Russian fort. I waited, but when ye didn't show up last night, I started gettin' nervous. Would of been a bad business if I just sat by while Bill Beard's kid got lost in the woods an' starved to death, now wouldn't it? So I moseyed down the river last evening, an' about sundown I smelled smoke—that an' some kind of chow cooking. Well, since I was already settled in for the night by then, I waited until first light, an' then I come looking for ye. What I caught sight of, though, looked like a pair of catamounts camped out by a crick side—them an' a pony. When I rode in, the cougars sidled off into the brush. If you've got 'em for protection, I don't guess they pay for their keep. Like a cup o' my special coffee, Mizz Beard? Pure coffee it is, except for some manzanita berries. Take it as a favor, I would, if ye'd put away that military ordnance. . . ."

"Samson Flowers! How in God's name did you . . . ?"

"Long story, long story. Ye ain't' fixin' to shoot me an' then stab me to death, are ye?"

Califia broke out laughing—waved her Elgin gun knife in salute, and stood up, holstered her weapon, and extended her hand to the old mountain man.

"Where are your friends, Samson—Greenwood and Beckwourth, I mean?"

Flowers shrugged.

"Never can tell about those two coons. When I left 'em, they picked up with Walkara the Ute and Pegleg Smith—only Caleb Greenwood, he don't cotton to Walkara, so he rode north to find his son, Johnny, at Sutter's Fort. Beckwourth, Smith, and Walkara, they said they was going to steal every horse in California as wasn't tied down with a chain, an' then they was figurin' to herd the bunch o' them back to Taos. I told 'em if they tried that, why Alvarado'd likely catch the lot of them an' stretch their necks. But Jim Beckwourth, he never listened to anyone, not in his life."

"Steal horses? You Americans pretty much play by your own rules, don't you?"

"Most o' the time. But as ye can see, Mizz Califia, I'm law-abidin', an' besides, I owe a bundle to your pa and your Uncle Raymondo. Like I told ye down to Cahuenga, they give me a job years ago when nobody else was willin' to do it, an' that allowed me to get on my feet so's I could mosey back to the Rocky Mountains to do some serious trappin'. That's all gone now, though. Europeans give up on beaver caps, an' they weren't too many o' Brother Beaver's kin left in the streams anyhow. I guess we catched 'em all, sure enough. So now I'm here an' looking for a job."

"If you're through babbling, Samson, I'd be pleased to drink your . . . coffee."

Flowers obliged, handed Califia a cup of the brew, winked, and pointed down the beach. The two cougars were happily engaged in stalking shorebirds.

"So you're looking for work? Have you ever done any logging? I mean, it's hardly the same as trapping furs, you know, and . . ."

"Guess I could learn, if it came to that. But what I had in mind—I figured ye'd need a hunter, someone to bring in meat for that gang o' tree killers you got. I may not be much of a logger, ma'am, but I'm a hell of a good shot. At one time or another, I've been camp hunter for Ogden's bunch, an' for Bill Sublette on one of his trips upriver, an' for Weyeth, as well. An' o' course, I been feedin' myself for the last thirty years. Your boys'll work harder if they've got fresh meat on the table, I'll lay odds on 'er."

"A camp hunter? Well, yes, all right, though I'd figured to assign those duties as necessary. . . ."

"You wouldn't want me cuttin' trees on account I don't know nothing about 'er, now ain't that right? By the same token, ma'am, you shouldn't hire no *greenhorn* an' give him a Hawken rifle an' expect him to do a *man's job*. You need game for your log butchers to chow down on, then give me the job. Remember, I worked for your pa and your uncle before you an' your brother was even born. . . ."

"All right, Samson Flowers, you're a hunter."

"Knowed that, knowed that all along. Question is, am I the hunter for Miss Boss?"

Califia laughed.

"Reckon ye is, ol' hoss. But one o' us is going to have to learn to speak English, or Spanish, or at least something that sounds like an honest-to-God language."

Samson Flowers got to his feet. He was considerably taller than she'd remembered—well over six feet. He tipped his head back and squinted, then extended an arm out to either side, stretched, yawned, once again revealing his missing tooth.

"Your pony's stove up," Flowers said. "Rock bruised hoof, or some such thing. Anyhow, you can ride behind me on my mule, an' we'll trail the mare. Juan Pescadero, he's a good fellow. Was genuine concerned about ye. That's partly why I decided to head up the coast an' find ye."

"The mare picked up an arrowhead—must have been lying in the trail, waiting. I think she'll be all right, though. Your mule strong enough to carry the two of us?"

Flowers rubbed his nose and then scratched at his lower lip.

"You sure got the damned prettiest gray eyes, Mizz Califia," he said.

"Do you have to spit all the damned time?" Califia demanded as they rode upstream beside the Russian River, past the Pomo village of Chalanchawi across the water. "When the wind's blowing, the spray comes back on me."

"I'll tell the wind to stop blowin', then." Flowers laughed.

The mountain man stared across the tidewater river, finding momentary pleasure in the effect of a million bits of silver light gleaming from the surface. In the village, he could see a few squaws grouped together—apparently intent upon butchering out a deer or an elk and placing strips of meat onto a drying rack. Brown-skinned children chased madly after one another. An old man stood not far from the women, pointing across the river to where Samson and Califia were riding along, the mare in tow.

Ain't nothing we've done has much touched the way they live— just kind of timeless, with the seasons passin' by, an' people dyin' and little ones gettin' born. . . .

"Chewing tobacco—that's a vile habit. The rest of your teeth are going to fall out, and then your tongue'll turn green. I'll have to declare a holiday while we bury you—and that's one man-day lost for every timber beast in the camp."

She felt . . . easy . . . toward Samson Flowers; and yet there was something about the man that annoyed her, just as had been the case at Cahuenga Pass during the battle against Micheltorena's forces. Perhaps she felt toward him as . . . well, as she might have felt toward a brother much older than Calvin. But at the same time she was quietly infuriated by the way he *presumed* things. How was she to have such a man working for her? True, he'd be off in the forest a good deal of the time and therefore out of her hair, but nonetheless. . . .

"Goddamned regular little momma hen, ain't ye?" Flowers demanded after the mule had jolted its way a few more yards. "Lady, this mountain hawg's old enough to be your pa. Besides that, you're riding on *my* varmint. Didn't Seagull an' Bill

Beard teach ye no manners? Children are damn well supposed to show respect for their elders."

"Mr. Flowers, I believe you said you were interested in being my camp hunter. Have you forgotten already that I'm in charge? Am I supposed to pay you for showering me with tobacco juice? Good heavens, act civilized!"

"It's *civilized* ye want? That's for coons what live in Philadelphia or Boston or London or some such. You get civilized, you get jails an' churches an' everybody afraid to do anything on account that somebody else might not like 'er. Ye pay taxes an' worry about whether they's a bridge in the right spot an' whether the schoolmarm's actually got a boyfriend off in another town an' she's going to see him on Saturday afternoons, an' is that goin' to have a bad effect on the children in her schoolhouse? Okay, so maybe you got a point. I guess I could spit downwind, considering. But about that job—when the time comes, you want to tell me just whar to plunk the deer as I haul 'em in? Truth is, I jest sort of come up hyar to help ye out—kind of an obligation to Bill an' Raymondo, so to speak. World I was brought up in, young ladies was supposed to stay home an' tend to crocheting an' so forth—until some young buck come along an' took 'em off their daddies' hands, anyhow. After that they was supposed to cook meals an'. . . ."

Gatogordo and Ponchita loped past the limping mare and the mule and the two humans. Flowers' animal, not yet used to mountain lions as trail companions, snorted and took a half-step sideways.

"Spread their legs on demand? So that's how you see women, is it? Let me tell you something, Samson Flowers. You may pride yourself on being a hunter, but I'll wager half a month's pay that I can beat you fair and square in a shooting contest. Chalk a six-inch circle to the side of a redwood, and we'll use Hawken rifles at a hundred paces. I'd offer a footrace, but as you say, you're as old as my father—and I'd be taking advantage."

Part of Flowers' mind was elsewhere—as a result of a lifetime of enforced habit—his eyes looking ahead for sign—sign of anything at all—his hearing attuned to the various familiar sounds of the forest—his sense of smell analyzing the air he breathed. In the world where he'd lived most of his life, to be inattentive to even the smallest things was very likely to end up dead. Those who learned the lesson survived, the others didn't.

Perhaps he should have ridden with Walkara and Smith and Beckwourth. Those boys would take in a handsome profit—if they managed to get that herd of horses clear to Taos. If not, then they'd find something else to keep them happy. Such men, and he included himself, were essentially no more than grown children with an immense thirst for play.

"*Spread their legs* sounds like some St. Louis trollop," he said, "willin' to take on any nigger for money. Before ye cut me off, young lady, I was going to say *have babies.* Wagh! It's the way o' nature. If grizzly mommas didn't have cubs, they wouldn't be no more grizzlies after a time. Argue me that one. . . ."

Califia felt the blood come to her face. She wished desperately that she'd not been obliged to accompany Samson Flowers on the mule. For one thing, the poor creature's back was about ready to break, and for another thing, she sometimes found it necessary to place her hands on Samson's shoulders so as to steady herself.

"Anyhow," Samson continued, "how much are ye payin' me? Be good if I knew how much I was gettin', if you see what I mean."

"Perhaps I should walk the rest of the way to camp. Why do you have to be so damned argumentative, Mr. Flowers?"

He turned half around in his saddle, grinned, the missing tooth highly noticeable.

"Heck," he said, "it's okay to call me *Sam* or *Samson*, either one. No sense being all formal. Ye don't want me hailin' you *Miss Beard*, now do ye?"

"*Miss Beard* will do quite nicely, sir. Either that or *Miss Boss*."

"Have it your own way, then. Have it your own way. Ain't that your pet carrion crow up yonder? Just before I rode off to find ye, the old feather duster was perched on the chuck wagon, an' I kinda coaxed him down for some petting. I noticed he was missin' a glide feather on either side, just like that one there. . . ."

Surprised, Califia studied the form of a big bird the former fur trapper was pointing to. It was sailing on wind currents several hundred feet up. Then the vulture swooped down, circling about, using its broad wings as brakes, and, fanning and hissing, El Buzzardo alighted on Califia's shoulder.

"Like I thought," Samson chuckled, spitting tobacco juice. "Now back to what I was sayin' before ye got onto the issue o' my personal habits. I admit these here Russian River redwoods are healthy enough to make planks an' all. But when I come across the Sierra with Joe Walker an' his bunch, we seen some redwoods as would put these hyar to shame. I'm talkin' trees twice the size o' the biggest ye got in the Coast Mountains. Make these'ns look like kindling or summat."

"You really take me for a fool, don't you? In the first place, you weren't with Joe Walker—because that was 1870, and you were in Oregon country, trapping for Dr. McLoughlin and the H.B.C. In the second place, I've been to the Sierra Nevada—and I've seen the big trees. Yes, they are *big*, but not all that much larger than the coast redwoods, when one gets right down to it. Not as tall, either."

Flowers chuckled.

"Mule," he said, "she's touchy, this one. An' a pack o' wild varmints to back her up, just in case. In the first place, Miss Boss, I damned well was with Joe Walker. I can tell ye everything that happened, first to last. An' in the second place, *some of them* Sierra redwoods sure as blazes is twice as big around as the best o' the coast trees, an' a different—how do ye say?—a different species to boot. I don't know what trees ye saw, but ye didn't see all of 'em, that's for sure. The ones I saw was *large*. When was ye in Sierra, anyhow? Bill Beard took ye thar, did he?"

"No, no. Not that it's any of your damned business. My cousin and I rode over there—nine years ago. The Indians shot Homer in the back, and he nearly died. . . ."

Flowers nodded.

Just ahead was the point where the river reached tide level— the green current streaming out in a long vee, settling into the wider channel. Another four miles to the logging camp. . . . Clouds were beginning to blow in off the Pacific—just thin streamers so far, but a storm was likely. It would be another month before the rains would stop for the summer, one of those long, dry, hot California summers—hot everywhere except right along the coast and inland as far as the fogs were able to get. That was the realm of mists, the area where the redwoods grew. The old red-barks liked moisture, that was certain. . . .

"Seems I heard something about that," he said. "But with regard to the trees. Don't your people—the Ohlones, I mean—don't they sort of figure the great big fellas are like sepulchres, something o' the kind? The souls o' the Ancients are inside 'em? In any case, ye ought to leave the big'ns alone. Ain't right nohow to cut down trees what ye don't need. Raymondo, he's a man who's read every book in the world. He could tell ye. Some of them granddaddy redwoods was already alive, most likely, when Jesus Hisself was born, an' maybe long before that. Ain't right to cut down trees what ye don't need. That's part o' the reason I run out on your pa an' Raymondo close to thirty years back—all them stumps just sitting there, bleedin' an' cryin'. Afterwards, after we'd finished with an area, the birds wouldn't sing no more. I tell ye, trap a few varmints, an' the next year they'll be just as many as before—if ye don't take too many, I mean. But cut down a whopping old tree, an' even a century later she won't be growed back. An' maybe it won't never grow back. I seen some o' what the boys have done up in Maine and over to Minnesota country. Ain't forest fires or high winds able to cause so much outright destruction as what a bunch o' tree butchers an' their axes an' oxen can do. Ain't just *against* nature—it's outright *war* on nature. Fencin' an' plowin' the land's one thing, but killin' the big trees, that's another."

Califia was astonished—a side of Samson Flowers' nature that she hadn't even suspected.

"Furthermore," he continued, "runnin' a damned logging camp ain't no proper thing fer a young fe-male to be doin'."

Califia laughed. "I assure you, sir," she said, "I am not at all a *proper young fe-male*."

Samson pursed his lips and sent a long stream of tobacco juice off to the side of the trail, and El Buzzardo, startled by the sudden action, lifted into the air, powerful wings rowing him upward toward the sun.

"Could of fooled me, then," Samson replied.

CHAPTER FOURTEEN

Bullwhackers and River Pigs

[1845:]

CALIFIA'S FALLERS WORKED from springboards six feet above the ground, using wide-bitted hand axes as well as double-length whipsaws as a means of taking down two-hundred-foot-tall redwoods. The big trees, with a tendency toward being fragile, required *beds* of slash and lopped foliage—and if the cutters were sufficiently skillful, the giants tilted slowly, slowy at first, and then gained momentum as they fell, hurling themselves to earth at last with a terrible rush of noise and flying debris, coming to rest in the preconceived places. If a tree missed its bed, then occasionally the trunk shattered, rendering an indeterminate portion useless except for the making of shingles.

Once a tree was down, then the *buckers* worked along the upper log, hewing away branches—and next using misery whips to saw the log into lengths of either sixteen or thirty-two feet; but on the greatest of the trees, some of these sections were too massive for the *bullwhackers* and their oxen to skid to the river, and so it was occasionally necessary to split them into halves by means of boring holes and filling these with gunpowder. Once the sections of log were rolled free into the Russian River, however, they became the essential property of the *river pigs*, men whose specialty it was to herd the timbers together into rafts or to move with the logs, sometimes on top of them and sometimes along the riverbank with them, downstream to Sutter's mill.

Califia and Juan Pescadero were able to design and build a check dam at a narrows in the stream—one sufficient to impound a small lake and then to release the water all at once, so that the logs, singly or in rafts, were carried down the Russian River on the back of a flood, to a place where John Sutter's men had constructed a sawmill to produce lumber for the lucrative and ever-expanding foreign trade, as well as for the construction needs of his inland empire of New Helvetia. A percentage of the cut, by agreement, was left to Olivo & Beard, to market in whatever way they wished.

Bill Beard had first utilized the check-dam method on the San Lorenzo, years earlier—a method he, in turn, had learned while working with his father on the Nuthegan and the Black Branch, in Vermont.

Sam Flowers fit in gracefully with life in the logging camp, professing not to know how to handle an axe and indeed successfully avoiding all contact with the labors of timbering. But he proved an adept hunter, and, with the aid of various Pomo boys from Chalanchawi village, he was able to supply Califia's men with a generous sufficiency of fresh meat. Furthermore, owing to his contacts with the Indians, he was often able to trade for such things as dried salmon and salmon flour, and acorn cakes, as well as basketwork hats that fit almost like Viking helmets, quantities of dried native tobacco, and wild onions and parsnips.

As provider of whatever *grub* the local area might afford, and as purveyor of properly outrageous tall tales about his times among the fur brigades in the High Shining, Sam Flowers was indeed a great favorite among the timber beasts. To be on Sam's good side was to assure oneself of choice cuts of meat, rolls of Pomo tobacco, and other delicacies.

Flowers had a particular knack for getting under the boss lady's skin, and the occasional dialogues between these two provided a species of entertainment—something generally lacking in the dark redwood forest along the Russian River.

On several occasions Califia offered to allow Samson to

draw his wages, but somehow or another, the hunter never did. If things got a bit out of hand in terms of his uneasy relationship with Miss Beard, Samson merely stayed away from camp for an extra day. His return, however, invariably meant a plentitude of fresh meat. Some of the boys would engage in eating contests, and any number of the fellows could put away three pounds or so of half-cooked venison or elk at a sitting.

One of Flowers' stories concerned *boudin* contests when Bridger's Brigade was staying with the Doogooriga Shoshones. A buffalo's intestine would be cleansed and toasted until not quite crispy. The middle of the rope of flesh would then be marked, and a handkerchief tied to the spot. The contestants proceeded to eat, each from one end, toward the middle. Whoever reached the handkerchief first was declared the winner.

Whereas Califia's men didn't actually try out the contest routine, they did come to perceive the venison and elk *boudins*, properly roasted over the coals, as a great delicacy.

Both Bill and Calvin Beard visited Califia's logging camp, and so the elder Beard was reunited with Sam Flowers, his Bull of the Woods from nearly thirty years earlier.

"Hoo-raw for the shingler!" Flowers whooped as Bill Beard rode into camp.

Beard dismounted, and he and Samson began whacking one another on the back.

"Workin' fer your kid this time around, old hoss!" Samson blurted. "Quite a little lady, this'un. Runs a tight ship, she does. Works the lads half to death, and yet by God they love it. . . ."

When Flowers and Beard had finished pounding at one another, Calvin extended his hand, and the two men shook— not with great enthusiasm, on either side.

"Met Calvin hyar an' Califia too when we whupped Torrejon, down south. Bill, I heard ye was in thick with Vallejo an' Castro an' Alvarado, all three. Way things is goin', mebbe ye'll end up being gov-nor of Alta California. Well, they could do a sight worse. An American gov-nor's a good idea, I'm thinking, since they's more and more Yanks comin' in to California all the time. A new bunch arrived at Sutter's Fort just before I come over hyar. With summer, they's like to be a hundred new men—an' women, too.''

Bill the Sawyer nodded.

"We'll live to see Alta California as part of the Union—one of the States. I believe it. First Texas, and then Oregon and California. There's a fuse on the powder keg, and it's getting shorter all the time. Oregon country, that'll sure as hell be American, and maybe Western Canada as well. Jefferson knew it all along, and that's why he sent Lewis and Clark to the Pacific. Polk's into it with the Brits right now. It's like Monroe said—the United States is *bound* to expand to the Pacific. After that we push Russia off our continent. . . .''

"Manifest Destiny," Flowers agreed. ''I read that somewhar—mebbe in one o' them Back East newspapers Sutter gets from time to time—him or that Mormon coon, Sam Brannan. He a friend of yours, Bill?''

"I'm afraid I haven't had the pleasure. A crony of Sutter's, is he?''

Califia and Juan Pescadero had just returned from a brief survey of the next logging site, half a mile upstream. The Lady of the Wild Creatures, her black rooster following along behind her, embraced her father and Calvin.

"How's Mother? When you get back to Hotochruk, you tell her how much I miss her. Now that you're here, Dad, I realize that I'm utterly homesick. Calvin—have you and Juanita had any more children while I've been away?''

Calvin grinned

"Possibly, possibly," he replied. "We've just brought the old *Don Quixote* down from Oregon country. Sis, we've seen Oregon pines—the same kind of firs we've got here, actually—and Sitka spruces as big as most of our redwoods. McLoughlin has a thriving lumber industry going. We've learned a few things—even Pop agrees with me.''

"I guess Cal's right," Bill Beard said. "If a man doesn't learn from his competition, the competition's bound to eat him alive. I figure it's about time that we modernized a bit. . . . I see Rory Sunrise is still with us. Where's the buzzard and those worthless lions of yours, *hija mia*? Samson didn't shoot them, did he?''

Flowers guffawed.

"I have to work twice as hard, just to keep the cougars fed," he grinned, showing off his missing tooth to best advantage. "El Buzzardo, he's content with what's left over."

Beard shook hands with Juan Pescadero and asked how things were going.

"I would not have believed it," Juan replied, "but seeing is believing—*con el ojo y con la fe jamás me burlaré*. Miss Califia, she knows how to make the men do whatever she wishes. They labor even harder because they are working for her. . . ."

Califia smiled demurely, nodded.

Having witnessed McLoughlin's methods at first hand, and having noted that indeed he could find no fault with them, Bill Beard told his daughter he was now ready to make adjustments in his previous logging procedures. After observing his daughter's Russian River camp, Bill the Sawyer talked the matter over with Califia, who, in turn, gave instructions to Juan Pescadero, her bull o' the woods. What could be done along Puget Sound and the Williamette River, after all, could be done in the mountains of California as well.

The new methods worked—would be incorporated into operations on the San Lorenzo and elsewhere. As Bill Beard remarked to Calvin while the *Don Quixote* made for open water, out through the shallow coastal fogs and into bright sunlight, after taking on a cargo of freshly cut redwood at the mill John Sutter's men had built, "Son, we're by Gawd letting some light into the swamp, no question about it."

Calvin, signaling for additional sail on the foremast, looked questioningly at his father.

"How long until a hundred other logging companies are at work in our mountains? How long can the redwoods last? They don't go on forever, after all."

"Way beyond our lifetimes, Cal, way beyond. A hundred years, maybe even a century and a half—maybe forever. They're growing all the time, and new ones sprout up from the areas we've cut over. It's hard for a man to look ahead, into the future. Maybe if H.V. ever comes back from Europe, he can figure 'er out. All that education's got to be good for something."

"You think he's going to return, Dad?" Calvin asked.

"Now that he's married, you mean? Could be we were wrong in keeping those two apart—Homer and Califia, I mean. I'm beginning to wonder if your sister's actually going to find her a man to keep her warm in bed. Truth is, I don't think she's even looking."

Up ahead, a number of big brown pelicans were diving from the sky, wings back, hitting the ocean water with sharp splashes and then reemerging into the air, gulping fish, the strong wings beating foam behind them.

Summer came, and, since Calvin was en route to Hawaii, Bill Beard and Raymondo Olivo transported the first load of lumber (in one of Martin's schooners), their projected voyage running from Russian River, south to the Golden Gate and into San Francisco Bay, through Carquinez Strait, up the channel of the Sacramento to the mouth of the American River, and up that tributary stream a short distance to a landing below Sutter's Fort. Samson Flowers was selected to accompany the voyage—since he knew the river channels fairly well, not from shipboard experience but from having ridden the trails from New Helvetia to Rancho Vallejo on several occasions.

Samson bid Califia adieu and expressed the fond wish that she and her men and her menagerie wouldn't starve to death during his absence.

"By the grace of fate and all the souls imprisoned within the great redwoods, we'll survive. Father, are you certain you want this man for a guide? I'm not certain he knows north from south."

"Ye heard anyone claim that Sam Flowers ever got lost? Whar'd ye get such a rumor, anyhow? This child knows every crick an' hill between hyar an' the Sand Hills o' Nebraska, by Gord. Well, most of 'em, anyhow. . . ."

With the cargo of redwood stowed in the hold, Bill and Raymondo worked their way out of the Russian's tidewater channel, across the bar, and southward toward Point Reyes.

Heretofore, Captain John Sutter had been using Fort Ross itself as a source of lumber, dismantling nonessential buildings constructed by the Russians and transporting the materials of which the structures had been built to New Helvetia.

The Petaluma mill might have provided a more convenient

source of lumber, but Olivo & Beard had sold out their interests in that operation to Thomas W. Larkin, the American consul who'd been their partner all along. Despite the heavy drinking of his half-brother, R.B.R. Cooper, the venture prospered, and Larkin had a lucrative contract to provide redwood of various grades to Panama and Columbia. With Larkin intent upon gaining sole possession of the Petaluma mill, Raymondo Olivo and Bill Beard had been able to negotiate a handsome price for their interest.

"There'll be plenty of markets for everyone," Bill Beard insisted. "Besides—with Coop in charge, the venture'll go belly-up inside of a year—unless, of course, R.B.R. gets his addiction to spirits under control."

"I have a better idea," Raymondo Olivo said.

"Is that supposed to be news? What in hell are you talking about, Raymondo? Just jabbering to hear your own voice?"

Beard grinned and clucked his tongue.

"Hermano Sancho, how many times must I tell you? Men do only those things which are designed to make them either more rich or more powerful, and so it is with Señor Larkin. Now he will attempt to sell his redwood to Señor Sutter, and we will be without a market. You see how things are?"

"So—what's your *better* idea?"

"Simple," Olivo replied. "First we offer his men a higher wage to come work for us again, and then we burn down Señor Larkin's mill."

"It's a thought," Bill Beard admitted.

"So now we deliver lumber to New Helvetia. Well, perhaps Señor Sutter will be able to cease and desist from the *unbuilding* of Fort Ross. In another year, there would be no more Fort Ross. Already he's transported all the animals and tools and even gateposts and smithy and tables and cabinets. . . ."

"Makin' good use of 'em, too," Flowers put in. "The Cap's got his fort set up like a regular little hive o' factories—an ironworks, chandlery, tannery, even a winery. He started the booze mill right off, his first year up thar—had his men gathering wild grapes along the river. Now he's got vineyards an' orchards an' the whole shootin' match. Must have learned it all in Switzerland, I guess. . . ."

Along the winding river they traveled, through a delta region of numerous sloughs and islands, the interlaced channels of the Sacramento, lined with tules and willows and great spreading cottonwoods. Egrets and cranes and herons stood about in the shallows, occasionally bobbing their heads to spear unwary fish, while mud hens and ducks and even swans floated serenely on the still, clear water. A few range cattle made their way about through tall grasses to the northwest of the main channel, and at one point the schooner passed a pair of gold-colored grizzlies who were happily dining on the flesh of a calf.

But as the double-master worked its way northward along the Sacramento, past a triple branching that separated Grand Island from River Island, no more longhorns were to be seen. As a result of a continually expanding hide and tallow trade with American merchant sailors, the Californio ranchos had spread this far inland, and yet no farther. To the north lay Sutter's land of New Helvetia. Summer heat brooded heavily above the river, and by late-afternoon twilight, swarms of mosquitoes and gnats caused the crew to curse and douse themselves with a variety of substances, most of which were but minimally effective.

Before sundown they used a long hawser to moor their craft to a huge white oak dominating the eastern bank of the channel, and Samson Flowers went hunting. Within an hour he'd managed to bag a young male tule elk, and soon the haunches were roasting above a roaring fire fueled by chunks of driftwood the previous winter's flooding had left to dry in bands along the high-water mark. Raymondo brought out a pair of wine flasks, the vintage of Salinas Valley, and these were passed around.

Wind continued to blow from the south the following day, a wind that Raymondo opined had a scent of the ocean about it, and shortly after noon they reached the mouth of the American River and proceeded up the lesser stream to Sutter's embarcadero, where, with assistance from some of Sutter's tame Maidu Indians and Sandwich Islanders, they proceeded to unload their cargo of planks and beams and boards.

Between his absence during the revolution and his subsequent business at Fort Ross, Sutter discovered that the wild Indian bands in the foothills, Maidus and Miwoks, had begun to strike back at the establishment of New Helvetia—and not even the presence of their semidomesticated brethren as paid workers on Sutter's lands prevented the men of the outlying villages from stealing cattle. Indeed, some of Sutter's *own* Indians had apparently gotten into the habit of slipping away with their cousins and joining in on the marauding parties.

John Sutter was patient in his efforts to persuade his former workers to return to their responsibilities, but his patience was at an end when a band of Maidus made a raid on the rancho of his good friend Thomas Lindsay, who was killed in the course of the battle that ensued. Lindsay had served with Sutter in the attempt to retain Micheltorena as governor.

The Indians drove off some three hundred cattle, though no one had any idea what they intended to do with the animals. Some believed the Indians had been led by a professional cattle thief, one who intended to slaughter the lot of them and to transport hides and tallow down the Sacramento to Yerba Buena, where an interested American merchant was certain to be found.

Without saying so, Sutter wondered if the hands of Señores Castro and Vallejo might not have been in on the matter, but the Captain was hardly prepared to move against those two powerful individuals—and particularly not, considering the outcome of the recent war.

With Flowers and Beard and Olivo and their men now at the fort and able to enforce order in his absence, Sutter deemed it safe to proceed against the Maidus. With twenty well-armed men, White and Indian as well and all experienced fighters, he gave pursuit, picked up the trail of the stolen animals, and overtook the thieves as they herded their ill-gotten cattle southward toward the San Joaquin. The Indians were also armed, a fact which clearly implicated *someone or another*, and a hard-pitched battle followed.

Sutter regained most of the cattle, but he lost three men, including Juan Vacha, his clerk and loyal friend.

As Sutter remarked to Beard and Olivo upon his return, "I was, as usual, the first to charge, and a number of arrows pierced my clothing. Yet I escaped without injury. . . ."

Sam Flowers listened, nodded, and thought to himself that

the operation had the marks of Walkara and Jim Beckwourth all over it—except that those worthies were supposed to be back in Taos or Pueblo—and, of course, if it *had been* Jim and Pegleg and the Ute, there was simply no way Sutter would ever in hell have gotten the longhorns back.

Beard and Olivo were making preparations for their return voyage when Pierson B. Reading brought in word of yet further Indian troubles.

"Raphero of the Mokelumnes," Sutter explained to Beard, Olivo, and Flowers. "*Vor fünf Jahren oder etwas*, this Raphero of the Mokelumne Miwoks, he has supplied me with many of my best men. *Und* now? He has gone on the warpath and has threatened to massacre the farmers, and to burn their houses and wheat fields. This is the work of Jose Castro. That man is jealous of my growing importance, and so he has chosen this as a means of embarrassing me. He wishes the governor to believe *Ich bin* unable to keep the Indians of my district under strict control. *Jawohl*, yes—but Castro will be disappointed. I will make a show of force. . . ."

The words Sutter uttered in anger were not merely empty assertion. Within the hour he'd called up every available man at the fort and issued them arms. With Reading as his second in command, Sutter led his hastily assembled troops out of the gates of the fort and headed south once again, toward the Mokelumne River.

In Sutter's absence, Bill Beard, Raymondo Olivo, and Samson Flowers took the opportunity to ride back into the Sierra Foothills, past Sam Brannan's little settlement at Mormon Bar and on up the southern branch of the American River to Ko-lo-ma, a Maidu village located in a narrow valley between high ridges dotted with digger pine and oak, as well as some ponderosa and fir. In a world where there were no redwoods, Bill Beard remarked, one could conceivably make do with such timber as was present on either side of the river.

As they continued their venture upcanyon, however, the forest became thicker and the conifers more dominant, of several varieties.

"The great big *redwood* trees," Samson remarked, "are up high, on the ridges. These hyar Sierra are one of the damn strangest mountain ranges in the world. If it weren't for the river canyons, they'd be close to flat—well, slanted eastward, at least. They be redwoods hyar, don't ye believe otherwise— only high up, like I say, hidden away in glades an' ravines. The trees is there, but how a coon'd get 'em to water is more than I can figger. An' the rivers what come down out of the Sierra—they ain't much now, not by mid-summer, but when the rains hit, the cricks get ungordly big, for a fact. . . ."

Beard and Olivo took Flowers's yarn with more than a grain of salt. Yet, was not what he'd said essentially the same account Califia and H.V. had given, years earlier, in the aftermath of their abortive elopement?

The present, however, was not an auspicious time to explore so extensive a mountain range—said to be nearly three hundred miles long and eighty miles across and of very considerable height in places. But already there were a handful of wagon trails across the backs of the mountains, and a small but steady flow of emigrants from the American East was finding its way into the great fertile valley of Alta California.

Still, without question these mountains were clothed with extensive forests, with great stands of cedar, ponderosa pine, and the nearly ubiquitous fir McLoughlin called *Oregon pine*, a species that was now properly denoted *Douglas fir*, after the Scottish botanist who'd explored the forests of Western Canada and the Oregon country during the twenties and thirties but who was now dead, gored to death in Hawaii by an angry wild bull. Douglas had observed that the tree was not a pine at all, lacking the proper kind of needles. It wasn't a fir because its cones had bracts and grew downward instead of upward. And it was clearly not a member of the hemlock family. It must be then, he reasoned, a species and a family entire unto itself.

The Sierra forests also contained another of David Douglas's discoveries, a five-needled white pine with cones up to two feet in length—a tree, as they'd learned from workers at Mormon Bar, called *sugar pine*, a name apparently given in response to the *sweet aroma* released when the wood was cut into. Others said the sap was sweet—and that, if dried, it produced crystals of sugar. Beard was highly skeptical, however.

Sugar pine sap tasted like regular pine pitch to him, and he wasn't about to try to sweeten his coffee with turpentine.

Raymondo laughed at the idea of Douglas *discovering* the trees. Indian people, he insisted, had known about every tree and bush in the forest for thousands of years. Europeans, he sneered, never believed a thing had been *discovered* until one of them saw it for the first time.

"Were there not people in America already when Columbus sailed across the Atlantic? If so, then perhaps those people discovered America, and not Señor Columbus. But the truth is that Indian people have always been here on this continent. I think the Europeans must have lived here once also, a long time ago, before the beginnings of civilization, but then they went away. After many centuries they came back again. . . . I do not believe those dates that Ussher and Lightfoot have calculated—that God created the world in 4004 B.C. Perhaps that was simply one of the times when Old Man Coyote changed things around a little bit. The Ancient Ones lived much longer ago than that. . . ."

Beard gave thought to his partner's theory of discovery and demographics. He'd heard the objections before, several times before. And—after all—perhaps Raymondo was correct. How could one know about such matters?

"Anyhow," Bill the Sawyer said, "prospects for West Coast logging, and prospects for Alta California itself, both look good to me. Here, for instance, we've apparently got an immense forest, but no market for timber. We'd have to get our goods down to the Sacramento River or the San Joaquin and then ship the stuff to the same places we do now. If the Big Valley ever starts getting settled, however—I mean, if New Helvetia, for instance, attracts enough emigrants, then we've got market a-plenty. . . ."

"That will not happen," Olivo replied, "not so long as Mexico continues to control our destiny. We have just gotten rid of Torrejon and his *cholos*. Perhaps we must also free ourselves of Pico and Alvarado and Castro, even though they are good men, fair-minded, and just. We must not continue to be tied to the apron strings of Mexico, *consido a faldas de Mexico.* We must be our own nation, separate from the others. We are better off, Sancho Beard, independent of your United States as

well. We can be a nation, a great and powerful nation someday. Are we not larger than England or France or Spain itself?"

Bill Beard nodded.

Samson Flowers spat a stream of tobacco juice.

"Hate to hear a coon talk like that," he said. "The Yanks is
goin' to take over, no question about 'er. At the present rate,
California'll soon have more Americans than *Gente de Razón*.
With Texas an' all, the United States is bound to go to war
with the Meskins. Then whar will ye be?"

Olivo burst out laughing.

"We will be cutting down trees, just as always. Whoever
wins the war, the *vencedores* will need lumber in order to build
back whatever houses have been burned down or blown up
with cannon fire. Either way, *compañeros*, we will be the win-
ners. But not the Indios. . . . They will die, they will vanish—
even Pelican Doctor's Hotochrukmas will eventually vanish.
The Ohlones and Pomos and Maidus and all the others, once
they had a good way of living. But the sun has gone black in
those skies, and now the Indios are caught between the powers of Mexico and the United States. I used to be Indio, but
what am I today? Just an old man who dreams of independence for his motherland."

"Gawddamn it, Raymondo, don't go getting all sentimental.
We got to be thinking about how we're going to supply lumber
to Sutterville and Monterey and San Jose. People keep coming
here, and as long as that's the case, it's our obligation to provide them with the boards to build their houses."

Samson Flowers spat again.

"They's already too many people in California, if ye wants
my opinion. Once a place starts growin', that's nowhere a real
man wants to be. Time to head out for Canada, mebbe. But
right now, we got to find us a place to make camp for the
night—some kind o' meadow. The ponies is hungry. We been
pushin' the critters pretty hard."

Beard squinted westward. The sun was indeed dipping low
toward the horizon.

"Lead on, faithful guide," he laughed.

By the time Beard, Olivo, and Flowers returned to Sutter's Fort a week later, the Captain himself had also returned—and had already put the head of Raphero on display near the main gate.

Sutter's venture had almost come to grief. On reaching the Mokelumne River, he'd ordered his men to construct a raft sufficient to carry supplies across the river, which was still running fairly high from melting snows far back in the recesses of the Sierra Nevada. The raft capsized, with the resultant loss of numerous firearms and most of the ammunition. But Captain Sutter was not to be denied. He ordered his troops onward, following the Mokelumne back into the hills. There he discovered Raphero's stronghold. The attack was immediate, and the Indians were thrown into panic and disarray. Raphero was captured, and Sutter returned directly to his fort. The Indian chief was given a brief trial and sentenced to death by hanging. The execution was carried out that very afternoon, with all the fort in attendance, and afterward the chief's head was severed and placed on display, as a grisly warning.

Without further ado, Bill Beard and Raymondo Olivo weighed anchor and turned the prow of their two-master downriver, heading for San Francisco Bay and the Pacific Ocean—and on to the Russian River and the loading of yet another cargo of redwood.

As for the fifty-some-odd-year-old Samson Flowers, veteran of many campaigns both in and out of the beds of women and father of at least a few half-breed children scattered throughout the North American West, he found he'd quite actively been missing the presence of one Califia Beard.

It damned well bothered him.

Pescadero motioned and yelled at the same time, and as he did so the head *bullwhacker* threw a lever on the portable steam boiler, gear wheels turned, and a big winch line went tight: yet another *turn* of logs rolled down the bankside and into the already timber-filled waters behind the Olivo & Beard Russian River check dam. Almost immediately the *river pigs*, men who'd elected to make their livelihood by means of herding about logs in the river, were at their work, their *tin pants*, heavy waterproof canvas britches, slick and shining in late August sunlight.

The boss lady, as certain as ever that there was no task so difficult that she herself couldn't perform it—certainly not so long as mere males were able to do it—was out on the river, among her men, peavey in hand, shouting instructions and working side by side with her crew. The men had learned, whatever presuppositions they might have held, that Califia Beard was not merely the boss's daughter but in fact the boss herself, a powerful will and a skilled manager of the timber camp.

Flowers lounged on the riverbank, whittling a stick and watching Califia as she worked with the river pigs. He watched her lithe form as she balanced on a floating log, her men attempting to form up a deck. He watched as she suddenly turned half around, glancing across to where he reclined, and then slipped, fell. Even when he heard her cry out, he still didn't realize anything was seriously amiss. But then her men began to shout, leaping from one log to another and converging upon the spot where the boss lady had gone down.

Good Christ in the morning! Califia! She's pinned between them damned logs—one false move, an' she's crushed, broken up an' spit out. . . .

Instantly Samson was on his feet and running, leaping down from the embankment into the water, pulling himself up onto a log.

"Pescadero!" he thundered. "Gord-damn it, Juan, get yore Meskin ass down hyar! She's caught between timbers!"

Men stood about, not doing anything, staring down to where Califia was indeed pinned between a pair of four-foot-thick poles, one arm caught behind her, held just below her breasts, unable to move, unable to do more than gasp out a few words. . . .

"Give me that damn peavey!" Flowers yelled, snatching a river pig's hook-ended pry bar away from him. Then he was standing beside her, shoulder-deep in the river, peavey hooked to the butt end of the log, and he was moving it, straining, pulling the damned thing free by main force.

Califia reached up, and strong male hands grasped her and pulled her out of the water and up onto the half-formed log deck. She shook her head, gasped for breath, and pressed her hands against her ribs in an attempt to determine if anything had been broken.

She looked up, past the men around her, and could see Juan Pescadero coming down the slope at a full run. She could also see Samson Flowers hoisting himself out of the water.

"Thanks . . . thanks, Sam," she said. "For a minute there I thought I was finished . . . wasn't paying attention to what I was doing . . . damned foolishness on my part. I believe you saved my life."

"Among the nations," he said, "that'd mean you're my slave—until ye exchange the favor. . . ."

She stared at him.

That grin with the tooth missing. That wretched grin. . . .

CHAPTER FIFTEEN

Venture North

[1845:]

THOMAS A. LARKIN, United States Consul in Monterey, was officially informed he was to do everything possible to block the designs of any foreign power upon the land of Alta California. Furthermore, he was to promote public sentiment in all ways likely to prove conducive to an eventual annexation of California to the United States. Larkin had received a confidential government communique to this effect in the middle of October, 1845.

A month earlier John Slidell of Louisiana was chosen to proceed to Mexico City for the purpose of offering up to forty million dollars for New Mexico, California, and the Rio Grande boundary for Texas. By November, however, the proposed offer had been somewhat altered. Slidell was appointed Minister to Mexico and authorized to inform the Mexican government that the United States was willing to assume all American claims against Mexico (these amounting to at least six million dollars) in exchange for the entirety of Mexican territory to the north and east of the course of the Rio Grande, east of the headwaters of this river to the forty-second parallel, and north of the forty-second parallel. Furthermore, the United States offered to purchase New Mexico Territory for five million dollars. In addition, the Americans were willing to pay twenty-five million dollars for California.

Before the year was out, word would arrive that the Mexican government had, on principle, refused to receive Slidell—inasmuch as the Mexicans had agreed to receive only a commissioner, not a Minister.

President James K. Polk clearly reaffirmed the Monroe Doctrine, opposing further European colonization of North America as well as any European attempts to maintain a balance of power in the region. In short, the United States was on the verge of yet another vast addition to its territorial holdings.

In New Helvetia, meanwhile, John Sutter's troubles were hardly over—even after the *Injun problems* were more or less solved and Raphero's head was on display beside the main gates. A dry spring and the failure to plant resulted in what amounted to a full-scale crop failure, but the master of the Sacramento Valley maintained his front toward such creditors as Vallejo, Larkin, and Marsh.

In a letter to Larkin, he wrote, *All my debts will be paid, and I will have a very large amount left over.* He planned in several locations to divert water from the American River, to the end of irrigating his wheat fields and of turning the wheels of flour and lumber mills he intended to build—work on the former project to be performed by Sam Brannan's Mormon settlers, and the latter by a crew under his friend and partner, James Marshall. Further, Fremont, an American officer, had recently crossed the Sierra Nevada and had told him of *plenty of Beavers . . . never disturbed before by trappers.* Sutter planned to send out a trapping brigade to the Sierra. As to the establishment of a lumber mill relatively close to his settlement at New Helvetia, Sutter wrote to Larkin, *A great Advantage for this Establishment is that we have the best quality timber close by. It is only thirty miles from here where I have 9 white Men and 10 Indians employed, sawing the best Kind of pine, making shingles of pine and Cedar. . . . In this Cedar and pine wood I intend to build a saw-mill. . . .*

Rains fell as the California autumn wore on, and in the stands of redwood along Russian River, operations slowed in the face of the difficulties involved in skidding logs through increasingly heavy muds; finally Califia, recognizing that the end of the season had indeed come, sent word to Sutter's mill on the lower river that after one final run, operations would be suspended until spring. Before taking on cargo, Calvin Beard (now back from Hawaii) was to bring the *Don Quixote* to the head of tidewater to pick up all but a handful of timber beasts, these to remain at the site through the winter (under the direction of Sam Flowers).

Califia, along with Juan Pescadero, Gatogordo and Ponchita, El Buzzardo, Rory Sunrise, and several horses and oxen, would later proceed to Rancho Vallejo, crossing there via Mariano's barge ferry, and so on to the San Lorenzo mill and ultimately to Hotochruk village—and a reunion with Seagull and Bill, Calling Owl and Raymondo.

This first year of operations on Russian River had proven successful indeed; Califia and Juan discovered a workable method of taking down all but the greatest of the trees—quartering the logs, sectioning them, moving them downslope along skid roads formed of side-by-side barkless Oregon pine poles, with yoked pairs of oxen chained in tandem to either side of the skid trough, and *corduroy* or cross-pole road put in place to give the animals more certain footing as they strained and heaved against the masses of the big timbers they moved.

With camp now quiet and equipment stowed away for use in the spring, Califia Beard began to feel a genuine reluctance to begin her journey southward to Pelican Doctor's village. What lay to the south was known, after all, while to the north rose mountain range after mountain range, uncharted lands—lands of the wild Pomos, Wappos, Yukis, and Wintuns. Up there somewhere, according to all the stories, was the *great white mountain* of Waiiaka . . . or Ieka . . . which sailors insisted they could sometimes see from a hundred miles out into the Pacific—a mountain that was reported to be a peak of fire, like the giants her father and brother had seen in Oregon country, both north and south of the Columbia River.

Furthermore, stories persisted of stands of redwood more extensive and more huge than anything thus far discovered—perhaps up where the Russian River began, perhaps even far-

ther north than that. But where was the trusted companion
who'd go there with her—who'd be willing to search out whatever secrets the land to the north might hold?

"Homer Virgil, damn you!" she said. "How in the hell am
I ever going to be able to *see* Shasta if you're off in England,
drinking tea with sophisticated ladies—and making love to your
refined, fragile little wife? Coyote's doings, I guess."

Rory, the small black rooster, as if sensing his mistress's
discontent, came scuttling across the framed-in tent that served
as Califia's quarters, did a brief courtship dance for her, and
fluttered up into her lap.

Ponchita, asleep on a pallet across the tent, beside Gatogordo, looked up momentarily, took in the brief rustling of
feathers, yawned, and once again closed her eyes. Gatogordo
groaned softly in cat fashion, caught up in dream. Califia noted
a rising of the fur along his spine, this followed by a wistful
sigh. Then he began to make half-audible nursing sounds.

"We never grow up, do we?" Califia asked the rooster.

The bird cocked his head and stared at her—the intense
round black pupil surrounded by amber-orange iris, the eye
unblinking. Only when she began to stroke the feathers on his
throat did Rory Sunrise close his eyes.

"I want to know what's up there," she told him. "Yukis
and Wintuns and beyond them the Achomawis—Worrotetot's
people, Blackbeard the great warrior—rumor that he's half
White, like me. . . . And what about the trees? Do they just
keep on getting larger and larger? Surely there's got to be a
limit somewhere. You're ready to go with me, ehh, Mr. Spurs?
And what about the faithless felines? Are you two interested
in a bit of exploring?"

Gatogordo no longer nursed in his sleep, but the wide,
powerful paws were working on the pallet, making bread, just
like a tabby.

"Ye wants to go hellin' around the Coast Range? If this child
says no, ye'll jest head off on your own account, because that's
the kind o' hardheaded female ye be, Califia Beard. Likely I'd
end up having to come fetch yore bacon out o' the fire anyhow, so that wouldn't give me no peace. All right, all right,
I'm yore man, then. Ye want to take a gander at Shasta Butte,

why I'm the nigger as can take ye thar. With them two over-
growed catamounts trailin' along behind us, I guess the Injuns'll grant us some powerful *medicine* an' leave us the hell
alone. By now they's all pretty much into their winter villages
anyhow, with enough acorn meal an' salmon to hold 'em. If
not, I guess they'll go under, since that's the way o' things. So,
Miss Boss Lady, when we set to ride?"

Califia stared westward, across the still Russian River's tidewater channel. From five miles off she could see a blue plume
of smoke going up from the sawmill's burner. Sutter's men
had logs enough to keep them going another month or two,
and after that, with perhaps a month of shutdown time, the
Olivo & Beard logs would start floating down the channel to
saltwater again.

At the moment, a conclave of bald eagles, golden eagles,
ospreys, and red-tailed hawks were spiraling, playing wind
currents, taking time off from the long days of hunting and
simply enjoying themselves. The spring nestlings would be out
on their own by now, more or less self-sufficient hunters, and
thus the parent birds were free to enjoy an interval of leisure.
Califia smiled. It was wonderful, she thought, simply to be
able to observe such a spectacle.

Then she turned to Samson.

"Why is it," Califia queried, "I'm already certain I've made
a mistake in asking you to be my guide?"

"Natural enough, natural enough. Females is knowed to be
helpless, an' so, being o' sound mind, ye looked around and
found a *male* to ride ahead with ye and point out the path-
ways. Hellfire, I've been lookin' out for one female woman or
another all my life. Ain't no sense changing now. If men don't
take care o' the ladies, they're like babes in the woods. I tell
ye, Califia Boss Lady, it's a *turrible* responsibility."

"Have you seen El Buzzardo? He flew off about nine this
morning, just after Cal set sail, and I don't think he's back
yet."

"Ye worry more about that garbage-eatin' oversize crow
with a ugly bald neck than any normal person worries about
money an' fame an' things of that sort."

"Possibly. But the vulture's promised to take care of a certain job."

"Job, ehh? Contracts with buzzards, is it? An' what in blazes might that be?"

"He's promised to pick your bones clean, Mr. Flowers, after I nail you dead-center with my Hawken."

Flowers grinned, winked.

"Shucks," he said, "ain't no buzzard's going to peck my bones. They're buzzard-proof, that's what. Comes of years an' years of eatin' roast vulture—she's a great delicacy among the Cheyennes. No, ma'am, I sure ain't seen that bird, not since breakfast. . . ."

The strange caravan moved northward, with Califia Beard and Samson Flowers and two mountain lions and a turkey vulture and a small black rooster and two extra saddle ponies and a pair of packhorses ascending the Russian River to its source. They continued into the drainage of another considerable stream, this one flowing east to west—very likely the Eel River, according to Flowers. They turned downcanyon, moving westward—until the stream, drawing in tributaries with each consecutive canyon, began flowing almost northward, parallel to the coast.

For two days a steady rain fell. Flowers threw up a shelter at the base of some vertical spires of rock along the river, cinching a saddle blanket from above and below. Califia attacked a downfall cedar lying athwart the canyon wall and produced a quantity of dry firewood. She grumbled about not having a misery whip and a maul with her so that she might section a number of rounds and split them to the desired sizes, but with no more than a shingling hatchet, she was able to accomplish her purpose. Despite the rain and the fact that the saddle blanket dripped, Samson and Califia soon had a satisfactory fire burning beside their shelter.

Buzzardo came in for a portion of raw venison and then, with his crop full, he retired to the crown of a Douglas fir across the river. Rory Sunrise, who'd been riding on Califia's pommel for the previous three or four hours, was wet and churlish—but now, perched as close to the blaze as was prudent, he resolutely set about attending to the task of preening his feathers.

The two lions quickly settled down under the shelter, and

by the time Samson had the lines tight, he could see that nothing less than an act of *Gord* or the authoritative voice of Miss Boss would be sufficient to dislodge the felines. When Califia informed the cougars that they'd be required to move, they did so grudgingly.

Califia knelt beside the fire, the long braid of her hair dripping down her back. She stirred a measure of crushed coffee beans into a pot of steaming water and glanced over at Flowers.

"Well, at least we ain't goin' to starve," he muttered. "An' I guess the tabbies ain't all that bad, nuther. Ye say they'll hold still for bein' pillows? If this damned rain turns to snow, I expect I could put up with 'em for bed partners. A coon gets to be my age, he ain't so picky."

Califia glared at Samson, shook her head.

"Why must you keep harping on being old?" she asked. "You don't act old—hell, Sam, you don't even act grown-up most of the time."

The mountain man tamped tobacco into his pipe and used a flaming sliver of cedar to light up. He puffed, snorted, let smoke trail from either side of his mouth.

"Tobacco mixed with dried bear dung?" Califia asked.

"Sure enough, sure enough. Ye want to try 'er? I know it ain't ladylike, but . . ."

Califia smiled.

"I've been waiting for you to ask," she said.

"That a fact?"

He handed her the pipe. She took it, arched one eyebrow, and then placed the bit between her teeth. From the way she sucked on the thing, Flowers knew immediately that his employer had smoked a pipe before—perhaps even often.

"Not bad," she said. "So you think you're up to sleeping with a mountain lion, do you?"

"A man ought to be willin' to try anything at least once."

For whatever reasons, Califia found it necessary to lower her eyes. She felt the blood coming into her face, and she resorted to coughing—as though she'd breathed smoke too deeply.

————

Along the full extent of Russian River, they'd found dense stands of redwood interspersed with ponderosa pine and Douglas fir, but on the fourth day they entered into some truly astonishing stands, and for the following two days, much to their amazement, there seemed always to be some prodigy even greater or taller than anything they'd seen as yet—trees they estimated at well over three hundred feet and whose trunks at the base were perhaps twenty feet or more in diameter. Samson Flowers had never, in fact, been along this upper drainage of the Eel before—and had never beheld such trees.

"Hope to Gord," he grumbled, "that you an' your pa an' your uncle Raymondo don't take it into your heads to cut trees like these hyar. It's bad enough what we been doin'. Every time one o' them big fellas goes over, I figure everyone involved in 'er is going to have to spend time in *purgatorio*— ain't that how ye Catholics call 'er? I'm jest saying what I think is all. Ain't right, ain't right nohow. It's as bad as fencin' off the land the way they've done some places, an' plowing up the sod, an' building cities. I tell you, cities is the curse o' the human race. A time will come, take note now, Boss Lady, the time'll come when they's going to be cities all over hell itself, jest the way she is around New York an' Philadelphia an' Boston. Then ye'll look back an' wish to old Coyote Hisself that ye never took it into yore head to cut timber no way. Plowin' the land an' planting crops, that's a sin, sure enough. An' cutting down the big trees when they's no need for it, that there be another sin. There's no reason to listen to Samson Flowers, though. No one ever has. Me, I can see the future after a fashion, and I don't like what I see, I'll say that much. . . ."

"I swear, you're the most bullheaded, most contentious man I've ever met. How are we to make a living otherwise, answer me that? The number of trees that we can cut'll never make a difference to the forest as a whole. It's too big for us to harm it, just like the ocean's too big for us to hurt it either."

"Beggin' yore pardon, Miss Califia. I don't pretend to be no genius, not like your pa and your Uncle Raymondo. Me, I'm just a mountain hawg, destined to get scalped by some burnt-up Blackfoot, in case I ever mosey back that way. But even this child can see what's as plain as the nose on your . . . no, on *my* face. Ye cut down trees like some o' these, and she's going to take a while to grow back. I counted rings on some of those stumps there on the Russian, an' I tell ye, it makes a man humble. A couple of the big stumps was nigh to a thousand years old—unless trees grew different in them days. *Them redwoods ain't goin' to grow back, no sir. Not unless we're willing to wait around for a thousand years or so.*"

Califia heard what Samson was saying. Indeed, she'd had similar thoughts herself. Homer Virgil, he'd foreseen the same horrible eventuality—and maybe, in the final analysis, that's why he'd gone away, so as not to be involved in the destruction of the black forests of California.

They continued on up the coast from the place where the river they'd been following debouched, passing by several Indian villages situated close to the ocean, and then crossed open prairies and skirted a large, almost completely landlocked harbor—one that Califia could see immediately was certain someday to prove a center for lumbering, providing only that sufficient population should find its way to these remote shores. Samson and Califia kept their distance from several more villages but used the field glasses to observe a group of men hewing and burning out a canoe perhaps twenty-five feet in length. Other canoes of similar size were ranked along the beaches, above tidewater.

When Califia and Samson reached a freshwater lagoon separated from the ocean only by a narrow band of sand dunes, they turned inland, cresting a wide ridge, and then moved down into a forest that reached out to either side of a wide, fast-running creek. Here the trees were of utterly amazing proportions, as though each were actively involved in outstripping all its fellows in a silent but desperately mad quest for sunlight and growing space.

"Some of these trees must be nearly four hundred feet tall," Califia remarked as they pushed on through zones of light and shadow. "Absolutely astonishing. . . ."

"If a coon comes back after a lifetime . . . will they still be hyar? I guess so. Hell, as far as we are from civilization, could be no one'll ever find 'em, not unless we guide 'em in. Places like Connecticut an' Massachusetts—and Missouri, for that matter—them I can understand; I mean, ye pile up the stones into boundary walls, and ye cut down the trees just to get at the dirt, to plant crops and that sort o' thing. Whatever's *wild* has to go because it's the enemy. Foxes an' chickens don't mix, at least from the chicken's point of view. This hyar's sort of like we're ridin' through Gord's own garden, ye know what I mean?"

Califia thought about *Gord's garden*, smiled, nodded. There was actually a bit of the poet in Sam Flowers.

"If the logging ever comes this far north, perhaps we'll make the area into a preserve. But I think you're right. There's plenty of land around the Bay and out into the Sacramento Valley. With the harbor back there . . . possibly Dad and Uncle Raymondo could convince Castro to push through another land grant. Way up here, who'd object? If we're still in California, I mean. You have any idea about the Indians—I mean, which tribes live here?"

Flowers shook his head and flicked the reins against his horse's neck. The creature responded by proceeding at exactly the same pace as before.

"Guess we're still in California, all right, but I ain't certain. In any case, we ain't crossed Klamath yet, an' that one flows down out o' Klamath Lake, in H.B.C. country. When we get close to Shasta Butte, they won't be no mistakin' it. Might be the biggest mountain in the world, for all I know. In any case, I seen some big'ns, and they don't measure up. Oh, they's Hood up in Oregon country, an' the Tetons an' Long's Peak an' Pike's Peak over in the High Shining, but I'd guess Shasta's bigger. When we get thar, you tell me if I'm right."

"Bigger than the Sierra Nevada?"

"That's different. The Sierras is all kind of *one mountain* what's four hundred miles long, so it don't count. Shasta, she just stands out thar all by herself."

As they proceeded upslope, Samson caught wind of something—a faint, unpleasant odor that he recognized immediately.

"Somethin' dead. Deer, most likely."

As they rode on, the smell grew stronger. Then they saw it—a dead grizzly, with a single vulture perched on its side, the avian head disappearing again and again into the body cavity, emerging, swallowing.

"Ain't that yore varmint?" Samson asked.

"El Buzzardo!" Califia called out. "What in heaven's name are you doing?"

The big bird looked up, neither sheepish nor defiant. He swallowed several times.

The bantam rooster, perched on Califia's pommel, lifted his head and crowed.

They passed beyond the long ridges where the forest changed from nearly all redwood to a mixture of Douglas firs, ponderosa pines, white pines, and live oak and black oak. Flowers was certain a fast-flowing river they reached wasn't the Klamath—not large enough. This stream they followed eastward, upriver, and into the interior of the Coast Range.

Some days the skies were leaden, and rain fell. At other times they encountered thick, dripping mist. Between storms, temperatures dropped, and ice formed on puddles and bunches of coarse grass and young willows along the river.

The farther they went, the less rainfall the land evidently received—so that in places whole mountainsides were only half clothed in forest. There was snow on the canyon rims—and at times they found it expedient to resort to the high country, in deference to occasional villages along the river—these the Wintuns, Flowers theorized, a wide-spread denomination whose language was related to that of the Ohlones, as well as the Yokuts, the Maidus, and the Miwoks. These people, while reputed to be peaceful and without firearms or horses, were nonetheless known to be extremely resentful of White intrusion into their lands.

For three days they rode southeast; then the river made an abrupt turn to the north, and Samson Flowers knew for the first time exactly *whar in hell* he was.

"Trinity," he said. "I should of knowed it—only the damned thing was running the wrong way. Sutter's campañero, old P.B. Reading, he's got a rancho across the divide eastward, right at the long end of the Sacramento Valley—whar the river comes down out o' the hills. Beyond that, it's all mountains an' forest, clear up through the Siskiyous an' over to the Warners."

Califia studied her chart of extreme northern Alta California. She shook her head emphatically. Either the map had been composed by a dreamer who'd never been near the area, or she and Flowers weren't at all where he said they were. Perhaps both things were true.

"Let's say I take your word for it. Okay. But where's this *Waiiaka*, Mt. Shasta? It's supposed to be Old Man Coyote's lodge. Now I suppose you'll tell me that God's big song-dog has apparently moved since you were here last."

"Nothin' o' the sort," Flowers snorted. "Ye be the *Lady o' the Wild Things*. Ast yore two overfed mountain lions if I ain't right. Animals know by instinct. Only humans has to learn every damned thing they know."

Up ahead, on a moss-covered boulder beside the hissing waters of the Trinity, Ponchita was ensconced, tail trailing down the rock, twitching.

"Lead on," Califia laughed. "What choice do I have? If you're trying to lure me off into the forest, Samson Flowers, so that you'll be able to take advantage of me, I think we've probably come about far enough. . . ."

"Never even thought o' such a thing," Flowers replied, frowning. "First place, Bill the Sawyer'd nail my hide to a redwood tree. Second, this nigger's got *honor*. Way I see it, that sort o' thing's up to the ladies. Look now, Miss Boss. About two days o' riding upriver from hyar we'll cross a pass an' head down to the headwaters of the Sacramento—one o' the branches, anyhow. Three streams come together to form the Sacramento—one from the west of Shasta Butte, one from the south, and one from out o' Goose Lake in the high desert. That'n's the longest but it ain't the biggest, at least not most of the time, I reckon. Anyhow, we'll be into *Okwanuchmu* an' *Achomawi* territory, whar Warrotetot, old Blackbeard, is chief. We was talkin' about him, if ye'll recollect. Them Injuns like to fight, them an' the Klamats. So I figger we'd be wise not to go any futher, not when they's just two of us. Of course, with them cougars o' yours, Blackbeard might decide ye was Coyote's Daughter or summat, an' worship ye. But the chances is he'd burn this child alive, jest like the damned *Rikaras*."

"The *Rikaras* burned you alive? No, never mind. Let me get this straight, Sam Flowers. We've ridden for God-knows how many days to get here. Are we going to be able to see Mt. Shasta? It didn't used to be all that important to me, but now it's a matter of principle. I can't die happy if I don't see that cursed mountain."

"Kinda hard not to see 'er," Flowers laughed.

CHAPTER SIXTEEN

The Old Bull

[1845, 1846:]

THE MOUNTAIN, VISIBLE now from a pass north of an astonishing rocky formation Flowers called Castle Crags, shone brilliantly in bright December sunlight, its high crown and massive lateral peak cloaked in purest white, snow that appeared perpetual, much of it glacial ice, a mountain so big it simply dominated the landscape, a giant among mountains, a titanic presence, films of gray cloud trailing from the summit and giving almost the appearance that the mountain was contemplating volcanic activity, an awakening of contained magmatic fires that had formed this collosal formation, this prodigy. . . .

Flowers gestured with an outreached hand, but said nothing.

Califia tried to think of words worthy of, utterance. The Pacific Ocean was huge, infinitely greater than this one snow-capped mountain, but somehow from a purely human perspective a mere ocean was nothing at all. The vast sprawl of the Coast Ranges through which they'd ridden—these, too, were great. But now that she saw Shasta, her entire sense of proportion was changed. Even with all her anticipation and growing doubt about the reality of *Waiiaka*, to have emerged from a stand of fir trees high on a mountain and to have gazed off to the east—and to have seen what at first didn't seem real at all but only a kind of vision engendered by her own wandering mind. . . .

Shasta!

A chill north wind was blowing as they made camp beneath overhanging limestone from whose base a spring trickled between bandings of fern. They built a fire pit out of chunks of stone and quickly gathered knots and broken sections of pine, cedar, and juniper—fuel sufficient to last the night. Waiiaka began to pulse with color—thin orange darkening to crimson, as the setting sun cast red light that was amplified by the snowy peak.

Califia set a haunch of venison over the flames, and sparks went up into the crepuscular hour. After a time only the crown of Shasta remained visible, a summit of dark red set against darkness. The first stars appeared along the eastern rim.

Samson Flowers rummaged through the saddlebags, cussed a couple of times when he failed to discover the object of his search, and finally let out a whoop.

"Beginnin' to doubt my own memory," he called out to Califia. "But hyar it is—honest-to-Gord High Shining *arwerdenty*, or at least the fixin's of 'er. . . ."

Flowers held up a bottle.

Pure alcohol—not even drinkable unless cut four to one with water, tea leaves, coffee, tobacco, juniper berries, and, so the rumors went, both buffalo dung and grizzly blood.

"If that's what I think it is, Sam Flowers, you'll go blind if you even sniff it."

"Hell no—I'm tellin' ye, Miss Boss, this be the genuine article, my last one, too. Got 'er from Louis Vasquez over to Jim Bridger's fort, a year an' a half ago—just before I started west with Fremont an' them. Been keepin' 'er for a special occasion, and I reckon this'll do. If you ain't interested, then sip yore coffee an' let me be. . . ."

"Who says I'm not *interested*?"

"Wal, now, that's more like it. We'll drink to the by-Gord discovery of Shasta Butte. We'll mix 'er in the coffeepot. Thar's juniper berries up over the rise, if I can get to 'em, an' I can spare an extra plug o' tobacky. The whole genius o' the thing, ye see, is in the makins."

"No deer dropping or bear flop," Califia said. "And no mountain lion piss either. Besides, the kittens won't hold still for it."

Flowers twisted his face in mock disappointment, the missing front tooth noticeable between his bearded lips.

"Then how about buzzard droppins?" he asked.

"If you want a drinking partner, *Señor Florears*, then you'll have to forgo the more exotic ingredients. The coffee's fine, and the tobacco's okay, but let's stop there."

"Wal, I wasn't plannin' on hunting down no grizzly, not after dark anyhow. All right, *Señorita Patrona*, hyar she goes. . . ."

Flowers poured alcohol into the half-full pot of coffee.

Shasta vanished into the darkness, and Samson and Califia gorged themselves on venison and drank coffee laced with white lightning. The rooster scratched at the edge of the firelight, pecking for the cracker crumbs Califia had tossed him. El Buzzardo roosted in a broken-topped ponderosa, and the two lions, more or less sated from some kill of their own earlier in the day, paid minimal attention to the roasting meat— begging for handouts merely because that activity constituted appropriate behavior in a Confucian sense and because it was a matter of feline honor to do so; but soon they retired to a secluded niche in a tangle of willows and young aspens.

"The children are in bed," Califia laughed—thinking as she spoke of the difficulties half a dozen youngsters must pose to Calvin and Juanita on those instances when the sailor came home from the sea.

"Plumb tired out, I guess. Wal, this child too, for that matter. That wind's getting colder by the minute. Could be the temperature's goin' to hit zero tonight. . . ."

Califia drank off the strong mixture, laughed, and motioned for Flowers to refill her cup.

"There's a new world ahead of us, Samson. This particular wind's cold as holy hell, but there's another wind blowing— blowing for all of California, I mean. Big changes—and it's just a matter of time, too. Once we're officially an independent

nation and pull in half a million settlers, then the world will
have to sit up and take notice."

"Wagh! That many damned foreigners, an' they won't be
space for no honest men. Got to have elbow room, for Gord's
sake. Have another shot o' *arwerdenty*, Califia, old gal. Look
hyar now. Ye go fillin' this country up with settlers, then this
child'll head off for Canada or Utah Territory, mebbe up onto
Snake River somewhar."

"Mr. Flowers, you're unsocial. With half a million people,
we'll have genuine cities—and all those cities will need lumber
to build their houses—timbers for their business buildings and
hotels and—"

"Crazy as yore basic hound with a nose full o' quills."
Flowers shrugged. "Is that what you an' yore pa wants? Sell
lumber till the damned cows come home? Cut the trees an'
kill off all the wild varmints an' set cobblestones into every
mule trail an' fence the land until they's nowhar a child can
go without steppin' on *somebody's propity*? No sir, not this
coon. I left all that behind once, an' I sure as hell ain't goin'
to let 'er cotch up with me. They's already too damned many
ranchos, an' too damned many longhorn cattle where they
ought to be herds o' antelope an' elk. I been a trapper, so ye
might say I'm as guilty as the next nigger. But I'll tell ye—just
because a thing's *wild* don't make it *bad*—no sir. Truth is, it's
the dead opposite. The Injuns have lived hyar forever, an' they
ain't done as much to the land as you an' me an' the boys
have done, loggin' these past few months. Think on it, Califia.
Think on it."

"Great Christ, Samson, trees'll grow back. . . ."

"Not the big ones, no sir. You're jest lyin' to yourself if ye
believe that. Ast Pelican Doctor what he thinks about 'er . . .
if he ain't dead by now, I mean. He ain't, is he?"

"Wasn't when I last saw him. Let's don't argue anymore,
Samson Flowers. I'm half drunk. Yep. So fill up my tin cup.
Then let's get some sleep. Tomorrow we head south—back to
the San Lorenzo. I've learned what I wanted to learn about the
Coast Range and the Siskiyous—or are these actually the Sierra
Nevada? No matter; there are forests to last a thousand years,
I've seen that much."

"You ain't never seen what a crew o' Michigan loggers can

do to a patch o' woods, no matter how big. Five years, an'
they'll lay her level. I promise it. One more drink, Califia.
What do ye say?"

At length they found their way to their separate bedrolls,
and Califia Beard lay there in the darkness with Rory Sunrise
perched on her stomach, the bird visible by guttering firelight,
its feathers fluffed out for warmth against the chill. Califia was
half of a mind to keep her wits clear and half of a mind to
give in to the alarming sensation that she was being sucked
into a whirlpool.

"The cold's comin' down from Canada," Flowers growled.
"Out on the Bighorn, I've seen 'er drop down to fifty below
an' then some. . . ."

He rose, heaped wood on the fire, and then turned back to
his bedroll.

"Here," Califia half whispered, "come lie with me. We'll
bundle—so we won't freeze to death. That's all—I don't mean
anything else, Samson Flowers. After all, you're old enough to
be my father. . . ."

"True enough, true enough," the mountain man replied as
he gestured with a nearly empty coffeepot in his hand. "Try
one more swig—It'll keep yore blood flowin'."

Then they were lying together. Whether it was the *arwerdenty* or something else, Califia found the warmth and even
the odor of this *male animal* in her bed more than just a bit
pleasant. At some point, perhaps an hour later—after the rooster
had inexplicably crowed and the fire had died to orange-red
coals—the man and the woman embraced, mouth to mouth.

My God, Califia Beard, what on earth are you up to?

But a different kind of intelligence had taken over, a species
of intellect that abhorred the very notion of denial, of restraint,
or reasonable action. Samson's big hands cupped themselves
over her breasts from behind, and he nibbled at the nape of
her neck. She moaned softly and was surprised to realize where
it was her own hand had wandered.

After a time the rooster grew impatient. He was wary of
having a human creature roll over on him, and he retreated to
the foot of the bedroll.

Samson fumbled with her clothing, and Califia reached
down to uncinch her britches. She slid them down so that one

leg at least was unencumbered. Then she undid the lacings on
the man's leathers. She laughed as he groaned—she grasped
his cock.

"It's too cold to play games," she whispered, her voice gone
husky. "Come into me, Samson Flowers. I want you to . . .
make love to me . . . to hump me."

"You sure? Califia, I want you damned bad—but yore pa
an' yore uncle, they'll have me strung up, sure as buffler dung.
Pardon me—this child sort of put that bad."

"I'm my own woman," she replied. "I'm the only one you
have to answer to. Come into me, damn it, or I swear I'll rape
you, Sam Flowers. . . ."

*She stood high as a mountain somewhere in the Sierra, and she
felt cold and alone—more alone than ever before. Everything she'd
believed in, everything she'd worked toward—all had crumbled,
vanished. Even her animals were gone, and the landscape was
strangely desolate and hostile. She watched as the stream she stood
beside waned and went dry, fish flopping listlessly among dark-
colored stones, gasping, dying.*

*Then Pelican Doctor was there beside her, looking more old
and frail than she remembered.*

*"What is it, little one?" he asked, and she began to laugh—
because she was taller than he. "I've done the wrong thing," she
replied. "I've made the wrong choice, Grandfather. Why was it
necessary for you to send Homer away? Even if he and I could not
have been man and wife, couldn't we have been cousins, as always?"*

*"It wasn't I," Pelican Doctor said. "Even though you and H.V.
were born of twin sisters, there's no law to prevent you from being
husband and wife. First Man and First Woman were brother and
sister, and they were also man and wife. It was they who begot
the Ancient Ones. Even though brothers and sisters no longer
marry, cousins sometimes do—unless one of the shamans has a
medicine dream which prohibits such a thing, and that wasn't the
case with you and Homer Virgil. Ohlone numbers diminish. Perhaps now it's time for cousins to marry so that our people will
survive."*

"Then why was he sent away, Grandfather?"

"Calling Owl's son was fated to journey to the other world—to

learn the medicine of the people who live there. Raymondo spoke of this thing for many years."

"Will H.V. return?" Califia asked, her voice trembling.

"Perhaps, perhaps it will be so. But he's already taken a wife, Little Cal. Now it's time for you to take a husband. You need a man who's strong, just as you are. You need a man you won't be able to twist and bend to your will. Once, generations ago, you'd have been a warrior woman—a shaman—a leader of the people. But now everything is changed."

Pelican Doctor pointed to a spot across the tumbled boulders of the mountainside, a place where several twisted, wind-deformed junipers grew. Sunlight spilled through the foliage of these trees, and Califia thought she could detect a man standing there, half obscured by greenery and half simply insubstantial.

"H.V.?" she gasped, and then turned quickly to Pelican Doctor for affirmation.

Her grandfather had been transformed into a creature half man and half coyote—a manlike being with a song-dog's head. He wore a battered sombrero and somehow managed to hold a pistol in either hand. He yipped several times and then threw back his head and howled.

"H.V.?"

"It's me, it's Samson hyar," a male voice replied from out of the close, cold darkness. "Ye was havin' a bad dream, Califia. Mebbe we drunk a spot too much arwerdenty. . . . Go back to sleep now. Sun won't be up for another hour an' more."

She pressed close to her lover, took comfort in his strength, in his simple male presence, his self-assured good nature. She had wanted, needed, had to have a lover, and she'd chosen him and taken him. It was sufficient. It was good. She had no regrets.

When the white dawn burned from the east and the giant mountain of Shasta became evident, Califia realized that its entire configuration was changed. The ancient volcano was in eruption!

No—it had blown up, it had hurled the upper third of its snow-clad mass into the sky.

Why had she heard nothing—no sound?

She studied the mountain, slowly realizing that clouds had wrapped themselves about it, a great vortex that shrouded both summits. As the sun rimmed higher above the horizon, these clouds began to gleam, to shimmer.

She saw lightning flash from the cloud to the mountain—distant, so distant she never did hear the thunder she knew would have to follow.

On the second day of the new year Califia and Samson passed by Pierson Reading's rancho at the northern terminus of the Sacramento Valley, learned the proprietor was attending to business at New Helvetia, and proceeded to Peter Lassen's somewhat less elaborate ranch on Cottonwood Creek. The good-natured Lassen was indeed at home, treated them well—though as a committed cattleman, he was somewhat taken aback by the presence of presumably *tame* mountain lions. Lassen inquired concerning the health of Raymondo Olivo (whom he'd met a year earlier), and he shared with them the news that Fremont and his sixty American regulars apparently were not of a mind to submit themselves to the authority of General Castro. Larkin was on Fremont's side, but Castro had nonetheless directed the American officer and his *armed band* to stay away from the coastal settlements.

Lassen was glad to be able to converse with a representative of the well-known Olivo & Beard lumbering operations—since he, too, intended to establish a mill—hoping to utilize spring floods to float logs down from the extensive forests of pine and Douglas fir which grew among the Bolly Peaks to the west of his rancho. As settlers arrived in the northern valley, there'd be a quick market for lumber. Lassen had already acquired a small sailing craft equipped with an auxiliary steam engine, one capable of operating in the shallower waters of the upper Sacramento. With this vessel he'd transport saws, gears, fly-wheels, and other necessary equipment upriver from New Helvetia—though how long it might be before the machinery arrived around the Horn from New Haven, Connecticut, he didn't know.

It was evident that Lassen was curious as to the relationship between Califia Beard and Samson Flowers. Beyond one or two probing questions, however, he didn't push the point, though it was clear that he perceived the two of them—she with her zoo in progress, he not unlike such Rocky Mountain fur trappers as Beckwourth, Carson, or the Greenwoods (father and son alike)—as eccentrics of the first water.

The night they spent at Lassen Rancho, Califia and Samson slept in separate rooms, since they deemed it wise, in light of Peter Lassen's strangely bourgeois scrutiny, to maintain appearances. Once on their way south, however, the two found reasons sufficient for sharing one another's sleeping rolls night after night.

"Ye realize," Flowers complained in the aftermath of one of their lovemaking sessions, "that a hoss my age could be subject to *go beaver* real sudden, trying to keep ye happy in the sack, I mean. All my life I figgered the ladies didn't really *like humpin'* an' only did it to keep their men grinnin' and willin' to keep on workin'. Besides, who ever heard of a mare what wanted to ride her stallion?"

"Liar!" Califia laughed. "If there are any women who *don't like it*, why that's because their men haven't got any sense— or because they're ashamed to tell their men what to do. Males have to be taught, whereas we women have an instinct for this sort of thing. Don't you just *hate* having sexual relations with me?"

"Never heard it called that sort o' thing before, but by Gord, Califia, ye've got the most unholy *appetite for screwin'* this child has ever seen."

"Tell me when you get tired of it, Sam Flowers. If you want your water cut off, this lady will be happy to oblige you. . . . "

"Could we at least tell that damned turkey vulture not to stand around on one leg an' watch? A rooster an' two mountain catamounts is bad enough. I feel like some old buffler bull that's been dragged back into the herd an' put to stud again."

"An old bull with a nice . . . hump," Califia laughed. "Is my bull hungry?"

"A *turrible responsibility*," Flowers lamented, not for the first time.

The romance, long in coming, flared and quickly funked. By the time Califia and Samson had reached Sutter's Fort, the entire month of January had passed, and the frenzy of mating had become somewhat more calculated, more psychologically demanding. Califia and Samson, in short, were at each other's throats almost constantly.

First he wanted to get married, at least if that arrangement met with the approval of Bill the Sawyer.

Then she grew angry that he should be concerned about the matter of Beard's blessing—or anyone else's blessing, for that matter, other than their own.

Next she insisted that John Sutter had full authority to legalize their wedded bliss, but Samson opined that no *legal preachments* were necessary, since no such ritual was followed among either the High Plains tribes in whose lands he'd been a trapper or among the Costanoan peoples—the Ohlones, Califia's own people. In short, Samson Flowers would be damned if he'd allow any *civilized Whiteman* to pass moral judgment on him.

By the time he relented on this point of cultural loyalty, she decided that heretofore she'd done quite nicely without the encumbrance of a man, and she didn't really need or want a half-educated bear telling her how to think about politics, business, or the tilt of a redwood tree. Furthermore, with one tooth missing, Flowers's grin was positively unsightly.

She was a *Gorddamn hardheaded bitch*.

He wasn't sufficiently sensitive to her need to have (at the very least) a rooster, a vulture, and two mountain lions.

He had other wives back among the Cheyennes and the Gros Ventres.

She was forever talking, both asleep and awake, about her cousin Homer, and he wasn't about to compete with *no leetle runt what reads books to other lettle runts for a livin' an' besides lives halfway around the world into the bargain*.

He lacked any kind of ambition and had no concern for the lumbering business.

She was already married to *a gang of timber beasts an' Gord-awful river pigs an' the like*.

He was a sonofabitch.

She was a bitch pure and simple.

And so they parted company.

Califia didn't wait for passage downriver for herself and her animals but rather proceeded posthaste on horseback, arriving at Hotochruk village a week later. Gatogordo and Ponchita, foot-weary though they were, immediately recognized that they'd returned to familiar territory and struck out on a hunt and were gone for several days—only to slink into the village, sleep for a day or so, and then disappear into the forest once more.

Rory Sunrise attempted to exercise dominance over every hen in the village and found himself in confrontations with roosters that had been no more than mere striplings when he'd left. Soon all the roosters were fighting among themselves, and young boys were standing around, cheering. Rory, surveying the confusion he'd engendered, flew to the crown of Calvin's house and crowed lustily.

El Buzzardo winged off toward the ocean, where he doubtless hoped to discover a dead seal and perhaps the company of a few old comrades.

Bill Beard pretended to be furious with his daughter but relented quickly. Seagull insisted on a full account of the interval of nearly a year. Calling Owl had four letters from Homer Virgil, and these Califia dutifully read aloud to her aunt, though she strongly suspected that Calling Owl had already heard them a dozen times or more.

Raymondo and Bill were eager to renew operations on the Russian River but were disappointed to learn that Samson Flowers would apparently no longer be working for them. Juan Pescadero had broken a bone and would be laid up for at least two months. A young pine, of all things, had *barberchaired*, buckling backward off its stump, in the process snapping Juan's leg just below the knee. As to questions about the former Olivo & Beard hunter, Califia replied that Sam Flowers was a vagabond by nature—that the idea of a steady job was antithetical to him.

Calvin and Juanita had Califia to dinner in their *log mansion*, and dinner was a long ordeal of young children (number indeterminate) climbing into her lap and asking the same questions over and over—and of listening to Juanita (no longer precisely the same fresh-faced child Calvin had taken to wife ten years earlier) babble about the exploits of her young ones: who had learned to talk, who had learned to read, who had gone sailing with Calvin, who had been engaged in various brawls with Hotochrukma boys.

The recently acquired *Don Quixote II*, a double-master with a steam-engine drive, was ready to weigh anchor from Santa Cruz to transport crew and supplies back to the Russian River operation. Spring rains would soon be past, and it was time to return to the business of felling timber.

Leaving Calvin's house, she met her grandfather—though certainly not for the first time since she'd returned.

"Where is your husband?" the old chief asked, squinting at her.

The eyes in his wrinkled visage were concerned, and he asked the question as though he knew something that he in fact had no way of knowing, since she'd said not a word to anyone with regard to what had transpired between herself and Samson Flowers.

"I don't have a husband yet, Grandfather," she replied.

"Then it will happen soon," he said. "I've dreamed this thing twice now."

Califia and her crew and her menagerie (larger now, since Rory had insisted on taking along the Lady Broodsalot, his own true love) and her father and uncle, as well as horses and oxen and various supplies, set sail on the *Don Quixote II*: Calvin Beard, Captain. When the craft put in at Yerba Buena, Bill Beard returned to the ship with a copy of the following proclamation:

> Fellow Citizens: A band of robbers, commanded by a Captain of the United States Army, J.C. Fremont, have without respect to the laws and authorities of this department daringly introduced themselves into the Country and disobeying the orders of Your Commander in Chief and the Prefect of the District by whom he was commanded to march forthwith out of the limits of our Country and without answering their letters he remains encamped at the Natividad, from which he sallies forth, committing depredations and making scandalous skirmishes.
>
> In the name of our native Country, I write to you to place Yourselves under my immediate orders, at Head-

quarters where we will prepare to tame the ulcer, which should it not be done would destroy your independence and liberty for which you all always sacrifice Yourselves, as will Your Friend and fellow Citizen.

—José Castro

Calvin, Bill, and Raymondo nodded, handed the document to Califia.

"Just a matter of time," Raymondo said. "*Al fin y al cabo*—when all is said and done, it's inevitable. The United States of America, it will try to swallow California and perhaps Mexico also."

Don Quixote II continued north to the mouth of the Russian River, delivering some equipment to Sutter's mill and taking Califia and her crew on up to the head of tidewater.

Whatever the state of relations between Mexico and California and the United States, it was time for the *timber beasts* (these individuals—mostly Yanks, but also some Indios and a few Sandwich Islanders—who'd found their way across from New Helvetia to the San Lorenzo) to sharpen their wide-bitted axes and begin to bite through heavy, fibrous bark and close-ringed, oxide-colored wood. It was time for the calling out of *timmmburr!* or *ma-der-o!* and the tilting to one side and the rushing to earth of trees that had been centuries in the growing. If some of these shattered upon impact, why, that was to be expected, even when beds of brush were meticulously constructed ahead of time.

Broken logs, in any case, could be converted into shingles, for which there was always a sufficient market.

CHAPTER SEVENTEEN

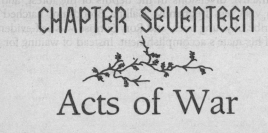

Acts of War

[1846, 1847:]

REDWOODS, PINES, AND cedars were coming down. Ingenuity, lines, winches, oxen, and sheer stubbornness managed to put the check dam back in place against the force of a springtime current, and log rafts were being formed up by the river pigs. Califia brought along a couple of young Ohlones to act as camp hunters, and although these youths were skillful enough at tracking and tolerable good shots into the bargain, between them they were unable to provide the plenitude of game that Samson Flowers had formerly delivered so punctually.

Califia's logging operations seemed headed for a second season of grand success. If the men occasionally grumbled at Miss Boss's edicts—seeing her as a relentless taskmaster—they nonetheless accorded her almost religious reverence. Califia Beard's presence within the camp had the salutory effect of causing men who might not otherwise even bathe in the course of a month to swim regularly, to wash their twill and flannel shirts, to shave from time to time, and even to tone down their crudely colorful lingo when the *Lady* was close about.

Califia's famous pair of *tame catamounts*, though they appeared in camp upon occasion, had apparently discovered more attractive diversions in the depths of the forest, and so came to visit less frequently. Gallina Broodsalot hatched an instant tribe of young ones, and Rory Sunrise was self-evidently proud of his mate's accomplishment. Instead of waiting for the first hint of false dawn, the small black rooster now regaled the darkness with his crowing—almost in the fashion of a determined New England town crier.

El Buzzardo, however, had discovered no committed playmates amongst his *brethren* on the blue afternoon skies, and he continued to roost close to the community of loggers and to make faithful inspections of the camp garbage dump. Neither were strips of meat, set out to dry on racks, exempt from the ravages of his crooked beak.

In short, everything was relatively under control—with matters running along in their greased grooves so smoothly that the ongoing tedium of days conspired to render everyone *fat, stupid, and happy.* Califia Beard, in spite of her best intentions in the opposite direction, found herself thinking again and again of *that bullheaded, unpredictable, language-mutilating, gaptoothed refugee from a beaver pond.* In retrospect, Califia decided, Samson Flowers did have one or two redeeming traits. In the first place, as she now reflected, she felt at home with him—even if she had difficulty in getting along with the rockheaded, obnoxious bastard. Secondly, she enjoyed his odor—musky, leathers bloodstained under God-knew-what conditions, knife wound on one cheek, one scar on his belly and one just under the collarbone, both from having *attracted a mite of galena,* a raspy and yet strangely mellow voice, powerful arms which, when she slept within them, made her feel ridiculously like a little girl, a willingness to make love when offered even the slightest bit of encouragement, and a shameless, self-satisfied appetite for doing one or two truly outrageous things of which she'd grown quite fond.

Was it her nature to *ruin* all relationships with male human animals? Or was it that Fate held a grudge against her, providing hints of satisfaction but ultimately denying the full term?

John Sutter realized events in Alta California were moving inevitably, relentlessly toward a moment of no return. For six months that self-important, strutting Fremont (and his men) had proven both an embarrassment, stemming from the Yank's defiance at Gavilan Peak, and the cause of divided loyalties. However much Sutter might sympathize with the American cause, the fact of Fremont's presence served to dilute those sympathies.

When the American officer subsequently moved north, stopping at Lassen Rancho and, under the leadership of Kit Carson, butchering perhaps a thousand Yana Indians for presumably having taken three of Lassen's cows, Sutter was not pleased. Then Fremont bought horses from other renegade Indians, the Wintuns, animals that had most likely been driven away from Sutter's own range several months earlier.

Later word indicated that Fremont and Carson had proceeded as far north as Klamath Lake, where they'd foolishly engaged a much larger force of Klamat warriors armed both with bow and arrow and H.B.C. fusees. Only desperate maneuvers had allowed the Yankees to get back across the river and away from the wrath of those warrior kings of the high desert.

"Meaner'n by-God Piegan Blackfoots, an' smarter, too," Kit Carson was quoted as saying after he and the others had managed to extricate themselves.

Archibald Gillespie of the United States Marine Corps showed up at New Helvetia, with letters from Secretary of State Buchanan, Senator Thomas H. Benton (Fremont's father-in-law), and apparently verbal instructions from President Polk himself. Upon learning that Fremont was not at Sutter's Fort, the military courier rode north immediately, intent upon finding the American military commander.

On the one hand, Sutter really didn't like the presumptuous Fremont at all and on a personal level might have been pleased if the Klamats had left *Herr Johnny* for the carrion crows; but on the other hand, Fremont in some way or another represented the government of the United States—and the master of New Helvetia was clearly of the opinion that the future belonged to the United States.

In a letter dated May 12, 1846, Sutter remarked to General José Castro: *I think this gentleman is an officer of the United States Army. . . I told him this and he replied that he formerly was, but that he now has retired from the service. Who knows? It is my opinion that Señor Gillespie is a courier for Captain Fremont and who knows but that he may have important dispatches from his government?*

The second week in June a gang of *Bostons*, some twelve buck-skin men led by Sutter's friend William Ide and the American Ezekiel Merritt, committed the first act of war. Presuming Mariano Vallejo and his soldiers might move against the growing band of mountain men and settlers, a threat José Castro was known to have made, Merritt and his companyeros took the offensive and proceeded to *liberate* a herd of horses being driven from Sonoma to Monterey. Merritt, a loyal American, then rode to Fremont's encampment near the base of Estawm Yan, otherwise known as the Yuba Buttes or Sutter's Buttes, and made the commanding officer a present of the equines.

Perhaps Fremont, with his well-armed band of regulars, would be willing to provide protection.

But Merritt, a veteran of several battles against High Plains Indians, wasn't finished yet. Indeed, the idea of fighting a war in behalf of his native land began to compel his imagination. Furthermore, so long as Vallejo remained the commander of Mexican forces, it was altogether probable that he would now feel obliged to round up the Yanks and expel them from the province. With some fifty men (Samson Flowers among them), William Ide and Ezekiel Merritt staged a surprise raid on Sonoma, the Americans quickly enforcing their claims to military victory by means of raising a new flag above the town plaza, a pennant decorated with the drawing of a California grizzly. The Americans had the good fortune of being able to take a very considerable prisoner—none other than Mariano Vallejo, along with other nobles of the *Gente de Razón*, Vallejo's relatives.

The *Bear Flag Rebellion* was now a fact, and Alta California was declared a *free and independent state, in no way subservient to those sonsabitches in Mexico City.*

A second confrontation followed quickly, the morning of June 24th—the Battle of Olampali, named for a nearby Pomo village. Twenty American settlers blundered into contact with Captain Joaquin de la Torre and his Leather Jackets. There was an exchange of long-range gunfire, and the result was one Californio killed and two wounded, while the Americans suffered no casualties.

Fremont realized that he was obliged to act. He and Kit Carson and their men moved down the valley to Sutter's Fort and were allowed entry. The prisoners from Sonoma were also brought into the fort and kept there under house arrest—including Mariano Vallejo, his brother Salvador, a military aide named Victor Prudon, and the latter's brother-in-law, one Jacob Leese. Sutter allowed the prisoners to eat with him and to walk with him in the evening, without benefit of guards. Within a few days Fremont complained that Sutter was dealing with the men as though they were guests, not prisoners of war.

"Nonsense, *Herr Fremont*, nonsense. These are men of property—they will not attempt to escape."

"Sutter, don't you know how to treat prisoners of war?"

"*Jawohl*, indeed I do, Captain Fremont. I have been a prisoner myself. But if you do not approve of my actions, then take charge. . . ."

The prisoners, at length, were put into the hands of John Bidwell, who dealt with them exactly as Sutter had.

Whatever the political extremity, Sutter was unable to perceive Mariano Vallejo and his family as other than friends.

Word came that the United States and Mexico were officially at war, and directly Commodore John D. Sloat arrived off Monterey and, on the morning of July 7th, with two hundred and fifty sailors and marines, came ashore, marched to the Spanish Custom House, and raised an American flag—proclaiming that *henceforth California will be a portion of the United States*. . . .

The sloop *Portsmouth* took control of San Francisco Bay, and the American flag was raised above the plaza at Yerba Buena. Lieutenant Joseph Revere of the *Portsmouth* took a party and moved on to Sonoma, where the Bear flag was lowered and the United States flag was raised. Following this ceremony, an American emigrant named Scott was given an American flag and directed to ride to Sutter's Fort and to raise Old Glory at sunrise, July 11th.

John Sutter wrote in his journal:

A long time before daybreak I had the whole Fort alarmed

and my guns ready. When the Star Spangled Banner slowly rose on the flag staff, the cannon began and continued until nearly all the windows were broken. Some of the people around the Fort made long faces, because they thought they would have had a better chance to rob and plunder if they had remained under the Bear Flag. The Sonoma prisoners, not knowing what was going on, were greatly surprised. I went to them and said: "Now, gentlemen, we are under the protection of this great flag, and we should henceforth not be afraid to talk to one another. . . ." They all rejoiced that the anarchy was over.

The American conquest of California was still far from complete. Pio Pico and his brother Andres were united in their determination to resist the *Gringos*, and the settlements south of the Tehachapi Mountains remained loyal to Mother Mexico.

Eight days after Sloat took Monterey, he was replaced by Robert F. Stockton, who proceeded to promote Fremont to major and to put him in charge of the California Battalion, including a group of Walla Walla warriors who'd come south from Oregon country on a revenge-taking, but whom Sutter had induced, with a promise of pay by the United States Government, to fight against the Californios. Stockton then ordered Fremont to prepare to march southward along the coast toward the Los Angeles Pueblo, where he would eventually join forces with General Stephen W. Kearny, presumed to be marching overland from New Mexico.

Stockton's naval force would also proceed to Los Angeles, intending to strike quickly and so occupy the pueblo and thereby preempt any use of the facilities by Andres Pico.

Sutter's Fort, with the Americans in control, was the only fortified place in the Great Valley. Here the Yankee settlers came in for protection against forces commanded by General José Castro and against whatever wild Indians Castro might be able to enlist in his cause. Volunteer companies were recruited, trained, and outfitted to fight against Castro's Leather Jackets or against Andres Pico's men, these reportedly encamped in the mountains near Los Angeles.

John Sutter, though he had clearly allied himself with the Americans, was nonetheless somewhat suspect, simply because he had formerly attempted to keep Micheltorena in power. Fremont took no chances whatsoever—and proceeded to place a subordinate, Edward Kern (the designated *artist* of the expedition) in official command at the fort—an act which annoyed and indeed deeply offended the owner of New Helvetia. Adding insult to injury, Kern proved to be almost completely incompetent as a leader—and Captain Montgomery of the *Portsmouth* was eventually obliged to dispatch one of his own officers to the fort—to give poor Kern instructions in matters military.

When it became abundantly clear to Samson Flowers that Sutter was not to lead a force southward but instead to remain at the fort, the mountain man saddled his trail pony, loaded the saddlebags of a pair of packhorses, and made tracks for the Olivo & Beard logging camp on Russian River.

The truth was, he damned well missed the company of Califia Beard. Perhaps under normal circumstances she'd had enough of him, but circumstances were no longer normal. Surely there was to be a bloody battle ahead—not just some little exercises in military gamesmanship such as the civil embroilments of California. No, this time, *sartin as bears shit in the woods, by Gord,* they were going to have a genuine contest. After all, this was Mexico against the United States, and the fate of half a continent hung in the balance. Men were going to get *sent beaver,* and afterward there'd be something worthwhile to sit around a camp fire and talk about. Therefore, Califia Beard would want to be present. She liked excitement as much as he did, and she'd be *powerful disappointed* if the whole thing happened, and she didn't even know about it. What good was a war if a body didn't even know there was one? By the time Calvin or Bill the Sawyer or Raymondo Olivo brought word from Santa Cruz, the whole shootin' match would likely be over.

Two days of hard riding took Flowers across the valley and up Putah Creek and over to the stinking springs and on to the redwood forests along Russian River.

"Caaaaal-lifiaaaa!" he bellowed as he galloped his horses into camp. "It's by-Gord war! The Yanks has taken Monterey an' Sonoma an' Sutterville! Fremont needs volunteers. . . ."

Califia recognized the voice and was more than a little

pleased to hear it when in fact she'd supposed she'd seen the last of Sam Flowers, supposed that she'd driven him off and turned him forever against her. She gestured helplessly toward Juan Pescadero, now more or less healed and once again at the northern camp.

Juan grinned, winked at the boss lady.

"*Una afortunada desgracia, Señorita Califia*—perhaps it is good that Flowers has come back. You speak of him almost constantly—I think you must actually be fond of him. . . ."

"The way a dog's fond of a tick on its snout," Califia replied.

But she'd already stepped out of her small office a hundred yards back from the river and, hands on hips, was grinning as she watched Flowers on horseback, standing up in the stirrups, and waving his ancient Hawken flintlock.

In September Califia and Samson, accompanied by a dozen timber beasts who were of a mind to join the fighting, rode south toward the San Lorenzo mill. The Lady of the Wild Things left behind her mountain lions, as well as Rory Sunrise and Gallina Broodsalot—but with specific and pointed instructions to Juan Pescadero and to all the men in camp. Gatogordo and Ponchita were to be fed when they showed up; furthermore, should it subsequently be discovered that Broodsalot or Rory or any of their sixteen offspring had been put into a pot, she, Califia, would personally flay alive the offending chicken-eating cannibal.

El Buzzardo, sensing his mistress was of a mind to desert him, stayed close about the camp and went circling along when Califia and Flowers and a dozen loggers set out along the trail that led toward Carquinez Strait, where a ferry would take them across the mile-wide channel.

As luck would have it, the *Don Quixote II* was in port at Santa Cruz, and the village, as well as the neighboring settlement of Branciforte, was buzzing with rumors. Word had it that Fremont was well on his way to the Los Angeles Pueblo, that Stockton's naval force had occupied the pueblo, and that Gillespie and fifty men under his command, left to control Los Angeles, had been surrounded by the residents and taken prisoner. Before surrendering, however, word had it, Gillespie managed to send a messenger named Juan Flaco Brown to contact Stockton, if not in Monterey, then in San Francisco, as Yerba Buena was now being called. Brown narrowly escaped the Angelenos and rode nearly nonstop, covering five hundred miles in an amazing five days. Stockton, but recently arrived in Monterey, departed southward once again, the exhausted Juan Flaco Brown soundly asleep below deck.

Seagull and Calling Owl were of the opinion that the crazy Americans and the crazy Mexican Californios should be allowed to kill one another without the assistance of Olivo & Beard. Pelican Doctor, now approximately a hundred years old by his own reckoning, though somewhat younger than that as Bill the Sawyer and Raymondo Olivo calculated matters, suggested that there was often advantage in allowing camp dogs to fight, but that one had to be careful not to attempt to separate them—for fear of being bitten. If the *Boston dogs* killed all the *Spanish dogs*, so much the better. Already the great-winged condors had vanished from the skies above the Santa Cruz Mountains, and that was doubtlessly because there were far too many Whitemen of both sorts. Whitemen killed the deer and elk and replaced these animals with long-horned cattle. Then they butchered the cattle and sold the hides and the tallow and put the meat into casks of saltwater. Nothing was left for the condors to eat, and so they had gone away to places where there were no cattle.

"Regardless what Pelican Doctor says, we can't just sit around and smoke our pipes and theorize about what's going to happen," Bill Beard exclaimed.

"Alas," Raymondo put in, "though our people are as brave as grizzlies, we cannot hold off these *Norteamericanos*. William Fur-Face, I see now that you have been right all along, and therefore I think that we must sail south and stick our iron into the fire. If we stay here at home, comfortably out of danger, what will we tell the grandchildren when we are old men? Perhaps it will not be such a bad thing to be a part of the United States."

Bill Beard laughed.

"Hell, Ray, we're old coons already—or haven't you been keeping track of the years? Of course, I hold my age better than you do. Well, Captain Cal, my boy, how soon can we set sail?"

Calvin shifted his chair about, took a sip of whiskey, and stretched out his long legs.

"The ship's ready right now. I've got a partial cargo of tools, rice, beans, and leather goods aboard—those and a few crates of printing equipment for one of John Sutter's cohorts—Brannan, the Mormon elder, who wants to start a newspaper or some such thing. We've already got one newspaper in Monterey—the *Californian*. How many do we need, for Christ's sake? But there's no need to unload. Califia's got herself and Flowers and twelve others. We can easily recruit a hundred and arm them as well. Plenty of room for everyone. Let's sail with the morning tide."

"I am afraid," Juanita said, "that this time you will not come back, Calvin Beard. You'll turn me into a widow, and our children will starve to death. . . . "

Flowers winked at Califia, then nodded toward Juanita.

"Leetle Señora Beard, you've got a point—except that nobody ever gets kilt in California wars. Ye know that. The lads jest sort of shout at each other from opposite hilltops an' maybe kill a mule or so if the powder for the brass cannons ain't wet. Then they shake hands an' get back to their business."

"True enough," Califia said. "But this time it sounds different—it's not just a matter of sending Micheltorena back to Mexico City. What if Mexico dispatches an army?"

"Looks like the Mexicans have got their hands full already," Calvin remarked. "Here in California, we're on the fringes of things. If we didn't fight at all, matters would likely settle out just about the same."

"I have heard," Raymondo said, "that your General Kearny and the Regular Army Dragoons are on their way from New Mexico. The *Norteamericanos* have occupied Las Vegas in New Mexico, and Texas is already part of the United States. General Zachary Taylor and his army have invaded Mexico, and Santa Anna is ready to negotiate for peace. . . ."

"Texas, an honest-to-Gawd state!" Bill Beard agreed. "Admitted to the Union just after last Christmas—while Califia and Samson were helling around up by Mt. Shasta. . . . Another year or so, and Alta California'll be in the Union, too. Mark my word."

"*Manifest Destiny*," Calvin said. "I figure the United States is eventually going to swallow up all of Mexico and all of Canada and Russian Alaska to boot. Wait and see. . . . That's what H.V. said, too, in his last letter."

"So marked, so marked," Raymondo agreed, at the same time rubbing his hands together. "Perhaps we should drop anchor in Monterey—to find out if our old friend Jean Paul Martin would wish to go along for the grand adventure—perhaps Larkin as well, if Señor Consul did not already accompany Fremont. We shall be able to witness the making of history."

"Let's sail with the tide, then," Califia said, patting the knife pistol she wore strapped to her leg. "Nothing against Pico and his brother, you all understand, but the way I see it, the future of Olivo & Beard lies with the United States of America, and besides . . ."

Samson Flowers laughed, slapped his leg.

"An' besides, ye like excitement. It's yore nature. Most likely ye wants to shoot a few Leather Jackets."

Califia glared at the mountain man and then glanced out through the window. She made note of El Buzzardo perched near the crown of a canyon live oak.

"Why do I put up with you?" she demanded. "Just don't get in my way."

Gillespie signed his name in behalf of the United States, promising to withdraw his men to San Pedro and to depart from California in expeditious fashion. Before that inglorious departure, however, Stockton's reinforcements arrived and the battle for control of Los Angeles was resumed.

Not Leather Jackets from the Mexican army but rather Californio ranchers and vaqueros commanded by José Carillo, men skilled in horsemanship though poorly armed with carbines and homemade willow lances, turned back Stockton's naval force, harrying the Americans in their retreat to San Pedro by means of numerous rounds from a single small brass cannon which a Mexican woman had hidden away at the time of Stockton's initial entry into Los Angeles. A vaquero named

Ignacio Aguilar was said to have fired the cannon with a lighted cigarette. *The Battle of Old Woman's Gun* was, as later reported, "a victory for California horsemen, powder made at San Gabriel, and a salute-firing cannon from the plaza."

The Picos were jubilant—indeed, so was Abel Stearns, an American rancher whose loyalties had shifted almost totally to the side of the Californios he'd lived among for twenty years. While it may have been true that Mexico was both heavy-handed and even disdainful of the rightful needs of the relative handful of *hidalgos* and *mestizos* and *immigrantes* who constituted the *Gente de Razón*, nonetheless it seemed to Stearns and the Picos and many others that these *Gringo Bostons* were both damned high-handed and utterly ignorant with regard to the way matters stood in California.

But Fremont was close, so rumor persisted—perhaps even then in the act of crossing the Tehachapi Mountains, and General Kearny's Dragoons were moving in from across the Mojave Desert to the east. Such was the situation when *Don Quixote II* dropped anchor in San Pedro Harbor, gathered whatever intelligence was available, and then sailed on to the south—to San Diego, where Stockton's ships were waiting.

As matters turned out, Kearny's force didn't arrive until the twelfth of December—his troops half starved, exhausted both from the desert crossing and from a series of encounters with Andres Pico and his men at San Pascual, some thirty miles northeast of the mission. Kearny's men, though mounted on mules and horses that were in terrible condition after the sands and rocks and creosote brush and Joshua trees of the Mojave, charged several times. Pico's horsemen retreated and then doubled back upon their pursuers. In the hand-to-hand conflicts that ensued, Kearny lost seventeen men, with another nineteen wounded. The Californios suffered no loss of life, and as was later learned, a mere handful of their men were wounded.

Kearny, in possession of the field of battle and therefore able to claim a *victory*, was in actuality cut off, the only viable route to San Diego blocked. Fremont and Stockton had previously sent Kit Carson eastward, with dispatches for Washington—and with directions to make contact with General Kearny along the way. Carson met the general on the Rio Grande below Socorro and showed Kearny Admiral Stockton's official message that American control of California was established; as a result, the general had ordered most of his command back to Santa Fe. Fortunately, however, Kearny convinced Carson to guide him through to San Diego.

Now the canny little mountain man, taking Lieutenant Edward Beale with him (as a matter of military propriety), was able to outflank the positions held by the Californios and make his way to San Diego, where Beale notified Admiral Stockton as to what had happened. Stockton sent Carson and Beale back to San Pascual, accompanied by some two hundred marines and soldiers. At the approach of the American reinforcements, Andres Pico saw fit to withdraw—and General Kearny was able to complete his journey to San Diego, arriving at the mission on December 12th.

After the near-disaster on the desert, Kearny and Stockton required two and a half weeks to get their mounts and weaponry back into proper order.

What in hell had happened to Fremont? Lost in the Coast Range, his men smitten with cholera? Had José Carillo managed to recruit a new and larger force than the one he'd commanded at the Battle of Old Woman's Gun?

On December 29th, however, the combined forces of Kearny and Stockton, together with the Olivo & Beard *timber beast brigade*, set out on horseback from San Diego, the six hundred American regulars and one hundred loggers encountering very little sustained opposition along the way.

On January 8th, 1847, the Americans found themselves at the upper ford of the San Gabriel River, with a force of Californios under José Maria Flores facing them from the opposite bank. Flores's men began to fire, and the Americans, in a panic, fell back.

"Come on, coons! Ain't no time to stop now!" Kit Carson sang out as he urged his mule into the river, firing and loading as he went.

"Hooraw fer the mountains!" Samson Flowers yelled, following that with a piercing rendition of the High Plains war cry, "Hoo-ki-hi!"

Califia, ignoring her brother Cal's plea for common sense, plunged her own pony into the San Gabriel, firing her repeating pistol as she moved ahead.

Above the melee one could hear Kearny's bass voice, raging and sputtering.

The Olivo & Beard loggers, seeing the two mountaineers and one lanky female (whom they revered as Miss Boss) charging across, took heart and pushed ahead, with the military following. José Maria Flores's men, disconcerted, withdrew—and within a matter of minutes the American force had made its crossing—miraculously, with no casualties whatsoever.

The following day at the ford across the Los Angeles River, Flores' men were once again in position, but this time the Americans did not so much as hesitate—and the Californios, greatly outnumbered, hastily pulled back.

El Buzzardo, whatever grandiose visions he may have had of dining upon the flesh of men fallen on the field of battle, was obliged to settle for a horse that had broken a leg and had to be disposed of, a calf apparently killed by a mountain lion and worked over both by a family of coyotes and by half a dozen rival vultures, and the decomposed carcasses of brown seals the tides had washed ashore.

CHAPTER EIGHTEEN

Aftermath

[1847:]

JANUARY 10, 1847, witnessed the raising of Old Glory above the plaza in Los Angeles, with Kearny and Stockton in attendance. The actual taking of the pueblo and the surrounding area was an anticlimax, inasmuch as the officers fully anticipated a direct confrontation with Andres Pico and his skilled horsemen—something beyond the minor skirmishes with Flores and his men at the crossings of the San Gabriel and the Los Angeles Rivers. Nor did Flores attempt a stand at the pueblo. Word had it that he'd resigned his authority to Andres Pico and departed, posthaste, for the district of Sonora.

Where was Pico himself?

Possibly he and his men were encamped in the Tehachapis, to the north, or closer at hand, in San Fernando Valley.

"You an' yore buzzard up to a leetle exploration?" Flowers asked.

"I take it you've got an idea where we might find the Californios?"

"Pre-zactly. Call it the *intuition of a mountain hawg*. Ye up for it?"

Califia, with El Buzzardo perched comfortably upon the

caved-in crown of her sombrero, glanced across the parade grounds to where Bill Beard and Raymondo Olivo and Brother Cal were rubbing elbows with Kearny and Stockton and Gillespie and the other officers, as well as half a dozen priests and perhaps twice that number of minor Californio functionaries. Even the wealthy Abel Stearns was among them, the American-turned-Californio having now readjusted his loyalties so as to cause himself and his family the least amount of difficulty during the time of governmental transition which clearly lay ahead. All things considered, the little gathering was amicable.

"You're right, Mr. Flowers. We don't really belong here, do we?"

"Time was when ye wasn't so damned formal, Califia."

"Time was when I still thought you were capable of acting like a human being, but I should have known that was just for show."

"Gord-damn it, ye want to ride with me or not? This child's heading out, one way or the other."

Disturbed by his mistress's sudden, agitated head movements, El Buzzardo began to fan his big wings. A moment later he flew, rowing his way upward, perhaps to investigate three or four other vultures circling about, off toward the seashore.

Was she beginning to soften toward him? In truth, did she really remember just what it was that had driven the wedge between them? Had she and this ungainly, long-legged, gaunt, gaptoothed, bearded, scraggly-haired refugee from the fur trade actually contemplated the crime of matrimony? In her imagination, for the smallest portion of an instant, she could feel him, aroused, thrusting into her—could remember the sound of him afterward, snoring blissfully and sounding for all the world like a grizzly in a cave, asleep during a winter snowstorm high in the mountains. Then she was vexed with her own mind for betraying her, and vexed with her body as well—or with some variety of intelligence down in the female center of her being, an intelligence that from time to time demonstrated its independence. Surely, surely if she merely wished to endure an act of mating, there were available more likely and more comely men than Samson Flowers. . . . Men, damn them, had a great advantage upon those occasions when the madness of desire overcame their better judgments—they could simply bed any one of those women who were happy to accept a few coins. Why was there no similar cultural marketplace available for women? Was it unnatural, after all, for a woman simply to desire a man? To want the white fire? Califia's cheeks were suddenly flushed, tingling. She looked away—hoped Flowers sensed nothing.

"All right, all right. I guess I've got nothing better to do," Califia replied. "Where are we headed?"

Sam nodded. He was shading his eyes—gazing after the soaring, dark shape of El Buzzardo.

"Up the coast, naturally, past Palos Verdes an' on to Monte Pinos an' Tejón Pass. If Andres Pico's still got his *jinetes* with him, could be he's fixin' to ambush Fremont an' them."

"I heard Stearns say Pico's most likely in the San Fernando. . . ."

"Could be, could be. But why'd he do that? She's not a good place to fight, as I recollect, an' if Fremont be comin' over the mountain. . . ."

"Perhaps our friend Fremont's gone back to Sutter's Fort. How could he possibly take this long to get here?"

Samson shrugged.

"Run afoul of them damned Yokuts, mebbe, or the Chumash. Expect we'd best tell yore pa what we're up to. I shore don't want old Bill thinkin' I kidnapped his daughter."

"Mr. Flowers," Califia replied, "you suffer from delusions. You and your friend Kit Carson together couldn't take me anyplace against my will. Truth is, I could drill the both of you at fifty yards. Keep that in mind."

Samson grinned. For whatever reasons, Califia had risen to the bait.

"Wouldn't invite Carson in on 'er," he said. "Problem with Kit—well, he's too short to be any good at kidnapping. By Gord, now that I think on it, mebbe you an' me ought to kidnap Old Kit. . . . I mean, hellfire, ye're a good foot taller than any normal female."

Califia closed her eyes and rubbed at her temples.

"Get the horses," she said at last, "and I'll tell Dad and Uncle Ray where we're headed."

———

The man and the woman, trailing a pair of packhorses behind
them, reached the Pacific just north of San Pedro and rode
along the sand for a couple of miles, neither speaking, neither
exactly certain why it was the two of them were going anywhere . . . together.

Then, as the wind shifted, an odor of rotting flesh became
apparent.

Flowers motioned, pointing. Half a hundred vultures and
two or three giant-winged condors were moving in from various quadrants, evidently intending to converge at some point
not too far on up the wide, yellow, pebble-strewn beach.

Samson and Califia urged their ponies ahead.

Lying there, just beyond an outcropping of worn and
mussel-laced boulders, half its body laved by incoming waves
and half exposed to the soft, warm sunlight of California winter, was the carcass of a whale, its back encrusted with bar-
nacles, just as though it were the hull of a wrecked schooner.
*Except that the back actually seemed to be moving with a life of
its own.*

Vultures, several dozens of the birds, hooked their beaks
down, scooped quantities of fat, lifted their heads, swallowed—not even when a condor alit on the dead whale did
the congregated turkey vultures do more than grudgingly move
aside, and at that with a bad-natured flapping of wings.

Perched near the dead gray whale's blowhole, wings fanning, throat muscles working as he gorged himself with blub-
ber, was El Buzzardo.

"Goin' to take more than a few sweet words to coax His
Nibs away from that there lunch," Samson chuckled.

At the mouth of Topanga Canyon, Samson decided to turn
inland. Just a hunch, he insisted—but what if Andres Pico
didn't have ambush in mind at all and simply wished to make
formal surrender to Fremont rather than to Kearny and Stockton, whom he'd met in battle and who might not be feeling
completely charitable toward him and his men?

As the two riders emerged into the rolling hills of San Fernando Valley, Samson pointed toward a thin haze of smoke
to the north—too diffuse to be a signal fire, but possibly the
result of several cooking fires.

"Pico?" Califia asked.

"Reckon, reckon. An' mebbe the California Battalion an' Johnny Fremont hisself. . . ."

They urged their ponies ahead now; but when they drew close, Samson suggested they leave the animals behind and move in on foot—to make survey of the situation and not take chances with their own freedom. Together they crawled onto the rim of a small bluff and peered into the hollow below, while El Buzzardo took this opportunity to come flapping in for a landing, wings spread wide.

"Swear to Gord, that critter's goin' to give this child a heart attack yet. He's jest like a damned owl—ye cain't hear him comin'. Good thing them ain't Pieds Noirs down thar—or we'd have our asses in slings, I tell ye. The whole secret about spyin' is, nobody's supposed to see ye doin' it."

"Buzzardo," Califia whispered, "they won't have noticed. But they can hear you bellowing clear back to the Los Angeles Pueblo. . . ."

Flowers grunted, studied the scene below.

There was an obvious military encampment, though the troops hardly appeared to be United States regulars. Some were mountain men, while others were Indians, some with rifles, some with bows and arrows. A few wore uniforms that looked suspiciously like Sutter-issue. And Californios as well. . . .

"Pico's hyar," Samson said, nodding. "She's all finished except the buttonholes. Let's fetch our ponies an' mosey in."

"You're certain?" Califia asked. "How can you be so damned certain?"

"They ain't shootin' at each other, are they?"

"All right. You've got a point."

"Damned rights. Jest like I always said.

"Wal, would ye look at this. . . ."

But this voice came from behind. Califia spun about, revolver drawn.

"Sam Flowers—that be you behind the whiskers? What in hell ye doin', coon? Who's yore lady friend—Califia Beard, ain't it? We done met when we was cookin' Micheltorena's bacon for 'im, though mebbe she don't recollect. Still got the garbage-eater, I see."

"Caleb Greenwood!" Samson sputtered. "Ye sneak up on a nigger that way, an' yo're subject to get yourself kilt."

"Wagh! Could of had ye both dead to rights," Greenwood replied, grinning.

He had something he could hold over Flowers's head for years, if either of them lived that long, and he knew it.

Greenwood had ridden south from Sutter's Fort—mostly out of sheer curiosity, wanting to know how the war was going beyond the Tehachapis. He had news from the north, as well. A late wagon train got itself stuck in the mountains when ten feet or so of snow fell in the course of a few days, isolating George Donner's party beside a lake on the east side of the pass. Sutter saw trouble coming and sent Charles Stanton over the mountains, and with him some five pack mules loaded with dried beef, flour, and the like. Stanton met the Donners at Truckee Meadows, mid-October. They moved on up into the Sierras, and that was when the heavy snows fell.

Sutter had been planning another rescue mission at the time Greenwood left to head south, so what had happened to the emigrants, he didn't know. But Pico, Greenwood informed Califia and Samson, had surrendered to Major Fremont, and already the peace treaty was signed, just that morning, in fact— January 13th, the Year of Our Lord, 1847. So peace had duly broken out; for all intents and purposes, California was now a *by-Gawd official part of the New-Nighted States of America*. Fremont had been obliged to fight several minor battles on the way south, but beyond that he'd pretty much taken his own sweet time. When Andres Pico's messenger met Fremont under white flag, at Tejon Pass, only then did the major realize the Californios wished to surrender.

Fremont and Pico and their men met near the hamlet of San Fernando, and the leaders quickly drafted the *Cahuenga Capitulation*, signed and hence made official on January 13th. The war was over, so far as California was concerned, and the articles establishing the conditions of both victory and defeat included no vindictiveness—no punishments were either threatened or provided for, and conciliation was the unifying spirit.

Fremont greeted Samson Flowers, pounding his former hunter and scout on the back and bidding him welcome to the *New California*. Flowers, in turn, introduced Califia Beard, at the same time recounting the story of how he and Kit Carson and Califia had charged across the San Gabriel and into the face of Flores's troops' rifle fire.

"Kit's supposed to be in Washington, D.C., for God's sake—Stockton and I sent him there with dispatches, under orders. How in the devil . . . ?"

"Met up with Kearny on the Rio Grande, I guess, an' the General convinced old Kit to show 'im the way to California."

The Pathfinder's close-set eyes gleamed with what Califia took to be minor annoyance. Then he touched his fingers to his mustache and nodded.

"Well, I suppose a general outranks a major, at least. If Stockton and Kearny have matters straight between them, that's all that matters. So—Mr. Flowers. Give me a complete rundown, if you will. Have Stockton and Kearny retaken Los Angeles or not? Andres Pico's told me most of the story, but I want to hear it from one of our own. Pico had Kearny pinned down out on the desert?"

"Yup, that's it. But Carson an' a coon named Beale slipped through and got to San Diego with the news. Then Stockton sent out a couple hundred sailors an—"

Fremont turned to Califia, smiled.

"Señorita Beard, is it? Your father and uncle are in business with John Sutter—one and the same? Yes, I thought so. Tell me—should I believe a thing our good friend Samson tells me, or is this simply another of his monstrous fabrications? With gentlemen like Flowers and Greenwood over there and even my good friend Carson, one never knows how much salt to take. . . ."

Flowers managed to finish his account in relatively brief fashion, and Fremont thanked him and turned to matters more pressing. The weapons taken from Pico's recruits were stacked like cordwood on a mule wagon, and conqueror and conquered alike prepared to ride south to the Los Angles Pueblo, where the document of surrender would be delivered to the commanding officers of the Western Expeditionary Forces.

Three days later, as fate would have matters, Admiral Stockton (with the full authority of the United States Government) elevated John C. Fremont to the rank of lieutenant colonel and appointed him Governor of California.

Why Califia decided to ride north with Samson Flowers she would never know—but the decision was made. Furthermore, at the time at least, it felt right. Caleb Greenwood agreed to deliver a letter from Califia to her father.

She'd proceed across the Tehachapis and up the Great Valley, detouring eastward into the Sierra Nevada with an eye toward discovering stands of yellow and white pine, as well as cedar. There were now ranchos well established in the valley—Visalia, Madera, others along the lower San Joaquin—a river certainly large enough to accommodate schooners, if logs could be floated down such mountain rivers as the Stanislaus and the Mokelumne and of course the upper reaches of the San Joaquin itself.

Years earlier, she and Homer Virgil had made a venture back into those mountains, and now Califia was of a mind to see the mountains once again, even though the higher ranges would be locked deep in winter snows.

Samson Flowers had been with Fremont and Carson when those worthies actually crossed the Sierra in winter—and, according to Sam at least, he'd been back into the mountains on numerous occasions. He claimed to know the pass above Truckee Meadows where those Donners were stuck until the spring melt. He'd seen the lake that Fremont dubbed *Bonpland*, though the Washo Indians called it *Dá-o* or *Ta-hoe*. Sutter, Brannan, Bidwell, Reading, and their ilk chose to believe the big lake didn't exist at all, except in Fremont's imagination. Fremont claimed Lake Bonpland was the source of the American River, but Sam didn't think so—and never had. Flowers claimed to have seen the lake four years earlier, when he accompanied Fremont and Carson and half a dozen others to the peak of a mountain on the way across the Sierra.

Califia and Samson rode north, their packhorses trailing behind them, and in some ways the journey was almost like their venture to Shasta. The hard feelings, the annoyance with one another, the trivial arguments which more than anything else had caused them to part company, now seemed to both of them simple foolishness. After all, Alta California was suddenly a part of the United States, and the future was bright. Possibly even Baja California would be American territory before this war was concluded.

Furthermore, Califia and Samson decided they still *liked* one another—agreed on the matter. It wasn't an issue of mutual tolerance at all. They damned well enjoyed being together.

When the gray skies of late January brought light rain, they took shelter as best they might, but when the sun shone, together they explored the shores of Buena Vista and Tulare Lakes, shot geese and roasted the flesh, provided El Buzzardo with such a quantity of fresh meat that the big bird all but lost interest in searching for carcasses. They managed to spear salmon and even to net a sturgeon that must have weighed eighty pounds—then, not knowing what else to do with the monster, Califia turned him loose; they took delight in stampeding a herd of tule elk that doubtlessly numbered in the tens of thousands. They rode hell-bent in pursuit of the big ungulates, shouting, firing pistols; they observed blue herons and egrets fishing in the shallows of marshes, and along a wooded stretch of a stream their map did not indicate, they watched a pair of sandhill cranes engaged in a territorial war, thrusting and parrying artfully without once ever making contact—a strange dance performed without witnesses other than two humans, who were hardly concerned with the outcome so much as the performance itself, and one vulture, who'd happily have picked the bones of either of his fellow avians.

Califia and Samson discussed the probable future of California and wondered how attractive this land might prove to potential emigrants from the East. Already the trail westward to Oregon was receiving fairly heavy use, and settlers were trickling down to Sutter's Fort as well. With such great, open distances on all sides, however, Califia and Samson found it difficult to imagine the land as being any way other than it was at present—empty.

With time at their disposal—and no place in particular that they had to be—Califia and Samson passed by the Visalia and Madera ranchos, saw long-horned cattle grazing the prairies for several miles in either direction, a scattering of Indio vaqueros tending the animals; then they explored the canyon of the Merced River as far eastward as mid-winter snow levels would allow.

Once into the foothills, the river veered sharply, flowing through a canyon from north to south. Ten miles farther on the canyon reversed itself once again, apparently rounding a long ridge, now south to north, now once more east to west. White oaks, blue oaks, cottonwoods, and grassy or chaparral-covered hills gave way to forest, the often contorted digger pines at first and then ponderosas and Douglas firs. Rocky canyonsides rose two thousand feet and more to what appeared to be heavily forested plateaus.

The river itself, wide, slowly meandering stream though it had been out in the valley, was here a roaring monster of gray-green water, snaking about great fractured-off boulders, pouring through long vees of whitewater.

Winter sundown came quickly in the canyon bottom, even though light gleamed from the rims high above. Then the sky off to the west, beyond a jagged ridge, flamed intense crimson-to-gold among horizon-wide bands of cloud. El Buzzardo, who'd been circling above them for most of the day, came spiraling down as soon as he saw his humans ready to make camp, the vulture spreading his wings wide and alighting in the crown of a small digger pine.

If he exercised patience, El Buzzardo knew, Califia would feed him.

"Chill in the air," Flowers remarked as he scooped out a fire pit in a bank of damp sand on a rock shelf some ten feet above the constantly chuckling Merced River.

"Must have been a flood a couple of weeks back," Califia said. "At least we've plenty of firewood. You're not thinking snow, are you? From the looks of the vegetation, I wouldn't suppose. . . ."

"Never can tell. Sutter says it snowed once right thar at the fort, in the middle of the valley. Them mountains up above us, they make weather. She might be clear as a bell anywhar else, and by Gord it's rainin' up high—or snowin', for that matter, an' right in the middle of summer, too—jest like back in the Tetons an' the High Shinin'. Anywhar in the mountains this time o' the year, though, an' all bets is off."

"I trust we're not going to get snowed in like those poor devils Greenwood was talking about, are we? What in hell would we do to keep warm, Sam? Let's see—first off, I could cut your hair, and then. . . ."

Flowers fluffed up a pile of digger pine needles and lit them—then placed half a dozen year-old cones into the sputtering flames.

"Fixin' to be Delilah, are ye? Well, time was when that problem didn't bother us," he said, glancing at her sideways, winking.

"I was thinking the same thing, Sam. I don't suppose that. . . ."

Flowers blew on the fire, coaxed it for a moment longer, and then stood up. Without saying anything further, he strode over to where he'd left the saddlebags dangling from a stubby oak branch. He dug around inside, whistling a bit as he did so.

"What in hell are you looking for? I've got the haunch of *carne de venado* right here. . . . "

Flowers found what he sought, held the container aloft.

"Whiskey? You've a bottle of whiskey, and you haven't said anything until now?"

"Didn't seem proper," Samson replied, grinning, making full display of his missing front tooth.

In a way, Califia thought, the gap-toothed grin fit Samson perfectly. On anyone else it wouldn't have been attractive in the slightest.

"Get the venison to roasting, woman," Flowers laughed. "This child's powerful hungry."

She lay on a pallet of fir boughs, and the blankets were pulled up about her. She wore nothing, and he too was as naked as the day he was born. The fire, close beside where they lay, was burning brightly—a sap-laden bole of digger pine heaped with limbwood and cones and chunks of alder and oak the river had brought downcanyon and deposited on a broad shelf of slate below their campsite. They lay side by side and drank from the bottle—the liquor, which didn't even taste all that horrible, was like fire inside her. She watched the stars in the sky above—they dimmed, they vanished. Clouds were moving eastward, a storm in off the Pacific, yet another in a long succession of winter storms.

The temperature was above freezing, even this far back into the labyrinthine Sierra, and so the precipitation would once again likely come in the form of rain. Sam handed her the bottle. As she sipped slowly so that her mouth wouldn't go numb, Sam ducked his head under the covers and began to lick at the nipples of her breasts. He was already erect—she could feel the male hardness rubbing against her leg.

He nursed at her the way a calf nursed its mother's teats. Was that true about males? They wished to be mothered, they wished to consume the milk of the mother?

"Poor Sam," she whispered, "I'm dry as a barren doe. There's nothing for you there."

He lifted his mouth from her, squeezed both breasts with his hands.

"O' course there is," he said, half audible with his head beneath the blankets. "Right nice leetle udders, an' not so leetle, either."

"You have a silver tongue, Samson Flowers. Damned if you don't."

"Thank ye, thank ye. . . ."

"I'll stop your blabbering," she said, ducking under the blankets and fastening her lips to his, then biting at his chin hairs, demanding to be kissed. When he slipped his tongue into her mouth, she felt the hair rise along the nape of her neck—felt herself go hot and slippery between the legs.

"I want you, Sam. Come into me—it's been . . . so long . . . I've never stopped wanting you to make love to me."

"Only if ye'll let me marry yore pretty ass, right an' proper."

"You have such a way with words."

"Gorddamn it, will ye marry me? Hold still now an' let me get this thing o' mine into yore. . . ."

He was scrambling about, trying to get up on top of her without casting off the bedroll into the camp fire—and not having very good luck.

"All right, you gray-bearded barbarian, I'll marry you if you insist. I should think there'd be an easier way for a lady to get. . . ."

Possibly Samson had drunk a bit more whiskey than was

good for him. He nearly twisted sideways, directly into the blazing fire pit.

"You lie down—flat on your back," Califia ordered (surprised at the thick sound of her own voice), "and let me. . . ."

"Jesus o'mighty an' all Gord's sons. . . . "

She grasped him with both hands and bit softly at the tip of his silly instrument and then, hesitantly, took him into her mouth.

The bedroll slipped to one side—fortunately, not into the fire—and Califia, intent upon what she was doing, hardly even noticed the soft, soft droplets of rain that had begun to fall— drops which were nonetheless like small needles into the flesh of her back, buttocks, and legs.

When they awoke in the morning, the world about them was blazingly white—three inches or so of snow on everything— boulders, firs, digger pines, oaks. But the sky was clear, the sunlight warm. Wet snow fell from the branches, and the horses stamped about, creating circular areas of slushy, red-brown mud.

El Buzzardo was still in the digger pine, where he'd apparently spent the night. The tree's thatch was covered with snow, but the vulture wasn't. Instead, he appeared to be standing on tiptoes, fanning his big black wings with the gray-white underfeathers, motion designed to evaporate moisture, all but hypnotic.

The man and the woman sat up, stared at one another's nakedness, and then began to laugh. They rose and dressed, and Sam set about readying the ponies for the ride back downcanyon. Califia built up the fire, and they ate cold venison and drank hot coffee. Buzzardo came down from his tree and demanded breakfast as well.

On the way out of Merced River Canyon, Samson and Califia ran across tracks in the snow—Indians, mostly on foot, a few on horseback.

"The Yosemites, I'll bet," Samson remarked, "a mountain branch of the Yokuts. Their chief's a coon named *Tenieya*, or was last I heard. A couple o' Sutter's Miwoks was tellin' me about him. Got a secret valley up yonder somewhere, so they say."

"Is that where we're heading? Sutter's Fort?"

"Reckon so. Anything special? Want to head due west, to the San Lorenzo? I thought ye told Bill the Sawyer ye'd meet him at Russian River, as soon as the weather was decent."

"All depends upon whether you really want to marry me, Sam Flowers. Or was that just so much talk last night?"

"Reckon this child does want to get hitched at that, Miss Boss."

"Then Sutter can *hitch* us. He's got the authority."

"Reckon, reckon. By Gord, the world don't look half bad today, does it?"

CHAPTER NINETEEN

Yellow Seeds in
the Sand

[1847, 1848:]

CALIFIA AND SAMSON made their way to Sutter's Fort, and the King of the Sacramento welcomed them—provided hospitality—and, as an officer of both the former and the present governments, officially bound them with the legal entanglements Sam called *the crime of matrimony*, though he was grinning broadly as he made the pronouncement and proceeded to place his big hands beneath Califia's derriere and lift her off the ground—to the amusement and applause of all.

There was no great celebration, however, because of the unfolding horror of what had been happening a hundred miles to the east, among the deep snows of the High Sierra. Caleb Greenwood had told them the first part of the story. By the time the drama would finally play out, Califia and Samson would be back with Juan Pescadero, at the Russian River encampment. John Sutter himself, on his way to Fort Ross, would tell them the remainder of the saga of bravery, starvation, and cannibalism.

Though Sutter sent Stanton with assistance, the party led by George Donner was fated to a most horrible tragedy. On the

19th of October the previous fall, Sutter's man, along with two Indians and some five pack mules, met the party at Truckee Meadows. By the end of the month the emigrants reached the eastern shore of Truckee Lake (now called *Donner*), and here they were overwhelmed by heavy snows. Several attempts to hoist their wagons up the icy boulders of the pass proved futile, and so the would-be Californians built crude shelters and waited for better weather—though it should have been evident to all that the only hope lay in the advent of an early spring. Storm followed storm, the snows reaching fifteen feet in places as the Snowy Mountains lived up to their name, and the party grew desperate. Twice during November a handful of the pilgrims attempted to cross the pass, hoping both to conserve food and to summon help—and yet another attempt was made in December. Ten men and five women fought through snows on makeshift snowshoes, and five weeks later the survivors stumbled into a friendly Maidu village. Two had lost their lives, including Charles Stanton, whom Sutter had dispatched in the first place with help for the party.

The Maidus guided the thirteen to William Johnson's rancho, and Johnson took the exhausted and half-starved pilgrims to Sutter's Fort.

In February, Sutter sent a rescue party of seven, each man with a heavy pack full of food on his back. Moving ahead doggedly, the *good angels* reached the lake. The occupants of the makeshift cabins were starving—they'd eaten porcupine flesh, oxhide, shoes, belts, alder bark—and finally they'd resorted to devouring the emaciated remains of those who'd already starved to death.

Fifteen children and eight adults were taken back across the pass and down through the seemingly endless snows of the Sierra to the Sacramento Valley and Sutter's Fort. Two more died en route, and more most certainly would have perished but for the good fortune of their meeting a new relief expedition on its way across the mountains—this group headed by a man named James Reed, who'd previously been banished from the Donner Party because of his having been involved in a stabbing. Reed's party provided the twenty-one survivors with food and medical assistance.

Reed and the others moved on into the snows and reached

Truckee Lake on the first of March; two days later, taking with them a man, two women, and fourteen children, they began the trek back to Sutter's Fort. As they made their way down the South Yuba River, a heavy snowstorm hit, immobilizing them for a week. They built a fire on a platform of logs, and the fire slowly sank into a pit of snow. Reed brought in a supply of firewood for the pilgrims and started down the mountain in search of help. He encountered yet another rescue team, who ministered to the party and then hurried on toward the pass.

The emigrants were huddled at the bottom of the pit the fire had melted in the snow. Three more were dead, and portions of the bodies had been hewn away and eaten.

Part of the rescue team undertook to move the frail, exhausted emigrants to New Helvetia, though only two were still able to walk. The remainder of the team pushed on over the pass and down to the lake. Many were dead of starvation, and a mere four were sufficiently hale to attempt the trip across the snow-choked Sierra—three being the children of George and Tamsen Donner, the leaders of the party. George and Tamsen and Lewis Keseberg were left behind.

A month later the final rescue group reached Truckee Lake. By then only Keseberg was alive—a man reduced to the condition of a savage beast, both mind and conscience apparently numbed by the horror of his means of survival.

Forty-five in all, out of eighty-seven, lived to reach the Sacramento Valley. Captain Sutter, true to his generous nature, had both funded the rescue attempts and provided food and shelter for those who managed to survive the white hell of the Sierra.

Back in 1818 Great Britain and the United States had agreed to a joint occupation of the Oregon country, but by the 1840's this solution was no longer workable, and in 1844 the Democrats under Polk made *fifty-four-forty or fight* a central portion of their campaign rhetoric. Apparently one war at a time was sufficient for most Americans, however, and the Treaty of 1846 was worked out, with Britain giving up all claims to land south of the forty-ninth parallel, thus for the first time establishing a continuous boundary from Atlantic to Pacific between the

United States and the British Dominion of Canada. Dr. John McLoughlin, H.B.C. proctor and spiritual father of the Northwest, was appalled to find his timber operations as well as his home and various business enterprises well within Yank territory. McLoughlin had become, *de facto*, an American citizen.

Another huge area was added to Empire America, west of the Louisiana Purchase and south of Oregon Territory. The Treaty of Guadalupe Hidalgo brought to an end the hostilities between the United States and Mexico, at the same time adding to the territories of the United States an area nearly as large as that acquired through the Louisiana Purchase. If all the lands acquired from Mexico were considered a purchase (since Mexico was given payment), then the vast new additions cost something like four cents per acre. In addition, the treaty clearly obligated the Americans to verify titles to all lands held via Mexican and Spanish land grants, and Fremont and the other military governors who followed insisted the United States act in good faith.

Reality, however, was to produce significantly different results from those which might have been expected. For one thing, the American courts could not seem to comprehend why such huge tracts of land should have been awarded for the purposes of cattle ranching—or, in the case of Olivo & Beard, for timbering operations. Good fortune, however, smiled upon William Beard, still officially a citizen of the United States. Thus, title to the tracts of redwood forest to the north of Santa Cruz, to the west of Petaluma, and along the Russian River passed official scrutiny, while many other claims either did not or got bogged down in court procedures.

Many of John Sutter's lands were ultimately to be disallowed, including his huge *Sobrante* grant.

The reason was simple.

Gold.

A few yellow seeds which Jim Marshall picked up out of the sands in the millrace of the sawmill Sutter was having built near the Maidu village of Ko-lo-ma—these seeds were to change everything that had been known in California.

In late July of 1846, the 450-ton ship *Brooklyn* arrived in Yerba Buena. On board were a group of Mormon emigrants—in excess of a hundred children, seventy women, and sixty-eight men—religious exiles who intended to establish a colony somewhere in California. This group proceeded up the Sacramento River to Sutter's Fort, and ultimately established a village a few miles upstream on the American River—Mormon Island, as the place was called.

A second group of Latter Day Saints arrived in January of 1847, a military group, the *Mormon Battalion*, drawn from Iowa and elsewhere in the Middle West. They'd left Fort Leavenworth in August and marched to Santa Fe and subsequently on to San Diego, arriving after the fighting was concluded. Once disabled, these men intended to join Brigham Young at Salt Lake, and they set out for the Mormon heartland in July of 1847, their route taking them up the San Joaquin and on to Sutter's Fort.

Reaching Truckee Lake—or Donner Lake, as it was now called—they met Sam Brannan, the Mormon elder, who was on his way back from Salt Lake. Brigham Young's colony, Brannan told the men, had scant food on hand, an amount barely sufficient. Those who had neither families waiting for them in Salt Lake nor provisions sufficient to last them through the winter ahead were to remain, temporarily, in California. Thirty of the men turned around, returned to the fort, and were taken into the employ of John Sutter—to labor on the building of a new grist mill at Na-to-ma, powered by water from a *river-turning* some three miles above the mill, and on the construction of a millrace for the American River sawmill to be built at Ko-lo-ma under the supervision of an experienced sawyer named James Marshall, one who'd worked briefly for Olivo & Beard at San Lorenzo. Sutter required lumber to build his gristmill, and pine and fir would find a ready market both in the vicinity of the fort and in San Francisco, as Yerba Buena was now called. Quite evidently, the demand for lumber in California was destined to increase steadily for the foreseeable future. Olivo & Beard had bought out Sutter's interest in the Russian River mill, and though he continued to secure lumber from this source, it was clear to him that a productive mill closer to hand would be a great advantage.

By early September of 1847, Sutter had a crew of twenty-five, a few of them Maidu Indians, most of them Mormons, at

work on the project—with Jim Marshall supervising, and with
Mrs. Wimmer, wife of one of the Mormon laborers, providing
services as camp cook.

Raymondo Olivo received word that his son Homer Virgil had
been awarded the degree of Master of Arts from Cambridge
University. H.V. had already engaged in a career as a teacher
in a British preparatory academy and had married a young
lady named Roxanne Breton. The two of them, H.V. said in
his letter, led a life both civilized and content. In England,
cosmopolitan land that it was, the matter of his Spanish-Indio
heritage was no issue at all. He was assumed to be Mestizo
and was known to come from an extremely wealthy family in
a mysterious land once explored by the great Sir Francis Drake,
somewhere to the south of the present British-American port
of Astoria, in Oregon country.

Because of its far-flung empire, the British had become
rather fond of these *native* individuals who came from all
around the world to study at the great English universities—
since it was, after all, the fate and the destiny of the British to
civilize the peoples they'd conquered or with whom they found
it convenient to maintain commercial relations.

But now, with his education truly completed in the eyes of
the world, Homer Virgil was thinking very seriously about
returning to California, a part of the growing empire of the
United States of America, that fiercely independent outgrowth
of British colonial methods, the difficult and burgeoning nation
with whom the British had already been forced to wage two
inconclusive wars.

At first Roxanne, whose family had lived in Caernarvon,
Wales, since the early 1600s—a merchant-class family, one
branch of which owned half a dozen coal mines—had been
staunchly opposed to the idea of venturing halfway around
the world to California. At length H.V. had put the "Western
adventure" in the light of being a visit of perhaps a year or
two at the most, and on that basis Roxanne concluded she'd
be willing to accompany her husband. Perhaps it was even
possible that some sort of commercial arrangements might be
made, so her uncle, Jarvis Breton, the owner of a wholesale

house in Bangor, suggested to her. Mutual profit, after all, could only render Roxanne's marriage the more stable.

Raymondo Olivo studied his son's letter over and over—and, of course, shared its contents fully with Calling Owl and Bill Beard and Seagull. Even the aged Pelican Doctor was obliged to listen to multiple readings of the missive.

Homer Virgil was returning to California—date uncertain—but the reality was quite certain, at least in Raymondo's mind. The well-educated but self-taught Raymondo couldn't have been more pleased. Not only had his son, whom he'd all along regarded as his prize pupil, succeeded at Cambridge, but now that son was intent upon returning to the land of his birth, the loyalty to a land and to a people and to his father and mother sufficient to draw him back.

It was true, certainly, that Bill Beard's son Calvin was also a great success—captain of several craft, a skilled navigator, and a canny businessman. Calvin would be the eventual *booshway* of the Olivo & Beard holdings, and not too many years down the line. Both Raymondo and Bill were approaching sixty. Though that was hardly an age to think of retirement, still, the sailing of ships, the loading of lumber, the operation of sawmills, and the running of timbering camps—these were the occupations of younger men. Olivo and Beard—together they would oversee their little business empire, with Calvin in effect running the show.

Raymondo reflected on how oddly things had turned out, for it was his niece Califia who'd become the *bull o' the woods*, the one who ramrodded felling operations and made her loggers toe the line, men who'd rather drink than make love and who'd much rather do either than take orders. Whatever magic it took, Califia possessed it.

With Homer Virgil returning to California, returning as a profoundly educated man, what was to be his place in the ever-growing business world Bill and Raymondo had hewed out during the course of half a lifetime? It would be appropriate for such a man as Homer Virgil to teach in a university—and perhaps Olivo & Beard, a few years down the line, would be able to establish and endow such an institution. Jean Paul Martin, now seventy and in failing health, had once or twice spoken of such a thing—a kind of monument to the land they all loved. Surely Larkin could also be persuaded, and possibly even John Sutter could be made to see the great good that might eventually come from the establishment of a university where the giant redwoods grew.

Or possibly one should lay one's plans on a somewhat smaller, though no less important, scale. The impact of the Spanish and the Mestizos and now the Americans and foreigners of all sorts—upon the Ohlones and the various other Indio peoples—had already been massive. Few, too few of the Indian villages remained in the old way, in the *wild*. As more and more civilized people came into California, fewer and fewer of the peoples—Ohlone or Pomo or Wintun or Maidu or Miwok or Yokuts—would be able to survive in the ways of their ancestors. They would have to become civilized at last. And they would need schools to help them make this profound transition. If only Homer Virgil were willing to put his wonderful European education to such a use. . . .

Calvin Beard commanded several craft capable of navigating and transporting significant cargo along the relatively shallow waters of the Sacramento and lower San Joaquin. With these craft he supplied Sutter's New Helvetia operations and hoped to haul return cargos of pine lumber to San Francisco and San Jose, as soon as Sutter's new sawmill got into operation.

With logging operations more or less at winter standstill, due to the heavy rains that seasonally beset the Coastal Mountains, Califia and Samson accompanied Calvin on an upriver supply run to the growing settlements of Sutterville and Sutter's Fort. Skies were heavily overcast, and a soft valley rain was falling as the *El Sancho*, a double-masted, side-wheel-driven steamer hissed its way past the northern end of Grand Island and into the wider channel above. Calvin stood at the wheel, pipe clenched between his teeth, and gave two quick blasts of the steam whistle, the noise sufficient to send aloft several dozen Canada and snow geese from the shallows along the eastern bank.

"Beautiful birds," Califia remarked, speaking more to El Buzzardo than to either her husband or her brother.

The vulture, perched on a bridge rail, was apparently neither disturbed by the squeal of the whistle nor interested in a burst of gray and white wings through the damp afternoon. Members of his own race, he was rather certain, were clearly superior not only in flying ability but also in those qualities which defined avian beauty.

Samson Flowers grunted. With nothing else to do, he'd been indulging in a reminiscence—with Joe Meek and the boys at the Battle of Pierre's Hole. The good, healthy smell of black powder in the air, horses screaming, men yelling out in victory or singing their death chants. Those were times, by Gord, when life was truly worth living. He'd been younger then, much younger, and much more able to do whatever damned thing he felt like. Yes, a good deal more free as well. There was much to be said for married life and responsibility and the like, but part of him had already grown weary of the whole business. Part of him just wanted to be back there, out in the High Shining.

Califia was one hell of a woman, and that was a fact. But possibly, just possibly for Samson Flowers, at this point in his life, she was if anything too much of a woman. Califia and a jug of *arwerdenty* made one amazing combination, and there were times when he fairly well believed the old chestnuts were going to explode. All in all, it wouldn't be such a bad way to die. But maybe a Siksika arrow in the throat wouldn't be so bad either. Samson didn't suppose there was any one *really good way to go beaver*, but maybe they knew something, the old chiefs who staked themselves out, a cord binding them to their own lances thrust into the earth as a challenge to their enemies, a bald assertion that *I would rather die than retreat, and I'm by-Gord prepared to do jest that, so you fellas come on in and let's have at 'er.*

Get right down it to, maybe whiskey itself was the way to go—damned right, and let one's buddies bury the carcass *out thar*, where the winds whistle among the pines before a winter storm, and where black bears and catamounts might come wandering through, yes, an' sniff a bit an' think in the way varmints think, *there was a man.*

But not tame catamounts.

Getting tamed was all right, but there was somehow something about it that wasn't *all right* either. Still, if it had to happen, Califia was sure as hell the lady to have it happen with. Maybe that was the trouble. In the case of a normal woman, a coon could just up an' leave whenever he was of a mind to do 'er. Califia, most likely, she'd come track a feller down.

Only that wasn't the way it happened, if one worried about those details called *truth*. He, Samson Flowers, he was the one who'd come grinning back, unwilling to let go of this most astonishing of all female-women. Why? Because without her he couldn't sleep, and when he was awake, he couldn't stop thinking about her.

But after that they went and got hitched.

In early January of 1848, Califia, Samson, Calvin, and John Sutter accompanied Jim Marshall up the South Fork of the American to the site of the new sawmill, whose construction was nearing completion. Califia surveyed the structure and then rode into the hills, from whence the logs would come—to be skidded down by means of draft horses in heavy harness. Many pines were of decent size, but because of the lay of the land, no elaborately prepared skid roads would seem to be called for. Once at the river, the logs could be floated to the mill, winched out of the water, placed in a cold deck, and then pulled into the mill by means of a steam-driven winch.

Compared to the great stands of redwoods, the timber here was actually sparse, but nonetheless seemingly of high quality. The ponderosa and sugar pines were much more resilient than redwood, less prone to shattering upon impact as they fell. One big problem that Califia could see quite clearly lay in the fact that Jim Marshall, jack-of-all-trades though he was, lacked the experience necessary to be the *booshway* of an efficient sawmill and logging operation. But the man was full of energy and wasn't one to be daunted by a difficult job, and so perhaps Sutter's new enterprise would be a grand success after all.

Marshall himself stayed on at the mill with his crew, which was presently at work on the millrace, and Califia, Samson, Calvin, and Sutter returned to the fort, with El Buzzardo scouting the blue skies ahead, staring down from great heights for any sign of a dead deer, antelope, or longhorn.

'You are happy, *ja*, *Frau Flowers*?" Sutter asked Califia when the two of them had fallen somewhat behind the others. "Or is there something wrong with this new marriage of yours?"

"Nothing I can't handle, John Sutter," Califia replied, a bit more annoyance in her voice than she'd intended. There was no reason, after all, to be short with Sutter. On the whole she was fond of the Swiss-German, and she'd found him to be a businessman with a sense of ethics. He had his flaws, of course—his *harem* of Indian women, for instance. It was doubtful his *real* wife and his children would ever arrive from Europe, though Sutter spoke of this event as being a certainty.

"I will not pry, then," Sutter said. "But you don't appear happy, Califia, *sehr traurig*. I'll drop the subject immediately if you say so."

Califia glanced ahead to where Samson and her brother were riding, the two engaged in animated conversation.

"Sam's a good man," she remarked at last, "though it's possible he simply wasn't cut out for marriage. But hell, that's true of me as well. Uncle Raymondo says I'm Artemis, the huntress in those old Greek tales, and Artemis is a virgin by her very nature—all of which goes to show you how little my uncle understands me, dear man though he is."

"Samson Flowers, your husband . . . he doesn't . . . make love to you?"

Califia burst suddenly into laughter.

"That," she replied, "is not precisely the problem."

"*Ach, ja*, I see what you mean—I think. Well, perhaps you should consider taking a lover, in any case. Perhaps you want sophistication. . . ."

Califia winked at Sutter.

"Why, sir," she said, "whatever do you mean?"

Even to speak so lightly, so flippantly, did no more than increase the tightness of the fist that pushed against her vitals.

Before the *El Sancho* was ready to voyage back down the Sacramento to San Francisco Bay, Jim Marshall found his *yellow seeds* in the Ko-lo-ma millrace. The mill boss had left a sluice gate open at night to allow the water to flush away sand and gravel. When he walked the length of the ditch on the morning of January 24th, he saw something that caught his attention. He sent his half-Maidu companion Jake, *Pine-nut-eater*, to get a frying pan, which he subsequently utilized to work a bit of sand from the edge of the ditch.

Gold, sure as hell. . . .

That night Jake's wife dreamed that the mountains were melting, and that the Whitemen called Wawlems laughed insanely as everything was changed, as the Indian peoples were butchered or died of a hundred different diseases or were dressed up like Whitemen and began to live like Whitemen.

It's only a dream, Ooti, dearest one, only a dream. You have read my thoughts but have found only confusion. I do not think anything bad will happen. Jim Marshall is my friend. . . .

The worthless yellow metal that was in all the streams, too soft to be good for anything: this was what would drive the Wawlems crazy, and soon the Whitemen would cause the mountains to melt and they would surely cut down the sacred tree, Ootimtsaa, the great oak of the Beginnings of All Things, and hew it up into slabs and planks there at the mill. . . .

"No," Jim Marshall insisted, "I'm not a quitter. I contracted to do a job for the Cap'n, and I shall do it. The men will begin cutting logs when the equipment arrives—if I have to put them in chains to get them to do it."

John Sutter didn't believe it at first. Who could have believed it? Gold lying all over the damned place? The mill workers, including the virtuous Mormons, would spend their spare time ripping up segments of riverbed. Bigler, one of them, was to write later: *We knew we were getting pretty fair wages for our labor on the mill and it was sure pay, while on the other hand there was a risk to run . . . when Sunday came, down into the tail race we would go . . . we could pick and crevice with our jack and butcher knives, and we hardly ever failed to get three to eight dollars and sometimes more . . . still we were fearful to venture, and besides the mill was so near completed, we finally decided to stick to the mill until she started.*

Sutter obtained *aqua fortis* from his apothecary and applied it to Marshall's yellow lumps, but the acid had no effect. Then he went to his *Encyclopedia Americana* and read about gold. He was convinced. Thereafter Sutter prepared twenty-year lease papers to which the leaders of Ko-lo-ma village fixed their marks—a lease giving Sutter official control of all the land up and down the American River in either direction from the mill—except that the newly appointed military governor, Colonel R.B. Mason, dismissed the document as invalid, since Indians were not allowed to enter into leases or any other legal arrangements.

CHAPTER TWENTY

To Hell With
Logging

[1848, 1849:]

CHARLIE BENNETT, THE mill worker Sutter chose to take the document to Monterey, told numerous individuals about the gold at Sutter's Mill and furthermore, in delivering the lease document, plunked down a poke full of nuggets for Mason to admire. In Benicia, Bennett listened to Ed Pfister talk about the coal on Monte Diabolo, and so, scornfully, Sutter's man displayed the contents of his buckskin pouch. In San Francisco, Bennett told Isaac Humphrey, a Georgian with gold-mining experience. Humphrey was convinced. In Monterey, Charlie Bennett told everyone willing to listen.

In a letter to Mariano Vallejo, dated February 10th, Sutter spread the Gospel of Gold himself: *I have made a discovery of a gold mine, which, according to experiments we have made, is extraordinarily rich. . . .*

Sam Brannan learned of the gold as well—learned indirectly from Jacob Wittmer, who'd been told about it by one of the Wimmer children and who'd proceeded to do a bit of panning himself. He'd stopped at Brannan's Mormon Island store, close by the American River between Sutter's Mill and the Fort, and paid Brannan's partner, George Smith, for a drink—with a pinch of gold dust. Brannan hurried up from San Francisco, was quickly convinced of the genuine nature of the strike, set his own men to working, and a second strike was made.

Returning immediately to San Francisco, Brannan sauntered along Montgomery Street, hat in one hand and a bottle of gold dust in the other, all the while roaring, *"Gold! Gold! Gold on the American River!"*

By March 7th, a month and a half after the initial find, Sutter wrote to a friend that . . . *my entire staff, laborers and overseers alike, have joined the rush to the foothills and left me only the sick and lame behind. Mein Gott, what will come next?*

Pierson Reading, George McKinstry, and young Edward Kemble, editor of the *California Star*, took passage upriver in May, aboard Leidesdorff's schooner *Rainbow*, destination Sutter's Fort.

Kemble was impressed by the land and the mill, but made no mention of gold. In the May 20th issue of the *Star*, Kemble was obliged to write, *Fleets of launches left this place on Sunday and Monday, closely stowed with human beings . . . was there ever anything so superlatively silly? . . . all sham . . . a takeoff . . . got up to guzzle the gullible.*

But a new city of tents was assembled all about the valley where Sutter's Mill stood nearly completed and utterly useless. Already ships in San Francisco Bay rose and fell with the tides, unattended, crewless. *Gold in the mountains!* Men dug and hacked at the cutbanks and moved boulders by sheer force of human will, and again and again significant quantities of gold were found. A few feet of river gravels became dear real estate, and those who spent their days up to their asses in cold water were more than willing to kill to protect what they presumed theirs by right of claim.

Tem-diyoko, the moon of new fawns, brought with it numerous pleasant sunny days, while blue lupines and golden poppies rioted. The rare mariposa lilies blossomed, as did kitten ears and larkspurs. Redbud splashed the hillsides, and wild mock orange blossomed near the river. Violence flared, and the miners rose up to *murderate those thievin' Injuns.* As a consequence the Maidus of Ko-lo-ma and Tu-meli villages were nearly annihilated in one happy night of killing and raping and burning. Marshall's man Injun Jake, known to his own people as Pine-nut-eater, was dead. His twin infants were murdered, and his wife Ooti was raped and left for dead—though as fate would have it, she would not only live but lead the survivors on a series of *revenge-takings* that would strike fear into the hearts of miners throughout the land which would become known as *La Veta Madre*, the Mother Lode. But for now it was different, and when the sun rose the next day, there were many bodies strewn across the meadows.

Oleli Coyote and Pano the Grizzly looked down on the scene. They shook their heads, lolled their tongues. Yet there was nothing they could do as they observed the spirits of those who had passed out of life start up from the mutilated corpses and begin their trek to the peaks of Estawm Yan and the High Meadows, from which they would step off onto the path leading to the Spirit World, their names not to be spoken again.

Already the condors had flown away to the southern mountains, while far to the east, a continent away, a human flood was about to be loosed.

The Olivo & Beard timbering operations continued to bring down redwoods, cedars, firs, and pines and to convert them into shingles, beams, boards, and finished lumber, with the market for such products steadily improving and even leaping ahead as the stream of emigrants into California began to swell. While all this was going on, the word concerning discovery of gold spread like the proverbial wildfire. To those for whom *gold* was a compelling idea, the result was no less than utter madness and a frenzied search for sudden riches beyond all comprehension.

Bigler and others from the mill at Ko-lo-ma discovered better *diggins* upriver. Marshall found gold at Liveoak Bar and, despite the massacres of just a few weeks earlier, was able to engage Miwok Indians to mine for him. Isaac Humphrey the Georgian set to mining not far from the mill and soon contrived a workable *rocker*. Bidwell, visiting Coloma, realized there were similar deposits of gravel near his Chico Rancho, and he in turn hired Indians to sluice for gold on the Feather River. P.B. Reading made similar observations and set Indians to work along Trinity River. At one point on the Feather, six men from Monterey and fifty Indians extracted two hundred and seventy three pounds of gold in less than two months. On the Yuba River, the first five prospectors earned some $75,000 in three months.

Sinclair at the forks of the American.

Mormons at Spanish Diggings.

An Irishman at Yankee Jim.

Weber on the Stanislaus and the Mokelumne.

At Dry Diggings, a.k.a. Hangtown, the average was from three to five ounces per miner: *". . . the 300 Hangtown men were the happiest in the universe."*

At Knight's Ferry on the Stanislaus three men using picks and knives took out an average of $200 to $300 each day.

Antonio Coronel, working the Tuolumne, produced some forty-five ounces the first day, while Chino Tirador used a horn spoon to clean out a ledge, producing so much gold he could barely lift it.

One man found a nugget that weighed a full pound.

Another worked eight days and took out fifty-two pounds of gold. . . .

In May only a few hundred miners were at work, but by mid-summer the number had grown to three thousand or so, and by year's end the number would be in excess of ten thousand.

The miners were Indians employed by Whites and Whites who'd deserted from Governor Mason's command, seamen who'd jumped ship from vessels anchored in San Francisco Bay and Monterey Bay, and not a few respectable Californios who'd also caught the fever endemic within the earth of Alta California. Prospectors came pouring in from Oregon, Hawaii, and Mexico.

Califia Beard Flowers, singing at the top of her lungs, peavey in hand, rode a raft of redwood logs downriver, and Samson there with her, cold and grumpy and wet from having slipped off the raft as it careened on the wave of released water from the check dam, yes, and all but drowned himself. Even his bag of tobacco was wet, and when El Buzzardo came swooping in, thinking to land on his head, Samson actually toyed with the idea of vulture soup—steaming hot and laced with liberal portions of birdflesh and onions and potatoes and creek lettuce.

Christmas was but a day or two away, the year drawing rapidly toward its finish. A long, relatively rainless autumn had allowed the Olivo & Beard timbering operations to continue until late, and only now, with the first rains and subsequent frosts on the flats beside Russian River, had Califia elected to call a halt to cutting.

Calvin waited at tidewater, where Juan Pescadero was directing the loading of lumber into a steam-equipped schooner, *La Dulcinea*, which would also transport Califia's men back to Santa Cruz, where they'd find ample rum and whiskey and the company of the professional señoritas at Branciforte, as well as at several other area establishments. Possibly a few men would disappear in the general direction of the goldfields and not return with spring, not until they'd had their fill of prospecting, at least.

The boss lady elected to stay on at the encampment for another week or two. After that she'd think about traveling south to visit her family. But right now she had to attend to her flock of thirty bantam chickens, the offspring of Rory Sunrise and Dame Broodsalot. Independent though the birds were, if left unattended, they'd likely be decimated by coyotes and foxes—predators that kept their distances so long as humans were present. Furthermore, the two mountain lions were off on a hunt—except that this time it was quite possible that one or the other had found a mate somewhere among the high ridges, a lion unwilling to venture to the *dreaded place* where trees were being felled.

Califia stood at the raft's "prow," very much like some Viking heroine—had Samson thought about it or known enough about such matters as to have been able to think about it. But what he did think: *Damned peculiar female, that's all. I should of had 'er with me that time at Pierre's Hole when Joe Meek an' Muckaluck an' Godin an' Pete LeBlueux an' gimpy Milt Sublette took on half the Injuns in the Northwest. Give 'er a chance, an' she'd be a by-Gord Pine Leaf, that's what. Only instead of takin' Siksika ha'r, she skulps the forest—gets her jollies watchin' them big redwoods go over, even if the damned things bust all to hell an' so she cain't even use 'em. It's time for this coon to head for the high country, no question about 'er. . . .*

"So tell me about Beckwourth," Califia said to her husband. "He's back in California, him and that Pegleg fellow? How long's he been there at Sutter's Fort?"

"Cain't say, not for sure. John Greenwood jest claimed Beckwourth an' his pa, Greenwood's that is, was fixin' to get into the gold-thing, one way or the other."

"Give a shove, Samson! We don't want to end up on top of those rocks ahead. Here—the two of us together. . . ."

"Seems like to this child, would have made more sense to of built the Gord-cursed mill up whar we're cuttin' timber."

"John Sutter wanted it here."

"Now your pa an' Raymondo own the thing, why not move 'er upstream? A nigger could get drownded ridin' logs this way."

"And float the boards to where Calvin can pick them up?"

"Why·not?"

"Tell me about Beckwourth—and those Reed murders. What did John Greenwood say about those?"

Flowers fussed with a half-formed and still-wet cigarette, attempting several times to light the thing before cursing and tossing the wad of damp paper and tobacco flakes into the river.

"Wal, Reed married Maria Antonia Vallejo, yore kinswoman, an' they had one kid an' was expecting another. But ye know that."

"True, true."

"An' others. They was livin' at San Miguel, along with an old Injun feller an' his grandson, as well as a midwife named Josefa or some such. Pio Pico hisself must of sold Reed the mission buildings or part of 'em. Anyhow, Peter Raymond an' three other Irish Yanks an' a Injun asked for lodging. A couple days later the five of 'em started hackin' folks to death—even the children and the Black man who was paid to cook. They fetched Reed with a rifle ball an' the others with axes. Jim Beckwourth, he come across from Santa Fe with Pratt, an' then he started totin' mail dispatches, and he come to the mission an' found the bodies. So he rode like hell to Monterey an' reported the thing to Leftenant Sherman an' then to Colonel

Mason, who sent out Leftenant Ord an' the soldiers. Beckwourth must of went along for the ride—an' they caught up to Raymond an' his compañeros an' stretched their necks. After that I guess old Jim went off to the mines to find Caleb Greenwood an' Pompey Charbonneau, the same as got born when Lewis and Clark went across to Astoria. Pompey, Clark sent him to Germany to get educated, sort of like yore cousin Homer, an' he come back—stopped in at Sutter's Fort. Him an' Beckwourth went to school together in St. Louis, though ye cain't always believe Beckwourth—a sorry liar if ever thar was one. Truth is, only Bridger an' one or two others can outyarn him."

Califia used her peavey to push off against a small raft of four logs, freeing it from a willow tangle along the bank. They were moving into relatively quiet waters, and the mill and the *Dulcinea* were dead ahead.

The Argonauts began to pour into California even before the Sierra snows had melted. They came by boat, some around the Horn, some across Panama, and some from the west coast of South America or from Hawaii or even from the Orient. The siren cry of *gold!* was sufficient to draw fortune-seekers from half around the globe. San Francisco was growing steadily, though news of a rich new strike might, over the short term, cause an evacuation of the fledgling city. Sacramento City was also growing—not where Sutter hoped to see a thriving settlement, but rather just to the south of the confluence of the American River with the larger Sacramento—*Nem Seyoo*, as the Maidus called it. In any case, new buildings were going up. Sutter gave in to the inevitable, sold lots to those who wished to build, and accepted notes of credit for many of the sales.

As for Sutter himself, he'd been partaking of the bottle a great deal more freely than was good for him, and according to some he was half drunk most of the time. Nevertheless, he continued welcoming one and all to Sutter's Fort, and there were many among the visitors who were happy to take advantage of their host's compulsive generosity. Sutter's son, John, Jr., arrived the summer of 1848, boarding his father's ship, *Sacramento*, for the voyage upriver. The twenty-two-year-old discovered his famous father was in danger of losing his immense fortune, and soon he convinced his paternal parent to allow him, the son, to take over the business and to handle and account for all monies. Young Sutter brought together Sam Hensley, Pierson Reading, and Jacob Snyder—to establish a mercantile called Hensley, Reading & Co. John, Jr. proceeded to sell lots along the river for $500, while those close to the fort went for $250. He appointed Peter Burnett as financial advisor and held a public auction for town lots, thus enabling him to pay off the most crucial debts of the King of the Sacramento River.

The elder Sutter was furious with his son, and within a fairly short time, the two men were not even speaking. But for a while things looked good indeed. J.A. Moerenhout, French consul in Monterey, wrote of Sutter's Fort that . . . *all around the courtyard inside, it is divided into chambers and rooms, eighteen by thirty feet in width . . . now all is occupied and let for gold.* Sutter himself had moved out of the main quarters and rented those also—and the enterprise in total was bringing in some $2,000 to $3,000 per month, the rooms constantly filled by men on their way to the mines.

The industries Sutter founded were at a standstill, and the crops remained unharvested. Tannery and wood and metal shops were empty, and the vaqueros left their herds behind and went off to search for gold. The cattle wandered unattended, and many of them were shot and slaughtered, the meat taken to the mining areas for market.

Early in 1849 Sutter was offered $40,000 for his more-or-less deserted fort, and the offer was accepted. Leaving his grand enterprise behind him, he moved north to the Hock Farm, whose two-story house had been built by Sutter's friend, John Bidwell. Sutter no doubt sought quietude and tranquillity in the company of a few of his female Indian servants.

But Fate plays a strange game of cards. At this point Sutter's sour-faced wife arrived, a woman he hadn't seen and with whom he'd hardly communicated for the past fifteen years— and with her came a daughter and two more sons, as well as Mrs. Sutter's sister, a certain Mrs. Schlaffi, and Mrs. Schlaffi's son.

No one was more cognizant of the massive changes occurring in California than was J. A. Sutter.

La Dulcinea hissed and puffed its way northward along the tree-lined Sacramento River, as Calvin Beard left Sacramento behind and passed by the mouth of the *Río de Las Plumas* and onward toward Lassen Rancho a few miles south of Red Bluff, a tiny settlement that was generally regarded as the limit for even a small oceangoing craft. Peter Lassen had attempted to establish a sawmill, though without much success. One of his attempts to bring equipment upriver from Sacramento resulted in his craft going aground and ultimately sinking, with consequent loss of everything, including a six-foot circular saw that was to be the feature of his operation. Now Lassen invited the more experienced Olivo & Beard people to survey his holdings, with an eye toward entering into some sort of collaboration, such as had been done with Lassen's friend, Sutter.

The timber along Cottonwood Creek proved to be more than sufficient—a mixed coniferous growth of Douglas fir, ponderosa pine, incense cedar, sugar pine, and white fir. From a logger's point of view, the eastern Coast Mountains, known here as the *Yolla Bollys*, provided everything except redwood.

As the men rode back toward the rancho, Peter Lassen suggested an alternate site—near the mouth of a little river which flowed into the Sacramento from the east, feeding down from the vicinity of the mountain called Lassen's Butte. Not more than a few miles back up the little river, which issued through a remarkable canyon, there were endless stands of ponderosa—far more than in the Yolla Bollys. Since pine was generally considered the finest wood for construction, relatively light and durable and extremely strong, perhaps a logging venture drawing upon the east-side forests would be more appropriate.

As was evident to Calvin and Samson, however, Peter Lassen had other matters on his mind at the present—he seemed almost to be going through the motions. Heavily in debt and in fear of losing his rancho, the pioneer was now giving thought to blazing a new emigrant route into California—one which would bring pilgrims in at the northern end of the Sacramento Valley. True, Red Bluff was indeed a long way from the mines of the Mother Lode, but gold had been discovered to the north—with Reading's Wintuns making strikes both on the Trinity and along the Sacramento itself.

With *La Dulcinea* moored at a makeshift embarcadero, Calvin Beard and Samson Flowers proceeded on horseback along the banks of the now meandering Sacramento to the extreme northern end of the valley, past Ide's Rancho and on to the holdings of P.B. Reading and the half-born settlement of Shasta City, which boasted a couple of stores, a livery, a Lutheran church, a small, half-finished jail presided over by *Alcalde Reading*, and a poorly stocked hardware store. News of the strikes had already drawn in several hundred souls, and Reading was on the verge of becoming an extremely rich man. Land sales and selectively awarded grubstakes, though similar practices had done virtually nothing for John Sutter, were working for Reading. There were far fewer miners, and because of the smaller numbers, it was possible for the King of the Upper Valley to keep a handle on things.

After riding with Reading and viewing his holdings, Calvin Beard was ready to head back to Lassen Rancho, but Samson Flowers shook his head.

"Hate to tell ye, hoss, but this child ain't goin' back jest yet. Much as I try, I'm jest no good at stayin' put, plowin' the same old forty month after month. Wagh! I spent most o' my life wanderin', trappin' and huntin'. Goes against the grain, somehow, for me to set still. Hellfire, Califia, she don't need me to do the huntin' for the crew. The boys'll manage jest swell on their own. Anyhow, Cal, I believe I'm goin' to try my hand at prospecting."

Calvin nodded his head and ran his fingers over his waxed mustache. Even before he started, he knew he was wasting his time trying to convince big Sam Flowers that he ought to get back into harness. It wasn't gold that was in the man's eye, not that exactly. But one might call it gold, since whatever it was, it amounted to the same thing.

"Up the Trinity?" Calvin asked.

"Reckon. Mebbe even across the mountains an' over onto the Klamath. Might be gold thar, too. Seems to me the gravels looked purty much like the ones hyar an' on the American. A coon never knows until he looks. Me, I'm not getting any younger. I figger I'd best look now, while I'm able."

"None of us is getting any younger," Calvin agreed. "What should I tell Califia? I mean, you *are* coming back after a bit, aren't you?"

"Hell yes, hell yes. O' course I am. It's jest like I say—I need to look around for a spell. No way of knowin' what's back in them Siskiyou Mountains until a coon takes a gander."

"But damn it, Samson, you married the girl. Sis hasn't driven you off, has she? Make certain you've thought this thing through before you do something both of you are likely to regret. When you're together, you always seem happy enough. Jesus Christ, I've always kind of envied you. . . ."

Sam Flowers made a gesture—a gesture of helplessness.

"I'm old,"he said. "Old enough to be her daddy an' yours too, Cal. Truth is, I'm pushing sixty—an' that ain't the youngest cat in the woods. Maybeso Califia ought to be thinkin' about finding a buck her own age, more 'or less. I *love* her, ye know that. Gord-damn it, she deserves better'n me. With me up hyar, minin' for a spell, it'll give Califia a chance to think things over. Mebbe we kind of trapped each other, I don't know. But right now I'm of a mind to see what's back in them mountains. Califia an' me, we rode part of 'em together, an' this child won't ever forget. You tell her that, will ye, Cal?"

Calvin Beard studied the older man's eyes. They were pleading and at the same time defiant.

It was no use, and he knew it.

The need for lumber increased at an astronomical rate, and the mills of such as Olivo & Beard, Larkin, Sutter, and others were simply not able to generate boards and timbers in sufficient quantities. The time was ripe for outside investment and exploitation. The demand for boards in the mining districts was so intense, for flumes and bracing and sluices and the like, that eventually even Sutter's Mill at Ko-lo-ma was torn down, board by board, and used in the pursuit of the *worthless yellow metal*.

Absurd though it was, the merchants of San Francisco, Monterey, San Jose, and other cities resorted to ordering lumber from the American East—with material arriving from Maine, by shipboard. Once the *Rush* was in full swing, New England merchant captains began to bring not only gold-seekers around the Horn, but cargoes of lumber. The barkentine *Suliot*, dropping anchor at San Francisco early in 1849, boasted passenger berths made of hemlock costing $10 a thousand in Maine, once in California to be dismantled and sold for $300 a thousand.

But here in the Coast Range, where the forests stretched on seemingly without end, opportunities abounded for men of vision, and entrepreneurs emerged. The would-be loggers proceeded to stake out huge tracts of forested land, just as Raymondo and Bill the Sawyer had done, and soon the air was rent with the cries of steam-driven circular saws large enough and powerful enough to process many thousands of board feet of lumber every day. Systematic exploration was under way, with paid *timber cruisers* estimating, taking notes, working on maps, and laying the battle plans for what was to follow. Olivo & Beard as well would cruise the Coast Range, the Yolla Bollys, the Siskiyous, and the Sierra Nevada itself—looking to the future, looking to find sites where the big logs might be gotten down, whether by means of skid roads or wooden-wheeled wagons drawn by oxen or by flumes, to rivers sufficient to float them. Califia, who seemed hardly disturbed by the news that Samson had elected to remain in the vicinity of Shasta City for the winter, engaged Juan Pescadero and half a dozen young Hotochrukmas, and set out to explore the mining region—in search of lands to claim or buy for timber, not for gold.

Bill Beard and Raymondo Olivo, leaving Calvin shoreside and in temporary control of the entire Olivo & Beard operations, took their wives and two or three Yankee timber fallers and rode north from Sacramento, toward the Trinity, Salmon, Scott, and Klamath rivers. For Seagull and Calling Owl, the journey was an adventure. To leave the village and its concerns behind! If it should occur, Bill Beard thought to himself, that they happened to run into a certain Samson Flowers, why possibly a bit of strong-armed logic might be used to bring this rascal back to his senses and hence to his wife. If a man undertook to marry the daughter of William Beard, by Gawd, that man had responsibilities that he was damned well going to live up to.

With the discovery of so much gold, nothing was ever likely

to be quite the same again, however, and they all knew it. Come spring, emigrants from the East would be pouring in, wave after wave. While Bill Beard and Raymondo Olivo could merely surmise the ultimate impact, they could feel the changes in the air.

Pelican Doctor was having bad dreams of late. . . .

Beard and Olivo could not know that William and Frederic Talbot, Andrew Pope, Cyrus Walker (a relative latecomer), John Dolbeer, and Allen Corzine would find their way West and in the long run challenge Olivo & Beard supremacy in the woods, and yet the longtime friends could certainly imagine that sufficiently financed, ambitious, and energetic men would emerge as rivals. Nature abhorred a vacuum, and the vacuum was present. The winter of '49 would see Talbot in San Francisco, his brig the *Oriental* loaded with house frames, shingles, heavy timbers, and sixty thousand board feet of sawn lumber. But the Talbots, Pope, and Walker would go north, establishing their mills along Puget Sound, ultimately shipping finished timber south to California. Corzine and Dolbeer, with the lure of gold in their eyes, would cross a continent, fail in their mining ventures, and turn to the kind of work they knew best—the felling of timber. With men such as these, the last and greatest portion of the *Big Clearing* would be under way. And yet, no matter how many giant trees were cut, the loggers would never believe their efforts amounted to more than a bit of scratching into the immensity of the stands. *Timber! Timmmm-burrr! I tell ye, there's no end to these ungodly dark woods.* . . .

PART THREE

THE CALIFORNIA TRAIL

CHAPTER TWENTY-ONE

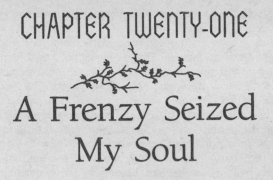

A Frenzy Seized My Soul

[1848, 1849:]

BY AUTUMN OF 1848 San Francisco was half deserted—the same story at all the settlements. The men were gone to the gold-fields. Military personnel deserted. The contagion spread. Shovels formerly priced at one dollar now sold for fifty. Indians were hired to mine—those who had not been *extirpated*, to use government lingo. Some four thousand men were at work in the auriferous zone, half of them indigenes.

On August 19, 1848, the *New York Herald* had announced to the nation the discovery of gold in distant California. A Sacramento Valley settler wrote to relatives in Illinois: "We in this country live and move on beds of the richest minerals. . . . We have them for picking up. . . . Plenty for all, for years to come." The *New York Journal of Commerce* quoted the Alcalde at Monterey: ". . . men . . . open a vein of gold just as coolly as you would a potato hill." Colonel Mason, military governor of California, delivered his official report, and on December 5, 1848, President Polk told the second session of the 30th Congress: "The accounts of the abundance of gold in that territory are of such extraordinary character as would scarcely command belief were they not corroborated by authentic reports of officers in the public service."

It was official and not simply a matter of further wild tales from beyond the frontier. The entire nation was thrown into fine stew, and thousands upon thousands sold possessions and homes and prepared to set off westward. The *New York Herald*, January 11, 1849, reported, "Poets, philosophers, lawyers, brokers, bankers, merchants, farmers, clergymen—all are feeling the impulse and are preparing to go and dig for gold and swell the number of adventurers to the new El Dorado."

By February 28th of 1849, the first shipload of gold-seekers had arrived in San Francisco. More would come, many more—eighteen thousand miles around Cape Horn, or to Panama and through the sweltering jungles of the isthmus and thence by steamer to San Francisco, or by canal and horse and wagon and riverboat to Independence or St. Joseph or Council Bluffs and thence westward across plains and mountains and deserts and more mountains. . . .

Coinage of gold dollars and twenty-dollar double eagles was authorized. General Zachary Taylor, Whig, was inaugurated as the twelfth President of the United States, Millard Fillmore his Vice President, and John M. Clayton his Secretary of State. President Taylor sent official messengers to the people of California and of New Mexico as well, urging the formation of governments. In Congress the seats were divided almost equally between Whigs and Democrats, and a small band of Free-Soilers provided a balance of power. Controversy over slavery raged on.

On June 15, former President Polk lay dead in Nashville, but the Gold Rush his announcement provoked continued to gain momentum. Men from the cities or the small farms of the American East, men ignorant of the wilderness, read Fremont's *Journal* and other accounts and purchased many guns, a practice encouraged by the U.S. War Department, which offered to sell pistols and rifles and ammunition at cost to those who would emigrate to California and Oregon. With Mexico defeated, American claim to the land was clear—for the sum of fifteen million dollars, the United States had gained, along with its victory, more than seven hundred thousand square miles of territory—as specified, upon the signing of the Treaty of Guadalupe-Hidalgo.

Emigrants who picked the overland route had their choice of two main trails—the Santa Fe and the Oregon-California. By year's end, California's population would stand at more than a hundred thousand, with eighty thousand of these being gold-seekers.

Hulking Benjamin Goffe, lately the Professor of Literary Puritanism at Yale University, was headed for California—not to seek gold, but rather to write a book dealing with the trials and tribulations of those who actually sought the precious metal. For some days now, nearly two weeks in fact, he'd been traveling in the company of a charming young couple, husband and wife, whom he'd met on the Erie Canal—a young pair intent upon reaching California, just as he was.

The woman was perhaps twenty-three or -four, thin, dark-haired, blue-eyed, graceful, polite, and highly attractive—and Ben Goffe, idly fantasizing about this *objet d'art*, found himself wishing the lady were unmarried and that he were perhaps fifteen or so years younger—and a bit less of a horse, plus blind to boot without his thick glasses (he carried two extra pairs about his person at all times). Roxanne Breton Olivo was a native of Caernarvon in Wales, daughter of a successful businessman—a wealthy burgher, one who never intended for his daughter to marry a Californio, or for that matter to leave Jolly Old England at all.

The young British woman's relatively short and brown-skinned husband was the more interesting of the two, albeit less sexually attractive, at least to the former Yale professor of literature and distant relative of Goffe the Regicide from the time of the Puritan Revolution in England and furthermore an habitual heterosexual by both practice and inclination. The husband appeared to be to one side or the other of thirty and clean-shaven, with very little facial hair in the first place. His name was Homer Virgil Olivo, as Ben learned from talking with the young people, and he was a *bona fide* fellow scholar. Olivo held a master's degree from Cambridge and had for some years taught both at a preparatory school and at the university itself. Olivo was, he'd confided to Goffe after they'd been traveling and taking their meals together for several days, a full-blooded Ohlone Indian, native of California, and scion of a wealthy family. Homer's father and his uncle, the latter a former Yankee merchant sailor who'd been sent to and graduated from normal college, were partners in a highly-successful timbering venture and were the holders of three valid Mexican land grants. Both men, Olivo said, had married members of the Hotochrukma tribe—sisters, in fact, twins.

Now the Olivos were on their way to California—*a bloomin' visit, just that and no more,* as Roxanne added quickly. A glance into the husband's intense eyes, however, told a different story. Olivo was going home—and was intending to stay there, even if he himself didn't as yet realize this elemental fact of his own nature.

It was just past noon, August 1st, 1849, when H.V. Olivo and his wife Roxanne and Benjamin Goffe debarked from a steamer called *Mizzip Dowager* and set foot in St. Louis, Missouri, a thriving and rapidly growing young metropolis of nearly seventy thousand souls. The *Gateway to the West* was a sprawling, ugly place—parts of it old, but most of it new—and everywhere an air of frenzy, an air of the unfinished. The place, Ben Goffe remarked as a matter of mutual interest, had been established as a fur-trading post back in 1764 by two Frenchmen, Linguest and Chouteau, though those worthies had certainly never dreamed of the frenetic energy that would eventually manifest itself in this city that styled itself as the *Queen of the Frontier.* Indeed, St. Louis was complete with an opera, a grand cathedral, and a Catholic institution of higher learning, St. Louis College.

As the three of them strolled along, up from the waterfront toward the litter of brick and board buildings among which they trusted they'd be able to find reasonable accommodations, they observed the astounding diversity of human types, both male and female: men wearing Indian-cut leathers and beaver hats, knives slung from their waists, pistols, and often a rifle over the crook of an arm; dandies, gussied out in the latest fashions, clean-shaven and hard-eyed men who where, almost certainly, professional gamblers, the smooth-talking pirates of the Mississippi; farmers and their families, expressions

suspicious, clothing obviously homemade; merchants; black-
smiths; town rowdies; proper churchwomen in full skirts of
gray and tan, women who walked straight ahead and kept
their mouths pursed. And there were gangs of ragtag children,
their clothing patched and patched again, some of the girls in
tomboy attire. Gentlemen, whether riding or walking along,
were often enough accompanied by their Colored servants.
Other Blacks, apparently free men, entered and exited from
mercantile shops and grocery stores.

"Canterbury pilgrims to the power of ten," Olivo remarked—and Goffe nodded, adjusted his thick glasses, and
grinned.

They took note of sullen-eyed young women, faces painted
and hair elaborately coifed and ribboned—some of them
laughing gaily and haranguing passersby, others standing quietly and looking neither to the left nor the right, waiting.

Roxanne glanced at her husband, mostly to see whether
he'd taken notice of the professional female scum.

There were old men with ragged gray hair and polished
wooden canes—Indian women, some clothed in traditional
tribal fashion, others wearing ill-cut American garb—French—
English—Irish who had doubtless left Ireland as a result of a
potato famine and so found their way to Missouri—Germans
who'd had enough of revolution and so had booked passage
to the New World as a consequence of the reestablishment of
the Old Bund—Mexican Spanish—Southerners—New Englanders. Here were the brawl and confusion and intermingling of
sexes and ages and nationalities and human types—and all in
a muddy city on the banks of the great Mississippi, a town
where no one seemed to stay very long.

After dinner H.V. and Ben retired to the *El Sombrero Saloon &
Watering Hole*: *H. Mudd, Prop.* Here a stranger introduced himself—an individual who appeared the absolute prototype of the
Eastern newspaper cartoonist's view of the man of the Western frontier. Farnsworth "Bully" O'Bragh's costume had about
it an air of unique authenticity—a worn, shiny buckskin coat,
leather dark in places with impregnated grime and grease and
possibly even blood. His face featured striking green eyes and
was covered with a profusion of white, stringy hair. A red

band encircled the forehead, and from beneath a battered black felt hat hung three tightly woven pigtails. The remainder of his getup consisted of buckskin leggings, cross-laced, and moccasins. A broad-bladed butcher knife hung in a battered scabbard from a wide belt, as well as a Colt Dragoon revolver.

O'Bragh informed Olivo and Goffe that they would need a guide—and that he was the man.

"Ye see, I been out thar *recent*. Found me some gold, too, even if I weren't lookin' very hard. Me an' old Isaac Humphrey, we was ridin' together for a spell an' come to Ko-lo-ma in March o' forty-eight, jest about the time Bidwell was thar, pokin' about for Sutter hisself. Isaac, he'd mined gold over in the Cherokee lands, near Dahlonega, an' so he showed the locals how to use a gold pan an' a rocker. Couple weeks after I left, Penryn an' Johnson an' them massacred a whole Maidu village, but they'll get theirs after awhile—ain't that right, Ben? McCain, that's what they'll call ye an' yore Injun lady, leetle *Ooti*."

"Why is it," Goffe asked, "that I have the distinct feeling I'm dreaming, and you're part of my dream?"

O'Bragh leaned forward, knitted his brows, and motioned with his empty hand.

"Leetle secret, jest amongst the three of us. Truth is, I don't exist. Never did. But ye ain't dreamin', nuther one o' ye. Anyhow, I'll see to it ye get to Cali-forny, safe an' sound."

Olivo and Goffe exchanged incredulous glances.

"Thar at the table wih Monte Lil," O'Bragh continued, "them two's Al Corzine an' John Dolbeer. Jest kids, so to speak, but they're on their way to Cali-forny too. Corzine's from New Brunswick in Canady, an' Dolbeer's from New Hampshire. Both o' them's spent a few years in the loggin' woods, an' now they've decided to strike it rich in the goldfields. Crazy, ain't it? I mean, the way a man tries to outwit fate an' all. They ain't no way o' doin' it, an' that's why I come to help ye."

"Been married seven, eight, mebbe a dozen times in all. A fella gets older, he starts losin' track of things that don't matter much. First time was when I went upriver with Lewis an' Clark, by Gawd. Leetle gal named Fool's Hen. She was a sweet one, I'll tell ye. *Hidatsa*, she were."

"Farnsworth O'Bragh," H.V. laughed, "you're full of hot air. I've read the journals of that expedition, and I'm sure Ben has as well. I don't recall your name being listed—not mentioned at all. To put the matter simply, you weren't there, unless you've changed names. In any case, that was more than forty years ago. . . ."

"By the great green Gawd, who says I weren't? I done led them coons clear down the Columbia River, except we called 'er the *Oregon* at the time. Them boys was liars if they say different. Like I told ye fellas, my name ain't *Farnsworth* except in a legal way. It's *Bully*."

Goffe glanced at Olivo, shrugged, and pulled three cigars out of his jacket pocket. He offered one to H.V. and one to O'Bragh.

"Well," Ben chuckled, "I suppose you don't have to worry about either of those worthies contradicting you—since Lewis had been dead for forty years and Clark for about ten. Perhaps the journalists were guilty of a minor omission in the personnel list."

"Mebbe so," O'Bragh replied, biting off the end of his cigar and lighting up. "Guess I was just testin' you boys. Now Clark, he turned to surveying after a time. Laid out the town of Paducah, Kentucky, for a fact. That was part o' my old stompin' grounds. Both them coons is gone under, an' a world's gone under with 'em."

H.V. raised his glass of whiskey in a toast.

"Here's to Lewis and Clark."

"Wagh!" O'Bragh snorted. "An' hyar's to the gold in Californy. Tell ye what ye want to do—a metal pans' better'n a Meskin *batea*. Even a damn fry pan's better. But the rocker box, that's the way to go. A coon can mine a thousand dollars a day with no more than a pan, but a rocker box'll double yore take. Boys, this old coon's tellin' ye the truth."

Homer Virgil and Ben studied O'Bragh's wrinkled, intense face, and almost supposed they saw small glintings of fire in the mesmeric green eyes.

"Time was," O'Bragh went on, "when every coon in the mountains blamed young Jim Bridger for goin' off with Fitzgerald an' leavin' Hugh Glass thataway. But it's because they didn't know no better, mebbe. They wasn't out thar at the time, if ye catch my drift, lads. Aw hell, I'd of probably done different. Me an' Hugh had been compañeros, to tell the truth. But listen—out yonder a dead man ain't worth nothin', no sir. An' that's what Hugh was after that sow grizzly tore 'im up. Major Henry hisself figgered it. But jest the same, he left Fitzgerald and leetle Gabe thar to watch over 'im until he went under official. Nobody could of figgered anything different was goin' to happen, not the way Hugh was chewed up. The Major, he couldn't keep his whole party thar, not with the murtherin' Rees up an' spiling for a fight. Ye ain't goin' to sleep on me now, are ye, Homer?"

H.V. cleared his throat, glanced at Goffe.

"Fact is," O'Bragh continued, "I took note that yore eyes was closed."

"Just concentrating on your story, Farnsworth."

"His name's *Bully*," Ben Goffe whispered.

"Right, right. Ye both got to remember what I'm sayin'. Wagh! Otherwise she's all jest a waste of time, pure and simple."

H.V. took another pull from the whiskey jug and nodded.

"Couldn't agree more," he said.

"Okay," O'Bragh went on. "So like I was sayin'. If either one o' them niggers was to blame, it was Fitzgerald. Bridger, he was jest a greenhorn, more or less. Seventeen years old, I'd guess. No more'n a cub."

"So," Goffe interjected, "instead of staying with Glass until he died, Bridger and Fitzgerald left him to die and went back downriver."

"Yep, that's what happened all right. Only Hugh, he weren't ready to *go beaver* yet. No sir, an' he come back from whatever place that old sow griz sent him, an' thar he was, all busted up an' lyin' on top of the beastie's hide—because Hugh had actually kilt her, an' the boys skinned her. No food, no water, no knife, no horse pistol, no Hawken by Gawd."

"Weaponless?" H.V. demanded. "The bastards left Glass weaponless?"

"Darned rights. Leave a gun with a dead man, an' the Red Divvils find it, an' later they use it to put a coon under. So it's like ye done murthered yerself, slicker'n buffler squat—an' I mean *green* buffler dung, not the dried-out kind folks use for camp fires an' the like."

Goffe stretched, nearly fell over backward from his chair, the latter creaking and complaining under his weight.

"So what'd Glass do?" H.V. asked. "Let's get on with this fabrication, Bully, my friend."

"Ain't no *fabrication*, ye Gawddamned fool. Now Ben hyar, he's half man an' half bear an' jest as blind as a bear without them glasses. But you—you don't have no glasses, an' you're still blind. Listen up, now, Homer Olivo. Old Hugh, he set 'is own leg somehow an' then started crawlin'. Ate grasshoppers an' worms an' maggots an' snakes. Outgrowled some wolves, he did, an' dined on a leetle buffler they'd took down. An' by Gawd he made 'er all the way back down to Fort Atkinson. Ye any idee how far that be?"

"Not the slightest," H.V. replied.

"How do you happen to know all this?" Ben Goffe asked.

"Hundreds of miles, that's what. But old Hugh made 'er because he was about the toughest coon what ever come to the High Shinin' or to the plains either, for that matter. What were that other question?"

Goffe passed the whiskey jug to Bully, who took a long drink and snorted, wiped at his mouth.

"My question," Goffe said, "concerned the matter of verisimilitude versus mendacity. Ergo, how do you know any of this tale is true?"

"True!" O'Bragh yelled out. "I'll tell ye true. Every child in the mountains has knowed about 'er for close on to thirty years. An' we got to keep tellin' the story over an' over because that way it's like old Hugh's still with us somehow."

"Dead, then?" H.V. asked.

"Yep. Gawddamned Rees finally got him. Porkypined 'im with arrows an' left 'im on the river ice, up by Fort Union. Sixteen years back, it were.

"Pass the whiskey, Mr. O'Bragh," H.V. said. "Then I think this particular *greenhorn's* going to head back to his hotel and get a good night's rest."

"Mon frère, mon frère," the *booshway* of the lot sang out, *"vous et moi,* we must do this thing. I am, how you say, *the bull of*

the docks. You can break this old man's arm, *peut-être*, but my arms, they are bigger, *non*? Come, we wrestle now."

There was trouble in the air. Corzine and Dolbeer edged closer to Goffe and Olivo—men they at least recognized from on shipboard. The rivermen, on the other hand, looked willing to slit a man's throat for a fifty-cent piece.

"Advise ye to let well enough be, *Monsurry Frogs*," O'Bragh said. "Big Ben hyar, he was jest foolin' with this child. Be careful or Benny'll be snappin' yore tendons out o' yore arm. He's more than half bear, I'm tellin' ye. . . ."

"*Enfant de garce*, we shall see, we shall see. . . ."

The Canadian proceeded to take O'Bragh's place at the table, across from Goffe, and once again the hands locked, muscles tensed, and the match was on.

"Can he do it?" Dolbeer asked H.V.

"Professor Goffe will hold his own, I assure you."

"A professor is he?" Corzine asked. "What's he profess?"

"English—seventeenth century literature."

"That right? Have to watch what I say, then. When I was in school, I never liked parts of speech. Jesus—look at that!"

Ben Goffe, not at all taking to the French Canadian's manner, gritted his teeth, twisted with all the strength at his command, and quickly pinned his opponent's wrist to the table.

"Pig of a Yankee storekeeper, you cheat!" the Canadian cried out. He grabbed for a whiskey jug and promptly flung it at Goffe's head.

With that action, the inevitable fight was under way.

"Wagh!" Bully called out. "Ye dumbass dunghead of a French river scow! By the Great Blue Jesus an' all me other Irish ancestors, that ain't no way to wrist-wrastle!"

At this point John Dolbeer picked up a chair and crunched it across the head and shoulders of one of the rivermen, who groaned and fell into what was already a sea of kicking and sprawling humanity.

A sprinkling of mountain men had been in the saloon all along, both the real articles and the pretenders, and these individuals immediately lunged forward to confront the small army of *mangeurs du lard* who had seemingly appeared from out of the woodwork. Shot glasses skided across the floor, and playing cards flew into the smoke-filled air.

"Not my goddamned mirrors, not again!" H. Mudd shouted, emerging from one of the back rooms, flailing his arms about as if to bat down any projectile that might be aimed at the objects that were his pride and joy.

Monte Lil was cursing with gusto sufficient to turn the air blue. A pair of town toughs, neither mountain men nor rivermen, had fallen sideways in their struggles—across the table where Lil and her victims had been gambling. Then someone grabbed at Lil's hair, and the shining black locks came off, revealing shorter, almost matted gray-white beneath the wig. Except that no one was paying any attention.

Dolbeer and Corzine leapt into the fray, hurling punches at whomever happened to be in front of them. Ben Goffe drove a big fist into a random face, and the individual spun about, stunned with the force of the blow he'd received. O'Bragh was waving a knife back and forth and at the same time screaming what sounded like an authentic Indian war cry.

Two unpleasant-looking individuals dived at H.V., and Olivo, in turn, picked up the arm of the chair Dolbeer had broken across a riverman's back and began to wield it like a club, striking one man full in the mouth, producing an eruption of blood and flying shards of teeth. The second attacker stumbled, and H.V., now well entered into the spirit of the evening, dealt the man a stunning blow with the side of his foot.

Homer looked across the room—saw Goffe lifting a pair of men by their shirt collars, soundly cracking their heads together. The two groaned and went cold at Ben's feet.

Then half a dozen were on Olivo, and he went down under the combined weight of his assailants—but as he fell, he saw old Bully attempting to come to his aid, flailing back and forth with the flat of his butcher knife. Someone else had a knife. The point gouged into H.V.'s forearm, the wound no so much paining as merely numbing the flesh. Next, with astonishing luck, Olivo was able to slip out from under the heap of writhing and cursing humanity that had covered him. He stood up, backed away.

The melee was getting serious.

Ben Goffe was on all fours, crawling about under the tables, groping for something—his glasses. H.V. saw the spectacles, as yet undamaged, in one corner, and he moved quickly, picked them up.

The table Goffe was under broke with the weight of several bodies, and Ben was pressed to the floor.

Grunting. Cursing. The heavy sound of flesh impacting flesh. O'Bragh and his war cry. Other war cries. Then a succession of pistol shots, these followed immediately by the sound of plate glass shattering and cascading in bits and slivers to the floor.

"God curse you all!" H. Mudd shrilled in a long wail of anguish.

A coal oil lantern, struck by a hurled shot glass, exploded, and suddenly a pool of flame danced on the floor.

In the aftermath of the brawl and subsequent fire that nearly burned down *El Sombrero*, O'Bragh, Olivo, Goffe, Corzine, and Dolbeer found themselves standing under a street lamp several blocks distant. They spoke briefly of the difficulties of the trail ahead, and then O'Bragh was gone—slipped off into the August darkness.

"The old man was right about our needing a guide," Allen Corzine said. "We're two months late in starting, maybe more. Unless we make record time, we're subject to have to winter in Salt Lake City, out on the desert. I come west to find gold, not to work for some good Mormon farmer."

"You think the old guy actually *knows* the California Trail?" Dolbeer asked. "Where'd you run into him, anyway?"

H.V. shrugged.

"There in the saloon tonight. I thought perhaps you two knew him from somewhere. If he was on the *Dowager*, I sure as hell didn't see him."

"I've read about emigrants riding mules instead of horses," Dolbeer said. "So maybe he does know what he's talking about. But if he's already taken off, then what good's it going to do us?"

"It's past midnight, Homer Olivo! How dare you desert me in the midst of this awful hole in the wilderness? Back in England, you never treated me this way. I don't think you love me anymore, and perhaps you never loved me at all. I've seen enough of your America to last me for the rest of my life. It's not too late, Homer. For all that's happened, we could jolly take passage back on that wretched steamer and go south to New Orleans and from there back to New York City. As things are, what's ahead of us? By your own account we may meet with wild Indians, and there are few if any accommodations along the emigrant trail, not for the next fifteen hundred miles! For all you've told me about Alta California, matters are scarcely any better there. How could you have gone off and left me this way in a city filled with thieves, murderers, charlatans, and prostitutes? Do you think I'm blind? That I didn't see them?"

H.V. grinned. Roxanne was damned lovely when she got her back up. Her intense blue eyes were blazing beneath a sable crown of carefully formed curls. The lip rouge she'd put on, possibly in anticipation of his return to the hotel room, was slightly smeared in a way that he found most appealing, most sensual.

"Oh come with me and be my love, and we shall all the pleasures prove," he sang, seeking at the same time to encircle her slim waist with his arm.

"Don't you try to bloomin' sweet-talk me, Homer. Why did I ever agree to come with you? Why'd I ever marry you? We've seen nothing but . . . barbarians . . . for days on end, and even your friend Goffe seems to me about half savage— hardly civilized at all. How do I know you yourself won't turn *savage* once we've left the frontier behind us? The scar on your back, the one you say came from an arrow . . . perhaps you've been a *wild Indian in disguise* all along! Well, I can ride a horse if I have to, and I'm no stranger to difficulties of all sorts—but this St. Louis of yours is horrid. I wish to return to civilization!"

H.V. lifted Roxanne and carried her toward the bed. She struggled, mostly for effect, kicking and flailing at him with her fists closed, the pastel-blue silk of her evening dress clinging to her well-formed body. But now she was laughing.

"Don't think you can just make love to me and everything will be all right again, Homer Olivo! Is that all you can think of? I swear, I'll turn your water off for good if you leave me alone this way again!"

"I thought you said you wished to peruse the tome of the fair *Pamela*," H.V. said. "I merely allowed sufficient time for your reading. Is Mistress Pamela still writing letters to one and all? Where does she get so much ink, so many sheets of paper, and envelopes sufficient? In truth, I think she's hoping that lecherous Squire B. will slip unseen into her chambers. . . ."

"Reprobate! You don't love me at all—it's only my body you want. I'm just a plaything to you. . . ."

"And a handsome plaything at that." H.V. chuckled, placing Roxanne upon the bed and leaning over her, slowly, deliberately unbuttoning her bodice.

"I'll quite turn your water off, Homer, that I will. . . ."

H.V. kneeled beside the bed, placed his lips to the nipple of one breast, and slipped his hand beneath the blue silk that concealed her smoothly shaven pubic area.

Goffe lay exhausted on the lumpy bed in his hotel room and drifted into fitful sleep—and into a dream that was a duplication of the discovery which had led to his resolve to seek out a better world than the one he'd shared with his beautiful young wife, Etta.

He tethered his horse behind a clump of sumac and walked the familiar footpath that skirted the swamp, just above a high-water mark defined by those times when fierce winds and rains of a southern hurricane wandered too far north and drove the tides back into Farm River's mud flats, producing a lake several miles across, one that took a week or more to drain completely into Long Island Sound.

Ben approached the cottage, intending to spy inside from beneath the honeysuckle-draped, eastward-facing bay window. Still sixty yards from the cottage, he saw the door open and an unexpected male figure emerge. He threw himself flat among fringe-topped licorice stalks, parted the sweet-smelling vegetation sufficiently to be able to observe the intruder's movements—a man dressed in black, his white choke-collar visible even from this distance.

"Don't need my damned glasses at all," Ben thought. "It's that young Catholic priest from East Haven. . . ."

Now a woman appeared, and the priest turned back, went to where she stood, and the two locked in fervent embrace.

"Etta. She's been bedding the Pope's child, right in my own goddamned hideaway. . . ."

The priest walked off quickly—whether he felt any guilt in the matter one couldn't say.

Ben was tempted to continue, to spy on his wife from the nook beneath thick growth of honeysuckle vines—then, when she emerged from the cottage, to grab her by the hair and backhand her a few times, battering her into unconsciousness. His male rage, hurt pride, and gnawing jealousy were intense—and he even considered throwing her down among the weeds and having his way with her.

Cuckold! Cuckold!

In this moment she was inexplicably desirable, and he felt a powerful need to repossess what was his. But he did not feel desire in any usual sense. The impulse was to strike out, to force himself upon her, to humiliate her just as she'd humiliated him.

"Great God," Goffe muttered between clenched teeth, "what if she's got more little priests inside? What if she's servicing them one by one?"

He felt black shame as he uttered the words, and he realized his own voice was barely recognizable. It wasn't Benjamin Goffe, scholar and professor. No, it was something dark, hard, wild, fiercely male, without conscience or scruple. He was having trouble breathing, and he could feel a pulsing sensation in his ears. His face was hot, damp with sudden perspiration.

Etta, goddamn you to hell, I love you! I loved you once, and you threw the love back into my face. My beautiful one, my precious, my whore of Babylon. . . .

He backed up, turned, crawled away from the sick-sweet aroma of green licorice, got to his feet, and began to run along the footpath whose every twist and turn he knew by heart—from the endless comings and goings of boyhood. Sunlight blazed in the oaks and maples before him, blazed in the air out across Farm River Swamp, shimmered through clouds, gleamed from the wings of a flight of blackbirds that twisted into a knot in the air before him and then burst apart, a sensation of oneness, a single dark being of feather and blood, shattered as the birds darted every which way, slipping about and then disappearing beyond the tall-standing cattails that lined the shore of the small river.

My fairest though unprotected flower. . . . Mea culpa, mea culpa, mea culpa. . . .

CHAPTER TWENTY-TWO

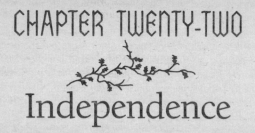

Independence

[1849:]

LONG, TWO-FORKED river, the Platte rises on both sides of the front range of the Rockies. The South Platte draws down from the snows of the eastern face, from the mountains now called Elbert, Lincoln, and Evans—these peaks as yet unnamed, still sleeping at the time when the "Californians" moved west. The North Platte, inscribing a huge bend around the Laramie Range, sucks at the snows of Hague's Peak and the high granites of the Never Summer Mountains and the Park Range. From the headwaters of the North Platte to the eventual confluence with the Missouri, the river is nearly a thousand miles in length.

"A mile wide and a foot deep," the mountain men liked to say. But in times of extended winter rains, the Platte becomes a gray-brown monster, sweeping all before it as it pours down from the back of the continent and races eastward through the sea of grasses, short grass and tall grass, a land without boundary or dimension, limitless sky above the unending undulations of prairie.

Redbud, daisy, golden Alexanders, birdsfoot violets, prairie rose, spiderwort, purple milkweed. Bunchgrass, sweetgrass, bitter grass, gamma grass, big bluestem, Indiangrass, switchgrass, cordgrass.

Sandhill cranes, whooping cranes, white pelicans, meadowlarks, prairie chickens, crows, ravens, vultures, ospreys, eagles, hawks.

Blacksampson and butterflies.

Raccoons, coyotes, wolves.

Wild petunia, lead plant, goatsrue, black-eyed Susan, coreopsis and compass plant, butterfly milkweed. Bullthistle and sagebrush.

Blackbirds everywhere, solids and redwings.

And along the streams: willows, cottonwoods, oaks, elders. Cardinal flower, foxglove, bottle gentian, Riddell's goldenrod, twigbrush. Blueberries, strawberries, blackberries, wild plum.

Frogs, lizards, snakes.

Buffalo, grunting, snorting—enormous, curious, unpredictable animals. Still millions upon millions of them as the nineteenth century reached its midpoint. On the Santa Fe Trail in 1839, Thomas Farnham passed for three days through land "so thickly covered with these noble animals, that when viewed from a height, it scarcely afforded a sight of a square league of its surface." Farnham did some calculations and concluded that the buffalo covered an area a little larger than Rhode Island.

Scant rain, and the land swelling upward to sagebrush and creosote brush and juniper and prickly pear.

H.V. Olivo, his wife Roxanne, Benjamin Goffe, Allen Corzine, and John Dolbeer all booked passage upriver aboard the steamer *Missouri Princess*, the fare per person a nominal ten dollars. This craft would transport them some three hundred and seventy-six miles up the Missouri River to the town of Independence, at the eastern terminus of the California, Oregon, and Santa Fe Trails.

At length the time to go on board had arrived. The *Princess* was nearly loaded for her upriver journey and was crowded with more than two hundred tons of freight and over a hundred passengers—Yorkers, Yankees, Buckeyes, Wolverines, Hoosiers, gamblers, swindlers, drunks, and various characters that appeared to be cousins of Bully O'Bragh—though the latter wraithlike individual was nowhere in sight.

H.V. entertained a mental image of the white-bearded old scarecrow on muleback, heading for the far mountains.

H.V. and Roxanne repaired to their quarters, a small, single cabin with an overview of the main deck and the river and beyond. At last the steam whistle had screamed five times, and the sternwheeler was out into the channel and under way, back up the Mississippi and past Mosenthein Island and Columbia Bottom to the point of Portage Des Sioux, below which the muddy waters of the Missouri and the relatively clearer flow of the Mississippi, joining, flowed side by side and unmixed for a few miles. Here the *Missouri Princess*, her steam whistle roaring to mark the signal moment, slipped inside the current and entered the mouth of the Muddy River, proceeding upstream past three considerable islands—Cora, Pelican, and Bryan by name—as well as several smaller willow-and-maple-entangled spits of land in the river.

"Olivo," H.V. said to himself, "it's real now—if it wasn't before, not even crossing the Atlantic, not even on the canals and stagecoaches and river scow down the Mississippi from Illinois. I'm on my way home to California, a somewhat reluctant Welsh wife in tow. But once we're there, Roxanne'll adjust. She's a good soul, even if she does make a bit of fuss at times. . . ."

H.V. looked out his small cabin window at the crowded main deck, almost every square foot of it taken up either by cargo or by emigrants who'd chosen not to pay for better quarters. Already a number of men were playing poker—the foolish ones falling directly into the hands of those who made their livings with cards.

H.V. glanced at Roxanne, who was already absorbed in her copy of *Pamela*. He remarked that Ben Goffe was also out on the deck, apparently engaged in spirited conversation with other passengers, but there was no response from Roxanne other than a faintly-discernible nod. His wife, he realized, had retreated into her own private world and hence was oblivious to his presence.

He took out his journal, and began to write:

H.V. *Olivo's Journal, August 3, 1849:*

In coming down the upper Mississippi, I first knew what a truly great river looked like—for there is nothing in California and nothing in England to compare with it. Perhaps the Rhine in Germany is of comparable size, but the portions of that stream which I have seen were bounded by buildings and other human clutter, and thus it did not seem impressive at all—rather somewhat predictable, like the Thames in London.

Passing the mouth of the Missouri a short distance above the fledgling metropolis of St. Louis, suddenly the great river of North America had grown to twice its former size, perhaps more. For I've already concluded that the Missouri is actually the main stream and not the subservient affluent. If the Big Muddy River (as some denominate it) lacks the grace and dignity of the so-called Father of Waters, it's a powerful and at times treacherous being. Even now, in mid-summer, the waters are constantly riled, as though heavy rains were falling in the lands from whence the current arises. That would be, I presume, the Rocky Mountains that we've all heard so much about and which I keenly look forward to seeing, though I truly doubt they're any match for the Alps of France and Switzerland or the High Sierra of California. Truthfully I remember little of my ill-fated adventure into those mountains. From my present perspective, however, no peaks are visible—for the fabled continental divide lies more than a thousand miles due west of my immediate location—and, as the charts indicate to me, nearly three thousand miles if one were to follow all the hooks and loops that the River Missouri describes in its course.

In truth, the land through which the rivers flow at present shows few if any signs of a Western Frontier. We pass by areas dotted with many small farms, these separated at intervals by zones of forested banks and densely shaded coves where small streamlets enter the Big Muddy River. It is only in and about these latter that any sense of genuine latent wildness exists. There are no conifers at all. Lumber is apparently imported up the Mississippi from the New England woods or down the river from the headwaters of the river. Indeed, I saw numerous timber barges on the Mississippi on the way to St. Louis.

At times I worry as to whether Roxanne will indeed be up to the overland venture which lies ahead of us—undeterminate, countless miles westward to California, a California which is, as my father has written me, much changed from the land I remember—the land where I grew up with my cousins Calvin and Califia. Presuming a successful crossing, I worry as well about how Roxanne and Califia will get on with one another. It's doubtless a good thing that Califia has finally married, though I'm not truly certain how I feel about that matter, either.

Why is it we're never quite ready for what's about to happen? Perhaps when I'm older I'll be more temperate in my assessment of the future—yet I wonder if our traveling companion, Professor Goffe, approaches this overland journey with any less trepidation than I. . . .

Though it's said to be a wife's duty to accompany her husband wherever he may be obliged to go, nonetheless I fear Roxanne's heart is so firmly attached to England that she'll never be fully satisfied until we return—and that's something, after all, that I'm in no position to predict. My family found means to send me to Europe for an education, and now I feel honor-bound to return—and somehow to give back a little of what I received. I know my father hopes to see the establishment of a school for the Indian people—perhaps with the assistance of territorial government—and surely statehood cannot be far away, not now that gold has been discovered and half the world, or so it would seem, is of a mind to go there. Institutions of learning are bound to follow—indeed, the United States seems even more set on the goal of universal literacy than England itself, a condition doubtless owing to the fact that no entrenched class system is in place, other than the obvious social evil of Black slavery. It remains true, however—in America there is no Nobility other than that which establishes itself through its own performance.

The voyage upriver to Independence was several days longer than anticipated, for the ship was beset by nearly a full day of howling winds and torrential downpours. At one point the *Missouri Princess* came aground on a sandbar hidden beneath the roiling current of the Muddy River, and the passengers were obliged to raft ashore, leaving only the captain and his mate aboard, along with a melange of wagons, supplies, farm animals, and four passengers too ill to be moved. There had been some talk of cholera on shipboard, but the mate insisted that it was no more than a matter of loose tongues and wild rumors. The ship's doctor nodded agreement. In any case, the officers were able to extricate the lightened steamer from the sand, and the slow journey against the Missouri's insidious brown current continued.

A few hours after the passengers were once more aboard, one of the boilers ruptured, a steam-release valve tearing loose. Necessary repairs could not be accomplished until noon the following day.

In all, the journey upriver, amounting to approximately three hundred and seventy miles, took seven days, lacking a few hours—an average of little more than fifty miles a day.

"Bully O'Bragh and his wretched mule could have made it overland in not much longer," Goffe remarked to H.V. as they bade farewell to the trouble-plagued *Missouri Princess*.

Dolbeer told them that the ship's doctor himself was down with the cholera, and that one of the four who'd been sequestered in the infirmary was close to death.

H.V. glanced at Roxanne and at Ben. Cholera was a dread plague—one that spread God-knew-how. Thousands had died of the disease in St. Louis just a year earlier—according to common word. It was possible, then, that everyone who'd been on the *Princess* might be infected.

"I suppose," Ben said, adjusting his thick glasses, "that we'll muddle on as always, inasmuch as we have no other choice in the matter. What say you, Mr. Olivo?"

"It's a sorry trade, a bad joke all around," H.V. replied.

"Must you men forever be so morbid?" Roxanne demanded. "Mr. Dolbeer doesn't really know a blessed thing. He's mouthing rumors, nothing more. . . ."

Roxanne, H.V. realized, was in fact not looking at him or Ben as she spoke. He glanced in the direction her gaze seemed to indicate.

Allen Corzine, perhaps twenty yards distant, was engaged in animated conversation with a red-haired, freckle-faced young woman whose breasts, one might say, were *prodigious*.

Single men—and that included the likes of Corzine, Dolbeer, and even Ben Goffe—were permitted to patronize such trade, if they saw fit. Besides money, the only payment might be a free-floating guilt and, of course, venereal diseases such as syphilis, gonorrhea, and chancre. Knowledge of the danger, however, never seemed sufficient to deter males from indulgence—was even the doubtless profound Benjamin Goffe able to resist temptation once it was put into his way?

And yes, H.V. recalled, there had indeed been times when. . . .

But Roxanne. Was it simple fascination on her part, observing a male of her acquaintance attempting to enter into a love-for-payment arrangement, or was she actually staring at Corzine himself? The man was, H.V. reflected, quite good-looking and something of a smoothie, a kind of rough-hewn ladies' man, so to speak.

Perhaps it was permissible to *contemplate* interdicted behavior, provided only that one refrained from acting out the contemplations. But did Roxanne's protestations of love and loyalty not preclude her from *looking* at other men as she seemed now to be looking at the twenty-five-year-old former logger from New Brunswick in Canada?

Hold your imagination in tow, Homer Virgil. You've got enough real problems ahead of you to occupy your time more than sufficiently.

The season was late indeed, and they had no leader—no one to guide them westward to the fabled land of gold.

Goffe and Olivo, after making the purchase of a team and a cart, drove to a farming area a few miles from the ragged little city and made inquiries about supplies and more horses. From a farmer who'd come from South Carolina originally, Goffe bought a ten-year-old plow horse—a Percheron dubbed *Old Blue*. Mumbling something about "O'Bragh's advice," Ben paid for the ungainly animal and for a saddle as well, though the cinch had to be extended to fit.

The two men purchased quantities of such things as flour, bacon, coffee beans, cornmeal, salt, dried beans, and rice. After a long day of equipping their outfits, they returned to the rooms they'd taken at an inn called the Noland House.

H.V. sat in a wooden rocker and glanced through the week-old copy of the *St. Louis Statesman*.

On page three was the following notice:

Six Negras For Sale. Including a Woman of twenty-three years, experienced for the house. A girl aged seventeen, likely & a good worker. Three farmhands, aged 43, 49, & 50. A Boy, 12 years old. All are Blackskins & are healthy & full warrantee. These may be seen at 41 Box Elder St., between Noon & Four. Priced Reasonable.

"America," he thought, "my country now, though I hardly know you—my country because a war between two nations with claims to California was settled in favor not of the one who built missions and set up ranchos, but the one with the greater military force and ultimately the greater dream and the greater ambition. And now this insanity of gold. . . . All right, America, then. The hope of the civilized world, a land where any man is free to strike for liberty, free to forge his own destiny by means of the labor of his own two hands—unless, of course, he's Negro or Celestial or Indian like me. Then the rules shift somewhat. The beautiful, fatally flawed nation, the empire in progress. . . . And out there along the Pacific, though hardly anyone has as yet realized it, there are forests of such Promethean proportions as to create riches far, far beyond all the hoopla that this Gold Rush portends. But time will tell the story. My acquaintances Corzine and Dolbeer, for instance, have left logging behind, or so they believe. My crystal ball tells me they'll miss the gold and discover redwood instead—because someone's bound to come along who'll invent machinery sufficient to fell those giants. . . ."

The band of emigrants who'd assembled outside the village of Independence was still far from ready to begin its westward trek. Olivo, hoping that once he was out on the trail Roxanne would cease her whining and raging and so give him some peace, was not of a mind to wait any longer. Ben Goffe was of a similar mind, though obviously for quite different reasons. Corzine and Dolbeer, similarly, claimed to be all for heading westward immediately.

"What in hell do we need a guide for?" Corzine asked. "We're none of us blind, except Big Ben here when he's misplaced those glassed of his. No offense, Mr. Goffe, no offense. I mean, it's not as though the trail branched in a dozen differ-

ent places, is it? We've got maps, and we've got rolling stock—
and for the time being, at least, we're blessed with good
weather. I vote that we head out."

H.V. was aware that the process of taking on supplies and
of working out the political considerations for a journey to
California, a journey made in concert, would take far longer
than the amount of time required by reasonable necessity.
Goffe agreed. Both men had spent enough time serving on
college committees over the years to know that an apparent
commonness of purpose would almost certainly be fractured
into numerous personal purposes, all at loggerheads, as soon
as any joint-action group was formed.

The present was clearly not the time for such bickering. It
was a time for action.

"I thought O'Bragh was planning to meet us up here," John
Dolbeer said. "He might have been a good one at that—but
since he's not here, I suggest we pool our wits and head west.
Maybe we can find a guide *out there* somewhere."

H.V. glanced at Dolbeer and then at Corzine and then at
Roxanne. Was it his imagination only that his wife spent an
inordinate amount of time studying Allen Corzine?

*That damnable crystal ball of mine—I keep seeing trouble ahead
with this fellow. I'm not so sure it's a wise plan to pitch in with
these two—a long way to California, and many, many opportunities. . . .*

At length Olivo and his wife and Ben Goffe left the big fire
around which the future citizens of Oregon were holding forth
and, making themselves as comfortable as they could within
the Conestoga they'd purchased jointly, fell asleep listening to
the gruntings and bodily moanings of oxen and horses and
that docile giant of an animal, Old Blue.

"That Percheron's just like you, Ben," H.V. laughed. "I tell
you, fate's been at work. Let's get some sleep."

Goffe got himself settled, felt a momentary flash of envy
toward Olivo lying there close beside his young wife, tried to
remember what it had been like when he and Etta had actually
slept in the same bed, gave up on that, and drifted into a
hypnogogic state wherein all manner of strange images floated
up—among these the half-formed vision of Old Blue, clad in
academic robes, standing tall and square-shouldered in one of

the Yale lecture halls and presenting an extremely dull lecture on life among the Houyhnhnms.

At some time before dawn Goffe's snoring awoke Olivo, who at first imagined he was hearing some distant and regular thunder. Then he rose and took a few strides from the wagon for the purpose of relieving himself.

"My God, how many stars there are," he whispered, staring upward at the wide sweep of the prairie heavens. He was certain he'd never seen so many stars before—not even when he was a boy, back in California—except perhaps that time when he and Cousin Califia, the two of them in love, the kind of first love that's oblivious to all difficulties and so sets out to satisfy itself at whatever cost, when they two together crossed the Big Valley and ventured into the river canyons of the mysterious Sierra Nevada. There, in those mountains, H.V. was certain he'd seen, if anything, even more stars than the multitudes which presently burned in pure darkness overhead.

A protracted *yip-yipping* and wailing filled the night, the sounds of what seemed to be fifty or more animals.

"Prairie wolves, God's little dogs, the coyotes," H.V. thought. "Their cries—different from those of timber wolves. . . ."

He experienced a strong sensation of time flowing about him, time like a wind—a dozen years back, the song-dogs on the ridges above Stone Face Falls, there at Hotochruk village on Big Creek in the Santa Cruz Mountains. He had to remind himself that the sounds he was hearing were almost certainly not generated by fifty animals at all, but rather by four or five. That ululating sound—a mated pair howling mouth to mouth. . . .

H.V. returned to the wagon and slipped in past the considerable mound of the sleeping Benjamin Goffe. The night was chill, and H.V. drew a heavy blanket about his shoulders. Roxanne was sleeping profoundly, and he didn't wish to disturb her. He breathed deeply in the darkness and decided to light a cigar.

Shortly before dawn John Dolbeer and Allen Corzine rode away westward.

"I'm in no position to say you nay," Captain Frederick Culhain replied. "Perhaps you gents and the lady would care to join me for lunch? When a man's got a dream, then he's got to follow it. Tell me, though—both of you are college professors and I gather you're fairly well fixed. To leave England and New England respectively, I presume your reasons must be compelling. Me, I'm a professional soldier—but you gents? So I'd like to know—why have you set out to seek the Realm of King Midas? There's danger from the Indians, particularly to your wife, Mr. Olivo. The dangers of the land itself are too well known and numerous for me to list them. Why would anyone give up *everything* for no more than a chance at some great lottery of fate?"

Goffe chuckled and shook his head, his glasses nearly slipping off his nose.

"It's a long story for both of us," he replied, "But you should know that Professor Olivo here is in fact an authentic, full-blooded Indian from California. His father and uncle are owners of what I gather is the largest timbering operation in the territory. So he's merely going home. Me, I've left a few . . . troubles . . . behind me and am intending to write a book and thus secure my fortune."

"I'm keeping a journal myself," Culhain said. "Thick glasses. What happens if you lose them or break them along the way?"

"Two pairs of extras in my luggage," Ben replied. "I presume there are lens-grinders in California."

"Of course, of course," Olivo laughed. "We're not utter barbarians out there, after all."

Culhain studied the faces of both men and then nodded.

Noon of the following day found the Olivos and Ben Goffe well behind Captain Culhain's "C" Company Regulars—for the oxen, even with a lightly loaded wagon, were still no equal in speed to the mounted soldiers.

The sun floated, silver-yellow and disklike, at the apex of a huge and cloudlessly blue sky, and the heat over the uplands above Blue River was intense. But they pushed on ahead, H.V. flicking a lash over the backs of the oxen at times, angry at the big animals for lolling their tongues out so conspicuously, angry as well at Old Blue and the other horses for attempting to bite through their braided leather lead ropes. At length, realizing the folly of attempting to keep up with Culhain's troops—or, more precisely, of attempting to catch up—they relaxed, eased off on the animals, and finally (an hour past noon) came to a small swampy area where a water hole had been dug out. The oxen and the horses drank deeply.

Ben Goffe urged the animals away from the water, fearing they'd become bloated.

"Companions," he said to the creatures, "we most sincerely apologize for the way we've treated you. It was our own foolishness, not any fault of yours. Hereafter we'll simply proceed at our own speed, Cattle of the Sun. Culhain will certainly camp well before sundown, and so perhaps by traveling a few extra, leisurely hours, we'll draw abreast of our leaders. What say you, equines and ungulates?"

Old Blue worked his jaw back and forth as he chewed a mouthful of dry cordgrass, blinked his eyes, and seemed to nod. The other horses brought their ears forward, but the oxen looked sullen and out of sorts—as though perfectly aware that humans had for centuries been in the habit of lying to beasts of burden.

The afternoon wore along, and H.V. squinted up into an oppressive expanse of blue sky, noted half a dozen large, circling birds, and guessed them to be vultures. Beyond an occasional clump of dwarfed oaks in the seemingly endless and undulating sea of dry tallgrasses, the vultures were the only sign of life. The plains glittered yellow-white in the heat, and H.V. shaded his eyes and mopped a red kerchief at his forehead.

"This is a fine place you've brought me to, Homer," Roxanne hissed. "Why is it I always listen to you and do what you say, and then regret it later? There are *lions* out here, isn't that true? My mother and father pled with me not to accompany you to America, and now I realize they were right all along. In addition to everything else, this wagon jolts me to death. I'll be an old, worn-out woman by the time we reach your California!"

"Maybe we ought to abandon the wagon and see if we can convert the oxen into pack animals," Ben suggested. "As it is, the horses aren't doing us a whit of good."

"Possibly we neglected to read the footnotes in some of

those books that told us what to expect along the Oregon Trail," Olivo mused.

The Conestoga jolted its way forward, with the oxen seeming to aim themselves at every chuckhole and rock in the well-worn roadway. Roxanne was cursing under her breath—though doubtlessly cursing in ladylike fashion.

"It's going to be a long trip to California," Ben said.

H.V. burst out laughing.

They drove their animals onward until the prairie sun dropped westward, beyond the farthest undulating wave of tallgrass and broken rock, sunset flaring an immense and dreamlike redness across the face of the earth. Then, realizing they should have stopped a mile or so earlier where the wagon trail crossed through a swale with a running stream and a grand canopy of cottonwoods, they halted, watered the animals from the oaken barrel in the rear of the wagon, and proceeded to make a fire.

Roxanne complained about the dust and made a point of sneezing and coughing several times, but then, as H.V. was preparing to brew coffee, she took the task away from him and proceeded without further comment. Once the coffee was ready and they'd drunk a cup or two of the steaming liquid, everyone felt better about their situation. They ate cold meat and a portion of a loaf of bread.

"Riders coming in!" H.V. said, pointing back down the trail to where four shadowy figures emerged into the thin circle of firelight described by the camp fire—two horses with riders and another pair of pack animals.

"Goffe and Olivo—is that you?"

Corzine and Dolbeer.

The pair of former loggers and future prospectors for California gold brought their mounts to a halt and sat expectantly in their saddles; then Roxanne invited them to share what was left of the supper. Once the invitation had been proffered, however, the two dismounted quickly, partook of hot coffee and cold meat, set their animals to grazing, and threw down their bedrolls.

Roxanne's spirits, her husband noted, had clearly improved. H.V. was beginning to wonder if, indeed, he'd made a mistake in not returning to California *solus*. After all, while he had no compelling urge to put a .44 slug into Allen Corzine, it was possible that Fate had exactly such an action in mind. In the long run, *honor* could very well require a duel.

John Dolbeer was in fine fettle, however, and let them know right away that he and Corzine were not proposing themselves as traveling companions. They'd rejected the notion of either the sodbusters or the argonauts as trail-mates and had decided to go it alone. With an extra horse apiece, they'd concluded, they'd be able to make the best possible time along the emigration route and thus reach the pass through the Sierra Nevada in advance of winter storms.

"Provided, of course," Corzine said, "that the white stuff don't start falling before summer's actually over."

"We'll play it as we go," Dolbeer agreed, "but I think we've got a first-rate chance to make it across, free and clear. For you folks, with that big wagon and all, I'm not so certain. Why limit yourselves with the Conestoga? Since you're not hauling furniture or farm equipment, why . . . ?"

"We're beginning to think that way ourselves," Ben admitted.

Dolbeer inhaled another cup of coffee and then withdrew a banjo from his saddlebags. He sat down on his sleeping roll and plunked a few notes.

"John's going to serenade you." Allen Corzine grinned. "If you get tired of the bellowing, just say so. . . ."

Dolbeer began to sing—his voice untrained and yet quite melodious:

> *I've got a mule, her name is Sal;*
> *Fifteen miles on the Erie Canal;*
> *She's a good old worker and a good old pal,*
> *Fifteen miles on the Erie Canal. . . .*

"Don't know why we gave up on logging," Corzine confided. "The truth is, it wasn't a bad life. John and I didn't actually know each other then, of course, since I was felling up in Canada, and Dolbeer was in New Hampshire until he moved out to Sault St. Marie in Michigan country, where Isaac Stephenson had bought areas of timber on the Escanaba, the Ford, and the Sturgeon rivers—a dollar and a quarter an acre, or so I heard. Guess I ought to let John tell his own story, huh?"

"Is it possible to buy land just for the trees that grow on it—at a dollar and twenty-five cents?" Roxanne Olivo asked. "Is the land worth anything, then, after you've cut down all the trees?"

"For farming or running cattle?" Corzine asked.

"Standard price, standard price for government stumpage." Dolbeer shrugged. "New England timber was something, but hellfire—it's one big forest from the western end of Lake Erie to the western end of Lake Superior and beyond. By God, there's money in logging, I'll tell you. If Allen and I don't take to gold-mining, we're thinking about investigating the Oregon woods. Must be some need for lumber on the West Coast, especially now, with everybody's cousin heading there. One way or the other, we figure to get rich."

Corzine laughed. "We'll be rolling in money by the time we're thirty, and when we're as old as Ben here, we'll own half the West Coast."

"Damned right," Dolbeer agreed. "We can have our own state."

"Well, nonetheless," Ben Goffe grumbled, "this old blind man's going to get some sleep. You young fellows can draw up your maps, but it's been a monstrously long day, and I suspect we're going to have a steady diet of such days until we reach California. Roxanne, you and H.V. take the wagon— I can put my bedroll up next to the big cottonwood. . . ."

Olivo dreamed, but nothing came either rationally or sequentially; in bits and pieces, rather. Himself in front of a class of faceless scholars, himself being hunted by Leather Jacket soldiers, Micheltorena's cholos almost certainly, and the buckeye bushes were in profuse blossom, white wands of flame touching here and there against green hillsides high up among the ridges of the Santa Cruz Mountains, larkspurs and mariposa lilies and the small wild hairy-petaled yellow tulips called kitten ears. Himself as a child, lost in a wilderness without definition or direction, huge canyons splatched with manzanita and yew and digger pines, sun and moon in opposite quadrants of the heavens, then soundlessly vanished into a thick gray hazelike rain. He observed as loggers, hundreds of them, leaped gracefully up onto springboards and began to cut into the red-gray boles of redwood trees, and he came slowly to the realization that each man was dressed identically, and each had the same expression—no, more than that, each had the same face. And the face was his own. Then he found himself listening to cries of birds and knowing certainly he had no idea what kinds of birds they were—even though he was aware he'd once known them all, knowledge now lost to him, intimate knowledge of the wilderness (and his birthright) but taken from him by the polite norms of Englishmen, so civilized and proper and yet, when the hour was right, among the most bloody and violent of humans. And thus he, H.V. Olivo, was able to attend his own funeral, listening to an obscene oration in which the minister alternately trampled upon the cross and inveighed against the California Indios, assuring one and all that corrupt individuals such as H.V. Olivo would ultimately roast in the fires of dread Infiernos. A serpent coiled next to him, the snake wearing glasses and nodding wisely. H.V. heard himself saying over and over again, "I'm sure as hell not dead, that's not me they're burying—you can see I'm not dead, can't you?"

His own protestations awoke him, and he sat up in the darkness. Roxanne continued to sleep, blankets bunched about her throat. She too was dreaming, and her breath came in short gasps alternating with muffled whining sounds. H.V. reached over to touch her, felt her stiffen, pull away from him. He lay back down and stared at the canvas top of the Conestoga, faintly visible—if indeed that too were not merely a product of his imagination.

When the first gray-silver light came, the stars vanishing well in advance of the emergence of the sun, everyone was up and about in preparation for the day's ride. H.V. started another small fire and set the pot of coffee to brewing. Cold meat and coarse bread would round out the breakfast.

Ben Goffe was still attempting to make friends with Old Blue the Percheron, the animal shaking his great head back and forth and displaying large, square teeth. The oxen rolled their lips and snorted, so that small bursts of vapor rose from their nostrils. The horses stamped their hooves on the beaten sod.

Mid-morning brought them to a fork in the trail. An irregularly printed sign, set up on a post with a heap of rocks about its base, read *California this way*.

"Culhain and his troops probably spent the night here," H.V. remarked to Ben Goffe, the latter now riding Old Blue. The Percheron waved his head back and forth, nose toward the west, and whinnied.

From no great distance came an answering cry—the braying of a mule. Then another and another, until the air was filled with a chorus of mulesong. H.V. looked up the trail and discerned both a rider on muleback and a pair of pack mules as well.

"Come along, ye Gawddamned fools!" the rider yelled at them. "Ain't no point in dwadlin' if ye wants to get to Californy!"

"I believe it's the Ancient Mariner," H.V. said to Goffe.

"O'Bragh!" Ben yelled. "Is that you?"

"Of course it's me, ye damned Yengway idjit! Who else would be hyar, waitin' for ye?"

"The old duffer from the bar fight?" Allen Corzine asked. "How in the name of Sweet Jesus?"

O'Bragh used his knees to clap the mule's sides, and the creature began to half-step sideways toward the Conestoga and the three mounted riders. Goffe ran his fingers through his hair and began to laugh.

"Farnsworth, my friend," Ben Goffe said in greeting. "I can't tell you how glad I am to discover that you really exist. I'd half convinced myself that you were part of a bad dream. . . . "

"Wal, that's exactly the way it is, for a fact. Life itself's a dream—ain't ye figgered it out yet? You an' Homer thar, both of ye professors an' all, but don't know nothin'. Ye got bad memories, both o' ye. An' the two tree butchers with ye? Well, all's the same."

"Right, right," H.V. said quickly. "Your name's *Bully*. No offense intended. We're glad to see you, whatever the circumstances. If you know the trail, we're in need of a guide. What do you think, Ben?"

Goffe adjusted his thick glasses, pushing them back onto the bridge of his nose.

"I guess we can make it worth your while, Mr. Bully. Is there some sort of paper to sign or . . . ?"

"Paper ain't worth nothin'. A coon gives his word, that's enough."

"John and I aren't buying in on the old guy's services," Corzine said. "He's going to be more bother than he's worth—that's how it looks to us. Olivo, your wagon's too slow for our blood. We want to get through the mountains before winter hits."

"Yep, that goes for me." Dolbeer nodded. "Not that we don't enjoy your company, you understand. But we've got some serious mining ahead of us, and the sooner we get there, the sooner we can get started."

"You mustn't go off alone," Roxanne protested. "We're few enough as is—and strength's in numbers. You two can't mean. . . ."

"Wasn't planning to ride with you more than a day or two anyhow, ma'am," Corzine shrugged, "though the thought's downright tempting."

"It figgers," O'Bragh said, unsheathing his thin-bladed skinning knife and picking at his teeth with it. "Truth to say, folks, this nigger's surprised to find ye out this far. Me an' Porcupine hyar was on our way to Independence. Thought mebbe ye'd be needing a guide, all right. I know the trail, every bend an' twist of 'er from hyar to Sutter's Fort. You want to hire this Irish Vulture or not?"

Ben Goffe allowed Old Blue's reins to sag, and the oxen shifting in their traces, snuffling at whatever weeds and stubble were within reach.

"What are your wages, Bully?" H.V. asked.

"One way or the other," Corzine said, "count us out. We're not nursemaiding any old coots. We'll see you in California, if you ever get there. . . ."

Corzine tipped his hat toward Roxanne and winked. Then he and John Dolbeer readied their mounts and pack animals in preparation for heading out.

"You can't just let them go!" Roxanne protested to H.V.

"They're grown men, Roxy, and they've got their own decisions to make," Olivo replied. "Now then—about the matter of wages, Mr. O'Bragh?"

The old mountain man nodded, spit through his teeth, put the skinning knife away, and snorted.

"Room an' board an' a leetle grubstake when we gets to the goldfields, I reckon. Now that's cheap, Sonny. Look at 'er this way. The room comes free, an' I figger to do most of the huntin'. So it probably won't bust ye to take this child on. Old as I am, could be I won't be needin' any grubstake, nuther. But if I keel over out in the desert somewheres, ye got to promise ye'll dig an honest-to-Gawd Christian grave for me an' pile rocks on top. Loves coyotes, that I do. But I don't want the leetle brush wolves gnawing my bones, no sir."

H.V. glanced across to where Corzine and Dolbeer were cinching their saddles. For a moment Olivo toyed with the idea of pushing Corzine into some sort of confrontation—pistols, say, at close range. The sonofabitch clearly had eyes for Roxanne. . . . Then he nodded at Ben, noted agreement in the older man's eyes, and turned to Bully.

"It's a deal, grubstake and all. You want a signed contract, Farnsworth, old fellow?"

"Ain't yore word no good?"

Allen Corzine and John Dolbeer, confident of their abilities to handle themselves along the trail, rode out on their own, intent on catching Culhain and his troops. As for H.V. and Roxanne Olivo and Ben Goffe, they soon came to realize the old *Irish Vulture* was in fact, just as he advertised himself, an expert wilderness man. That O'Bragh knew the trail was beyond question—every watering hole, every grove of cotton-woods, every gully, and every outcropping from the Wakarusa River to the Big Blue to the Big Sandy to the Platte. In the evenings Bully would venture off for a short time and inevitably return with game, sometimes an antelope, sometimes a deer, sometimes a brace of turkeys or three or four rabbits or fool's hens.

"Further west," he said, "they's still lots an' lots of bufflers. Folks, I've seen herds of 'em what would take three, four days jest to pass by. I tell ye, there be millions of 'em out thar. Jest don't go pissin' yore pants, lads. Excuse me, ma'am—I'm jest a bad-tongued old coon an' cain't hep it. Time we get up-country, they ain't no way of missin' 'em. Besides, what would the four of us do with a whole damned buffler? No point in carryin' meat when we can hunt it whenever we needs 'er. No sir."

CHAPTER TWENTY-THREE

South Pass

[1849:]

O'BRAGH WAS FOR abandoning the rig and for selling the two oxen at Fort Kearny, but H.V. insisted that Roxanne might not be up to riding horseback.

"Mules, lad, mules. Cows ain't no good but for eatin', real cows nor ox-cows nuther. An' truth to say, they ain't much good for that. Homer, we could be makin' a lot better time without the Conestoga, however much the missus likes it. Winter comes in fast out hyar, an' we're losing good time. Jest seasons, an' them's July, August, an' winter. August be about finished. Ye ought to be able to figger 'er out for yourselves, by Gawd."

H.V. discussed the matter with Roxanne, and the lady concluded she'd be *damned for a London slut* if she'd give up the Spartan luxury of her wagon. O'Bragh shrugged, slapped Goffe on the shoulder, and signaled for the group to move forward. At one point they actually overtook a small band of sour-faced sodbusters, and twice they met groups on the way back—men, women, and children, disillusioned—short-tempered, and beaten.

By late afternoon on the final day of August, 1849, with the temperature running easily over a hundred degrees and the sun lancing mercilessly from an immensity of unmarred blue, they rattled and jolted their way down off the rims toward Fort Phil Kearny.

They slept within the walls of the fort that night, though whether O'Bragh slept or not, H.V. had no idea—for Bully had slipped away just after the evening meal, whether to drink with some of his old mountain companions or to consort with the band of Oto Indians whose small village was assembled just outside the fort itself.

When morning came, O'Bragh did not deliver the expected string of arguments against keeping on with the wagon. Indeed, the old man seemed simply eager to get back on the trail, and Goffe, who had by this time become keenly sensitive to O'Bragh's sudden shifts of mood—periods of what seemed to be depression but lasting for no more than an hour or two of silence—thought best not to question the guide.

Once out of sight of the fort, and with perhaps half a thousand Mormon emigrants visible—many on foot and a few in Conestogas, plus some on horseback, moving along the Mormon Trail to the north of the broad, shallow waters of the Platte River—O'Bragh pulled Porcupine about and waited for Goffe and the Olivos and their oxen to come abreast.

"Guess ye was wonderin'," Bully said simply, "so I'll tell ye. Got family among them Otos, this child has. Had a wife with 'em once, but she's gone to the Spirit World. Name was Wilted Daisy, an' by Gawd that woman could make love all night long, an' that's a fact. After half a year with Wilt, I was a full three inches shorter, an' I ain't talking about height, nuther. Excuse my language, ma'am; it's sorta like I cain't hep myself. Think I probly got it from my Paw. Anyhow, we damned near screwed ourselves to death, we did. She an' me got us two kids. That's who I was visitin' last night. Growed up, of course."

Goffe raised an eyebrow and looked at H.V.

"Two kids in six months?" he asked. "How's that work, Farnsworth, my friend?"

"Not in six months, ye damned fool. I was jest explainin' that . . . Aw, hell, they ain't no sense in talking to dunghead idjits, an' that's a fact, too. Pardon me, Miss Roxanne. I'll try to keep a fit tongue in my head."

At their guide's urging, they traveled from dawn until dark, with Bully forever complaining about how the Conestoga was slowing them down. He predicted rainstorms, howling northwest winds, and sudden blizzards followed by subzero cold. Despite such prognostications, however, the first and then the second week of September flowed on, weather holding under cloudless blue masks and temperatures that reached a hundred degrees by mid-afternoon.

Goffe would wipe at his thick glasses and shake away the beads of perspiration that formed at the tip of his nose and along his chin and that matted a fresh growth of beard about his mouth, cheeks, and throat; then he'd wrap a blue bandanna around his forehead to absorb the sweat. Bully, after a few days of observing the big man's problems with afternoon sun, presented him with an old black felt hat. O'Bragh himself then donned a beaver cap, from all appearances as old and worn as the felt.

"Injun Divvils wouldn't recognize me in that *civilized* headgear anyhow," he said. "Don't want no heathen Cheyennes nor Pawnees nuther shootin' their old friend the Irish Vulture, no sir."

By twilight either H.V. or Goffe accompanied Bully on short hunting forays—a new adventure for the big man, a renewal of nearly forgotten skills for the Cambridge-educated California Indian. Once on foot in the gathering darkness, Bully inevitably managed to find game. At the same time, experienced teacher that he obviously was, he was instructing the two college professors in the arts of stalking and shooting. O'Bragh himself came equipped with a fifty-caliber Hawken flintlock and a matching Hawken flintlock pistol. As to the percussion weapons that H.V. and Goffe carried, O'Bragh considered these *sufficient if ye don't run out o' caps.*

Trajectories, ranges, the proper loads of black powder for this and that kind of hunting—Bully was expert at all of it. His combination of skill and instinct in stalking game, H.V. had to admit, was little short of phenomenal. Perhaps Farnsworth O'Bragh didn't lie as much as the traveling companions previously supposed. Possibly Bully's tale-telling amounted simply to an overly zealous elaboration of the truth. As to the fairly considerable string of scalps, these kept folded away in the saddlebags and bought out only upon occasion (as for Roxanne's benefit), to recount a particular battle or to emphasize a point—well, at least four of the twenty-three were the hair of Whitemen, and that was something that bothered Benjamin Goffe. The Indian scalps, on the other hand, hardly seemed real—no more than a pair of alligator shoes seemed real, or a leopard-skin stole, or a boa of maribou or ostrich feathers.

Roxanne was fascinated and at the same time utterly repelled.

H.V. considered the matter. Wildness, after all, was no stranger to him—he'd grown up in an Indian village, and he'd cut his teeth on hunting and wandering about among mountains where the Spanish Californios never set foot. But O'Bragh represented a different sort of wildness—and a violence that was inimical to H.V.'s nature. The guide had throughout his lifetime apparently been at one with both wilderness and violence, with the result that both conditions seemed to him as utterly normal and inevitable.

But H.V. remembered stories Pelican Doctor had told— warfare among the villages, one expedition northward to fight with the Pomos, prisoners disemboweled or burned alive. . . . Yes, but such things were tolerable back in that indeterminate world that existed before Raymondo Olivo and William Beard came to live among the Hotochruks—before the Mexican Spanish and their string of missions, their attempts to Christianize the Ohlones, their attempts to cut them off from their *savage past*. As to which was better, who could say? With civilization came restrictions, rules, laws, wagon trails, cities, steamships, jails, forests hewn down, mountains swarmed over in the quest for gold.

"The wildness is catching me," H.V. thought as they rode slowly back to their camp that evening, a freshly killed doe slung over a pack mule's back, odor of the gutted carcass insistent in his nostrils. "And I'm not altogether certain whether I hate it or love it beyond all reason. . . ."

That night, as wolves howled nearby, their cries answered

by a shrill chorus of coyotes, H.V. rolled over, face-to-face with Roxanne, and grasped her by the hair—drew her mouth to his. Inexplicably, her momentary resistance to this sign of intended lovemaking was no more than that, and after an instant she opened her mouth and clung to him. Sexual fire flickered through both of them, and Roxanne half whispered and half cried out *hurry, for God's sake hurry!* as H.V. struggled to remove the restraints imposed by layers of nighttime clothing.

When he entered her, Roxanne clamped her teeth onto his shoulder and began to scrape her fingernails down his back in tempo to his repeated thrusts. In her mind a volcano's crater welled up with either fire or blood and was on the verge of overflowing when H.V. shuddered to a stop, and she let out a long wail of disappointment—disappointment that what had been so often promised, the thing of which she had dreamed so often, was once again denied her.

She feigned sleep, and after a few moments H.V. rose, pulled on his clothing, and slipped out of the Conestoga. In his absence, she held the breath tight within her and reached down to where trickling flame was once again rising, a small, intense fountain between her legs, and she touched it and moved her fingers rapidly, moaning softly as she did so.

Outside, H.V. relieved himself as he stared into the starlit darkness from whence the cries of the wolves and coyotes issued. A few feet distant, across the embers of the dying fire, he could see the large, inchoate mound of Benjamin Goffe, asleep on his side, snoring quietly.

"By Gawd, Sonny, ain't the song-dogs somethin'? If this child lives another hundred an' twenty years, he ain't never goin' to get used to it or tired of it nuther. . . ."

On up the Platte they moved, overtaking and leaving behind one band of pilgrims, whose leader assured them that Dolbeer and Corzine were a full day ahead. At the point where the wide, shallow river branched, the emigrant trail continued along the south bank of the South Platte for an additional fifty miles and then crossed the big stream and moved away to the northwest, reaching North Platte at Ash Hollow. Across the river they'd occasionally catch sight of yet more bands of Mormon pilgrims, the well-orchestrated migration keeping to the far side of the river, out of range of possible conflict with whatever *Oregonians* or *Californians* might also be working their way westward.

"Saint Brigham'll force that desert out thar to bloom, by Gawd, jest to spite my old companyero, Jim Bridger, if nothin' else. Jim promised him five hundert dollar for the fist bushel o' corn he could raise—an' I don't think Gabe's paid him yet. This child figgers Brigham's of a mind to set up a whole new country, separate from the United States, jest like he'd told everybody. Mebbe the time'll come when the shootin' match busts loose. My friends back in Kain-tuck, they's always talkin' about it. South'll go one way, Mormons'll go another, an' mebbe the Injuns'll finally have had enough an' band together. If they do that, they can still run yore basic Long Knives right out of the Shinin' Mountains an' the High Plains. The Injuns could do er' all right, an' mebbe they should. Me, I'm of two minds on the matter, but I jest might side with 'em if it ever starts happenin'."

H.V. nodded, took what Bully said with the usual fistful of salt, and slapped the lines over the backs of the oxen. He recalled comments his father and Califia had both made in letters—about the Mormon Battalion and Sam Brannan and the other Saints in Alta California. In the long run, it was altogether possible that Brigham Young's vision was the greatest of them all. Sutter had envisioned a new country, all right, but nothing on the scale of what the patriarch of the Latter Day Saints imagined. Sutter's vision might even have come to pass had it not been for this Gold Rush—a madness that had already drawn, according to reliable estimates, nearly a hundred thousand people into the goldfields.

Then, thinking on the matter further, H.V. yelled out, "O'Bragh! We haven't even *seen* a single wild Indian as yet. The way you keep talking, Roxanne's going to start thinking they're all over the place."

"They is, they is, lad. Wagh! Mebbe we ain't seen hide nor hair of 'em, but that don't mean they ain't seen us. By the Lord's Potato, they'd have to be plum-ass blind not to spy old Ben hyar—unless, o' course, they figger him for a kind o' movin' hillock. No sir. Probably been close enough to count

the hairs in that new growth o' beard the Professor's sprou-
tin'."

Rims along the river now and upthrustings of land from place
to place. At Ash Hollow they'd seen a hundred wild turkeys
and nearly an equal number of pronghorn antelope bounding
away, the birds half flying and half running, the antelope appearing to do the same.

*Ancient Ruins Bluff. Court House Rock. Jail Rock. Chimney
Rock. Dome Rock. Scott's Bluff. . . .*

The sea of grasses gave way in places to short grass and
sagebrush, creosote, thistles, large areas of sand and broken
stones. Still the heat bore down each day, with gusts driving
fine particles of sand. Ben removed his glasses, wiped at his
eyes, and swore silently. It was mid-September, and Bully kept
talking about a time of cold setting in. Instead the days remained uniformly oppressive, the heat a bit drier than it had
been a hundred miles back, but otherwise unchanged.

Goffe's mind drifted.

*July, August, and Winter? I'd give a dollar and a half for some
of that winter right now. In Connecticut the trees are beginning to
turn color, the first flamings of red in the leaves of oak and maple.
Indian summer, rain squalls once in awhile, perhaps a first frost
on the fallen leaves in the mornings. . . . My friend Olivo, I'm
afraid he's got real troubles with that lady of his—not my kind of
difficulties, not yet, but it could come to that. Corzine—she couldn't
keep her eyes off him. She's thinking about England as well—her
home, a long way from here. Me, I'm searching for a new world,
and Homer's going back to the place he was raised. But Roxanne's
in exile. Why she's come along at all's a mystery. . . . Perhaps
she's not so different from Etta. Maybe it's what we do for a living—used to do, that is. We marry our God-cursed books. . . .*

They reached Fort Laramie, a former fur post recently purchased by the United States Government for use as a permanent military post, central headquarters for the protection of
emigrants along the Oregon and California Trails. Old Glory's
fluttering red, white, and blue topped a tall staff.

"Wonderin' about Injuns, was ye?" O'Bragh chuckled,
drawing Porcupine to a halt in prospect of the military post.

"O' course, H.V. hyar's as Injun as a man can get, I suppose, but that's different. Ye're Injun in blood, but a damn sight Whiter'n I am in every other way. This nigger finds hisself ridin' with a pair o' professors, by Gawd, an' one's Injun. What's the world comin' to?"

H.V. gazed across toward more than a hundred hide lodges set up in small groupings just to the east of the fort. Young warriors were riding their ponies about at breakneck speeds (reminiscent, Homer Virgil thought, of himself and Cal and Califia when they were kids), leaping from one side of their mounts to the other (something only Califia had ever been able to do properly), riding backward, grasping braided loops in their ponies' manes (something he and his cousins had never even thought of) and slinging themselves sideways and nearly beneath the pounding hooves. Indian women were clustered about in groups, not all that different from life in Hotochruk, curing meat and making pemmican, scraping hides, talking. Children ran wildly all over the fields, their dogs leaping and chasing.

Blue-coated soldiers rode in formation to either side of a huge drayage cart loaded with split firewood. Other Indian children followed along, pointing and laughing. There were stacks of buffalo hides, brought in—as O'Bragh said—for bartering. A knot of women spread out to its full extent a bolt of bright red cloth, utterly pleased with their recent purchase.

H.V. shook his head.

"Life's different for the tribes out here, that's certain," he said. "There's no resemblance to what we saw in St. Louis. These people have *freedom*."

"For a fact, for a fact," Bully agreed. "What do ye think, Benny? They's Cheyennes, a leetle tradin' party, most like from Leg-in-the-Water's bunch."

"A grotesque name," Roxanne said. "And everybody's half naked. . . . Hasn't your government sent out Christian missionaries to help these people?"

"There have doubtless been missionaries," H.V. said. "In California the church enslaved the people—but not Pelican Doctor's village. That's where I grew up, love, as you know."

"In something . . . like this?" Roxanne asked, a note of incredulity in her voice—as though she were seeing her husband for the first time—as though all the things he'd told her about his family and his upbringing and the people to whom he owed his allegiance were only now fitting into place, making sense. She was horrified.

"Leg-in-the-Water," O'Bragh explained, "he's the big war chief, ye see. The Cheyennes could take Fort Laramie any time they was of a mind to do 'er. It ain't the Yanks what control the Plains, not by a shot. If the Red Divvils wasn't good-natured an' curious, wouldn't be a wagon train as would ever cross over, an' that's a flat fact."

Roxanne heard but didn't accept the guide's assessment. The British, after all, managed quite nicely to control indigenes all over the planet. This being the case, surely even the Americans would manage somehow—if the stakes were great enough.

Ben Goffe nodded and gazed beyond the fort, westward. Far along the skyline, unnoticed until this moment, rose the mountains—high and some sixty miles or more distant. One peak, loftier than the others, was due west.

"The Rocky Mountains," Goffe mumbled. "Bigger than anything I've ever seen before."

Ben thought of the dark form of Mt. Katahdin in Maine, of Mt. Lafayette and Mt. Washington in New Hampshire, of Mt. Marcy in New York.

"Nope," O'Bragh chuckled. "Them's the Laramie Range. Some calls 'em the Black Hills, but that ain't right. Black Hills is north of hyar an' a mite easterly. The big fella, that's Laramie Peak. She's ten thousand, mebbe more. I climbed up thar once, years agone, for a look around. Can see a long way—I recollect that much."

"Then where in blazes *are* the Rockies?"

O'Bragh grinned.

"I'd of thought you two pro-fessors would of studied yore maps some. Don't worry none. We'll be gettin' thar. Wagh! The thing about children—impatient as hell, all of 'em."

H.V. Olivo's Journal, September 16, 1849:

We arrived at Fort Laramie yesterday after an overland journey of more than a month. The trek would have taken longer, but we were able to hire an extremely competent and experienced guide, one Farnsworth O'Bragh, former mountain man and trapper, age indeterminate but certainly not under sixty-five. The venerable trapper has elected for reasons of his own to take Roxanne and me and our friend Goffe under his wing, and we are much the better for it. O'Bragh insists that Roxanne and I must get rid of our wagon and rely instead on mules, such as he has, for carrying equipment. Roxanne will be hard to convince. I believe she's long since decided that her husband's a sheer madman intent upon getting both of us killed by wild Cheyennes—a people, in fact, encamped here at the fort. It's true that we're late in making our way across the mountains and deserts, but thus far the weather has been favorable. Perhaps O'Bragh is one of those persons who invariably presumes the worst; thus anything less dire may be seen as a blessing.

Earlier in our marriage, Roxy and I were quite happy—content on the pittance I made as a tutor and occasional drafts of credit from my father halfway around the world. It grieves me to say that we are not that happy now. Indeed, I shouldn't be astonished if, once in California, Roxanne decides to return to England via shipboard. Hopefully she'll be placated by the mild climate, the beauty of our ocean and forests, and the fact that my family is relatively wealthy and thus able to afford a few of the amenities.

Fort Laramie no doubt has seen the likes of the Sublettes, Henry, Ashley, Chouteau, Bridger, Fremont, and Carson—the latter pair passing through on their way to intervene in the internal political squabbles of California, and so to make the place of my birth an American province. But now the post's owned by the Army, and the garrison here is under orders to protect the emigrant trails, including great numbers of Mormons, who have their own trail to the north of the river.

The land we've passed through is huge, of an unbelievable conformity in most places, marred first by the rising of hills of sand along and to the other side of the Platte, and later by numerous dramatic formations of stone, some of them several hundred feet above the surrounding countryside. These rocks serve as landmarks and appear to be erosional remnants of some earlier age, sometime during which the entire plain must have stood at a height at least equal to these present-day tow-ers. Wildlife is especially abundant. While I've as yet seen only a few small bands of North American bison, there have been endless numbers of deer, elk, antelope, wild chickens, turkeys, cranes, herons, vultures, hawks, and eagles. My cousin Califia would be in her element here—in the sense of her fascination with wild creatures, I mean. Four times we've actually sighted grizzly bears, more silver and white to their fur than the California variety, and if anything somewhat larger. Frontiersmen, true to their reputations, are much given to whimsical lying.

My friend Ben Goffe, a physical giant of a man and yet one with a poet's sensitivities, is going through a process of grief with regard to his own wife—almost as though the woman had died. He does not speak of the matter, but I gather something of genuine import came between them, thus precipitating his decision to remove to California. All in all, he's a most unlikely emigrant. However, his great physical strength makes him a formidable opponent for any man—and his intellectual vision and capacity for intuitive leaps should combine to allow him a very real degree of success in California. I must admit that I feel drawn to the man—as one might be to an older brother or a favorite uncle. There are probably not many like him in California, and I hope we'll be able to keep in touch once we've arrived.

Misty rain drifted in from the northwest. Roxanne sipped at the coffee Bully brought her, set the tin cup aside, and held her hands out over the little camp fire.

"The brew tastes odd this morning," H.V. remarked.

"O' course it do. What this child means is, it jest tastes the way it ought to. I put in a leetle mountain seasonin', so to speak."

"What sort of seasoning, Mr. O'Bragh?" Roxanne asked.

"Couple of things. First, ye put in willer bark strips, dried or green don't make too much difference. Good for the arthritis, it is. An' then comes the second in-gredient."

"All right, all right," Ben snorted, rising and taking a sip from his cup.

"Dried buffler dung, o' course. Wagh! Ain't no coffee worth a damn without 'er. . . ."

Roxanne looked stunned—as though she'd been lashed across the face.

"You put in *what*?" H.V. said after spitting out a mouthful.

Ben stared at what remained in his own cup, shrugged, and decided that whatever Bully had added to the mixture probably wasn't poison. The old man, after all, was pouring himself another.

"Children, children," O'Bragh continued, "I figger ye ought to get some proper duds if ye can afford 'em. Post in the fort'll fix ye up with a buckskin coat an leggings. For moccasins, the best thing's to find an old Cheyenne woman to make 'em for ye, but we ain't got time. Unless, of course, ye'd be interested in winterin' with the Cheyennes an' headin' on to Cali-forny when the snows melt out next spring. Miss Roxanne, skirts has been fine so far. They look real good on ye, an' this child's not complaining. Get ye some britches, heavy shirts, an' a felt hat. If you folks wants to get on across, then you an' H.V. have got to sell that scow o' yours an' dress in a way that's practical."

Roxanne Olivo frowned and turned away.

"I suppose you're going to tell us it's snowing in the mountains right now," Ben said, wrinkling his nose so as to lift the spectacles for an instant.

"Of course it is, ye dunghead. Pardon me, Miss Roxanne. But what in the sweet hell did ye think it were doin'?"

"Snow—in the middle of September?"

"Yep. Listen now. We started upcountry late, an' ye knowed it. Too late. What with that be-Jesus wagon of yours. . . ."

"The Mormons aren't stopping," H.V. noted.

"Nope, they ain't, for a fact. But them folks is jest moseyin' over to Salt Lake. We got six hundred miles of desert after that an' then what could be the worst of all."

"Homer an' Benny!" O'Bragh called out. "Come on over hyar. This old-timer be Big Mouth, an' the two sprouts are called Whirlwind an' White Frog—Morning Star war chiefs all three, an' damned good men to know if ye're ever through these parts again, by Gawd."

H.V. and Ben came forward, nodded, uncertain what to

expect. To their surprise, however, the Cheyennes spoke English—and they did not seem inclined to scalp anyone.

"Our friends, the Pawnees," White Frog said to O'Bragh, "sometimes they have bad habits."

"It is because Antoine Behele leads them," Big Mouth said, the pronounced wrinkles about his eyes and mouth even more noticeable as he spoke, "and he is a Whiteman in his blood."

"What ye coons gettin' at?"

"Two men who say they know you," Whirlwind replied. "The Pawnees have them captive—they were going to burn them to death for attempting to rape a young squaw who was bathing alone in the river. But when Antoine Behele learned the men were friends of yours. . . ."

O'Bragh scowled with puzzlement.

"What be their names?" he asked.

"Corzine and Dolbeer," White Frog replied.

"Jest as well. Them two was up to no good from the start. Make a fair bonfire, most like."

"Can anything be done?" Goffe asked, somewhat taken aback by his guide's apparent lack of concern.

"Rape a young squaw?" H.V. asked. "How could that have happened? Two Whitemen on their way to California—why would they? Allen and John had gold on their minds. . . ."

"My friends hyar, they got horse dung for brains," Bully grinned. "What ye say, White Frog? They any way o' buyin' them two coons out o' their trouble?"

"Perhaps," he said. "The squaw is one that no man really wants. She's married to Behele's nephew, Gray Elk, who is willing to sell her to your friends if they'll take her away from the village. The young Pawnee Loups men believe Sar-a-wit to be pretty, but no one can get along with her. In every village there seems to be such a woman—sometimes more."

"In other words . . . ?"

"In other words," Whirlwind replied, "our friend Behele will allow Corzine and Dolbeer to go free and not be burned to death if the Irish Vulture will promise to take the two of them and Sar-a-wit away from his village. If those men truly intend to go to the Western Ocean, then they will probably never come back. If they take Sar-a-wit with them, then Gray

Elk will be able to marry a woman Behele captured from the Apaches."

Bully yawned and shrugged.

"Way I see it," he said, "yore friend Gray Elk can hitch up with that Apache gal no matter whether the other'n stays or goes. Warriors can have as many squaws as they can afford— ain't that so, now? Always has been that way."

"True, true," Big Mouth said. "But this woman refuses to allow another woman into the lodge. Gray Elk could kill her, of course, but then the Apache girl might not wish to marry him—and besides, others in the village would not like it. The Apache is Behele's captive and lives in his lodge, but his own wives do not want her there. . . ."

H.V. nodded.

"Sounds pretty complicated to me," he said, *sotto voce*, to Goffe.

"So," Bully snorted, "we got to bargain with them savitches to haul Corzine an' Dolbeer's asses away an' not let them or the woman go back. This gal we're talkin' about—is she Pawnee, or . . . ?"

"She was gained in battle," old Big Mouth said. "She was a captive, like the Apache girl."

"Only now she's married to Gray Elk," Bully nodded, "she's got tribal rights, same as anyone else."

"Yes," White Frog said. "If you will do that, then Behele's Pawnees will not have to burn the two Whitemen or turn them over to the squaws for torture."

"Wagh! Burnin's better, no question. Lads, what do ye say? I'm workin' for the two o' ye, so she's got to be your decision, one way or t'other."

"I'm not especially pleased to have Allen Corzine as a traveling companion again," H.V. said, "but I don't suppose we have any choice in the matter. Once we're to South Pass or thereabouts, I presume the two of them will be off on their own again."

"And likely leave their playmate with us," Goffe said. "This business of passing a lady around from one to the other, according to convenience, hardly strikes me as the Christian thing to do."

"Well," O'Bragh said, "them two ain't altogether bad coons,

an' another female might give Miss Roxy a friend to talk with. . . ."

White Frog nodded.

"Yes," he said. "Sar-a-wit speaks English very good. I think maybe she will be glad to go with you to the lands near the Western Ocean."

"Your friends search for gold also?" Big Mouth asked. "There is gold in our mountains. We could show you where to dig, if that's what you wish. Then the Irish Vulture would be able to stay with us this snow and not go searching for the Big Water."

"The Vulture could ride with us when we go to kill all the Crows," Whirlwind added.

"Bloody heathens!" O'Bragh growled. "I told ye, I ain't goin' skulp-huntin' no more. An' if I've told ye once, I've told ye a hundred times: show any Whiteman whar's gold, an' they won't jest be ridin' through yore lands no more. They'll be building towns an' diggin' up the hills, jest like they're probably doing in Cali-forny."

"How much digging could a few Long Knives do?" Big Mouth asked.

"How many beavers can they trap? Answer me that one. Damned near got all of 'em, now didn't they?"

H.V. *Olivo's Journal, September 18, 1849*:

Determined to reach California before the year is out, we have finally concluded that Mr. O'Bragh is indeed correct—we'll be able to make much better time without our Conestoga. Roxy is not pleased, but even she sees the reality of the impingements of time. We proceeded forthwith to the Fort Laramie trading post, where we sold the wagon and acquired a string of mules and a pair of riding ponies, complete with saddles, saddlebags, etc. Between us Ben Goffe and I had brought along two crates full of books, and these we presented to the fort's commandant. As much as the thought pained us, we could see the folly of attempting to transport an additional couple of hundred pounds any farther westward.

Fortunately, the best of my books—that is, those which I'd

found reason to annotate or those from which I taught my classes—are in storage in England, prepared for shipment to California, should I elect ultimately to remain in the land that brought me wailing forth. As to this matter, much depends upon Roxanne. It's my hope, however, that she'll find Alta California to her liking. Much time has passed since I was last there, and much has transpired—revolution upon revolution and then the American occupation. Statehood, all insist, is inevitable; but at present a battle rages in the American Congress as to whether California is to be admitted as a free state or as a slave state.

The three of us—myself, Roxanne, and Ben Goffe—are now clad in frontier-style clothing, primarily leathers crafted by Cheyenne women, and the old Irish Vulture has us wearing moccasins. For me, the present change in costume is in effect a reversion to childhood, in general if not in particular. For Roxanne and Ben, however, the change in clothing marks something much deeper. In all truth, I believe my wife could grow fond of such garb.

"Ye'll get used to 'em, coons," Bully told us—though my attempt to translate his *mountain-yard* patois may leave something to be desired.

The soldiers have already picked up our wagon and oxen, and the quartermaster is due to arrive presently with our mules and trail ponies. We've kept only a handful of our books, and these for special reasons. Goffe was unwilling to part with his *Milton's Complete Poems* and *Fremont's Journal*, while Roxy has clung to her *Pamela* and two or three novels by Scott and a few others by the Bell brothers—Charlotte, Anne, and Emily Brönte. I myself have held back only a beautifully bound edition of *Don Quixote* for my father, a volume with the Spanish on recto and English on verso.

We are due to leave first thing in the morning, with a detour to the southward so that we may attempt to extricate the unfortunate Corzine and Dolbeer. My assessment of the former as having a roving eye was apparently not inaccurate, given the nature of the trouble he's in. If matters rest as Big Mouth, Whirlwind, and White Frog say, the salvation of our erstwhile traveling companions depends upon our willingness to take a squaw named Sar-a-wit with us. Possibly some good may come of all this.

The four of us went downriver from the fort—for the purpose of some target practice. I was pleased to discover that my skill is not diminished. Some things, apparently, once learned are never forgotten. Ben Goffe had clearly used weapons before but displayed no great skill. Roxanne complained that her Colt pistol *jerked too much*. I doubt that she'd ever in her life fired a weapon. Bully insists the skill is necessary as we move on through areas where roving bands of Indians may well prove less friendly than those we've encountered thus far. A certain scar on my back reminds me the danger is quite real. Furthermore, all the High Plains Nations are armed to one extent of another with both pistols and rifles, in addition to lances and bows and arrows.

The sun burst through, and within the space of time it took to ride westward but a few miles from Fort Laramie, the gamma and sweetgrass-patched sandy soil was damp and fresh-smelling; the air alive with the odors of wet vegetation and resins of evergreen, the source of the latter a long stand of scrub cedars along the rim near of the meandering North Platte; the sky opened completely, leaving only a few streams of vapor drifting southward from the high, humpbacked monolith of Laramie Peak.

The upper two thirds of the mountain, to the great amazement of the Olivos and Goffe, was completely white, evergreens along its shoulders draped with snow, the high rock faces glittering, the darker hue of granite visible in only a few places.

"O'Bragh!" Ben called out, "you were right, as certain as thunder. My God it's beautiful, just beautiful. . . ."

Bully turned on his mule, looked back at the two men and the woman who followed him.

"Folks," he said, "ye've got to stop doubtin' me word. If a nigger cain't trust his own guide, then he's in deep trouble. Mebbe I don't never tell the truth, but I don't lie nuther, this child doesn't. Listen now—Miss Roxy, ye hear what I'm hearin'? Homer Virgil, what about you?"

The three of them became aware of a sound that reminded them of thunder—or, Ben thought, of a steam locomotive coming down the tracks, the *New York, New Haven, and Hartford*.

"What is it?" Roxanne cried out. "The ground's shaking!"

"Bufflers! Come on now, let's get to movin'. Up thar on the rim, mebbe we can see what's goin' on. . . ."

With Goffe astride his Percheron and the Olivos on their trail ponies, Bully guided his charges toward the cedar-lined heights. Astride Porcupine, Bully reined in his mount once he'd reached the rim—and then extended his arm outward, his index finger pointing emphatically toward a herd of bison—several thousands of the big red-brown animals, and all in motion at once, the entire herd caught in a frenzy so that the whole seemed to be, in some utterly inexplicable fashion, a single organism of inchoate extent and form, running, running, plunging ahead with wild force and astounding speed, strangely silent and heading southward across the rolling upland toward an undefined destination.

H.V. Olivo's Journal, September 23, 1849:

The "squaw" whom we've agreed to take with us and who's been riding with us for the past several days, apparently in full agreement with the idea of emigrating to California (since that's where she was originally bound, a year ago, before fate intervened), is in point of fact a black-haired, violet-eyed, highly attractive White woman—one taken captive in battle (a party of emigrants had refused to provide Pawnee warriors with "presents"). This particular confrontation with regard to right-of-way along the trail resulted in half a dozen Indian deaths and the demise of the entire party of pioneers, with the single exception of Sarah Witt, whose odd violet eyes seem to have fascinated those who took her prisoner. Subsequently the woman was given to Gray Elk, and he took her for a wife.

However, Sarah, a girl of perhaps seventeen or so, is of a sulky disposition (shall we say) and tends to fits of wild temper—something we've already had occasion to observe. Sarah apparently never did consummate her marriage to the redoubtable leader of the Red Shields and insisted on sleeping on the opposite side of their lodge. When Gray Elk decided to take a second wife, the Apache girl of whom the Cheyenne chiefs had spoken, Sarah flung her husband's prized medicine shield into the fire pit.

I have at least part of this tale from the mouth of the Irish Vulture himself, and he in turn got it from his friend Antoine Behele, a French-Spaniard captured by the Pawnees many years ago but now their war chief. Other portions of the story I've gotten from the principals themselves.

Gray Elk (possibly in desperation) had gone on an extended horse-thieving party against the Comanches to the south and so was absent from the village at the time when Allen Corzine and John Dolbeer stumbled onto the young woman in the act of bathing. Seeing a Whitewoman so disposed, they followed their baser instincts and called out to her. Sarah, in turn, began screaming wildly, and within moments a dozen Pawnees had come to her rescue, in the process taking Corzine and Dolbeer prisoner. The two men were bound to a post, and piles of dead brush and so forth were heaped about them in preparation for a torching.

At this point Gray Elk and his warriors returned to the village—and brought with them more than two hundred Comanche ponies. A celebration was in order, and for a time it was touch-and-go as to whether Corzine and Dolbeer would be released or made the focal point of the celebration. When Dolbeer in desperation mentioned O'Bragh's name, Behele intervened—and thus a message was sent to the Cheyenne chieftains at Fort Laramie—on the presumption that Bully could not be far behind, if Dolbeer was speaking the truth.

At the crucial moment, Sarah was not altogether certain she wished to return to the world of the Whites. She made it plain she was not willing to take either Corzine or Dolbeer as a husband. Indeed, she offered to castrate both men if either should lay a hand on her, and she demonstrated her point by drawing an *Arkansas toothpick*, as Bully called it, and making quick, darting motions with the narrow blade. Corzine assured her that such a thing was very far from his mind and that the same was true for Dolbeer. Both, he said, had sweethearts whom they fully intended to marry, as soon as their fortunes were secured.

"Then this girl'll go to California with you. But no funny stuff from anyone. When I want to hump with a fella, I'll do it. But it's my choice, no one else's. Back in Pennsylvania

Johnny Melthorp got me drunk on cider and tried to hoist my skirts. I used my uncle's goddam walking stick on Johnny, right between the slats, and he never tried to get funny again. I'm willing to work my share, though. I'll be glad to wash pans, do laundry, peel potatoes, or whatever you folks want. Maybe I can sleep next to Miss Roxanne, at least whenever she's not messing around with her husband. . . ."

South Pass: a wide trench valley between ranges, a rise just up from the Sweetwater River, meadows, the actual point of the continental divide difficult to determine, though some of the *Californians* consulted Fremont's Report and recalled that the pass was situated "between two low hills arising on either hand fifty or sixty feet." Nevertheless, if the passage seemed more like a narrow valley rising, all who crossed it must have realized the significance of moving ahead into lands that drained to the Pacific Ocean. South Pass was, without question, the point of no return.

In June of 1849, one emigrant planted an American flag at the pass. A few grown men actually wept. From there Pacific Creek flows southwesterly to Little Sandy and Big Sandy, the combined stream in turn a tributary to the Colorado. Beyond the pass, the going got tough, the trail branching at Sublette's Cutoff, the main route proceeding to Bridger's Fort (and another cutoff heading north) and on to Salt Lake City in the heart of Brigham Young's holy land of Deseret and thence to the north of Great Salt Lake and across Bear River, Little Malad River, and Deep Creek and on to Steeple Rocks near the headwaters of Raft River, there rejoining that portion of the trail called Hudspeth's Cutoff and on to Thousand Springs Valley and across to Humboldt River, a stream that works its way through the astounding desolation of Nevada to the little river's terminus at Humboldt Sink.

Another cutoff led west from Salt Lake City, the Hastings, rounding the point of Stanbury Mountains and crossing Great Salt Lake Desert, pure salt and shimmering mirages, inexplicable playas and muds that mired wagons, the Bonneville Flats—the Hastings Cutoff, Hastings the pamphleteer, luring gullible Easterners to California for years, even before the discovery of gold. The ill-fated Donners had bought it, struggling across the blinding white ancient lake bed, leaving equipment and dead animals in their wake, their eyes fixated on the distant pyramid of a mountain that would eventually be called Pilot's Peak—on their way to starvation and cannibalism, the party locked in terrible snows and cold in the Sierra, stranded there the winter of 1846 and 1847, a lake and a pass named in honor of the horrible fate that had overtaken them.

Sierra Nevada, the snowy mountains, these constituted a last great barrier on the trail to California, the trail to *gold, boys, goddamn gold everywhere*!

The party of seven reached South Pass on the fifth day of October, late in the afternoon, and H.V. rode off by himself as Bully and Sarah were cooking an evening meal of roast venison.

The basin was empty of human population, excluding themselves. But at a distance of no more than a hundred and fifty yards, with ears up and heads forward, a great band of pronghorn antelope stood at attention—perhaps three or four hundred creatures in all. For a few moments they watched the man on horseback; then, as at a signal discerned only by themselves, the antelope were in full flight, bounding as gracefully as jackrabbits—large, horned jackrabbits. And within a few moments more they crested a low rise in the floor of the half-frozen basin and were gone.

H.V. rode for a short distance in the direction the antelope had taken and then pulled his pony to a halt. To the north the Wind River Range already slept under the snows of winter, and, during the day's ride, he'd noted the mountains had been often obscured by bandings of dark clouds. Snow, no doubt, was falling up high—but along the trail there was no precipitation at all, and occasionally the sun came brilliantly through.

Now, however, the peaks burned a dull red-orange rising out of heavy shadows as the sky, banded with long wavings of cumulus and cirrus, flamed brilliantly.

"Astonishing," H.V. thought, "inhumanly beautiful. The Lord paints pictures like this where there's no one to see them—no one but a half-mad Indio-turned-English, riding mindlessly toward a fate he can only guess at. No, not the *Lord*. The only God worth praying to is the Dreamer, the one who conceived all this—deserts and mountains and heaving oceans to either side, glacial islands and tropical forests, Scottish moors and Swiss Alps and California redwood forests—the Dreamer, yes, and his incompetent henchman, Tío Coyote, who's characterized by whim and a black sense of humor, his mischievous nature—*Coyotl God*, the *Quetzalcoatl* of our Mexican brethren to the south—before they forgot who they were, at least—Old Man Coyote, vice-gerent to the abstract, dreaming, Creating Principle. Creation's imperfect, but the ultimate Creator's without flaw. In one swoop of sublime intuition, these Western Bedouins (and I am one of them) came effortlessly to terms with the presence of evil in the world, a world nonetheless engendered by an all-powerful, all-knowing, and moderately beneficent God, a Great Manitou, an Omnipotent Dreamer, neither enforcing nor permitting any Satanic principle. Nor is there need for such concepts as those of Sin Original or Fall from Grace, be that fall *fortunate* or otherwise. Within the *Gospel of Old Man Coyote*, the matter of an afterlife as well makes perfect sense and seems in accord with the world as it is, as it may be observed by any human creature conscious enough to look at it. Those who die simply wander off to a Spirit World, stepping from Pico Blanco or Monte Diabolo or some other convenient high place onto the Star Trail that leads across the night skies. There's no Hell, no Purgatory, no Heaven such as the Christians conceive of those realms. Humans and birds and even animals and fishes—and probably insects, reptiles, and vegetation—all these find their way to Other Side Camp, a strangely Platonic condition where life goes on endlessly. . . ."

Ben Goffe, or so H.V. construed from talking with the former Yale professor, was an exponent of free will, self-determination, and Protestantism—a disciple of John Milton, the great Christian scholar and poet. Bully O'Bragh, on the other hand, Whiteman though he might be, was a kind of fundamentalist spokesperson for Native American religious awareness, at least as that awareness existed on the High Plains. With the thought in mind of drawing those two worthies into a discussion of matters of God and Nature's God, then, H.V. thumped his heels to his pony's sides and set off toward camp, where by now Bully and *Sar-a-wit* would have dinner ready.

CHAPTER TWENTY-FOUR

Cali-forny

[1849:]

"O' COURSE THE varmints has got spirits," Bully said. "When we kill 'em, we pray for their souls, don't we? Danged rights. An' that's so they'll be able to get on into the Spirit World."

"As I understand the matter," Ben said, adjusting his glasses, "these prayers assist the animals in finding their way to the Happy Hunting Grounds so that they may eventually return as animals—again to be slain for food and clothing."

"Ye're gettin' it. Look now—it's the Spirit World, not no *Happy Huntin' Grounds*. You college pro-fessors made that one up. Spirit World's jest a different place, like this one sort of, but without no real boundaries. It's a place where coons go, is all."

Roxanne was staring at Allen Corzine, who was, in turn, staring at Sarah Witt. Sarah held one hand to each cheek and leaned forward.

Dolbeer was whittling on a stick—but exactly what he was carving was indeterminate.

"The good man goes there," H.V. said. "Pelican Doctor loved to tell the stories. Once in the Spirit World, the good person continues in goodness, enjoying his existence just as he had in life. Beyond all this, he isn't rewarded, and the Great Dreamer makes no demands upon his fealty. In fact he doesn't even ask for it. To tell the truth, the Great Dreamer isn't even there. But Other Side Camp has a head chief, just as the villages on earth do."

"She's probably all the same everywhar," Bully remarked. "Makes sense, don't it? If a coon's bad hyar an' now, he punishes himself. An' he goes on doin' the same thing in the Spirit World."

"And yet in this world," Goffe interjected, "those who are evil often seem to thrive—taking advantage of their moral superiors. The race is not to the swift, nor the battle to the proud, as the Preacher once remarked."

"This nigger don't have no truck with preachers. But if a coon's crooked enough, he can get rich," O'Bragh agreed. "Still and all, in an Injun village, *rich* ain't the same thing. One day a child's got ponies, an' the next day he don't. But if his companyeros trust him, why, that's worth summat."

"Through it all," Ben continued, "this *Omnipotent Dreamer* continues to dream? And he awakens from time to time with messages for Old Man Coyote, the latter charged with tending to the changes in the Grand Plan but often, having his own fish to fry, extremely careless in matters of manufacture. Imperfection, then, is caused by creative shortsightedness? Evil, as Christians know it, doesn't exist—has never existed. But some things are much better than others. . . ."

"Speak English, Sonny. This child never larned no Portagee, or whatever it is ye been talkin. But I'll toll ye this much—it's a damned sight better to hump with an experienced fe-male than with any scared virgin. Excuse me, ladies. Like I say, I was born with a bad tongue. But to continue—she's better to hump with either one than with your basic she-grizzly. Sow grizzlies, in turn, is better'n moose ladies, an' not so dangerous. One time this child married a griz an' lived with her for a year or more. We had us two . . . cubs, I guess ye might call 'em."

"Oh, horse pucky!" Sarah exclaimed, certain now that she'd been taken in. "I don't think you'd do such a thing, Bully."

"Of course he would," Corzine laughed. "Old guys like Bully'll screw anything if it's still warm."

"Mr. Corzine," Roxanne said, shaking her head, "your language is disreputable. There are ladies present. . . ."

"Excuse me," Corzine said quickly. "Never thought of it that way. But if you want to find fault with someone's lingo, then jump on O'Bragh."

"Figgered ye'd say that," Bully complained. "Hellfire, if you boys hadn't of said ye knowed me, ye'd of been charcoal by now, an' ye know it, too."

The sundown, with its astonishing beauty, was long since past—and the autumn heaven was shotgunned with stars, points of white against gray-blackness, but lighter in the southeast, where a full, pale white moon had just risen above the horizon. Night subsumed the glittering peaks of the Wind Rivers and transmuted the forms of clouds. A screech owl called out, *kit-kit-kit-kit-twirrrrrrr, kit-kit-kit-kit, twirrrrrr . . .*, and for an instant H.V. found himself translated backward through a haze of years, thirteen years back, to a night of August drought when tree frogs chittered, dry leaves rattled in close darkness, and a covey of quail let loose little red strings of question marks that shimmered in the darkness.

Hold me tight. I have dreamed this moment over and over, and yet I don't know what to do. I want you to . . . take me. I am yours. . . . It's time for me to become a woman now. A girl needs a teacher—you must show me what to do, Homer Virgil. I'll do whatever you tell me.

Was this, then, what he was returning to? The true and root and absolute reason he was being drawn back? He was returning to the place where he and his cousin had committed . . . what? Incest? Or merely a violation of that bond of trust which had united the two of them throughout their childhoods? H.V. realized tears were coming to his eyes. He excused himself from the little social group arranged about the fire and walked into the night—as if under necessity of relieving himself.

It was all . . . beautiful. Califia had been merely a part of it, a kind of metaphor of the wildness from which he had been banished some thirteen years earlier—banished into a world of civilized graces and civilized vices.

Behind him, bathed in moonlight, lay the drainage of the Sweetwater, a stream that, joining and joining, would ulti-

mately make its way to the Gulf of Mexico and hence into the
Atlantic Ocean. But before him, downslope a few hundred
yards, oozing from marshy springs, rose a stream called Pacific
Creek. These waters, Olivo knew, would flow on to join with
Big Sandy and Little Sandy and finally the Green River, the
Seedskeedee as O'Bragh called the river, a main branch of the
Río Colorado, which found its way through nearly endless
mazes of canyons to the Gulf of California, the Sea of Cortez,
and the Pacific Ocean.

Behind him lay the American East, the Atlantic Ocean, the
familiar, civilized world of England—England, that troubled island nation whose tentacles stretched out and were intent upon
securing the greatest empire ever known, a world of books
and manners and proper ways of doing things—a world that
had transformed him through the course of these past thirteen
years from what he had been, a kind of quaint *savage* out of
the pages of Jean-Jacques Rousseau, into the cultured, confident young professor of language and literature at Cambridge
University.

Ahead of him lay deserts and mountains and a land called
California, the homeland from which he had grown estranged,
a place where men were reputed to be plucking nuggets of
gold out of the sandy bars of rivers that flowed down from
the mysterious Sierra Nevada, the very place to which he and
Califia had attempted to flee. Perhaps fortunes in pure gold
had lain all about them. . . .

Homer Virgil Olivo found it strangely difficult to breathe.
He sucked in the brisk night air and wiped at his eyes. Suddenly aware that someone was close beside him, H.V. turned
about—even gave thought to drawing the Colt-Patterson revolver he wore strapped to his leg.

"It's a glorious night," Ben Goffe said quietly. "I feel as far
away from Connecticut . . . and my wife . . . as I imagine I
would if I were on a different planet. Do you suppose there
are places like this one on Venus or Mars, Homer?"

"Other Side Camp?" Olivo managed. "By God, Big Benjamin, maybe that's where it is."

"Christian or heathen," Goffe replied, "it would be a good
place. There's something about this huge, almost desolate land
that's sufficient to turn a man *ecumenical*."

The farther west they traveled, the more nearly obsessed O'Bragh became, the old man up before dawn each day and seemingly unwilling to halt even when darkness had fallen.

"Days is gettin' shorter," he kept saying. "Want to reach the goldfields, don't ye? Corzine thar does—I can see it in his eye. Quit moanin' in yore beard, Goffe. Wagh! Ye an' Homer fuss more'n any six old women."

In truth, of course, H.V. and Ben weren't fussing at all. Bully's predictions of the fierceness of mountain weather and its tendency toward sudden changes had been borne out more than once. Already they'd been obliged to push ahead through snow a foot deep in places. For this reason O'Bragh had elected to take Sublette's Cutoff to Soda Springs at the big bend of the Bear River rather than proceeding to Fort Bridger. Bully had been keenly looking forward to seeing Jim Bridger, a man he referred to either as *Gabe* or as *Blanket Chief*, and so the taking of the shorter route was apparently seen as a necessity.

The ground at Soda Springs was frozen hard beneath three or four inches of crusted snow. Here they met a wagon train, some twenty Conestogas and nearly a hundred human beings, their equipment in bad repair, their food supply scant, and their spirits low. Bully, H.V., and Ben talked briefly with the leader, a Virginian named Hodges—with the thought in mind that young Sarah Witt might be better off with the larger group. Indeed, Corzine and Dolbeer seemed engaged in a kind of competitive struggle with one another for Sarah's favor, and Bully feared trouble on down the line.

Yet another solution, Bully suggested to H.V., was that of convincing Allen Corzine, John Dolbeer, and Sarah all to attach themselves to the wagon train.

The surprise came from Sarah herself:

"Look here, Bully O'Bragh, you ain't fobbing me off on this bunch of sodbusters. Gray Elk and Behele give me to you and Homer over there, and you're honor-bound to keep me on. I'm doing my share, ain't I? Damned rights I am. And this girl's not of a mind to go to Oregon. It was a place like that I come from in the first place—nothing but farmers with no sense of excitement and no imagination. That's what got them all kilt, if you want to know the truth."

Bully looked stern, but Ben Goffe burst out laughing.

H.V. shrugged.

"Pet rattlesnake," he chuckled.

Corzine and Dolbeer, perhaps sensing the arrangement that was being discussed, strode quickly to the conference site. Corzine took off his hat and extended his hand to Hodges.

"Can't let her go," Corzine said, "no matter what O'Bragh has to say. I'm fixing to marry this little lady. . . ."

Dolbeer stared in disbelief at his compatriot.

"Are you astin me?" Sarah demanded.

"Guess I am at that." Corzine nodded. "Well—will you, or not? Maybe you'd rather have John here."

"He ain't ast me." Sarah grinned, glancing at Dolbeer.

Dolbeer seemed unable to think of anything to say.

"All right, then, I'll marry you, Allen. And I'll make you a damned fine wife, too."

To the astonishment of all present, the two of them just stood there, the diminutive, sandy-haired girl, hands on hips, staring up at the lanky, bearded Allen Corzine.

"Ain't you supposed to kiss the lady—or something of the sort?" Hodges asked.

"Not till we're married," Sarah said—and said so firmly that the matter could only be judged settled.

"Wagon master can hitch folks, cain't he?" Bully demanded.

"I have that authority," Hodges nodded. "But this has hardly been a sufficient engagement. The young lady just now agreed to the gentleman's proposal, and—"

"If you want me, Allen Corzine," Sarah Witt said, "then marry me now. I ain't damaged goods, even if I was married to old Gray Elk—because I wouldn't let him get into my britches, even though he threatened to cut off my nose. I told him if he tried to force me, I'd find a way of hacking off his plaything, and I meant it, too."

"You got a *Bible*?" Corzine demanded.

Bully gave Hodges some perfunctory advice about holing in for the winter and then, as if realizing his words were not being attended to, passed on some information about the existence of hot springs twenty miles to the west, on Port Neuf

River, a place were game might be expected to be more plentiful.

With that, and with the wedding of Mr. Corzine and Miss Witt a *fait accompli*, the small party pushed onward, taking Hudspeth's Cutoff to Raft River, where the Oregon Trail forked north and the California Trail drifted southward, upstream along Cassia Creek and thence to the headwaters of Raft River and on across to Goose Creek and thence to the Humboldt River, the *Mary's* as O'Bragh called it, a small desert stream whose branches rose high in the great stony wall of the Ruby Mountains west of Thousand Springs Valley.

The antagonism that had been growing between Corzine and Dolbeer, and which H.V. fully expected would intensify in the aftermath of the fair maiden's having chosen her champion, did not. Indeed, the girl and the two men seemed, if anything, even closer than they'd been before.

"Has the little hussy married both o' them?" Roxanne asked her husband as they lay huddled together for warmth—physically closer now than they'd been in quite awhile.

"Perhaps," H.V. replied, struggling to remain awake after the unexpected bit of lovemaking that Roxy had just precipitated.

"She's hardly a sufficient wife for Allen Corzine," Roxanne said. "For John Dolbeer—well, perhaps so. I can't imagine what came over Allen. . . ."

H.V. felt a momentary twinge of annoyance with his wife, her familiar use of Corzine's name, but the issue was not, he concluded, worth waking up for.

The date was now the first of November, 1849. Intervals of daylight were growing rapidly shorter, and the nights had become exceedingly cold. The few Indians they'd seen in this land of gaunt, bony mountains of red-gray rock and sparse vegetation seemed to H.V. the most miserable of creatures, their lodges often nothing more than overlaced heaps of brush above shallow pits in the earth. Any resemblance, Olivo thought, to the noble Cheyennes and Utes and Mountain Shoshones they'd seen earlier were purely coincidental—and the contrast to the Ohlones of Hotochruk village, as he remembered them, was equally stark.

"It's the land does it to 'em," O'Bragh said. "Ain't none of 'em had horses until jest a few years back, and mostly they ain't even got knives an' guns. Wicked with the bow an' arrow, though. Use rattlesnake pizzen on the flint tips, they do. More than one old boy's gone under because he underestimated a *Shucker*, I'll tell ye. By Gawd, they can live where nothin' else can, human or animal. Loves crickets an' grasshoppers an' grubs, they do. We never cotched beavers out hyar because the gawddamned Shuckers ate 'em all, for a fact. When Bonneville's bunch come through, Meek an' Walker an' them was lucky to hang on to their topknots."

For a short time, as they rode along through this half-frozen world, H.V. contemplated Rousseau's grand postulation of the *Noble Savage*, a concept that some in England and France had chosen to apply to H.V. himself, and one which might well apply in different fashion to the Cheyennes, for instance, but which seemed to have little to do with the Humboldt River Shuckers. Then, for a time, Olivo considered Thomas Hobbes, who insisted the basic condition of man and his temporal span was best described by the phrase *short, brutish, and nasty*.

"Why don't these people go somewhere else?" Goffe demanded. "They aren't obliged to live in this . . . wasteland . . . are they?"

"O' course not," Bully laughed. "Jest proves their *character*. I figger they like it hyar. Ain't no reason they'd stay, otherwise. Lads, right times of the year, an' these mountains is the most beautiful in the world, more or less. Desert's somethin' ye got to learn to love. I've seen the mornin' sunlight make the whole place seem like a soft fire was shinin' through things, by Gawd! No other place I know of whar it's that way, no sir."

"Farnsworth," H.V. laughed, "I believe there's actually a poet hidden back in your skull somewhere."

"What you just said—it sounded like poetry," Roxanne agreed, "except that it didn't rhyme."

"Poet?" Bully snorted. "Poet in a mule's ass-end. No offense, Miss Roxanne. Ye know how it is with me. No offense to ye, nuther, Porcupine, old beast. Didn't mean that, exactly. I'll tell ye, ye won't find me readin' none of that *Milton* stuff, no sir. Okay for ye, mebbe, but not for this child. Same's true for Wordswords and yore Lord Byron to boot. Besides, it don't take no poet to see that things jest *shine* sometimes—if ye know how to look at 'em, that is."

The conversation was halted due to the fact that they'd reached a point where it was necessary to ford the Humboldt, and the five men and two women drew up their respective mounts.

On the far side of the stream was an old woman. Apparently she'd been looking for pieces of firewood along the river's edge, but now she stood straight and watched the little band of emigrants.

H.V. glanced at Bully and realized the mountain man was entranced.

"By the green balls of Jesus, ain't she somethin' now? Thar's a proud woman if I ever seen one. She ain't no more afraid of us than a blue jay is of a crow. Lord, look how she holds herself, straight as any arrow. An' I got a haunch she's livin' by herself—leetle lodge up thar ain't big enough but for one. Ye see it?"

H.V. Olivo's Journal, November 3, 1849:

I write this in the most unlikely of places and, indeed, the most unlikely of times. Roxanne, wrapped like a mummy in red, is huddled beside the camp fire—sage and juniper wood, quite aromatic and something I might appreciate more under other circumstances. Ben Goffe is off walking—or possibly hunting, inasmuch as he's taken his rifle with him.

Allen Corzine and his new bride Sarah, as well as John Dolbeer, have left us behind and have gone westward toward California on their own.

The river before me is nearly frozen solid, for last night's temperature dropped far below the zero point, though how far I do not know, having no means of measuring. But it was a cold such as I have never before in my life experienced—the air extremely dry and numbing. When I awoke this morning just before dawn, I found that when I spat, the saliva froze almost instantly upon touching the ground. Benjamin Goffe looked almost the part of a huge St. Nicholas, for his breath had deposited ice crystals all over his beard.

The terrible cold has ameliorated now, and the temperature has risen to zero or so. For the sun is up, a thin white disk at first emerging from the back of the Ruby Mountains to the southeast, between high peaks known as Hole in the Mountain Peak and Ruby Dome. The sky is faultlessly blue from horizon to horizon, and the aspens along the frozen river are an intense hue of gold. These quaking aspens live up to their name, for even the slightest motion of the air sets every leaf into nervous movement.

The remainder of the world hereabouts, however, is an extended composition of gray and white, the latter being snow, drifted to but a few inches, in other places the land being swept quite bare, except for the endless growth of sage. The far mountains are purple at their bases and stunningly white higher up, where the snow appears to be of considerable depth. I doubt that it all melts, even during the summer.

Pronghorn antelope and deer are plentiful, having no apparent difficulty in securing forage in this hostile land. The long-eared western hares, jackrabbits, are everywhere in astonishing profusion. Despite the predations of coyotes and wolves and the local Indians, the numbers remain beyond counting.

This place, however beautiful, is no place to spend an early November interlude. The culprit is one Te-moak woman, in her sixties I'd guess, a widow whose husband died of rattlesnake bite several months past. She lives alone in the most wretched hut and is apparently waiting, in all good humor, for death to overtake her also and deliver her into the Spirit World. To complicate matters, however, Farnsworth O'Bragh has fallen in love with her, the lady's name being, roughly translated, *Rabbit-chaser*. Bully's determined that she must accompany us on our continuing journey to the land of El Dorado.

At present he's courting her, though I gather she's fairly determined to stay and await the Grim Reaper. O'Bragh's stubborn, and there's strength in that quality. I suspect he'll have his way with her at last. Here's a bit of his language, as nearly as I can render it:

"Gawd save me Irish soul, this child's in love again. Happens to me about this time every year, I don't know why. Seems like a coon ought to fall in love in the springtime. Guess my rutting cycle's out of whack, or summat."

Thus Ben Goffe and Roxy and I had the choice of going on ahead with Dolbeer, Corzine, and Sarah—or of waiting for Bully to accomplish his purpose.

In the meanwhile, I should record an account of a singular valley through which we passed some several days since. It's called City of Rocks, and it's marked by exceedingly numerous jutting formations of light gray decrepitating granite, the whole to the extent of two miles by perhaps half a mile. Earlier travelers have marked some of these, according to their fancies, as "Napoleon's Castle," "City Hotel," and "Sarcophagus Rock." Many are marked with names and initials of various emigrants, the letters simply scratched into the lichens or daubed on with tar. The day we passed through this place was gray and windy, with steam rising from the various formations—mist, I should say. At that moment, had I been allowed to rename the spot, I'd have called it CITY OF DIS. On reflection, however, I think I was most reminded of an ancient Druid remains, such as Stonehenge and other similar places in England. But this one, much grander in scale, was built by none other than Old Man Coyote, the ever-present creating principle in these Western lands.

The fire has burned down while I was writing—and so I must close this entry in deference to the practical necessity of gathering more fuel. Roxy's expression indicates that I must not put off the venture any longer.

H.V. Olivo's Journal, November 4, 1849:

It appears that Bully's suit for the hand of the fair Rabbit-chaser has prospered, for the two of them now declare themselves married and may even, for all they will tell us, be thinking of having children. It's no longer possible for anything O'Bragh does to surprise me, and indeed Benj. Goffe has declared the man officially among the Olympian *immortals.*

I spent a portion of the morning target-practicing—the drawing of my weapon from its holster and then the firing at a particular rock formation some thirty or so feet distant. There was a time in my life when I was fairly skilled at this sort of thing, and nearly as accurate as my cousin, Califia.

It is very difficult for me to come to terms with the reality of actually seeing her again, conversing with her, etc. What we shared more than a decade ago is gone and must not even be brought up, for the better of all concerned. Califia is married, as the last letter from my mother and father indicated, to a man considerably her senior—an old friend of Dad and Uncle Bill, as it turns out. But it will be odd for me to address her as *Mrs. Flowers.*

Presumably, we will leave within an hour or two, and so I had best attend to the horses and mules. Oddly enough, the mules have taken a great liking to Goffe's Percheron. At night they huddle close to Old Blue, who seems quite pleased with his status among them. The other horses, however, are not so sociable.

Though I have no great fondness for Allen Corzine, I hope that he and his wife are well—and of course John D. also. I harbor the odd intuition that our paths are fated to cross again, and possibly more than once.

By the 12th of November, the little caravan consisting of three men, two women, one very large horse, a pair of normal-sized horses, one mule named Porcupine, and several pack mules reached Lassen's Meadows, where Peter Lassen's northerly trail cut away from the Truckee-Carson route. O'Bragh, however, was having no part of the alternate route.

"First off," Bully said, "the damned fool's real name is *Larrson*. An' in the second place the man's a pure fool. If ye wants to take a good look at Black Rock Desert, then that's yore road. An' if ye've changed yore mind an' wants to go up into Oregon country, she's all right too. I'll tell ye whar it goes. North, that's where, an' crosses Fandango Pass, which ain't even the Sierra Nevada no more. Then it wanders around through one canyon or another, headin' almost straight south again, past Larrson's Volcano an' finally down to Larrson's Rancho. Coons what go that way finally figger it out, by Gawd. After goin' three hundred miles out of their way, they reach the *Rio Sacramento*. Then they find out she's still another hundred miles an' more to Sacramento City, an' close to another hundred from thar to the goldfields. No sir, we ain't goin' that way."

Goffe grinned at Bully's outburst.

"Did one of us suggest the northern trail?" he asked. "Professor Olivo, perhaps? Or are you listening to the voices of the birds again?"

O'Bragh took off his beaver cap, glanced at Rabbit-chaser, the latter's gaze fixated on her husband.

"Guess ye didn't at that. I done misjudged the lot o' ye."

"Well, straight ahead then!" H.V. laughed. "We're going through where the Donner Party froze to death, I take it, and ended up eating each other?"

"Sounds like jolly good sport," Roxanne said.

Bully whistled and slapped the stock of his Hawken.

"Now ye got the idee. She's not a bad pass so long as ye ain't pullin' wagons, an' the heavy snows ain't come yet."

"What's all that white stuff up on the mountains, old friend?" Ben queried.

"Snow, o' course, ye dunghead idjit. Didn't they teach ye nothin' at that there Yale College?"

On November 16th they reached Truckee Meadows, where they met a group of ragtag would-be *Californians*, forced to halt in the quest for the goldfields. The group's scout had come back with a report of twenty-foot snowdrifts choking the pass.

"Who's this *scout* o' yores?" O'Bragh demanded of the dark-haired, mustache-sporting individual named Lemuel Hollings.

"Fiddlehead Wilson's his handle," Hollings replied, "the stubbornest old sonofabitch I ever ran into. Said we should abandon our rigs and move ahead on snowshoes, for Christ's sake. Me and the boys didn't see it that way, and the old buzzard left us. He even demanded we pay him full amount of his contract—threatened to stick a knife into me. Well, we kept our word—as much as he did. Gave him half wages, and he rode off to the west, along with a couple of gents that caught up with us, them and a slick little piece of goods they were likely sharing. Probably all four of them are frozen stiff as boards up in the Sierra by now."

"Wagh!" O'Bragh grunted. "I know the coon, by Gawd, an' the other three as well. Ye should of listened to 'im, Hollings. Fiddlehead's as good a trail man as there be. Time ye wait for spring to cross the mountains, ain't goin' to be no gold left in Cali-forny."

"Gold's no good to dead men," Hollings said. "We heard about those Donners. We're thinking about heading south, around the mountains."

"She's a long way, but could be you're right at that. You boys don't happen to have no whiskey with ye, now do ye? I'll pay for it, United States money. Got a powerful dry, as it turns out. . . ."

Goffe shrugged and accepted the inevitable delay.

"Corzine, Sarah, and Dolbeer have apparently gone on across," H.V. told his wife, "even though word has it the snow's twenty feet. Looks to me like we've got problems."

"Too late on the trail," Ben agreed. "Well, we knew that all the time. The question is, what in the devil do we do now? Snowshoeing across the Sierra doesn't strike me as a viable alternative to. . . ."

"What?" Roxanne asked. "We can't very well stay here until March or April or whenever the snow decides to melt."

A big fire was set to blazing, and an entire antelope was roasted for the occasion. O'Bragh clearly intended to spend the evening regaling the greenhorn Argonauts with all manner of tall tales—bear-fights, Indian-fights, and the like. Bully, with Rabbitchaser sitting stiffly beside him and understanding precious little of what her husband was saying, cleared his throat, lit his pipe, and began to hold court. The official subject for the evening, as H.V. might have guessed, was that of various trappers and parties of emigrants getting stranded in the snow.

Roxanne listened with some interest, but H.V. was more concerned with the potential danger this gang of men—*gang of thieves was a better term*—might pose.

Bully, however, didn't seem concerned—or perhaps it was simply that the appeal of being the acknowledged raconteur was so great that danger hadn't occurred to him. At the point where Jim Clyman got lost in the snows for the second time, however, Roxanne began to doze off. H.V. nodded to Goffe and guided the nearly somnambulant Roxy back to the place where they'd pitched camp. H.V. checked the cylinder of his Colt-Patterson, placed the weapon where he could easily get at it in case of need, and lay down beside his wife. In fairly short order both of them were sound asleep.

When H.V. awoke shortly before dawn, a thin, cold rain had begun to fall. He rose, chewed on a piece of unleavened bread, and looked about for O'Bragh—half supposing he'd have

to stir the venerable mountaineer into life after the previous
night's late drinking and tale-telling. Rabbit-chaser was fixing
breakfast, warming strips of dried meat over the flames and
brewing a small pot of coffee—something Bully had showed
her how to do a week earlier and at which she was now quite
adept. Ben Goffe stood next to the fire, warming his hands.
But wherever Bully was, he was not close by.

"Off relieving himself," H.V. thought, "or else vomit-
ing. . . ."

Goffe moved over to check his equipment. He cinched Old
Blue's saddle, the huge horse nibbling his beard in the process.
H.V. joined the big man, and together they readied the remainder of the animals. With this task complete, they walked
back to the fire.

A few minutes later a somewhat wide-eyed Rabbit-chaser
gestured toward the camp of stranded miners. The men were
up and about, with Hollings and half a dozen others standing
together in a knot, staring fixedly toward Rabbit-chaser, Ben,
and H.V.

Roxanne, still somewhat dazed with sleep, walked toward
the fire—the idea of hot coffee very much on her mind.

"Trouble," Rabbit-chaser whispered. "Owl-face men want
something. . . ."

H.V. was surprised at the Te-moak woman's use of English,
for he hadn't previously heard her speak. Apparently Bully had
been using his spare time to instruct his new wife in the rudiments of the Whiteman's lingo.

"Where's Bully?" H.V. asked as he glanced over toward
Ben. "Does he know? What trouble, Rabbit-chaser?"

The Indian woman didn't look directly at him but whispered the word "money."

Hollings and his friends began to amble casually toward
the fire, spreading out somewhat so as to form a loose half-
circle.

"What's on your mind, fellas?" Ben called out, at the same
time trying to recall if the caps were in place on his Walker
.44 revolver, assuring himself they were, and wondering further if he actually had the nerve to use his weapon, should
necessity require it.

"Where's the old buzzard?" Hollings asked. "We figure you boys owe us something for last night. . . ."

"What did you have in mind?" Ben replied, lowering his right hand in case he should be required to go for his revolver.

"Depends on what you're carrying." Hollings grinned, at the same time withdrawing a pistol from his coat. "The little split, maybe—that ought to even things up. Me and the boys wouldn't mind using her for a spell. . . ."

Ben glanced at Rabbit-chaser and at H.V., the latter motioning Roxanne to stand behind him.

"We've got cash," Ben said. "Name your price and we'll pay it. You leave the young folks alone. Best you stop right where you are, Hollings. Come any farther, you'll have to go through me. . . ."

"Big talk for a blind man . . ." Hollings was saying when Olivo's pistol spit fire, the slug catching the Argonaut below the collarbone and sending him howling to the ground.

An instant later the heavy crack of a Hawken rifle sounded, and another miner sagged forward and sprawled motionless, face down on the frozen earth.

Ben Goffe had his weapon in hand and was firing, firing.

Men dived for the scant cover available. . . .

Olivo pushed Roxanne to the ground, shouted at her to stay there, and leaped forward to protect Rabbit-chaser—but Ben, displaying amazing agility for a man his size, was already between the Indian woman and any possible lead.

From the sage covered rim above the Truckee River's narrow flood plain, a puff of blue-gray smoke drifted into the air. Yet another miner went down, his leg lashing out, but only for a moment.

Jesus Christ—just like taking down buffalo, I suppose. . . .

Then Olivo was kneeling astride the fallen Hollings, Colt-Walker pressed to the side of the man's skull.

"Order them off!" Olivo shouted, "or I'll blow your goddamned brains out. . . ."

"I'm hit, boys!" Hollings yelped, "My goddamn shoulder's bust. . . ."

"Who's next, coons?" came the voice of Bully O'Bragh. "This child ain't lifted ha'r in a week or more, an' I'm gettin' downright edgy. . . ."

Bully appeared from a dry wash a few yards distant. Crouching with his rifle leveled at the stunned *Californians*, he moved with catlike quickness to where the wounded Hollings was attempting to rise. Within a moment O'Bragh had slipped the noose of a braided rawhide lariat about Hollings's throat and was half dragging the man toward Old Blue. He knotted the lariat about Ben's saddle horn and shouted, "Come on, folks, let's ride! Ain't no damned hos-pi-tality around hyar. Let's go find Cali-forny. Hollings, he's comin' with us, sort of like insurance. You boys want him back, best ye come look for 'im about a mile down the trail. Pore bastard seems to be losin' blood fast. . . ."

With Hollings half stumbling and half being dragged behind, the party of five was on its way out of camp. Bully, turned halfway about on Porcupine's back, kept his Hawken trained on the emigrants—and Ben and H.V., as well as they were able, followed suit. Hollings screamed in pain when he was yanked off his feet and dragged forward over the icy ground.

"My Gawd-damned coffeepot!" Bully yelled. "It's cost this child his damned coffeepot! Whar's this nigger ever goin' to get another one like it?"

Hollings screaming like a gut-shot lion, back on his feet, grasping the taut lariat with one hand, cursing and lunging forward to keep up with Old Blue's pace. The pack mules braying. Rabbit-chaser laughing and laughing, Bully's presumably lost coffeepot held up as she rode, and Roxanne screaming her lungs out, half in fear and half in high dudgeon. Now pistol fire from the camp, the shots missing but bringing on another round of braying from the stampeding mules. Old Blue rolled back his lips and clamped his big, square teeth together. H.V., riding just to the rear of Roxanne, turned and fired off three shots in the general direction of the camp. And Hollings falling once more, bellowing, bellowing, begging for mercy. . . .

True to his word, Bully stopped a mile or so from the camp and removed the noose from about Hollings's neck. With that he drew his skinning knife, mumbled something about what a man's face looks like after he's been scalped, and wavered the blade before the terrified man.

"Left to yore own devices," Bully said, "you probly ain't such a bad coon. Take my advice—get shed o' them others. You pull this kind o' thing in Cali-forny, the lads'll stretch yore neck sure."

"Dime quien es tu junta y te diré si haces yunta," H.V. added. "A man's known by the company he keeps. If you live with thieves, you die with thieves."

"Durned rights. Couldn't of said 'er better myself. Wal, it's been amusin'. This child ain't laughed so hard since Gawd died."

For a moment the group watched Hollings as he stumbled back toward his friends, and then Bully thumped Porcupine's sides. A cold rain continued to fall as they rode, and they kept to a fast, steady pace. But it soon became evident that they were not being pursued, and at length Bully signaled for them to slow down, to conserve their animals.

"Folks, the Gawd-awful Sierras is just ahead of us. Cain't see 'em because of the damned clouds an' such, but they's thar. Take my word on it."

Without even stopping for a noon meal (though Roxanne whispered complaints to her husband), they followed the course of the fast-flowing Truckee River, right back into its canyon.

Either he doesn't believe what the other scout said, or he's got a plan to put our animals themselves on snowshoes—and even that wouldn't surprise me. . . .

H.V. played the scene of the morning's violence over and over. Though it was possible, indeed highly likely, that he'd actually killed a man, the likelihood did not appreciably bother him.

Didn't feel right from the time we got there. I should have known, should have urged caution. Bully understands his business, but he's not infallible. That sordid little drama's got to serve me for an object lesson. There'll be more like Hollings. California always was a place where a man's his own law, and it sure as hell hasn't gotten any better. Once we get across the mountains, Bully will be heading off somewhere—because that's his nature, his life. . . .

As they rode ahead into the wet fog that filled the rocky canyon of the Truckee, O'Bragh was singing something at the top of his lungs. The words, H.V. surmised, were probably Shoshonean. Rabbit-chaser's people were cousins to the Shoshones. But then the guide looked back at H.V. and Roxanne, winked, and shifted to English:

> Oh, what was your name in the States?
> Was it Thompson or Johnson or Bates?
> Did you murder your wife and fly for your life?
> Say, what was your name in the States?
>
> Come all you Californians,
> I pray ope wide your ears,
> If you are going across the plains,
> With snotty mules or steers,
>
> Remember beans before you start,
> Likewise dried beef and ham,
> Beware of ven'son, dang the stuff,
> It sometimes is a ram.
>
> You must buy two revolvers,
> A bowie knife and belt,
> Says you, "Old feller, now stand off,
> Or I will have your pelt."
>
> The greenhorn looks around about,
> But not a soul can see,
> Says he, "There's not a man in town,
> But what's afraid of me."
>
> Oh what was your crime in the States?
> Was it thievin' or murder or rape?
> Did ye strangle a gal an' then shoot a pal?
> Oh what was your crime in the States?

"Bravo! Bravo!" shouted Ben Goffe from the back of his faithful Percheron, "bring on the Philharmonic!"

"Goddamn it, O'Bragh," H.V. yelled into the swirling fog, "where in the devil are you taking us? Is this the entry into the netherworld, or what?"

"Speak English, coon, how many times do I got to tell ye?"

"Do you actually know where we're heading?" Roxanne demanded.

O'Bragh laughed and winked at Rabbit-chaser.

"Course not. The Gawddamned pass is filled with snow. If Fiddlehead says it, then she's true. So we're lookin' for a different pass. Hollings an' them may go south, once he's patched up an' the others is buried. But the mountains is higher that direction. So we'll head t'other . . . ."

A tributary branch flowed into the Truckee from the north, and the party turned upstream without hesitation. As long as the affluent was flowing southward, it was running parallel to the main range of the Sierra. Toward the end of the third day of their ascent from Truckee Meadows, they crossed over a ridge where snow lay crusted to a depth of over a foot. More snow was falling now, sporadically, the big flakes drifting from the heavens like so many autumn leaves.

The group made evening camp among a dense hedge of gnarled junipers, the thick, aromatic foliage serving to keep wind and snow away from them and the dead branches on several old trees providing ready firewood, heavy with pitch and capable of giving off an intense, if smoky, heat.

Morning found the snow nearly twice its previous depth, and the animals had great difficulty in moving forward. Only Old Blue was able to navigate the white stuff with any ease, and so Ben took the lead position, thereby using the Percheron's huge hooves to trample the trail sufficiently for the other animals to follow. At length they descended into an extensive and nearly snow-free valley, and sundown brought them to the northern end of this basin—a broad, swampy, mountain-encircled plain where snow geese and Canadas huddled about on the banks and numerous antelope browsed, a valley whose meandering streams ultimately gathered together at the northwest extremity.

"*Río de Las Plumas,*" O'Bragh said, "it's got to be. Seen 'er on one of Fremont's maps, by Gawd, an' this child knew that must be the one Steve Meek told me about. Ye see, folks, old B'ar Killer Meek an' his brother Steve an' some other coons come this way back in the winter of '33, an' Stephen told me about whar they crossed the mountains. Deep snows up top

side, same as now. B'ar Killer wandered around until he found
him an easy way across. It pays to listen to the stories coons
tell—listen an' remember. Best thing is to have been thar once,
next best is to listen to the nigger what has. This hyar river
runs right down into the Sacramento Valley, past Sutter's *Hoch
Farm* an' the town o' Marysville. I been thar before."

"We trust your judgment, Farnsworth," H.V. laughed.

"Name's Bully, ye thief, an' ye know it well, too."

"What about Allen . . . and Sarah and John?" Roxanne
asked. "Do you think they found their way across, or. . . ."

"If they was with Fiddlehead, they probably headed north,
same as we did—only up Long Valley most likely, an' on to
Honey Lake. Larrson's Trail comes down through thar somewhere. But if Fiddlehead left 'em behind, then who knows?
All depends on how the snow lies."

"Perhaps we should try to find them," Roxanne persisted.

Bully shook his head.

"They done made their choice, Miss Roxy. A coon can only
do so much."

Ben Goffe took off his glasses for a moment, polished the
lenses.

"Well, are we or are we not actually in California?" he
asked.

"Hellfire, ain't the Gawddamned Sierra Nevadas in Cali-
forny? What bunch o' hills ye think we been trampin' through
for the past four days? Wagh!"

"California . . . ," Ben repeated, waiting for the sound of
the word to seem real. "Well, my friends, since I don't see any
gold nuggets lying about, I suggest we make camp while there's
still sufficient light. We'll build a big fire and shoot an elephant
for dinner. Wasn't I promised that I'd see an elephant on the
way to California?"

Roxanne looked puzzled. H.V. laughed softly.

"Elephant?" We've done been lookin' at the Elephant for
the last thousand miles, lad. Only mebbe ye didn't see 'er
through them stove plates ye use for spectacles."

The skies cleared, and the mountains about them glittered with
sunlight, the whiteness almost too intense to look at. But close
beside the rapidly growing river there was no snow; passage

was extremely difficult in spots, the pitch of the ground and the rocky canyonsides requiring them to work their way upward in places nearly to the snow zone. Nevertheless, before sundown they'd reached a small but thriving mining camp called American Valley, a settlement consisting of a hundred or so Whitemen, not a woman among the lot, and a Maidu village located just to the north. H.V. was interested to note, the following day, that the Indian men were hard at work, digging and washing sand, right alongside Whites. Some of the Maidus, he learned at the post, were working for the Whites, while others, more enterprising and having learned the value placed upon gold, were working on their own, having convinced a local drunk to file the claim in exchange for a quarter of the profits.

"These Maidu people," the post keeper said, "they're basically a peaceful lot, even though a few of their villages have been massacred down south. Well, there's room for all, at least at present. If you folks are heading toward Sacramento City, beware. Last month they had a bad outbreak of cholera—both there and in the goldfields. Sick men were being brought into the hospital by wagon, two and three at a time. For a while, sixty or so a day were dying—that's what we heard, at least—and most of the residents left town and run for their lives. I hear the walls of Sutter's Fort are sagging, the roofs are leaking, and half the windows are broken out. A damn shame, actually. A year ago the place was thriving, but prices were sky-high—onions, potatoes, and eggs were going for a dollar apiece."

"What about lumber?" H.V. asked.

"A dollar a board foot," the post keeper replied. "The boys have been tearing down buildings in Sacramento and elsewhere—just to get timber. We got a shipment of boards from Larkin's mill the other day, and it was all sold out inside of an hour. Rumor has it someone's going to open a mill up here, but so far it's just talk."

"Olivo & Beard," H.V. asked.

"Could be that bunch, all right. They've put in a mill at Lassen Rancho, not far from Red Bluff. Before this Rush is over, it could be the trees'll be worth more than the gold—only most are too damned busy digging to see beyond their own noses."

"Well, folks," Bully said, "I've done led ye to the goldfields, jest like I promised. She's an easy ride to Sacramento City from hyar—jest keep headin' downstream an' ye'll git thar. For Larrson's place, Homer, ye go north when ye reaches the valley. Me an' Rabbit-chaser, we're fixin' to lodge up hyarabouts. When we've found us a mule-load of gold dust, I figger we'll head back over to Fort Bridger an' visit with Gabe an' Vasquez an' Washakie for a time, who knows? Shame ye didn't get to meet them coons. It would of done yore hearts good."

Olivo and Goffe attempted to pay O'Bragh, but the old mountain man was adamant in refusal. He laughed and shook his head.

"Already been paid," he insisted. "This child ain't pore, no sir. Keep yore money. Chances are we'll see each other again after a time. When that happens, ye can buy the old Irish Vulture a drink."

The men embraced, and the women did likewise, an act initiated by Roxanne Olivo, much to the Te-moak's surprise.

There was no point in lingering, and everyone knew it. It had been a great adventure, but now the adventure was over. Still, after the long, long trek across half a continent, it seemed *wrong* to both H.V. and Ben that they should be riding away from this *graybeard loon* who had slowly and insidiously become one of the closest friends either had ever known.

"Ye an' that whale-sized horse is goin' to make quite an entrance at Sutter's Fort." Bully grinned at Ben. "Miss Roxy, ye got to promise to take care o' Homer thar. Git now, all of ye. Me an' my Rabbit-lady has got some serious fornicatin' to do. Ain't had no privacy since we got hitched, as it turns out. . . ."

CHAPTER TWENTY-FIVE

A Meeting With Samson Flowers

[1849, 1850:]

THROUGH SEPTEMBER AND the first half of October of 1849, a convention met in Monterey, and finally a California Constitution was formulated and adopted, one that prohibited slavery, and a month later the California Constitution, provisional and perhaps technically illegal, was nonetheless adopted by the voters—those who had remained in the settlements or who were willing to take time off from the gaining of their fortunes in the goldfields to vote—goldfield settlements where the men outnumbered the women by a ratio of five hundred to one and perhaps more.

The winter storms had set in, and in the Sierra the snow was accumulating, while among the forested ridges and hills below the high granite of the mountains, occasional heavy rains were welcomed after a long, hot, cloudless California summer. What had been dry ravines in August now contained quick streams. Forest fires, lit accidentally or with malice aforethought and left to burn as they would, were quenched, the blackened earth covered with a litter of dry pine needles and a scud of yellowed oak leaves.

Those who'd come west believing "Hell, it don't snow in

Californy, it don't even frost" were soon disabused of their notion. The *Río de Las Plumas*, the Yuba, the Bear, the American, the Cosumnes, the Mokelumne, and the Stanislaus became howling monsters that lashed and chewed their canyon bottoms, and the ground froze hard at nights and was turned to mire by day under the footsteps of the obsessed minors. Store-bought articles of clothing were priced in accord with the plentiful gold—if they could be had at all. Miners purchased clothing from the Indians if they could or, if not, laced together rough garments of green deerhide and continued digging and prying and panning, falling asleep at nights in crowded, drafty huts of brush and hand-hewn planks. The men sucked at bottles of whiskey if whiskey was available; they cursed the fierce rains and occasional days of sleet and wet snow.

But once in California, the men "rushed to the mines and went to work . . . without tents, many without blankets to shield them from the cold night air, living on pork and hard bread. . . . Hundreds had been stricken down by disease; many died, while others had been unfitted for work for the rest of the season. . . . "

John Dolbeer, Allen Corzine, and Sarah Witt Corzine had indeed accompanied Fiddlehead Wilson north from Truckee Meadows along the little-used Long Valley Trail—listening to but scarcely believing the old salt's repeated warnings about the deep snows in the mountains to the west. The Sierra, Wilson assured them, was considerably less formidable to the north, where they'd intersect with Lassen's *Death Horn* route, a trail that hardly deserved its foreboding nickname.

Wilson himself, however, wasn't bound for California, not even if Dolbeer and Corzine had been able to pay him. His destination was the valley of the Snake River and the post at Fort Hall, and he intended to reach that destination by way of Goose Lake and across the desert to Owyhee River and so on to the Snake.

Honey Lake, a considerable, if shallow, body of water, was largely frozen over when the foursome reached it. Camped at the terminus of the southern arm of the lake, however, was a small band of emigrants—others who had started late and had found the Donner Pass closed off by heavy snows. The group was being led by an individual named Emile Tucker, a rough, bearded fellow with a patch over one eye and tattoos of grossly deformed women on both forearms—a man who spoke in hoarse whispers. Several scars were visible on the backs of his hands and on his face as well, and no great amount of genius was required to comprehend that Tucker was (or had been) a knife-fighter.

"Suggest ye stay clear of that'n," Wilson said. "Susan River runs into the far end o' the lake hyar, and if you follers it up to its source an' keep heading west, ye'll pick up on one crick or t'other, an' that'll lead you right on down to the valley, between Bidwell's place at Chico and Lassen Rancho, most likely. You're after gold—and word has it that there's good diggins on the Trinity, to the west of Shasta City and Reading's hacienda. North on the Klamat as well—supposed to be some real strikes. That's what I heard, anyhow, but since I ain't no gold miner, how would I know? Best o' luck to you, an' if you ever runs into that O'Bragh character again, tell 'im Fiddlehead says a dead man ain't got no right being up and about and leadin' folks to California. The Vulture and me, we go way back. . . . "

Corzine bade Wilson farewell and ignored his advice. Instead he listened to Tucker's scheme about turning east onto the desert and there making contact with the Lassen Trail—northward to Fandango Pass, which either crossed the Sierra or the Warner Mountains, and Tucker wasn't certain.

The following day after lunch, with camp well established and the animals taken care of, at Dolbeer's urging Corzine mounted up, and the two friends rode toward the mountains to take a close look at the timber—mostly fir, the trees evenly formed. In addition there were pines with great yellow bark plates and cedars of considerable size. As former loggers, the men toyed with the idea of forgoing mining altogether and instead setting up a sawmill—provided only that the forests extended to the mining regions. Everything they'd heard suggested a paucity of lumber in the gold camps.

Word of the immense size of some of the trees in the Western forests had indeed reached both New England and Canada and the woods of the Great Lakes region, but Dolbeer and Corzine found nothing out of the ordinary about the trees close by Honey Lake—excepting a few patriarch pines perhaps five or six feet through at the butt, and larger than anything either of them had ever taken down.

By sunset they were back to the camp area. Fires were blazing, and haunches of venison and antelope were roasting, along with portions of mule meat, since one man's pack animal had broken a leg and had to be shot.

But where was Sarah?

"The damned little hellcat! John, you don't figger she's headed off on her own, do you?"

"I said all along you shouldn't leave her alone. Too many loose cannons around—and Sarah's a fine-looking filly, which is of course the reason you married her without ever thinking for a minute about how much it was going to cost you in the long run, you lunkhead."

"What are you saying?" Corzine demanded.

"I'm saying Sarah could well be in almost any bunk by now. A man gets one whiff of her and goes crazy, just like you did after O'Bragh pulled us out of the hot water with Behele's Pawnees. Our ponies are still here, at least, so apparently she didn't take off with the animals."

"She wouldn't leave without the horse I gave her," Corzine said. "I just don't figure she would have done that. Something's damned peculiar here."

"Sarah was listening to old Wilson rattle on. Could she have headed back southward, do you suppose, in the hope of meeting up with Goffe and the Olivos?"

"Don't be a jackass, Dolbeer. Not on foot she wouldn't. Damn it, just when things were working out good. . . ."

John Dolbeer studied the layout of the encampment. Something was wrong with the picture. Something was different now.

"Emile Tucker," he said finally. "Tucker's tent and ponies are gone—he's struck out for Black Rock Desert, just like he said. Two or three other tents are gone as well."

"Then sure as hell Sarah's with him—against her will or with it. My guess is," Corzine growled, "the sonofabitch has ab-ducted her. There's no way she'd have left the two of us—

not when . . . Most of the time I think she likes you better than she likes me."

"I believe," said John Dolbeer, "that Sarah was happy. My friend, is she worth fetching back?"

Corzine looked doubtful.

"Maybe, maybe not. Well, I suppose so. How many guns you figure the scar-faced bastard took with him?"

"I wonder how in hell he persuaded Sarah to tag along? She sure doesn't strike me as the kind who'd be willing to service a whole damned regiment."

"She can fend for herself, that much I know," Corzine replied. "If she ain't back on her own hook by morning, we'll fetch her. You up for it?"

John Dolbeer suffered from the *Sar-a-wit* disease, a malady that seemed to have but two cures. Since one of those was suicide, with no real satisfaction involved, that particular option was without appeal. He'd fallen hopelessly in love with the petite, wiry hellcat almost from his first glimpse of her, bathing bare-ass naked there in the river. She was a vision—violet eyes under a storm of raven hair—thin but with a pleasing width to her hips and a fullness through the breasts that no young lady her age and size ought properly to possess. In Dolbeer's mind, Sarah was like fire—a fire that moved about and spoke and ate and probably had all the normal human bodily functions, but one whose very touch melted that which it came into contact with. Fire was what he and Corzine had damned near ended up in, there among the Pawnees. But it was more than that—not merely a matter of appearance. The faint, faint *smell of her* was enough to drive a man crazy. He'd even remarked to Allen Corzine upon this characteristic of the woman-child his friend had so impulsively married, if one could refer to what had transpired as holy wedlock.

At first Sarah dealt with Corzine just as she had with Gray Elk—she refused to consummate her union. She liked things just fine, she said, with both Corzine and Dolbeer to protect her—and since she was legally married to one of the two, why, that was all the better. When Corzine protested that the husband had certain *available rights*, Sarah nodded and admitted that she'd read as much in a magazine once. Still, why any respectable lady would be willing to allow a man to *pump her between the legs* was more than she could figure, though it was certainly true that she herself greatly enjoyed being hugged and fondled. Still and all, menfolks were known to be perverted and also inordinately fond of their perversions—*sort of like they've all got red ants crawling around on their water faucets or something*. Corzine acknowledged the condition and claimed she'd *gotten the damned thing up and now he couldn't get it down without her, and wouldn't she be willing at least to give it a try?* Just holding it and rubbing it would probably be sufficient, but if she were willing and could see her way clear to take it into her mouth, why, that would be quite satisfactory. Surely, as her husband, he did have those *available rights*, and he'd heard of such matters being tried in a court of law, with wives being ordered *to give the devil his due* and *take it like a man*, so to speak.

It wasn't jealousy Dolbeer felt so much as pure envy. After all they'd been through together, wouldn't his friend Corzine at least be willing to share? Such an accommodation, Dolbeer knew well enough, was deemed by the world at large to be hugely unnatural—not even Mormons would countenance such a thing, though with relationships the other way around the Saints had no trouble, and in that respect they were just like the Indians themselves, permitting a man who was hale and sufficiently wealthy to take on as many woman as his circumstances allowed.

So Allen married Sarah, and in the world's eyes that was an end to the competition. John Dolbeer considered himself an upright and moral man, and so, difficult as it was, he attempted to accept the whims of fate and to ignore Sarah's fascinating smell.

But now?

Corzine seemed hardly more than annoyed that Sarah was gone, lured off into the desert by Emile Tucker, a man scarred and tattooed and likely wanted in the East for a host of offenses. Allen could and would do as he wished. But John Dolbeer had made up his mind.

He was up well before sunrise. Without waking Corzine, who was snoring peacefully and huddled in his bedroll, breath ris-

ing in small puffs of steam, Dolbeer set out in pursuit. When
the sun finally emerged above the translucent purple desert
rims, he was some ten miles from the encampment, and the
big, shallow lake was no longer visible behind him.

He followed fresh trail, complete with the parallel ruts of
Emile Tucker's buckboard, and he observed jackrabbits moving this way and that over the thin, patchy snow and among
clumps of sage and greasewood. Magpies perched on rocks,
and a big bobcat was hunting voles or mice.

Then, as he rounded a thirty-foot tumble of granite boulders—there was Sarah, Sarah on horseback and wearing the
gray sombrero Allen had given her. One of Emile Tucker's
horses trailed behind.

"I come to find you," Dolbeer said.

"Figgered you might. Probably I done hitched up with the
wrong horse. Why didn't Allen come? No, don't tell me. Shit,
I might be dead for all he cares. . . . "

"Why in God's name did you leave?"

"That sonofabitch Emile made me an offer what it didn't
look like I could turn down. I mean, he said he'd shoot me
an' the both of you if I didn't do what he said. I didn't scream
none because a bunch of folks was heading for the desert, and
I figured things would work out. But they didn't."

"My God, girl, it's good to see you—you're all right, aren't
you?"

"Guess so, but Emile Tucker isn't."

"What happened—I mean, how'd you get away?"

Sarah smiled, and John Dolbeer could feel the silver-gold
fire of her physical presence.

"We camped at the edge of the desert," she said, "and then
that sonofabitch Emile decided he was going to hump me. I
couldn't talk him out of it, John. Swear to God, I tried my best.
So finally he come at me, and I had to use my Arkansas toothpick on him a little bit. He started grunting and yelling like a
madman, saying he was going to kill me, so I done slit his
throat. After that I lit out and spent the night next to a big
juniper about five miles back."

A miserable two weeks later, John Dolbeer and Allen and Sarah
Corzine, along with a dozen or so other disheartened Argo-

nauts, made their way across heavily forested Hatchet Mountain and down Little Cow Creek to the head of the Sacramento Valley, to Major Pierson Reading's holdings at the boomtown of Shasta City, the self-styled *Queen of the Northern Mines*.

The fate of the unfortunate but no doubt deserving Emile Tucker had somewhat altered John Dolbeer's desire for the strange, dark-haired young woman who was, after all, married to his friend Corzine and therefore beyond his grasp. Somehow or another, *Sar-a-wit-* didn't smell quite so good as she had before—or possibly the simple awareness that she'd murdered Tucker and showed no remorse for her action had inexplicably altered his olfactory sense.

In any case, Dolbeer bade farewell to the Corzines and set off southward, thinking perhaps to make a stop at the Olivo & Beard mill at Lassen Rancho to look for work—or perhaps simply to continue southward to the Yuba goldfields or the American or the Cosumnes. After all, he'd crossed a continent with the idea of searching for gold. He'd already spent six, nearly seven years in the logging woods, and so he had a trade he could fall back on, should necessity dictate. But first he'd attempt to strike a lode.

Corzine, on the other hand, hit it off famously with Pierson Reading, Sutter's erstwhile compatriot and now himself quite a wealthy man who might well end up being governor of the State of California, in the likely event that California became an official state. Reading, who saw ambition in Allen Corzine's eye and who was furthermore just a bit taken by the significant *wild beauty* of his young wife, provided the couple with a grubstake and an untouched section of Whiskey Creek to work (with a percentage to Reading, who owned the land via Mexican land grant).

By the end of January of 1850, Corzine had constructed a log shanty, complete with an adobe and stone fireplace, and had actually equipped the structure with a hand-hewn table, a pair of unmatched chairs, and a relatively comfortable mattress stuffed with pine needles, cattail down, and sawdust.

With matters of domestic necessity attended to, Allen Corzine went to work shoveling muddy gravel from the bed of Whiskey Creek. Even given the fact of the generally mild California climate, snow lay deep on the mountains above, and tapestries of ice formed each morning along the stream's margins. His rubber boots leaked, and tallow, however liberally applied to canvas britches, failed to keep a man dry. One had to persist at the backbreaking work in a kind of frenzy—or freeze to death. Hands grew numb, and a man could smash a finger and not even feel it until five minutes afterward.

Three Irishmen downstream (another claim arrangement with Pierson Reading) took sick and within a week were dead, presumably of pneumonia, and miners for a mile around laid off half a day to see to it the *Micks* were buried properly. But others were sick as well. Some languished with the diarrhea or with the dread consumption. Reading sent in half a dozen Wintuns to work the claim of the dead Irishmen, but the Indians, presumably having harvested a considerable take of nuggets and dust, disappeared—didn't return to their village and indeed were not heard of again. Word had it they'd gone south to the Malakoff Diggings.

Corzine persisted, however, driving himself relentlessly and returning to his hovel and to the ministrations of Sarah night after night. He was finding gold, damn it, and a good bit of it, too. Sarah was impressed, and after Allen had drunk himself into a stupor and so had crashed out for the night, the girl with violet eyes would stoke up the fire (she herself had to split the firewood, since Allen was at work at the placer all day), sit at the crude table, and admire by candlelight the accumulated nuggets and fines her husband had panned.

Then one evening, after a particularly fruitless day spent shoveling muddy gravel and standing in icy water, Allen Corzine returned to his shanty to find it empty. Sarah wasn't there.

Corzine nodded, buckled on his Colt revolver, saddled up, and rode through a soft rain the five miles to the tent city of Whiskeytown. After a survey of several lantern-lit saloons, he found Sarah in the *Dewkum Inn*, quite drunk, sitting on the lap of a large, white-bearded man in worn and badly stained buckskins.

"That's my wife your paws are all over, old man. Sarah, get your ass up. Get your coat on. We're by-God going home. You, White-beard, if you weren't on the edge of the grave already, I'd gladly rearrange your face. Touch my woman again, and I'll do worse than that—feed your fucking remains to the crows. . . . "

"Simmer down," the barkeeper said. "The lady's had too much to drink, that's all. I take it you be the husband. Your family honor's intact, my friend."

"Stay out of this—it's between my woman and me, and the old coot here."

The man in buckskins, none other than Samson Flowers, easily lifted Sarah to her feet and then stood up. Tall and wiry and broad-shouldered, he grinned as he loomed over Allen Corzine, at the same time nudging the inebriated young woman toward her husband.

"Keep yore shorts on, Sonny. No harm meant. The lady sorta stumbled jest before ye come in, an' that's Gord's own truth. Ast anyone who was watchin'. She stumbled, and I caught 'er. Truth is, we ain't even been introduced. Furthermore, I was a married man the last I heard, though it's possible my lady's given up on me—since I ain't been home in a spell. Name's Sam Flowers, young fella. Mebbe you heard o' me. I ain't lookin' for a fight—been doin' that all my life, an' what's it got me? Young guy like you could probably handle me anyhow, even if you ain't the biggest coon in the world—no offense, now, ye understand. Have a shot o' whiskey, lad, an' catch hold of yore temper."

Sarah glanced at Corzine, saw the fire in his eyes, and, giggling hysterically, turned back to Samson Flowers.

"Don't leave me with *him*," she said, sticking her tongue out at her husband. "He'll jest start whippin' on me, like always. . . . "

"That what you do, lad," Flowers asked, "kinda cuff your lady around every so often? Ain't gentlemanly behavior, now, an' that's a fact. Says in the *Bible* Gord don't cotton to that kind of thing. *Repent, repent, for the time of the end is at hand.* Have a drink on this old mountain hawg, an' let's set things right. Tell you what. If you was hitched to the catamount I'm married to, she'd bounce ye on your head. I expect old Califia, she can whip most men—damned fast with a pistol, too. I tell you, you never saw anything like it."

Corzine reached out to grasp Sarah's arm, but the former Mrs. Gray Elk pulled back and flung herself in Samson's general direction. The buckskin man caught her about the waist, steadied her.

"Take yore lady home an' treat her right," Flowers said, using both hands to guide the tipsy Sarah toward Corzine.

Corzine reached toward his young wife, but she turned from him and slipped to the floor, laughing crazily as she sprawled there, her petticoats askew and her white lace corset showing.

Flowers winked at Corzine.

"Nice legs on the leetle gal. I envy ye, friend. Take 'er on home. I'll buy ye a whole bottle next time we run into each other."

With either a growl or the word *sonofabitch* uttered through clenched teeth, Corzine leaped toward Flowers, flinging punches as he came. Samson slipped to one side, and Corzine, off balance, slid facedown across the sawdust-littered floor of the tavern—thus occasioning a great deal of laughter from around the *Dewkum Inn*. The boys had seen Samson Flowers in fistfights on two or three previous occasions, and each time the venerable mountain man's opponent had ended up unconscious. Several patrons were of the opinion that Sam, old as he was, might yet make a career as a box-fighter.

Allen Corzine was now in a cold fury. He scrambled to his feet and launched a new assault against the long-legged mountain man.

Flowers picked up a chair in one hand and shattered the flimsy furniture across Corzine's head and back.

"Damn it, Flowers!" the barkeep howled. "I ain't going to have no stools or chairs neither the way you're going. You owe me, damn it!"

"Put it on the company tab." Flowers nodded. "One o' you boys get the lady to her feet. The *Dewkum Inn* ain't runnin' no peep show."

Corzine rose to one knee and drew his Colt revolver, held the weapon before him with both hands.

"Put yore toy away," Samson laughed. "Take the lady an' head on home, wherever's home."

The sounds of two pistol shots roared through the smoky, lantern-lit room.

Samson Flowers grinned, made a gesture indicating no harm had been done, and then crumpled to the sawdust.

The first shot had missed altogether, but the second had pierced Flowers's heart.

Major Pierson B. Reading, coming across from the site of a proposed sawmill at the village of Eureka, on Humboldt Bay to the north of the Eel River, took the opportunity to make survey of his mining leases along Whiskey Creek. He stopped in at the Corzine cabin—was surprised not to find the usually diligent Allen hard at work—was even more surprised to find Sarah alone in the cabin. Reading had made the presumption that Corzine had probably been temporarily drawn away from his pick and shovel by the violet-eyed young beauty to whom he was married. Even middle-aged and respectably yoked gentlemen such as Reading were not oblivious to Sarah's charms. Whether in men's clothing or dressed up fit to kill, this girl had an indefinable something about her that caused males to breathe more deeply in response to a definite speeding up of the heartbeat.

Reading rapped on the makeshift door, and within a matter of moments Sarah answered and invited him to come inside.

"Where's Allen? I stopped at the creek—actually, I don't think anything's been done there since the rain, and that was two or three nights ago. Is he sick, Sarah, or . . . ?"

She stepped close to him—closer, in fact, than he actually felt comfortable with.

"You ain't heard, Mr. Reading, sir? He tried to defend me over at the Dewkum Inn, an' now they've put him in jail in Shasta City. Plannin' on hanging him, I expect. But I've got gold here, and our share's enough to hire a good lawyer, if I can find one."

"In jail? On what charges?"

Tears were forming in the corners of the violet eyes.

"Murder, Mr. Reading. Allen got into it with old Sam Flowers—they was punching each other and busting up chairs and such. Then Allen shot Flowers, more by accident than anything else, and he just dropped dead. The sheriff says Flowers was married into that Olivo and Beard clan—hellfire, we done come across country with one o' them, a young college professor named Homer Virgil. But now Flowers's wife'll be coming to Shasta City, and so I reckon they'll hang poor Allen, all right."

Sarah was standing close to him, very close, and Reading could feel small droplets of perspiration on his forehead.

"This girl would do just about anything for you . . . if you could get my husband out of jail," Sarah said. "Allen says you *own* Shasta City and everything else hereabouts. You could own me too, Mr. Reading, sir. I love my man, but I want him out of jail. Can you help us?"

"I think so," Reading said, his voice unsteady as he watched, fascinated, while Sarah Corzine began to take off her clothing.

CHAPTER TWENTY-SIX

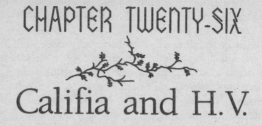

Califia and H.V.

[1850:]

THE MURDER OF Samson Flowers, if murder it was, went unpunished—despite Flowers's ties to the powerful Beard and Olivo families. The official word was that the killing occurred as the result of a fair fight—and hence there was no legal liability—since both Flowers and Corzine were, in effect, attempting to defend themselves and thus engaged in mutual acts of self-defense. Pierson B. Reading himself handed down the verdict, acting in the capacity of Alcalde, that "Mr. Corzine is to be given his freedom, without indemnity, forthwith."

For a time thereafter the Corzines were lodged in their own rooms in the spacious Reading Hacienda—and might have stayed on except for the jealous excesses of Mrs. Reading, who had taken an immediate dislike to young Sarah Corzine. But a bond had been formed, and Allen Corzine became a partner to the older, wealthier man.

"You're an experienced logger, Allen, is that right? Of course it is. I know you have in mind to make your fortune in gold, my boy, but a fortune's a fortune, isn't that so? I pulled your bacon out of the fire, so to speak, but there's a way for you to repay me. The price of lumber's higher than hell here in California—and that's outrageous, inasmuch as we have the most astonishing forests in America and probably in the entire world. What we don't have is men with the know-how to cut the trees and mill them. That's where you come in. I'll provide you with a crew of Wintun Indians and equipment. You ever seen redwoods, young fellow? You've logged back East, where the trees are toothpicks compared to what we have out here. If you've got the gumption for it, you can become a rich man, Allen Corzine, richer than you ever dreamed. Enterprise and marketing, Allen—I tell you. . . . That friend of yours, Dolbeer I believe? I recollect that he was a logger too—the pair of you worked together or some such thing? Where in hell did he go?"

By the time Califia Flowers arrived to pay her respects, the remains of the veteran mountain man had long since been laid to rest. Even persistent inquiries with regard to the identity of Flowers's killer, made by none other than William Beard and Raymondo Olivo themselves, resulted in the acquisition of but scant information. There had been a barroom brawl, Pierson Reading informed the partners and the widow, during which *a good time was had by all*, with numerous shots being fired at random, in accord with the overall celebratory mood, and in the aftermath Samson Flowers lay dead upon the floor. No one knew who might have fired the fatal lead.

Pierson Reading, a loser in the recent territorial governor's election, remarked on certain *lost ballot boxes* whose contents might well have won for him, but otherwise Reading took the workings of both fate and the political process philosophically.

"When these things happen," Reading confided to Raymondo Olivo, "there is naught we can do to alter events. In the larger sense, all our actions are predetermined. Who, for instance, could have predicted what would happen to your niece's husband? Yet, given the circumstances, it's apparent the sequence of actions was inevitable."

Raymondo nodded.

"We understand that you're setting up on Humboldt Bay— putting in a mill, *por casualidad*. So now we are rivals, is it not so?"

Reading offered Olivo a cigar.

"Surely, Mr. Olivo, there's room sufficient for all. We have, in the final analysis, no great shortage of redwood trees. There's a great and untapped market out there in the world at large."

Olivo lit his cigar.

"*Sí, sí*, the market is very great. I do not think, Señor Reading, that we will manage to bankrupt one another."

During the year of 1849, at least eighty thousand and perhaps a hundred thousand emigrants had poured into California, many to look for the magic of gold and many others with the intention of drawing a livelihood indirectly, from those who did the actual digging, sluicing, and panning. Such individuals would establish basic industries and services, among these the vital enterprises of agriculture, manufacture, shipping and overland transportation, and timbering.

H.V. Olivo had returned to California late that year, in the wake of the vast majority of fortune-seekers—but the following year the grand exodus from "civilized America" would continue. Nor would the flow of emigrants westward cease for many years to come.

In his journal of that year of '49, Alonzo Delano had written, *For miles, to the extent of vision, an animated mass of beings broke upon our view. Long trains of wagons with their white covers were moving slowly along, a multitude of horsemen were prancing on the road, companies of men were traveling on foot, and although the scene was not a gorgeous one, yet the display of banners from many wagons, and the multitude of armed men, looked as if a mighty army was on its march.*

Delano would be among those who opted for Lassen's Cutoff, the *Death Horn* route—across Black Rock Desert, into Surprise Valley, over the Warner Mountains, through basin and range country, past the volcanic dome of Lassen's Butte, and down canyon to the upper end of the Sacramento Valley—still two hundred miles distant from the thriving hub city at the confluence of the American and Sacramento rivers.

That same year J. A. Moerenhout, French consul at Monterey, had written, *The growth and importance this new settlement [Sacramento City] has exhibited are among the marvelous things that are happening in this country. . . . Now there is a town of 3,000 to 4,000 inhabitants there, with a quay lined with fine*

*buildings, streets laid out and with a large volume of business that
increases as communication with the placers and the interior becomes more regular and easy, and where . . . thirty-five ships were
at anchor, the smallest of which was fifty to sixty tons.*

In addition to the difficult overland routes to California,
including the Oregon and California trails, the Old Spanish
Trail, the Santa Fe–Gila Route, and the Southern Routes from
Texas and Arkansas, there were both sea routes and sea-land
routes. From the American East, those who came in quest of
the latter-day Golden Fleece could reach the land of their destination by a long, six-month sea journey around Cape Horn—
the route well established by New England seafarers who'd
been engaged in whaling or in mercantile trade with the Californios, exchanging manufactured goods of various sorts for
hides and tallow from the ranchos. These ships now outfitted
themselves to carry the "Californians" themselves, as well as
machinery, furniture, lumber, preserved foods, clothing, bolts
of cloth, and thousands of other necessary goods—though once
the vessels were anchored in San Francisco Bay, crews tended
to desert in favor of the goldfields, leaving the ships unmanned
and temporarily unable to return whence they came. In addition to the New Englanders, however, were ships of various
nationalities—from Hawaii, South America, Mexico, Russian
Kamchatka, and Europe.

Another route took its pilgrims to the Isthmus of Panama—
the Pacific Mail Steamship Company established regular service between New York and Chagres and then, once cargo
and passengers made their way across the jungle (where they
faced poor food, yellow fever, unpredictable storms, and
drinking water that did absolutely terrible things to one's insides), transported them to the Pacific shore, then on to San
Francisco. Other routes crossed Nicaragua or central Mexico.
In any event, a great problem lay in insufficient numbers of
ships available on the Pacific side—so that some emigrants
resorted to locally built sailboats or even dugout canoes to
continue their journey to San Francisco.

The riches of California! However backbreaking the toil of
mining may have been, and however fruitless for most, strike

after strike was made—and taverns buzzed with tales, often authenticated, of casually discovered nuggets of a pound, two pounds, six pounds, more. . . . Some men became hugely wealthy, but more often than not the real riches went to the lawyers, the merchants, the operators of utilities, the saloon keepers, the operators of whorehouses, the owners of sawmills, and the larger mining companies that were soon formed. By late 1850 the average miner, if such a being existed, was making little more than two dollars per day.

The miners poured themselves into their labors and often neglected to take time out even to cook their food or to attend to any kind of personal cleanliness. Men commonly lived in tents or shanties, drafty and leaky, and such clothing as was available tended to be inadequate. Notions of the *extremely mild climate*, advertised in various brochures that circulated east of the Mississippi, were quickly abandoned in face of the reality of torrential rains, flooding rivers, heavy frosts, and astonishingly deep snows that fell above three thousand feet in the mountains. Drifts in the Sierra sometimes reached thirty feet in depth, and temperatures in the valleys to the east of the range's crest sometimes dropped to thirty or forty below zero. There were those who were willing to argue with one and all that the area around Donner Lake was indeed the coldest spot on earth.

The mining camps themselves, at times of holiday at least, were violent but good-natured places. Even hangings, when they occurred, were times for celebration—though as to the celebration of what, God only knew. In Shasta City, for instance, the occasionally scheduled hanging was a public holiday. A condemned man was given the scaffold as a *bully pulpit*, and those who were about to have their necks stretched sometimes spoke for an hour or two or longer, delivering moral sermons or diatribes against all duly constituted authority or merely extended *apologias* of their own lives—with the approval of those assembled.

Frank Marryat wrote this account of the settlement of Murderer's Bar: *On the banks [of the river] was a village of canvas that the winter rains had bleached to perfection, and round it the miners were at work at every point. Many were waist deep in the water, toiling in bands to construct a race and dam to turn the river's course; others were entrenched in holes, like grave diggers, working down to the "bedrock." Some were on the brink of the stream washing out "prospects" from tin pans or wooden "batteaus"; and others worked in company with the long tom, by means of water sluices artfully conveyed from the river. Many were coyote-ing in subterranean holes, from which time to time their heads popped out, like those of squirrels, to take a look at the world; and a few with drills, dissatisfied with nature's work, were preparing to remove large rocks with gunpowder. All was life, merriment, vigour and determination, as this part of the earth was being turned inside out to see what it was made of. . . .*

Only *damnfools* attempted to cross the Sierra in winter, but there were those who did. As soon as the passes were open that next year of 1850, a flood of migration was on once more. The trails from St. Joseph and Independence and Council Bluffs were busy, and entrepreneurs set up ferry service at a dozen river crossings along the way. Cholera took an even greater toll than the previous year, and heavy rains over the desert put the regular wagon trail along the Humboldt River under water in numerous places. William Waldo and his California Relief Agencies, working largely in the interests of humanity, saved many hundreds from various sorts of disaster in the crossing of the Sierra.

With roughly equal numbers arriving by sea, the hotels and lodging houses in San Francisco and Sacramento were clearly insufficient to provide the required lodging. Owners charged exorbitant prices and put ten or even twenty men in a room. Meals cost an unheard-of $3 and higher, while a shot of whiskey commanded two bits or four bits.

In addition to the established cities of San Francisco, Monterey, San Jose, Sacramento, and Stockton, new communities grew quickly the length of the *Mother Lode*—places with names like Nevada City (Deer Creek Dry Diggins), Grass Valley, Placerville (Hangtown), Columbia, Sonora, Murphys, Downieville, and Shasta City. For the first few years, at least, these were to be settlements essentially lacking (if not devoid of) the civilizing influence of females. Some women, certainly, had come to California as part of the great wave of migration, but many of

these were business ladies, *professionals*, and not unduly concerned with etiquette and other varieties of propriety.

With the impact of sudden wealth from the mines, the
overall price structure in California was drastically altered, with
measurable impact upon that of the world at large. Lumbering,
agriculture, and commerce of all sorts began to boom as a
result of the sudden new wealth being gleaned from the mountains—from the Rogue River in Oregon to the Merced River in
California.

On the way south from Shasta City, William and Califia Beard
and Raymondo Olivo paid a visit to their friend and partner
John Sutter, who had lost much of his wealth and power and
who was now in residence at his Hock Farm, close beside the
Feather River, its banks lined with great oaks and sycamores.
On the west side of the river stood Sutter's home, constructed
of whitewashed adobe and surrounded by walls that enclosed
outbuildings and corrals and about a hundred acres of cultivated grounds. Seine nets were drawn across the river, providing a plentiful supply of fish. A rancheria was situated a few
hundred yards from the house, a village of some three hundred
Maidu Indians—quite tame, as Sutter remarked, not at all resembling the warlike *Pano* clan who occasionally attacked the
settlements of miners—a group believed to be engaged in an
extended *revenge-taking* as a result of the massacre of some
Maidu villages shortly after the discovery of gold.

Sutter, younger by eight years than Bill Beard and Raymondo Olivo, was now forty-seven and living the life of a
dedicated family man, his wife and other relatives residing
with him. Gone were the devoted Indian women who had, at
an earlier time, ministered to his needs. Sutter had even attempted to persuade longtime friend John Bidwell to marry his
twenty-two-year-old daughter, Eliza. But Bidwell was not of a
mind to commit himself in this fashion.

Sutter, as though in disbelief, read his guests the contents
of Bidwell's letter—a letter they themselves had delivered to
the former King of the Sacramento Valley, since they'd stopped
at Bidwell's Arroyo Chico Ranch on their way south.

John Bidwell conveyed his respect and affection for Sutter,
and yet he turned down the proposed alliance by marriage: *I*

desire to see you frequently, and to live, so long as we both may live, in terms of intimacy and friendship . . . but I cannot persuade myself to marry. . . .

Bill Beard and Raymondo Olivo presented Sutter with a draft in satisfaction of the final portion of the debt they owed him as a result of buying out the Russian River milling operations, and the Swiss-German, chronically short of cash these days, thanked them warmly. Even Frau Anna Dubeld Sutter made a genuine attempt at hospitality, and the longtime friends enjoyed a convivial dinner.

"*Ach, ja,* ladies and gentlemen, we grow older, all of us—except Califia, of course, who has apparently discovered the Spring of Youth. *Herr Beard,* your daughter is even more lovely now than the first time I met her—five years ago, was it not? *Wilhelm und* Raymondo, you are older than I—nearly sixty, *nicht wahr?* We have dreamed a strange dream here in Alta California, and we have seen our world move first one way and then another. Our fortunes rise and fall with the tides. As to the gold, who knows? One moment I owned my own country, and the next I am merely a candidate defeated in election. . . ."

"The courts are certain to rule in your favor," Bill Beard said. "Your title to the lands, after all, was quite official. If your deeds are not found to be valid, then none of ours are either."

"In that case," Raymondo suggested, "perhaps we must fight yet another civil war. I've always heard the Americans believe in rule by law."

"Perhaps it will be so," Sutter agreed. "For now, I suggest we drink a toast to the lovely Califia. She's experienced a tragedy, and yet she has borne it with great strength, great fortitude. I wish her deep happiness, for she deserves no less."

The glasses were raised *to Califia,* including the one held by Anna—but Anna, Califia was certain, didn't actually sip the wine.

Once there might have been a hint of something between me and John Sutter. But why would his wife suspect such a thing? Perhaps she's one of those women who're inherently jealous of all who might conceivably be construed a rival. Can't she see that I've no desire for intrigues? I loved Samson. . . .

Sutter spoke of the constitutional convention, called for the

previous September by the military governor, General Bennett
Riley, at a conclave held in Monterey. Learning that Congress
had adjourned without acting on the issue of statehood for
California, Riley had arbitrarily devised districts and called for the
election of delegates. Sutter had been one of four representatives
chosen from the area round about Sacramento—the others being
Sam Brannan, John McDougal, and Peter Burnett. The convention
went on at great length, with much heated discussion, chiefly
with regard to the issue of slavery, but eventually a constitution
was indeed devised, a pattern for a government of free men—and
a government for a state rather than for a territory. The issue of
state boundaries was also debated hotly—with some favoring the
Rocky Mountains as the eastern frontier, others the Sierra Nevada.
Ultimately, the general wisdom suggested excluding the Mormons of the Salt Lake area—since they were not, in any case,
represented at the convention.

When presiding officer Robert Semple became ill, Sutter
was asked to preside. He'd presented an address and had been
generously applauded by those present. Whatever had happened to his lands and was still happening to his cattle and
farmland, the *General* was revered as a founding father—one
whose acts of generosity were legend.

*Four years later, Juan Bautista Alberdi, father of the constitu-
tion of Argentina, would base his work on that of the Californians,
writing, "Without universities, without academies or law colleges,
the newly-organized people of California have drawn up a constitution full of foresight, of common sense and of opportunity. . . . "*

Ultimately, as Bill Beard, Califia, and Raymondo Olivo knew,
Sutter had been encouraged to run for governor and had con-
ducted a vigorous campaign. The election day on November
13 had been marked by extremely bad weather, and few voted.
Peter Burnett won with less than seven thousand votes. Sutter
received only two thousand some odd votes and finished
fourth in the final tally. Pierson Reading, also a candidate,
finished second, though in the aftermath it was discovered that
numerous ballot boxes from the north had been lost and hence
not counted. Burnett was declared the winner, but it was altogether possible that Reading should have been.

As they were drinking a glass of wine in the aftermath of
the meal, John Sutter mentioned the fact that he'd met a gen-

tleman named Benjamin Goffe, who'd told him of coming across on the California Trail in the company of one Homer Virgil Olivo and his wife Roxanne, a young couple whom Sutter presumed to be Raymondo's son and daughter-in-law.

Olivo and Beard had been expecting H.V. and Roxanne but had been under the impression the couple would arrive via ship, having rounded Cape Horn. They thanked Sutter for the information and made preparations for an immediate departure, with Santa Cruz as their destination.

Califia, still a bit numbed at having been summoned to visit the grave of her husband, could take little joy in the prospect of once again seeing H.V., her lover those many years ago, the one whom, in her heedless youth, she had presumed to spend a life with—H.V. who was now, by all the accounts Uncle Raymondo had received, quite happily married to the oh-so-proper Mistress Roxanne.

Whatever else might be the case, Califia reflected, she and H.V. had been the closest of friends. She mustn't allow her own despair to taint that friendship. If Homer Virgil were happy, then she, Califia, was happy for him. She resolved to make friends with Roxanne—and in no way to do anything which might present a hazard to that relationship. Indeed, the longer she thought the matter over, the more grateful she was that H.V. was at last back in California. If she had ever in her life needed a good friend, now was that time.

H.V. and Roxanne, had parted company with Benjamin Goffe and proceeded to make their way to Yuba City. After a few days of recuperation time spent in what passed for a hotel, the Olivos were able to book passage downriver to San Francisco. Based on information received at the offices of Olivo & Beard, the couple took a cabin on a schooner bound for the San Diego Mission—where, they'd been told, Raymondo was on a business venture, presumably to determine the feasibility of establishing a mill in the forested inland mountains.

Yes, Raymondo Olivo had indeed been there a month earlier, but he had long since departed for Northern California—with urgent business in Stockton. One associate was certain the elder Olivo had gone on horseback, in the company of a group of ranchers and cattlemen. Another man (sporting a handlebar mustachio) insisted Raymondo was with Captain Calvin Beard, aboard the new *Don Quixote*, bound either for Monterey or Nova Archangelisk in Alaska.

Roxanne became ever more cross as the weeks went on and H.V. was unable to make contact with his father.

"This is insane—all of it!" she insisted—and then burst into tears.

The absurdity of being back in California after so long a time—and still not having had a reunion with his family—was not lost upon H.V., who had seen his best intentions turned to naught but frustration and wasted time.

The utter ferment in California, he mused, could not have been made any clearer. Besides, why in the devil had he not proceeded directly to San Lorenzo or to Hotochruk? Most likely, that's where his mother would be—there with Pelican Doctor's people.

A ship, destination San Francisco, lay at anchor in the harbor, but all possible berths were already taken.

"Roxy, dearest, are you up to a three-hundred-mile horse-back ride?"

"Why is it, love, that I've got the bloomin' suspicion that I don't really have any choice? I'll do anything, Homer Virgil— only get us a house, for God's sake!"

And so they rode northward, toward the San Lorenzo mill and Hotochruk village.

At Roxanne's urging, H.V. immediately signed lease papers for a small, tile-roofed adobe in Santa Cruz—a building formerly used as lodgings for the commandant of the Leather Jackets, back during the days of Micheltorena and his detested *cholos*. The structure boasted a wide window consisting of multiple small panes of glass, a few of which were green and a few of which were the color of burgundy wine, and this window, constructed as a kind of bay, looked out over the ocean and across the black, teethlike rocks that were completely visible at low tide. A sandy beach spread away to either side of the rocks, and no more than a few hundred yards distant stood the old Catholic Mission.

H.V. had stopped at the San Lorenzo mill on his way to

Santa Cruz and so had spoken at some length with Calvin—
learning at that time of what had happened to Califia's husband and also of the whereabouts of his father, his uncle, and
his varmint-loving cousin. Cousin Cal was now the proud father of an apparently indeterminate number of little Beardlings.
Juanita, no longer the thin, pretty girl that H.V. remembered
from years earlier at Rancho Vallejo, was round-faced, dark-
eyed, and plump—and quite possibly pregnant yet one more
time.

In any case, financial arrangements were made, and H.V.
and Roxanne were enabled not only to take their lease but also
to acquire furniture (at inflated prices, since the impact of the
goldfields was being felt even here, more than two hundred
miles distant).

By means of hiring a small crew of local drifters and school-
boys, the Olivos were able to get moved in—a process Bully
O'Bragh had unwittingly simplified greatly when he'd insisted
that they jettison not only the bathwater but the baby as well—
in the interests of moving more rapidly toward their destination.

H.V. hoped to take Roxanne with him on a venture out to
Hotochruk village, the Ohlone encampment still there in the
same place after all this time, in the meadow beside Big Creek,
in the midst of a redwood glade at the center of which stood
the two intergrown giants that were, for all practical purposes,
one immense tree with a double crown.

However, Roxanne Breton Olivo, formerly of Caernarvon
in Wales, was not in a mood to traipse off anywhere further—
not to any Indian village, not even the one where her beloved
husband had been raised. After the long and extremely difficult
overland journey and the fruitless jaunts up and down the
length of California, she wished simply to rest—perhaps for a
month or more, and to read some good books, if such luxuries
were indeed available in so remote a place as Alta California—
and if they were published in civilized English.

H.V. was unable to change his wife's mind, and so he saddled his trail pony yet one more time and made his way northward along the coast, surprised to discover a tiny village named
Davenport perhaps a dozen miles beyond Santa Cruz, complete with a small Catholic church and gently sloping hillsides

devoted to the cultivation of vegetables and, of course, to the pasturage of cattle. The village, in fact, was no more than a quarter of a mile north of that amphitheater-like cove that the old *Don Quixote* had used as a doghole, for the loading of lumber by means of ropes and pulleys—and where, of course, he and Cal and Califia had so often come to swim, along with other Ohlone young people. For the first time in a long while H.V. had occasion to recall Spotted Fox's daughter, the smiling and firm-breasted girl called *Mariposa*, the Butterfly. It was hard for him to think of her as other than she had been there in the dawning of his world, all of them in their mid-teens.

And *Little Cal*, Califia—his cousin, with whom he'd first known what it was like to be a man. He remembered Califia inexplicably turning her young stallion eastward along the Zayante trail—himself following—and how one thing led to another until they found themselves high in the Santa Cruz Mountains, and the Pacific was far away and infinitely vast and gleaming in sunlight—and then sundown, and the two of them roasting ears of corn, and the mating cry of a screech-owl, *kit-kit-kit-kit-twirrrrrrrrrrrr.* . . . Then they were together, naked beside a small stream under August moonlight, Califia with those strange, intense gray eyes that always seemed to be looking completely through him, and yes, she had reached out to him, had drawn him to her, yes, and murmuring how *a girl needs a teacher.* . . . The days that followed, those glorious days of exploration, across the Great Valley and into the Sierra Nevada, a land of forests and canyons until they reached that garden of huge boulders, and then up a lateral canyon until ultimately they found themselves within a grove of gigantic trees that now, as he struggled to remember accurately, seemed far more like images out of some dream, distorted and made huge in accord with the needs of the adolescent to experience that which is truly heroic, more of that sort than true memories, trees he'd laughed about at the time, the *arboles gigantescos de California*, the magic grove, the Garden of Eden to which he and Califia, Adam and Eve, had attempted to return.

A great golden-furred grizzly sow and two young ones—the trio oblivious to the humans on horses and seemingly not even curious about them.

There he and Califia spent the night, making love again and again, goading each other on until sheer exhaustion overtook them. By the clear light of day, when they thought their senses had returned to them, they made their crucial error—they attempted to go back to their own people. Pursued by Yokuts . . . and then an arrow, a quick stab of intense pain in his shoulder, the wound not fatal but fatal to the wild and doubtless incestuous relationship between two who'd grown up essentially as brother and sister. . . .

Three miles beyond the *new* village of Davenport, H.V. rode inland along the course of Scott Creek (as it was now called) and then turned due east along Big Creek, the tributary stream.

A large, hand-carved sign had been posted at the mouth of the little canyon: *Olivo & Beard Property, Those with No Ostensible Business Here Are Instructed to Stay the Hell Out, on Penalty of Being Shot.*

H.V. grinned, nodded, and rode ahead. The sign's language was clearly the invention of Uncle Bill Beard, who had never in his life been able to say anything simply.

As he came to the place where the trail forded the stream, H.V. dropped the reins and allowed his pony to drink. When Olivo looked up, he realized someone was standing no more than thirty feet distant, just on the opposite bank of the creek. The old man—his appearance one of *extreme* age, in fact—wore a breech clout and calf-high moccasins that were cross-laced. The man's arms were heavy, sagging a bit with age but nonetheless apparently quite powerful, and tattooed with a series of wavy, parallel dots. From the distance of thirty feet, H.V. couldn't tell whether the stranger were smiling or not—for the man had evidently lost all his front teeth.

"Homer Virgil, is that you?" the burly old individual asked. "You have changed—you look like a Whiteman whose skin is a little darker than normal. You look much as your father did when he was a young man, though."

For a long moment H.V.'s voice would not come to him, and he was ashamed of himself for fear that he would begin sobbing like some adolescent girl.

"Pelican Doctor?" he managed. "Is that you?"

The chief laughed loudly.

"So, Homer Virgil Olivo, you have returned. None of your relatives is here but me—your father and your uncle and your cousin Califia are off in one of those places where the Yeng-ways search for gold. Come on across. Your pony will stand there all night if you don't tell him what to do. . . . "

PART FOUR

REDWOODS &
SEQUOIAS

CHAPTER TWENTY-SEVEN

Roses on the Klamath

[1850–1852:]

CALIFORNIA ACHIEVED STATEHOOD in 1850. President Zachary Taylor had died in the White House, ostensibly of cholera, the same disease that had taken so horrible a toll on the ranks of the emigrants to California. On July 10, 1850, Millard Fillmore was sworn in as the thirteen president of the United States of America.

A Senate select committee, headed by Henry Clay, reported three bills to the floor of the Senate—an Omnibus Bill dealing with California, the boundary and debt of Texas, territorial governments, a fugitive slave measure, and a bill to abolish slave trade in Washington D.C. A convention in New Mexico adopted a constitution establishing boundaries and prohibiting slavery. Some senators urged that the Missouri Compromise line extend to the Pacific, so that California to the south of Monterey would be open to slavery.

Then the Senate passed a bill establishing a territorial government for Utah, with no restriction on slavery. The boundaries for Utah would be the Rockies to the east and the Sierra Nevada to the west, with Oregon Territory to the north and New Mexico Territory to the south. The Senate also approved

a bill adjusting the boundary between Texas and New Mexico,
at the same time providing a payment of ten million dollars
to Texas. A further bill was passed, this one on August 13, to
allow California admission to the Union as a free state. Two
days later the Senate approved a measure establishing the Territory of New Mexico without restriction as to slavery.

The period of September 6–9 saw the House pass a combined Texas and New Mexico bill and the Utah bill, along with
the California statehood bill. On September 9th Millard Fillmore signed legislation making New Mexico and Utah organized territories, while California was admitted to the Union
as the thirty-first state.

The meeting between Califia Flowers and Homer Virgil Olivo,
as matters turned out, was both brief and formal—hardly what
either might have anticipated. They embraced carefully and
then stepped back, each making a point of not staring at the
other.

Roxanne Olivo and Califia sized one another up in the
manner of prizefighters, and Homer Virgil, consummately ill
at ease, was forced to recognize consciously what he'd known
at some deeper level all along: Roxanne somewhat resembled
his cousin. Tall, dark-haired, and possessed of keen blue eyes,
Roxanne was in some superficial way a smaller-scale model of
Califia. Smaller in stature, yes, and her blue eyes lacked the
intensity of Califia's nearly paralyzing gray stare. How could it
be that one who lived to discipline his mind had not realized
what he was doing—what it was that drew him to Roxanne in
the first place? Or was he afflicted by a poet's wild imagination?

Whatever the case, he was married, and furthermore he'd
brought his properly civilized wife halfway around the world
to this land of California. Without a doubt, he owed Roxanne
fidelity.

Delighted though she secretly was to see H.V. again after
so many years, Califia was determined not to allow her emotions to make a fool of her. She was a widow, after all, a
woman in black (no matter what colors she wore), and she
would act accordingly. Furthermore, matters at Russian River
required the Boss Lady's immediate attention, and Califia,

stunned by the fate of Samson Flowers, threw herself into her work.

Within a week, the small sidewheeler *Mambrino's Helmet* was loaded with equipment and foodstuffs, as well as a mother raccoon and eight cubs, Rory Sunrise and Dame Broodsalot, and ever-faithful El Buzzardo. Calvin Beard set his course northward from Santa Cruz, and Califia was on her way back to a reunion with her cougars, presuming the big cats weren't too busy to come visit for a spell.

After much talk with his father, H.V. concluded that the most likely place to establish a school for the Ohlones and other Indian peoples would be in the rapidly expanding young metropolis of San Francisco. Roxanne was not happy in Santa Cruz, not even with her odd window overlooking the sea. She brooded a great deal. She missed England. She wished to be in contact with those who were willing to talk about books and music. She could see no reason why she should be denied the pleasures of opera and ballet.

H.V. talked with both his father and his Uncle Bill—was surprised to learn the old partners, hardheaded businessmen though they'd become, were nonetheless committed to his idea of a *college of sorts* for the Ohlones and other Indian peoples.

The importance of redwood was not lost upon the newcomers, and rival logging operations sprang up. A barge tender brought a load of unevenly sawed lumber into San Francisco and began to unload on a wharf below Ed Williams's lumberyard. Williams observed the operation and became interested. Olivo & Beard lumber was one thing, but this man evidently had contacts with the mill of some newcomer.

"Where'd you get this stuff?" Williams asked.

"Bodega Bay or thereabouts. Captain Stephen Smith, he's got him a sawmill up in the Big Trees. That concern you?"

"Yes, good fellow, it does. Let's talk business."

Williams bought the whole shipment, and thereafter had occasion to speak with his friend, Harry Meiggs.

"If you haven't seen the trees, Harry, it's damned well time you did. Millions and millions of feet of redwood, and some of the trees so goddamned immense that nobody has any idea how to cut 'em down, and that includes Larkin's bunch and Olivo and Beard."

"What about Smith?" Meiggs asked. "He must have the magic."

"The truth is," Williams continued, "some of those trees are so damned big that twenty men couldn't reach around one. I figure they're the oldest living things, and I'll lay you odds that some of 'em were over a thousand years old when the Lord was born."

"Point of fact," Meiggs said, "I do know. I've been down to the Olivo & Beard operation on the San Lorenzo. You don't have to convince me. So how do we make some money out of 'em?"

"San Francisco's growing fast, and there's never enough timber. After the last fire, everyone in hell was screaming for boards. Martin brought three loads down from Russian River, and it still wasn't anywhere near enough."

Plans were subsequently laid, and Williams went east via the Panama route and on to Connecticut to buy the machinery and saw blades necessary to the establishment of a mill, all of which equipment had to be shipped to California by means of the Horn Route, so that a full six months passed from Williams's setting out to his return.

Williams and Meiggs chartered a small schooner under a certain Captain Lansing and, machinery aboard, proceeded up the coast, past Bodega and on up the Mendocino coast to Big River, whose channel narrowed very quickly, providing at best a minimal harbor—sufficient for a doghole, nothing more. They anchored the schooner as securely as possible, at the same time hoping the fierce gales of the previous evening wouldn't be repeated.

The following day Meiggs and Williams canoed their way up the Big River, a stream that soon developed into no more than a creek at the end of a tidewater channel. To either side great redwoods grew, and the stream banks were clotted with pink-throated azaleas and rhododendrons. Williams would write later: *The winter rains had not wholly ceased and the river banks were full, the slight ripples meeting the verdure of the shore, the tall redwoods with their great symmetrical trunks traveling toward the skies . . . and over all the hush and solitude of the primeval forest—all combining to impress upon our minds the beauty and truth of the poetical line—"The groves were God's first temples"—and as I recall the beauty of the picture, I cannot but regret the part it appeared necessary for me to enact in what now looks like a desecration.*

Work on the mill went forward, but storms and lack of experience combined to see to it that the winter was upon them before the roof was on—and as a consequence, the building was ripped apart by fierce gales. Williams was determined, however, and by the following April he and his men had their mill up and running—with a production of fifty thousand board feet per month. Back in San Francisco, Harry Meiggs was merchandising every stick of lumber he received.

Thus was born the Mendocino Saw Mills, a potent competitor to the long-established operations of Olivo & Beard, and with the new company was to come such innovations as railroad tracks along which oxen hauled lumber carts from the mill site to a clifftop overlooking the doghole, so lumber might be hoisted down to the deck of a waiting schooner.

With Bill Beard and Raymondo Olivo giving advice and counsel, the widowed Califia was encouraged to establish a new operation near the mouth of Klamath River, on the north coast. Klamath country represented the northernmost and some of the largest redwoods, but now Olivo & Beard was to find itself in genuine competition. Pierson B. Reading had established first one and then a second mill on Humboldt Bay, the initial facility close by the town of Eureka and the second at Arcata. Dolbeer and Corzine ran the mills, and these individuals, Mariano Vallejo insisted, had been bankrolled by Reading, who seemed intent upon making the entire northern portion of the state his private preserve.

Bill the Sawyer and Raymondo Quixote Olivo went to Monterey to visit their old friends Philip Larkin and Jean Paul Martin, the latter in frail health and, at his own surmise, not long for this world. Both Larkin and Martin warned the partners that Reading was fair-minded but a fierce competitor. If anything, the defeat in the gubernatorial election had somewhat embittered the man. In any case, Larkin and Martin agreed, in matters of business competition, Pierson B. was unlikely to take prisoners. He considered the northern portion of California to be his *stamping grounds*, and Olivo & Beard would be viewed essentially as foreigners intruding upon the terrain.

Because of widespread and intense mining activity along the Sacramento and its tributaries, and along the Trinity and the Klamath as well, thousands of outsiders had poured into the northern areas of the state. Reading might not be able to control this horde of essentially lawless individuals. The whole mining thing, in fact, was like so much glowing swamp gas. Tent cities were set up and just as quickly taken down—or burned or simply abandoned.

But timber was different, and timber was the game Reading had chosen to play—with Allen Corzine and John Dolbeer as his knowledgeable agents in the field.

Larkin, who'd had occasion to meet Corzine, was of the opinion that in the long run, Reading might not be the match of his young partner—the latter an extremely shrewd, extremely able individual. Furthermore, there were rumors that Corzine's stunning wife Sarah was the apple of Pierson Reading's eye, and that because of her influence, Reading was less than fully critical of Corzine's actions and decisions.

A weakness for the ladies, Larkin conjectured, represented Reading's one potentially crucial weakness. But of how many men might one have said the same thing? *The little god of love* had laid low the ambitions of more than one hero and was known to afflict even the actions of Father Zeus and nearly all the other Olympians, gods and goddesses alike.

Jean Paul Martin urged caution while at the same time encouraging Bill and Raymondo to expand their operations northward. Huge profits, Martin was certain, were to be made from West Coast forests—which had, as yet, been no more than scratched.

"This sickness, it is *fâcheux*, a weakness in the blood of my family, *mes amis*. And yet I have lived a good life—*oui*, and a fairly long one as well. I left my homeland behind and found a better land here in Alta California. I have no regrets whatsoever. *Non, non*, you must not interrupt me. I have thought this matter over, and the conclusion I have come to is correct. Such family as I have back in France, friends of me, they are of little significance. It has been many, many years. I had no children of my own, and so I chose to adopt you two, William and Raymondo. You have worked hard and prospered, and I have rejoiced with you. You have remained loyal to me and have never played the parts of the ingrates. With these things in mind, I long ago altered my will so as to make you and your three children my heirs. You have become wealthy through your own labors, and so my wealth is not truly important to you. But the time is close now when I must leave and go to the land of mists and darkness. Odysseus may have been able to return to the world above, but I shall endeavor to accept my fate. In any case, I wish you to have it, the *fortuné*. That is all I wanted to say. Gentlemen, we shall have a cigar and a glass of port, *non*?"

Early in 1852 Califia and Juan Pescadero got their own mill running—with Juan supervising that operation, while Califia headed the gang of timber beasts a few miles upstream along the river, where Olivo & Beard had managed to acquire timber rights to tracts totaling some fifty thousand acres—a virtual kingdom of redwoods.

Because Olivo & Beard land adjoined Reading's holdings, Califia agreed to a meeting with Allen Corzine—and, accompanied by Pescadero, rode south to Eureka for the purpose of discussions. As matters turned out, she had lunch at the Hotel North Coast with both Corzine and his old compañero, John Dolbeer—while Juan tended to business with the local blacksmith, since the mill was in dire need of extra blades for the trim saws. El Buzzardo, once again established as his mistress's primary traveling companion, awaited Califia's pleasure while perched atop a large yellow cedar perhaps a hundred yards distant from the elaborately decorated three-story hotel built completely of redwood milled at the Corzine operation, the latter established a year and a half earlier.

Reading had assured Corzine that Califia Flowers didn't know the identity of her husband's killer—unless, of course, rumor had made its insidious way to Santa Cruz.

Nonetheless, Allen Corzine hardly looked forward to the necessary meeting with his rival *booshway*. Given the tales he'd heard about her, how could he be certain she might not pull out a Deringer pistol and make a corpse of him, then and there?

But the engagement began pleasantly enough, and Corzine's courage grew. Indeed, he found himself decidedly attracted to this particular female, rival or not, so attracted that he had to be careful not to make a fool of himself. Califia's presence was nearly sufficient to cause him (at least momentarily) to forget all about Sarah.

Corzine, after offering a toast to Califia's *half-human, half-divine beauty*, made the proposal that Olivo & Beard sell its newly established mill and concentrate instead on logging operations. Speaking with the authority of Pierson B. Reading behind him, Allen Corzine offered forty-five thousand dollars, a fair price as Califia conceded, and offered further to purchase on a long-term basis whatever logs Califia's timber beasts might produce, provided only that these were rafted downriver just as though the mill had remained under the operation of Olivo & Beard.

Politely, and with an ingratiating smile, Califia declined in behalf of her parent company.

Allen Corzine glanced at John Dolbeer—the two nodding slightly in a fashion that Califia took to mean *Nothing ventured, nothing gained. If we want that damned river to ourselves, we're going to have to come up with something a hell of a lot more compelling.*

"Well," Corzine nodded, "what if we up the ante? Olivo & Beard has controlling interest in a considerable portion of forest, from Martin's Ferry downriver to Johnson creek—excepting, of course, the disputed areas around the Karok village of Pecwan. By grant and purchase, according to our accounts, you folks control close to eighty square miles. Califia, we're prepared to buy you out—mill, land, all operations, provided only that we can come to an equitable price—amortized over twenty years, let's say. Olivo & Beard will realize a considerable profit and—"

"I don't think so," Califia smiled. "We've been in this business longer than anyone else in California, and we believe in the future. Competition'll be good for both of us—Olivo & Beard and Reading, Corzine, and Dolbeer. If we're willing to cooperate, then very likely we'll be able to supply one another with logs as our respective stockpiles gain and recede. The state's growing rapidly, and the need for timber's immense—not only here, but in the East as well, to say nothing of Hawaii, South America, the Orient. Olivo & Beard is prepared to co-operate—as in the matter of making some sort of settlement with the Yuroks and Karoks and Hoopahs—but we have no interest whatsoever in selling out."

Dolbeer nodded and drummed his fingers on the table.

"The fact is, we fairly well have the market here in Eureka under control. That means you'll have to ship everything south—or north."

"Perhaps your local merchants will be interested by lower prices," Califia suggested, sipping at her wine. "In any case, we have a fleet of a dozen schooners at our disposal, all capable of taking on lumber."

"A dozen?" Corzine asked. "We understood you had seven ships, all told."

"Seven of our own," Califia replied. "Four others belong to Jean Paul Martin of Monterey, and a fifth we have on lease from Philip Larkin. Look, we're willing to provide transportation for you, gentlemen, provided we can reach agreement with regard to rates. . . . "

Corzine stared at the beautiful, rough-hewn woman before him and reflected on the vile irony of fate. How could such a thing have happened—in all the taverns of the Far West, how in hell had he managed to find himself involved in a dispute with Sam Flowers? What horrible species of predestination could have caused him to draw his Colt and fire . . . ? *Her mouth . . . sensuous . . . lovely . . . her name's just right too . . . Amazon queen of California, and Jesus Christ All-Mighty, I'm falling ass over teakettle in love . . . in lust at the very least . . . and by God I'm sitting here talking business and getting a damned hard-on at the same time. You son of a bitch, God, you destroyer of men's lives, you and your rotten sense of humor, hitching me to my little hellcat and getting me to think I'm almost happy, and then you show me this one, whose reprobate of a husband I just happened to kill in what could have been deemed cold blood and a hanging offense, if Pierson Reading hadn't taken a shine to Sarah and so decided to intervene and save my neck for a different kind of stretching. . . .*

Juan Pescadero listened as he and Califia made their way
northward, past the Dolbeer milling operation at Arcata and
onward to Big Lagoon and from there across the hills to Redwood Creek, where some of the greatest of the trees grew—on
government land. Here, at the foot of one particularly huge old
patriarch, Califia and Juan made camp, fastening an oilskin
tarp in place against an insistent though still light rain.

While Califia tended the horses and convinced El Buzzardo
to eat a quantity of dry bread, Juan found a deadfall maple
and flailed away with a hand axe, ultimately producing a fairly
considerable pile of firewood. He came ambling up the easy
slope and dumped his armload.

"Goddamn buzzard, he's all set for the night." Juan grinned,
taking note of the big red-necked bird perched on Califia's
saddle.

"I tell the Buzzard about how much fun his wild relatives
are having out there in the storm, but he's not buying."

"Dolbeer's mill—maybe we should have taken a closer
look," Juan said. "What I hear, he's using different kinds of
gears to drive his gang saw. Supposed to be more efficient—
faster."

"So I understand," Califia agreed as she blew on the sputtering flames. "He's a clever man, though he doesn't talk much.
Where's that canteen? Let's get some coffee going. Incidentally,
Dolbeer must have come across on the California Trail with
Homer Virgil—partway, at least. H.V. told me about him—an
experienced logger and also an engineer of some sort—naval
engineer, I think. Came to find gold but changed his mind.
Isn't that a strange twist of fate, Juan? Dolbeer and a friend
struck out on their own and were captured by Pawnees—probably Dolbeer and Allen Corzine, since the two of them ended
up being partners. H.V.'s guide, an old salt named O'Bragh,
once lived with the Indians and was able to negotiate a settlement that had to do with taking a bad-natured squaw off the
Pawnees' hands. I've forgotten now whether Homer said the
woman married Dolbeer or someone else. There was a professor named Goffe as well—H.V. and Goffe became close friends
during the journey, but now the man's rumored to be living
with some renegade Maidus to the east of Sacramento—near

Downieville and Grass Valley. That's a strange turn of events, to say the least—a professor turned renegade."

Pescadero was startled by this bit of intelligence.

"Dolbeer, *he's* one of them that rode with H.V.? You sure, Miss Califia? And that other *hombre*, Corzine, him too?"

"I'm not certain, but it's likely. They're both Reading's men—as you know. He bankrolled the pair of them in an attempt to drive Olivo & Beard off the Klamath. Now that we're here and ready for business, Reading wants to buy us off—or put us in his employ, one or the other."

"Goddamn peculiar, *se enreda la pita*. Señora Califia, I think maybe he is the one."

"What are you talking about, Juan? *One* what?"

"One goddamn bad *sonamabeech*, that's what. This Señor Corzine, the one you do business with—isn't he the man who shot Samson?"

Califia stared at her foreman—stared without saying a word. The string of seconds flowed on uneasily so that the interval seemed much longer than in fact it was. Califia stood up and faced Pescadero. The boss lady placed her hands on her hips and shrugged back the dark mane of her hair. When she spoke, her voice quavered.

"What are you saying? Tell me what you're talking about, Juan!"

For a moment Pescadero acted almost as though oblivious to Califia's imperative. He turned, reached into a packsack and withdrew a leather flask of wine, lifted it, tilted his head back, and directed a crimson stream into his mouth. He offered the flask to Califia, who shook her head.

"I hear it from a mill hand," Juan said. "Tommy, him who used to be blacksmith in Shasta City. The *hombre* who shot Samson, Reading got him out of jail, then sent him across the mountains to Eureka. All that happened two years back, when . . . fella who shot Samson, he was with Dolbeer to start with—then they split up. Must have come across from Missouri with Cousin Homer and the others. . . ."

Califia felt her face go hot.

"It couldn't be," she said. "God's got a damned bad sense of humor, but not even He would. . . ."

"Have wine, Miss Califia," Juan said, forcing her to accept

the flask. "What God we talkin' about? Coyote, he's the only one that matters—an' he's crazy in the head. Gets killed all the time and then has to come back to life."

Califia sprayed wine into her mouth, returned the flask to Pescadero, and sat down beside the fire.

"I know about Coyote," she said. "To tell you the truth, I think I was married to him—Coyote in one of his incarnations, at least. I miss Sam, I sure as hell do—even if I never was able to get along with him. *Gord-damnit*, that's what he would have said. Corzine? You think he shot . . . my husband? The three of us, we were just sitting there and talking and eating. You've got to be wrong, Juan. It just doesn't make sense. However it happened, and I know Samson was forever getting into brawls, there's no way that an Allen Corzine could ever have . . . even with blind luck, there's no way. . . . Not sit there across from the widow and pretend to be . . . friendly . . . as if he had good sense . . . and offer compliments and wag his tail like a goddamn puppy dog and want to enter into a business arrangement. . . . "

Juan glanced over at El Buzzardo, frowned at the bird, and then kneeled down to place some more wood on the fire.

"Crazy, huh? What does this old Mestizo know? I just tell you what Tom the blacksmith say to me. All them guys get drunk together—they don't know what's going on. Usually don't remember anything, either."

The following Sunday, shortly before the noonday meal, a horseman rode in, scattering a covey of bantam chickens, the chief rooster of this particular social organization apparently half of a mind to do battle with the newcomer. The horseman tethered his mount at the hitching rail and walked quickly to the unfinished log cabin where the *booshway* lived. He removed his hat and proceeded to rap on the door.

After a moment Califia appeared, studying the stranger who'd come bearing what seemed to be a present—a cluster of red roses, their long stems wrapped in waxed paper and tied with a red ribbon.

"Miz Beard," the courier managed, "these here are for you. I come all the way over from Orick this morning. I was careful with 'em, just like Mr. Corzine told me. . . . "

Califia stared into the man's nearly blank brown eyes, saw only confusion.

"Why, thank you—yes, thank you," she said, accepting the bouquet. "From Allen Corzine, you say?"

"Yes, ma'am. I guess there's a note tucked in between the flowers. . . . "

"Which you read, naturally?"

"No, ma'am, of course not. I wouldn't do that. I just do what Corzine tells me, that's all."

Califia nodded, smiled.

"Thanks. You must be starved. There'll be chow over in the bunkhouse in about half an hour—corned beef and beans and salmon cakes and coffee. Stay and eat your fill."

"Thanks, ma'am," the courier replied, backing up awkwardly before turning in the direction of the Olivo & Beard bunkhouse.

CHAPTER TWENTY-EIGHT

Requa and Pecwan

[1852:]

H.V. Olivo's Journal, May 2, 1852:

Roxanne and I have now moved into the log house that Father and Uncle Bill constructed at Requa, a Yurok Indian village that's long occupied this same spot on the north shore of the Klamath River (*Klamat*, as they call it) immediately inland from its mouth. The village is quite well established and figures in several Yurok legends I've been honored to hear. The Yuroks are a taciturn people by and large, but I've been able to gain the confidence of two of the tale-tellers, both of them quite old, one a man, the other a woman.

Klamat is generally translated as *generous river*, no doubt owing to the hordes of salmon that in season come in from the sea, though the word itself isn't Yurok at all but rather Klamath—those who live far upstream at *Upriver Ocean*, known otherwise as Klamath Lake, on the desert side of the Cascade Mountains, a northern extension of the Sierra but differing from those mountains in being volcanic. The greatest of the peaks is *Waiiaka* or *Ieka* or *Shasta*, the latter a term applied to the Indians of the region, who may more properly be named the *Sastees* or the *Achomawi*. Peter Lassen insisted I should be able to see the mountain from his rancho, but haze prevented that.

The peculiar thing here is that the Klamath Indians are apparently of the same language group as the Yuroks and their cousins the Karoks—though Yuroks insist Yurok and Karok languages sprang from a different source. What I'm much more confident of is the fact that these peoples are related to Indian groups along the Pacific coastal waters from here northward, apparently to the Aleutian Islands. Until fairly recent times, there's been a well-developed trade route operating, including a slave trade. I gather the Klamaths, a highly successful warrior people who once nearly did in Fremont and the indomitable Kit Carson, capture Modocs, to whom they also seem to be related, and sell them to the Karoks. I should put all this in past tense, of course. The Karoks in turn sold them to the Yuroks, who then awaited the arrival of the big Aleut canoes (capable of carrying up to fifty men). Russian domination of the Aleuts put an end to the practice.

Roxy wasn't happy in Santa Cruz, and her spirits didn't greatly improve while we were in San Francisco. Nor do I genuinely believe that our removal to this Indian village in the north will help matters very much. It's altogether possible our marriage is in its final stages. However much I care for Roxanne, I simply cannot and will not allow her to run my life. I'm not of a mind to return to Europe.

Olivo & Beard operations figure to thrive here along the Klamath River. We have extensive tracts of virgin forest, much of it redwood, and our mill can barely keep up with the stream of logs that Califia's men send down the river to Johnson's Flat below Pecwan. Barges are used to bring the sawn lumber west to Klamath Mouth, where Cousin Calvin's able to take cargo aboard his *Don Quixote III*, the most recent addition to his flotilla. He has a virtual navy of his own. This afternoon saw him on his way south once more, the hold filled with redwood and fir of high quality.

My job at Requa is to arrange for cargo and contracts for trade goods—for Califia's mill and logging operations, for trade with the Indian peoples, and for trade with the growing numbers of gold miners who work the upper Klamath and its tributaries. Their efforts, one notes, have badly muddied the river, even this far from the site of their activities a hundred miles inland, above Ishi-Pishi Falls.

Perhaps the school I wished to establish in San Francisco will prosper here, for the Yuroks are an intelligent and curious people with a strong sense of their own past.

Roxanne is not in the best of health. Not only is she somewhat frail, but she's generally unhappy with her life in this "howling American wilderness." Possibly her frailty is primarily within her own somewhat active imagination. What I know positively is that she accepted the remove to Requa with a kind of stoic fatalism. It would doubtless be a good thing if we were to have a child to bind our flagging marriage. For the past several months my presumed husbandly rights have been ignored. Her health, she insists, requires that she have her own room. There are other complications as well. Yesterday Roxy and I returned from a short venture upriver to the logging areas—a trip, I'm afraid, that left a very bad taste in my mouth. My wife and my cousin seem to despise each other on sight. That was the essential response the women had when they first met, more than two years ago, a kind of spontaneous reaction that seems to be triggered anew each time the ladies are together.

Roxanne sees Califia as an utter barbarian, I'm afraid, a freak of nature—a woman's body that happens to be occupied by a hard-driving male of the laboring class. The pet vulture, various and sundry house-chickens, and stories of tame mountain lions that come in to meet her when she returns to the Russian River operation—these things do not help. However absurd Roxanne's perception of my cousin is, there's apparently no changing Roxy's mind. The ladies exchange insults, and not very subtly, all the time they're together. I almost have the feeling they look forward to these confrontations.

To the extent that I'm able to judge accurately with regard to Califia's response to my wife, on the other hand, I should say my cousin thinks of Roxy as a spoiled child. Well, possibly that's true—but she's not so spoiled or helpless she wasn't able to endure the trek across the American continent—something, I'd venture to say, many women would be unable to do.

It's possible that each recognizes in the other a basic anti-type, an opposite—and further that there's even a hidden element of jealousy. What I experienced with Califia all those years ago—rather, what we experienced together, culminating with the arrow in my back and my near-brush with death— hasn't been altogether forgotten. Do I still feel attracted to my cousin? Do I dare to inscribe in this journal a truthful answer to that question, even though the privacy of my writing is kept inviolate?

The answer, of course, is *yes*. The *passion*, if I may call it that, is not of the sort that's likely to do more than remain hidden, an ember burning the length of a dead root even as the winter rains pour from the sky. But what of spring, and the time of warmer, drier days? I recall being shown a peat bog burning that time Roxy and I spent a week in Sussex, burning slowly beneath ground and killing the pasture above. The Little Corporal, Napoleon, said it best: *A man seldom remembers but never forgets his first love.* True enough, true enough. Here am I, acting as a company functionary in charge of God-knows-what, cargoes and records of lading and keeping tabs on production for Olivo & Beard, yes, and hence in repeated contact with Califia—so that the two of us are honor-bound to gaze upon one another and then to look away.

H.V. Olivo's Journal, May 14, 1852:

The world's a strange and unpredictable place. My friend Goffe, from whom I had heard not so much as a single word since we arrived in California, has learned of my whereabouts and contacted me via post—at the same time urging me into complicity with regard to a change of names and a consequent hiding of his former identity—a practice common enough among Californians. He's now living with an Indian wife named *Ooti*, or *Acorn Girl* (and indeed an entire Indian tribe as well), in the mountains east of Peter Lassen's rancho, close by the volcanic butte now generally called Lassen's Peak. The man who was Goffe has adopted the cognomen McCain—the *clan of Cain*, or so I'd presume the meaning to be, inasmuch as Big Ben's a devoted scholar of language and literature. Furthermore, he has a son named William True-Bear. I wouldn't have thought of a man Ben's age as finding a young wife,

Indian or otherwise, but a portion of me envies him. It's a great disappointment that I'm still childless—and subject to remain so unless I find a way to warm the cockles of Roxy's heart, as well as other portions of her anatomy. There was a time when we couldn't keep our hands off one another, but all that's changed now.

From various hints Ben drops in his letter, I'd hazard that he may have turned renegade for his wife's people, at least for a time. We've all heard of the death-dancing Pano Maidus; that *Grizzly Clan*, as it's been called, is resolutely intent upon exacting some grotesque revenge. The other Indian groups hear the rumors, and they too begin to think about striking back. Even Pelican Doctor laments that he's too old to go on a revenge-taking. In any case, Ben's secret is safe with me, of course—particularly since I don't actually share it and can only conjecture.

Ben *McCain* has set up a sawmill and is able to produce good-quality pine lumber—yellow pine and sugar pine, since the forest in that area is primarily of those species, but with Oregon fir and red and white fir mixed in as well. I've suggested to Califia that perhaps it would be in our best interest to take a trip to this place *McCain* calls Upper Eden. If there's any way of transporting sawn lumber down out of the mountains to the Sacramento River, Calvin will be able to take on occasional cargo, to the benefit of both parties involved. Pine lumber, after all, is in many ways a superior building material—stronger then redwood, if not as weather-resistant. Pines are good-sized trees, to be sure, and in general they offer fewer difficulties in terms of logging and hauling the logs into mill.

As to how this is likely to work out, I can only surmise. I must be careful. I mustn't allow myself to do anything dishonorable. Roxy and I have had many good times together, and in all truth I cannot blame her for feeling toward Califia as she does. Long ago I told her what happened between myself and my cousin—long before Roxanne and I were married. To employ the ancient cliché, one must sleep in the bed one has made; and if there are dangers, temptations I should say, why then *un gramo de previsión vale más que una tonelada de curación*. . . .

A final unhappy note: my idea of establishing a school here at Requa seems to be dying at birth. The Yurok leaders are concerned that the *medicine* of the Whiteman will infringe upon their own. Despite my skin color and beardless face, the Yu-roks are determined to see me as a *Boston Yengee*. It is possible that I've turned White and yet cannot see it?

H.V. Olivo's Journal, May 17, 1852:

I accompanied a new group of loggers upriver to the camp above Pecwan, some of the men miners who'd tossed their pans into the brush, and a few of them genuine loggers who've made their way west from Michigan. No doubt these individuals heard tales of trees ten times the size and three times the height of what they'd been cutting, inasmuch as accounts of our Western forests have long since reached the East, along with at least a few loads of redwood lumber carried around the Horn. Most Easterners laugh at the *tall tales* and presume them to be the lies of a Kit Carson or Jim Bridger; but those same stories must have been welcomed by the childlike imaginations of New England and Michigan timber beasts, tree butchers, buckers, and river pigs. Just as the redoubtable O'Bragh and Sam Flowers and others like them were forever dying of curiosity to discover what lay beyond the next range of mountains, so the archetypal logger couldn't be satisfied until he'd seen with his own eyes such forests as had as yet not echoed to the faller's axe.

I gather it must be deemed as a kind of competition—man against tree. In any case, one can imagine these *gentilhommes des tin pants* grinning and rising precipitantly from the split-log *deacon seats* of their respective bunkhouses (also know as *muzzle loaders* if they're so damned crowded the men have to slip into their bunks from the foot), packing and rolling up their *bindles*, and setting out for the fabled redwoods, Douglas firs, sugar pines, and ponderosa pines of the Far West.

At the time I was sent off to England to be educated and, of course, to effect a separation from Califia, lumbering in California and to the north in Oregon country was as yet a small-scale industry. Prior to the discovery of gold at Sutter's Mill, the *civilized* population of the West, including the British in Canada and Oregon and the Californios and Yankees in California, probably did not exceed a total of 25,000—few enough for so huge a land. But one must add to that the obvious matter of isolation, with nearly two thousand miles of mountains and deserts and plains separating the West from, let's say, the Mississippi River. Export to the East was essentially out of the question, and so our logging operations seemed fated to growth, dependent upon increase in local population. But worthless yellow metal in the river sands, the glowing petals of California poppies, and all was destined to change.

With the great influx of population into California, the doors were opened to a greatly expanded logging industry, and Olivo & Beard, its operation securely in place, grew rapidly. Competition from a hundred or so Corzine and Dolbeer companies was inevitable. In any case, some of the men I now led up the Klamath were those who'd previously worked in the pine and spruce woods along Manistique River in Michigan, as they informed me. They found their way to Eureka in the hope of getting work at one of the Corzine/Dolbeer logging operations. Nothing was doing in that quarter, but with luck they ran into Juan Pescadero, who'd come in to Arcata to fetch supplies. Olivo & Beard was in need of crewmen, and agreement was soon reached.

Several of these fellows were of a mind to provide musical accompaniment to our journey up the Klamath, and by means of free adaptation of a song that must have been native to the north shore of Lake Michigan, came up with the following doggerel, half chanted, half sung:

I arrived in Eureka the tenth day of May
To make my connection with a coach I did pray;
But got left in Arcata and this was my doom;
To pay a short visit to the Dead Man's Saloon.

I walked boldly in and stepped up to the bar;
A big-titted beauty says, "Have a see-gar."
So I took the stogie, sat down on a chair,
And the young thing come skipping and tripping round there.

She boldly flounced up and sat down on my knee,
She says, "You're a redwood axeman, that's plain to me—
You've brought down the big toothpicks, I surely do know
Since your muscles are hard from your head to your toe.

"Your shorthorn's as long as a Tennessee eel
And would frighten a grizzly dame with its deal:
But Mister I've tamed greater serpents than this,
So I'd suggest that you go take a quick piss. . . . "

The boys seemed to enjoy the irregular ballad and sang it repeatedly until one fellow suggested the Stan Hager song. The Michigan men were enthusiastic—and so the choral performance was renewed, again with extempore adjustments to a doubtlessly corrupt original text, so as to account not only for their present situation but also that of the mythical Stan Hager. The tune to the second ditty, I noted, was nearly indistinguishable from the first:

My name is Stan Hager where the white waters flow;
My name it's engraved on the rocks of the shore;
I'm a boy that stands happy on a log in the streams,
My heart was with Hannah, for she haunted my dreams.

I went up the Manistique some money to make;
I was steadfast and steady, I n'er played the rake.
Through Marquette and Ishpeming I'm very well known;
They call me Stan Hager, the pride of the town.

One day on the river a letter I received—
From Hannah, who told me that she was sure peeved;
She'd wed a young man who a long time had delayed,
And the next time I'd see her she'd not be a maid.

Then adieu to the Manistique; for me there's no rest.
I'll shoulder my peavey and I'll head out West.
I'll go to Eureka some pleasures to find,
And I'll leave my own Ishpeming darling behind.

So come all you jolly raftsmen with hearts stout and true,
Don't depend on a woman; you're sunk if you do—
And if you should meet one with a dark chestnut curl,
Just think of Stan Hager and his Ishpeming girl.

However, I couldn't for long keep my mind on the brainless good nature of the loggers and loggers-to-be. On horseback again, I felt as though reprieved from the cares that sometimes all but overwhelmed me—domestic matters that I shouldn't, of course, have reason to complain about. Pescadero and I exchanged pleasantries, with me riding alongside the laden buckboard he was steering, and then I drifted on ahead, intent upon absorbing the thousand various impulses of spring. Klamath River was wide and blue, with sunlight reflecting in brilliant crescents from an infinite number of points in its current, and in the broad green meadows which sloped gently toward the river, we discovered numerous elk, these interspersed with bands of deer—yes, and a few pronghorns as well. White egrets stood like so many stiff-backed palace guards along the water's edge, now and again joined by a blue heron—a bird whose great size never ceases to surprise me. Not even the few condors I remember from my boyhood could match the wingspread of a large heron—perhaps as much as ten feet from tip to tip. For all their size, the herons appear to be relatively gentle birds, and they work out their territorial disputes generally at long range, with a great deal of huffing and strutting and posturing. Strangely enough, they act as though they don't even see the egrets and lesser herons and bitterns—as though these birds were of some minor hegemony and beneath their notice.

The dark redwood forest grows to the river itself in places and to the bounds of meadows in others—redwoods almost exclusively, though with an occasional Oregon fir or ponderosa mixed in. These two latter varieties grow more luxuriantly high up on the long ridges of the Coast Range—presumably owing to less moisture or to more rapid runoff during storms.

Lights gleamed from the river, ungulates moved out of our path but didn't seem particularly disturbed by our presence, and the fishing birds continued their business in the Klamath's shallows—jabbing into the water, sometimes spearing an unwary fish, and then tilting back their long beaks to swallow their wriggling prey.

At length I drew my pony to a halt and waited for Juan and the gang of recruits to catch up.

Across the river from us, as we forded Blue Creek, we caught sight of a sow grizzly and three cubs—unusual, from what Pelican Doctor had told me. I wondered if perhaps this grizzly had somehow adopted a cub from a less matronly cousin—or if perhaps the mother of the third cub had died. Among the Ohlones there are no orphans, and possibly the same is true among the grizzlies.

One of the former gold miners pulled his rifle from its scabbard and proceeded to take aim at the griz.

"Don't shoot!" I shouted. "We're not paying you to terrorize the damned bears. You wound that old gal, and she'll hunt you down, sure as hell, and chew off your pizzle for lunch. Put the gun away. . . ."

"That an official Olivo & Beard order?"

"Consider it official."

"Yeah? Well, you don't look like no damned logging boss I ever heard of. Why should I believe your name's Olivo, anyhow?"

"Put down the rifle," I insisted, "or I'll be obliged to commandeer it."

"What the hell's that mean?"

I grinned, spat as far as I could in the direction of the river, and rode up to the troublemaker's side.

"Put your rifle away," I said softly, "or I'll break off your arm and beat you to death with it."

The miner eyed me suspiciously. He was taller than I and perhaps twenty or so pounds heavier. He grinned.

"You an' whose goddamn pappa?"

"Me and my little friend here," I replied, withdrawing my Colt-Patterson and waving the barrel back and forth. "Please understand—all of you—we need workers, and we pay good wages, higher than the Dolbeer men get. But there's no drinking on the job, and hunting's left to the man charged with that responsibility. You want to argue, just head on back down the river—and no hard feelings. When we get to the log landing, you'll meet your other boss—a boss lady, Bill Beard's daughter. Pescadero operates the mill, and Califia . . . Flowers is the woods boss."

"*Cow of the woods?*" one of the loggers asked. "What kind of tom-jack operation is this, anyhow?"

"We've been cutting timber since 1820, as a matter of fact," I replied. "First damned logging operation in California, and we haven't gone broke yet. Understand me, fellas, Califia's a special lady. She can likely outride, outshoot, and outsmart any man here. Nonetheless, if I hear of anyone causing her grief, that man's going to get buried."

"What a bunch of bullshit . . ." someone muttered.

A few yards distant was a small dead ponderosa with a dozen or more cones clinging to the upper branches. It appeared a fairly easy shot and a good chance to show off a bit, and I proceeded to fire four times—was fortunate enough to send three cones spinning through the air.

"Gunslinger, ehh?"

I whistled, shook my head.

"Never thought of myself in those terms," I said. "You want the truth, gentlemen? The truth is—I'm a damned English teacher, that's what."

This remark drew a general round of chuckling, and even the troublemaker grinned sheepishly—though whether it was because I'd admitted to the *female* role of English teacher or because I'd sent the cones flying I couldn't tell.

The gunshots brought Juan Pescadero on the run, the big Mestizo waving his own Colt in the air.

"Un ojo al gato y otro al garabato!" Juan yelled. "Look out! No goddamn gunfighting in my crew!"

"Just target practice," I said. "I was explaining about Califia—how she taught me to shoot. Did you catch sight of the momma griz?"

I pointed across the river to where I could detect the sow's hump as she moved off through tall grass and lilac brush. Juan glanced, nodded, and then holstered his pistol. He touched his fingers to his mustache and glared at the new men.

"Maybe we should *keel* someone just to make a point?" he asked.

"Not necessary," I replied. "Everything's under control. Let's get on to where the *big trees* grow."

I snapped the reins along my pony's neck.

H.V. Olivo's Journal, May 19, 1852:

The very idea of felling the big redwoods has begun to work on my mind. According to the philosopher, certain things may be regarded as *categorical imperatives*. Now I begin to think that cutting these magnificent forests must be indeed a negative imperative. *Thou shalt not fell these giants. Thou shalt leave the bloody trees alone. Thou shalt get the hell out of here lest I smite thee with lighting and earthquake and volcanic eruption and grievous boils and other lesions of the flesh.*

Whether I do or not, however, the logging business will go on. Califia was pleased with the new batch of recruits—especially with her skilled Michigan axemen. Running her crew short-handed, she hadn't actually been able to keep up with Pescadero at the mill. At least part of the trouble, as she explained to me, lay with the fact that many of the trees in groves closest to the river were simply too damned big to work with, and so it proved necessary to skid smaller logs down the hillsides, along cross-tied chutes that brought the timbers to where ox teams could deal with them. Driving oxen on a slope was an extremely dangerous business, since if a log should overcome its inertia and begin moving on its own, it was almost certain to override the ox teams, drover and all. Several animals had been lost in this way at Russian River, and at the same time, one bull-skinner had his leg crushed as he attempted to slash the oxen's tether lines to get the animals the devil out of the way.

Califia talked to the new men for quite awhile, explaining both what was to be done and what was not under any circumstances to be done. Chief among the prohibitions is the matter of proper and respectful treatment of the numerous banty chickens. Eggs, when discovered, are to be turned over to the camp cook. In no way are the chickens to be harmed. The black and red birds have, so to speak, proprietary rights. She held up both Rory Sunrise and Dame Broodsalot on her arm, and the expression on Boss Lady's face was quite serious.

"These two in particular," she said, "are old friends of mine—the father and the mother of their respective nation, and hence the source of many omelets. In a world where eggs are worth their weight in gold, the man among you who harms a feather on any avian head will be shot at first light and chopped up for chicken feed. My other friend, the vulture perched up here on the chuck wagon, that's *El Buzzardo*. We've been *compañeros* for many snows. As long as you don't leave chow lying around, and as long as you don't try sleeping on the job, then he's no danger. Fall asleep on shift, and El Buzzardo figures you're dead and starts pecking your eyes out. If he gets to be a pest, gents, tell me about it. Yell at him if you want, but don't throw rocks. I'm telling you—the man who harms one of my birds will be cut in half with a dull axe. Let's just say the boss lady's *dingy as an outhouse mouse* and let it go at that. You fellows have got your quirks, and I've got mine. When you have a few days off, ride on down to Eureka. Dead Man's Saloon's supposed to have a dozen *nurses* on the job at all times. You need nursing, they'll nurse you. But no *Karok orphan gals* and no booze here in camp. . . . "

Following the pep talk, an arm-wrestling match was held between Tommy the blacksmith and Califia—for the benefit of new crew members. Pescadero read the rules, *Texas Rules*, as he so eloquently put it. Once the match was under way, Califia grabbed an axe handle and pretended to belabor Tommy, then pinned his arm—to the sustained applause of the old hands.

"Winner and still cham-peen, by virtue of *hacerle a uno la pera y jugar sucio*," Juan declared, "*y por gracia de Jesús y Maria!*"

The meeting was declared over, and the men, tools in hand, were led out to where logging was in progress. The greenhorn miners and the seasoned Michigan loggers as well were given the rudiments of the art of cutting big trees and moving the logs about. Those who didn't learn quickly enough were subject to end up quite dead.

H.V. *Olivo's Journal, May 21, 1852*:

On Sunday, shortly before noon, a dispatch rider drew up before Califia's shanty at the log landing beside the Klamath, dismounted, and knocked on her door. This scene, I learned later, had occurred numerous times—always on Sunday. The rider came to deliver roses, roses probably cut from year-old bushes beside Allen Corzine's new house in Eureka, some forty miles distant—Corzine, whom I now knew to be the suspected killer of Califia's husband, had apparently encumbered approximately half of one employee's working hours (and no doubt extra pay to boot) for the explicit purpose of delivering flowers. In respect to pacifying a guilty conscience, men do strange things. I considered whether in fact I'd ever liked Corzine, and the answer was clearly negative. When he and Dolbeer were with us on the way up to Fort Laramie, Corzine insisted on flirting with Roxy. After O'Bragh rescued the two of them from Behele's Pawnees, Corzine was too busy trying to gain Sarah's favor to pay any further attention to my wife. Who, after all, could blame such trifling behavior? But the fact remained that I felt no warmth toward the man. Was it that Corzine was reputed to have shot Sam Flowers, a man I'd often heard of but never actually knew—a man who'd deserted Califia for the lure of booze and brawls—or was it that I felt jealousy, the same niggling anger I'd experienced toward Allen Corzine when he was being so goddamned *friendly* in Roxanne's direction?

H.V. *Olivo's Journal, May 22, 1852*:

On Monday morning, while we watched a pair of old hands gandy-dancing their way from one springboard to another until they were a dozen feet above the ground and safely upon a loosely constructed scaffolding and then resuming work on a massive back-cut which, when finished, would be considerably taller than the men themselves, their axes flashing through the filtered sunlight of the forest floor and *chunk-chinking, chunk-chinking,* I found myself telling Califia of my concerns. Her gray eyes flashed with excitement, and she brushed her long dark hair out of her eyes and laughed at me.

Lovely breasts . . . a woman's breasts beneath the loose cloth of a lumberjack's red flannel shirt . . . I must learn to prevent my imagination from wandering . . . to where it should never have been in the first place . . . a world past, a world ago. . . .

"England hasn't worn off yet, Homer. You think in terms of limits—everything small and tidy and in its place. The West's big beyond all schemes to tame it, and I don't think we ever will, not even if mankind should someday learn to harness the fires of hell itself. I leave the biggest trees, of course, since I'd be hard pressed to figure out what to do with them if we did fell them. I doubt the spirits of any Ohlone dead are up here, and the Karoks have nothing to say on the matter. Homer, when we were back at the San Lorenzo, you told me about that big friend of yours, the one from Connecticut—him and his Sleeping Giant Mountain? Come along, and I'll show you a real sleeping giant."

I wasn't altogether certain whether Califia had blown me a kiss—perhaps she did so without thinking, for she turned quickly and strode to where the ponies were tethered. Apparently I was supposed to follow.

We rode among redwoods, the forest replete with the odors of life—of ferns in great green clots scattered among the trees, of pink-throated azaleas in blossom, of yellow bush lupines in open areas where sunlight penetrated, and of flaring pink rhododendrons in the shady areas.

"What I want to show you, Homer, it's right up ahead here. Redwood doesn't rot—you know that. So this giant may have fallen hundreds of years ago, who can say? Some of the bark's still on it, but the rest of the log's turned white, the way they do when a river carries them out to sea and the sea plops them back up onto the beach—like that tangle of logs where we used to. . . ."

Califia stopped suddenly, her sentence in mid-career, and then she burst out laughing.

"Where we used to take off our clothes and lie there in the sun—when we were children, Homer Virgil. Don't you remember?"

"Nothing of the sort ever happened," I replied. "I am innocent of all charges."

Califia nodded.

"Your arrow wound—does that still bother you at times?" she asked.

"The wound—yes—at times. I can tell when there's a rainstorm on the way in, just like Pelican Doctor."

"Something good came of it, then," Califia said, drawing her pony to a halt. "There's your *sleeping giant*, right down below us. Eventually bits and pieces of foliage from above will bury it, I suppose. That will happen long before it rots. . . ."

An immense downfall tree lay there in the shade, among lesser, upright giants, and clumps of fern spurted from the zone where the bole lay on the ground like some long, gray sheaf of stone—with segments of red-gray bark still clinging.

"Come!" Califia called out. "We can ride our horses right up onto the whale's back—I've done it several times since I discovered the old fellow. I could have the men section the log and skid it to the landing. I'm certain the wood's still as usable as ever. But somehow the beast looks—what? Asleep, yes, asleep. It's been sleeping here for centuries, a gigantic whale out of water. The Karoks have a story about a whale that lived in a small lake somewhere back in these Siskiyous—but I think perhaps someone a long time ago came across this old tree and responded much as I do. It looks like a whale, don't you think?"

"*Very like a whale,*" I chuckled, quoting Shakespeare's Polonius and feeling vaguely, stupidly superior. It had indeed been years ago, my father made all three of us—Cal, Califia, and I—read and discuss *Hamlet,* and there followed a discourse upon what one might fairly attribute to the Bard and what was to be deemed simply the chattering of his characters. The scene came back to me—Dad and the three of us there in Hotochruk's medicine lodge of all places, sitting around a fire pit and talking about a British playwright who'd been dead and entombed for two hundred years.

Califia and I approached the fallen giant from its smaller end, where the trunk had no doubt snapped when a windstorm of the distant past had brought it down, perhaps even on the day that Shakespeare himself was laid to rest under his rhyming flagstone. Califia urged her pony forward, and the animal easily leaped onto the back of the log. I followed, and we moved toward the far end, where the great spreading bole flared with a tangle of roots that seemed to clutch at the air. With great caution we were able to turn our horses about.

"I come here sometimes in the moonlight," Califia said, "and lie down on my back, stare at the stars—the few at least that one can see between the trees. It's almost as though only part of heaven had been created."

"This place—time stops here. Don't let them cut up the log, Califia. For the few dollars it's worth after it's sawn into boards, we'd lose a spoke in the Great Wheel of Creation. Maybe this redwood's been here since Noah's flood."

"You don't really believe that . . . ?"

I shook my head, urged my pony toward the jump-off point.
"No. But why not think of it as a broken-off mast from
Noah's Ark?"

"Perhaps," Califia replied. "But I like my stranded-whale
idea better. I could never imagine how Noah built an ark large
enough for all the animals—two by two, and so forth. Perhaps
they had larger *cubits* in those days, just the way everyone
seemed to live about ten times as long as they live now. You're
a scholar, Homer Virgil. You'll have to show me . . . that . . .
someday. How big the ark was, I mean."

"Be happy to," I said as my pony balked, on the verge of
refusing to leap down, "as soon as you explain to me why in
sweet hell you're accepting those roses every week from the
sonofabitch who killed your husband."

Califia didn't respond immediately. Then, as we rode into
a sunlit area dotted with twenty or thirty great stumps, she
pulled on the reins and smiled.

"Allen Corzine? Why, Homer, he's a former friend of yours,
I believe. Perhaps I should challenge him to a shoot-out? I
thought about that. Samson had left me. He became an old
man quite suddenly, and after it happened he was never the
same. He resented me—and resented the hold he thought I
had over him. He wanted his freedom, and he simply took off
and didn't return. His message to me was that I should find *a
buck* my own age. I loved Samson, you educated toad, don't
you think otherwise! But he died the way he had to, the way
he was fated to die. There was no malice in it—I didn't know
for a long while, but I do now. A brawl over some floozy in a
tavern in Whiskeytown. Bullets started flying, and Samson
stopped one of them. Corzine was arrested and turned loose
for lack of evidence—so maybe he shot Samson, and maybe
he didn't. I'll probably never know, and I don't really want to.
For your information, Allen Corzine's married—and happily
married, from what I hear. Sometimes Allen and John Dolbeer
and I have business dealings—that's all there is to it. Dolbeer's
another of your trail partners. A bit of a coincidence, isn't it?
What happened with Samson makes things difficult—and Corzine sends roses up sometimes on Sundays. You want me to
apologize for what I can't control?"

I nodded, somewhat surprised by Califia's outburst, but no

less surprised at myself for having brought up the matter in the first place.

"*Sí, señorita*. I was there when Corzine got married—though whether he's still with the same lady, I don't know. About those roses—every Sunday for the last three months, from what I hear. How long do you think he'll keep it up?"

"Couldn't say. Some men are more persistent than others. Let's get on back."

"Allen's married to a young lady named Sarah Witt," I said. "Perhaps you recall the story I told everyone two years ago? The white woman who'd been captured by Pawnees—and since they didn't want her, they kidnapped Corzine and Dolbeer and negotiated their release on the grounds that we were to take Sarah with us."

For an instant Califia appeared genuinely puzzled. Then she shrugged.

"Maybe the famous Mrs. Corzine's a pureblind bitch—how would I know? I'm told she's quite attractive, H.V. She chose Allen, then. Perhaps you're a bit miffed by that? Of course, you're also married—to that *oh so proper* Dame Roxanne the Lion-hearted. One woman's not enough?"

At this point Califia spurred her pony and was off like a shot, disappearing across the clearing before I could even get my animal to moving.

*

II.V. *Olivo's Journal, May 27, 1852:*

I returned to Requa this afternoon (Saturday) to find Roxy in what appeared to be a deep depression. That mental state, however, altered quickly enough when I attempted to placate her. The argument that my trip was dictated by the needs of the company did little to "soothe the savage breast," for *savagery* is what Roxanne's melancholy soon turned into.

"Why did I ever leave England?" she demanded. "Why did I marry you in the first place? My father was right—a miserable bookworm with no other ambition and insufficient gumption to compete in the world of commerce, and an aboriginal to boot, even if you are a schoolmaster. . . . Why, Homer Virgil? That's what I want to know! Why have you dragged me off to this godforsaken corner of the universe only to leave me in the care of a couple of Yurok house servants while you go off whoring after that cousin of yours? Don't lie to me—she's never out of your thoughts. How dare you presume to deal with me in this fashion? I demand a divorce and a generous settlement—I demand that we return to England. Oh, Homer, I don't mean to talk like a common fishwife. Those days back in England, they were good, weren't they? Remember when we used to make love all afternoon and into the evening? A flask of mead and a nice coal fire burning in the fireplace. . . . Why don't you ever make love to me anymore? I have desires too! I. . . ."

When I approached her and attempted to take her into my arms, she rose from the sofa, slipped away, grabbed a pewter bookend, and hurled the thing directly at my head, missing by no more than a few inches.

"You bloody sonofabitch!" she howled as the bookend bounced off the wall and thudded to the floor. "Don't even *think* about laying your filthy hands on my arse—not after you've been with her! If it wasn't your cousin, then it was some dirty squaw you found along the river. I've had quite enough of you, Homer Virgil Olivo! When Calvin returns for his next load of lumber, I'm leaving with him. At least in San Francisco it's possible to lead a more or less civilized life. You can come with me or stay here, that's up to you. . . . "

Then Roxy was out of the room, slamming the door behind her.

Picking up the bookend, I took note of an empty rum flask on the floor beside the sofa. I grabbed from the shelf a new book, one that Uncle Bill had bought me before I came north to Requa—a double-volume edition in a cardboard dust case. Then I turned and left the house, slamming the door behind me. My pony was still saddled, for I hadn't taken time to tend her before entering the house and attempting to make peace with Roxanne. I'm certain the poor creature had been standing there in full anticipation of a rubdown, a curry comb, a clean stall, and a bucket of oats and corn, but such was not to be. For the time being at least, I'd had quite enough of Miss Roxanne and her temperament, and so, without being entirely certain where I was going, I crossed through Requa, with its communal lodge and its log and plank houses on the slope above the river, almost in the fashion of some quaint little village beside a loch in northern England or Scotland.

But this was a Yurok village on the Klamath River, and upstream not too many miles were a mill and a logging area and people with whom I could enjoy a reasonable conversation—though at the moment the image of Roxy's empty rum bottle was sufficient to suggest that I, too, might just wish to get roaring drunk. Unfortunately I had no rum, whether genuine British or a good Yankee imitation, but I did have a small bottle of very bad whiskey tucked into my saddlebags—*snakebite medicine* that required no snakebite. I reached back as I rode, found what I sought, and proceeded to take such a swig that my eyes hurt, my throat burned, and I was unable to breathe for a few moments. Then I snorted with pleasure and wiped at my eyes. With the late-afternoon sun brilliant and quite comfortable behind me, I made my way toward Pecwan. Nightfall overtook me at the Blue Creek crossing, and so I put my pony on the end of a rawhide lariat (instructing the animal not to eat the damned thing), threw down my bedroll, lit a camp fire, ate jerky and stale bread, and resolved to drink the rest of my whiskey.

After a bit I fetched the new book and settled beside my flickering fire to read. The novel was by a woman author who'd gained a bit of notoriety with this particular two-volume edition: *Uncle Tom's Cabin; or, Life Among the Lowly.* I could see immediately why Uncle Bill and Dad had been so intrigued with the book, sentimental though it was—for it was a response to the Fugitive Slave Law of 1850 and appeared to be the work of one who knew her material well and who had likely done a bit of research.

Uncle Bill had told me the book, published earlier this year and having just arrived in San Francisco, was a best-seller in the East, and in the South as well, though one would suppose for different reasons. The subject had great inherent interest, of course, both in its own right and because of the obvious comparison to the treatment of the Native peoples here in California and elsewhere in the lands west of the Mississippi— to say nothing of the hateful impact upon the Indian peoples from the time of the first settlements in New England, more than two hundred years earlier—or of the Spanish conquests in Mexico and in South America.

Is it always the case that those people with the more advanced technology are fated to dominate those with whom they come into contact—and to enslave them if possible and convenient? Machiavelli asserts that might makes right, and for all practical purposes I suppose he's correct.

H.V. Olivo's Journal, May 28, 1852:

I was enjoying my cousin's conversation when that damned Allen Corzine arrived—this time bringing his Sunday morning roses in person. He was startled to find me there—for indeed it had been some considerable while since we'd seen one another. Califia sensed immediately the hostility I felt toward this man who had once been my traveling companion, and she attempted to pour oil upon the troubled waters. I was having no part of it. However foolish I was being, I knew precisely why it was that I was acting in such a fashion. The green demon of jealousy had me. This sonofabitch Corzine had not only laid Samson Flowers in his grave, but now he was attempting to pay court to the man's widow.

Allen and I exchanged pleasantries with regard to Sarah and Roxanne, respectively, and then I suggested rather pointedly that it was altogether possible that his weekly roses weren't precisely welcome.

"H.V., what's got into you?" Califia asked when the two of us had a moment out of earshot of our visitor. "Allen's a business associate. Calvin's got a contract to transport finished lumber from the Dolbeer mill south to Monterey and Santa Barbara. You're annoyed by the roses? Look, Homer—if Allen chooses to play the fool with some notion of gaining my favors, why that's all to the advantage of Olivo & Beard. At least act decent to the man. Great heavens, you and your friends once saved his life—rescuing him from the Cheyennes. . . . "

"Pawnees," I said. "And that's just one of the mistakes I made with this fellow. He's got all the character and personality of a slug—or perhaps a rattlesnake. Don't buy his brag, Califia. He's not the harmless businessman you take him to be. He'd sell his mother's soul if there were profit in the transaction."

"You're being foolish, and you're being unpleasant. Relax a

bit. I can't imagine Allen's likely to stay very long. His riding up here this way is a real compliment. He knows I know about the incident with Samson—don't call it murder, H.V., it wasn't. Sam Flowers lived and died in accord with his own plan. Had it come to a shooting match, not Allen Corzine nor God Himself was Samson's match. It wasn't that. Tom the blacksmith was there—and he's told me the entire story. For the moment, however, we share these forests with Reading, Corzine, and Dolbeer. Unless we want an all-out war, we're best advised to get along, to make adjustments."

"What's happened to you, Little Cal?" I asked. "I'm not even certain I know you anymore. . . ."

I turned, strode out through the main room, where Allen Corzine was nervously smoking a cigar. I tipped my hat in Corzine's direction and scowled.

"It's too bad O'Bragh didn't leave you for Behele's men to burn," I said. "Take my advice, Corzine. Stay the hell away from Califia. She may not wish to put a round into you for the murder of Sam Flowers, but I don't feel so generous. Truth is, I could do it without thinking twice."

"What in God's name are you talking about, Homer? Did I say something to get you riled?"

"Nothing recent," I replied as I left Califia's log cabin. I slammed the door as I did so.

Slamming doors was getting to be a habit with me.

CHAPTER TWENTY-NINE

Business
Proposition

[1852:]

H.V. RODE DOWNRIVER, past the mill at Johnson's Flat, and then upslope through dense forest where a pair of spotted owls took flight, one bird circling back to its nest, far up in a red-wood. Olivo proceeded to the back of Pecwan Ridge, a narrow formation between Klamath River and Bear Creek. Here the forest was mixed, with occasional live oaks and madrones and Douglas firs. Along the very summit of the ridge few trees of any sort grew—rather there were areas of bunchgrass and glowing white stalks of blossoming bear grass, manzanita, kin-nikinnik, cascara, and toyon—the latter also flaring white clusters of tiny flowers that would become the bright red berries of California holly (as Americans called it) of late autumn and up to the time of the Nativity. William Beard had for years gathered the prickly, dark green leaves of live oak and inter-spersed these with fronds of toyon for the making of Christ-mas wreaths.

A pair of elk stood upwind and thus remained oblivious to his approach. Olivo watched as the two big ungulates rose onto their hind legs, almost like dancers in some ancient bal-letlike performance, moving about nimbly as they nibbled

trailing strings of Spanish moss. Then, directly as the creatures
became aware of human presence, they settled to all fours,
sniffed at the sunlight-filled air, and vanished downslope, in
the direction of Bear Creek Canyon.

H.V. was about to urge his pony forward when the ridge-
spine began to heave, not so that he could see it but certainly
so that he could feel it—even though he was on horseback.
The mount felt it too, neighing wildly, as though a bear or a
lion were close about. Earthquakes were nothing new—not
certainly to one who'd been raised in the Santa Cruz Mountains, where the earth was almost certain to tremor two or
three times a year, sometimes causing rock slides from ridge
to canyon bottom, but this sensation was different—and everything so utterly silent he wondered if his imagination were
playing tricks.

*The sun, directly ahead of him, flared suddenly and seemed to
fill the entire sky—this followed by waves of noise, as though all
the thunder over the mountains had spoken at once. Instinctively,
he turned his pony about—one thought in his mind, one thought
only—to get to Califia. If it was all ending, if it was all to be over
within a matter of hours or perhaps only a matter of moments,
then he wished to be with her, with her to stand witness as the
dark forests flared in arching crescendos of flame and a soft gray
snowstorm of falling ash. . . . But instead his pony balked and plunged
downcanyon, leaping over fallen logs, hurtling dry ravines, and coming
to a sudden halt in a meadow where lilies and pentstemons and
fireweed were blooming. The sunlight was pleasantly warm, and the
solar orb appeared in no way changed—brilliant and yellow-white in
the afternoon sky.*

*H.V. dismounted, dropped the reins, left his pony, and walked
as one transfixed—certain he could hear the voices of young
women—nymphs, perhaps—nymphs who haunted the woodlands
and who, though in some vague way related to the wielders of
power on high Olympus, paid little attention to those entities and
lived in harmony with the other creatures of the wild, who fre-
quented river bottoms and spoke to herons and egrets and laughed
and dived with the salmon on the way upriver to ancestral redds
and then laid and fertilized their eggs and died and made food for
bears, raccoons, possums—eagles, ravens, murrelets, ospreys.*

For a moment he saw them—naked young women with long

hair—but not blond, not as in the Botticelli painting—brown-skinned and dark-haired. They reclined upon a formation of stair-like stones, a spiral that rose to . . . nothingness. But they weren't women. They were coyotes. What had accounted for his astonishing error of perception?

They approached him—long-legged, loose-jointed, cowls of red-gray fur about their throats.

"We've been waiting for you, Homer Virgil," one of the coyotes said. "I suppose you've been busy reading books or some such thing, but at least you've finally gotten here. Our people will vanish soon—the Ohlones, the Yuroks and the Karoks, the Wintuns, Maidus, Achomawis, and all the others. You've taken on protective coloration, and so your seed will be safe and will wander on into the human future."

"Of course," said another, "you have to have a mate. That woman you brought over from England, the blue-eyed female, she's not going to bear you any children. It would be better for you to find one of your own kind."

"Roxanne can go to hell for all I care. I made a great mistake, and she's it."

"There was no mistake, Homer Virgil. Your father named you for a reason, though he may have been misguided. In some ways Homer's world was like ours, but Virgil's was civilized—with roads and government and all that, with schools and places of entertainment and subject peoples. Your father admired these men and others like them—I suppose, after all, they were storytellers, and that's what you will be as well. Are you surprised we know about these things?"

"But you said . . ."

"Yes. Coyotes mate with coyotes, not wolves or village dogs. You must find the right coyote, Homer Virgil. Among our kind, even sister and brother may mate. Pelican Doctor will tell you what to do."

"My grandfather—nothing's happened to him, has it? He's all right?"

"All living creatures grow old and die. That's the way of things. We coyotes are born over and over again, down through the generations. Humans are also born over and over. Pelican Doctor is very old, but he's also very wise. You must ask him while there's still time."

"What about trees? The giant trees? In my mind's eye I can see nothing but stumps, nothing but denuded mountainsides, hillsides slipping loose in the rains, fires turning the night into a glowing hell. . . . "

The coyotes glanced one to another.

"Pelican Doctor has seen the same thing," one coyote replied. "Perhaps this vision means something."

Then Olivo was back on the crest of Pecwan Ridge. He was astride his pony, uncertain what he'd seen—if indeed, he'd seen anything at all.

The words of the coyotes stayed with him, and matters that he'd more or less chosen to ignore or to keep out of the specific range of consciousness now demanded an audience. It was true. He had put on protective coloration—he was in effect disguised as a Whiteman, and because of his education and his family's wealth, he was able to operate quite nicely within the civilized framework that was being formed around the land of Alta California—a land which had held, until the devastations that accompanied the Gold Rush, perhaps more wild Indians than all the rest of the lands claimed by the United States.

During the past year or so three separate Treaty Commissioners had determined which parts of California might be utilized to bring Indians together. Some eighteen treaties had been formed—but then the United States Senate refused to ratify them. In most cases lands were not set aside for the occupancy of Native peoples. America, so the argument went, had won California from Mexico by virtue of military victory, and thus the land, all of it, was American by right of conquest. The Indians of California had become a dispossessed population, lacking the protection of either citizenship or law. Indians weren't allowed to vote, and neither were they to be allowed to possess firearms. They couldn't give testimony against Whites, and neither could they enter into commercial agreements or hold gold claims. With the passage of the *Act for the Government and Protection of Indians*, a thinly disguised legalization of slavery came into being—with Indians being placed on rancherias and all but owned by their White governors. Indian minors could be indentured, females to age fourteen, and males to twenty-five.

If it wasn't precisely legal to hunt Indians for sport, it wasn't precisely illegal either—and numerous massacres were effected. In other instances, whole villages died of diseases to which the people had no resistance. Wise Indians found a White protector—a drunk who could stake a claim—and the Indians worked for that man, half a dozen or so performing the labor and giving as much as three quarters of the gold to their White *benefactor*.

Bill Beard and Raymondo Olivo were the official governors of the Hotochrukmas at least in the eyes of the state—a state that was able to ignore the fact that Raymondo Olivo was in fact a full-blooded Ohlone, though one who'd achieved significant status and hence citizenship during the time of Mexican rule in California and who was, along with Beard, the holder of three Mexican land grants, as well as a good deal of forest land purchased with profits from logging and milling and shipping operations.

With a master's degree from Cambridge, then, was Homer Virgil Olivo still an Indian or was he not? Did a knowledge of Sophocles and Cicero and Spencer and Shakespeare exempt him from the inevitable fate of his people?

Among the Old Californios, there where many whose blood was largely Mexican Indian. Spanish heritage was more one of language than of blood.

The coyotes had promised offspring—offspring from the mating with another *coyote* like himself.

Pelican Doctor's people could no longer roam the land as they saw fit—and when Pelican Doctor died, perhaps there would no longer even be a village of Hotochruk. Perhaps the change had already occurred—with the school Raymondo had long since put into place, and its required skills of reading and writing and figuring—and with gainful employment at the mills, so that the Whiteman's currency might be used to purchase things which, in a former time, the people had either made for themselves or done without.

The Yuroks and the Karoks were essentially *tame*, as were the Hoopahs, as well as the Wintuns over in the valley. But back up into the Siskiyous the various tribes of Shastas con-

tinued to hold hegemony over their ancestral lands, they and the
Modocs and the Yana Indians in the canyon country to the west
of Mt. Lassen—some of the Paiutes as well, and some Washos.
But how long could this last? As soon as gold was discovered in
an area, the Indians were slaughtered or driven off.

Indeed, even the redwood forest land which Olivo & Beard
had bought along Klamath River was originally intended, by
treaty, for Indian occupancy. Now a lumber company had
rights to the forest, if not the land itself, and numerous Yurok
and Karok men were working for those who brought down
the giant redwoods.

How quickly the time of genuine wildness had passed
away. . . .

Once back to the village of Requa and to his own house,
H.V. tended his trail pony and made himself busy about the
stable area, even taking time to renail a stall slat that had come
loose—owing to the fact that the carpenters had apparently run
short of nails and had fastened the railings with a single spike
to either end. Perhaps the horse, pushing against the boards
in an attempt to scratch himself, had worked them loose. In
any case, H.V. picked up a handful of the square nails forged
at the smithy in Eureka and hammered two more into either
end. Next he looked about to see if anything else needed nail-
ing—or perhaps sawing or. . . .

He scratched his pony behind the ears and walked out into
the twilight made his way to the house.

A kerosene lantern was already burning in the living room,
but Roxanne wasn't there. H.V. called out to his wife but received no answer.

He proceeded to the bedroom—Roxanne's room now, since
she'd decided that she much preferred sleeping alone. The
door, he found, was fastened from within.

He called her name, louder this time, but still without answer.

*An unstoppered vial lying on a knickknack table at the corner
to the hallway. . . . The anodynes. Opium. The last he'd noticed,
the vial contained perhaps a dozen pills, and now it was empty.*

With a kick H.V. caved in the door, but there was no sign
of life in the darkened room. He found a lantern, lit it, held it

up. Roxanne was crumpled on the floor beside the bed—unconscious but breathing deeply and regularly, her dark hair framed about her delicately featured face. A wave of tenderness, affection, and concern came over him—something he'd not experienced toward her except fleetingly for more than a year now. How many pills had she taken? Had she taken them all at once? Had she intended suicide? He lifted her in his arms and carried her into the living room, while she, for her part, came partially conscious, the intense Welsh eyes opening wide—she was conscious enough to curse at him and flail away with both fists.

"It's me—your husband," he protested. "Roxy, wake up. . . ."

"I know who you are—you beast. Goddamn you Homer let me alone let me sleep I'm not going to fuck you anymore because I just want to die leave me alone goddamn you to bloomin' hell. . . ."

H.V. placed his wife in a chair, thought about slapping her face as a means of bringing her out of her stupor, decided against that course of action, and strode into the kitchen to set a pot of cold coffee onto the stove—which he proceeded to stoke with kindling.

But that would take too long.

With this self-evident fact in mind, he poured a cold cup of coffee and took it in to Roxanne—forced her to drink it.

"Goddamn you Homer I just want to die you son of a bloody bitch!" she said, spitting cold coffee across the room. "I'm Roxanne Breton from Caernarvon, and I hain't no wife of yours, and to tell the God's own truth, I should never have come here with no educated Injun. . . ."

Allen Corzine stayed on at the Olivo & Beard mill after H.V.'s departure. He was friendly toward Califia's men and acted genuinely fond of bantam chickens, asserting that back home in New Brunswick his folks had once supported a flock of more than two hundred banties—until they began to spread throughout the neighborhood and make a general nuisance of themselves. He would have continued with the story, how his father began a systematic slaughter of the creatures until the *chicken herd* was back down to a more manageable fifteen or twenty, but the look in Califia's eyes suggested the subject should be changed.

He knew a man once, he said, who kept falcons, including a red-legged hawk, but no carrion crows.

Califia informed him that El Buzzardo was a turkey vulture—and that vultures had acquired a bad reputation owing to their role as scavengers. In point of fact, she continued, El Buzzardo appeared to have a definite preference for fresh meat and was fairly good at stalking and catching mice, almost like a cat. It was true, however, that if he didn't like someone, he might very well vomit at his antagonist.

Corzine studied the big bird perched on the cabin's eave and wondered if he detected a spark of malicious annoyance. El Buzzardo ruffled his feathers, fanned his wings for a moment, and then began to preen.

Califia laughed, turned, and opened the door to her cabin. Corzine stared appreciatively at the outlines of the long-legged and well-formed woman's body hidden beneath traditional male clothing. He made particular note of the configuration and strangely attractive movement of *la derriere*, and felt a twinge of desire. He held his breath for just a moment, glanced up at El Buzzardo (still engaged in the ritual of feather-preening), and then followed Califia inside.

Califia Beard Flowers, what in Christ's name were you doing married to that old toad of a man I shot because Sarah was sitting there, half drunk, on his knee? You and Sarah, damned if you don't look alike—even though she's a shrimp, and you're bigger than a lot of men. Your eyes, gray, and Sarah's the color of the Platte River at sundown. What is it about black-haired females that gets to me? Olivo's wife's another—jet colored hair and blue eyes—Roxanne. Three women—they come in small, medium, and large—and I'm married to the runt of the litter, except in the matter of temperament and determination, and then Sarah might as well be a mountain lion or a griz. What God-awful fate was it that brought Dolbeer and me to that spot in the river where she was bathing—and what possessed us to try to jump her? Before we could turn around, there were Pawnee warriors all over hell. Dolbeer wanted Sarah more than I did—why in God's holy name didn't I let him have her?

For a moment Corzine toyed with an idea, a vision. He

could see himself standing above a recumbent Homer Olivo, the smaller man knocked down by a single blow of the Corzine fist. Corzine laughed and slowly drew his pistol, aimed at the fear-stricken eyes, thumbed back the hammer. . . .

It could come to that. He, Allen Corzine, was sure as hell not going to allow any Indian with a headful of books to stand in the way of his carefully orchestrated scheme, already in progress, of wresting control of the northern redwood forests from both Pierson Reading (a dull-witted man who could be had for a few nights of Sarah's company) and from the Olivo & Beard combine as well. He could easily deal with either Homer Olivo or Califia Beard Flowers separately. But both of them? The answer didn't lie in a bullet, however tempting that option was at the moment, but rather in getting Homer Olivo to pack up his *stunner* of a wife and return to San Francisco or Santa Cruz or wherever it was he called home. Back to England would do nicely.

As for Califia, she could be sweet-talked and conceivably even enticed into a partnership of sorts. If it were possible to changes horses in the middle of the stream, let go of Reading and take up with Olivo & Beard, making appropriate arrangements with Califia in the process, why. . . .

"So, Mr. Corzine," Califia said, motioning to one of the chairs at the kitchen table and seating herself in the other, "let's talk about the logging business. What's on your mind? Since I understand that you're a happily married man, I presume the weekly roses haven't been for the purpose of courting the Klamath River boss lady, but for some other purpose—a peace offering, perhaps? Let's put our cards on the table, Allen. What is it you want?"

Corzine attempted to stare directly into the intense gray eyes, found that he was unable to do so, and reached into his jacket pocket for a cigar.

"You mind if I smoke?" he asked.

"Not in the slightest," Califia smiled, fishing into her own jacket pocket for the makings. She rolled her cigarette one-handed, touched her tongue along the edge of the paper, and lit up.

Corzine burst out laughing.

"I'll be damned. Where'd you learn that trick?"

"My ex-husband," Califia replied. "The old guy you shot in the brawl in Whiskeytown. No—I shouldn't have said that. Strange things happen when fellows have too much to drink. Let's get down to business. Are you going to light that cigar, Allen, or not?"

Corzine swallowed before he spoke and then took a deep breath.

Califia listened intently, without expression, as Allen Corzine proposed a partnership between the two of them—an entity that would be separate from either Major Pierson Reading or Califia's father and uncle—a logging and milling operation to control the great redwood forests of the northern Coastal Mountains. The kind of partnership he had in mind, he continued, would engage only the two of them—not her brother Calvin and his ships, and not John Dolbeer. Call it *Eureka Lumber Company*. And, of course, it was obvious to both of them that they felt strongly attracted to one another—and so why not allow the proposed partnership to extend itself in the most natural manner—the two principals to be lovers as well?

Corzine was growing red in the face, and Califia, though enjoying his discomfort, nonetheless felt somewhat sorry for the man.

"A charming proposition," she replied. "What a shame that I'm obliged to refuse. Olivo & Beard is here on the Klamath River to stay. We've got rights to the timber, we've got the know-how, and we've got the manpower. You can inform the good Alcalde of Shasta City that Califia Beard's operation isn't for sale. How'd you manage to get the drop on Samson, by the way—or was it really just an accident, as I've been told? No, it's best that you don't say anything. It's not in the cards for us to be partners, Allen, but I'll be happy to cooperate with you and Mr. Dolbeer in a proper businesslike manner. I've accepted the roses and not hunted you down. Take that for what it is. When we met in Eureka, you and Dolbeer and I, I didn't know you were the one responsible for Samson's death. I learned afterwards. With regard to lumber, there's no reason we can't cooperate. You need someone to do the freighting for you, and my brother Cal's got his own small navy and is willing to do the job if the rates are right."

Corzine pushed back his chair, stood up.

The piercing gray eyes were now not quite so attractive to him.

"Perhaps I've overstepped the bounds of propriety," he said, "so let me make myself completely clear. The partnership I suggested—it could still work—it could still work if we wanted it to. Otherwise, I'm prepared to buy out the entire holdings of Olivo & Beard, everything north of Eel River—lock, stock, and barrel. As an officer of your family's company, you're duty-bound to make my offer known. We're willing to allow for a reasonable profit, just as I said when we met in Eureka."

Califia took a drag on her hand-rolled cigarette, blew smoke out through her nose, and squinted.

"I've never quite gotten the knack of that," she said. "Makes my eyes water. Allen, I believe the truth of the matter is that Olivo & Beard has resources sufficient to take on you and your friend Reading, right here in your own backyard, without undue fear of financial disaster."

"I'm under orders," Corzine said, "to drive you off the Klamath River. Major Reading is only one of my backers. We hold no malice toward your father and your uncle, but the Redwood Empire is ours—and we intend to do whatever's necessary to eliminate competition."

Califia also stood up—stubbing out her cigarette in the process.

"A minute ago you wanted to be my lover, Allen. You and I together—we were going to forge our own little empire. And yet now. . . ."

Corzine realized, quite suddenly, that he was being used—manipulated.

"I'll give you time to think about all this," he said. "We have the power to drive you off the Klamath, if it comes to that. Califia, I don't mean to be angry with you—I swear to God. I find you fascinating—desirable."

"Yet you send me roses that turn out to be, each of them, a threat—each a bullet wound spurting crimson, a rosebud unfolding. I like your style, I genuinely do."

With surprising agility Corzine moved around the table—taking her momentarily unawares—and pulled her to him, his mouth seeking hers.

She didn't scream—didn't yell—had no desire for any of

her men to come pouring in to the boss's shack and find her being pawed by a rival logging boss.

She turned her head to one side, avoiding Corzine.

"Bitch—I don't want it to happen this way—you're forcing me—I'll have you one way or the other, Califia. . . . "

Then he felt the gun barrel pressed against his chest.

"Back off," she said, her voice controlled but on the verge of breaking. "This is tempting as hell, Allen, all of it. I'd pull the trigger in a minute except for. . . ."

He backed away, hands held out before him in placating fashion.

"I'm sorry, sorry," he managed. "I thought you wanted. . . ."

"You were wrong about that, too, Mr. Corzine," Califia said. "Right now I suggest you be on your way. I believe our business is finished, for the present at least."

Corzine glared at her for a moment and then began to chuckle—the mirth growing, emerging as full-throated laughter.

"The lady smokes hand-rolled cigarettes and packs a Deringer. Maybe that's why Sam Flowers was making a pass at another man's wife. I could grab that toy, you realize, and have my way with you."

"You could also," Califia replied, "end up quite dead—or wounded in a place that would be most inconvenient later on. Things have gotten a bit out of hand, Mr. Corzine. Business folk aren't supposed to act toward one another this way. I absogoddamnlutely suggest you ride back to that new house of yours and your wife Sarah. Cousin Homer says she's quite a beauty. When my brother Calvin arrives next, I'll have him pay you a visit. Until then. . . . "

"You're making a great mistake, Califia. Like I said, I'll give you time to think things over, and then. . . ."

"Will you still send me roses? I've become quite fond of them, you pig's petootie. . . .'"

Corzine shrugged, bowed from the waist, turned, and left the cabin. He walked quickly to where his horse was tethered, mounted, and—not hurrying—began his ride upriver toward Martin's Ferry a few miles below the confluence with the Trinity River; from there he'd take the dog-back mule trail to French Camp Ridge and on across the jumbled coast hills and dark redwood forests to the Pacific Road and the fishing village of Trinidad.

These women who haunt my life—they're termagants and savages. I must be making sacrificial offerings to the wrong god or goddess—either that or I've got the world's worst luck. I'd have sworn Califia wanted it as much as I did—that she was ready for me to make my move. When it comes to males and females, males don't have a God-cursed chance. Another day, another dollar, another dollop of experience. What the hell do I do next?

CHAPTER THIRTY

Eden Garden

[1852:]

ROXANNE OLIVO SURVIVED her attempted suicide, if that's what it was and not merely a miscalculation with regard to how many anodynes might be ingested without consequent damage. The entire episode, as it turned out, was precipitated when Roxanne began to order about her Yurok housemaid. Not familiar with the contentious nature of Yurok psychology and utilizing the high-handed British method of dealing with underlings, Roxy gave summary orders that certain things about the house were to be permitted and others were not.

The Yurok girl, a teenager whose *White name* was Bitsy, raised her upper lip and displayed her somewhat uneven teeth in a way that was clearly not to be mistaken for a smile. Roxy ordered Bitsy to change her attitude. Bitsy began to huff and call out insults in Yurok, knowing full well that her mistress couldn't understand what was being said. After something of a shouting match, Roxanne slapped the Yurok girl across the face, and Bitsy replied in kind—then picked up the broom and began to strike Roxanne with it.

The confrontation was all over in a matter of moments, with Roxy hurling a carved soapstone figure of Poseidon in

Bitsy's general direction as the Yurok made her escape. Roxanne, utterly shaken by what had happened, proceeded to take
an anodyne and to drink a quantity of Russian vodka. An hour
or so later she swallowed the last two remaining anodynes.
When grogginess overtook her, she went into the bedroom,
carefully latching the door, and climbed onto the bed. At some
later point she dreamed Homer was trying to make love to
her, and struggling (in her dream) to escape him, she rolled
over onto the floor.

"I refuse to stay here in Requa. You're gone much of the
time, and there's simply nothing for a civilized woman to do.
I insist you allow me to return to San Francisco. At least there,
love, there are a few people with culture and taste. What have
you bloomin' done to me, Homer Olivo? I was a *lady* once,
and what am I now? You were a schoolmaster and a fellow at
the university—and now, what? A blasted functionary in your
father's company. . . . "

H.V. glared at his wife, but then nodded.

"All right," he said. Thereupon he rose, exited the house,
and went out to commune with his horse.

H.V. rode upriver, stopping by Johnson's Flat to visit briefly
with Juan Pescadero. He continued southeast along the Klamath to Califia's logging encampment above Pecwan. Califia was
pleased at his return, and each recounted to the other what
had transpired during the interval they'd been apart. H.V.
spoke briefly of his *medicine vision*, without detailing what it
was the chorus of coyotes had said to him, and went into
more specific detail with regard to Roxanne's ill-advised
method of dealing with the problems in her world.

Califia spoke as tactfully as possible of her encounter with
Allen Corzine—of the apparent determination on the part of
Corzine's backers, whoever they might be, to drive Olivo &
Beard off the Klamath—of the offer to buy, of the proposed
Eureka Lumber Company, with herself and Corzine as part-
ners, and finally of Allen's apparent infatuation with her and
his attempt to force himself upon her.

"What if you hadn't had the pistol?" H.V. demanded.

"In that case, most likely I'd have been obliged to do Mr.
Corzine some serious bodily harm. Homer, all I had to do was

yell—and my boys would have come running. They'd have cut
him to pieces, and El Buzzardo would have feasted for days."

"I was with that bloody bastard, off and on, all the way
from Independence," H.V. said. "When it was convenient, he
stayed with the rest of us—and when it wasn't, he was off on
his own."

"What about Dolbeer?"

"He went with Corzine. It's a puzzling business. My instinct
and my training as well tell me that John Dolbeer's not a fol-
lower, not by nature. Why he's allowed Corzine to call the
shots for him, I have no idea. Dolbeer had some schooling—
surveying, engineering, or whatever—and is clever as hell with
equipment. If he needed a thing, as like as not he'd make it—
invent it, you might say. After Bully O'Bragh managed to get
their beans out of the fire with the Pawnees—intercede with
Antoine Behele, that is, and negotiate their release—and Sarah
into the bargain—why, Dolbeer appeared to me to be the one
who was genuinely smitten with her. Naturally Corzine had to
make his play—and she, being nobody's fool and so attaching
herself to the one she believed might do the best for her, chose
Corzine. Allen was making advances to Roxy—did I tell you
that before? The truth is, I began to get damned jealous. But
then Corzine and Dolbeer took off on their own, and the next
thing we knew, word came that the Pawnees had them. Once
they were back with us, Corzine was too busy courting Sarah
to pay any attention to Roxy. Possibly I'd have been better off
if Sarah had never gotten into the picture, and Corzine had
wooed my wife away from me. It's over, Califia—I'm fond of
the girl, but I simply can't deal with her anymore. I feel like
the Ancient Mariner with a damned dead albatross around my
neck—do you remember the poem? Except that our guide,
Bully O'Bragh, *was* the Ancient Mariner. Ben Goffe agrees with
me—I'd like you to meet Ben. A fascinating man, former professor at Yale, and now proprietor of both a Maidu rancheria
and a lumber mill."

Califia stared at her cousin for a minute or more, nodding,
not speaking.

"Have you ever wondered what life might have been for
us, Homer, if we hadn't tried to come back? Whatever happened, it would all be so different—so utterly different. After

you were gone, after Uncle Ray had sent you off to England, Pelican Doctor and Calling Owl both talked to me. In *our world*, Homer, there's no reason we shouldn't have been allowed to . . . be . . . together. Some might have thought it bad luck, that's all—because our mothers are twins, not for any other reason. In the old days, Pelican Doctor told me, twins weren't permitted to live. Sometimes both would be killed—left out for the animals, right after they were born. In other cases the people would wait to see which one was the *human* and which was merely the *pretender*. Once that was determined, then the false twin would be slain—or abandoned in the forest."

"I think our own fathers were the ones most opposed," H.V. agreed. "Seagull and my mother spoke with me after I returned from England—almost apologetically. They must have told me a dozen times how relieved they were that I was married and happy, even if Roxanne and I didn't have any children as yet."

"Yes, children are important to the Ohlones. If one has children, then it's safe to die. Until then, it isn't. Even though Other Side Camp is a very good place, it's important that one leave children behind—those who'll remember . . . us . . . and perhaps tell stories about us sometimes, even if they aren't allowed to use our names. Juan Pescadero's Mestizo, raised by the church, and he believes in the Jesus God. Juan thinks children are important also, but not in the same way. I'm not certain I can explain it very well."

"I think I understand," H.V. replied. "The Greeks—Homer's people—their children were their immortality. Because we're conscious and can't really imagine what it's like not to be conscious, not to be, we have to find some way of believing we're going to survive the Big Darkness. Whatever happens hereafter, we want to leave children behind—simply because in that way a part of us survives. I understand, but I don't necessarily agree. I'm not sure I want to have a child with Roxy, for instance. The kid would doubtless inherit the worst in both of us."

Califia poured small shot glasses full of whiskey, and they made a toast—except that they never said what it was they were drinking to.

East of the father river, otherwise known as *Old Miss*, logging was largely a matter of one man versus one tree, but among the giant redwoods, the situation was quite different. No one dared called Califia Beard *Cow of the Woods* instead of *Bull of the Woods*, at least not while she was close about, but it was she who bellowed at six in the morning, "All out for the timber!" Furthermore, she decided which trees to fell, what sort of beds or cushions were to be constructed to reduce breakage, and what were to be the proper lengths for the logs to be bucked.

Here in the West, everything was constructed on a different scale—Brobdingnagian, to say the least. Because the bases of the big trees were swollen, so to speak, it made sense to perform the cut at some elevation above the ground. Pairs of axemen worked from scaffolds or, if truly skilled, from springboards five feet long and round-ended and metal-lipped so as to bite into the upper wood of a notch that had been cut in the trunk—to be wedged into place and balanced upon by the faller wielding his long-handled axe.

The paired axemen faced their partners across the front of the redwood some ten or fifteen feet above the ground and went to work on the undercut, blades flashing in rhythm, *one-two, one-two*, carefully hewn so as to be flat on the bottom and angled from forty to fifty degrees on the top—in all, cutting through about a third of the tree. Their performance, as H.V. might have noted, strangely resembled some sort of contrived, mythic dance.

From here the fallers moved their springboards to the tree's far side, where a horizontal cut was made just deep enough to remove support from the redwood—causing the tree to lean and then to fall on the side of the undercut.

When the tree began to go over, the woods rang to the cry of *Timburr!* At this point the fallers flipped their axes into the brush and made a hasty descent from springboards or scaffolding.

A terrific crash ensued as titans up to three hundred feet tall battered the earth, occasionally shattered into useless fragments or nearly that.

Olivo & Beard operations generally made a point of leaving the true giants, but a few trees with diameters up to twenty feet or more were felled just to prove it could be done. One such tree kept a pair of axemen busy for a full workweek. And the logs, once bucked into lengths of 16, 24, 32, or 40 feet, sometimes had to be split open by means of auger holes and powder—to get them down to reasonable size. The buckers, often working alone out in the brush, carried whiskey bottles filled with kerosene, these with hooks on them for convenience's sake, the *oil* used to clear pitch from the blades of bucking saws.

A new bottle for every quart of kerosene. . . .

The axes themselves were nearly four feet in length—the size necessary so as to allow the axemen to reach into the hearts of the trunks—but not even this added length did the job. Indeed, the fallers were required to stand inside the undercut in order to work back to the necessary imaginary line. The tools of the trade: *pickaroons, wood mallets, wedges, cant hooks, peaveys, corked boots, Boker jacks, broadaxes, falling axes, bucking saws, misery whips, oilcans, cross-tied cradles, skid roads, flumeways, the oxen grunting and snorting as the bull-skinners whooped and yelled and sweet-talked their charges. . . .*

Did the earth move?

Olivo & Beard enterprises, H.V. and Califia agreed, was certainly powerful enough to deal with Corzine and Dolbeer—whoever, along with Pierson Reading, was bankrolling them. Several great fortunes had already been made by means of gold-mining operations—with hard-rock mines going full blast in Grass Valley and Jackson and elsewhere, and with European investment pouring in. Sutter's star had faded, but Sam Brannan's had risen—indeed, Brannan himself was the apparent organizer of the San Francisco Vigilantes, a kind of outlaw citizen militia that directed itself occasionally against such *bandidos* as the famed Joaquin Murieta and at other times against Mexicans and South Americans who presumed to hold mining rights. Agriculture flourished in the valleys of the Sacramento and San Joaquin, and virtual empires were assembled, sometimes by means of absorbing former Californio ranchos and sometimes by means of abuse of the homesteading laws.

Could Thomas Larkin and Brannan and perhaps Talbot Green have joined forces with Reading?

Well, whatever was to come, in all probability the long-established firm of Olivo & Beard would more than hold its own.

H.V. spoke for the first time of setting aside the most magnificent of the groves of redwoods—an idea that sprang partially from his recent medicine vision and partly, he presumed, from Pelican Doctor's long-held opinion that the giant trees in some way contained the spirits of those who were long dead—and that Coyote and Condor and Grizzly would all be offended if such trees were harmed.

"Condor has gone away," Califia said. "Oh, they still circle over the Tehachapis and the Southern Sierra, but no one's seen one in the Santa Cruz Mountains for some time now—and I've never seen one near Russian River. I know that we're Americans now, and I accept that. But sometimes the things these *Gringos* do infuriate me. I've heard stories of men shooting condors for sport—and killing the grizzlies and the wolves, slaughtering the elk. Why isn't it possible to settle a land without destroying it?"

"I think you can lay that one to human nature," H.V. replied. "But about the redwood patriarchs. At first it would have done no good to cut down the biggest trees, even if Dad and Uncle Bill had been able to do it. We had no way to process such logs—unless, of course, a hundred men were hired to work with axes and wedges until a giant had been turned into shingles. But now the equipment's much better. Humans may not be trustworthy, but they are clever. Pescadero tells me Dolbeer's new gang-saw is capable of working a log ten foot thick, eight cuts at a time. He's rigged a new set of steam-driven gears so as to speed up the operation a great deal. Men like Dolbeer have restless, practical minds, Califia. They think in terms of belts and pulleys and steam pistons and the like—and what they can think, they find some way of building."

"What are you getting at?"

"Simple. At some point soon, those big trees everyone's been leaving alone are going to start looking profitable as hell. It won't take long—and then the old giants will be no more than some gigantic stumps and a faint memory in the consciousness of the future."

"There are too many of them, Homer," Califia said. "We must have millions. Surely, to the end of the world we'd never take them all. Not even the hundreds of thousands of people who've arrived in California since the discovery of gold have much affected the land. For God's sake, even this many people are simply dwarfed by the size of things."

H.V. shook his head.

"The forests of England are gone, all gone, Califia. There are still wild places over there, but precious little of forest or original wildlife, as I surmise, remains. On the continent, the same thing. Everywhere the woods have been hewed down to make boards or to use for firewood or simply to clear the land. And it all happened long ago. In Germany and Austria some forest remains—the fabled Black Forest, for instance. Peasants wander about gathering firewood—whatever falls in the way of dead limbs and such. Even the Alps, which are damnably magnificent mountains, they've long since been tamed, gentled if not fully civilized. However huge America may be, and certainly it is that, human will is determined to round it, to gentle it, to eliminate the very principle of *wildness*."

With the thought in mind of preserving selected groves, they rode upstream along Roach Creek and across the brushy summits of the Bald Hills, from whence they could view the Pacific Ocean perhaps a dozen miles westward, utterly huge and cerulean blue and beyond, heavy, swirling zones of fog, reaching outward toward the far Aleutians and Hawaii and distant Japan and Korea.

El Buzzardo had the sky to himself—with not so much as one of his own kind or a hawk or an eagle anywhere in sight—and he played with the wind currents, the tide of air moving from offshore and bringing with it the possibility of a rainstorm.

From the crest H.V. and Califia proceeded into the drainage of Redwood Creek—for there, as Califia knew, grew some of the most magnificent and tallest redwoods, several of which she'd estimated to be in excess of three hundred feet—a handful more than three hundred and fifty. Other groves, of course, each with its own giants, abounded both to the north, as beside Smith River, and to the south, along the Eel and Mattole

Indeed, the redwood zone, limited though it was to the mountains and canyons closest to the Pacific, a region of heavy fogs whose tiny beads of moisture precipitated and collected upon the foliage, dripping constantly to the forest floor a hundred, two hundred, three hundred feet below—this zone of redwood dominance extended from extreme southwestern Oregon along the seaward slope of the California coast and ultimately down the length of the dark Ventana Mountains beyond Monterey and the Big Sur River.

Scrub jays screamed as Califia and H.V. entered one particularly impressive grove, and a pair of wapiti caught their scent, glowered in their direction, and then loped away, gaining speed as they traveled. Along the big creek, rhododendrons and pink-throated azaleas were in riotous bloom, with the latter causing the air virtually to tingle with honeylike odor.

H.V. and Califia tethered their ponies and walked about, studying the various trees and guessing as to heights and probable ages. Certainly several of the redwoods, they agreed, must have been alive and well at the time Christ was born. The greatest trees, they presumed, were already growing when the son of Philip of Macedon conquered the greater portion of his known world, an empire that fell quickly to pieces upon the death of that young god-king, Alexander the Great. The Roman Empire in turn had risen, overcoming native Etruscans and controlling the entire Italian Peninsula and finally all those lands which surrounded *Mare Nostrum* and quite a few other lands besides. But mighty Rome fell, and the Western Empire dissolved or was dissected, bringing on the Dark Ages and the Holy Roman Empire and the rise of the nations of Europe and the Renaissance and ultimately the emergence of a *modern world*, with England's great and seemingly ever-expanding empire and Mother Russia's slow conquest of the huge Asian extent of Siberia.

In truth, the great trees were only a portion of the cousins' motivation for coming here—yes, and both of them knew it—yet neither said anything, neither so much as hinted at the ever-strengthening bonds of attraction, a fierce physicality and even sensual hunger that drew them together when they were little more than children and that now, in its reassertion, was pushing each into the arms of the other—after half a lifetime spent apart, and after a marriage apiece, hers terminated by an act of Fate or God or Whimsy, and his struggling along as two dissimilar people came to comprehend, in a way that would not allow self-deception or vague plans for the future or any other consideration, that they were of two separate worlds and two separate civilizations divided by the Old River Ocean and a continent that at least some of the Native peoples called Turtle Island.

It was late afternoon, and sunlight became ever more dim as fog rolled in from the ocean, inundating Redwood Creek Canyon and causing a thin precipitation of mistlike rain to swirl down from the high, verdant boughs of redwoods, so that if one looked upward, one felt moisture upon one's face.

El Buzzardo came swooping through the grove, and then, with wings held upward, he alit on a downfall alder close to where his mistress and her friend were standing. Almost immediately he went to grooming—and then looked up in accusatory fashion when Califia failed to step forward to assist in the process.

"The crown prince of the airways wishes to be petted," H.V. laughed.

Califia nodded and did as her offal-eating friend expected. The large, red-necked bird tilted back his crooked-beaked head and closed his eyes, as though in some sort of avian trance.

The fog wasn't chilly at all—but rather in some respects like a mysterious, enfolding blanket that served to isolate this realm of giants from all other possible realms. Without questioning the matter, without speaking, H.V. gathered dry wood and hollowed out a shallow pit beneath the overhang of a great, bent redwood that one might almost have supposed to be a kind of twin to the doubled redwood back at Hotochruk, where Califia and Homer Virgil had grown to adulthood.

As though the matter were all prearranged—as though they'd intended precisely this encampment from the beginning—Califia and Homer Virgil cooked a dinner and drank from a wine flask. El Buzzardo as well had his wine and a portion of the corned-beef hash and soggy, logging-camp-baked bread; then, after allowing himself to be petted by both Califia and her *male friend*, he vaulted effortlessly up into the overstory of the redwood forest and settled in for the night.

Sounds—almost those of a barking dog: *hoo-hoo-hoo-hooo-ah!*

Califia nodded.

"Big tree owl," she said.

"Not a screecher?"

"Screech owls like oak trees," Califia said. "And they don't bark. That's a spotted owl. Listen to it. . . . "

With foggy twilight falling about them and the details of things blurring together, Califia and H.V. clasped hands and walked to the stream, where they heard some angry, territorial shrieking and rasping on the part of a kingfisher. Several moments passed before they were able to identify the bird itself—perched on a clump of wild lilac close beside the stream and only barely visible in the fog, the dull blue of its feathers blending with gray so that at first what they saw was simply a white neck band, seemingly suspended in air.

"He doesn't wish to have an audience while he's fishing," H.V. said. "Perhaps we should return his creek bottom to him—terminate our lease, so to speak."

"Kingfishers are a pain in the . . . neck," Califia replied. "We're grown up now, Homer Virgil. We can do whatever we like—and no one about for twenty miles or more to say us nay. Do you have the nerve to go swimming with me?"

H.V. grinned.

"Being *grown up*, then, I presume we'll go into the water bare-ass naked, fog and all? We'll die of consumption complicated by the ague."

"Naturally. I want to see what you look like after all this time. Don't you wish to look at me?"

Califia affected a hurt expression.

"Little good it'll do," he responded. "The gray will turn to pitch black before we can get undressed."

"Perhaps, perhaps. I want you to take my clothes off, H.V. I want you to . . . What we had long ago—do you remember?"

An uncomfortable silence hung between them.

"I understand," H.V. whispered.

"You mustn't do anything you don't want to, though. Are you going to . . . defrock . . . me, or not, Homer Virgil?"

"A gentleman must always do as his lady wishes."

Califia laughed.

"Did they teach you that in England?"

He shook his head as he unbuttoned the green flannel shirt she was wearing—green that had lost all its color in the fading light.

"No. No, I think I always knew," he replied.

"Once we made a mistake," she said.

"And you wish to make the same mistake again?"

After that they ceased speaking. They clung desperately to one another, and mouth sought mouth. Across the stream the kingfisher ruffled its feathers and shouted at the blur of rhythmic movement.

They talked for a long while afterward, sitting beside the camp fire, at times almost enjoying the smoke that occasionally drifted into their faces, almost savoring the sensation—something shared, something revisited now after an interval of time that was neither long nor short but which now seemed to both as though it represented a path through the forest, erroneously taken—two paths, rather, that for a while remained close together and then radically diverged, one to a world where he was fated to be seen as the *gifted alien*, but alien nonetheless, she to a time of lonely though in some ways exciting self-determination, a woman succeeding in a male arena, succeeding by dint of sheer willpower and a sense of pattern and possibility that few males shared.

The horses moved about in foggy darkness, and at moments man and woman could hear the sounds of chewing—as the animals lipped at willow brush or gouged their blunt teeth into the succulent bark of young alders.

Redwood Creek, running smoothly through its channel, created a soft, inevitable music, and somewhere, possibly not too far away, horned owls called and mockingbirds chittered and trilled. Wind was blowing now, but huddled close about the camp fire, H.V. and Califia were only vaguely aware of it. Yet the huge trees, their red-brown and lichen-spotted boles rising indeterminately into firelight-suffused fog, groaned softly—reminding Califia of the sounds her pet cougars had sometimes made when the felines got up the nerve to lie beside a fire, their backs turned.

"It's crazy," she said, turning to H.V., "but suddenly I feel lonely—no, as though I've lost something, as though perhaps we've both lost something. I was thinking of my mountain lions. You remember that I wrote you about them. They went wild finally—almost wild. It's been a year since I've seen them— they came in to visit and stayed for a day or so. If they're still alive, and I imagine they are, they're in the mountains near our Russian River logging operation. They were brother and sister, H.V., and perhaps that's why they never mated. Do you suppose animals recognize such things at some sort of word-less level?"

He shrugged.

"So they left the comforts of the logging camp behind and went off to do their own hunting? Maybe it's just that they had to get back to their birthright in order to mate and have little ones. Vulture, cougar, kids who grew up riding horses on the beaches—who knows why we do what we do? As Pelican Doctor says, Coyote Man has whims. He does what he wants and thinks about it later."

CHAPTER THIRTY-ONE

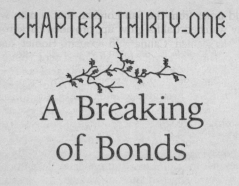

A Breaking
of Bonds

[1852:]

THE FOLLOWING DAY was unseasonably cold, with intense rain driving in off the Pacific. El Buzzardo's feathers were wet, and Califia and H.V. were both feeling guilty. They returned to Pecwan, and H.V. attempted an apology. Then he left the camp and proceeded downriver to Johnson's Flat. Here he shook hands with Juan, drank a cup of coffee, and rode off into a rain that alternated with occasional bursts of sunlight.

Rain or no, Califia insisted on taking a small crew of men out to work that afternoon. Far from her usual cheerful self, she climbed the springboards and began to belabor a half-finished undercut. The Michigan boys knew something was amiss, and they could guess that it had to do with the two-day trip the boss lady and her cousin had taken. The timber beasts at Olivo & Beard already knew a good deal about the good-looking *booshway* they worked for, and her love life was the subject of bunkhouse talk. They felt genuine loyalty toward this woman who worked side by side with her men, and yet they were puzzled to learn that Corzine, a rival booshway, had gunned down Califia's husband—even if the man and his wife weren't living together at the time.

One old-timer from the San Lorenzo mill, a man who'd at least partly watched Califia grow up, provided background information. It seemed Califia and Cousin Homer had been sweethearts. The family got wind of it and sent young Homer to Europe to get civilized. Now he was back—and what the hell did the lunkheads suppose was going to happen? Only thing was, Homer was married to an English lady. As to the rumor that Roxanne was a distant relative of the Duke of Monmouth, well, he wasn't sure about that part.

Now that the boss lady had actually spent some time with her *kissin' cousin* and had come back all down in the mouth, Califia's boys were genuinely concerned. More than one man had given thought to the possibility that he and he alone might fill the void in Califia's life, but such notions were never translated to Miss Beard. To do so would be to violate the code of Tin Pants Chivalry.

For the boss lady herself, however, things had become altogether too goddamned complicated—or *Gorddamned*, as her erstwhile lover and deceased husband would have said. *You sonofabitch, Samson, if you hadn't run off. . . . I was happy with you—why didn't you understand? I'm' still angry, do you know that? Not only do you take off to prospect, for Christ's sake, but then you turn around and do your prospecting in Whiskeytown, where else? And either you or that peculiar Coyote you follow decided the play was over, a long one but not long enough. You saw things when the wildness was still everywhere, the land unmapped, and got you an Indian family or two and found your way to California just in time to fall into cahoots with Pa and Uncle Ray and help them get started in their shingling business, then disappearing again and showing up when you got around to it, there in the Tehachapis in the thick of our revolutionary plotting against Torrejon—and I had eyes for Alvarado but changed my mind when he decided I was just some useless female along for the ride—you and Beckwourth and Greenwood, and then again coming to find me on the coast above Chalanchawi after I'd actually begun to take a fancy to John Sutter and was camped out with my cougars and El Buzzardo. You tangled up my life—but for all of it, Samson Flowers, you were one hell of a man, a horse, and you knew just what to do with a frightened female who was a woman in years but not in experience, and stars began to fall from the night skies because of the rough magic. Jesus Christ, Samson, even if everyone looked at us and thought about father and daughter, that didn't make any difference, and I would never have left you, never, and that crap about my finding a buck my own age was to infuriate me so as to give you the space you wanted, because what you really had in mind was to go off and die, like some old buffalo who figures his humping's over, only the method had to be that of getting shot—unless what you really had in mind was to pick up directly (since I hadn't fetched you) and head off to the Rocky Mountains to find Bridger and Beckwourth and Greenwood and Carson again, or maybe back to one of those Indian villages where you'd left family, because it simply wasn't in your nature to stay put for very damned long, no matter what woman you were with or how much she loved you, and I did love you, Sam Flowers, you sonofabitch. . . .*

Now it's all tangled up again. First there's this jackass of an Allen Corzine who may or may not have actually fired the shot, Samson, and he's been sending roses, so maybe he thinks he's the one at least, and he's either of a mind to run me out of the red-woods or get my britches down—because after all there's no way of knowing what kind of craziness runs through the mind of a damnfool male. Perhaps if I used my head, I'd go after Allen, presuming I could separate him from the child he's hitched to, because that way at least I'd be safe from—H.V. You mustn't be angry with me because I loved Homer first. You had others—you understand. Is Homer the young buck you wanted me to find? You knew he was coming back to California, and you simply walked away? But if you were so damned smart, Samson, didn't you realize Homer was married? This situation right now ain't merely complicated, it's impossible. The only way this lady logger can see to solve the problem is to run away from it, just like you did. You have to understand—with Homer it's like I'm a girl again—but it's not right, not right for a number of reasons. What in God's name have I gotten myself into?

Okay, then, the matter's settled. Juan Pescadero takes over up here in my stead, and I'll head south to Russian River. Gatogordo and Ponchita, are you still there, haunting the canyons and possibly even waiting patiently for your fly-by-night mistress to return?

"Time for a break!" Califia yelled, tossing her axe aside and jumping from the scaffold to a springboard five feet below and from there, with a long leap, to the ground.

At that particular moment, the boys agreed later, the boss lady definitely had a different expression upon her face. And those gray eyes of hers. . . .

Homer Virgil Olivo's mind was spinning. What had at the time seemed so simple and natural and *right* appeared now almost monstrous. He, a married man, had taken shameless advantage of his own cousin, a widow. True, two years had passed since Samson's murder, and Califia was presumably permanently separated from the man at the time, but that didn't really change anything. What mattered was the implicit will of the clan—wasn't that what it was, after all, that had sent him voyaging to far England in the first place?

Worse yet, he was married—to a British woman who'd had the bravery and extraordinary courage to accompany him across an ocean and across a continent on a journey of such difficulty as to boggle the mind. She had done it, succeeded, grown stronger. But now? He had repaid her by renewing an illicit relationship with Califia, renewing his own youthful folly.

Glorious crimson lashed through tides of cloud far out across the Pacific—the sun ellipsoid as it sank into fog banks, distorting, ultimately being swallowed. Thus it was nearly nightfall when he reached Requa, where he was astonished to find a half a dozen Yuroks at work, in the final stages of packing furniture, linens, dishes, cooking utensils, lamps, glassware, pottery, and of course all of Roxy's clothing.

"I'm leaving, Homer," the blue-eyed one informed him. "I'm going to San Francisco, since there's no other civilized place in your wretched California. I've contacted Mr. Corzine, who's been decent enough to arrange for passage aboard *H.M.S. Scotland Venture*, which will take mooring at the village pier tomorrow. You're welcome to come with me, if you wish. I won't stay here any longer—you call it *company business*, but the fact is you spend every possible moment with that sheep in wolf's clothing, *your own true love, la la*. I've some pride, Homer, and my star's not so totally hitched to your wagon as you may suppose. I'm willing to be your wife—in every sense of the word—but not here. As it is, I'm starving to death sexually—I'm not the cold fish you may think. Try to remember what it was like between us just three short years ago. We can find that love again, if you're willing."

H.V. stared at the crates ready for transport to the marina. He reached into his coat pocket and withdrew a cigar, bit off the end, used his thumbnail to pop a white phosphorus match, and lit up.

"Well, Roxy, this is a bit of a one-person decision, what?"

Hands on her hips and a red bandanna about her forehead, she glared at him.

"Jolly bloomin' right it is, dearie."

"In that case," H.V. replied, "let's have our new employees box my things as well. San Francisco, is it? You're right. Klamath River's altogether too confining. There's been some talk of establishing a College of California, as I understand it, and perhaps they'll have need of an experienced teacher. I suppose there can't be too many in California who've had my university teaching experience. Our old friend Ben Goffe, perhaps—but he's busy with other projects—a ranch in the mountains, not far from American Valley, where we came through. Do you remember, Roxanne?"

"You're willing to come with me?"

"Does it astonish you, love?"

The return to San Francisco did not go as smoothly as H.V. and Roxanne might have hoped. Together in close quarters on the little steam-driven schooner, and with no way of distancing themselves, the Olivos were drawn into one donnybrook after another—to the point where the captain, a New Englander named Thomas Barrington Bates, made not altogether jesting threats to throw both of them overboard.

Once inside the Golden Gate and onto the calm waters of San Francisco Bay, Bates brought the *Scotland Venture* into dock at the bustling embarcadero, where the Olivos and their belongings were quickly off-loaded. Bates shook hands with H.V., sent words of greeting to Calvin Beard (whom he had once met in Hawaii), tipped his cap to Roxanne, and turned back to his ship, where the stevedores were already at work, winching pallets of redwood from the hold.

After two days in an overcrowded hotel—two days spent

in attempting to secure a lease agreement on something liva-
ble—Roxanne threw a classic temper tantrum—her finest performance in the eight years she and H.V. had been together.
She'd had enough, she said, of her impractical and forever-
wandering husband—a man who appeared to enjoy forest solitude to her company. Perhaps, she suggested, the fact that
Homer Virgil was Indian had something to do with it. As soon
as he was back on his native ground, she yelled, his heart had
won out over his head, and his sympathies had reverted to
the aboriginal savages who lived in huts. San Francisco, furthermore, was a tinder heap—a charge with some truth to it,
since between 1849 and late 1851, most of the city's business
district had been burned some six times, culminating in the
so-called *Great Fire* of May, 1851.

From the beginning, San Franciscans demonstrated a perverse genius for rebuilding their ravaged city, each time recon-
structing on a more grandiose scale—for this windblown area
jutting north between the Pacific and the *Bahía* was fated to
be, they firmly believed, one of the world's great and famous
cities—the chief port and the cultural heart of California. Occasional earthquakes might rattle the buildings, and fires might
consume entire blocks at a time—but always the city would
rise again.

"I'm a savage, then," H.V. growled. "Is that it?"

"Essentially, yes."

"Not all that long ago, we must keep in mind, the Welsh,
Cornish, Irish, and British were all *enfants du bois*," he insisted.
"In gaining civilization, the whole lot of you have lost the only
thing that was ever important to you—or about you, for that
matter—and that was your connection to the soil itself. Earth's
a powerful goddess, and in the long run, her will is absolute."

"Powerful *goddess*, is it now? Homer, I'm beginning to suspect you're not even Christian, despite all your protestations
and your praying. In England, you'd likely have been one of
those old Druids who built Stonehenge—yes, and who cruci-
fied poor devils in oak trees, too. What do you Yanks know
about the *land*? In England, at least, we have lived in the same
place long enough to. . . ."

H.V. nodded.

"Indeed, I'd have been a Druid," H.V. agreed.

On the third day of their stay in the hotel, Roxanne decided that she wanted a divorce, immediately if not sooner.

On the fourth day she announced she was returning to England as soon as passage might be arranged. If H.V. wished to accompany her, why, that was fine. If she hoped for such a thing, she surely did not expect it. For herself, she was determined to go in any case. She'd had quite enough of *America del Norte* in general and of California in particular. She did not wish, she said, to be on the same continent with . . . a certain member of H.V.'s family.

One part of Olivo was heartsick the marriage had come to so sorry a state—that it was, indeed, breaking up like some unfortunate ship driven into shallow waters by a fierce Pacific storm and then chewed apart on the coastal rocks. This same portion of him was even tempted to return to England. Back to the life of the pedagogue. . . .

But quite another portion of his being was relieved and not at all inclined to follow this lovely, hysterical woman to whom he'd been married for some time now, married *sans* offspring.

Roxanne secured passage aboard a ship that would take her south to Panama. From there she'd cross the isthmus by barge and horseback, securing lodging and passage to England on a trans-atlantic clipper that would likely be in harbor at Colon.

H.V. made the necessary financial arrangements, drawing a sizeable sum from the Olivo & Beard office in San Francisco. With these funds he paid for Roxanne's return to her native land. He also purchased two horses, a saddle and saddlebags, a sturdy pair of high-topped boots, a Kentucky long rifle, and a few other incidentals. He left word for his father and uncle that he intended to see for himself the mining regions along the western slope of the Sierra Nevada, that region known generally as *La Veta Madre*, the Mother Lode.

Whatever grand, final scene Roxanne had planned for their matrimonial melodrama, H.V. was never to know. He didn't wait. Instead, with firm resolve, he took his horses aboard a ferry and crossed the bay to Oakland. From there he rode north, avoiding the main routes. He wanted to be alone, and these hills, forested with live oak and blue gum, provided the opportunity.

Blue gums were an alien species from Australia, but at this point who would have believed it? Long ago, so the story went, the Spanish planted the first of them, and the fast-growing *Eucalyptus globulus* spread like wildfire over the inland hills, where frost was infrequent. One variety of eucalyptus, or so H.V. had read, a tree called the mountain ash, was said on its native soil to reach heights nearly as great as those attained by redwoods.

A momentary fragment of his Pecwan Ridge vision flared, and he saw the Coast Range denuded of redwoods, Douglas firs, and pines—endless gardens of stumps—and then the remarkably fast-growing eucalyptus taking over, gum and stringbark and mountain ash, these planted to produce lumber for an emergent civilization—and he could see these new trees in turn being logged, crashing down amidst a rain of torn foliage and a heavy, medicinal odor of eucalyptus sap.

When H.V. reached the relatively bare, grassy hills that sloped toward Carquinez Strait, he took a ferry across and went to visit the aging Mariano Vallejo at the new but smaller mansion, somewhat to the north and west of the former residence. The entire rancho was diminished now, due to a combination of things—to Vallejo's having sold large portions of his land, to simple encroachment and squatting, and to several American court decisions regarding validity of land titles.

"*Señor Olivo, es fantástico!*" Mariano said. "How many years since I have seen you? Ah, you were only a boy then—and now you are a famous scholar who has been to England, to Cambridge—*por supuesto*. Only by two days you have missed seeing your cousin Calvin Beard, my *hijo-yerno*, so to speak—for is not Juanita Ortega like a daughter to me? He was here—he came downriver from Sacramento. *Sí, sí.* we are all relatives—we are all one family, *la familia, el linaje*, from the old Alta California which is no more. Well yes, *sí*, things change, and a man is a fool to resist that which is inevitable. Perhaps the future will remember us, who knows?"

He was alone now, but not the way he'd felt when dispatched on the great adventure to England. Shunted forth from his homeland though he'd been at that time, there had always been people about him, and he'd never had any real difficulty in forming relationships. At the university he'd become quite close with a handful of young fellows his own age, and of course, before growing serious about Roxanne, he'd enjoyed the company of a number of other young women.

Now that he'd return to California and indeed had been *home* for more than two years, it was time to learn the dimensions of the Mother Land—her rivers, her lakes, her inland mountains. Oh, a lifetime would be required to see even a small portion of the whole, but this plan of action was, for the moment at least, precisely what he had in mind.

He rode north, keeping essentially to the base of some arid hills on the western side of the Sacramento Valley—dry because of a rain-shadow effect produced by storms coming in and dropping a great deal of their moisture over the mountains. Thus, the eastern extent was semidesert, as would have been the floor of the valley itself except for the streams pouring down from both the Coastal Mountains and the Sierra Nevada to the east. The Big Valley was essentially a broad grassland punctuated by stands of white oak and valley live oak interspersed with willow and cottonwood. In some areas, herds of tule elk moved about, in others deer, and in others cattle—for in less than five years since the discovery of gold, small settlements had appeared up and down the Sacramento and San Joaquin valleys.

Far to the east were the Sierra Nevada, a series of high, white ridges with zones where the snows had already melted or were hidden beneath a cover of forest. Sutter's Buttes rose from the valley floor, dreamlike, the magical place of the New Creation, at least in the minds of the Pomo, Wintun, and Maidu peoples—the place where the Oak of Creation was planted long ago, before even the creation of humans. A great flood had drowned all the First People, and the Big Valley was filled with water—according, at least, to the stories. Since only Sutter's Buttes rose above the universal flood, it was to this place that the animals made their way and had a conclave beneath the Oak of Creation.

Out of damp clay, Coyote formed the People.

The dome of Wahgalu (Wahganupa, Mt. Lassen), high and white in the sunlight, became visible as H.V. rode northward. From his present vantage point, the Sierra appeared to be merely ridges, not essentially different from the Coast Ranges behind him, the Yolla Bollys, as they were known—the Yolo Mountains. But above the long blue weavings of the Sierra, Wahgalu rose, along with a cluster of minor crags, all of them snow-covered.

H.V. entertained the sudden image of a huge mountain of long ago, one that simply blew up—with Wahgalu forming in the aftermath of that amazing explosion which, if it happened at all, must have shaken the foundations of the earth.

Could such an explosion have been in any way related to the creation tale depicting the central valley as a kind of inland sea? Perhaps the earth tremorings so common in the mountains of Santa Cruz and in the vicinity of San Francisco had at some point caused a rupture between the ocean and the *Bahía* and so caused the inland sea to drain. Perhaps, he thought, it was impossible that what was now the Sacramento River originally flowed into the Pacific Ocean at Monterey Bay—for to the east of Monterey he'd made note of alluvial plains far greater than the Salinas and other small rivers might have accomplished on their own. Or possibly the entire thing was some portion of Noah's fabled flood. Flood stories, as he'd learned, were ubiquitous.

In any case, somewhere to the south of the mountain called Wahgalu lived his friend Ben Goffe—who now went by the *nom de plume* of Benjamin McCain. Why would Goffe have jettisoned his family name—one of which he'd seemed to be extremely proud—descended from that Judge Goffe who'd been signatory to the death warrant for the English king back in Puritan times?

> *Oh what was your name in the States?*
> *Was it Johnson or Thompson or Bates?*

H.V. turned his pony eastward, toward the long *massif* and its white, dominating peak:

Another mountain was also visible now—an even greater mountain, H.V. supposed, far to the north, a *considerable butte*, as Alonzo Delano had remarked upon first seeing Shasta—the Giant Waiiaka, or such Califia once described it, writing to him in a letter that he hadn't received until a week or so before he and Roxanne took passage for the New World.

But there, close beside Wahgalu, lived the half-blind Benjamin, married to a young Maidu woman. Stories had circulated about a revenge-seeking group of Panos, and their female leader, as well as a *big White bloke* who rode with them. Later accounts included a tall, thin, bearded individual with an uncanny knack for getting in and out of scrapes—one who, even through the inevitable distortions of such tales, sounded much like Farnsworth O'Bragh.

H.V. mused on the matter for a time.

"McCain, huh?" he said to his pony. "*Mala suerte!* Wouldn't it be something if all this wove together? I guess the Queen's Injun should go take a gander at *how the stick's floatin'.*"

CHAPTER THIRTY-TWO

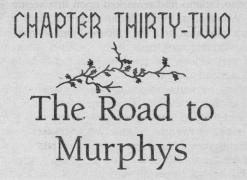

The Road to Murphys

[1852:]

H.V. Olivo's Journal, June 21, 1852:

I have not taken the time to write for the past few days. Among other matters, I've been visiting my old friends Ben and Bully and meeting Ben's young Maidu wife and of course his infant son, one William True Bear Goffe McCain, perhaps a year and a half old now and naturally already walking and talking, quite an active little fellow, and large for his age. With Ben his father, I suppose there's no great mystery; as the old cliche insists, the acorn doesn't fall far from the oak.

Truly I wish my own happiness were as full and complete as Benjamin's.

Farnsworth O'Bragh is unchanged—because, as he says, "Once a coon's dead, why, they ain't nothin' much goin' to happen after that." For reasons best known to Bully, he persists in the delusion that he's already died at least once and possibly more than that—but things that *need doing* keep waking him up. In any case, the mating with Rabbit-chaser seems to have prospered. The two are inordinately fond of each other.

Both Ben and Bully were disappointed to learn Roxanne and I have parted and that she's on her way back to Jolly Eld Angelond. Ben listened sympathetically and offered little in the way of advice, as was proper. Bully, however, assured me that I'd been freed from *a hurrible burden, lad, and after a time, ye'll see what this child means.*

Ben's wife is named *Ooti-du*, which, literally translated, is either *Acorn Girl* or *Female Acorn*. She's simply Ooti, relatively small, beautifully formed, mystically intense—a Kuksu shaman, a leader of the people, one whose medicine vision was such that the older priests were forced to pronounce it authentic. It's hard for me to conjecture that so generous a spirit as hers may in fact belong to the dreaded leader of the Panos, the erstwhile scourge of the mining camps. Whatever the case, Ben and Ooti are established at a place they call Upper Eden, and they have round about them a composite of two Maidu villages—a rancheria, with a good bit of industry built in. The McCain sawmill's capable of producing first-grade pine timbers, and in behalf of Olivo & Beard, I've entered into a contract with Mr. McCain and his clan (since he insists the Indians are part-owners, no matter the law) for four-by-six timbers, to be delivered to the bank of the Sacramento River just opposite the mouth of Willow Creek and Lassen Rancho. The arrangement should prove profitable to Ben and to Olivo & Beard as well.

Ben would like to see the establishment of a national reserve of some sort, to encompass those lands which lie immediately about the mountain of Wahgalu—a volcano and, I should think, still active—for there are numerous areas of hot springs and sulfur jets in proximity to the peak itself. Wild animals abound, including wolves, mountain lions, and golden grizzlies. Just as Califia has an absolute penchant for adopting animals, wild or otherwise, so Ooti is said to have adopted a pair of grizzly cubs and raised them to maturity. High up on the mountain we saw tracks in the snow, and Ooti pointed out a singularity in the small toe of one, so that she was certain the bear that made the track was one she raised.

We actually climbed the peak—Ben, Ooti, Farnsworth, and I. We rode our trail ponies to perhaps eight thousand feet, where we encountered heavy snowbanks. O'Bragh had fashioned an extra pair of snowshoes for me, and the group of us, with these basketlike contraptions on our feet, made our way up the last two thousand or so vertical feet, along an inclined route of perhaps three miles, to the summit—where, in fact, there was little snow at all, doubtless owing to the incessant winds.

I believe one can see half the world from up there. The experience was startling, astonishing. Mt. Shasta looms on the northern horizon and is considerably greater than Wahgalu, both in height and mass. I had the curious sensation I might simply take a run and leap across the intervening fifty miles and land amidst the snows of Waiiaka.

We three stood there, nodding and staring into the distance, just as though we had good sense. Then I pulled out three of the little cigars I sometimes smoke, and we all lit up and puffed away and stared some more at the immensity of the sprawling mountain and canyon country. Such vistas reduce cocky human awareness to its elemental proportions, and one feels a kind of unity with all that exists, both mineral and organic. Not even matters of the greatest significance to nations, not sickness and health, not life and death, make any difference. The mystery of the forest—and of the wildness—overwhelms all else. Indeed, I found myself wishing passionately I might eventually be laid to rest there on the mountain, with the rough lava rocks and the vastness of blue heaven and the wind that blows forever.

As we were on our way down, we felt an earthquake, though not of any great magnitude—but sufficient to start an avalanche, which went pouring down the mountain with enormous energy. I suppose the quake had something to do with the mountain's internal fires, banked for the present but certain to roar up at some indeterminate future moment.

No man, as the philosopher has said, can step into the same river twice. No, all's change, all's motion, all's process—whether we happen to be aware or not. In the face of this, as one comes to perceive, the momentary flaring of a human brain amounts to little more than a cipher. We humans are adept at the matter of survival, but I suspect that when we are all long since gone, the great silent process of nature, toward what ends we can only guess, will continue as always. Whatever we are, we aren't necessary to the ultimate purposes of the Vast Otherness.

Bully was ready to leave for the *High Shinin'* even before I arrived at Upper Eden and he delayed his departure in deference to me. Despite Ben's repeated invitations to stay awhile, I departed with Bully, and he and Ooti and I rode southward to a mountain valley rimmed on nearly all sides by peaks, the northern end of the Sierra—for north of that point the mountains are newly volcanic, and so are best thought of as part of the chain of snowcaps which extends through Oregon and Washington Territory, or so I've read.

In this valley, across which runs the new emigrant route from the high desert down into the Central Valley of California at the town of Marysville, we stopped at a trading post, one whose chief cook and bottle washer was none other than the legendary James P. Beckwourth, who discovered the pass and built the wagon road, expending perhaps $2,000 of his own funds in the process, but in the hope of being reimbursed by the city of Marysville—a vain hope, as matters turned out, for the town burned the night before Beckwourth led in the first of the wagon trains.

Among his previous adventures, Jim Beckwourth has been both an Indian chief and an Indian fighter, horse thief *nonpareil*, as well as compañero at one time or another of Califia's former husband, Samson Flowers. As I say, the old mountain man (young, actually, by O'Bragh's standards) discovered the pass just to the east of the valley and proceeded to blaze a trail into California, and subsequently established a ranch and trading post and livery here in the valley which bears his name. Naturally enough, O'Bragh and Beckwourth also knew one another—and soon the two of them were embracing like a pair of Russian generals and exchanging notes on mutual friends and acquaintances. I'd told Bully about the death of Samson Flowers, and Bully, guessing accurately enough that Samson and Beckwourth were acquainted, passed along the news.

"Gone beaver?" was all Jim, said, nodding.

In this I believe I sensed a grand fatalism such as might only be accepted by men whose values are so totally those of *this life*.

Beckwourth is a large man in his fifties, a Mulatto, whose

father was a First Family of Virginia aristocrat who fell in love with and married a slave girl. O'Bragh says Jim Beckwourth was for a number of years the *head war chief of the Mountain Crows*, during which period the Crows were the scourge of the mountains. Beckwourth, in turn, knows Pompey Charbonneau, of whom I've read in the *Journals of Lewis and Clark*. Charbonneau, like me, was sent to Europe to be educated— and, like me, he chose to return to the land which bore him, arriving in the Rocky Mountains before the expiration of the beaver trade. Beckwourth's of the opinion that Charbonneau is presently operating a hotel in Placer Dry Diggings, on the other side of the mountains—and that possibly he and I might have occasion to *palaver*.

Numerous Indians have congregated about Beckwourth's trading post and hotel (if one may call it that). In all appearances, one finds oneself in the midst of an Indian village. The lodges are constructed after the fashion of the Cheyennes and Pawnees out on the plains—and I suspect Mr. Beckwourth has acted as building supervisor.

A band of emigrants reached the valley while I was there— destitute, exhausted, on the verge of starvation. Beckwourth saw to their needs and said nothing of payment—and made loans, apparently, with little likelihood of their ever being repaid.

O'Bragh and Rabbit-chaser were of a mind to keep going— possibly to Fort Laramie or thereabouts—and so, with yet another wagon train making its way across Beckwourth's Valley toward the trading post, we parted company—Farnsworth and his lady friend to the east, across the low divide of Beckwourth's Pass, and I to the south, for I was intrigued by old Jim's tale of a huge lake hidden somewhere in the mountain fastness. Beckwourth was certain of the lake's existence because his Washo Indian friends had told him about it, and he was altogether certain these people never told anything but the truth.

Proceeding south from Beckwourth's Valley, I came upon the drainage of Little Truckee River. Two and a half years ago, Ben, Bully, Roxy, Rabbit-chaser, and I had followed that stream in the opposite direction as we searched for a less snow-choked route across the Sierra. A few miles farther I reached the confluence with the Truckee. Here I turned my mount upstream, following the Donner Trail into the mountains—at the same time supposing I'd been *had* by that tale of a great mountain lake—since now I could see familiar peaks ahead that I knew to rise near the emigrant pass.

But the Truckee turned northward, and I followed along for perhaps no more than fifteen miles when, to my utter astonishment, I reached the margin of a deep blue body of water that appeared to be at least twenty miles long and perhaps half that distance in width. The water was amazingly clear, and the mountains that rose all about the lake had held their snowpacks to mid-summer's day. In all the world I cannot imagine one could find a more stunningly beautiful prospect, and I wished *keenly* that Califia were with me—in honor, perhaps, of our own venture into the Sierra numerous years ago, 1836 it was—the time we found great redwoods whose foliage differs from those native to the Coastal Mountains.

I proceeded along the lake's western shore, passing one remarkable bay which, a mile or so in length, appeared to have been gouged out of the granite, possibly by ice, and above, to either side, dramatic monoliths, one of granite, the other of a reddish stone. The remarkable form of a cross of ice stared eastward across the lake.

The Washo story of *Mountain Lake* or *Fremont's Lake* is astonishing indeed, and so I give the following account:

It's said that there were once no mountains and no lake, but rather a fertile valley through which the Truckee River coursed westward, toward the Pacific. Those who lived in the valley were both peaceful and prosperous, but then a savage group from the north appeared, destroying and killing. Those who survived became slaves to their conquerors, and they were obliged to build a temple for the worship of the sun.

Next a great tidal wave swept in from the Pacific, and following this catastrophe came a greater one—with earthquake and volcanic fire. The immense convulsions continued, and a great mountain rose, spewing fire and ash into the sky, so that particles of gold rained down. The Truckee River now ran eastward, into an inland sea where today there's only desert. At last the center of the mountain collapsed, and the Truckee

River filled in the gaping hole in the earth, creating Lake Fremont.

The remarkable thing about this fanciful tale, it seems to me, has to do with the temple to a sun god—possibly an echo of something from the Toltecs or the Mayans or even the Egyptians, though if it were of the latter, we'd surely have to revamp our notions of ancient history.

Whatever the case, I discovered no signs of any such temple or, for that matter, of any actual human habitation. But is it not remarkable? With a heavily used emigrant trail to the north and another, as I discovered, just a few miles to the south, the very existence of this immense mountain lake is supposed conjectural—and is not described at all accurately by the various maps I've seen.

Once south of the lake, whose passage required the better part of a full day of riding, I reached the Carson Pass Trail and crossed to the western slope of the mountains, encountering no more than a few rapidly melting drifts of snow high on the mountain's back. Since I was on no particular schedule, I resolved to attempt, at least, to find my way to that place where Califia and I camped the year before everything changed for both of us.

H.V. *Olivo's Journal, June 27, 1852:*

I've continued my traverse westward and southward through the Sierra, down from the high rocks and into the zone of dense firs and sugar pines and river canyons where, as often as not, I discovered bands of men working the rivers and creeks, up to their waists in mud and water and a terrible look of greed and desperation on their faces. What all this frenzy of mining has done to the landscape in so short a time is utterly astonishing, and until the gold vanishes or becomes as commonplace as lead or copper, I presume the systematic devastation will continue.

I've begun to despair of ever finding that place, that very special place where Califia and I once lay together, young lovers beneath a burst of stars. Doubtless I'm still too far north, but the task is essentially one of finding a needle in a haystack.

The Sierra, to put matters simply, is enormous—hundreds of miles in length and eighty or a hundred miles across, all of it dissected, almost surgically, by remarkable canyons—such as that of the Mokelumne, the river I've followed down out of the high country.

In other ways I've most certainly rediscovered the spot Califia and I shared—yes, and a string of other places, other times. That was the age of our innocence, though we were intent upon doing the *forbidden thing*. As I rode, I found myself there again, the two of us, atop the Coast Range, with Monte Diabolo off to the north and San Joaquin Valley, vast and flat, at our feet—the Sierra Nevada far away, beckoning, beckoning.

We've cast our lot. I don't think there's any way back now, Califia. Do you regret what we've done?

Were those the words I actually spoke at the time, or do I merely reconstruct a species of presumed reality?

As yet I've seen nothing resembling a giant redwood. There are many yellow or incense cedars of significant girth and height, but on the whole these particular red-barked trees are hardly more than a hundred and fifty feet tall, and though their boles are often impressive, they in no way compare with many of the redwoods presently being felled—and certainly not with the giants along Redwood Creek where Califia and I. . . .

Perhaps it was a dream—the combined dreamings of a lonely girl and a lonely boy. Possibly the place we went to ceased to exist the moment we left it, even as it only came into existence when we desired and so entered.

And yet I do have that scar on my back. . . .

The lands of the Yokuts—and Califia and I spending that one night close to the abandoned village. We made love and afterward lay there listening to the crazed laughter of sandhill cranes and the astonishing and infinitely complex music of mockingbirds.

Then the Sierra, and we rode up that lateral ravine until we found ourselves in a dense forest—first dogwoods and alders and willows, and then that grove of giants, larger than anything either of us had ever seen.

Such trees contain the spirits of those who have died and have gone to Other Side Camp. Perhaps there were giants who lived in these mountains—and that's why the trees are so large.

The two of us then, together. . . .

A great golden-furred grizzly sow and two young ones . . . oblivious to the humans and seemingly not even curious. The mother bear and her offspring took their time, ambling the length of the giant grove and finally disappearing into the forest of pine and fir beyond.

Califia, goddamn it! This whole thing is so utterly insane! *Una afortunada desgracia,* as my father would say—it's a blessing in disguise, it's an ill wind that blows no good. But what good, what possible purpose in all this? When we've been together, we've been happy—blessed in happiness. Apart, we do foolish things—marry other people, for instance. Because in some vague way or another, Roxanne reminded me of you, Califia, and since I'm a very, very logical person, I married the woman. I cannot speak for you—perhaps you loved Sam Flowers—and truly I hope you did. No, I don't mean that. Even though he's dead, I'm jealous of him—God save my pagan soul for such pettiness, such meanness of spirit.

So, Califia, why aren't you here with me right now? We should both be searching for that sacred grove where light gleams in water—though perhaps humans, for the sake of their own sanity, should never be allowed to enter. Yet we entered. We were Adam and Eve, we were First Man and First Woman—and we didn't need Tío Coyote to show us how to mate with one another. We discovered that for ourselves—and, goddamn it, it was good.

My musings were cut short when I realized I'd ridden into a small but bustling mining encampment. Just downstream a bridge had been slung up, by means of logs and cables, across the Mokelumne. Once onto the road, I turned southward, passing through the settlement of Mokelumne Hill well before noon. I made my way along a well-used horse and wagon road to the town of San Andreas and from there to Murphys [sic] where I'm spending the night in a room at Murphys Hotel. The original name of the settlement, as I gather, was Murphys Ranch—without the apostrophe, since such matters of spelling and so forth are not deemed significant in the Mother Lode.

———

I thought I'd finished writing for the evening, but such was not to be the case. I've just met a fellow who's told me an interesting story—I had almost the same feeling as the night Ben and I met Farnsworth O'Bragh—that I'd been taken in tow by Coleridge's patented graybeard loon. The gentleman's name is Augustus T. Dowd, an employee of the Union Water Company of Murphys—as a hunter, to supply fresh meat to the workmen on the various canals used for gold mining.

Dowd was hunting, he told me, and wounded a grizzly. In the act of pursuing the beast, the hunter came into a grove of immense trees—the very sort, certainly, that Califia and I discovered during our *grand escape*.

"Surely," Dowd remarked to me, "I figgered it must of been some curiously delusive dream!"

To assure himself of their reality, he walked around several, administering to each a series of kicks. Once he'd returned to his camp, he told the boys what he'd found. Predictably enough, they all laughed—accused him of drinking when he should have been hunting. The boys hooted him out of the bunkhouse. Dowd said nothing further for a couple of days—resolved to put up with the chuckling and ribbing of the miners—one of whom asserted that Dowd's big-tree story sounded like *one of them thar lying tales Jim Beckwourth used to tell when he was running the general store in Sonora.* In a way, Dowd admitted, such a comparison was a compliment, since Beckwourth was known hereabouts as the world's greatest yarner.

Then came Sunday morning. Dowd announced, "Boys, I've done kilt the biggest Gawdamn grizzly that I ever saw in all the days of my life. I'm going to get me something to eat—and then I'll need some help bringing that beastie in. Matter of fact, we all best go."

Within a short while the gang rode out, Dowd as guide, up along Angels Creek to the crest and over to Antonio Creek Falls, then to the south branch, and up that ravine another couple of miles to some meadows. There grows the immense tree—along with a host of giants only somewhat less impressive.

Matter-of-factly pointing out the astonishing diameter and admirable height of the tree beneath which they stood, Dowd exclaimed, "Now, by the blue balls of Gawd, are you fellers willing to admit the truth of my big-tree story? This here's the griz I wanted you to see. Ain't she something?"

H.V. Olivo's Journal, June 28, 1852:

With the images of my interlude with Califia still in mind, certain now that Dowd's trees must be of the same sort as those we'd stumbled onto—and that, in all likelihood, there were many more such groves waiting to be discovered—I paid Mr. Dowd to take me upcountry. I was not the first, needless to say, that Augustus T. had led back into the forest to view the *Calaveras Big Trees*, as he so appropriately dubbed them—for this was indeed Calaveras County, *Skulls County*.

The trees are huge indeed—much larger than those Olivo & Beard have been felling—greater in girth if not in height than those in the *cathedral* grove on Redwood Creek. I examined the bark, the foliage, and the cones. The latter are extremely small, out of all proportion to so huge a tree—and the seeds themselves hardly more than grains of sand. Foliage differs significantly from the coastal redwoods (the latter somewhat resembling that of a fir) and instead is more of a gray-green and similar to the yellow cedars which grow in the Sierra and the Coast Range as well. With huge, red-gray, bark-encased boles rising upward as they do, the grove gives one a sensation of having entered into some ancient temple, constructed not to honor Zeus or Apollo or Athena, but rather Dionysus and all other nymphs and satyrs and dryads who inhabit the wild areas of the earth.

I urged Dowd to secrecy, for as I suggested, such trees must grow in but few places in the world, and hence they ought to be preserved so that they may be enjoyed and contemplated by human creatures for centuries to come. In the *Good Book* we read of the cedars of Lebanon, and yet those cedars are long since vanished—all but a very few, or so I'm told. The same must never happen to these magnificent redwoods of the Sierra Nevada.

As I gave thought to what amounted to national preserves, enclaves of the primordial condition of nature, I envisioned immediately that big blue lake in the mountains, Lake Fremont, the place the Washos call *Da-o*, which also ought to be preserved in its pristine condition, as well as the area around Wahgalu (Ben McCain's dream) and a thousand other places here in the North American West—places in New England as well, and along the spine of the Appalachians and long stretches of the Mississippi and the Missouri and the Rocky Mountains and Salt Lake and the deserts and . . .

Perhaps, I concluded, it was a lost cause—lost before even being proposed. Even if one could present such schemes, such beautiful dreams of preservation, to the Congress of the United States, they are destined not to be fulfilled. My own assessment of the nature of mankind leads me to suspect that once the existence of the groves were known, it would not be very long before the thought of felling a few of the hugest trees would occur. If there are indeed extensive stands of these monsters, then perhaps logging makes sense—with strict adherence to the rule of preserving for posterity these prodigies of nature.

Was it not in the minds of my own father and my Uncle Bill, more than thirty years ago, that a similar scheme hatched? *Let's cut these babies down and turn them into shingles. Good market in Monterey.* . . . I myself am no less than one of the primary heirs to an empire founded upon the felling of the giants.

Utility on the one hand and aesthetics on the other—or is it perhaps far more than mere aesthetics? In destroying the wilderness, after all, it's possible that we're also destroying ourselves.

"Afraid it's too late, Olivo," Dowd grinned, lighting the small cigar I'd offered him. "They's already been gents up here who've got ideas about turning them redwoods into lumber, if redwoods is what they be. Here in the goldfields, boards is at a premium. Homer, if a wagonload of lumber from one of your pa's mills shows up, the whole lot's sold before the boards get unloaded. Eggs and shovels and boards, not necessarily in that order, are in genuine demand—just like anything is when they ain't much to go around. I'd say a Bigtree Rush is probably already as good as under way, just like a gawddamn Gold Rush, so to speak. Speculators are likely sending out their teams all over the Sierra to see how many Bigtrees there be. Hellfire, I may just go into the tree-cutting business myself. That's how

your folk got rich, ain't it? Can't be no harder than mining for
gold—or hunting meat for a gang of scurvy canal diggers, for
that matter. Way I see it, Olivo, I've kinda got me some fin-
der's rights."

I stared intently into Augustus Dowd's brown eyes—eyes
that looked to me at that moment strangely like five-dollar gold
pieces.

H.V. Olivo's Journal, June 30, 1852:

Since I could think of no other reasonable course of action, I
decided to take the matter directly to Governor Peter H. Burnett—even though, so far as my logic would lead me, the
mountain lands and therefore the forests upon them must certainly belong to the Federal Government, and not to the state
at all. From what I knew of Burnett, I didn't really suppose
that he'd be willing to act, not during the continuing frenzy of
the Gold Rush and the rapid settlement of what was once the
peaceful territory of Alta California. At the same time, I was
aware that Burnett knew both my father and my uncle and
had doubtless done business on more than one occasion with
Olivo & Beard and, in any case, would wish to placate the
son of Raymondo Olivo.

Dowd drifted across the dusty street and in through the
swinging half doors of the Murphys Hotel, and I, for my part,
proceeded to my room, got my few belongings together, and
returned to the hitching post. I mounted my horse and, with
my pack animal following, I made my way out of town, with
Sacramento my destination.

The government of the State of California had been moving
about since the beginning, but Sacramento had become the
unofficial capital city. San Jose was designated in 1849 for the
first session of the legislature. This year, however, the legislature convened at the town of Vallejo, on a site provided by
Mariano Vallejo himself. When the quarters proved inconvenient, the government chartered a riverboat and moved "lock,
stock, and gavel" to Sacramento, the gateway to the Mother
Lode.

Two days after leaving Murphys, I found myself seated

across a desk from Governor Burnett, each of us smoking a Cuban cigar. Burnett listened to me, heard me out, and stroked his chin whiskers; whereas he had the appearance of thoughtful concern, it was obvious he was merely humoring me. The governor no more comprehended the nature of the Big Trees of the Sierra than did those water workers in Murphys—before Dowd made up his bear story and so tricked them into looking for themselves.

"Redwoods in Calaveras County?" the governor asked.

"Yes—but bigger than the Coast Range trees, possibly the biggest trees in the world."

"I thought our . . . normal . . . redwoods were the largest."

"Possibly taller, but definitely not bigger. You'll need to see these giants in order to believe them."

Burnett pursed his mouth and tapped a forefinger to his lower lip.

"An entire forest, Mr. Olivo?"

"I don't know," I replied. "But yes, a small forest at least—and groves in more than one place. Back in 1836 my cousin and I . . . Governor, what I do know is this: those trees need protection, for otherwise someone'll decide to start cutting them down."

Burnett puffed his cigar.

"Perhaps I'll send a fact-finding group over to Calaveras after the legislative session's finished," he suggested. "Tell me, Homer, how are your father and your uncle? It's been a while since I've seen either of them. I understand your company's got a few troubles with its operations up north, on the Klamath—Larkin, Stearns, and Reading, I mean—the Corzine and Dolbeer combine. I understand there's a new lumberyard over in Stockton—a fellow named Asa Simpson, I believe. Did you come down that way, by any chance?"

I shook my head.

"Well, in the long run competition's good for everyone," Burnett said, rising from his chair.

CHAPTER THIRTY-THREE

Pelican Doctor's Judgment

[1852:]

H.V. PUT SACRAMENTO behind him. He took a ferry barge across the river and proceeded westward through the sweltering, mosquito-infested marshes of the *Nem Seyoo*'s flood plain. The Coast Range rose ahead, long and purple against the cloudless summer sky. Once, H.V. reflected, the Central Valley had been the realm of wild Indians and tule elk. Now there was a sprinkling of new farms close behind those few creeks that made their way down from the *montañas secas*, their courses plotted by bands of oaks and cottonwoods.

To the south rose the distinctive dome of *Monte Diabolo*— Mt. Diablo, as it was now indicated on the maps.

At the valley's margin, H.V. turned into *Arroyo de las Putas* and rode into the mountains—from high, brushy or barren hills, quite dry—to stands of *madroña* and oak with beards of trailing Spanish moss—to stands of pine and fir. Beyond the first swellings of the Coast Range lay Napa Valley, with its considerable vineyards, and then another series of long ridges, these spotted with redwood and fir. Round about Santa Rosa the land looked quite civilized, all things considered, and in places intensively cultivated, with pastures demarcated and Hereford cattle grazing. Beyond yet one more wave of ridges, H.V. reached Russian River Canyon and the deep redwood forests that clearly showed signs, here and there, of the operations of loggers—Califia's men doubtless chief among them.

Visions of the essential calm of the English countryside passed through H.V.'s mind, and he shuddered. Was that condition of almost total human utility, of human omnipresence, to be California's fate as well? And the fate of the world's unexplored zones—the mysterious interior of Africa, the far north of Canada and Russian Alyeska, desert reaches of the Australian Outback, the infinite green tangles of the Amazon, and the mighty spines of the Sierra Andes and the Himalayas? For three centuries California had slept—or dozed, rather, and the scattering of Mestizos and Spanish, the missions and their impact upon the Native peoples, the ranchos and the herds of long-horned cattle, an occasional Yankee or British trading vessel anchoring at Monterey or Yerba Buena—even Herr Sutter making his way into the interior and taking with him his dream of New Helvetia: none of that, truly, had greatly affected the land. But now, in the aftermath of this astonishing curse, *gold*, came all manner of change—with wagon after wagon crossing the passes, shipload upon shipload of humanity arriving at San Francisco.

Something further, something even more devastating and far-reaching: the Gold Rush was precipitating a Timber Rush, and the implacable forces that had systematically removed the forests of Europe and had been for a century and more at work on the forests of New England, the South, and the Great Lakes region were now hacking away at the redwood, pine, and fir forests of the Far West.

Surely it was all too damned big for human midges to have any appreciable impact upon it—the wilderness too trackless, too immense.

Forests of stumps, stumps as far as the eye could see. . . .

The Russian River operation. Could Califia possibly be here? She'd spoken of making a trip south, yes, in the immediate future. Perhaps the plan was to no other purpose than that of putting distance between the two of them—something Roxanne's precipitant decision to remove to San Francisco had obviated.

With regard to the Sierran redwoods, he was certain Califia would see eye to eye with him as to the necessity of doing something to preserve the trees—possibly an acquisition on the part of Olivo & Beard. The need for lumber in the Mother Lode was clear and immediate, and just possibly with the opening of a new mill or two, the felling and sawing of pine and fir might not only go a long way toward satisfying the desperate need but, handled properly, could be worked so as to set aside the Calaveras Big Trees and other groves as yet undiscovered.

If Califia were not at Russian River, then he'd ride south to San Lorenzo to talk with his father, Uncle Bill, and Cousin Cal—if the latter were not aboard any of half a dozen *Don Quixotes*, bound for Panama or Hawaii or Chile. One way or the other, though, something had to be done. What he really desired, he realized, was for all these accursed *Outsiders* to go back to whatever worlds they'd come from. Having returned from exile, he was becoming outright territorial. But since the eventuality of exodus and diaspora was relatively unlikely, and since he was resigned to the certainty California would never again be the mystery and the splendor it had once been, why, at least a man might attempt to save some trees that happened to be *muy goddamned grande*.

Early July heat lashed at the redwood groves along the diminished current of Russian River, and the logging camp was empty—empty, at least, except for "Chef" Apfelkopf, who was busy at the cookshack, working out his meal schedule for the next week—a schedule that would have to be considerably different if any more *unheimlichbastardfires* broke out. The last blaze started, inexplicably, halfway up the ridge, and some of the boys were obliged to spend two days up there, extinguishing the wretched inferno, while the others were turned into a kind of mule train, hauling buckets of water up to where the fire was more or less contained. Apfelkopf, of course, with all too little help, had been required to tote chow to the tin pants dandies.

"Next time," he reflected, "*Ich bin getempted* to roast a few of the wretched bantam chickens that run all over the camp.

The insolent black rooster, he'll be the first to go—except, of course, that he *ist Frau Blumen's* special pet."

In any case, the fire hadn't been the chickens' fault. Indeed, "Chef" had a suspicion one of the young buckers (there were half a dozen wet-behind-the-ears New Yorkers in camp now) started the blaze as a kind of diversion from the tedium of drawing the misery whip back and forth across sections of redwood and fir.

Fire was not a good thing to play with. Whereas the redwoods themselves seemed oddly resistant to flames, the other species weren't—and a yellow wave could run through a logging camp with all the devastation of a raging river in Michigan after the breaking of spring ice. The previous summer, a few miles up the canyon, a fire burned for two weeks, charring several thousand acres—so that very little survived, whether animal or vegetable, other than the big redwoods.

The hundred or so camp chickens went off into a wild chorus of cackling and crowing, and Apfelkopf stepped outside to see what was the matter.

"Where's the crew?" a stranger asked. "I can't seem to rouse anyone. I take it Califia—Califia Beard—she's here in camp, isn't she?"

"Chef" turned quickly, regarded the oddly clad stranger—Indian or Mexican from appearances, a man of medium height and build and wearing black denim pants, a chambray shirt, a buckskin jacket, and a silk stovepipe hat. The bulge under his long jacket indicated a weapon.

"Ich spreche kein English, Herr Bandido. Ich been nur ein, how you say? *Ein cook."*

"Sondern Ich been kein bandido," H.V. grinned. "I'm Homer Olivo—one of the *booshways.* Sorry to startle you, my good man—*es tut mir leid.* Come now, since you're the cook, you must be able to sling English as well as hash. What the hell's going on?"

Apfelkopf glanced once again at the lump under the jacket, nodded, smiled without commitment.

"Herr Olivo? I'm sorry—we haven't met before. I thought you were *ein* gunman who'd come to rob me—*ist* Sunday and everyone's gone. The boys are at the Injun village at the mouth of the river—Chalanchawi. They play the hand-game with the

chiefs—and besides that, one old boy's set up a kind of drinking emporium and whorehouse. Califia, she doesn't approve,
but since the boys got accustomed to Sundays with the Injuns
while she was *im nord*, she let it go."

"Interesting," H.V. said. "So where's Califia?"

"Upstream from *dem skidweg*, above the check dam. She
goes there to read, I guess. Anyhow, she don't want company.
But you're family, so that's different, *nicht wahr*?"

"Upstream, you say?"

"Maybe half mile *oder etwas*. You know about cougar, ehh?
Probably *die* Boss Lady's got that cougar with her. Damned
thing's *so gross wie eine Kuh*."

Califia swam easily across the clear river, stood up when she
reached the shallows, used both hands to twist the water out
of her long, dark hair—and then stood there in the sunlight,
hands on hips. Water droplets on her shoulders, arms, breasts,
legs—glintings of light, tiny points of brilliance so that she
appeared to H.V., crouching now behind cover of willow and
alder, more like a goddess than a mere unclothed female of
human persuasion—like the Botticelli Venus, but changed, altered so as to approximate reality while yet, through subtle
chemistry of light splintering through beads of moisture, more
nearly configuring the ideal, the Socratic-Platonic *idea of woman*.

*The hair dark, of the earth, not fragile and blond—no graces
close by to receive her, no oyster shell and no translucent Aegean
waters behind her, but only the still surface of Russian River blazing in white afternoon sunlight, and the heavy green of redwood
forest, green everywhere excepting one slope beyond the stream
where most of the trees have been felled, and even there simply a
different sort of green as young redwoods compete for space and
light with ceanothus brush (no longer blooming this time of the
year) and buckeye and Douglas firs and black oaks.*

On a shelf of gray-black slate projecting into the water was
a large mountain lion, a creature doubtless weighing in excess
of two hundred pounds—ears fully alert, tail switching from
moment to moment—the creature having assumed a stance
that might have been interpreted as a crouch to be followed
by a leap.

That had to be it, H.V. thought, one of those lions she'd

written him about while he was in England—one of those she said had reverted to the wild and were roaming the redwood forests, coming in perhaps once in a year to renew the primal bond with the female human being they apparently regarded as their own mother—or as an old and valued friend.

H.V. wanted to shout—to call out to this woman who'd long been for him the very epitome of the opposite sex, the one who most nearly embodied some precious portion of his own inner nature—the gray-eyed Eve who was, in some way or another, Divinely interdicted fruit. At the same time, he found he could barely breathe—as though he'd somehow blundered into the midst of an ancient Greek myth, or into some vision Coyote had permitted him, even though he believed himself fully awake and in contact with the rocks and the air, with the earth upon which he knelt.

He mustn't, he realized, disturb this moment—he must not, by an assertion of his presence, take this instant away from Califia.

"*Gatogordo!*" she called out. "Fat Cat! Come swimming with me!"

After speaking these words, she splashed water at the cougar, turned, and leaped backward into the river.

A kingfisher, perched atop a tangle of blue willow on the far bank of the stream, called out in agitation—the rasping, chattering cry of the insane blue bird with its white collar. The kingfisher screamed a second time and then took to the air, skimmed the surface, and disappeared beyond a tumble of boulders.

The mountain lion squinted as the spray hit him—and then he, too, leaped into the water and swam with consummate ease toward the far shore. Califia, beneath the surface, came up behind the big cat and grabbed hold of his tail—so that he turned in mid-stroke and came back toward her.

"Slowpoke!" she cried out, laughing and spitting water and then launching shoreward once more, the cougar in pursuit.

H.V. remained hidden until Califia emerged from the river, repeated the ritual with her hair, and strode to the bank, where a red towel was draped over a sprawling wild grapevine. After a turn or two about the pool, the cougar also emerged, leaping up and shaking its fur as energetically as a dog might have done. Then, suddenly, the lion was staring toward the cover of brush and young trees behind which H.V. remained hidden. Whether the summer currents of air had shifted slightly or he'd inadvertently made some movement that caught the mountain lion's eye made no difference. His presence was known.

Califia, intuitively understanding the cougar's change in posture, pulled on her britches and a blue denim shirt. She dressed without excessive hurry, but she buckled on her pistol before she bothered to pull on stockings and boots. With seeming casualness, she walked to the far side of the slate formation and, weapon in hand, crouched behind it.

"Chef Apfelkopf, is that you? Who's got business with Califia Beard?"

H.V. stood up, his hands in the air.

"A fine way to treat the man who loves you," he complained.

"Homer Virgil? What in God's name? How long have you been hiding up there like a damned peeping Tom? I ought to shoot you as a matter of principle. . . ."

"Fire away," he said, "I'm coming down. Fat Cat, is it? Tell him I'm harmless, Califia."

The mountain lion had now retreated—gliding over the rocky formation to crouch down beside his mistress.

"Somehow," she said, "I don't think you have too much to worry about—not from this great coward here, at least."

Califia accompanied H.V. to Carquinez, where they were ferried across the gleaming strait dividing Grizzly Bay and San Pablo Bay, both of these simply portions of the larger *Bahía del San Francisco*. From there they rode east of the Berkeley Hills and crossed the low mountains on the Altamont Pass Trail that led down to Santa Clara and San Jose, from thence across to the San Lorenzo Mill—with both of them feeling in some strange way they were repeating a portion of a venture they'd made sixteen years earlier, the return from that venture into the Sierra.

This time no Yokuts arrow nearly took his life, and this time they were not children guiltily returning home—to await whatever judgment their parents might decide to make. Califia had listened to his account of the Calaveras Big Trees, and she agreed with him—just as she agreed about the wisdom of preserving the cathedral-like grove on Redwood Creek—yes, those, and many another.

"There's great irony," she said. "Our family was responsible for founding the timber industry in California. Olivo & Beard is responsible for a good portion of the lumber that's been used to build San Francisco, Sacramento, and other towns—rival timber operators have followed our example. What we've done, they've done. Larkin, Stearns, and Reading? So that's where Allen Corzine and John Dolbeer got their funding. Once we were partners with Larkin, and now I suppose we're commercial enemies. As this land grows, H.V., there'll be more and more logging outfits—you know that. I suppose it's time to get some rules in place—through the legislature, if possible, so that the really *big* trees will be spared."

"How do you suppose our fathers are going to respond? To acquire the land where the Big Trees grow—that makes sense in terms of the business, but it sure as hell doesn't make sense to buy stumpage in order not to cut it. We can put in mills over there that will more than finance the preservation of whatever Big Trees we can manage to protect—presuming there are any left to protect by the time we get all this worked out."

El Buzzardo came flapping down, landing this time not on his mistress's shoulder but atop H.V.'s silk stovepipe hat.

"Guess he's finally decided I'm safe," H.V. grinned.

"Okay. But am I safe? How do you answer that, Homer Virgil?"

He reached up with one hand, stroked the turkey vulture's wing.

"Does he have any bad habits I should be aware of?"

"Just the usual. What about *us*? We're both miserable when we're apart. The years when you were in England, I could almost accept that. But now you're returned to California— good God, H.V., it's more than two years since you've been back. Now Roxanne's returned to England. . . ."

El Buzzardo took off once more, catching a wind current and spiraling upward, upward, until he was little more than a small, curved black line against the blue, high above the redwood-forested ridges beyond Los Gatos.

"We gave in to the wishes of our family," he said. "I suppose they were looking out for our best interests—that, and my father's dream of sending me to Europe for an education. I can't lay it all to him—it had become my dream, as well. But you could have come with me, Califia. . . . "

"No," she replied. "You had to leave, and I had to stay. We both had certain lives to live—and without them, we wouldn't be here, together now. We were little more than children at the time—and didn't realize we in fact had a choice to do whatever we wished. Or if we understood, we believed the price was banishment. But are we free now? Or are we forever to be denied—like characters in some tragic novel? Roxanne's gone, H.V. She's deserted you. Will you ask for a divorce? Even that detail makes no difference, of course. We could go on living separately but not far apart and. . . . "

"To hell with that," he said. "Our family's simply going to have to accept our judgment. The law doesn't prohibit us, and, damn it, I think I'd enjoy living in the same house with you."

She laughed—laughed strangely—and when she turned back toward him, tiny but quite intense fires were burning in the strange gray eyes. It wasn't important that they were ignited by the afternoon sun beyond the pass, which was rapidly sinking, to extinguish itself in the Pacific.

"No doubt you'd grow tired quickly enough," she said. "I've become cantankerous in my old age—I've got certain habits, and I insist on sleeping on my own side of the bed."

"Which side might that be, *Aphrodite Kallipygos*?" he demanded.

"What in hell does that mean?"

He laughed.

"That you have beautiful . . . eyes," he said.

"You'd best be telling the truth. I'm going to look it up in your father's huge dictionary."

"You still haven't answered," he said. "Which side of the bed?"

"The *right* side, of course. Are we going to talk to our parents—or just go ahead and do what we want to do?"

"In all likelihood, they'd find out eventually. So I suppose we should try to convince them that our *medicine vision* is valid. What was it Pelican Doctor told you—I mean, about the traditional way of the Hotochrukma with regard to twins? Pelican Doctor—he's not necessarily opposed to the idea of our getting married?"

"Yes, no," Califia replied. "Because we're the offspring of twin sisters, some would say it's bad luck for us to . . . Once, a long time ago, when twins were born, either both would be left out for the animals to devour, or else just one would be— if they could figure out which was evil and which was good."

"Highly enlightened. If our mothers weren't twins, then, there'd have been no problem. At least any children we might have won't be so definitely *overbred*. Hell, the ruling classes of Europe have been inbreeding for a thousand years, and look at them. Well, I suppose that's not the best example. Even the Three Wisemen, the *Magi*, were the result of sons impregnating their mothers—for religious purposes—to wit, the creation of beings who could speak with the vision of the gods, whether they fully understood that vision or not." -

"Homer Virgil, you make this sound quite academic and quite horrible. The way I see it, even if we were brother and sister—even then, if we were in love, we should live together. If that's what you and I want, then that's what we should do. We've already wasted half our lives. . . . "

"Are we strong enough?" H.V. asked. "I mean, we may still be obliged to go off together, to sunder our ties with our family. My friend Benjamin has taken a new last name. We can do the same thing, if it comes to that."

For a long moment the man and the woman studied one another.

"Yes," Califia said.

"All right, yes. We'll speak with our family, then. . . . "

The partners, the San Lorenzo foreman said, had gone to Monterey—inasmuch as word had arrived that Jean Paul Martin was dead, possibly of pneumonia, possibly of heart congestion. With this news, H.V. and Califia rode until darkness, up Boulder Creek and along the old Olivo & Beard mule road across the mountains, beneath the point of Eagle Rock, and thence down to the north branch of *Arroyo Grande*, Big Creek, where they camped for the night. They built a small fire and sat side by side after a dinner of jerked venison, scorched camp bread, and coffee.

Neither had known Jean Paul Martin well, and yet the man, always something of a mysterious figure, was in one way or another a member of the family. H.V. and Califia were aware that it was Martin's financial assistance, many years earlier, that had allowed Raymondo and Bill the Sawyer to get started— or at least that Martin gave the partners generous assistance. Whether they actually knew the man or not, then, it was still as though someone in the family had died.

Pelican Doctor was very old. Would he, too, die soon? Or would he perhaps really live to see the century mark?

The night was filled with the cries of mourning doves and screech owls and, from somewhere up on the ridge, what sounded like the laughter of a sandhill crane. Along the creek a pair of night herons chittered.

The inevitable happened, resurgence of the life force, and soon Califia and H.V. were lying together, locked in the naked embrace in the moonlight, with warm July darkness flowing about them and the sound of the stream, low with drought that had troubled the Coast Ranges, running softly in its stony bed, sounding at times almost like bells, tiny bells, possibly of obsidian or quartz. The hunger of time spent apart drove them on, goaded them on, until darkness flared, tingling with lights, and carried them into dreamless sleep, still joined in one an- other's arms.

In the morning Califia woke H.V. by chewing on his wrist.

"Have you turned cannibal?" he asked, attempting to throw off grogginess.

"You're on my side of the bed," Califia insisted. "Remember? I explained all that. . . ."

"I'll show you about which side of the bed," he muttered, knotting his fingers into her hair and pulling her mouth to- ward his.

"You lie still!" she said. "Last night you rode me every way from Tuesday, and now it's my turn. If you think women don't like to ride, Homer, then you know nothing about our spe- cies."

"*Species*, your ass, lady."

"That's possible. Now lie still and let me work. . . . "

Eventually, though, they decided they were hungry—for the more usual kind of food, and they devoured whatever had been left over from the night before. The venison was neither better nor worse, but the camp bread was such that not even El Buzzardo would touch it—El Buzzardo, who'd observed patiently from the branch of a California laurel while the mistress and the male friend went through their highly elaborate mammalian mating ritual. No doubt the vulture was feeling a bit self-satisfied in the knowledge that vulturine patterns were far more predictable and reasonable—consisting of a dance in which both male and female participated, with the female then squatting down, wings extended, while her Chosen One trod upon her back.

H.V. and Califia packed their saddlebags, mounted their ponies, and continued downcanyon to the forks and past that to a point where they were obliged to lead their horses along a narrow hillside trail, so as to get past the waterfall. There many years earlier, Pelican Doctor had pointed out the rock face, a natural sculpture of a chief staring northward, northward, Pelican Doctor said, in the direction from which the First People came, long ago.

The creek was low, and the beautiful falls, a raging torrent during winter, was now a mere whisper, a white veil sifting down from the stone trough high above, more like a mist than a waterfall, in places simply gliding over the heavy black rock of the cliff to the pool below.

Half a mile above Hotochruk they came upon a young woman who was in the act of setting a woven fish trap.

"Mariposa!" Califia said from the back of her horse. "It is a beautiful day—it is a beautiful day to do anything. How are your husband and your little ones?"

The Butterfly Woman deftly set the basket in place, put stone on top of it, and climbed up the bank so that she was standing between H.V. and Califia—bare from the waist up, her ample breasts tattooed elaborately, and her cheeks as well. The voluptuous figure of girlhood was voluptuous still; though she had gained weight, she wasn't nearly so heavy as most Ohlone women in their thirties.

"It's good to see you—to see both of you. Only yesterda

ve were all young together, and now the years run by, just as
his creek runs. I am worried that it might go dry this year.
He who was my husband, Califia, he's gone now, and I mustn't
mention his name. He began to cough at the time of the new
winter moon, and when spring came his spirit wasn't able to
defend itself any longer. He has gone to Other Side Camp. I'm
well but very lonely because he has left me. I have my two
children, though, and perhaps I'll marry again when the time
is right."

Califia suggested that Mariposa should ride with her on the
horse, back to the village, and the woman agreed. With a bit
of assistance she was immediately mounted behind.

When they reached the village, both Califia and H.V. noted
there were fewer lodges.

"My husband wasn't the only one who died," Mariposa
explained. "But others have moved away—to Santa Cruz. Some
of the men sell their women to the Bostons, and then use the
money to buy whiskey. These aren't good times for our people. . . . "

They dismounted before Pelican Doctor's lodge, but the
chief was not there. Tethering their horses, H.V. and Califia
left Mariposa and walked across the meadow to the two small
log cabins that Beard and Olivo had built for their wives and
themselves—for those occasions when the partners and their
mates were actually in residence at Hotochruk.

Seagull and Calling Owl and the chief saw who'd arrived,
and the twin daughters and Pelican Doctor came out through
the front door of the Olivo cabin. Califia and Homer Virgil
each embraced *mother*, and Homer shook hands with the burly
old chief.

"You two will get married, is it not so?" Pelican Doctor
asked. "I dreamed this thing for three nights, and so I was
certain. I've already told my daughters what will happen."

For a moment at least, H.V. and Califia were speechless—
the chief's presumption surprised them.

"You wouldn't object?" H.V. asked, knowing that if the
chief were agreeable, his daughters would also be—and that
the son-in-laws, whatever they might have thought privately,
would very likely also come around.

"Of course not," Pelican Doctor said. "My daughters and I

have discussed the matter. Perhaps finally my other two grandchildren will give me great-grandchildren, just as Calvin and Juanita have done. But you'll have to hurry to catch up."

Seagull and Calling Owl nodded agreement.

"We heard from Raymondo that Roxanne has returned to her own land. Raymondo told us that three weeks ago, Homer Virgil, shortly after you took money from the San Francisco office to pay for her passage. You see, those who live in Hotochruk village know what's happening in the world outside our canyon."

"No disagreement—no disapproval?" Califia asked.

"Would it do any good?" Pelican Doctor demanded, winking.

"I suppose not."

"We have been wondering," Seagull said, "how long this would take. Isn't that right, my sister?"

"Bill and Raymondo will arrive tomorrow, or perhaps the day after," Pelican Doctor said. "Then we must all talk. When two people look upon one another in such a way that no one else seems possible—and when they have already tried to follow the old ways, as they supposed the old ways to be, then it is right they should be together. This is my judgment, and I'll tell Raymondo and William that I've thought about the thing for a long while, and my dreams tell me it is right."

CHAPTER THIRTY-FOUR

God's Own Trees

[1852:]

TREES, H.V. REFLECTED, trees greater in height and girth than any other species in the world, and that included the mighty Douglas firs that grew in the Coastal Ranges and in the Cascades of Oregon and Washington country and on up into British Columbia—such were the two varieties of redwoods to be found in the mountains of California. While he'd never seen the Douglas firs to the north, H.V. had talked with loggers who'd worked in both places and so were in a position to make proper judgment. In particular he'd spoken with a couple of fellows who'd come down from Puget Sound and the Columbia River—men named Rian and Duffs. They'd brought an old California sidewheel steamer called the *Santa Clara* south to Humboldt Bay, where they beached the leaky craft and proceeded to use long leather and canvas belts as a means of transferring power from the ship's main shaft to four saws they'd set up on the beach. The ship's cabins provided a bunkhouse, the dining room a mess hall. More to the point, this highly unorthodox sawmill was able to turn out up to forty thousand feet of rough lumber on a good day—if the lads with the axes and misery whips and teams of bulls were able to cut and transport the requisite number of logs to the mill site.

Even to such as Rian and Duffs, who'd worked in the great fir forests, the redwoods were *something else.* Trees in normal stands might run from three to ten feet on the butt, but giants of fifteen and even twenty feet were hardly uncommon. The big ones, of course, were more than just profitable to bring down and mill into lumber. Such trees offered the timber beasts a genuine challenge. By actual ring count (a tree normally adding one ring per year), the smaller redwoods were between four and eight hundred years old, while on some of the greater trees the ring count went to two thousand and beyond. H.V. himself had counted one monster stump Corzine's men had taken down a mile or two from the mill town of Eureka. *Two thousand three hundred and twenty-seven years old!* The tree was four hundred and seventy-five years of age when Jesus the Nazorean was born. Rome had not yet truly risen when the seedling first sought sunlight, and even Socrates had yet to live and die.

Rian put the matter succinctly: *These trees is older than Jesu H. Mackinaw. . . .*

How old were the Sierran Big Trees? Until one of the great ones was cut down, H.V. supposed, there'd be no way of telling. One might hazard a guess, however. Presuming similar growth rates, these *big* redwoods could well be in excess of three thousand years. Nor was there any reason to believe he'd seen the greatest of them. . . .

What perversity of human pride would allow a logger to sink his axe into such a tree? Yet, he had to admit, to watch one of the giants fall was indeed an experience one was not likely to forget. He'd observed Calafia's men in careful preparation, making a *layout* or *bed* for a tree that measured in at nearly three hundred feet. The tree came down with terrific force, causing the ground to shake, almost as though an earthquake had struck. When the redwood gave its initial mortal shudder, the loggers scrambled down from the scaffolding, flinging their axes ahead of them. The one whose job it was to detect this movement wailed *Tim-burrrrr!* The top trembled, and after a moment came a dry, tearing, splintering sound that began slowly and then came with a rush, drowned out momentarily by the careening plunge of torn foliage ripping against the crowns of neighboring redwoods. The tree fell, gaining speed, until it flung itself recumbent upon the layout, almost perfectly on target, heaving and shuddering as a rain of needles and small branches followed the massive bole to earth.

The boys in the cookshack, more than a mile distant, claimed the dishes rattled on the shelves after that baby came down.

H.V. and Califia counted the rings—making note of the scar from a fire in 1616 (if their count was correct), the year both Cervantes and Shakespeare died, and another in 1775, the year before the Declaration of Independence. A more recent fire, which they calculated to have occurred in the year 1817, had scorched the tree at just about the time William Beard jumped ship at Yerba Buena and proceeded to make his way south to San Jose, where he met Raymondo Olivo.

"Fate was at work that year," Califia smiled, touching the tips of her fingers to the mark of the most recent charred band.

"If only," H.V. said, "we had some way of knowing in advance. . . . I mean, knowing what it is that Fate's planned for us."

William Beard and Raymondo Olivo, returning from Monterey the next day, were delighted to discover their respective children in attendance at Hotochruk—though Olivo made a point of expressing at least polite disapproval of the fact that his daughter-in-law Roxanne had departed California for England a month earlier and that it was only by way of the grapevine and the San Francisco office that he'd learned about this family rupture.

"You, Raymondo," Pelican Doctor said, "you never like that girl anyway. *Thinks her shit don't stink.* That's what you said to me. Now she's gone back to some place far away, and you pretend to be unhappy about it?"

"I never spoke such a thing, Homer," Olivo muttered. "This old Indian, he has bad bad dreams, and when he wakes up, he thinks the dreams are real. As long as Roxanne was your wife, Son, I liked her just fine."

Bill the Sawyer broke out laughing.

"Sent her packing, did you, H.V.? Well, the truth is, she'd

never have been happy here in California—so there's no great loss, even if Sancho Raymondo now pretends to think otherwise."

"You admit it, then?" Olivo demanded. "All these years we have spent together, and finally you admit that you considered yourself to be the Don Quixote all along, while I was merely your faithful Sancho Panza?"

"Slip of the tongue, companyero, a slip of the tongue. I want to hear about these Leviathan-like trees H.V.'s been moaning about. Redwoods, you say? In sufficient numbers for us to set up logging and milling operations? From what I gather, though, you're more interested in putting them into some kind of preserve than in converting them to lumber."

"Homer and I saw such trees in the Sierra many years ago," Califia said, "when he and I . . ."

"Ran off like a pair of love-sick pups," Bill Beard said, finishing his daughter's sentence.

"Uncle Bill," H.V. said, "we're fixing to run off again—unless we can get the family's blessing. Califia and I . . . we love each other. We want to be together. I guess we've always wanted that."

William Beard and Raymondo Olivo stared at one another—not really startled by the words that had just been spoken, but not actually expecting those words either.

"This is truly what you wish . . . both of you?" Raymondo asked.

"That is what we both wish," Califia replied, staring first at her uncle and then at her father.

"Have you spoken to Seagull and Calling Owl?" Bill Beard asked.

H.V. and Califia both nodded and, without realizing they'd done so, reached out to clasp one another's hand.

Like a couple of guilty kids, damned if they're not! Hell, I'm for it if it'll make them happy. Life's too short to follow all the rules all the time. Most of 'em most of the time's sufficient. But will Ray buy it?

For his part, Raymondo turned to Pelican Doctor—whether because he was not himself certain what he should say, or whether he was simply deferring to the greater authority of the shaman and head chief of his people.

"These two, my grandchildren," Pelican Doctor said, "they've spoken to me about what they wish—to become as man and wife together. I have already told them that I had considered the matter. I've rehearsed my dreams so that I was certain I understood them. Three nights I saw the same thing— Califia and H.V. standing there, and a little boy dancing between them. The child is a symbol of their marriage. I looked into the faces of all three, and I saw they were happy with one another, just as a family should be. When a man and a woman look upon each other as these two do, it's wrong for the old people to stand in their way. That's what my dreams have told me."

"You actually had such a dream?" Raymondo asked.

"Would I tell my son-in-law such a thing if it were not so?"

Raymondo's face had hitherto been a perfect mask of seriousness, but now he began to grin.

"It's true, he said, shrugging, "I never much liked Miss Roxanne. Since she was my son's wife, however, I said nothing. But now she's gone away—she's deserted Homer Virgil, and I don't think she intends to return to California. Even the Catholic priests would have to say that desertion is sufficient grounds for divorce."

"Therefore H.V.'s damned well been divorced," Bill the Sawyer said.

"Yes, that's so. On the other hand, I have always loved my best . . . Sancho's daughter, and I would be proud that she should also be my daughter-in-law. There's only one law here at Hotochruk, and we are it. It's up to us as a family to determine what's right and what's wrong. Pelican Doctor has visioned this thing as *right*, and he's our purest authority."

"Then we have your blessing?" H.V. asked.

"You have always had that," Raymondo Olivo replied.

"About those Big Trees," William Beard said, "I'm going to propose that the two of you worthless kids hightail it over to Calaveras and see what you can do about buying up sections of land with the patriarchs on them. It turns out Ray and I have just inherited a bit of money. Jean Paul Martin left the two of us something over a million dollars in liquid assets. The Mother Lode's the fastest-growing part of the state, and the miners over there are howling for lumber. By all accounts the Sierran forests are mostly pine and fir, as well as some cedar. There's no point in our saving money for our old age, since we're old already. I say we go into business over there, maybe in Murphys and Sonora both, and in the process we spare whatever trees we're of a mind to."

"I wish Calvin were here," Raymondo said. "If we're to give the money to these two *worthless* ones, we should give part of it to Captain Beard as well, is that not so? He, after all, has his own family to support."

Bill Beard nodded and winked at Pelican Doctor.

"Don Quixote has always been in favor of keeping things in the family," he said. "Well, there's enough to go around. When Cal gets back from Chile, maybe we can buy him a new gold-plated anchor or something. One way or the other, I think Jean Paul would have approved. He had faith in this land, and he had faith in us."

Free from parental restraint, Califia and H.V. returned to the Sierra Nevada. But now, strangely enough, each night of their journey they felt (but did not speak of) the old interdiction, which was self-evidently still with them. In camping for the nights, they were careful to place their sleeping rolls several feet apart. However much they may have wished to lie in one another's arms, neither seemed willing to make the first move. As a result, each was beginning to entertain doubts as to the wisdom of their announced intentions.

Had it been, all along, the simple attraction of that which was prohibited, forbidden, unapproved?

Upon reaching Murphys, H.V. and Califia learned that Augustus Dowd, amazingly enough with the backing of Dolbeer and Corzine, had set up his own logging company and was in the process of felling the biggest of the Calaveras trees.

The cousins dismounted and walked to where Dowd was standing. El Buzzardo, perhaps hoping for some treat out of the saddlebags, swooped in, wings spread, and stumbled to a landing. Perhaps fearing to appear clumsy, the big bird scratched at the duff and pretended to look for insects—a habit he'd picked up from Rory Sunrise and the other bantams.

Dowd—"Jim," as his men called him—was apparently no-body's fool. Upon first contact with Corzine's agent, the discoverer of the Calaveras giants had proceeded hell-bent-for-leather to Stockton, where the Federal Bureau of Lands and Claims had established an office. Using virtually every dime of his own money, Dowd had obtained stumpage rights to five square miles of land, from McKay's Point northward to the Little Mokelumne River and southeastward to a promontory to be designated thereafter on federal charts as *Dowd Hill*. A forty-acre mill site was sold outright, near the head of a creek to be designated *Mill Creek*. No mention was made, naturally, of any Big Trees—though, as Dowd pointed out to H.V. and Califia, even if he'd described the giants in detail, he'd have accomplished nothing more than to cause the federal agent, a not very bright little man with a balding dome and waxed mustache, to think him *daft*.

Timber rights, the agent explained, were for timber only. In the event of discovery of gold or other valuable minerals, mining rights, as with claims or government land sales, would take precedence. "California," the agent said, "is built upon a foundation of gold. Some of the boys say, *You find it where it ain't*. And that's why the matter of relocating the aboriginals is such a problem. We never know where gold's going to be struck next, and so it simply isn't safe or reasonable to set aside tracts for Indian reservations—not when gold might be found there a month later. As to timber—why, we've got an unlimited supply of standing trees. Elsewhere in the country timber's become a staple crop, so to speak, and perhaps it will be here as well, eventually."

In the eventuality of conflicts deriving from multiple usage of the land, the agent went on to say, mining interests would be deemed primary—and Dowd would be given recompense in terms of equal stumpage elsewhere in the general vicinity, but close enough to his mill site so as to be practical.

Dowd lit a hand-rolled cigarette and grinned, first at H.V. and then at Califia.

"I knew Corzine or one of them might try to head me off at the pass, so I got to the pass first. Corzine's Larkin and Stearns's man, ain't' he? You understand, Olivo, if you folks had offered me a grubstake on the right terms, I'd have been glad to do business with ye. Still might be, since I've got the upper hand, so to speak. But I needed help—cash money to get a mill set up and to hire workers. So I established my right to the trees—that way I had some bargaining chips. Corzine hisself and four of his men showed up, and we went into a partnership—with Augustus T. Dowd holding sixty percent, by God!"

"Where's Corzine now?" Califia asked. "We're old friends."

"So I understand. Well, now. Don't guess it's any great secret. Mr. Corzine headed for Monterey—to make arrangements with Larkin, most likely. An' his men rode off on a scouting expedition—looking for more Big Trees, o' course. I expect that's what you'll be doing, too. Well, it's fine with me—I'm just a little fish. These is the Big Trees I found, and this is where I figger to make my fortune. . . . "

Dowd's fallers, H.V. and Califia learned, had been working for the past two weeks or so on a three-hundred-foot giant with a diameter of nearly thirty feet.

"Yep," Dowd said to Califia, "the way I see it, they ain't never been anybody in the history of the world who ever cut down a tree as big as this one—because, for one thing, just maybe this here's *the biggest damned tree that ever lived.* You're Bill Beard's daughter, ehh? You an' Corzine and Dolbeer, you're in a tussle up on the Klamath, from what I understand. Well, that ain't no affair of mine. I never thought I'd get a yen to go logging, but this here's something else. They must have some kind of special book for keeping track of world records, don't they?"

"Possibly so," H.V. admitted, at the same time shaking his head. "What's the good of felling the old giant—even if you manage to do it? When it hits the ground, it's going to break up into a hundred sections."

"Figure so?" Dowd asked, turning to Califia. "How'd you happen to adopt that buzzard, anyhow? Until now, I don't suppose I've ever met anyone with a tame buzzard."

"Found him on the ground when he was a chick—having a standoff with a gray squirrel. He only had about half his feathers at the time—must have fallen out of the nest, though I never figured out where it was, exactly. I intended to climb up and put him back, but fate decreed otherwise."

"Understand they vomit, kind of like a weapon."

"No more than porcupines throw their quills. I've seen El Buzzardo spit up his stomach contents when he's frightened. I suppose it might be seen as a hostile act. Not the most pleasant smell in the world, depending upon what delicacies he's been ingesting."

Dowd nodded, at the same time looking skeptical.

"So you think the big fella'll bust up when it hits the ground?" he asked Califia.

"That's possible. With the coast redwoods, we lay out a bed for the trees—otherwise they sometimes shatter. Of course, it takes skill to put the trees down where they're supposed to go. Your method of felling, Dowd, it's a bit unusual."

"Couldn't think of no other way—so we got the smith to make us the world's longest augers, and we started drilling. When she's ready to go, we'll use wedges and even blasting powder if we have to. We been drilling for fifteen days now. . . ."

"You figure this one's the biggest tree in the forest?" H.V. asked.

"Couldn't say. Well, the boys did find one that's bigger, but God Hisself took that one down—a long while back, as things appear. There must have been one hellacious windstorm, or maybe the tree was leaning, and it was a year of real heavy rain, and over she went. Most of it's hollow—a man can walk right through her!"

"We'd like to see it," Califia said. "Can you take us there—or at least point us in the right direction?"

"Be pleased to, ma'am," Dowd replied.

They walked less than half a mile through the forest of giants when, amidst lesser trees, they came to the uprooted monster—a truly immense tree that had been felled by some fit of nature, years earlier.

El Buzzardo had perched on the crown of Califia's sombrero—the black hat already marked with the stains of bird droppings.

"This is one tree Olivo & Beard can't be accused of butchering," H.V. laughed. "The Old Fellow upstairs, he's the villain of the piece. . . ."

"More than three hundred feet long," Dowd said, "and

about a hundred and ten feet around its base, as near as we can measure—with the log half sunk into the ground that way, I mean. Ain't she something?"

A crude ladder had been placed against the hollow giant's side, and the three of them climbed up, scrambled into the massive roots, and stood there, surveying the open pit beneath, a pit from which the great roots had been torn.

"How'd ye like to of been here when this baby went down?" Dowd demanded, grinning. "Just thinking about it makes a man want to . . . well, you know. Excuse me, ma'am, I near got carried away there, I guess. But you know what I mean, don't you, Olivo?"

"Afraid I do," H.V. replied.

"Damned if they ain't God's own trees. . . . "

H.V. nodded.

"Possibly that's something we should keep in mind, Mr. Dowd."

With only a moment's preliminary flapping of wings, El Buzzardo vaulted upward, rising to the sparse crown of one of the nearby giants, where he settled in, appearing quite territorial.

H.V. and Califia rode toward Sonora—uncertain both as to where they were going and as to whether in fact they'd been through any of this country during their earlier trek, before the coming of the gold miners, before the building of roads and towns and the digging of mines and the cutting of trees. Though much of the primal Sierran wilderness remained, the presence of Occidental humanity had largely transformed the general appearance of the land. Nor was their crude map helpful in terms of what they were seeking. Various rivers were indicated as coming down out of the Sierra to the east, all named and with roads and outposts and towns indicated, but the region of the Sierra itself was largely blank—or drawn by a cartographer with more imagination than actual information.

At the *Miner's Rest Saloon and Hotel*, H.V. and Califia introduced themselves and asked questions about known groves of Big Trees similar to those Dowd had found above Murphys. The barkeep related in typical gold-country fashion the account of a drama of the previous year, just after Jesse Tanner struck it rich on the Stanislaus. With *lead* in his saddlebags, he'd ridden to Coarse Gold to marry the girl he was in love with—a tame Indian named Manzanita Huerfano. She, however, had run off—after having been raped by a man named Piedra, and was reported to be living with the Yosemite Indians, in a secret valley located somewhere back in the mountains. Word had it she'd turned renegade and that she'd robbed at least one stage.

Tanner gunned down Piedra and set off in search of Manzanita. That night a saloon burned to the ground, and the Mariposa Battalion was activated—the boys riding off in pursuit of both Tanner and Chief Tenieya's Yosemites, or *Ahwahnee-chees*. While the boys did manage to round up Tenieya and his Indians and take them to a rancheria in the low hills, they never caught up with Tanner and Manzanita—for certainly those two were presumed together, if they hadn't killed each other.

"What," Califia interrupted, "has all this to do with Big Trees?"

"Lady," said the barkeep, "you folks asked, an' I'm just passing on the story, that's all."

"Two more whiskeys," H.V. said, attempting to placate the bartender and keep him talking. "This valley where the chief was caught—that's the *Yosemite* we've all been hearing about. Am I right?"

"O' course," the bartender said, arching one shaggy eyebrow at Califia, "I was just getting to that part. There's waterfalls a mile high, and trees bigger than anything Dowd ever saw. I ain't been up thar yet, o' course, but the boys what has agrees with me. Ye got a map? Okay, then. Some of them Big Trees is on the Tuolumne, but there's a lot more all over the Sierras. Yosemite Valley's on the Merced, an' both rivers are south of here. You folks with Olivo & Beard, ye say? Planning to build some sawmills, I'll bet. Good idea, too. Boards are scarcer than hens' teeth. Every time there's a new strike, we got to build us another town. Going to cut some o' them Big Trees, are ye?"

Not far from the South Fork of the Tuolumne, Homer Virgil and Califia urged their ponies downslope through an impressive stand of sugar pines and ponderosas. Beyond these trees lay a lush green meadow where more than two dozen mule deer browsed—until the sound of human voices and the snortings of horses brought them to instant awareness. The cervine faces turned toward the riders: ears, like so many gloved hands, stood at attention. Then all—does, bucks with antlers still in the velvet, yearlings, spotted fawns—were in instant motion, the herd vanishing into a stand of immense redwoods on the far side of the clearing.

Far away, high against blue mountain sky, El Buzzardo and another vulture circled back and forth.

"Is this the place—is it possible that we've found it?" Califia asked.

H.V. sat his pony, lit a short cigar, puffed thoughtfully.

"I don't know, Little Cal. Time blurs the memory—we'd have come in from over there, I suppose, where the meadow drains westward. We came up that side canyon—do you remember?"

"My memory isn't blurred, Homer Virgil. As to whether this is the same place, that's not the real question."

He puffed, grinned.

"What is, then?"

"The question, you educated jackass, is us. What are we? Since we left Hotochruk, we've pretended to be a priest and his attendant nun. I wasn't cut out for nunhood, I tell you. Pelican Doctor cleared us of any and all restraints, and our family presumes we've gone off on a prenuptial honeymoon with business overtones, so to speak. So here we are, back where we once humped each other blind, and we haven't so much as held hands. Oh, I'm not saying it's your fault, Homer. To tell you the truth, I'm scared to death . . . that we might . . . I don't know."

"I've thought it over," H.V. said.

"Indeed?"

"Yes, Califia, I have. You're right. This is the same place whether it is or not. If sixteen years ago was Eden, and the Lord of Hosts kicked us out in no uncertain terms, then just possibly it's better this spot isn't the same as before. It can be our sacred bower, and that's what matters. Consider, though we laid claim to the grove on Redwood Creek, and as soon a we did, we both started feeling guilty as a pair of thieves. We could hardly wait to get away from each other—to put distance between ourselves and what we knew to be true."

"And that is?" she asked.

"We . . . like . . . each other."

"You sonofabitch, Homer Virgil. I swear, I'll make you pay for that rotten remark. Tell me the truth!"

"All right, have it your way. I love you."

She threw back her head and laughed. The sunlight was full on her face, glinting in those strange, intense gray eyes and gleaming from her dark hair. She turned to him, her lips forming a kiss, and began to unbraid her hair.

"Bitch!" he said.

"Bastard!" she replied. "Who in hell ever gave you the right to go whoring off to England and leave me behind? You probably had lots of them—simpering little rosy-cheeked English women."

"No, not many. A few hundred I suppose. . . . "

"Lying reprobate!"

"I haven't the slightest idea why I should be getting an erection right now. . . . "

"As I recall," she said, "there's a lovely glade back in among those trees. Perhaps your jerky wishes to be nibbled on. You know damned well this is the same spot, you sonofabitch, Homer Virgil Olivo!"

Califia kicked her heels against her horse's sides and let out a blood-curdling whoop. In a moment she was racing madly across the meadow toward the grove of Big Trees.

H.V. smiled, nodded, and stubbed out his cigar on the scarred surface of his wooden saddle horn. He studied the sky, detected the distant black specks that were El Buzzardo and his new acquaintance.

"Just stay up there, friend," he muttered as he urged his pony ahead.

CHAPTER THIRTY-FIVE

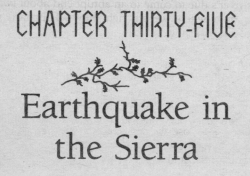

Earthquake in the Sierra

[1852–1855:]

TOGETHER THEY RODE south along the contours of the big hills
to the edge of Merced River Canyon—not a particularly remarkable gorge and a clear disappointment after the talk they'd
heard about magnificent Yosemite Valley. Instead of sheer
granite walls and thundering waterfalls, they found a sharp
vee-shaped canyon with occasional granite outcroppings and
mixed forest of pine, fir, cedar, and black oak.

"Nothing unusual about this place," H.V. mused. "Perhaps
we're too far downstream."

"I'd guess the river to be running almost due south. That'd
put us about here," Califia replied, pointing to a spot on the
map they carried, a document they'd purchased in Stockton
on their way across the San Joaquin Valley, but one printed
in 1850 in Boston, Massachusetts. "Do you suppose we can
trust cartographers who've never been to this part of the world?
Where do you suppose the lads got their information?"

"I wonder what the odds are against *any* damned map-
maker ever having been within a hundred miles of here," H.V.
shrugged. "The source was doubtless a hand-drawn chart sent
East by some drunken miner. In any case, according to our

map, the river's due to come to an abrupt end about two miles upstream from where we are right now—if, in fact, we *are* where we are right now."

"It's certain," Califia said, "this maker *de mapa* didn't know about any Yosemite Valley—since it's not indicated. Shall we proceed, Señor Pathfinder?"

"Your logic's without flaw, Lady of the Rueful Countenance. This trail along the river's been used—and recently—within the last day or so. Folks must be riding up to see things at first hand. Well, I suppose we can spare a few more hours—find ourselves a pool to camp by. We're close to a full moon tonight. We'll swim and frighten the kingfishers out of their nests. . . . "

"We've never made love in the water, Homer Virgil. Are you willing?"

"If you promise not to drown me in a fit of ecstasy, Little Cal, I'm up for damned near anything."

"My handle's *Califia*, you lout! I'm Queen of the Amazons. Please show respect. . . . *Prove* you're *up to the task*. . . . "

"I apologize, *Tamer of Vultures and Mountain Lions*. Onward."

As Califia and H.V. crossed a great jumble of boulders and loose till, the canyon before them opened into a narrow valley whose floor was thickly forested. To the south rose a set of magnificent spires, while on the north side of the valley crouched a huge granite monolith. Waterfalls thundered down from either side. As they proceeded, awe-struck by the grand size of things, there were yet other waterfalls. One on the north, H.V. was certain, fell at least two thousand feet. Farther ahead stood a sculptured granite dome, a mountain in and of itself, one of gigantic proportions, virtually bare of vegetation, with the face toward the valley giving the appearance of having been sliced by a titanic broad-bladed axe that could have been wielded by no one less than Tío Coyote himself.

"What could have caused such a thing?" Califia asked, turning to H.V.

He shook his head.

"The Mysterious Other," he said after a few moments. "The great and unsolvable mystery of the creation. Something seems

to have rubbed all these cliffs to shining—almost the way the
sea polishes the pebbles on the beach at Grayhound Rock."

"A great flood?"

"I don't know. Cambridge didn't teach us such things—
although the geologists had their theories. Ice might do it—if
one could imagine ice thousands of feet deep, glaciers such as
in Greenland or on the mountains of Alaska or at the bottom
of the world. In the winter the snows of the Sierra Nevada are
deep, twenty or thirty feet even, according to the stories. But
it's a far cry from that sort of thing to the immense quantity
of ice necessary to carve this astonishing trench. To have lived
in such a place—Tenieya's people must all have been natural
philosophers. . . . "

"Look," Califia said. "Riders ahead of us—up past the oaks!"

"They've come in search of the same thing we have. The
mystery, the awe, the wonder. They've got easels set up—
painting pictures, for God's sake!"

"We did well," Califia mused, "to keep searching. Whatever stories we've heard, they were nothing compared to this.
I've seen Shasta, and that must be one of the greatest mountains in the world. But this place, Homer, it's huge. It's as
though God Himself formed it in the beginning for Adam and
Eve—that's one Bible story that's always fascinated me. Except
for the sinning. Truly, that part of it never made sense."

H.V. shook his head, and he and Califia urged their horses
into the still, shallow waters, crossing for no other reason than
to avoid contact with other humans, intruders into this place
that should have been reserved for Coyote Himself—in case
the god ever had need of solitude.

Under a full moon, its white torch magically captured on the
surface of the river, a man and a woman swam together,
ripples trailing as the swimmers made their way across a
wide, shallow pool. When the two reached the far side, they
slipped out of the water and sat close together, staring back
to where a camp fire blazed, throwing up occasional sparks
and a trail of smoke that moved over the water, low to the
surface, drifting upstream toward great granite domes that were
also revealed by moonlight, silver-black against a star-glut.
Downstream, a few bullfrogs rasped mating cries, each praising

is particular portion of riverbank in the hope a female would gree with him—and they would mate, with eggs deposited here in the shallows, a clutch of speckled mucus.

A loon cried out, its quaver penetrating darkness and prompting a fox above the valley to break into a series of *yip-p-yippings*.

Not far from the camp fire, high among the upper branches an incense cedar, a large bird tucked its head beneath a ing—while close by the fire were the paired forms of coyotes, doubtless in search of mice darting from one clump of grass another on this night of the full moon, but drawn instead y odors of food, drawn in to where human creatures had just cently been eating, to look for scraps or for some greater ize not put carefully enough away, not secured against pre- ation. But now the coyotes sat on their haunches, both snuf- ng the air and gazing across the river's still water.

Then, had someone been close by, that person might also ave noted motion up in the cedar, a beaked head coming it, the bird suddenly alert, vulturine senses both aware of e coyotes and at the same time attempting to determine the ource of odd, faintly discernible, rhythmic swishings of shal- w water—from across the river—and the murmurings of Cal- a's voice and the voice of the other one, the man.

Mating sounds. Human.

We are wedded now, husband and wife," they might have id as they rode northward on their way to some unfin- hed—that is, barely begun—business in Calaveras.

A short distance from Sonora the vulture grew agitated and w away. Califia pointed to a pair of shapes against the sky, o big birds in a spiral, gyrations of forms.

"You suppose he's discovered a special someone?" she said Homer Virgil.

"Possibly. But it's the wrong time of the year for vultures be courting. Perhaps the old boy's simply found a fair- ather friend, *al nopal lo van a ver sólo cuando tiene tunas.*"

"A short-term arrangement?" Califia laughed. "*Atáscate ora que hay lodo*—gather ye rosebuds while ye may, El Buz- rdo. The Big Darkness overtakes all of us when we least pect it."

"You suppose that's the same compañero old carrion crow
found as we were riding south?"

"H.V., you don't really believe that's a male friend, a buddy
he's flying with? Look at the grin on his crooked beak. . . ."

"What amazing eyesight you have, my dear."

"Yes. It's required of women."

The following day they reached the Calaveras grove, where
Augustus T. Dowd was happily directing operations. Auger
holes had now been driven into the giant tree all the way
around—twenty-two days since the onset of the project, Dowd
said. Wedges were set deep into the great tree by means of
battering-ram logs suspended from the trunk, and still the patriarch refused to topple. Surely, however, the end was near.
The men were in a state of excitement, wanting to witness the
astonishing event.

"Good to see you again," Dowd said, grinning. "Where's
your garbage-eater?"

"Wandering around, wandering around," Califia replied. "I
try not to worry about the bird, though I hope he's got enough
sense to stay out of that tree you and your boys have venti-
lated. Looks to me like a bit of wind might bring it down."

"So," Dowd said. "What brings you back to my humble
tree butchery?"

"Not sure I'd be so quick to call it that," H.V. laughed.
"You and your lads have done your best, and she's still standing. . . ."

"So it is, so it is. But there's nary a tree that can't be felled,
and that includes this one. We'll fill those auger holes full of
powder if we have to—and blow 'er off the stump. What do
you think of the lean, Miss Califia? Have we got the layout in
the right place?"

Califia studied the tree and then squinted at the thickly
stacked brush and side-by-side heaps of young Douglas fir.
She nodded finally, nodded and winked.

"A first-rate job. I salute you."

Dowd grinned even wider.

"Coming from the lady what's known as *Cow . . . Bull of
the Woods*, I take it as a genuine compliment."

"*Cow* of the Woods, is it? Where in hell did you hear that

llen Corzine, I'll bet. Next time I see that miserable sonofa-
tch, I'm going to put a load of bird shot into his ass-end!"

"Excuse me, Miss Califia. Truth is, I never learned when to
ep my yap shut and when to open it. Mr. Corzine, he didn't
ean nothing bad when he said it—seems to respect you a
od deal, truth to say. Anyhow, I don't figure you and Mr.
livo come up here to admire a tree that won't fall down. So
hat is it on your minds?"

"You're right. We've got an offer to present—in behalf of
livo & Beard. We've got authorization to make a better prop-
ition than you received from Corzine and his bunch. In
ort, we're willing to buy out your stumpage leases—your
tire sixty percent of the operation—five times what you paid
r it. Then we cut you in for a percentage of the whole busi-
ss, according to the number of board feet milled. You take
salary as our mill director here in the Sierras."

"Don't know about the salary part, Olivo, but I'm listening.
e way I see it, these here Big Trees are worth a pile of
ugh—and like you say, they're all mine. Corzine's money
st sets up the mill and hires me a crew and pays me some-
ing for my trouble."

"It's not in our interest to have Corzine, Dolbeer, Reading,
rkin, Stearns, and the rest of California involved in Sierra
gging," H.V. said. "You're probably about ready to break for
nch—it's past noon. Let's go sit and have a drink and a
ndwich or two and talk business. We'll make it worth your
ile, Dowd."

Augustus T. raised one shaggy eyebrow, nodded.

"Best proposition I've had all morning," he said. "You got
y more of them little cigars? What's this about Larkin and
forth? The only deal I been trying to cut's with Corzine,
o loaned me some money. The trees is still mine, all of
n."

"Naturally," H.V. said, fumbling in his jacket and produc-
g an unopened box of little cigars.

Dowd made note of the Colt-Patterson, almost like a gun-
nger's weapon, in its tie-down holster, hanging easy on
mer Olivo's hip. A story, rumor actually, about Olivo gun-
g a man down over a game of cards—or was that someone

else? Having already made the slip about *Cow o' the Woods*,
Dowd decided wisdom lay in leaving well enough alone.

"Where's your chuck wagon?" Califia asked. "This lady's
half starved."

Dowd squinted at the Big Tree, the ring of auger holes quite
distinct from the distance of fifty yards.

"Beans is ready!" he bellowed at his crew. "Two hours off
for lunch today!"

With Augustus Dowd leading, Califia and H.V. and the four
crew members trailing, the group made its way through the
thick noontime heat to a shady glen perhaps half a mile from
the great, doomed tree—a place where clear water trickled from
a bankside and pooled amidst bunches of sweetgrass and a
couple of young red willows. Water striders skated on the
surface. Dowd and his crew had erected a table hewn from
fallen redwood, while the two benches were fabricated of segments of split sugar pine fitted out with crisscrossed legs.

At the edge of a fire pit surrounded by jagged chunks of
slate and a few ovoid quartz *river eggs* was a pot of beans and
bacon. Dowd grabbed his one-pound can of pepper and sprin-
kled black flakes over the beans.

"Almost done," he laughed after he'd tested a spoonful.
"Guess they won't kill us none. Kind of crunchy—good jaw
exercise."

The chuck wagon (not equipped with a cook) was an old
Conestoga, its canvas sails weathered and patched. Inside were
logging implements, a brand-new pair of calked boots (*corks*),
a wood-and-steel Boker jack, a half-empty hundred-pound
burlap bag of pinto beans, one small barrel of gunpowder and
another of cornmeal, a cracker barrel, two unopened gallon
jugs of what appeared to be maple syrup (but probably wasn't)
and a metal *hope chest* for bacon, smoked venison, chunks of
suet, and what might pass for sausage.

"I call 'er a hope chest," Dowd explained as he stirred
beans that had been simmering for the past two hours, "because me an' the boys sort of *hope the damned bears aroun'
hyar won't be able to rip 'er open.*"

Califia and H.V. chuckled dutifully, and Dowd put the fix-
ings into a big speckled coffeepot, scooped up water, set the

pot against the fire, and began to ladle out beans and bacon rinds.

The loggers sat down at the table—as if in anticipation of being served, inasmuch as there was a woman present.

"Aren't they cute?" Califia purred. "Just like children—waiting for their mother to feed them. . . . "

"Come fetch your gawddamned chow!" Dowd yelled. "What in hell's got into you coons?"

"We was trying to be polite," a six-foot-five, three hundred pounder named Tiny explained. "Don't get all lathered, Jim. Me an' the boys, we take the message."

"Ought to be able to wedge over the big gal this afternoon," Skinny Tom said—an individual as tall as Tiny but weighing certainly not more than half as much. "Why she hasn't gone already is beyond me."

"Trees we had back in Illinois," Tiny said, "hell, I could wrestle 'em down. The goddamn things around here, they don't even belong in this world."

"That's the truth," Skinny Tom agreed. "But no tree can stand up if all that's holding it is *air*, for Chrissake, not even the world's biggest redwood!"

"About the deal," Dowd remarked, pouring Califia a cup of half-brewed coffee and then setting a cloth sack partially filled with lumps of brown Hawaiian sugar in front of her. "Let's get down to cases. What precisely is Olivo & Beard prepared to pay me in the way of genuine United States money?"

Califia watched, smiling, as Skinny Tom inhaled his bowl of beans and then ladled out a second helping. Tiny, on the other hand, had seemingly lost interest in the beans. He ambled over to the chuck wagon and foraged in the cracker barrel.

Forbes and Placer Eddie sipped coffee and lit hand-rolled cigarettes.

"Trouble with the Calaveras woods," Placer Eddie sighed, "is that it's such a long way down to Angels Camp, an' that's where the nearest cathouse is. Pardon, ma'am, but you know—a fella needs company once in awhile."

"I suppose so," Califia agreed. "How'd you get your name, Eddie? I'll bet you came to California to make your fortune in gold."

"Hell, ma'am, I struck it rich, as a matter of fact. Up north on the Yuba River—just above the Washington diggings. I was on my way down to Nevada City with my poke when a damned Meskin in a tall hat rode out onto the trail and told me to reach for some clouds. I acted dumb, and the sonofabitch shot me in the leg. While I was bleeding all over everything in sight, he took my gold and hightailed it. After that, I sorta lost heart, you might say. Anyhow, I had enough of Washington, and so I come down this way. My tin ran out, and that's when Jim Dowd here ast me if I'd ever felled a tree."

"Don't believe nothin' he says," Forbes grumbled, and then formed an O with his lips and sent up a perfect series of smoke rings.

Skinny Tom drank the last of his coffee, said something about going back to look at the tree, and strode away from the shady grove, the dull green of his suspenders standing out against his dirty red shirt.

At that auspicious moment El Buzzardo streaked in under the cover of the trees, flared out his wings, and settled onto the table.

"It's a gawddamn eagle!" Tiny exclaimed, grabbing for a peavey.

"Harm a feather on that noble bird's head," H.V. cautioned, "and my lady's subject to ventilate your hide, big fella."

"Ain't no eagle," Placer Eddie said. "It's the damned tame red-neck buzzard, that's all. Watch out he don't spit all over you!"

The vulture investigated what remained of Forbes's bowl of beans, rejected the idea of eating any of them, and hopped onto the ground, strutting over to Califia to be petted.

"Now, if that ain't something!" Dowd drawled. "Tell me, Miss Califia, about how you and Homer here are going to make me a rich man."

H.V. lit a cigar, nodded.

"All right," he said. "You've got rights to five square miles of timber. That's thirty-two hundred acres, more or less, in case anyone ever got around to surveying the land. I imagine you paid—what? Fifty cents an acre for stumpage?"

"A dollar an acre," Dowd howled. "I knew I couldn't trust

ye. Olivo & Beard ain't no different than Corzine and his
crowd!"

"Call it a dollar, then," H.V. continued. "We'll pay you . . .
oh, four dollars an acre. That'd be twelve thousand, eight hundred."

Dowd sipped at his coffee and raised a shaggy eyebrow.

"Five dollars," he said, "and the stumpage is yours."

"Four dollars," H.V. insisted, "and we pay off what you
owe Allen Corzine. That, and you go to work for us as mill
foreman. Top wages, Hoss. We'll bring in the equipment we
need to set up the finest sawmill in the Sierra. What do you
say?"

"Don't know as I really want to be no mill foreman. . . . "

"What were you planning to do with Corzine's money,
then, if I might ask?"

"Well, hell, I was willing to do it for a little while, anyhow.
I sort of figured he'd buy me out when we actually got started."

Then the earth heaved, and El Buzzardo went streaming upward in a clatter of wings—in a beeline for clear space above.
Empty bowls on the table became momentarily airborne and
clattered along the redwood surface and dropped over the edge.
The tiny pool where the water striders were peacefully attending their business drew up at the center in a spontaneous wave
and splashed back down. The veteran Conestoga creaked and
slipped sideways, and Tiny, just in the act of getting to his
feet, found himself lifted and then laid out sideways, as though
he'd been struck by a runaway horse.

"What in God's name?" H.V. cried out once he'd caught
his balance.

"Goddamn earthquake!" Dowd said, "They's probably more
coming!"

Califia had been kneeling by the fire—just about to pick up
the coffeepot. The ground wave nearly caused her to tip forward into the coals. But now she stood up, grabbed H.V.'s
somewhat battered stovepipe hat, and put it on.

"Mr. Dowd," she smiled. "I do believe your gigantic tree
just went over."

Augustus T. Dowd wore the mask of a stricken man.

"My *tree*?" he howled. "Bat shit, ma'am, but that just plain

damncertain ain't possible. Excuse my French, but I'm tellin'
you Satan's own truth. Sure as pissants, that were an earthquake!"

"Whar's Skinny Tom?" Tiny asked as he scrambled to his
feet.

Then they were all running—running to that spot in the
forest where the patriarch stood, scaffolding up on its sides
and auger holes all around.

Only it wasn't standing anymore.

Whether a chance gust of wind had applied the finishing
touch, or whether the remaining core, stressed and splintered
by the action of the numerous wedges driven home by impro-
vised battering rams—whatever the case, the monster had indeed come down and had broken off sizeable sections of a
couple of its neighbors in the process, heaving its mass almost
opposite the intended direction and now lying shattered and
largely unusable across a narrow ravine.

A deathly silence hung over the forest, and the air was
heavy with midday heat—rich with odors of resin and torn
foliage. Then, at last, blue jays began to shriek, gray squirrels
began to chitter streams of profanity, and the process of nature
was restored. The humans, gasping and panting, stood in a
group, stared mutely at the prodigy, and at the same time
attempted to grasp the significance a few unobserved moments
had created.

*Skinny Tom, did you at least look up and see the hurtling
immensity and so experience an instant's awe-struck wonder before
a massive limb, careening toward you, the ultimate widow-maker
even if you hadn't even thought about getting married yet except
possibly for that one little blond whore in Angels Camp, the one
whose pink nipples stand at attention astride half-formed breasts,
when that widow-maker swatted you just as you might have swatted a mosquito or a gnat while you were eating that last goddamned bowl of Dowd's wretched beans?*

Tiny, a man not precisely designed for running, was the
last to arrive. His round face, fringed with red beard, was
streaked with sweat, and he struggled for breath. He glared at
those who'd reached the fallen tree before him.

"God . . . damn . . . Forbes, whar's Skinny Tom? Damn . . .

fool come over here just a few minutes . . . before that *earthquake* set me . . . on my considerable ass!"

A sick feeling went through Califia. Three summers earlier, at the Russian River operation, she'd lost a man when a redwood barberchaired.

"Tommy, you lanky sonofabitch . . . damn it to hell, where in the name of the Holy Old Mackinaw are ye?" Tiny bellowed as he moved with astonishing agility about the fringes of crushed limbs and gray-green foliage. Forbes and Placer Eddie followed immediately in a frantic search for what was sure as hell the crushed remains of a human being down under a grotesque sprawl of foliage and limbs, some of the latter three and even four feet thick and splintered all to blazes.

"He's over there, on the stump!" H.V. shouted.

All eyes turned to where a tall, thin individual with green suspenders over a dirty red shirt stood astride an auger-pitted stump nearly thirty feet across.

"Son of a bloody bitch!" Skinny Tom yelled. "I didn't even get to see the miserable whale go down. . . . "

"Where in Mother McCree's hell was you, Tom?" Dowd demanded. "We thought you was turned to red pulp down underneath the. . . ."

"Goldarn it, no!" Skinny Tom laughed. "To tell the truth, I was off in the kit-kit-dizze, takin' a crap. For a second there I thought I must of let loose with the world's biggest goddamn. . . ."

Then everyone was laughing hysterically.

Augustus T. Dowd decided not to remain in the logging business.

"Gents," he said to his crew of four, "these hyar are your new boss men—well, one's a boss lady, as we can all see, and a fine-lookin' female at that. As for me, I'm going to do something easy, like find gold or marry a millionaire widow-woman what don't have no bad habits. What good's a tree the size o' this'n if she don't even have the common decency to let a man watch her fall? I tell you, there ain't no pleasure in it."

Money changed hands, and Dowd was officially bought out. Two months later, after negotiations had broken down, Corzine and Dolbeer accepted payment, with interest, of the amount they'd advanced the discoverer of the Big Trees, and Olivo & Beard set up a mill for the purpose of turning Sierra Redwoods to lumber—though they discovered quickly enough that the wood was quite brittle and clearly inferior to the coastal variety. Thereafter the three new mills in the Sierra concentrated on ponderosa and sugar pine, and business was good.

Homer Virgil Olivo and Califia Beard Flowers were officially wed while standing atop a huge stump close by San Lorenzo River, with their entire family present, including old Pelican Doctor, who afterward remarked that he would now be able to die happy. Even Calvin and Juanita and their eight children were present, and Calvin gave H.V. the advice that he shouldn't allow his underclothing to be kept in the same drawer with his wife's.

"I finally calculated true north," Cal said, "but by that time we already had six kids, so we figured, what the hell?"

Raymondo and Bill the Sawyer both got drunk on vodka Calvin brought back from his venture to Kamchatka.

Raymondo washed out a bronze spitoon and placed it on his head.

"Mambrinos' helmet, ehh?" his partner asked.

"*Eres lengualarga,* friend Sancho," Olivo growled. "As always, you talk too much. . . . "

The twin sisters, Calling Owl and Seagull, sat next to their respective husbands and sipped at a mixture of vodka and grape juice.

Logging, milling, exporting—all branches of Olivo & Beard prospered, and H.V. turned his attention to the cause of preserving the greatest of the Big Trees, both in the Coast Range and in the Sierra, writing a steady stream of missives to state and federal officials. He and Califia visited the new capital city of Sacramento, and H.V. was asked to address the California State Senate.

By 1855 support for preservation of the redwoods and Sequoias (as they were now called, named to honor the Cherokee alphabet-maker) was growing, but other matters occupied the government, and still no action was taken beyond a commitment to accept and hold in public trust certain tracts of forest land donated by Olivo & Beard and others, though without sufficient provision to protect other groves from private logging operations.

On a national level, the question of the extension of the institution of slavery dominated America's attention, and when President Pierce withheld federal intervention in the free-soil controversy, political conflict turned into bloody civil conflict in Kansas. Ralph Waldo Emerson proposed to the Anti-Slavery Society of New York that slavery might be ended by means of offering full payment to the slaveholders, a proposal that was not seconded.

Longfellow published *The Song of Hiawatha*, and the Union continued its inexorable drift toward Civil War.

In Santa Cruz, California, Califia Beard Olivo, a month before her thirty-seventh birthday, gave birth to a child—a little girl, whom the parents named Lupine.

Califia held her infant to her breast and smiled at Homer Virgil.

"I'll get you a son the next time around. I promise."

H.V. Olivo laughed and lit a short cigar.

"What man in his right mind would wish for a son if he could have a daughter instead?" he demanded.

EPILOGUE

Old Paul & His Blue-Nosed Baby Girl

[1990, 1989, 1966:]

IF WE COULD prove the existence of Bigfoot in the Siskiyous—and if we could transplant a few members of the family to all other mountain ranges in Western America, then we might just be able to preserve what precious little remains of the once endless and magnificent wildness.

Don't worry, Bigfoot, old fellow, your secret's safe with us.

In all truth, we're waiting for Don Berry's character, Webb, to come flopping along, sour-faced and cynical, observing how it is that civilization's kind of like a disease that just keeps spreading, a blight upon nature, *against nature*.

Webb, we'll stand there with ye—only by Gawd we're going to blow a few of them settler folk to hell before we go under. Let the vultures keep on circling. Maybe Mt. Shasta will come to our aid. Possibly the great tectonic plates will decide it's time to shift a few hundred miles.

Or one could be reasonable. One could accept the inevitable. One could admit that the American Wilderness is already simply a strange, beautiful memory stuck in the corner of sapient consciousness, to be touted in movies but not otherwise honored at all.

Reality, the wave of the future: a Western American tree farm. Years ago poet William Everson said he was bracing himself against the prospect of a computerized ecology, with every coyote in the brush rounded up for its semiannual rabies immunization shot.

Now that the cold war is seemingly over and what former President Reagan called the *Evil Empire* appears in the process of self-dismemberment, perhaps it's time for the human race to consider the possibilities of continuing to live on Spaceship Earth. What are the necessary conditions?

In an all-day session with the Department of Fish and Game, U.S. Forest Service, and a cross-section of environmental and resource groups, Ken Payton observed in the *Sacramento Bee*, forestry board members said they were trying to determine whether they indeed should protect certain species. Judge Buffington in Humboldt County ruled that the Forestry Board has the duty to decide whether wildlife is threatened and whether society's need to cut old-growth timber outweighs the risks to wildlife.

But some critics say such species as spotted owls, fishers, marbled murrelets, and some types of salamanders and frogs are being used as surrogates for the hidden agenda environmental groups have of stopping altogether the harvest of old-growth trees. There it is. The bottom line. The very dregs. Just exactly what's going on. Goddamn it, what little old growth remains is precisely the point. The forest ecosystem is utterly changed when we leave checkerboards of mature trees alternating with clear-cuts—the symbiosis diminished. I don't mean to be reactionary and antigrowth and all that, but you see, spotted owls or no spotted owls, a dozen years down the pike, if we continue to cut, the old growth will be gone. Right now we still have it within our capacity to preserve what's left.

A timber consultant for Pacific Lumber Company tells us it's unrealistic to put off cutting old growth on the Plumas National Forest simply because of some purely hypothetical need to protect a hundred and fifty spotted owls. In any case, this same individual contends, available data show no support for the contention that the spotted owl is headed for extinction.

Praise the Lord and pass the ammunition.

Spotted owls? If them birds have got any spunk at all, they'll figure out how to adapt. We all got to adapt. If not, the great horned owls'll get us.

Tie a yellow ribbon to your ann-ten-knee. . . .

However, common sense tells us we could gut the Endangered Species Act without harming anything. We can have our spotted owls (if we want them) and a little old-growth timber as well. There are two possible solutions. Since the spotters stick to the old growth in order to protect themselves from their enemies, the horned owls and the barred owls, we could simply eradicate the horners and the barreds. Doubtless, however, Friends of the Earth or one of those other groups would be onto our case with regard to that extirpation—and would be insisting that the HO and the BO also deserve to be designated as *threatened*.

Let us move, then, to possible solution number two, to wit: train spotted owls to live in deserts. The birds can nest in piles of rocks and catch mice and rattlesnakes for a living, thereby increasing the desert's value as a tourist attraction. Owls will certainly be less bother than those Nevada wild horses the good old boys have been trying to wipe out.

Judith and I drive Highway One south toward Santa Cruz—no, toward Swanton, a town that never really existed in any real sense, though numerous company men once lived there in company-owned shacks. For half a century now and perhaps more, the redwood forests in this area of the Santa Cruz Mountains have been owned by Big Creek Lumber Company. Farther inland is Big Basin, where portions of the primeval coastal forest have been set aside within the boundaries of parks. The area isn't quite so popular as the long and highly dramatic seacoast, sweeping away toward the Ventanas to the south, but the trees nonetheless attract a very considerable number of visitors from the nearby metropolitan area of San Francisco and the sprawling Bay Area urban zone.

We turn off Swanton Road and enter Big Creek Canyon, a place where two huge redwoods grow side by side, their roots intertwining, even as their trunks abutt one another, fuse. Here in a former California Division of Forestry fire station, live he grand old man of California poetry, the poet of the San oaquin, the poet of Kingfisher Flat—William Everson.

We have, many times, built an open-pit fire beneath the wo great redwoods—have cooked dinner—have discussed literature and ecology and Joaquin Miller and Robinson Jeffers and Jim Beckwourth and . . .

A light rain has begun to fall—more mist than rain. Tonight we take supper inside.

Judith and I have done a bit of editing on Everson's volume of interpretive analysis concerning the death of J.F.K., a book written twenty-five years ago, when the poet was still Brother Antoninus. Now, a quarter of a century later, perhaps the time has come round for publication.

After dinner I step outside, turn toward the giant sisters, walk to them, stand under their outspread boughs, place my hands, palms out, against rough, stringy bark.

I hear voices, far off, far off. Pelican Doctor. William Beard. Raymondo Olivo. Three children growing up, perhaps even managing to climb into the huge branches of these trees. . . .

The creek sings in its bed.

Joaquin Miller once made reference to *the endless black forests of Northern California,* but now we realize just how finite, how vulnerable to being ended they are. In Joaquin's time, however, men had only just begun to think seriously about harvesting the forest, the ultimate clearing of the swamp. Oh, farther east they'd thought of it, all right, and the boys with axes and peaveys were already working their way westward. Paul Bunyan and his river-pissing ox. . . .

I wish I'd had the chance to see it back then. I have my imagination and my books, of course, but it's just not the same. In those days, things had a *shine* to them, and the forests were indeed endless for all practical purposes—out-and-out robdingnagian, for a fact.

What must it have been like, being there? What must it have been like to have accompanied Joe Walker when he crossed the snow-choked Sierra Nevada that time in 1833 and have come down to lay eyes on Yosemite Valley far below? Zenas Leonard kept a journal:

Some of these precipices appeared to us to be more than a mile high. *Some of the men thought that if we could succeed in descending one of these precipices to the bottom, we might thus work our way into the valley below—but on making several attempts we found it utterly impossible for a man to descend, to say nothing of our horses.*

So Walker and the boys discovered the Yosemite (though some still debate the matter). And wouldn't you know it? He and his men stumbled into a Sequoia grove as well:

Along the base of this mountain it is quite romantic—the soil is very productive—the timber is immensely large and plenty, and game, such as deer, elk, grizzly bear and antelopes are remarkably plenty. . . . From the mountain out to the plain, a distance varying from 10 to 20 miles, the timber stands as thick as it could grow and the land is well watered by a number of small streams rising here and there along the mountain. In the last two days travelling we have found some trees of the Red-wood species, incredibly large—some of which would measure from 16 to 18 fathoms round the trunk at the height of a man's head from the ground.

It's arguably true that the massive Sequoias have attracted more attention than any other feature of the Sierra Nevada. The public's first response was one of *being had*, yet another *tall tale from the compulsive liars of the West*. But once the authenticity of the giant trees was established beyond cavil, they were granted a reverential awe. A few titanic presences were cut down for no other reason than their size. Bark shells of whole Sequoia trunks were transported to New York or London and there put on display. On such whimsy, perhaps as many as four trees greater than the General Sherman were hewn to earth in deference to an incredulous world—four of the most massive living things since the dawn of time itself. On the stumps square dances were held. On one a small hotel was erected.

The vision of Pelican Doctor, the vision of H.V. Olivo. . . .

In my own dream I stand astride a bare ridge in the California Coast Range—though whether this particular mountain is one of the Yolla Bolly peaks or a Trinity Alp, I'm unable to determine. The sprawl of mountains about me, however, has been considerably foreshortened—or else I've been given powers of vision not normally my own. Indeed, I can see quite easily to

e broad Pacific Ocean, and likewise I can see across the
entral Valley to the slopes of the Sierra Nevada.

I'm horrified to witness *The Grizzly Giant* going down, and
want to cry out in meaningless protest. But other trees are
lling all about me—as if our present technology existed for
o other purpose than to fell the giants that yet remain.

I don't know how much time passes as I watch, but during
e interval of my witness, cities arise in the Valley, and the
r is transformed from pellucid to smoky haze—whether from
e exhausts of automobiles or the emissions of factories and
nerating plants or from the burning of rice stubble or piles
slash in the mountains themselves.

Even as I take note of the risings of cities in the Valley, I
alize that the forests have been systematically stripped from
e mountains of this land I love, from the Siskiyous in Oregon
d extreme Northern California to the long Coast Range ex-
nding southward past San Francisco and Monterey to the
entanas and beyond, to Santa Barbara and the Tehachapis,
ere curving inland and finally northward, the high granite
aks of the Whitney and Palisade massifs, the Yosemite, Ta-
e and the Gold Country, Lassen and mighty Shasta and on
ck to the white pyramid of Mt. Pitt (a.k.a. Mt. McLoughlin)
Oregon.

Other great forests stretch northward into Canada along the
ines of the Cascades and the Oregon Coast Range and the
ympics in Washington, those dropping off into the waters
Puget Sound and the Strait of Juan De Fuca.

But the forests are gone. . . .

Brush and raw earth remain—yes, and countless men and
men in green and tan uniforms are busily planting seedlings
in rows, the mountains laced with roadbeds set in place to
ilitate future harvesting.

In my dream I hear a terrible roaring off to the west, and I
n to stare.

Out of the Pacific a giant has risen, a titan form, a bearded
an in a red flannel shirt with sleeves rolled to the biceps,
spenders, a wool cap with black curls flowing out from un-
r it, high-topped calked boots. The man is singing and at
e same time juggling perhaps a dozen or so double-bitted
ling axes.

Ocean water pours down from his shoulders, and as he strides toward the land, tidal waves are formed—waves that strike the coast and pour back up into the seaside canyons.

Another titan arises: a gigantic blue ox whose horns are as wide as the Columbia River, and whose ebony hooves appear to be afire.

It's none other than Old Paul & his blue-nosed girl, Babe the gigantic ox.

Paul's voice comes like thunder.

What's this? Well now, what's happened hyar? By golly, Babe, it looks as if some leetle bureaucratic termites armed with machines and the like have taken down all the trees. When we was hyar, doing things by hand and all, there was timber to last a thousand years. Now they've done it. Human critters are simply not to be trusted; an' that's the rock-bottom word. Can ye figger it out, Babe? What in hell we goin' to do now?

The huge ox shouldered out of the ocean, accidentally stepped on a town or two, shook her hide so as to cause a minor hurricane, and then lifted her tail and pissed a goodly river.

For Paul's part, he began flinging his axes at cities called Sacramento, Salem, and Olympia. Then, with a snort that sounded like thunder itself, one of those times when Father Zeus was in a real snit, Old Paul muttered something about *gentlemen with foreheads villainous low what lives in Washington Dee Cee,* and with that he stomped across the Coast Range and the Valley and disappeared easterly, beyond the Sierra Nevada.

Me, I knew I wasn't having a normal kind of nightmare and so I woke up. I reached for my glasses and turned on the lamp.

I guess there's more than one kind of swamp that needs have some light let in.

"Go back to sleep, Bill," Judith mumbled. "We don't have to get up for another three hours."

She was right, of course, but I knew I wouldn't be able sleep anymore that night. The mind, once aroused, refused be placated.

———

thought about autumn, 1966. I was pushing thirty at the
me, a would-be poet driving a year-old Plymouth. I took a
rief unauthorized leave from my college teaching position and
und myself speeding up the California coast north from Bo-
ega Bay—heading for Eugene, Oregon, and possibly a beer or
wo at Maxie's Tavern. With luck I wouldn't miss more than
few days of classes. Accumulated sick leave would cover me.

Somewhere north of Fort Bragg, I checked my watch. Two-
-nine. Shortly thereafter I pulled to the deserted highway's
houlder, parked, shut off the slant-six, folded down the rear
at, got into a sleeping bag, utilized one of my shoes as a
llow, took two or three swigs from a jug labeled "Red Moun-
in," and listened to the rain.

I thought of a poem called "Savant's Lament":

> Goddamn it.
> Goddamn it.
> Goddamn it.
> We do not know
> A single Goddamned thing.

What I did know: the war in Vietnam was heating up,
hile at home aberrations named Speck and Whitman had
ained headlines for their respective mass murders. The past
ummer had seen racial riots in cities across the nation. James
eredith had hiked from Memphis to Jackson in an attempt
 encourage Blacks to register to vote, and now that the col-
ges were in session again, different kinds of riots were under
ay.

On the bright side, the first photograph of Earth as seen
 an electronically controlled camera on temporary duty
 the vicinity of the moon had been transmitted back by
tellite Orbiter I. Blue and white. Striking—though neither
dwood trees nor human beings were visible. Distance
esn't diminish a problem as one fellow said, but it does
markably put things into perspective: from two hundred
d forty thousand miles, *Middangeard* appeared much as
no doubt always had.

With at least a few of the world's problems as yet unsolved,
ell asleep while frenzies of wind-driven rain drummed the

Barracuda's roof, all but muting the sound of surges against a coastal headland perhaps a quarter of a mile distant.

Dawn light awakened me. I got out of my car, stared into a foggy drizzle, detected faint salt odor in the wet air, and then pushed my way through dripping willows and bush lupines into the drainage of a small, reawakened creek.

That was when I realized I'd fallen magically into a portion of the precise dream I'd had as a child, twenty years earlier when I'd first seen a redwood. But this was different—and experienced a distinct impression of having intruded, of having accidentally wandered into an arena where my presence was certainly not desired and at best was merely tolerated.

I stood in a microcosm: an amphitheater-like formation, kind of natural church—in some vague way appropriate to this Sunday morning. All around me were huge redwood stumps, some of them as much as twenty feet tall. Holes had been bored into their sides, holes spaced two or three feet apart and describing rings about the lichen-spattered bark of trees that had long since vanished but whose astounding presence remained, nearly tangible in this early dimness. From the top of one redwood stump, a considerable Douglas fir was actually growing, a tree perhaps seventy feet in height, its roots twined down through the stump itself until they reached mineral soil.

For whatever reasons, I found myself short of breath. I shivered. Laughed. I strode about from one oversized stump to another—at the same time attempting to envision human midges working from springboards (the bore-holes in the stumps bearing mute testimony), mere humans who'd managed to fell these great redwoods.

Like stepping into a myth, discovering the myth to be more than the men who dreamed it in the first place. Truly, these were the works of giants. . . .

But was I speaking of the long-dead loggers or the vanished trees or merely those platformlike remnants? I walked about aimlessly for a while longer, and then sat down in wet duff at the base of the largest redwood stump in the phantom grove. I realized I felt like a very small child who comes self-consciously aware in a mysterious world of adults. I took spiral-bound pad out of my jacket pocket and jotted down few lines so that I'd have some written record of what I experienced—against that eventual moment when I'd attempt to work the whole thing into . . .

At length I nodded, rose, surveyed the area one last time, and then pushed my way out through a veil of wet brush. The willow leaves, I noted, were beginning to turn yellow.

About the Author

BILL HOTCHKISS was born in Connecticut in 1936, the elder son of William Henry Hotchkiss and Merle Bertha [Stambaugh] Hotchkiss. At the conclusion of World War Two, the family moved to the West Coast, first to Medford, Oregon, and finally to Grass Valley, California, in the Mother Lode Region. Here the author grew up, attending public schools and graduating from high school in 1954.

A university scholarship and summer employment with the U.S. Forest Service took him to U.C. Berkeley and a B.A. in English in 1959. The following year he received an M.A. from San Francisco State University, and further graduate work led to M.F.A., D.A., and Ph.D., all in English, from the University of Oregon.

Hotchkiss and his wife, poet and novelist Judith Shears, live in seclusion either in Woodpecker Ravine, near the end of an unpaved former logging road, some eight miles from the town of Grass Valley, California, or alternately, on Munger Creek, near the metropolis of Williams, Oregon, in the Siskiyous. Their present menagerie consists of two dozen or so bantam cross chickens, a pair of button quail, three domestic turkeys, two wild turkeys found hitchhiking near Siskiyou Pass, six cats, three dogs, a skunk that persists in living under the house, and several Steller's jays whose job it is to harvest cherries, in season. Visitors include a pair of pileated woodpeckers who are fond of dogwood berries, a young doe who used to live in the house but who has

now liberated herself into the wild and returns sometimes at night to eat dry dog food, a flock of approximately thirty crows who roost in a nearby Douglas fir,
and an occasional raven, coyote, or porcupine—the latter
engaging in some sort of perverse professional arrangement with the three aforementioned dogs.